THE
PUSHCART PRIZE, XXIII:
BEST OF THE
SMALL PRESSES

BEST OF
THE SMALL
PRESSES

The PUSHCART PRIZE

1999

XXIII

Edited by
Bill Henderson
with the Pushcart
Prize editors

PUSHCART PRESS WAINSCOTT NY

Note: nominations for this series are invited from any small, independent, literary book press or magazine in the world. Up to six nominations—tear sheets or copies, selected from work published, or about to be published, in the calendar year—are accepted by our December 1 deadline each year. Write to Pushcart Press, P.O. Box 380, Wainscott, N.Y. 11975 for more information.

Acknowledgments

Selections for The Pushcart Prize are reprinted with the permission of authors and presses cited. Copyright reverts to authors and presses immediately after publication.

Distributed by W. W. Norton & Co.
500 Fifth Ave., New York, N.Y. 10110

Library of Congress Card Number: 76–58675
ISBN: 1–888889–09–8
        1–888889–13–6 (paperback)
ISSN: 0149–7863
First Printing, November, 1998

Manufactured in The United States of America
by RAY FREIMAN and COMPANY,
Jamestown, Rhode Island 02835

In Memoriam:

WILLIAM MATTHEWS (1942–1997)

INTRODUCTION
by BILL HENDERSON

In the autumn of 1964, I was a would-be great American fic-
tioneer with a mustache like Faulkner's. I lived in Paris near the Sor-
bonne in a seventh floor walk up garret with a skylight. Rent was $1.40
a night, and my daily food budget was about the same. I cooked on a
propane camping stove on the floor and bathed once a week, by ap-
pointment, in the one hotel bathtub. Toilets were located on various
stair landings and back copies of *Le Figaro* and *The International Her-
ald Tribune* were used liberally. Toilet paper was a luxury. Many other
would-be great American fictioneers lived in that old hotel at 22 Rue
du Sommerard. The typewriter racket was our song of hope.

Now a room in that hotel rents for $140 a night. There's a toilet in
each room, and an elevator. The young writers have disappeared;
Hemingway would find no moveable feast in Paris. He couldn't afford
even one meal at today's prices. He'd have to sleep by the Seine and
beg for change from the tourists. The bottom line rules in Paris as
elsewhere. It is a museum city.

Back in 1964, I wrote a short story in that garret. I had already written
several stories and a novel, and had been rejected without comment.
Even disdain would have been preferable to the usual "not right for
us." In those days *The Paris Review* still maintained an office in Paris.
Lacking the postage, I walked my most recent story a few miles
through the city to *The Paris Review* offices, one room, as I recall, up
a flight of stairs. I dropped off the piece—a tale about a wacky, dreamy
suburban kid that resembled the author a bit—and walked back to my
attic hole in the sky, expecting nothing.

Because the hotel lacked any kind of reliable mail delivery system,
I collected letters at the American Express office on Place de l'

Opéra, a good five mile round trip hike that I made daily. In a few weeks, I received a note from *The Paris Review* with my story enclosed. "Dear Mr. Sonnabend" it began. "We liked parts of your story. We would like to see more of your things." It was signed by a lady whose name I have forgotten.

I leapt across town and bounded over a Seine bridge, my soul buoyed by this faint praise that perhaps wasn't even meant for me, but for the real Mr. Sonnabend who was also receiving a letter addressed to Mr. Henderson. No matter. That rejection slip kept me going for another six years of form rejections from dozens of book and magazine publishers until I sold my first tale to *The Carolina Quarterly* for $75. Somebody had cared. Somebody at *The Paris Review* had cared enough to send me a personal, handwritten note!

* * * * * *

Then, as now, George Plimpton is the spirit of *The Paris Review*. I had a chance to talk with George early in 1998 before a reading to celebrate the publication of *Paris Review's* #144 and #145. We met at the Lansky Lounge, an establishment deep in New York's East Village, somewhere off of Delancey Street. To locate the Lounge you needed a flashlight and a genius cab driver. The cab driver I was blessed to hail; but lacking a flashlight we circled for quite a while before we discovered the street number for the Lounge and I made my way down an alley past trash cans to a likely door, which, fortunately, opened into a dark room where red wine cost $6 a glass and a dozen tables were crowded with people waiting for George, and his readers. Richard Howard, poetry editor for *The Paris Review,* introduced the poet, John Drury, and John came forward to read. Unfortunately, the Lounge was so dim that John couldn't see his text as printed in the *Review.* Somebody produced a small lamp. John couldn't both read and hold the lamp, so George stepped forward. Seated on a stool next to John, George held the lamp high. The poem was long. Ten minutes into the poem, lamp still high, George closed his eyes, meditating on the words, I figured. The poem still had a ways to go, a half hour to be precise. George seemed to sway a bit. I worried about him. Was that lamp-holding arm about to collapse? Perhaps a polite cough to John would have alerted him to the need for a change in lamp bearers?

But George, eyes closed, never lowered that lamp a fraction. He was, for that evening, poetry's statue of liberty.

I suggested to my friend, Rick Moody, the next reader, that we seek volunteers to raise the lamp for his reading. Luckily, the Lansky Lounge came up with some emergency lights and the evening was salvaged without further heroics.

George Plimpton, the lamp holder—an ancient symbol of course, but perpetually true about people like Plimpton and hundreds of small press editors who keep the lights on in our bottom line-fixated consumer utopia. Here's a bit of what was happening in publishing during the same general period of time as the events at the Lansky Lounge, just in case you have forgotten.

Random House, one of the few remaining large publishers of thoughtful books was purchased by the German giant Bertelsmann, A. G., which already owns Bantam Doubleday Dell (which includes Anchor, Dial, Delacorte and Broadway Books). Not so long ago Bantam, Doubleday and Dell were also independent firms before being snatched up and penned together. Now Bertelsmann owns not only Random House, but also its divisions: Knopf, Times Books, Modern Library, Everyman's Library, Vintage, Pantheon, Crown, Schocken, Ballantine, Villard, Del Ray, and Fawcett. Over a dozen formerly separate publishers are now one amorphous blob in Bertelsmann's deep pocket.

Other houses recently purchased include Holt, St. Martin's and Farrar, Straus and Giroux (owned by Holtzbrinck, Germany) and Penguin, Viking, Dutton and Putnam, (snapped up by Person P.L.C., England). And the list goes on and on.

Of all the major independents only W. W. Norton & Co. (Pushcart's distributor) and Houghton Mifflin remain.

Little new needs to be lamented about the magazine publishing world. Long ago all of the major journals, with few exceptions, converted to diet, sex and celebrity and the merry jingle of silly coins.

But there's a strange hope in all this: the giants of commerce on the one hand, too exhausted to dream of anything but cash, and the world of the zines, chapbooks, literary journals and books on the other hand. Ignored by the monied crowd, small press authors and publishers are blessedly free from the temptations to write for the consuming mob. In the small press universe you can actually attempt to tell the truth in an essay, or dream a dream in a poem or story. That perhaps is why this universe thrives in an age of emptiness. The worse it gets out there, the better it is in here. For the twenty-three years that I have published this series, the quality of the work—and the quantity too, have soared. Why? Nobody wants to buy us! We are blessedly alone: what's the bottom line on a guy who thinks it's his duty and just good manners to hold up a lamp for 40 minutes for a poet in an obscure funky room in a "lounge" nobody can find? To paraphrase Janis Joplin, there's nothing left to lose. No money here at all. And that's freedom.

* * *

As usual, there are many people to thank this year. And many people to remember: Bill Matthews in particular. When Bill died suddenly and too soon last year, the paperback edition of *Pushcart Prize XXI,* which he had helped edit with Pat Strachan, had been out only a few months. It was a terrific selection of poetry and a huge thankless job of judging he and Pat did. Our world is not the same without him. Bill's last small press poem will be found in the pages that follow.

This year's poetry editors are Marilyn Chin and Molly Bendall. They read thousands of poems and somehow survived the task and assembled a wonderful and varied selection.

Marilyn Chin is the author of *The Phoenix Gone, the Terrace Empty* (winner of the PEN Josephine Miles Award, 1994) and *Dwarf Bamboo* (nominated for the Bay Area Book Reviewer's Award in 1987). Both books have become Asian-American classics. She is currently a professor in the MFA program at San Diego State University.

Molly Bendall's poetry collection, *After Estrangement,* won the Peregrine Smith Poetry Prize in 1992. Her forthcoming collection, *Dark Summer,* will appear from Miami University Poetry Press soon. She won the Eunice Tietjens Prize from *Poetry* magazine, and the Linda Hull Memorial Prize presented by *Denver Quarterly.* She teaches at the University of Southern California.

Both Marilyn Chin and Molly Bendall have appeared frequently in past Pushcart Prize issues.

As always, my special thanks to Tony Brandt, our essays editor for many years. Not a single preposition or article or comma that is askew gets by Tony's cool eye. Cant hucksters beware. Thanks also to readers Jennie McGregor Bernard and Leigh Nastasi and to Rick Moody and Marvin Bell, roving editors who know the territory. And without Hannah Turner, nada.

*   *   *

Every year I am elated about the new writers and presses that are reprinted and honored here. In PPXXIII, as usual, most of the authors are new to the series. Also, we welcome the following presses for the first time: *Artword Quarterly,* Cleveland State University Poetry Press, *Event, New American Writing,* Red Hen Press, *Seneca Review,* and 9 x 9 Industries.

Altogether 68 selections from 42 presses as nominated by hundreds of editors and by our 217 staff *Pushcart Prize* Contributing Editors are included in our annual celebration.

If you are interested in glitz and buzz, this is one party you should pass by.

If, pilgrim, you seek a hint of the holy, and a taste of the hilarious, plus the acquaintance of some of the world's best writers, read on.

THE PEOPLE
WHO HELPED

FOUNDING EDITORS—*Anaïs Nin (1903–1977) Buckminster Fuller (1895–1983), Charles Newman, Daniel Halpern, Gordon Lish, Harry Smith, Hugh Fox, Ishmael Reed, Joyce Carol Oates, Len Fulton, Leonard Randolph, Leslie Fiedler, Nona Balakian (1918–1991) Paul Bowles, Paul Engle (1908–1991), Ralph Ellison (1914–1994) Reynolds Price, Rhoda Schwartz, Richard Morris, Ted Wilentz, Tom Montag, William Phillips, Poetry editor: Lloyd Van Brunt.*

CONTRIBUTING EDITORS FOR THIS EDITION—*Rita Dove, Ellen Wilbur, Susan Bergman, Sabina Grogan, Albert Saijo, DeWitt Henry, Carolyn Kizer, Thomas Sayers Ellis, Joe Ashby Porter, Rane Arroyo, Tom Paine, Michael Kaniecki, C. S. Giscombe, Richard Kostelanetz, Daniel Stern, Katherine Min, Lewis Hyde, Pat Strachan, Susan Wheeler, Robert Phillips, Philip Booth, Daniel Orozco, Edward Hoagland, Cleopatra Mathis, Kristin King, Ruth Stone, Sherod Santos, Caroline Langston, Rick Bass, Philip Dacey, Dan Masterson, Melissa Malouf, Julia Vinograd, Rebecca McClanahan, Jane Hirshfield, Mark Halliday, Jessica Roeder, Ron Tanner, P. H. Liotta, Maxine Kumin, Karla Kuban, Walter Pavlich, Jim Daniels, Jewel Mogan, Sharman Russell, Carol Snow, Marie Sheppard Williams, Jane Miller, Eugene Stein, Carl Dennis, Richard Tayson, Karen Bender, H. E. Francis, Stacey Richter, Kathy Callaway, David Lehman, Michael Waters, David Baker, D. R. MacDonald, Kim Addonizio, David Jauss, Joan Murray, Diann Blakely, Joshua Clover, Richard Jackson, Lynne*

14

McFall, Jim Simmerman, Rosellen Brown, Mark Irwin, Philip Levine, Jay Meek, Harold Jaffe, Tom McNeal, Pinckney Benedict, Maureen Seaton, Robert Schirmer, Maura Stanton, Gerald Shapiro, S. L. Wisenberg, Thomas E. Kennedy, M. D. Elevitch, Eleanor Wilner, Brenda Miller, Susan Mates, Sam Hamill, Richard Garcia, CyrusCassells, Mike Newirth, John Allman, Joyce Carol Oates, Stuart Dybek, Tony Ardizzone, Donald Revell, Stephen Dunn, Dana Levin, Gary Gildner, Kent Nelson, George Keithley, Ann Townsend, Edward Hirsch, James Harms, Robert McBrearty, Sigrid Nunez, Lloyd Van Brunt, Tomaz Salamun, Pamela Stewart, Campbell McGrath, Henri Cole, Lois-Ann Yamanaka, Edmund Keeley, Clarence Major, Andre Dubus, Debra Spark, Antler, Sylvia Watanabe, Christina Zawa-diwsky, Erin McGraw, Donald Rawley, Mary Ruefle, Eamon Grennan, Raymond Federman, Jim Barnes, Jack Marshall, Claire Davis, James Reiss, John Daniel, Dennis Vannatta, Michael Bowden, Joan Swift, Kay Ryan, Rachel Hadas, Gordon Weaver, William Matthews, Marilyn Hacker, Robin Hemley, Gerry Locklin, Arthur Sze, Billy Collins, Philip Appleman, Lee Upton, Brenda Hillman, Jane Cooper, Steve Yarbrough, Jack Marshall, Arthur Smith, Laura Kasischke, David Romtvedt, Mark Jarman, Janice Eidus, Agha Shahid Ali, Chard deNiord, Mark Cox, Robert Wrigley, Tony Hoagland, Molly Giles, David St. John, John Drury, Colette Inez, Gibbons Ruark, Dorothy Barresi, Brigit Kelly, Lloyd Schwartz, Melissa Pritchard, Vern Rutsala, Elizabeth Spires, Michael Heffernan, Stanley Lindberg, Josip Novakovich, Henry Carlile, Stephen Corey, William Olsen, Elizabeth Inness-Brown, Barbara Selfridge, Mary Peterson, Sharon Solwitz, Wally Lamb, David Rivard, Sandra McPherson, Laurie Sheck, Karen Fish, Kenneth Gangemi, Martha Collins, David Wojahn, Jean Thompson, Michael Stephens, Reginald Gibbons, Michael Martone, Timothy Geiger, Michael Dennis Browne, Stuart Dischell, Ralph Angel, Robert Pinsky, Lou Mathews, Sandra Tsing Loh, Manette Ansay, Andrew Hudgins, Steve Stern, JoEllen Kwiatek, Christopher Howell, Roger Weinbarten, Ha Jin, Carol Muske, Naomi Shihab Nye, Thomas Lux, Tom Filer, Christopher Buckley, Ed Ochester, Jennifer Atkinson, Michael Collier, Linda Bierds, Tony Quagliano, Richard Burgin, Gary Fincke, Bin Ramke, Susan Moon, Len Roberts, C. E. Poverman, Marianne Boruch.

CONTENTS

THE
PUSHCART PRIZE, XXIII:
BEST OF THE
SMALL PRESSES

AS KINGFISHERS CATCH FIRE

fiction by COLUM McCANN

from STORY

> *As kingfishers catch fire dragonflies draw flame.*
> —*Gerard Manley Hopkins*

A FLOCK OF KINGFISHERS arrived the evening Rhianon Ryan died, in the middle of a winter so cold that other birds froze in the air. Thousands of them came on a brief and noisy migration with a gunning of wings, making it seem that the northern lights had arrived in the sky, iridescent blue and salmons and corals and emeralds and the fabulous yellows of a thousand converging beaks. They came with a marvellous bobbing action in the air, like a shoal of flying fish. It was the strangest thing—apart from Rhianon—to have ever happened to the small Roscommon town.

The kingfishers appeared from the south, low-flying and rapid, casting tenacious shadows over the farmlands. They swooped down on rivers and fed on fish found in icy water. Farmers on tractors shaded their eyes, women at storefronts held up umbrellas to keep off the bird shit, children stood in the town square and let the birds alight in their arms, teenage boys took out rifles that they would never use. Still the birds kept coming, letting out a high sound, like a musical keen. They lined the awning of the cinema. Gathered in the eaves of the dole office. Congregated near the video shop. Perched on goal posts in the football field. They even sat around the rims of beer kegs at the back of pubs. For the whole of that night and the following day, until Rhianon was buried, the town was stunned into silence, watching kingfishers as they burst their colours through the air. Her funeral was carried out, but talk of Rhianon was overshadowed—even at her wake the missing gaps in her life were not filled with the chatter of the locals, but with talk of how the strangest aurora had visited the town.

Rhianon left Ireland on a mail boat bound for New York in the spring of 1950. It was her nineteenth birthday and by the time she wrote her first letter, three months later, there were so many rumours about her the townspeople were a little disappointed, at first, to find out the truth.

She was, she wrote, on her way to Korea with American soldiers to help nurse democracy into the world. Rhianon had always cared for the sick and the dying. At the age of eight she had climbed the wall of the local lunatic asylum with a pair of scissors in her hand. The following morning the employees were amazed as old women with no teeth suddenly rose from their beds with beehives and bouffants. Bachelor farmers slicked back pomade. Young lunatics were proud of their short-back-and-sides, carrying tiny mirrors around in their overalls. Every Saturday after that Rhianon was seen in the asylum garden giving free hairdos, carefully applying lipstick, clipping nose hairs, twirling cotton sticks in ears to take out wax. Some of the local people came to get their hair done, although they were always relegated to the end of the queue. During the week she bicycled to the houses of the sick and listened to their life stories as she gave them makeovers, rinsing their hair, chopping stray ends, taking away straggly fringes. She even took a short apprenticeship with the undertaker, dressing the dead, but the dead didn't tell interesting stories, so she soon gave up on that.

Everyone hailed her as she cycled along the curvy grey streets, with her pellucid blue eyes under a giant umbrella of electric red hair.

A party was held for her outside the local cinema on the day she left, and people came from miles around to wish her farewell; a line of them gathered under a red-and-white canvas tent to get tips on the latest makeup. Young men scribbled their addresses on the inside flap of cigarette packages. Old women listened carefully to hints about how to stave off wrinkles. Rhianon chatted with everyone, but was too shy to make a speech—she simply stood at the cinema door and hung her

24

head as the townspeople clapped. A car beeped impatiently to bring her to the mail boat.

When she left, all colour seemed to drain itself out of the town, down through the rain gutters, along into ditches, and out to the lowlands, leaving the streets pale and monochromatic.

When the first letter arrived, the people imagined Rhianon in nurse-whites, landing in Korea in a plane with a giant red cross on the side. World atlases were hunted out of libraries and youngsters located the port of Pusan where she said she was going. Great consternation rose up when the butcher claimed that Koreans were apt to eat dogs. A whiparound was made to send food to Rhianon, fruitcakes and long-lasting soda bread, with a stern warning: *Stay away from meat, girl!* Pictures of General Douglas MacArthur were clipped from papers and the talk was of whether the North Koreans would sweep further south or not. Her mother hung an American flag outside Rhianon's cottage, and it flapped through rainstorms.

Rhianon, for her part, began to send letters as long as skirts.

Helicopters flew in low, she said, carrying the injured. Korean women in the rice fields were shaped like sickles, backs bent into their work, stopping only to stare upwards at the flying machines. The canvas flaps of tents blew in the wind. The hospital was a symphony of moans. Soldiers screamed about the loss of their legs or arms. Bags of plasma were scarce. She had no time for hairdos and not an ounce of makeup was to be found anywhere. At night the scratchy voice of Nat King Cole came over the radios. American soldiers sat around and smacked chewing gum in their jaws. The Yanks called her "Popsicle" because they said she looked like a long white stick under an icicle of red hair. When evenings fell, mosquitoes raved delightedly around her and she had taken to drinking spoonfuls of vinegar to keep them at bay. Another Irish nurse had come down with malaria. Rhianon was nursing her. Don't worry about the meat, she wrote, there wasn't a dog in sight. The most abundant wildlife was kingfishers, tons of them, radiant and mysterious—they were often seen to dart around the camp, dropping the seeds of plants, then flying off again. At night bats flitted above the rice fields and somehow made her think of home, the movement of shadows on the land. She always signed off by saying that she would write again soon and drew a love heart underneath her name with a squiggle coming out at the end of the heart, like a tail of a tadpole.

25

The letters were carted by the postman around the town and people gathered in the tiny cinema, before Cagney appeared in a rerun of *Yankee Doodle Dandy*. Rhianon was discussed before the curtains were pulled back from the screen. Women wearing head scarves and brooches leaned into one another earnestly. Boys refused to believe that Rhianon didn't eat dogs. Men talked about the latest reports from the newspapers. And then one afternoon her letters burst into tropical bloom when Rhianon wrote that she was almost in love with a dying man, and people whispered of her affair even through the appearance of Hollywood stars in khaki uniforms re-enacting World War II.

The soldier, Rhianon said, had so much shrapnel in his body that he could have been a fallen meteorite, heavenly in the way he shoved his stubby arms to the sky as if he wanted to return to the patient black Korean night and utter some final rage. At evening the man gave off a glow in his army bed, the magnetism of the metal in his body attracting every packet of light in the tent around him. In the beginning the soldier had smelled of DDT—so much lice on his body that the tiny parasites had blocked out the light, but when a doctor doused him in insecticide he began to give off faint glimmers. Even the surgeons noticed the aura hovering around him, some of it coming from a sucking chest wound, more of it seeming to emanate from his eyes. They put it down to hallucination or perhaps chemicals—but Rhianon put it down to sainthood. He was the only one of her patients who didn't mind dying. He told her that there was a dignity to a good death, that to die well was the only thing a man could do honestly in life. Having almost fallen in love the soldier was happy to die. The *almost* was important to both him and Rhianon—to them love was like innocence, once you became aware of it, it was gone forever. Rhianon wrote, under a bare bulb where moths careened, that she sat by the soldier's bed—a metal frame with green canvas—and held his hand, feeling the light flow into her. The soldier smiled back under the cloth, a slow and spectral smile. In the distance firefights cleaved the oriental sky. Days piled themselves into weeks. Rhianon sometimes wasn't sure if he was already a ghost or not, so she broke the rules and kissed him gently on the lips to make sure he was still alive.

Under the soldier's bed, in a bucket filled with ice, lay three of his mangled fingers.

He had lost the fingers in a firefight near Inchon, when a grenade landed in the branches of a tree. Two hours later an army unit found him lying on the ground, full of shrapnel, staring at his fingers spread out on his emergency blanket. He had been holding the detached fingers to his mouth every hour, trying unsuccessfully to spit the drying blood back into them. He was placed on a stretcher. The fingers were brought into camp with him, in the pocket of his fatigues, a trinity of remembrance. The doctors cast them into a bin, but Rhianon rescued them and tucked them into her nurse-whites. She placed blocks of ice in a bucket every evening, carefully packing it around the dismembered flesh. Each morning the vicious heat of that Korean summer turned the ice to water and the fingers lay there, floating, speaking of love and collapse, turning blue and black, the demise of another summer's day.

The fingers didn't give off any light but Rhianon was afraid to let them disintegrate. She picked them up one by one and fastidiously placed ice around them.

"I have only one wish," the soldier told Rhianon one morning during the rainy season. "Bury my fingers in a place where I was young, and someday you must return to see what grows there. Promise me that. You can do whatever you like with the rest of my body, but my fingers must be buried and you must return to see what grows." Rhianon wiped the soldier's brow, from which light continued to fulminate.

When the letters arrived there were long novenas hailed to the heavens of Roscommon; rosaries were incanted at fieldside grottos; yellow votive candles were lit at the back of the church; the cinema was packed as Rhianon's mother read aloud the letters; some of the townspeople stared at their own fingers in a sad empathy for the unknown soldier. The complexion of gossip was changed. Talk of Rhianon was a grand diversion from idle chat about the weather, baking formulas, and the disastrous milk yields. The postman swished on his bicycle through puddles, from house to house, carrying news. Some of the villagers even felt their own hearts creaking as they heard about the bold and inky handwriting. *My soldier will die soon, I am sure of it. The tent is full of light. I'm not sure what I will do without him. With all my love, Rhianon.*

It was soon decided that the soldier was an American corporal, tall, beautiful, with hair so slick and blond you could skate on it. The hillside he spoke of was probably somewhere in Nebraska or the Dakotas. He was a rancher's son, people imagined, hence the request for the finger burial—to see what would grow in the soil of his youth.

27

His eyes undoubtedly held the chimera of blueness. He had probably been a hero in battle, maybe raging through the firefight with another soldier carried on his back, or pitching a grenade at an advancing line of Chinese communists, or gallantly planting a flag on a hill. He would have a quintessential American name—Chad or Buster or Wayne—names that invoked movie stars who were capable of rising from the ashes of their celluloid dying. And he too would rise phoenix-like from his hospital bed, recover fully, return one day to the country town with Rhianon on his arm, down Main Street, past the butcher's shop without a second glance, waving his fingerless hand at passersby, using the good hand to fling his hat to boys on the bridge.

Mrs. Burke, the dressmaker, made a white taffeta gown for Rhianon's return. Hurley, the publican, promised a free keg for the celebration. The funeral director said he might even jazz up his hearse with white ribbons for the imminent wedding. Rhianon's mother rehearsed recipes in her mind—potatoes roasted in a bed of rosemary, flanked by a slicing of fresh carrots. And when Rhianon scribbled a single-line note that she was coming home, the excitement in the town was paralysing.

When Rhianon returned in the spring of 1953—a warm day when yellow bunting was hung from townhouse windows—there was no blue-eyed soldier at her side.

She walked down Main Street, her hair unwashed and strung like strawberry jam on the top of her head, a hand over her belly where a child had begun to show. People came out to greet her, uncoiled from their houses like a giant rope, but they were shocked at the sight of the bulge in the smock. They shook her hand and welcomed her, told her how beautiful she looked, but soon drifted off, disappointed. Shouts from the doorway of the pub melted down into whispers. A gramophone in the window of a house was turned off and a needle slowly scraped across a record. The yellow ribbons were slack in the breeze. "There's no soldier with her," the butcher incanted from his shop counter, "there's no soldier with her at all." Somebody mentioned the word "whore." At a curve in the road near the river, Rhianon's mother slapped her daughter's face and that night the dressmaker sent a small plume of smoke above the town, burning the taffeta gown in an old oil barrel.

Rhianon wandered around the town in a daze, telling the story to anybody who would listen, gently whispering that instead of the blue-eyed baby boy of an American corporal, she was carrying the bastard child of a black-haired Korean soldier who, when he died, had set off a backwards meteor shower over the landscape of his country, huge streams of light rivering upwards to the sky from some hillside where digit-shaped flowers burst out every spring in his memory. Nobody asked about the fingers and Rhianon didn't say a word, although a van arrived from Dublin at her cottage carrying a giant fridge that nobody had seen the likes of before, with a freezer section on top, to which Rhianon attached a strong lock.

Her son, Jae Chil, was stillborn, Rhianon bought a twenty-acre farm, dug him a plot in the easternmost field, arranged him for burial, said a few Confucian prayers over the mound, dressed herself in mourning-black from that day on. Two deep furrows inveigled themselves into the corners of her mouth, where she deceived her sadness by forever smiling.

She tended to a herd of twenty cows with a dog she called Syngman and was often seen driving them down a laneway, a stick raised high in the air, her Wellington boots covered in dung. She came to town carting pails of milk in a baby pram. She was still beautiful, walked tall and unburdened, offered her cosmetic services to the undertaker who tentatively avoided her, hid himself in a back office when she came calling. She could be sometimes seen on the grounds of the asylum arranging the hair of patients as they sat in white garden chairs by flower beds, but for the most part she lived out the tedium of her days without bothering anybody, just working away silently in her fields. She didn't talk about Korea, although there were times when she was heard gibbering in a strange language to herself. Sometimes children sneaked up to her house and tried to peer in the windows. When she came out, in black apron with baking flour on the front, they ran away. Rhianon would stand at the door and stretch her arms wide, questioning them, almost imploring. From a safe distance the children would point at her and make a slant of their eyes, but she simply shrugged and waited until they left, the children bored by her seeming indifference.

On a few occasions, when travellers came through, she'd invite them to stay. They said that Rhianon seemed to always have words dangling on the very edge of her lips, but they couldn't figure out if the words were to be swallowed or shared. In the end the old woman said nothing, just sat with her guests and watched the sunsets slide by.

Rhianon stopped selling milk, only came into town from her farm when there were electrical blackouts and she would run frantically through the streets seeking anyone who had blocks of ice they could give her. She tore at the roots of her hair—corrugated now into rows of grey—and ran back with plastic bags of ice to her cottage, a quirk soon forgotten when new, more reliable pylons were erected all around the country, leapfrogging through the lowlands. There were rumours, of course. She was hiding the soldier in a back bedroom. She was saving to make another trip to Pusan. She was going to get married to one of the lunatic farmers. But the rumours were tame, and like the ice, Rhianon herself might well have been forgotten but for her final trip to the undertaker on a freezing Monday morning when, at first, nothing stirred in the deep cyanic vault of the sky.

She arrived in a floral dress, the black of mourning jettisoned for some reason. She stood at the undertaker's desk, twisting a curl around her finger, and said she would arrange herself for her own death, thank you very much, which would be on the following Wednesday.

"Absolutely no frills," she said.

"None?"

"Not a sausage."

"Pardon me?"

"None at all."

She handed him a bundle of money in old currency and said that her clothes were not to be touched, nor her pockets rifled, nor her fingers uncurled, nor her eyelids closed, nor her face made up in any manner or means, and definitely nothing should be done with her hair. Word of the gesture slipped around town and dozens of locals followed the undertaker on his trip to check on Rhianon.

It was the coldest day of the year. Berries had shrivelled on hedges. Puddles had been seduced by ice. The people came on foot and, as they negotiated the long laneway to the cottage, the distant flocks of birds appeared to the south. Men and women stopped in their tracks, lifted up their anorak hoods and removed head scarves for a better view. Children whistled through their teeth. The skein of kingfishers seemed endless and the people were mesmerised by the sight, almost frozen to the spot.

Only the undertaker, rubbing his fingers like money, went into the cottage. Rhianon was found in bed, propped up by four pillows, a natural death, her feet frozen to the bedstead, her eyes open, her face painted, a curious look of contentment on her. A cup of green tea lay on her bedside table. There were no notes. She was lifted into a coffin hurriedly and arrangements were made, while outside the townsfolk still stared upwards.

The kingfishers continued their onslaught, a salvo of them through the Roscommon sky, with a liquid movement of their wings. A silence descended, like that of a half-forgotten prayer. Instead of going to the wake—Rhianon had prepared whiskey and sandwiches and left them on the kitchen table—the group of people stood outside and saluted the wash of colour. Even the gravedigger looked as he slammed his boot on the blade of the shovel to lift the first clod of soil for the coffin. He kept straining upwards to see as the hole got deeper and deeper.

The birds left when Rhianon was laid down into the ground, in a plot she had prepared beside her son.

The locals walked home, chattering amongst themselves about the fabulous sight. They weren't even angry that two whole days had to be spent cleaning the bird shit from all the windows of the town and sweeping feathers from the ground. A smell of ammonia hung for weeks. Everyone waited for another visit of the birds, but it never came.

They all stayed stupidly unaware of the three shrivelled fingers that lay in the hip pocket of Rhianon's burial dress when they dropped her down into the ground. It never even crossed their minds that the Korean soldier had found the place of his youth, and it was only the following spring, when exotic oriental azaleas burst up wildly around the old woman's grave, that the townspeople pondered the idea that the kingfishers hadn't arrived for them at all.

Nominated by Story

31

A HEMINGWAY STORY

essay by ANDRE DUBUS

from THE KENYON REVIEW

In my thirtieth summer, in 1966, I read many stories by John O'Hara and read Hemingway's stories again, and his "In Another Country" challenged me more than I could know then. That summer was my last at the University of Iowa; I had a master of fine arts degree and, beginning in the fall, a job as a teacher, in Massachusetts. My wife and four children and I would move there in August. Until then, we lived in Iowa City and I taught two freshman rhetoric classes four mornings a week, then came home to eat lunch and write. I wrote in my den at the front of the house, a small room with large windows, and I looked out across the lawn at an intersection of streets shaded by tall trees. I was trying to learn to write stories, and was reading O'Hara and Hemingway as a carpenter might look at an excellent house someone else has built.

That summer "In Another Country" became one of my favorite stories written by anyone, and it still is. But I could not fully understand the story. What's it *about?* I said to a friend as we drove in his car to the university track to run laps. He said: It's about the futility of cures. That nestled beneath my heart, and displaced my confusion. Yes. The futility of cures. Then everything connected and formed a whole, and in the car with my friend, then running with him around the track, I saw the story as you see a painting, and one of the central images was the black silk handkerchief covering the wound where the young man's nose had been.

Kurt Vonnegut was our neighbor. We had adjacent lawns; he lived behind us, at the top of the hill. One day that summer he was outside on his lawn or on his front porch four times when I was outside, and we waved and called to each other. The first time I was walking home from teaching, wearing slacks and a shirt; the next time I was wearing shorts and a T-shirt I had put on to write; then I wore gym shorts without a shirt and drove to the track; in late afternoon, wearing another pair of slacks and another shirt, I walked up to his house to drink. He was sitting on his front porch and, as I approached, he said: "Andre, you change clothes more than a Barbie doll."

Kurt did not have a telephone. That summer the English Department hosted a conference, and one afternoon a man from the department called me and asked me to ask Kurt to meet Ralph Ellison at the airport later in the day, then Mrs. Ellison at the train. She did not like to fly. I went up to Kurt's house, and he came to the back door. I said: "They want us to pick up Ellison at the airport. Then his wife at the train."

"Swell. I'll drive."

Later he came driving down the brick road from his house and I got in the car and saw a paperback of *Invisible Man* between us on the seat. The airport was in Cedar Rapids, a short drive. I said: "Are you going to leave the book there?"

"I'm teaching it. I thought it'd be phony to take it out of the car."

It was a hot afternoon. We left town and were on the highway, the corn was tall and green under the huge midwestern sky, and I said: "They didn't really ask for both of us to pick up Ellison. Just you."

"I knew that."

"Thanks. How are we going to recognize him? Do we just walk up to the only Negro who gets off the plane?"

Kurt looked at me and said: "Shit."

"We could just walk past him, pretend we couldn't see him."

"That's so good, we ought to do it."

The terminal was small and we stood outside and watched the plane land, and the people filing out of it, and there was one black man. We went to him and Kurt said: "Ralph Ellison?" and Ellison smiled and said: "Yes," and we shook his hand and got his things and went to the car. I sat in the back and watched Ellison. He saw *Invisible Man* at once but did not say anything. As we rode on the highway he looked at the cornfields and talked fondly of the times he had hunted pheasants here with Vance Bourjaily. Then he picked up his book and said: "It's still around."

Kurt told him he was teaching it, and I must have told him I loved it because I did and I do, but I only remember watching him and listening to him. Kurt asked him if he wanted a drink. He did. We went

33

to a bar near the university, and sat in a booth, Ellison opposite Kurt and me, and ordered vodka martinis. We talked about jazz and books, and Ellison said that before starting *Invisible Man* he had read Malroux's *Man's Fate* forty times. He liked the combination of melodrama and philosophy, he said, and he liked those in Dostoyevski too. We ordered martinis again and I was no longer shy. I looked at Ellison's eyes and said: "I've been rereading Hemingway's stories this summer, and I think my favorite is 'In Another Country.' "

He looked moved by remembrance, as he had in the car, talking about hunting with Vance. Looking at us, he recited the story's first paragraph: " 'In the fall the war was always there, but we did not go to it any more. It was cold in the fall in Milan and the dark came very early. Then the electric lights came on, and it was pleasant along the streets looking in the windows. There was much game hanging outside the shops, and the snow powdered in the fur of the foxes and the wind blew their tails. The deer hung stiff and heavy and empty, and small birds blew in the wind and the wind turned their feathers. It was a cold fall and the wind came down from the mountains.' "

When we took Ellison to his room on the campus, it was time for us to go to the train and meet his wife. Kurt said to Ellison: "How will we recognize her?"

"She's wearing a gray dress and carrying a beige raincoat." He smiled. "And she's colored."

Wanting to know absolutely what a story is about, and to be able to say it in a few sentences, is dangerous: It can lead us to wanting to possess a story as we possess a cup. We know the function of a cup, and we drink from it, wash it, put it on a shelf, and it remains a thing we own and control, unless it slips from our hands into the control of gravity; or someone else breaks it, or uses it to give us poisoned tea. A story can always break into pieces while it sits inside a book on a shelf; and, decades after we have read it even twenty times, it can open us up, by cut or caress, to a new truth.

I taught at Bradford College in Massachusetts for eighteen years, and in my first year, and many times afterward, I assigned "In Another Country" to students. The first time I talked about it in a classroom I understood more of it, because of what the students said, and also because of what I said: words that I did not know I would say, giving voice to ideas I did not know I had, and to images I had not seen in my mind. I began by telling them the story was about the futility of cures; by the end of the class I knew it was not. Through my years of teaching I learned to walk into a classroom wondering what I would say, rather than knowing what I would say. Then I learned by hearing myself speak; the source of my speaking was our mysterious harmony with truths we know, though very often our knowledge of them is hidden from us. Now, as a retired teacher, I mistrust all prepared statements by anyone, and by me.

Still, after discussing "In Another Country" the first time with Bradford students, I did not go into the classroom in the years after that, knowing exactly what I would say about the story. Probably ten times in those eighteen years I assigned "In Another Country" and began our discussion by focusing on the images in the first two paragraphs, the narrator—who may be Nick Adams—bringing us to the hospital, and to the machines "that were to make so much difference," and I talked about the tone of that phrase, a tone achieved by the music of the two paragraphs, a tone that tells us the machines will make nothing different.

The story shifts then to the Italian major. He was a champion fencer before the war; now he is a wounded man whose right hand is shrunken; it is the size of a baby's hand, and he puts it into a machine which the doctor says will restore it to its normal size. Neither the major's hand nor the major will ever be normal. The narrator's knee is injured and the small proportion he gives it in the story lets us know that it will be healed. I told my students, when they were trying to understand a story that seemed difficult, to look at its proportion: the physical space a writer gives each element of the story. "In Another Country" moves swiftly from the futility of cures, to what it is that the physical curing cannot touch, and, yes, the young man who lost his nose and covered his face with a black silk handkerchief is a thematic image in the story, but it is not in the center of the picture, it is off to the side.

In the center of this canvas is death. That is why the narrator, though his knee will be normal again, will not himself be normal. Or perhaps not for a very long time. After the first hospital scene he tells of his other comrades, the Italian soldiers he walks home from the hospital with; all of them, in the war, have lived with death. Because of this, they feel detached, and they feel insulated from civilians and others who have not been in the war. The narrator is frightened, and at night moves from the light of one street lamp to another. He does not want to go to the war again. So the story now has moved from the futility of

35

cures back to war, where it began with its opening line and the paragraph that shows the lovely pictures of Milan; while, beneath that tactile beauty, the music is the sound of something lost, and the loss of it has changed even the sound of the wind, and the sight of blowing snow on the fur of animals.

A war story, then; and while the major and narrator sit at their machines in the hospital, the major teaches Italian grammar to the narrator. I cannot know why Hemingway chose Italian grammar, but my deepest guess is that his choice was perfect: two wounded men, talking about language, rather than faith in the machines, hope for healing, or the horror of war. I am not saying they ought to be speaking about these things. There are times when it is best to be quiet, to endure, to wait. Hemingway may be our writer who has been the most badly read. His characters are as afraid of pain and death as anyone else. They feel it, they think about it, and they talk about it with people they love. With the Italian major, the narrator talks about grammar.

Then the story moves again, in the final scene. Until now, it has seemed to be a story about young men who have lost that joy in being alive which is normal for young and healthy people, who have not yet learned that within the hour they may be dead. The story has been about that spiritual aging that war can cause: in a few moments, a young soldier can see and hear enough, taste and touch and smell enough, to age his spirit by decades while his body has not aged at all. The quickness of this change, of the spirit's immersion in horror, may cause a state of detachment from people whose lives are still normal, and who receive mortality's potion, drop by tiny drop, not in a torrent.

But in the story's final scene, the major furiously and bitterly grieves, scolds the narrator, then apologizes, says that his wife has just died and, crying, leaves the room where the machines are. From their doctor the narrator learns that the major had waited to marry until he was out of the war. His wife contracted pneumonia and in three days she was dead, and now in the story death is no longer the haunting demon of soldiers who have looked into its eyes. It is what no one can escape. The major reasonably believed he was the one in danger, until he was home from the war. Then death attacked his exposed flank, and breathed pneumonia into his wife. The story has completed its movement. A few notes remain: softly, a piano and bass, and faint drums and cymbals; we

36

cymbals; we see the major returning to put his hand in the machine. He keeps doing this.

Two years after I retired from teaching, and twenty years after that last summer in Iowa City, I was crippled in an instant when a car hit me, and I was in a hospital for nearly two months. I suffered with pain, and I thought very often of Ernest Hemingway, and how much physical pain he had suffered, and how well he had written about it. In the hospital I did not think about "In Another Country." I thought about "The Gambler, the Nun, and the Radio," and was both enlightened and amused, for always when I had talked about that story with students, I had moved quickly past the physical pain and focused on the metaphysical. Philosophy is abundant in that story; but I had to live in pain, on a hospital bed, before I could see that bodily pain deserved much more than I had given it. Always I had spent one fifty-minute class on the story. I should have used two class sessions; the first one would have been about pain.

A year after my injury, in a time of spiritual pain, I dreamed one night that I was standing on both my legs with other people in a brightly lit kitchen near the end of the day. I did not recognize any of the people, but in the dream they were my friends; one was a woman who was deeply hurting me. We were all standing, and I was pretending to be happy, and no one could see my pain. I stood near the stove. The kitchen door to the lawn was open, and there was a screen door and, from outside, Ernest Hemingway opened it and walked in, looking at me across the length of the room. He wore his fishing cap with a long visor He walked straight to me and said: "Let's go fishing," I walked with him, outside and down a sloping lawn to a wharf. We went to the end of the wharf where a large boat with an inboard motor was tied. Then we stood in the cabin, Hemingway at my right and holding the wheel with both hands; we moved on a calm bay and were going out to sea. It was dusk and I wondered if it was too late to go to sea, and I had not seen him carrying fishing rods, and I wondered if he had forgotten them. But I worried for only a moment. Then I looked up at his profile and knew that he knew what he was doing. He had a mustache but no beard and was about forty and still handsome.

The next night a writer's workshop I host gathered in my living room. When they left I sat in my wheelchair in the dining room and remembered my dream, and remarked for the first time that Hemingway had his head, and I had my missing leg, and the leg I do

37

have was no longer damaged. Then I remembered reading something that John Cheever either wrote or said: During one long dark night of the soul, Ernest Hemingway spoke to him. Cheever said that he had never heard Hemingway's voice, but he knew that this was his voice, telling Cheever that his present pain was only the beginning. Then, sitting in my chair in the quiet night, I believed that Hemingway had come to me while I was suffering, and had taken me away from it, out to sea where we could fish.

A few months later, in winter, I wrote to Father Bruce Ritter at Covenant House in New York and told him that I was crippled and had not yet learned to drive with hand controls; that my young daughters were no longer living with me; that I hosted, without pay, a writers' workshop, but its members could afford to pay anyone for what I did, and they did not really need me; and I felt that when I was not with my children I was no longer a useful part of the world. Father Ritter wrote to me, suggesting that I tutor a couple of high school students. In Haverhill there is a home for girls between the ages of fourteen and eighteen. They are in protective custody of the state, because of what people have done to them. In summer I phoned the home, and asked if they wanted a volunteer. Someone drove me there to meet a man in charge of education. A light rain was falling. At the home I looked through the car window at a second-story window and saw an old and long-soiled toy, a stuffed dog. The man came out and stood in the rain and I asked him what I could do. He said: "Give them stories about real people. Give them words and images. They're afraid of those."

So that fall, in 1988, we began; and nearly eight years later, girls with a staff woman still come to my house on Monday nights, and we read. For the first seven years I read to them; then they told me they wanted to read, and now I simply choose a book, provide soft drinks and ash trays, and listen. One night in the fall of 1991, five years after my injury, I read "In Another Country" to a few girls and a staff woman. This was the first time I had read it since my crippling. I planned to read it to the girls, then say about it what I had said so many times to students at Bradford College. I stopped often while reading the story, to tell them about images and thematic shifts. When I finished reading it, I talked about each part of it again, building to my explanation of the story's closing lines: "The major did not come to the hospital for three days. Then he came at the usual hour, wearing a black band on the sleeve of his uniform. When he came back, there were large framed photographs around the wall, all sorts of wounds before and after they had been cured by the machines. In front of the machine the major used were three photographs of hands like his that were completely restored. I do not know where the doctor got them. I always understood we were the first to use the machines. The photographs did not make much difference to the major because he only looked out the window."

Then because of my own five years of agony, of sleeping at night and in my dreams walking on two legs, then waking each morning to being crippled, of praying and willing myself out of bed to confront the day, of having to learn a new way to live after living nearly fifty years with a whole body—then, because of all this, I saw something I had never seen in the story, and I do not know whether Hemingway saw it when he wrote it or later or never, but there it was, there it is, and with passion and joy I looked up from the book, looked at the girls' faces and said: "This story is about healing too. The major keeps going to the machines. And he doesn't believe in them. But he gets out of his bed in the morning. He brushes his teeth, He shaves. He combs his hair. He puts on his uniform. He leaves the place where he lives. He walks to the hospital, and sits at the machines. Every one of those actions is a movement away from suicide. Away from despair. Look at him. Three days after his wife has died, he is in motion. He is sad. He will not get over this. And he will get over this. His hand won't be cured but someday he will meet another woman. And he will love her. Because he is alive."

The girls watched me, nodding their heads, those girls who had suffered and still suffered. But for now, on this Monday night, they sat on my couch, and happily watched me discover a truth; or watched a truth discover me, when I was ready for it.

Nominated by David Jauss, Joyce Carol Oates

THE LECTURES ON LOVE

by EDWARD HIRSCH

from THE PARIS REVIEW

1. Charles Baudelaire

These lectures afford me a great pleasure,
so thank you for coming. My subject is love
and my proposition is a simple one: erotic love,
which is, after all, a fatal form of pleasure,
closely resembles a surgical operation, or torture.
Forgive me if I sound ironic or cynical
but, I'm sure you'll agree, cynicism
is sometimes called for in discussing torture.

Act One, Scene One: The score is "Love."
The setting of a great operatic passion
At first the lovers have equal passion.
but, it turns out, one always seems to love
the other less. He, or she, is the surgeon
applying a scalpel to the patient, the victim.
I know because I have been that victim
though I have also been the torturer, the surgeon.

Can you hear those loud spasmodic sighs?
Who hasn't uttered them in hours of love?
Who hasn't drawn them from his (or her) lover?
It's sacrilegious to call such noises "ecstasy"
when they're really a species of decomposition,

surrendering to death. We can get drunk
on each other, but don't pretend being drunk
puts us in a sudden death-defying position.

Why are people so proud of that spellbound
look in the eyes, that stiffening between the legs?
Example One: She ran her hand down my legs
until I felt as if I'd been gagged and bound.
Example Two: She no longer gave me any pleasure,
nonetheless, I rested my hand on her nude body
almost casually, I leaned over and tasted her body
until her whole being trembled with pleasure.

The erotic is an intimate form of cruelty
and every pleasure can be used to prostitute
another: I love you, so I become your prostitute
but my generosity is your voluptuous cruelty.
Sex is humiliation, a terrifying game
in which one partner loses self-control.
The subject concerns ownership or control
and that makes it an irresistible game.

I once heard the question discussed:
Wherein consists love's greatest pleasure?
I pondered the topic with great pleasure
but the whole debate filled me with disgust.
Someone declared, *We love a higher power.*
Someone said, *Giving is better than receiving,*
though someone else returned, *I prefer receiving.*
No one there ever connected love to power.

Someone actually announced, *The greatest pleasure
in love is to populate the State with children.*
But must we really be no better than children
whenever we discuss the topic of pleasure?
Pain, I say, is inseparable from pleasure
and love is but an exquisite form of torture.
You need me, but I carry the torch for her . . .
Evil comes enswathed in every pleasure.

2. Heinrich Heine

Thank you, thank you ladies and gentlemen.
I have had myself carried here today
on what we may call my mattress-grave
where I have been entombed for years
(forgive me if I don't stand up this time)
to give a lecture about erotic love.

As a cripple talking about Eros,
a subject I've been giving up for years,
I know my situation (*this time he's
gone too far!*) is comical and grave.
But don't I still appear to be a man?
Hath not a Jew eyes, etc., at least today?

I am an addict of the human comedy
and I propose that every pleasure, esp. love,
is like the marriage of the French and Germans
or the eternal quarrel between Space and Time.
We are all creeping madly toward the grave
or leaping forward across the years.

(Me, I haven't been able to leap in years)
and bowing under the fiendish blows of Time.
All that can distract us—gentlemen, ladies—
is the splendid warfare between men and women.
I don't hesitate to call the struggle "love."
Look at me: my feverish body is a grave,

I've been living so long on a mattress-grave
That I scarcely even resemble a man,
but what keeps me going is the quest for love.
I may be a dog who has had his day
(admittedly a day that has lasted for years)
but I'm also a formidable intellect of our time

and I'm telling you nothing can redeem Time
or the evident oblivions of the grave
or the crippling paralysis of the years

except the usual enchantments of love.
That's why the night hungers for the day
and the gods—heaven help us—envy the human.

Ladies and gentlemen, the days pass into years
and the body is a grave filled with time.
We are drowning. All that rescues us is love.

3. Marquis de Sade

This is the first time I have given a lecture
on my favorite subject—the nature of love—
so thank you for courageously inviting me.
I hope you won't regret having invited me
when you hear what I think about erotic love.
These are provisional notes *towards* a lecture

since what I've prepared are some observations
which, forgive me, I will not attempt to prove
but which I offer as subjective testimony.
What I *will* claim for this evidentiary testimony
is its forthright honesty, which I cannot prove.
I offer you the candor of my observations,

and I trust I will not shock you too much
(or too little) by revealing the deep abyss
at the heart—the vertiginous core—of love.
We will always desecrate whatever we love.
Eroticism stands on the edge of an abyss:
Sex is not enough until it becomes too much.

Love is erotic because it is so dangerous.
I am an apostle of complete freedom who believes
other people exist to satisfy my appetites.
I am not ashamed to pursue those appetites
and I have the will to enact my cruel beliefs.
The greatest *liaisons* are always dangerous.

Exhibit Number One is an innocent specimen.
My niece has a face aureoled by grace,

43

a guileless soul, and a lily-white body.
I like to masturbate all over her body
and to enter behind while she says grace.
Her humiliation is a delicious specimen.

Exhibit Number Two takes place in church.
I sent my valet to purchase a young whore
and he dresses her as a sweet-faced num.
(Do I have any compunction about this? *None*.)
In a pew I sodomize the terrified whore
until she becomes a member of my church.

It takes courage to be faithful to desire—
not many have the nerve. I myself feed
from the bottom of a cesspool for pleasure
(and I have fed from her bottom with pleasure).
I say whosoever has the courage to feed
from the ass of his beloved will sate desire.

Please don't leave. My doctrine is *isolism*:
the lack of contact between human beings.
But strangle me and you shall touch me.
Spit in my face and you shall see me.
Suck my cock and you taste a human being.
Otherwise we are the subjects of isolism.

Forgive me if I speak with too much freedom.
I am nothing more than an old libertine
who believes in the sanctity of pleasure.
Suffering, too, is a noble form of pleasure
like the strange experience of a libertine.
I would release you to a terrible freedom.

4. Margaret Fuller

Thank you for attending this conversation on love.
I am going to argue in the Nineteenth Century
a woman can no longer be sacrificed for love.
The Middle Ages are over, ladies and gentlemen,

44

and I am going to argue in the Nineteenth Century
we are not merely wives, whores, and mothers.
The Middle Ages are over, gentleman. And ladies,
we can be sea captains, if you will.

We are not merely wives, whores, and mothers.
We can be lawyers, doctors, journalists,
we can now be sea captains, if you will.
What matters to us is our own fulfillment.

We can be lawyers, doctors, journalists
who write ourselves into the official scripts.
What matters to us is our own fulfillment.
It is time for Eurydice to call for Orpheus

and to sing herself into the official scripts.
She is no longer a stranger to her inheritance.
It is time for Eurydice to call for Orpheus
and to move the earth with her triumphant song.

She is no longer a stranger to her inheritance.
She, too, leaves her footprints in the sand
and moves the earth with her triumphant song.
God created us for the purpose of happiness.

She, too, leaves her footprints in the sand.
She, too, feels divinity within her body.
God created us for the purpose of happiness.
She is not the betrothed, the bride, the spouse.

She, too, feels divinity within her body.
Man and Woman are two halves of one thought.
She is not the betrothed, the bride, the spouse.
The sexes should prophesy to one another.

Man and Woman are two halves of one thought.
They are both on equal terms before the law.
The sexes should prophesy to one another.
My love is a love that cannot be crucified.

We are both on equal terms before the law.
Our holiest work is to transform the earth.
(My love is a love that cannot be crucified.)
The earth itself becomes a parcel of heaven.

Our holiest work is to transform the earth.
Thank you for attending this conversation on love.
The earth itself becomes a parcel of heaven.
A woman can no longer be sacrificed for love.

5. Giacomo Leopardi

Thank you for listening to this new poem
which Leopardi has composed for the occasion:
he regrets he cannot read it here himself
(he is, he suggests, but a remnant of himself),
especially on such an auspicious occasion.
He has asked me to present you with this poem:

Poetry Would Be a Way of Praising God if God Existed

Deep in the heart of night
I stood on a hill in wintertime
and stared up at the baleful moon.
I was terrified of finding myself
in the midst of nothing, myself
nothingness clarified, like the moon.
I was suffocating inside time,
contemplating the empty night

when a bell rang in the distance
three times, like a heart beating
in the farthest reaches of the sky.
The music was saturated with stillness.
I stood listening to that stillness
until it seemed to fill the sky.
The moon was like a heart beating
somewhere far off in the distance.

But there is no heart in a universe
of dying planets, infinite starry spaces.
Death alone is the true mother of Eros
and only love can revivify the earth.
Look at the sky canopied over earth:
it is a black sea pulsing without Eros,
a world of infinitely dead, starry spaces.
Love alone can redeem our universe.

6. Ralph Waldo Emerson

Thank you for coming to this lecture on love.
I have been told that in public discourse
my true reverence for intellectual discourse
has made me indifferent to the subject of love,
but I almost shrink at such disparaging words
since I believe love created the world.
What else, after all, perpetuates the world
except enacted love? I savor the words.

The study of love is a question of facts
and a matter of dreams, a dream that matters.
Lovers are scientist studying heavenly matters
while their bodies connect the sweetest facts.
Please don't blush when I speak of love
as the reunion of two independent souls
who have drifted since birth as lost souls
but now come together in eternal love.

There can be no love without natural sympathy.
Let's say you're a hunter who excels at business
(I'm aware this may be none of my business)
but for me it doesn't arouse much sympathy.
Let's say, however, you drink tea in the morning
and like to eat apple pie for breakfast;
we both walk through the country very fast
watching the darkness turn into early morning

and this creates a mutual bond between us
that leads to a soulful sharing of sabbaths.

The heart has its jubilees and sabbaths
when a fiery lightning strikes between us.
I do not shy away from the subject of sex
which is, after all, a principle of the universe
(it is also, alas, a principle of my verse)
since we are bound to each other through sex.

Look how the girls flirt with the boys
while the boys slowly encircle the girls.
The village shops are crowded with girls
lingering over nothing to talk with boys.
Romance is the beginning of celestial ecstasy,
an immortal hilarity, a condition of joy:
civilization itself depends on the joy
of standing beside ourselves with ecstasy.

Love is a bright foreigner, a foreign self
that must recognize me for what I truly am;
only my lover can understand me as I am
when I am struggling to create myself.
So, too, I must love you as you truly are—
but what is that? Under your cool visage
and coy exterior, your advancing age,
I sense the young passion of who you are.

The lover comes with something to declare—
such declarations affirm the nature of love.
Here is what the lover says to his love
in the heat of passion, this I declare:
My love for you is a voluptuous world
where the seasons appear as a bright feast.
We can sit together at this delicious feast.
Come lie down with me and devour the world.

7. Colette

My young friends, this is the final lecture,
though not the last word, on the subject of love,
so thank you for listening. It is my pleasure
to address a passion I know something about

(which is something, forgive me, I can't say about
all the previous lecturers)—not just pleasure,
but the unruly depths we describe as love.
Let's call our tête-à-tête, "A Modern Lecture."

My mother used to say, "Sit down, dear,
and don't cry. The worst thing for a woman
is her first man—the one who kills you.
After that, marriage becomes a long career."
Poor Sido! She never had another career
and she knew firsthand how love ruins you.
The seducer doesn't care about his woman,
even as he whispers endearments in her ear.

Never let anyone destroy your inner spirit.
Among all the forms of truly absurd courage
the recklessness of young girls is outstanding.
Otherwise there would be far fewer marriages
and even fewer affairs that overwhelm marriages.
Look at me: it's amazing I'm still standing
after what I went through with ridiculous courage.
I was made to suffer, but no one broke my spirit.

Every woman wants her adventure to be a feast
of ripening cherries and peaches, Marseilles figs,
hothouse grapes, champagne shuddering in crystal.
Happiness, we believe, is on sumptuous display.
But unhappiness writes a different kind of play.
The gypsy gazes down into a clear blue crystal
and sees rotten cherries and withered figs.
Trust me: loneliness, too, can be a feast.

Ardor is delicious, but keep your own room.
One of my husbands said: is it impossible
for you to write a book that isn't about love,
adultery, semi-incestuous relations, separation?
(Of course, this was before our own separation.)
He never understood the natural law of love,
the arc from the possible to the impossible . . .
I have extolled the tragedy of the bedroom.

We need exact descriptions of the first passion,
so pay attention to whatever happens to you.
Observe everything: love is greedy and forgetful.
By all means fling yourself wildly into life
(though sometimes you will be flung back by life)
but don't let experience make you forgetful
and be surprised by everything that happens to you.
We are creative creatures fueled by passion.

Consider this an epilogue to the lectures on love,
a few final thoughts about the nature of love.
Freedom should be the first condition of love
and work is liberating (*a novel about love
cannot be written while you are making love*).
Never underestimate the mysteries of love,
the eminent dignity of not talking about love.
Passionate attention is prayer, prayer is love.

Savor the world. Consume the feast with love.

Nominated by The Paris Review, Sherod Santos, Arthur Smith, Susan Wheeler

THE REVENANT

fiction by EDWARD FALCO

from THE SOUTHERN REVIEW

FIRST, A TEENAGE GIRL FLASHED ME at a Marilyn Manson concert. I had agreed to take Vee, my daughter, only reluctantly; I didn't want to spring for a pair of twenty-five-dollar tickets and take her to the civic center way over in Roanoke for the concert. I didn't know much about fourteen-year-olds' music, but I knew enough that there was no way I was going to let her go alone—and it was either that or tie her down. So I found myself at a Marilyn Manson concert, and while I was there among several hundred tough-guy teens waiting for the show to begin, this girl flashed me.

She couldn't have been more than fifteen. She wore a bright red choker. I was standing a few feet away from Vee, at the edge of a crowd that thickened into a knot of bodies near the front of the stage—which appeared to be about a mile and half away. I must have looked like a security guard or a bouncer, standing rigid with my arms crossed over my chest, watching the crowd intently, my eyes going back and forth from Vee to the intermittent spectacle of someone lifted over the throng and passed along on waves of hands until he or she fell, usually head first, into a gap in the tight surface of bodies. I'm six three, 280 pounds, built solid. I've always worked out, since I was a boy in Brooklyn and discovered I could avoid trouble if I looked like only a fool would mess with me. The kids were keeping their distance and looking elsewhere—except for this one girl. She was about eight feet away, her back to the stage; and she looked right through me, the line of her vision crossing my body about neck level. The way her eyes were focused, it was like I wasn't there, though she couldn't help but see me.

She was looking at me. She had short hair, a thin, attractive face, and a lanky body. No breasts to speak of. A black T-shirt with the word HOLE in plain white lettering enclosed in a white circle. Baggy pants she seemed to swim in. A dazed, I'm-not-here look in her eyes.

We stood there, she with her hands thrust deep in her pockets, I with my arms crossed over my chest. We were two points of silence in a mass of squeals and shouts that coalesced to a hollow din. I had just looked away from her, back toward Vee. I was feeling an uncomfortably familiar anxiety, one I hadn't felt in a while, but had almost every waking moment in Vietnam; a pervasive sense of danger somewhere within what I was seeing but invisible to me, as if the source were going to suddenly materialize and I had better be looking in the right place when it did. I couldn't quit scanning, searching. When I turned back toward the girl, she pushed her pants down to mid-thigh and pulled them up again quickly—and then just remained there staring through me with that lost look. It happened so fast I wasn't sure it happened at all, but the image burned itself instantly into my memory. She wore black panties that narrowed to strings across her hips and contrasted sharply with her fair skin. The triangle of black fabric was pulled to one side and ran in a dark line down the center of a sunny thatch of blond hair. My mind reacted to the sight like a strip of film. She was both the camera snapping the picture and the picture itself. I registered the image, and it remains burned in place to this moment.

I wondered if she expected me to do something. I had turned fifty the week before. She was a child. I looked into her eyes. Her gaze remained blank as she backed into the crowd and disappeared.

Vee approached me. "Do you have to just stand here like this?" Her face was bunched tight with anger, her lips a thin line, her eyes squinting.

"Deals' a deal," I said. We had agreed on everything beforehand. She could come to the concert as long as I came with her. She could stand with the crowd rather than sit in the stands, as long as I was nearby and she stayed near the edge. No going anywhere near the mosh pit. This was, after all, a band in which every performer was named after a serial killer. I said, "Just pretend I'm not here."

"Right," she spit out, and stomped away.

A moment later the lights went down, and an evening of almost unbearable sound commenced. I couldn't believe the volume of the music. Literally, it was shocking. The sound pummeled me, every thump of the bass a jab to the body. Relentless, overwhelming sound. After three hours, I was exhausted—and pissed off. When the lights finally went up and the general din resumed, I headed for the exit with Vee, who seemed to have forgotten momentarily how upset she was that I had insisted on taking her to the concert. She was pumped up, like all the other kids filing out of the civic center in a thick stream of dyed hair and pierced body parts. She floated along a few steps in front of me, and I could see her searching the crowd, hoping to find someone she knew, someone with whom she could share her excitement.

Then the next thing happened.

A group of three guys and one girl came along, walking against the flow of the crowd, and the girl recognized Vee. She squealed and took Vee by the hand and pulled her out of the line. The boys apparently didn't know Vee. They scowled and stood back and waited. I stepped out of the crowd, and one of the boys looked toward me and our eyes met. The girl was chattering about the concert and embracing Vee, who appeared slightly nervous and awkward. The boy said, "What are you looking at, Fuckhead?" and then he spit on me. He might have been sixteen, maybe seventeen. A high-school kid. He was scrawny, almost as tall as me, and like many of the boys that night, he was shirtless. He was built wiry and tight. I leapt toward him, and the fool stepped into my punch. One instant he was standing, full of himself; the next he was out cold on his back, bleeding from the nose and mouth. I grabbed Vee roughly by the arm and pulled her away.

Vee never said a word to me that night. Nothing. In the car on the way home she sat in the backseat, silent, for the hour-long drive. I didn't ask her who the girl was. I didn't ask her anything. Something was going on. First a girl flashed me; then I knocked out a kid; a boy; and by the time I was sitting in the dark of the car, driving home on a narrow country road under a bright full moon, I knew something was happening.

When I first got back from Vietnam, I wasn't all together—though nothing much happened to me there. Compared to some other guys, to most other guys, I was lucky. I saw some things, yes. And there were images that seemed to hunt me, stalking me and coming vividly to life when I least wanted to see them; the wrecked, bloody face of my lieutenant; the body of a young woman draped over a tree limb like an article of clothing hung to dry. She was naked. Something happened when I saw her. I came upon her in a small clearing, slanted shafts of sunlight filtering through a porous roof of leaves. I walked right up to

53

her. Her breasts were small, barely developed, the nipples puffy. I couldn't help looking at her, noticing the shapeliness of her calves and thighs, my eyes focusing a long moment on her sex. Her throat had been cut in a fat red line from shoulder to shoulder, and there was a circle on the ground where the dirt had soaked up her blood. And there were other things, other images . . . But it was six months maybe, at the most, that I was messed up, before I got it together.

I dealt with it. You can let things destroy you, you can let them eat you alive—or you can *master* them, you can *command* them. And you can get on with your life.

I was twenty-four when I got home. I had been to college; I had my degree. Useless, granted. In anthropology. A no-name college. But I had finished. I had done my turn in the service. Six months, maybe, I was a mess, before I met June, my first wife, and put my life together. I got a decent job with the phone company, which turned into a decent career. With June's work we made enough money to get a nice house. We did OK. I did OK. The marriage didn't last, but I'm not alone there. At least we never had kids to make it more complicated.

Those six months though . . . It feels like I spent most of them driving. I couldn't get myself together. I just couldn't. Nights, I'd wake up at four A.M. Every night, weeks in a row. Most nights, my stomach would be aching, a deep, generalized pain, a cramp that wouldn't let go. I'd take a shower and let the hot water run over my chest and stomach. I can see myself in that narrow box, which was lined with white tiles and had a bright light that shone into it so that my memory of it is this bright vision: my pink, naked body, the wide bulk of it leaning back so that the top of my head touched the tiles and the pulsing stream hit my belly. I'd writhe under the hot water. It helped, but not enough. Eventually I'd dry off and dress and get in the car and drive till the pain finally stopped, which usually took three or four hours. I drove thousands of miles that way. Thousands.

After I married June, I never had another four A.M. stomachache. They just stopped. I had gotten my life going again. I was back on track. Things went well with my job. I got raises and promotions. If I ask myself now whether I was happy then, I can't answer. I think I was happy. I know I wasn't tortured anymore by Vietnam, which I came to think of as a place where my life had gotten derailed for a brief time. I got past it. Even when June left me, I handled it OK. She had gotten involved with a consciousness-raising group. They thought of themselves as feminists. I thought of them as a group of angry, unhappily married women, and I was upset and worried when June took up with them. Turned out I was right to be worried. Suddenly I was getting the whole antimale litany, night after night: I was uncommunicative, unresponsive, an insensitive lover, and on and on. She lives in Washington state now. She's married again and has two boys. She sent me a picture once. Her husband wore a yellow ascot.

But a couple of months after she left, I met Marcy, and everything was back on track again.

The night of the concert, Vee fell asleep sobbing. Marcy and I could hear her from our bedroom, where we lay side by side, rigid and awake, both of us looking at the ceiling. Vee is our only child. Marcy couldn't believe I had knocked out a high-school kid. "You humiliated her," she had said when I told her.

My stomach hurt. It was a warm night, mid-May. The windows were open; the ceiling fan revolved lethargically. Marcy lay beside me with her eyes open. She's a big woman, almost as tall as me. She's vulnerable and acutely sensitive at times, which is precisely how she doesn't look. She appears to be stern and angry. A disciplinarian. The third-grade teacher everyone hated. It's worry that makes her look this way. She worries about everything.

When Vee finally stopped sobbing, Marcy said: "She just wants to be alive. She just wants to live her life."

"Really?" I turned on my side and leaned close to her. "The kid spit on me," I said. "He *spit* on me."

Marcy crossed her arms over her eyes. She turned away.

I hovered over her, and I realized my hand was clenched into a fist. I wanted to hit her. I had never struck a woman, and yet I knew what I was feeling. I wanted to grab her by the throat. I wanted to hurt her, and the desire to do so swelled within me like something wild that needed to be turned loose.

I slid away, got out of bed. I put on clothes and went out the sliding glass door to our bedroom deck. The air was still. It was a little after one, a Friday morning. Our deck looks out over a line of suburban backyards: maple trees, elms, basswoods, oaks, all surrounded by neatly mown grass, picket fences, red-brick patios and walkways. Our nearest neighbor had just put a stone bench under the oak in the center of his yard, with an in-ground light illuminating the area. All the houses had sentry lights that stayed on all night, relegating the darkness to corners and the shadows of things. Most nights I would have thought the view was peaceful and quiet, ordered and lovely; but that night I found the stillness frightening. I was sweating, and I felt like I needed to run. I needed to get out of there. The stillness was suddenly somehow loud. The lack of movement felt like lack of air, felt like I was suffocating. I couldn't breathe right. I shook my head and tried to laugh it off, but I found that my eyes were full of tears. I was crying. I was crying, and I hadn't realized it.

I don't have the words to explain the intensity of what I felt out there on the deck that night. It was if this feeling had come out of nowhere, risen up out of the stillness, this terrifying sense, like fear multiplied and squared. I absolutely did not know what was happening. I thought for a moment that I might have been drugged—but the only thing I drank at the concert was a Pepsi, and that out of a can. The feeling was huge; it altered the world. I had this sense that everything I saw was painted on a canvas: the world itself was a painting on a canvas, and I could see it wavering. I could see the corners beginning to curl. I laughed. I wiped tears out of my eyes with the back of my arm. From inside, Marcy called my name. "Jeff?" she said. "Jeffrey?"

I went into the bedroom and knelt beside her.

"You're crying," she said. She looked scared.

I shook my head.

"Yes you are," she said. She wiped a tear off my cheek.

"I'm going for a drive."

"A drive?" She sat up. She looked startled. "It's one in the morning!"

I explained as best I could. I told her something was happening, I didn't know what. I needed to get in the car and drive. She tried to dissuade me. She tried to get me back into bed. She wouldn't let go of my arm until I yanked it away from her. Then I took my wallet from the night table and the car keys from the hook by the kitchen window, and I drove away with Marcy standing in a pool of yellow light outside our front door, her hands clasped together as if in prayer.

Friday evening found me sleeping fitfully in an Atlanta hotel. I had driven through the night without much thought to where I was heading, and by the time the sun came up I was in Georgia, following the signs to Atlanta. In the car, in the dark, driving in the company of massive tractor-trailers, I had cried for a few hours before falling into the soothing, hypnotic trance of long-term driving. I didn't know why I was crying. I didn't know what I was doing. I was just driving, moving. In the morning I thought about stopping to call home, but I didn't know yet what I would say. I thought I might have had an anxiety attack out on the deck. I thought that might explain it. Something about the concert—the overwhelming noise, the girl dropping her pants, my hitting that kid—had brought it on. I needed to ride it out. I'd be fine. And by the time I drove into Atlanta, I was feeling a lot better, though still shaky. I got off an exit that led to Spring Street, and Spring Street led to a parking garage, which led in turn to a high-rise hotel, where I checked in and took a room on the twenty-first floor.

The key to my room was a card with a magnetic strip. When I slid it through a slot on the door handle, a green light came on, and the door unlocked. Inside I found a massive bed and a writing table, and a back wall that was all glass and led out to a narrow balcony overlooking the city. I stood on the balcony a while and gazed upon the cityscape: the intertwining strips of highway clogged with morning traffic, the array of tall buildings, including one that looked like a spaceship perched atop a column. It reminded me of something out of the Jetsons. I felt good out on the balcony, a dry breeze ruffling my hair. I was definitely feeling better. There was nothing of the panic from the night before. I went back inside and pulled the curtain, darkening the room. I stripped and got into the bed. In a few moments I was sleeping.

By the time I woke up, it was dark again; and when I opened the curtains, I found a nighttime panorama. The spaceship building was a soft blue circle surrounded by the glittering lights of the skyline. Long lines of red and white tail- and headlights moved along the highways. Twenty-one floors up, the noise of traffic was the principal sound; a loud, windy rush. As I stood on the balcony watching and listening, I felt as though I were waking from a very long sleep. And I *was* just waking from several hours of restless sleep—but it felt like something more than that. It felt like Rip Van Winkle. I said aloud, "Sleepy Hollow." Then I thought about Marcy and Vee, and for a moment I was out-and-out shocked at myself, at what I'd done, getting in the car and driving away from them, abandoning them. What could they be thinking? I wondered if they might not have called the police by now. In seventeen years of marriage I had been a model of loyalty and faithfulness—and then I just up and disappear. What could they be thinking? What was *I* thinking?

I went back into my room, sliding the glass door closed behind me, shutting out the traffic noise and replacing it with the loud drone of a fan. I sat on the bed and picked up the phone, intending to call home, intending to apologize to Marcy, intending to explain that something had happened to me, something I didn't understand. I had panicked

57

and fallen back on an old habit of driving, and I had wound up here in Atlanta, in this hotel where I was calling from, and everything would be OK, would be fine, I'd be home again in a few hours. I was sorry. I was very sorry. I picked up the phone, carefully read the directions. I punched 8 for an outside line; then I hit 1; then I entered my area code; but by the time I got to my number, I knew it wasn't over, whatever it was that was happening, this wave that had picked me up and was carrying me along. I put the phone back in the cradle. I straightened myself out and left the room. Then I was back in my car and driving around downtown Atlanta.

The evening was just beginning. Men and women strolled along city streets, looking like they weren't going anywhere in particular. I guessed because of the hour that most of them were heading to dinner somewhere, some restaurant. I drove around for a couple of hours, looking. At one point I found myself driving through a series of poorly lit, empty streets, a place in the center of the city but hidden away somehow; useless reality, back streets, back entrances to buildings. I was driving slowly, had been driving slowly all evening. I probably looked like I was cruising, looking for action, because a man walked out of the shadows in front of the car and motioned me to stop. He was dressed in beige pants with red shoes and black shirt under a bright yellow jacket. He was an explosion of color walking out of the dark, and it wasn't hard to guess what he would offer if I stopped: drugs or sex, sex or drugs. I didn't stop. I drove past him, and when I came to an entrance ramp, I took it.

The highway was thick with traffic. I imagined someone looking down at me from a hotel balcony: now I was one of the gliding lines of red and white lights. I drove for a half-hour, forty-five minutes, and then exited, meaning to turn around and head back to the city, maybe back to the hotel. I was thinking that I had to call Marcy. I had to at least let her know I was OK, even if I couldn't tell her what I was doing because I didn't yet know myself. I could at least call her. I could at least try to explain. I drove by a shopping plaza where two police cars were parked with blue lights flashing in front of a long, windowless building that looked like a factory or a bowling alley. The parking lot in front was crowded. Along the curb, there was a line of motorcycles. While I watched, the police put two guys into the back of a car and drove away. A small group of young men in tuxedos walked through a thick red door into the white building. Over the door, in red neon script, were the words: *The Gentlemen's Club*. I pulled into the lot. One of the tuxedos came back out and stood alongside the door with his arms crossed.

I guessed it was a strip bar, a club with exotic dancers, girls who stood on your table and took off their clothes while you gawked. Why I pulled into the lot then, why I parked and got out of the car and started for the entrance, was a mystery to me. I wasn't especially interested in sex. I hadn't been in many years. In high school and college, I was interested enough. Those years, the late '60s, sex seemed all anyone was interested in: it was as if the whole nation entered adolescence simultaneously. Sex this and sex that, on television, in movies, in books and magazines. I slept with several women then, though I couldn't remember many particulars. It had been almost thirty years. A couple of years into my first marriage, desire just about disappeared. June and I had sex maybe once every couple of months, and then it was fast and, as June loudly complained years later, unsatisfying. With Marcy, the lack of much desire for sex was one of the things that made us compatible. Ever since Vee was born, it had been a once-in-a-blue-moon thing.

So why was I stopping at a sex club? I didn't know. Best I could make out, it was like a wave I was riding, and that was where it took me. I walked past the guy in the tuxedo, who nodded pleasantly. I passed through the red door into a place that was like nothing I had ever seen. I felt as though I had walked through a crack in the culture's armor and wound up in a place where all the rules were in suspension: the place was Dionysian, Bacchanalian. Music screamed. Women stood on tabletops, naked or on their way to being naked. More women strutted around the barroom. In a far corner, elevated a few feet above the crowd, a black mechanical bull bucked and swayed, impaled on a silvery hydraulic tube, ridden by a woman dressed only in her skin and a mane of waist-length red hair that flew around her with the gyrations of the bull. When I first saw the bull and the woman, I stopped and gaped. I think my mouth might have actually been hanging open. While I watched, a boy climbed up and handed some bills to a guy in a tuxedo, and the bull stopped bucking for a moment while the boy settled himself in the saddle. The dancer stood in front of him grasping the pole in both hands, her feet wedged under the saddle, her waist at the level of the boy's head. A large group of young men began to yowl and hoot, and then the bull began to buck, tossing the boy forward and back. With each forward toss, the dancer thrust her pelvis toward the boy, who was pulled away from her by the motion of the

59

bull; and with each backward toss, the boy would lunge for her sex, his mouth open, while she expertly kept herself inches away. The more the bull bucked, the louder the crowd yowled.

I watched for a while, until the pure shock of what I was seeing dissipated, and then I made my way toward the bar, above which a woman was swinging on a trapeze suspended from the ceiling, taking off her clothes one article at a time and tossing them down onto the bartender to the amusement of the drinkers. I stood for several minutes behind a guy with a Semper Fidelis tattoo on his bicep, until a waitress in a tuxedo jacket and a bikini bottom approached and took my order for a drink. She explained that all the tables were currently occupied, but as soon as one was available, I could take a seat. A dancer would come and perform for me. Until then I could stand and watch or I could sit and watch. She pointed to a line of cushioned benches that ran along one wall. When she walked away, I saw that she was wearing a thong. I watched her until she was out of sight, then carried my drink to the back of the room and took a seat on a bench.

I observed the scene—attractive women walking around in various degrees of nakedness; mostly very young men, boys really, shouting and waving bills at the women, who came to them and let them place the bills under garters; naked women gyrating on tabletops, swinging from trapezes, riding mechanical bulls—with an attitude somewhere between numbed shock and amusement. I didn't know what I was doing there, at The Gentleman's Club. I was watching. I was having a drink. In a minute, I thought, I'd get back into my car and drive to the hotel, and I'd call Marcy and tell her I was coming home. I took a sip of my drink, about to put it on the floor, slide it under the bench, and head out; and then I noticed that across from me, maybe ten feet away, where a dozen guys were sitting in a line on the bench, there was a waitress. I assumed she was a waitress because she was wearing the same tuxedo outfit as the girl from whom I had ordered my drink. She had a cute, girlish face, with short dark hair cut in a bob, and she sat on the bench with the line of men, chatting with the guy next to her. A girl dressed in jeans and a T-shirt sat on the floor at her feet, between her open legs. While the waitress chatted with the guy, the girl on the floor nuzzled between her legs. From the motion of the girl's head, she appeared to be licking the waitress. Every once in a while she'd stop, and she too would talk with the guy, as if taking a momentary break from what she was doing to throw in a few words of conversation. This was so strange it shook me up. I began to feel frightened and anxious again—because I found it hard to believe that what I was watching was actually happening. Now and again the waitress would close her eyes and throw her back against the wall and hold the girl's head in her hands, pulling her deeper between her legs. This was in a crowded barroom. This was with scores of people milling around. Part of me wanted to cross the room and touch them, just to see if they were real. Instead, I put my drink on the floor and walked casually out of the bar.

Outside, I felt wildly disoriented. I stepped into the spring air, out of the wailing music and into the parking lot of a place that looked like any suburban mall anywhere, and for a moment I couldn't remember where I was; and before it came back to me—Atlanta, The Gentleman's Club, the hotel—I was pale and sweaty and nauseated. In the car, back on the highway, the feeling evolved into fear as intense as it was at home the night before on my bedroom deck. My arms were stiff, and my body was tight and cramped. I drove back to my hotel and got undressed and lay a long while naked under the covers. I was sweating. There was something physical going on inside me. I didn't know what it was. Through the glass I could hear the muffled sound of the traffic, like a reminder: *you're in Atlanta; you're not at home,* and I'd have to think to remember how I got where I was. I felt as though I were coming apart, as though something inside me was unraveling, something that had once been wound tight and secure.

I lay in bed for hours, willing my mind blank, before the fear began to dissipate. It happened slowly. It ebbed out of me. It left me feeling opened up and vulnerable. I was wide awake. It was a little after one in the morning. I told myself that I was having an episode of craziness. That was the only way to explain it. An episode of weirdness. I wished it weren't happening, but it was. I'd figure it out. I'd handle it. I'd ride it out, and then I'd get it together again, the way I always had, the way I knew I could. I kicked off my blankets and turned on the light, and I was startled by the sight of my naked body stretched out on the bed. It must have been a very long time since I had looked at myself naked. I felt as though I were confronting a stranger. My body was pale and doughy, an unhealthy hue of white. I touched the soft mound of my belly and pushed my fingers into the thick mat of hair that surrounded my penis. The room was bright. The sheets were white. I touched my eyes and my temples and my cheeks, as if I were a blind man trying to recognize someone. I touched my knees and my thighs and the place under my scrotum where my legs came together. I held my scrotum in the palm of my hand, and my penis rose quickly, stiff and hard, and

61

I looked at it swollen there against my stomach with something like a sense of wonder. I couldn't remember the last time I had masturbated. Not in years, many years. I sat on the edge of the bed and pondered the possibility of masturbating like a man considering the terms of a difficult equation; and while I thought about it, the erection disappeared.

I went out on the balcony. I stayed there a long time, naked, looking over the city. It's awfully hard to explain this. It was like, out there, I was in a maze, and I was trying to find the right turn. It's like there was a problem set before me, and I was experimenting with solutions. Only I didn't understand the problem. I couldn't see the maze. I knew I had to do something. I had no idea why or what. People out of their minds talk about wires implanted in their heads, controlling them, making them do stuff. That's what it was like. I was not in control. Things were moving me; I felt like a marionette—but in some way I knew that I myself was the hand pulling the strings making me move. I went into the room, and the way I remember what happened next is this: I sat on the bed, intending to call Marcy, to call home. I hesitated, trying to figure out what I would say, how I would explain myself to Marcy and Vee, and while I was hesitating, I pulled out the night-table drawer, where there was a thick phone book, a Yellow Pages. I opened it at random and found myself looking through several pages of advertisements for escort services. Now, this seems hard to believe, the way so much of what happened seems incredible to me now. But that's how I remember it. I opened the Yellow Pages, and I was looking at ads for escort services.

The one I called wanted to know where I needed an escort at three in the morning. I said it was a private party. I said it was in my hotel room. When she asked what kind of an escort I wanted, I said young. When she asked how she should dress, I said casual. I said jeans and a T-shirt would do. I said thin is preferable. I said she doesn't have to have much in the way of breasts. She laughed. There's a switch, she said. Then we worked out the payment. I gave her my credit card number. When I hung up, I went back out on the balcony. I didn't bother to get dressed, and a half-hour later my escort arrived. I opened the door in response to her knock. She took one look at me, and a smirk crossed her face. She made a sound somewhere between a snort and a laugh, then sauntered past me into the room. She said, "Not much for formalities, are you?" She gestured toward the door, which I was holding open, and the look on her face said *Well? Are you going to close it?* I closed the door and leaned back against it, and for a moment we just looked each other over. I asked for young, and they sent young: she looked to be in her early twenties. She was small, maybe five three, five four at the most, with heavy, round breasts that pushed against the fabric of a black, official Disney World Minnie Mouse T-shirt. Minnie was pictured in bright red and white, her arms akimbo and a look of reproach on her face. There was a caption; I forget what it said. At first I was upset about the size of her breasts—but it passed.

I cleared my throat. I didn't know what to say. I was standing there naked in front of a stranger, and I remember that I didn't feel awkward at all. I looked into her eyes. She had a face that would have been beautiful if it weren't marred by toughness, by an orneriness that made her look as though she might turn her head and spit on the floor at any moment. She had short black hair that lay flat over her forehead and angled down toward the back of her neck, barely covering her ears. She had dark eyes and a round face. She stood with her arms crossed under her breasts and one knee bent, adding to her I'm tough, I've-seen-everything look. All she needed was a toothpick between her teeth to complete the image. "Well," she said, her voice gentler than her appearance, "at least I know you're not a cop." She had a southern accent. I couldn't tell if she was putting it on or not. She said, "Where are you from, honey?" She sat on the bed and started to take off her shoes, which were sneakers, white. Nikes. When I didn't answer, she went on. "You know," she said, "what you want will be another 250 in cash. That's over what you've already paid." She paused then, watching me, one leg crossed over the other, holding a sneaker dangling from her finger by its heel.

I said, "What is it I want?" I thought she might know something I didn't.

She made that laugh-snort sound again. She said, "You have the money, darling? It has to be cash."

I shook my head. I didn't. I didn't have anywhere near 250 in cash.

She put her sneaker back on. She said, "Well, you better get dressed then. For what you paid, I'll go have a cup of coffee with you. That's all."

"That's OK," I said. "You can go. I don't know why I called."

She looked perplexed. "Honey," she said. "You're stark raving naked. Why do you *think* you called?"

"I don't know," I said. "You can just go ahead and go." I walked past her, toward the balcony. When I slid open the glass door, she said

"Wait," and she got up from the bed and touched my arm. I stopped. I stood in the open door with a breeze blowing comfortably against my bare skin.

"What?" I said, "You can go. I'm sorry I called. Honestly. I don't know why I did." I covered my eyes with my hands. I sighed. "I'm out of my mind," I said. "I'm having some kind of period of craziness or something." I rubbed my eyes. "You can go," I said. "Really. I'm sorry."

She stepped back and looked me over. She seemed partly annoyed and partly troubled. She said, "Do you . . . Is it that . . . I mean, do you like women to see you naked?"

I shook my head.

"I didn't think so." She looked down. "You don't appear especially excited."

"Go ahead and go," I said. "I'm sorry . . . " I looked down at myself. "I'm sorry I'm naked," I said. I gestured toward the door, and then I turned my back on her and went out on the balcony.

I stepped to the railing, grasped the wrought iron in my hands. I was looking down. At the moving lines of red and white lights. I looked directly below me, at an empty side street, dark in the moonlight.

She came out on the balcony behind me. She took my arm in her hand and pulled me toward her, turning me around to face her. She lost the southern accent. "Honey," she said. "You're not going to do anything crazy, are you?" She said, "You're not thinking about jumping or anything, are you?"

"No," I said. "I'm not thinking about jumping." My voice was shaky.

She took my arm. She touched me gently. "What is it with men?" she said. "What happens to you guys?" She touched my cheek. "Come here," she said. She stepped into me. She put one of my hands on her back and held it there, then put my other arm around her shoulder. "Dance with me a while," she said. "It'll make you feel better." She pressed her cheek against my chest. She held me in her arms, and her body began to sway, moving gently from side to side.

I only resisted for a moment. Then I leaned into her.

"I like dancing," she whispered. She touched the back of my neck with her fingertips. "Dancing always makes me feel better."

I tried to say something in response, but I couldn't talk.

"That's OK," she said. "Just dance with me."

I did. We danced an hour or more, silent at first but then talking a bit back and forth. By the time she left, the Atlanta night was fading into paleness, and the outlines of buildings were emerging from the dark. She told me her name was Sally. She told me she had two children, the first when she was fourteen. She told me that she loved dancing—just standing someplace alone and swaying to whatever music she could conjure. Something about it, she said.

After she left, I got in bed and fell asleep soundly.

When I finally got home, no one was there. I had driven back to Virginia through downpours and thunder. In North Carolina, with dusk coming on, I saw a lightning bolt hit a telephone pole, sending pieces of a transformer sailing in flames. By the time I pulled up in front of my house, it was late, and there hadn't been a storm for a while, but the wind was still gusting the way it does in thunderstorms; quiet for a time, then building and building right to the edge of being frightening. It didn't take me a second to figure out no one was home. There were no lights on. The driveway was empty. I had taken off and disappeared for thirty-six hours without so much as a phone call. I figured Marcy was in Alexandria with her sister. I could see her there at the kitchen table with her sister and her sister's husband, and her parents, who lived nearby, and maybe even her sister's husband's parents, who lived two houses over. They were all close. *We* had all once been close. I imagined them sitting around the table, talking: a family conference, the proffering of support and love. Vee would be upstairs with her cousin. There'd be music on. She'd probably still be talking about the concert.

Once inside, I wandered through the house, going from room to room, picking up things here and there—a knickknack, a picture, a book—and looking it over as if it held a secret I had forgotten. I opened the fridge and rummaged through it, rearranging bottles and red and blue food containers. I found an unopened plastic bottle of water. I broke off the cap, then held the bottle over my lips and squeezed it, shooting a jet of spring water into the back of my mouth. It tasted good. I took another long drink and carried the bottle with me to my bedroom, where I sat on the bed and noticed for the first time the envelope on my pillow. It was beige, same color as the bedspread. It blended in. Had I turned on the lights, I would have seen it right away. But I hadn't. The house was mostly dark.

I didn't open the envelope right away. I knew there would be a letter inside. I figured I knew most of what it would say. As soon as I walked into the house, I knew that everything had changed. I could feel it. Like an emptiness. In one sense it was sudden. In another, it was a long time coming. I went out on the balcony and stood in the gusting wind. I left the door open, and the wind blew into the house. I could hear curtains rustling. In another room, a door slammed. I was just beginning to have the faintest glimmering of what was happening to me. Now that I've gone back over things many times, I have some better ideas. But then, on the balcony, I was struggling. I felt as if I were closing in on something, as if the first pieces of a puzzle were about to fall into place. I knew it started with the concert, with the girl, and I reviewed what had happened, picturing her, and it occurred to me then I might have imagined the incident. Not imagined it: hallucinated it. It occurred to me that I might have created her—though I can still see her image vividly. She was like a switch that triggered the whole episode. I thought I might have taken down that girl from her tree in Vietnam, clothed and altered her and placed her among the concert crowd. She would have been the right age. I thought, maybe, twenty-five years ago her naked body was like a switch that turned off something inside me. Maybe, I thought, twenty-five years later she returned. I'd believe she was a ghost, if I believed in ghosts, which I don't. But if I did, I'd be convinced of it. Picture her. Think of how silent she was. Her small breasts. Her red necklace like the tattoo of a wound.

I wanted to push the notion out of my mind, and for a time, that night, I did. I got rid of it. It was a crazy idea. I had nothing to do with that girl's body winding up draped over a tree limb—or no more at least than anyone else who was alive at the time. As far as what happened to her was concerned, I might as well have not been there. I might as well have been protesting the war in front of the Pentagon. I had nothing to do with it. I wasn't there when it happened. I had no idea who did it or why. It was just something I saw. I was on patrol, and I saw it, and that was all. I had no more direct involvement than some hippie in San Francisco, some priest in New York, anyone who was alive in 1969, anyone who's ever paid taxes, or shopped in a supermarket, or laid down fifty bucks for a pair of jeans. I would have stopped it if I could. I wasn't there when it happened. It was just something I saw, passing by.

But seeing it did something to me. That much was clear. That much, out on the balcony that night, I accepted. It was like the first piece of a puzzle had fallen into place. I'm still working on it. It's a puzzle about the body—my body, that girl's. There's a connection. It's not about guilt or responsibility, though that's there, that's one of the pieces. But it's something different, it's something more. My hand and hers. My throat and her throat. Our bodies. The music did something to me: the volume and the intensity. The violence did something, my punching that boy. I didn't understand then, I still don't entirely now.

But that night in my empty house, when I first realized I might have hallucinated the girl at the concert, it was electric, sparks were snapping inside me. The wind gusted, blew through the house. For a moment I sensed the beginning of fear: it was like a fist closing around my heart. Instead of running, I let my body rock a little bit. I let it sway. That helped. That made things better. In Atlanta, while I danced with Sally, the city blazed around us, the blue light on the skyline turning lazily, the red lights of the cars merging into a glistening line that looped and spun. When we turned, the stars and the moon whirled. At one point in our dancing, I pressed my lips to Sally's hair and whispered that I loved her. It was crazy, I knew it. Immediately I said, "I'm sorry. I'm so sorry." She rubbed my back. She kept dancing. She said. "It's OK, really. It's OK." She kissed my chest. I held her. I held her tightly, and I blessed her. I blessed her and begged her forgiveness, holding her tightly as we danced.

Nominated by Steve Yarbrough

GRANDMOTHER, DEAD AT 99 YEARS AND 10 MONTHS

by WILLIAM MATTHEWS

from POETRY

Everyone cheered her on
like a race horse
to make a hundred,
but when I asked
how she felt, she said,
without pause, "Old."
Two by two the young
with their ambitious
jitters bought the houses
her friends died out of.
The village ate and ate
and cleared its plate.

"Dearie, what are you doing
here?" her husband asked me
one Thanksgiving long ago
(thirty years?) in the garage,
each of us bearing a flute
of champagne, Veuve Clicquot.
I loved him and so told
the truth. "Hiding." "Me, too,"

he said; "I want to bring
us all together here,
but the garage is part of here."
And too soon he was dead.

Like the widow Clicquot
she amazed the menfolk
and, more gallingly, outlived them,
including two of her three sons.
Tough as a turtle, everyone
said, but if she fell on her back . . . .
She'd lost control of her
bowels, checkbook and legs,
and everyone cheered her on.
I raised a glass
to her truant kidney
and to oblivion.

Nominated by Diann Blakely, Richard Jackson, Laura Kasischke, Philip Levine,
Gibbons Ruark, Arthur Smith, Michael Waters

THE TURKEY STORIES

essay by JULIE SHOWALTER

from NEW ENGLAND REVIEW

1. *Baby Turkeys*

Baby turkeys, unlike puppies or kittens, are most charming during their first days—bright-eyed and energetic, soft and fluffy, ready to take on the world they just pecked their way into. They feel like powder puffs when you hold them against your face. Their hearts vibrate a staccato and their cheep is sweet in your ear.

They arrive in a heated truck packed in heavy cardboard boxes stacked ten high. The boxes are divided into sections, twelve sections per box, ten turkeys per section. As you take the turkeys out of the box, you do three things: you count to make sure the hatchery hasn't shorted you, you pinch off the snoot, and you check for defects.

The snoot is a growth at the top of the beak. In a full-grown tom, it is red, elongated, hanging off one side of his beak and ending with a bulbous growth that looks like a half-filled water balloon. The snoot evolved because it attracts females. When a tom struts and displays his tail feathers, the snoot becomes blood red.

But male turkeys on a farm don't need to attract females. Most of our toms would be killed long before they reached their sexual prime. Those who survived to mate were supplied with all the females they could handle. If they didn't handle them properly, artificial inseminators were called in to help them out. So the snoot was useless. Worse, it was harmful. Even when there are enough hens to go around, the toms strut and threaten each other. They fight by grabbing each other by the snoot and pulling. You could lose a valuable breeding male to infection that way. Or to tripping over his own snoot.

But when turkeys are less than a day old, the snoot is tiny, like a protruding blackhead. You can pinch it off with your thumb and fingernail, pinch thousands off in a day and your fingers won't even get sore.

I was ten, my sisters seven and eight, the first time we got baby turkeys.

Defective turkeys are those whose feet don't open right, who have an eye that's clouded over, a wing that droops. "They won't live," Daddy said. "The other turkeys will kill them." Animals always kill the weak and malformed in their midst. "Better to kill them now," he said, and he picked up a turkey with only one eye and threw it hard against the wall. The turkey fell dead to the ground. "See," he said, "Quick. No pain."

But we could imagine the turkeys' terror, and we loved the soft baby turkeys. "Let us keep them," we said. "We'll take care of them."

"Suit yourself," Daddy said.

We got an egg box that was big enough to hold twenty babies and deep enough they couldn't jump out. We put sawdust in the bottom and a light bulb for heat on top. We covered the box with a plaid tablecloth and put it at the foot of our beds. When Mother came home from work, she shook her head. "They'll learn soon enough," Daddy told her.

That night the room was filled with a green light filtered through the tablecloth, the smell of fresh sawdust, the cheeps of tiny birds.

The next day three of the birds were dead. We carried them to the gulch where Daddy burned everything that died.

The third day the turkeys spilled their water and turned the bottom of the box into pulp.

The fourth day the room started to smell like the brooder house.

The fifth day the turkeys started sprouting feathers and losing their cute, fuzzy look.

The sixth day, we found the one we called Droopy pecked to death.

We told Daddy, "You were right, we can't raise them."

"Suit yourself," he said. "Now take care of them."

We started by throwing the turkeys against the wall like Daddy had done. But we threw like girls. And besides, our hearts weren't in it. The turkeys hit the wall, squawked in pain, and fell dazed to the floor. We cried and we threw them again. Soon, we discovered the most efficient way to kill a week-old turkey. Hold it by its legs and swing its head as hard as you can into the exposed wooden wall studs. If you

71

don't flinch or pull back at the last second, this kills them on the first try.

By the time we were in high school, it was a game. As we unpacked the baby turkeys, Daddy pointed to a spot on the wall and we'd see who could come closest to hitting it.

2. *Debeaking*

When turkeys are ten weeks old they have to be debeaked so they won't peck each other to death. You herd them into a small area a hundred or so at a time. Then they are caught one by one and handed over a fence to the person running the debeaking machine, a hot blade brought down on the turkey's top beak with a pedal.

The first time we debeaked, I asked Daddy, "Does it hurt them?"

"Nope. Not if you do it right. It's like clipping fingernails." But the smell wasn't like clipping fingernails. It was like burning flesh.

In my family, my sisters and I did the herding, then took turns catching and handing turkeys to Daddy. Bend at the waist, grab a turkey under the wings, lift the three-pound bird over the fence to Daddy. Bend at the waist, grab a turkey, lift. Over and over until the pen was empty and it was someone else's turn.

I was the oldest and always took the first turn. Then, once when I was twelve, I said, "I'll do the next batch too. If I get tired later, one of you can take my turn."

Daddy snorted, "That's Julie all over. Planning to take it easy when it gets hot and everyone's tired." I was the daughter who would rather read than jump rope, who got A's in math but couldn't throw a ball. In some families that would have made me the scholar. In our family, it made me the lazy one.

I vowed I'd show him. I caught the second pen, then said to my sisters, "You just herd. I'll catch. I'll let you know if I'm tired."

Bend, grab, lift. The turkeys throw up on you. They shit on you. Feathers in your nose. Bend, grab, lift.

Daddy said, "That's a thousand. It's the record. Let your sisters catch now."

"No. I'm not tired," He'd never be able to call me lazy again. This day would change everything. My sisters would look at me in awe; my father would be proud.

Bend, grab, lift. Two thousand. Bend, grab, lift. Three thousand. Six thousand.

Lunch break sitting in the shade, my legs were hopping. I bent over them to weight them down.

After lunch, "I'll keep going," I said.

There were thirteen thousand turkeys. If I could catch every one my life would be different. If I could catch every one, Daddy would see my worth. The scales would fall from his eyes and he'd say, "Yes, you are my favorite. I love you most." Bend, grab, lift. Ten thousand. Ten thousand times three pounds. Thirty thousand pounds of turkeys I'd lifted. Nine thousand pounds to go. Bend, grab, lift. My hands were bleeding. It didn't matter. Fifteen hundred to go. I bent, my back locked. I staggered. If I fainted, died, Daddy would say, "I didn't realize." Mother would never forgive him.

"I can do it," I said. "Let me do it." I was crying, "Please let me finish." My sisters were laughing at me. Maybe Daddy was too. It didn't matter. I was better than all of them. I'd finish this job.

And I did. I caught every one. Official count, twelve thousand nine hundred and forty-seven. While Daddy and my sisters put away the machine and took down the temporary pen, I leaned against the wall, dizzy, every muscle jerking now. Most of the turkeys were eating, walking around, pecking at sawdust, at each other, like nothing had happened. But there was one in a corner, hunkered down, trembling, staring blankly ahead with its stupid turkey eyes, in shock. As I watched, a drop of blood formed on its beak—cut too short, not cauterized properly. The other turkeys cocked their heads at the bright color, walked toward it. "Put that bleeding one in the sick pen," Daddy said, "before the others start pecking at it." While one of my sisters took care of it, he put his hand on my shoulder. "Good job, girls," he said.

We headed back to the house, my sisters running ahead, challenging Daddy to race, then him chasing them with a bucket of water. Me alone behind.

3. *The Night 3,000 Turkeys Died*

The day before the night that three thousand turkeys died, we moved thirteen thousand turkeys to the range. I was fourteen then, still three years away from leaving my family and the farm.

73

Turkeys spend their first sixteen weeks in a heated brooder house, temperature held constant the first week at eighty-five degrees, at seventy-five after that. When they are sixteen weeks old, they are put outside to range in fenced enclosures. A flock of thirteen thousand needs about ten acres on the range.

By the time the turkeys have been in a brooder house for sixteen weeks, the air is filled with the ammonia, feather particles, and dust. The stench is overwhelming. After an hour in the brooder house, your chest hurts for a day. You can contract disabling diseases from working only a week in a poultry house. Tiny barbed pieces of feather dig into the tissue of your lungs and never let go. But we didn't know that then. Sometimes we wore handkerchiefs over our faces. Most times we didn't.

Our farm was small and we brooded more turkeys than we could range ourselves. Usually giant trucks with crates came at night and we worked until dawn herding turkeys to the end of the brooder house, catching them, handing them up to the men waiting on the side of the truck.

This time we were keeping the turkeys ourselves. Daddy decided we would herd them to the range. It looked simple enough. We made a temporary chute of wire fencing that ran from the double end-doors of the brooder house, fifty yards to the pen. We would get behind the turkeys in the brooder house, shout, wave old shirts and gunny sacks at them, and they would run out the doors, through the chute, into the pen. And that's the way it worked in the first brooder house. The first turkeys hesitated at the door, walked out cautiously, then moved through the chute and dispersed. The rest followed. It took about an hour. Daddy was pleased. "Let's work straight through," he said. "We'll be done by ten."

We moved the chute to the doors of the second brooder house. When we threw open the doors at the end of the second house, it was nine in the morning. The sun streamed in the open doors on turkeys that had never seen direct sunlight.

The one thing you can count on with turkeys is that you never know how they are going to react. I've seen turkeys clamor against a fence trying to get into a range fire. I've seen them rush toward a screaming child trying to kill it, seen them run from a screaming child, spooked and terrified.

These turkeys didn't want to go into the sun. As we pushed from behind, they compacted. It was like an old adventure movie where the

74

walls are closing in. But there was no wall at the end, only a patch of sunlight which the turkeys would not touch. We yelled louder, waved our cloths, kicked at the ones in the rear. Finally, Daddy walked through the solid carpet of turkeys to break the log jam at the front. He stood at the edge of the sunlight, lifting the turkeys three or four at a time with his feet. Stirring them with his legs, forcing them into the sun.

Suddenly, they broke free. As stubbornly as they had refused to go into the light, they now rushed toward it. They ran in a panic, piling on top of each other, knocking down the temporary fence. By the time Daddy could get the doors closed, at least a thousand turkeys had escaped and were running free on the farm, onto our neighbor's farm, into the road.

We didn't own the turkeys. We raised them for a company that owned the hatchery, the feed mill, the fleet of trucks that delivered and loaded the turkeys, the processing plant. We got a portion of the profits, if there were profits. With a thousand turkeys gone, there would be no profits on this flock. Sixteen weeks of Daddy working fourteen hour days, of my sisters and me working along side him any time we weren't in school. All for no pay. No money at all for another sixteen weeks.

It took us eight hours to round up the escaped turkeys. Four of us trying to track down a thousand birds that had the whole world in which to hide and run from us. The sun beat down, and the air was thick and humid. We stopped once for water, and my sister Billie, the youngest of us, just eleven, vomited from the cold water hitting her stomach after hours of sun, heat, and dehydration. As she lay on the ground, shaking and holding her stomach, I hated her for being the one too sick to continue. But even she was not too sick. We all went on. She got an extra five minutes to rest, but we all went on.

At six o'clock, we rebuilt the chute. We opened the doors, and the six thousand remaining turkeys, the sun now low in the sky behind them, walked through to the pen.

We cleaned up. We ate supper. And we went to bed.

That's the day we had before the night three thousand turkeys died.

At midnight Mother woke us up. "We have to get to the pen. Daddy needs us." We had been too exhausted to hear the storm. We ran out in the driving rain. Flashes of lightning showed Daddy picking up turkeys and throwing them, one after the other.

75

When people learn I grew up on a turkey farm, they invariably ask, "Is it true? Are they really so stupid that they open their mouths in the rain, look up at the sky, and drown?" The answer is yes, some of them do that. They are that stupid. But that's not how three thousand die in one night. They die because they are scared and they huddle together in their fear. They climb on top of each other, trying to get close, to find protection in the mass of bodies, and they suffocate. We called it piling. It wasn't unusual for a loud noise to cause a pile in the brooder house. If there wasn't someone to pull them off each other, fifty could die because someone slammed a door.

But this was worse than any pile we'd seen. Turkeys who'd never spent a night outdoors, panicked by thunder, lightning, and rain in sheets. All we could do was pull them out of the pile and throw them away from it. They would run back, still seeking the comfort of the group. After a while, sliding in mud, grabbing soaked turkeys, throwing them, grabbing more, you don't know if the ones you are throwing are dead or alive. You don't care.

Maybe we saved some.

The next day, the sky was cloudless and the sun bore down on us again. We picked up dead turkeys, throwing them onto the back of a flatbed truck. Daddy drove the truck into a field far from the house.

Three thousand dead turkeys sitting in the Missouri sun for two days

The company that owned the turkeys had them insured against acts of God, so we couldn't do anything until the insurance inspector had seen them. He came, a man from town in a white shirt and tie who held his handkerchief over his face when he got close to the truck. He made no pretense of counting, just stood there gagging.

After he left, Daddy shoveled the turkeys into Dead Turkey Gulch. He poured gasoline on them and struck a match. They burned for days.

Nominated by Sharon Solwitz, S.L. Wisenberg

THANKSGIVING

by MARTÍN ESPADA

from PLOUGHSHARES

This was the first Thanksgiving with my wife's family,
sitting at the stained pine table in the dining room.
The wood stove coughed during her mother's prayer:
Amen and the gravy boat bobbing over fresh linen.
Her father stared into the mashed potatoes
and saw a white battleship floating in the gravy.
Still staring at the mashed potatoes, he began a soliloquy
about the new Navy missiles fired across miles of ocean,
how they could jump into the smokestack of a battleship.
"Now in Korea," he said, "I was a gunner and the people there
ate *kimch'i,* and it really stinks." Mother complained that no one
was eating the creamed onions. *"Eat, Daddy."* The creamed onions
look like eyeballs, I thought, and then said, "I wish I had missiles
like that." Daddy laughed a 1950's horror-movie mad-scientist laugh,
and told me he didn't have a missile, but he had his own cannon.
"Daddy, eat the candied yams," Mother hissed, as if he were
a liquored CIA spy telling secrets about military hardware
to some Puerto Rican janitor he met in a bar. "I'm a toolmaker.
I made the cannon myself," he announced, and left the table.
"Daddy's family has been here in the Connecticut Valley since 1680,"
Mother said. "There were Indians here once, but they left."
When I started dating her daughter, Mother called me a half-black,
but now she spooned candied yams on my plate. I nibbled
at the candied yams. I remembered my own Thanksgivings
in the Bronx, turkey with *arroz y habichuelas* and *plátanos,*
and countless cousins swaying to *bugalú* on the record player

or roaring at my grandmother's Spanish punchlines in the kitchen,
the glowing of her cigarette like a firefly lost in the city. For years
I thought everyone ate rice and beans with turkey at Thanksgiving.
Daddy returned to the table with a cannon, steering the black
iron barrel. "Does that cannon go boom?" I asked. "I fire it
in the backyard at the tombstones," he said. "That cemetery bought
up all our farmland during the Depression. Now we only have
the house." He stared and said nothing, then glanced up suddenly,
like a ghost had tickled his ear. "Want to see me fire it?" he grinned.
"Daddy, fire the cannon after dessert," Mother said. "If I fire
the cannon, I have to take out the cannonballs first," he told me.
He tilted the cannon downward, and cannonballs dropped
from the barrel, thudding on the floor and rolling across
the brown braided rug. Grandmother praised the turkey's thighs,
said she would bring leftovers home to feed her Congo Gray parrot.
I walked with Daddy to the backyard, past the bullet holes
in the door and his pickup truck with the Confederate license plate.
He swiveled the cannon around to face the tombstones
on the other side of the backyard fence. "This way, if I hit anybody,
they're already dead," he declared. He stuffed half a charge
of gunpowder into the cannon, and lit the fuse. From the dining room,
Mother yelled, *"Daddy, no!"* Then the battlefield rumbled
under my feet. My head thundered. Smoke drifted over
the tombstones. Daddy laughed. And I thought: When the first
drunken Pilgrim dragged out the cannon at the first Thanksgiving—
that's when the Indians left.

Nominated by Ploughshares, Susan Wheeler

HAPPINESS

fiction by BHARATI MUKHERJEE

from DOUBLETAKE

M Y FATHER WAS dying of cancer, but he hung in long enough to se-
lect a groom for me out of Aunt Flower Garland's short list of three.
The night before he passed away, he gave me his last advice and bless-
ing. He said, "In the areas I can control, namely financial security and
temperamental compatibility, I have hedged all bets. Happiness in
marriage? That, even I can't guarantee."

He rejected the candidacy of a physics professor in Tulsa, Okla-
homa, and a dentist in San Leandro, California, in favor of Arjun. The
physics professor had a grandfather who had nearly won a Nobel prize
in quantum theory, and the dentist's family owned a profitable phar-
maceutical company, but Arjun had a Ph.D. in electrical engineering
from Columbia University. Columbia was where my father would like
to have studied, if his father, so the story went, hadn't died of a rup-
tured appendix at (even by the local standards) the premature age of
twenty-six. My grandmother, two aunts, and father owed their second
start in life to the generosity of a maternal uncle, who, being a relative
from the maternal side, of course was under no obligation to take them
in. This uncle, who had five daughters and three sons of his own, paid
for the weddings of my Aunts Flower Garland and Leafy Vine, and,
when my father turned seventeen, arranged an apprentice job for him
with an engineer friend at a hydroelectric plant an overnight's train
ride from the city.

"And as the Calcutta Chamber of Commerce knows," my father was
fond of saying, and he said it always in English, "the rest is very much
history, isn't it?"

In his anecdotes, he gave his youth Dickensian twists and darkenings, not all of which I believed, probably because by the time I was born he'd made one fortune in lumber up in Assam, and another down in Andhra in steel. In a previous incarnation, Horatio Alger had to have been Bengali.

My father and I were very close, closer than most fathers and daughters in our traditional neighborhood, Mother having died of an overnight fever when I was three. I can't visualize Mother since there are no photographs of her, no likeness for me to have had framed and hung on the wall next to my late grandfather's and grandmother's portraits above the altar of gods in the room of worship, but her presence or absence persists in my brain as a faint stain of melancholy.

A week before my father died, Arjun, whose full name is Arjun Kumar Roy Chowdhury, flew in from New York on a two-week vacation from his job—he was a vice-president in charge of operations research at an electronics company—interviewed the women on the Roy Chowdhury family's short list of bridal candidates that he thought he might survive a lifetime with on the basis of photo, bio and relatives' preliminary impressions, and picked me. I need to believe that his family's short list was longer than my father's.

Given the long lines for immigrant visas at the U.S. consulate, Arjun was impatient to get the legal formality of marriage over with before he returned to New York at the end of his two-week leave, but we, Ghoses, insisted on letting a respectable time lapse between celebration of funeral and wedding. I don't call it *my* wedding, or Arjun's and my wedding, because the bride and groom played the least assertive roles during the lawyerly dowry negotiations, the by-fax-and-priority-mail transcontinental preparations, and the long, complicated, exhausting pre- and postnuptial ceremonies. We fasted when we were told to, we bathed with turmeric paste in Ganges water as prescribed, we played the laid-down games auguring connubial contentment, and when, toward the end of all the chants by the Brahmin priest and the vows in Sanskrit by Arjun and my maternal great-uncle, the dramatic moment came for the veiled bride to lift her head and look into the groom's eyes, we both managed I'm-ready-for-whatever-adventure smiles.

Two days after the wedding, the day known as *bou-bhat*, which I later translated into English for Karin Stein, my neighbor in Upper Montclair, New Jersey, as *the day the bride moves to her husband's house and cooks rice perfect enough for him to eat, because if the rice is too crunchy or too sticky she'll be sent back in disgrace to her parent's house,* Arjun and I boarded an Air India 747, and, strangers safety-belted into side-by-side seats, headed for instant intimacy.

Within a month of making my home in America, I learned how wise my father, the Cheetah of the Calcutta Chamber of Commerce, had been to hedge those bets that he could. At social gatherings, like the Tagore Society evenings in the Bannerjees' split-level in Chappaqua, New York, or at the organizational meetings of the Bengali Heritage Preservation Association in the Dases' condo in Queens, I sniffed out heartache and heard deceit. I picked up words and phrases that I hadn't been taught by Aunts Flower Garland and Leafy Vine: Creedmore, Prozac, shelter for abused women, defenestration.

Comfortable living and decent conduct had been taken for granted by my family. I was grateful that the Ghoses hadn't been deceived by the Roy Chowdhurys. Arjun hadn't lied about his degrees, his salary, his stocks and bonds holdings. He owned the Tudor-style house in Montclair, and the black BMW we had been shown photos of. And he owned things I hadn't seen before: a refrigerator with an ice-water faucet set in its door, a convection oven, an outdoor gas barbecue grill.

The more personal habits and peeves revealed themselves enticingly to me. For instance, every night before coming to bed, he dropped two Alka-Seltzer tablets into a highball glass of water, said, "Plop, plop, fizz, fizz, bottoms up! Prosit!" and gulped the noisy drink down while pinching his nose. I got to look forward to chasing the antacid grains off his lips with my tongue. It made me feel uninhibited. Who cares about long-term happiness when the tongue is tracing, teasing, tormenting, in fulfillment of its own, distinct destiny?

Arjun and I made our voluntary accommodations. At the dinner table, I learned to taste the differences between chardonnay and sauvignon blanc, and pretended preferences for merlots and pinot noirs and contempt for all California cabernets. He cut back on pork and beef. I filled him in on Indian politics: he'd missed so much of which party leaders had defected and why, and which cabinet ministers had been arrested and on what charges among the usual frauds, graft, currency violations, embezzlements. He reciprocated by dictating which senators and Congress representatives I was to trust and explaining the glories and ghastlinesses of the American two-party system. Politics was bedtime story. It didn't matter that I didn't have a vote in this country, that I hadn't voted in any election in any country. I still think of politics as love's foreplay.

Give and take; take and give: that was the flow of our intimacy. Arjun liked to make money, and he liked me to spend it. I did. I drove the BMW—bigger, shinier than in the photos I'd been shown—to the malls, and displayed what money could buy when, late in the New Jersey night, he came through the front door, carrying a briefcaseful of work he had yet to get through. It wasn't about being pliant. My father taught me, through example, that self-worth based on cashworth is the shortest cut to tragedy.

"Class and conscience," my father said, "go together like a washerman and his donkey. Class is the washerman, but he has to follow the path that his stubborn donkey takes, isn't it?"

My father's analogies were not for me to question. In his adolescent days as apprentice laborer, he'd composed a notebookful of morally uplifting couplets in Bengali, the point of all of which was, cultivate your conscience so that money and rank may not lead you astray.

I have followed his advice by never buying insurance. I wouldn't shed a tear if a burglar broke into the house while Arjun was in the Softron, Inc., offices in Manhattan and I at the cosmetics counter at Bendel's, and made off with a van-load of our belongings. But I have followed his advice for lascivious reasons. Penury neither alarms me nor goads me to covetous ambitiousness. Money, in my marriage to Arjun, was the consensual currency of intimacy. All around me in suburban New York and New Jersey, love was ending in sleeping pills, straitjackets, fatal automobile accidents. Not love, not loyalty, but steel-tipped intimacy, so sharp and thrilling that it has entered and exited before you have touched the wound, felt the pain: that intimacy was our strength. Forget the prenuptial haggling between the Roy Chowdhurys and the Ghoses. To each other we made no promises. We gave and took freely, greedily. We demonstrated large-hearted poor sense instead of self-interest. There should have been time for me to let my father know that before intimacy, happiness in marriage pales.

This is the way that our most special night happened. What does it matter which year, which season. It was a weeknight like any other weeknight in our American life. Arjun came through the front door, which the previous owner, whom Karin Stein remembered as "a moody Middle East type, don't ask me from where exactly, except that he was definitely not from Israel," had fitted with chimes that tinkled out a bar or two of what Karin identified as "It's a Most Beautiful Day"; he dropped his umbrella in its ceramic stand, hung up his all-weather coat in the hall closet; he thrust a cold, heavy bottle of champagne instead of the usual chardonnay against my bosom, grabbed me in a bear hug, and whispered, "Tonight we celebrate!" into the Austrian crystal necklace, which was what I had bought from a just-opened boutique earlier in the day.

"Celebrate what?" I assumed a bonus or promotion, or, for Arjun, more pleasing still would be a stock market coup. My role in our partnership was to draw the answers out of him.

"Who cares what?" He popped the cork right there in the hall, and with the champagne foaming down the sides of the bottle and leaving sticky droplets on the wood floor, dragged me in a bear hug to the kitchen.

A finicky housemaker would have blotted clean the champagne trail while Arjun was reaching for the fluted glasses I'd stuck way in the back of the highest cabinet shelf. They were still in the manufacturer's box. I'd bought them at a going-out-of-business sale in Paramus Mall. Arjun was a Glenfiddich drinker. Wine collecting was a hobby with him. He'd made a wine cellar out of what had been the last owner's woodworking shop. "Forget carpentry," Karin scoffed when she came over for our first wine-tasting party, "the guy was making bombs. Don't you hear any funny ticking noises when you're in the basement?"

A woman with good sense would have first turned off the gas flames under the pots of Basmati rice and goat vindaloo, then attended to whatever adventure destiny had lassoed.

"Let me guess," I laughed. "I've never seen you this happy, so it has to be something special."

Arjun pulled two champagne flutes out of their box, and held them under the kitchen faucet. I'd forgotten they were etched with a cloudy circlet of leaves and rimmed with a bright thin band of gold.

"So happy," Arjun retorted, "that I'm not complaining about having to rinse dishes."

"We aren't in Calcutta anymore." I tore off squares of paper towels and held them out to Arjun. Rolls of parch-tongued paper towels, packages of thick, crisp bond paper into which no insect bodies have been processed: those are the American marvels I prize.

"Try telling that to your Chappaqua friends. You think Prafulla Bose comes home at eight and does the dishes?"

He crumpled the dry paper squares and tossed them in the garbage. The track light aimed at the sink caught the bright slitheriness of water coating the inside of each flute.

"You've been nominated Most Valuable Functionary by your CEO."

"Don't even try," Arjun said. He poured the champagne carefully into a glass for me.

I had watched him pour wine before, but I hadn't noticed, really noticed, his wrists. I'd admired his fingers before, told him many times how movingly delicate I found them on a man who claimed to abhor painters and poets. The wrist that rotated with the bottle neck had the showy, arrogant sureness of wrists of the concert pianists I caught by chance on cable channels. "All right, you're a secret gambler, and you've just made a killing." I arced my body to kiss that confident wrist. So what that my head knocked the filled glass out of his surprised grasp.

"A gambler?"

I heard his shoes push aside broken glass. He was thinking of my feet, not his tile floor. I don't wear shoes or slippers at home. I didn't in Calcutta where our floors were of cool marble or stone mosaic, and I didn't in Upper Montclair with its oak, tile, lino, and wool-blend wall-to-wall.

"You don't mind drinking a toast to gambling?" He poured champagne into the second flute.

"Plop, plop, fizz, fizz!" I whispered. "Bottoms up!"

"Prosit!" he whispered back.

I took a gulp, he an assessor's sip. "How much, Arjun?" I was thinking how large a sum I would have to find creative ways for spending.

"Every asshole gambler should be so lucky to have you as a wife."

Then he whirled me into the living room with strides that resembled waltzers' on colorized, afternoon movies on TV, humming tunes I didn't know and at the same time wriggling out of his suit jacket, stiffening his spine and outstretched arms, tightening his buttocks.

It wasn't natural clumsiness that kept me stepping on his champagne-dampened shoes. Like most young women on my block, I took years of weekend classes in Tagore-style singing and dancing. Aunt Leafy Vine keeps my certificates in the vault compartment of her most secure cabinet, which by the way is made of steel manufactured in one of my father's factories. I am no more and no less physically graceful than the other Tri-State Bengali wives who have volunteered for bit parts in Tagore's drama *Red Oleander*, which the Tagore Society intends to stage next October.

That night I tripped, I kept tripping, stumbling, apologizing, because I couldn't feel the beat to his hummed tune. He rose on the balls of his feet: I thumped with my heels as though I was wearing dance bells on my ankles. He covered the available floor space with wide swoops in circles; I concentrated my energies on the slightest movements of finger joints and neck muscles. I had danced duets as Radha the Milkmaid to a girl-cousin's Krisha the God Biding His Time as Amorous Goatherd in family theatricals. But in those duets, Radha and Krishna never touched. Nobody led, nobody followed. There wasn't any need to. Power was shared by god and mortal. We improvised the depths of the lovers' passion, but never the way their love turned out. That was the trouble, I told myself. I had no way of telling when the humming and the prancing would come to their natural close. There were no scripted roles, no sage-revealed unalterable storyline, no faith that through dance I might discover the simple secret of cosmic chaos.

"It's no good," Arjun said.

He let go of me, suddenly, and I fell back into his favorite chair, a massive leather rocker, embarrassed at my own ungainliness, but thankful the ordeal was over while he hummed, whistled, twirled around the room solo.

"See how easy it is?"

I heard relief, not taunt, in Arjun's question. From the rocker, the posture and the footwork did seem easy. "I think my problem is I'm not hearing what you're hearing, I'm not *feeling* what you're feeling."

"What am I feeling?" he dipped his head back to ask his question, but by the time I answered, "You're feeling good, very good," he'd waltzed away to the farthest corner of the living room.

For another hour I watched, cowering at the unself-conscious celebration of . . . what was it that he was celebrating? What had he gambled on? How destructive could his winnings be? Was I a witness to bliss or lunacy?

When I went to bed that night, he was still dancing.

The next morning he left home at six-thirty as he always did to catch his commuter train. I haven't seen him since. I did find a note, an orange Post-It actually, stuck to the neck of the champagne bottle. It said: *There is another woman, but that's not the reason. Arranged marriages carry no risk. I know you'll react to my leaving, and to a gambler, certainty is boring. Ciao! Have a happy life.*

That was seven years ago. The changes in my life are mostly invisible. I still have the BMW and the house on North Fullerton Street. Karin Stein is still my friend, but she chucked her law practice for a bearded baker somewhere in the Northwest. She sends me postcards with grease stains. Last year I talked myself into starting law school.

Night classes, not Harvard or Yale. All the same, it's exciting work, and I am a hardworking student. My father's failure to arrange a lasting marriage has alchemized into new strengths and excitements. Now, for instance, I stay awake nights arguing the legal rights of frozen sperm or defending UFO-borne alien scientists against charges of rape. Are UFO abductions and orifice penetrations punishable crimes in U.S. courts? For amendments to immigration bills, do "UFObacks" fall into the category of undocumenteds? Is Arjun physically as well as legally dead? In American English is self-esteem a synonym for happiness?

Nominated by Doubletake

THE BOOK OF THE DEAD MAN #87

by MARVIN BELL

from POETRY

1. Accounts of the Dead Man

The dead man likes it when the soup simmers and the kettle hisses.
He wants to live as much as possible at the ends of his fingertips.
To make sense, to make nonsense, to make total sense, lasting sense,
ephemeral sense, giddy sense, perfect sense, holy sense.
The dead man wants it, he requires it, he trusts it.
Therefore, the dead man takes up with words as if they had nowhere
in mind.
The dead man's words are peacock feathers, bandages, all the
everyday exotica ground under by utility.
The dead man's book foresees a flickering awareness, an ember at
the end of the Void, a glitter, a glow beneath the ash.
The dead man's book is the radical document of time, nodding to
calamity and distress, happy in harm's way.
To the dead man, the mere whistling of a pedestrian may signal an
onslaught of intention.
The dead man calls his spillover a journal because it sounds helpless
and private, while a diary suggests the writings of someone
awaiting rescue.
The dead man doesn't keep a diary.
The dead man sweeps under the bed for scraps, pieces, chips, tips,
fringework, lace, filings and the rivets that rattled and broke.

His is a flurry of nothing-more-to-give, the echo of a prolonged note
struck at the edge of an inverted bowl.
Now he must scrub his brain before a jury of his peers.

2. More Accounts of the Dead Man

The dead man has caused a consternation, but he didn't mean to.
He was just clocking his pulse, tracking his heart, feeling his way.
He was just dispersing the anomalous and otherwise scouting the
self-evident and inalienable.
It was just that sometimes he couldn't stand it because he was happy.
It was the effect that he effected that affected him.
Some say it was his fervor for goose bumps took his breath away.
Some say it was the dead man's antsiness that put him in the dirt.
Some say he was too much the live wire, the living will, the holy
spirit, the damn fool.
His was a great inhalation, wanton, a sudden swivel in the midst of
struggle, a death dance with demons and other dagnabbits.
The dead man was well into physical geezerhood when he came to a
conclusion and declared his independence.
At once he was chockablock with memories, the progeny of design
and of blooper, boner and glitch.
He had his whole life to live.
When there is no more beseeching or gratitude, no seats remaining
on the metaphysical seesaw, no zero-sum activity, no acquisition
that is not also a loss, no finitude, then of course the dead man
smiles as he blows a kiss through the wispy curtain of closure.
Some say the dead man was miserable to be so happy.

Nominated by Jennifer Atkinson, Richard Jackson, David St.John

SPLINTERS

fiction by MELVIN JULES BUKIET

from THE PARIS REVIEW

HALF AN INCH LONG, an eighth wide, flat as parchment, sharp enough to pierce and pain anyone of mother born, the gray section of wood sat upon an ecclesiatstical purple matte between a gold-leafed garland of frame. The catalogue copy with its photograph on the cover read: "Documented, Authenticated Piece of the True Cross, First Sale in Two Thousand Years."

Other religious artifacts were grouped together in Barkeley's annual theological auction: silver kiddush cups that had belonged to Sigmund Freud, African fetishes, a ruby-studded Buddha, an original papal bull, a sheaf of correspondence between Reinhold Neibuhr and Teilhard de Chardin lamenting the discovery of Peking man and celebrating the birth of Niebuhr's daughter and several mosque-size prayer rugs from Mecca. Assembled over the year from many sources, the estimated value of the collection was nearly seven figures without calculating in the priceless designation of the True Cross.

The regulars in Barkeley's grand salon fidgeted nervously. Some re-knotted their rep ties, others foraged through Florentine handbags that bulged as if their material's breadth was presumed to be a reflection of their material depth. These people were accustomed to paintings and furniture, rare stamps and coins, property, jewelry and even golden records and pop memorabilia. They laughed when John Lennon's sweaty T-shirt went for sixteen thousand dollars the year before. But no one was laughing now. There was something about this round that made them uncomfortable in their familiar seats, and the characters Lot 78 brought into their domain under Barkeley's domed rotunda were too unsavory for their elite tastes. The odors in the room had clearly not been atomized.

First there were the priests. Traveling in strength for mutual protection from modernity, four of them represented the monastery that was relinquishing its claim to ownership (perhaps *caretakership* was a better word) of this universal treasure in return for a substantial check that stood for another kind of faith. It was their first time in New York or, for that matter, for most of them, out of Sardinia, and they belonged in the elegant surroundings as much as a flock of crows. Dressed in black robes, they were balanced on the opposite side of the room by several Hasidim, who might have been residents of the temporal city, but had never been seen in Barkeley's tony precincts. Wearing jackets and fur-trimmed hats, their beards brushing the glossy cover of the catalogue, the Orthodox Jews were there for the sixteenth-century Torah, and an intricate model of the golem of Prague.

At least a portion of the rank scent drifting among the audience came from a Cypriot gentleman who unwrapped a crinkly wax-paper package containing a liver sandwich and munched contentedly in the front row, while a pale man, Scandinavian Lutheran to judge from his gaunt, albinoid features, sat on the aisle, his long feet extended like crutches. Together with others in the room from more exotic locations beyond identification, they might have inhabited a Mideastern souk more fitly than parlor society.

Barkeley's had always been international in stature and tenor, but the usual foreigners came in discrete waves, the result of historical trends. Japanese tycoons bought art in the eighties and German industrialists invested in precious coins when their economy boomed while Australian land barons in the grip of subequatorial social inversion contended against each other for Chipppendale highboys to furnish their vast outback ranches. More recently, the newly prosperous Mafia leaders of Russia had been spotted purchasing letters or documents signed by delegates to the first American Continental Congress. Only time would determine if their investments were wise or whims.

Unlike these waves, the olio on hand for the theological auction was simultaneously too diverse and too concentrated for the regulars to type—not a United Nations but a Divided Faiths. Whereas the Japanese and the Russians seemed to wish to purchase respectability along with objects of value, and the Germans and the Australians had the grace to aspire to Barkeley's definition of class, this crew's concerns only coincidentally overlapped the house's. Their raucous jabber, like

90

a mob down at the docks buying spices in bulk lots from the Levant, showed their uncouth manners. Worse, their criteria for judgment were not temporal, but eternal.

A rotund Nigerian man in a porkpie hat idly flipped through the catalogue's introductory essay, "The Ecstasy of Faith in an Era of Faith in Ecstacy," by Dr. J. Rittenour, Professor of Comparative Religion at Hunter College, extended monograph for sale at Barkeley's office.

The Hasids glanced with irritation at a middle-aged woman in a green blouse who sat next to them. They did not raise their eyes high enough to perceive her coppery red hair or the gold chain that dangled against the pale freckled flesh inside the V of her silk shirt. In the Hasids' homes, as indeed their entire world, the sexes were rigorously separated, but this was neither their home nor their world. They might as well have been in Rome, and had no choice but to do as the Romans. Even if they were inclined to move away, they couldn't; by then every seat in the cavernous room was filled.

One man in the back row tapped impatiently, waiting for the object he had come for to be brought to the rostrum. His name was Mark, and so far as he knew he bore no relation to the apostle.

•

A line of credit for the man in the back row had already been arranged, its cap deemed "upon discretion of bidder." Since such designations were rather unusual, his presence had been brought to the attention of the auctioneer through a coded mark on the seating chart that showed the locations of likely ringers.

Forgetting, or choosing to ignore, the years in which his credit was not so excellent, Mark took his distinction in stride. Son of a White Plains dry cleaner, urged but never convinced to believe in a vague suburban Judaism, the sacraments of which were lox and pastrami, Mark had been a mediocre student at Boston University during the late 1960s, where the tastes of the era had led him from drugs to loud music to science-fiction novels about robotic dystopias and time warps. Indeed, it seemed a dystopian time warp when his father simultaneously shook his hand and informed him that the bucks stopped upon receipt of a diploma. Reiterating his dogma once more upon being introduced to Mark's faculty advisor, whose academic gown could have used a good cleaning, the graduate's father said, "I've bought all the books I'm going to."

91

Summoning the range of worldly skills he had mastered in four years at college, Mark thereafter clerked for the better part of a decade at a used record store in Somerville until he found himself thirty, married, baffled and balding, and returned to science fiction in his spare time, first for escape and then for sustenance. Scribbling nights in the basement of the house he couldn't remember buying, but vividly detested—its proliferating weeds, stuttering boiler, and mortgage—he produced a novel about a world where people were born at thirty and grew younger until they died at birth. Lo and behold, it sold.

Whatever small talent Mark brought to knocking off conceptual, post-apocalyptic thrillers, he was fortunate that there seemed to be an insatiable appetite for the genre, which he could, in his own small way, satisfy. His books were brought out by a second-rate San Francisco publisher. They paid him well enough to keep at bay his insufferable and by now, thank God, ex-wife and unpleasant daughter, but not so well as the pirated editions he saw one day cheek by jowl with the UFO section in a New Age bookstore in the Berkshires paid someone else. There, as if captured in one of his own alternate universes, Mark scanned a volume that was unmistakably his long-since remaindered *Journey to Eternity* condensed, divested of superfluous plot and rebound with a glowing light on the cover.

Two days later, his attorney from the divorce had filed an injunction against further distribution of the volume as well as a demand for royalties. The latter never did materialize, but the injunction was granted and a new version of *Journey* incorporating the editorial revisions of the spiritual pirates was mailed to a cynical New York literary agent who understood the lure of faith. Republished yet again, the book began to sell under Mark's own name, and, no longer confined to the secretive realm of the plagiarized, it soared from specialty to mainstream bookstores. Under the category of "Inspirational Literature" it simply refused to stop selling, no matter the belated savaging of critics who hadn't deigned to notice it the first time around.

Had *Journey* been the stuff of the author's own soul it might have proved a difficult act to follow, but since Mark was a hack from the get-go, he was able to tailor his vision to a new suit, and came out with four more *Journeys* in quick succession, each one lodging as fiercely as Mont St. Scipelli on its rock on the best-seller lists, and that was just the beginning.

•

"Ladies and Gentlemen, please take your seats," the auctioneer announced, and began the patter that would carry them through the long afternoon. In rapid succession he disposed of kiddush cups and Judaica, letters, rugs and bronzes until he said, "And now, for the lot you've all been waiting for . . . "

•

Playing with his name, the king of spiritual prose realized that the letters reconfigured also spelled Karma, well nearly, so he eliminated *Journey's* western orientation, retooled the essential core for a different market and tapped into yet another vein of transcendence. This way he gained readers—or, more accurately, adherents—from Back Bay to Bombay.

A writer not so much by as of inspiration, the reminted Mark Karma asked his agent why they bothered to cut in the publisher. He was a brand name; he didn't need any cute animal on the spine to sell his books. He opened his own publishing house and took in other authors under the one eye imprint. Then he cut out the agent.

Unconcerned about the dubious verification of high literary culture, Mark hired preachers, signed them to the kinds of overreaching contract he had once been subject to, and sent them off to hustle their wares on the road, renting some of the same auditoriums he remembered from his rock 'n' roll days, selling cartons, truckloads, of books and T-shirts and lunchboxes so the believers' children could "take their faith to school."

He purchased a chain of suburban newspapers and some radio licenses and turned them into the print and broadcast venues that *Time* magazine lambasted in a cover story on "The New Religiosity." Allegations of anti-Semitism were hurled at the magazine for referring to The God Network's founder as one "whose head, viewed from the rear, resembles a poppy seed bagel with an unusually large hole."

"Not inaccurate," Mark said, as he searched for more lucrative investments. Why pay the satellite company a transmission fee, he asked his new lawyer, and began negotiations to put his own artificial comet bearing the one eye logo into the astral plane. Then he fired the lawyer who worked by the hour and bought an in-house attorney all for himself. Eventually he needed an entire crew of attorneys, all dressed identically in three-piece suits and vests and ties bearing the one eye emblem.

•

"Do I hear fifty thousand dollars to commence the bidding on this remarkable relic from the foundation of Christianity?" The auctioneer caught the eye of the man in the back row. "Yes, I have fifty thousand dollars."

•

Sections and segments of the cross ranging in size from the tiniest chip to enormous planks were treasured in abbeys and monasteries as well as national libraries and private, aristocratic vaults from Lisbon to Istanbul. One huge chunk was in deep storage at the Hermitage, while others were scattered in priestly redoubts as far afield as São Paulo and Cambodia, where a society of Jesuits brought one as their group talisman in the seventeenth century. The joke, attributed to Twain after his European tour, but probably as old as the hills, was that if all these pieces were set together they would form a cross as large as a clipper ship. Healthy or sacrilegious skepticism was the only proper scholarly attitude towards relics.

•

"I have an opening bid of fifty thousand dollars. Do I hear one hundred?"

•

Despite rational disdain, however, these relics had exercised an undeniable fascination for more years than science had been the cult of the West. The relics fell into several categories. First there were the man-made artifacts, such as crucibles and shreds of holy garments, but others were organic, the more gruesome the better. Bones and shriveled organs commanded the highest veneration, but toenails of prophets and teeth of saints, locks of hair, and, in one case, a nose, were also worshipped in any church that maintained a claim to antiquity or authority. Nevertheless, in the hierarchical realm of the sancti-

94

fied, there was nothing to compare with the pieces of the cross itself, and within the realm of cross pieces, there were none to compare with the one from Mont St. Scipelli.

•

Money poured in so swiftly that the Karma Corporation had a difficult time managing its cash flow. Mark purchased other companies, which also gushed income. From publishing and broadcasting, he moved to real estate to railroads and provided venture capital for other innovative young entrepreneurs, until all that was worth Mark's time was to invest in national currencies.

"After all," he said, "the dollar has one eye, too."

Fortunately, this limited vision didn't stop him from shorting the dollar on the Capetown exchange and nearly breaking the Federal Reserve when the notes plunged—at least partially because of his action.

•

"Back to you, Sir. Yes, I have one fifty. Do I hear two hundred?"

•

Then came the more difficult question—what to do with his money? Not charitably minded, not particularly hedonistic, the man needed a hobby. He began to collect, not houses, not horses, not painting; well, some paintings. Not Renoirs of sentimental bourgeois in the garden, and surely not the vulgar expressions and abstractions of his contemporaries, but Titians, Giordanos, El Grecos, portraits of cardinals, saints and then, the font of visual artistry in the West, paintings of God in His many incarnations.

"The deity's been good to me," he said.

•

Without a doubt, the particular splinter on the cover of Barkeley's catalogue had been in the possession of the Scipelli brotherhood since the early tenth century, when Julian Despasse, illegitimate son of Henry, Comte de Navarre, Knight Hospitaler, brought it back from Jerusalem. Perhaps he was intending to convey it to Malta, several

95

hundred treacherous nautical miles to the north, but felt mortality boiling inside his swollen blood vessels and delivered it instead to the monastery that sat on a jagged outcropping of volcanic rock on the seaward edge of Sardinia in return for the funeral he required three days later.

Julian's second, unwelcome and invisible gift—plague—nearly decimated the monastery before it ran its decade-long course—or curse. The end of the epidemic was attributed to the mystical curative powers of the piece of the cross its original victim had brought, although perhaps it was blame rather than gratitude the segment of wood deserved.

•

Art went an inch in the direction of satisfying Mark's own inchoate yearnings. He bought madonnas and crucifixion scenes, and then, after a moment of inspiration, he set his two eyes upon the objects which inspired the artists.Discreet inquiries about the Holy Grail and the Ark of the Covenant were sent abroad, but the best research revealed those objects to be merely legendary. The only things from the age of faith that indubitably existed in the modern world were the relics. Mark was almost shocked when a Madison Avenue antiques dealer offered him St. Peter's left sandal and intimated that an ankle bone might also be available.

"You mean you can buy that stuff?"

"With all due respect, Sir, you can buy anything."

"Well, of course. I should have known."

And he plunged in. At first, he bought his share of ankles and fingernails and teeth, and toyed with the idea of attempting to reconstruct Jesus, but was brought up against unfortunate biological lacks—tissues did not endure so well as bone. Besides, the sacred body parts were tainted by the very humanity of their origin. It was the spiritual object nonpareil that lured him. It was the cross.

•

Before Julian had rescued the precious relic during the Crusades, it had been kept safe by an Islamic clan that had received it from an Essene tribe they had obliterated several hundred years earlier. Yet even under the reign of the infidel, the wood had been cherished; in fact, it was the fame of the splinter of Haroun Tell that led Julian to lay siege to its keeper's castle. The siege lasted seventeen months until the besieged had exhausted all the water in their cisterns, all the blood in their horses, and all the meat of their dead. Then when they opened the gate, Julian and his men marched in, and demanded that the heathen leader bow to him. So the Turk abased himself before his captor, and Julian's sword neatly severed his befezzed head.

Alas, Julian was not a visionary. If the conqueror had saved the bloodied repository of Allah consciousness, he might have been able to sell it as a relic to the Arab world, and create a new touristic industry, but instead he threw the wide-eyed, olive-skinned prize to the dogs.

•

The bidding—translated via large-screen monitors into all the major currencies in which the bidders were likely to be proficient—escalated swiftly. The Cypriot threw up his arms in disgust at a quarter of a million and stormed theatrically out of the room, but peeked back in. A further round, to 300, priced out the taciturn Swede who had been a prominent bidder at the early rounds. Likewise the three-hundred range eliminated all but three bidders, two in the room, and one on the phone.

Rumor swept Barkeley's as to the identity of the bidders. A Saudi sheikh was apparently one; at least he was nodding intently, either bidding or napping. Allegedly the phone was connected to a foundation established by Christendom's wealthiest peer, the owner of a chain of athletic shoe stores in California. The third was clearly a Jew, in the back row.

Mark was slim He wore corduroy pants and a vest that smelled faintly of tobacco. Sporting a short ponytail with the remains of his hair, he looked rather like the student he had once been, but he had the deep-set eyes and sweeping curve of nostril that made him instantly identifiable to either fellow Jew or Jew-hater, as he waved his fan with the number 18 upwards again and again, making 325 into 350, 425 into 450, and on.

•

Leaving a garrison behind to be devoured in turn by heat and disease, Julian boarded ship back to the civilized Christian world he had set off from a half dozen years earlier. All he bore was the precious splinter and a faint swelling in his groin. Flea-bitten and infected, he was welcomed at the harbor of Mont St. Scipelli when he displayed his gift and buried in a sarcophagus in the same nave as the cross itself, a signal honor.

Despite the historical fact that everyone who touched the piece of wood from its first presumed user forward died, the cross was enshrined behind the Sardinian altar. There it remained, the pride of the monastery for a millennium as medieval pilgrims flocked to behold and benefit from its mystical emanations. According to legends as well publicized as the flacks of the era could do with their primitive means, sans fax, the limp walked after viewing the cross, and the dumb spoke. The blind, vouchsafed a precious touch, saw, and a thousand other healings for every ailment from leprosy to infertility were claimed for the cross of Mont St. Scipelli.

•

The auctioneer paused to wipe a linen handkerchief across his brow. The bidding had slowed to $25,000 increments, and he thought it was a moment to build suspense to compensate for subsiding momentum. "Do we know," he asked, "how rare and special, how utterly individual a commodity we have here?"

•

Sadly, come modernity, the glamour of the thing began to wane.

Early on, other relics appeared at less inaccessible venues, making the arduous journey to the island fortress less necessary. Disdain their competition as the Scipelli fathers did, make sly insinuations that other fathers in other cellars steeped their ersatz relics in sacramental wine to simulate the patina of blood, their scorn had little effect on the appeal of their rivals. At less guarded moments, the Scipelli brothers might even admit to jealousy of a thorn in the abbey directly across the waters, a day trip by mule from Naples. On the other hand, the faithful who made the seaborne passage were usually better-heeled than the peasants on mules, and therefore more likely to leave some portion of their fortunes to the monastery that inspired them. Scipelli remained one of the richest castles in Christendom for centuries, until faith itself began to lose its appeal.

•

Auctions have patterns, and different people use different strategies. Some bid by regular steps and then jump to frighten the competition. Others lay low, cagily silent until all but one other bidder is out, and then enter the fray, hoping to shock and dispirit the one who felt the prize within grasp. As for Mark, he just kept his hand up, and intended to keep it there until everyone else put theirs down.

The representatives from the monastery murmured among themselves. Even the goatish sheikh would have been preferable, but their hopes centered on the anonymous phone connection. They hovered breathlessly at every pause from the Barkeley's employee on the line to California. They had done what was necessary, but they dreaded the consequences. A Jew had not entered their calculations.

Abominably, satanically, wealthy, the shaggy, shabby mogul in the back row might buy it for vengeance, to fling the trauma of his tribe into the ocean, or, worse, take it back to the Holy Land to donate to some Jewish museum for display among that stubborn tribe that refused to acknowledge the Lord who sprang from their blood and gave his own blood to redeem the irredeemable. For all anyone knew, he might simply drop the priceless piece of wood that bore the stain of divinity into a pulping mix at one of his factories and truck it out on a spool the size of a sequoia trunk to be printed upon by one of the hundred papers he owned: tawdry headlines today, spread under bird cages tomorrow. The same newspaper that chronicled the sale of the cross might actually contain it, and no one would be the wiser.

It was an atrocity, an outrage. But it was too late to remove the item from auction. The brotherhood had signed a contract with Barkeley's. Once the minimum upset bid (confidentially, pricelessness was defined in the papers as $50,000) had been reached, the sale was to be considered final—unless they bid themselves, and paid Barkely's ten percent commission. That commission alone was now past their grandest expectations of the entirety.

•

Diderot. Rousseau. Even if the enrollment of the church remained steady, the ardor of its parishioners' passion diminished, and by the advent of the enlightened eighteenth century, the descendants of the pilgrims to Mont St. Scipelli were reluctant to make the difficult trip. Still

99

the worst was yet to come. First there was Darwin and railroads, then Marx and psychology, each like a rabbit nibbling at the verifiability of doctrine, and then Hitler, and the bombing of the monastery by benevolent Yankee Flying Fortresses. The sedentary fortress had been used as an Axis command post in the latter days of World War II in a last-ditch effort to retain the Mediterranean and mount a southern naval offensive.

Now the time had come to heal the physical wounds of the war and the gradual deterioration of centuries. Roofing and repainting were dreadfully overdue. More importantly, if new acolytes were to be enticed to devote their lives to Scipelli's mission, it was vital to replumb the premises and purchase computers, perhaps replace the straw sack mattresses with Sealy Posturepedics since the days of mortification were history. Finally, after much painful deliberation, the sad time had come to send the monks' blessed glory and one clear asset off for auction.

•

What Barkeley's auctioneer in a silver-striped waistcoat did not know was that the seedier religious artifacts dealers on five continents were already well-acquainted with Mark since he had already purchased every other remnant of the cross that had come up for sale on the secondary market. Most of these relics were of clearly bogus provenance, but he didn't mind. His capital seemed endless, and though he was willing to haggle, he always, always, ended up with the merchandise. After all, what price was too great for something priceless? After acquiring a particular large section from a Palestinian terrorist, he sat with his French representative over celebratory arrack in an Alexandrian hotel bar. The thing itself sat between them.

One sip too many of the pungent liquid, and the dealer confessed his suspicions. Perhaps he was hoping to steer his well-heeled client in the direction of more prime merchandise, or perhaps he took unaccustomed pity on the victim.

Mark just laughed. "It doesn't matter."

"But . . . "

Lifting up the object, Mark said, "Each of them has been the subject of faith, no? Perhaps it is the faith of the forger if no one else. But wouldn't Jesus say that the forger's—or sinner's—faith is more valuable than the saint's?"

100

"But . . . "

"Besides, who says the real thing was, well, real? Are you telling me that you believe?"

"Of course not."

"Good, then get them. Any of them, as many of them as you can. I want them all. I want IT." He idly plucked at the grime underneath his fingernail.

•

The woman in the green blouse was the first to turn around. Staring was contrary to auction-house etiquette, but her perusal was so frank that it transcended gawking. It was not merely curiosity, but a form of judgment.

•

And so, though he didn't know it, the Cypriot, among others, scoured the Mediterranean basin on Mark's behalf, but fewer and fewer of the pieces of the true cross were left. Mark had purchased everything available, and when they were officially unavailable for a reasonable or unreasonable sum, he employed yet another, more delicate agent to hire a contingent of trustworthy thugs to scale walls, crack safes and remove the sacred splinters, leaving carefully fabricated forgeries in their place. Sometimes he later purchased his own forgeries to avoid suspicion. In this way, Mark had acquired the entire continental horde of wood chips, ranging from modest to more brazen timbers. Only Mont St. Scipelli's was untouchable.

Since one fright (lightning, fire) in the fifteenth century, a cadre of monks dedicated themselves to sleeping on the flagstone floor beneath their treasure through eternity. The Scipelli fragment was therefore as continuously well-tended as Lenin's tomb. Mark pondered a guerrilla assault upon the monastery, but that spiritual castle that Allied planes were compelled to bomb into submission could be breeched by no less a force. Disdaining the common morality, Mark knew that even he could not wage unilateral war against one of the pillars of the Church. He had to wait, and bide his time—until modernity compelled an outright sale. But until that day, this day, arrived, he had much to accomplish, and did so. He waved his fan, turning 750 into 800.

•

Once purchased or pilfered, the sections were shipped with extreme care, more care than insurance since loss was inconceivable, back to the Jew. Houses everywhere, at home no place, Mark chose the least of his dwellings to receive his wares. It was the one atop the Manhattan tower from the roof of which an antenna bounced the signals of the God Network into the heavens. Sitting on a white sofa in a white living room—he liked white; it dirtied so easily—he contemplated the glow of the city below, each corner an illuminated cross in the city of a million intersections.

One eye to his empire, he sat with his horde, some in elaborate frames, others in slim wax-paper envelopes, some under glass, some like the infamous Hermitage plank that had required the assistance of the remains of the KGB to liberate, leaned up against the wall like a carpenter's scraps. An enormous glass conference table sat in the middle of the room. Carefully Mark set his collection upon the glass.

•

The excitement in the room was palpable. The regulars had long since forgotten their disdain for the newcomers. They were united in their fascination with the process and their amazement at the result. Agape at the expenditure, which had not yet reached its limit, their eyes jerked back and forth from bidder to bidder to the Barkeley's employee holding up the eight-inch square rectangle that would be transferred after the bidding was over to one of those contending so fiercely for its acquisition.

Of course, from anywhere in the room but the auctioneer's pulpit, the splinter itself was invisible. Only its purple matte shone with the intensity of its contents. It was as if the furious bidding was for the frame alone, its substance an afterthought. Yet there, upon closer examination sat the tiny piece of wood that several human beings were willing, avid, delirious to exchange for a king's ransom, so the others in the room assumed it must be worth something. In short, they believed.

•

Twain was wrong; pieced together they would not make a clipper, a mere rowboat perhaps, or a four-pronged life raft on which to weather the harsh storms of this world's sea. They all sat on the long glass conference table along with the tools that had been delivered to the private suite at the top of the office tower as per the boss's instructions along with a crate of Elmer's yellow wood glue and another crate of epoxy wood filler.

For a moment, he felt like he had as a child in his family's Westchester basement, eyeing the rack of tools his father kept on a pegboard over the washing machine. Or perhaps the sensation was more akin to moments of struggle during the creation of his first *Journey* when he was attempting to place the words in proper alinement. Now, however, it was the greatest jigsaw of all time in front of him that would, he was confident, reveal a sum far greater than its constituent parts.

Humming tunelessly, the incongruous magnate in the grip of obsession painstakingly attached each to the other. He still didn't know why he was so consumed, but Mark had never especially questioned the path his life had taken; he merely set to the task, and did so now. Some pieces fit immaculately, clearly of a unit once upon a time, while other crude fragments had to be forced into blunt configuration with their peers. Mark overlayed one to the next, filling the gaps between two enormous rectangular arms with dabs of putty and filler.

Not a boat, but a cross, eighteen feet long, ten wide. Piece by piece came together over months of laborious trial and error, but in the back of Mark's mind he was always waiting for the centerpiece that would bind the two arms together forever. Now it was for sale.

•

Unaccountably the bidding went over the house's expectations, despite its coy word *priceless*. Price was on everyone's mind at Barkeley's. 700 became 750, 800 became 850 until the auctioneer paused dramatically and said, "Do I hear one million?"

Mark waved his card with the same mild irritation as if he was swatting a fly.

The sheikh turned around in his seat and made a salaaming gesture of respect as he ceased his nodding.

The auctioneer turned to the telephone. The employee taking the call wiped sweat from his brow and said, "Two million."

Mark didn't pause to blink. He said "Three."

The voice on the other end of the phone was apparently silent. The assistant hung up.

The men from the monastery cringed.

"Three million," the auctioneer cried, lifting his gavel. "Going once, going twice. . . ."

·

Who made the cross? In response, one might ask who was the best known carpenter in Jerusalem?

It was radical speculation, perhaps, but the answer Dr. J. Rittenour suggested in Barkeley's catalogue was expected to create a stir in religious/archaeological circles by asserting that the cross was the work of Joseph, and the famous final cry of the creature or creator— whatever he was—depending upon its beam was addressed not to a heavenly, but an earthly father.

"Forgive them," he said, "for they know not what they do."

And then his head collapsed upon the internal beam of his breastbone.

·

"Four," the woman in the green blouse announced.

Every face in the room turned in her direction. For the first time Mark looked at the competition. She stood up and strode to the back of the room. "Every Christ needs his Judas," she said. "Or Judith. Here's my card." It read: Dr. J. Rittenour.

She left the room.

·

Junked at the site after the body was removed, the twin timbers lay askew, in a heap along with others that had carried less divine passengers. And how could one tell them apart? By the workmanship.

That night a barefoot child in a burlap garment snuck among the trash, searching for a coin or necklace or anything of any value that might be bartered for a scrap of food in the marketplace. He heard the wailing of the mourners at the edge of the hill, and saw the flickering candles of those who prepared the body for the interment from which three days later . . . maybe.

Perhaps it took a child to make the leap into metaphor. Considering the pain of the believers, he suddenly understood that more valuable than gold, to them at least, might be the physical embodiment of the memory of their Lord and the anticipation of their salvation. He pried at the huge timbers and then leaped back in pain.

Tentatively, he approached the cross again, but the second he touched it, the fire in his hand flared. The boy could not see in the dusk, but he could feel the jagged edge of wood emerging from the ball of his thumb. He pinched the wood between the long, filthy nails of his other thumb and forefinger, extracted it, and fled.

•

Pandemonium exploded in Barkeley's as the echo of the auctioneer's gavel faded. Junior employees hurried to their positions to conclude the afternoon's business and stringers from newspapers rushed to phone in the unexpected story. The regulars huddled in stunned acknowledgement of the financial clout of faith while dealers jabbered amongst themselves and the brothers from Scipelli sank back in their padded seats, relieved yet as uneasy as their hosts had been at the start of the auction. They felt as if they had witnessed a miracle, and it did not feel good.

•

The boy carried his prize to a small encampment south of Jerusalem, hard by the Dead Sea, as Julian would carry it forward a millennium in the future. There he traded it to the tribe for a melon and the believers tossed the holy item into a clay jug with some ancient—even then they were ancient—manuscripts and attempted to live the life their master had decreed.

•

Mark sat at home and looked at the card. He still sought the unlimited now that even the sky was ablink with his satellite. The only terrain left to conquer was the ineffable, the ethereal, the other, something beyond the atmosphere, something celestial. For a second he almost laughed to realize that he felt the same cravings that his inane books apparently satisfied across the globe.

He knew that she had bought the piece of cross for either of two reasons: to keep it, or to sell it to him. Barkeley's would take its commission on the four million, not bad for ten minutes work, but the auction house was heretofore eliminated from any further transaction. Had the both of them remained in the room bidding against each other they might have gone to five, six, seven million, who could tell? If he was willing to pay one more penny than she was he would still have it, not in the auction room, but elsewhere.

•

The keepers of the splinter by the inland body of salt water eventually died, but not before they told their children about their legacy. Those children in turn told theirs, who told the Turks who slaughtered them as Julian would slaughter their Turkish descendants ages into the future.

And all of their bones bleached in the sun and crumbled to desert dust.

•

Midnight, contemplating his loss, the doorbell rang and Mark knew who it was. A person whose eight-figure check was good at Barkeley's had the wherewithal to detect his secret address. He dismissed his servants and buzzed in the woman with the green shirt.

"Call me Judy," Dr. Rittenour said. She didn't look like a woman with four million dollars to spend, but, then again, neither did Mark appear to be such a man.

"Wine?" he asked with the sophistication that came naturally with vast wealth, and ushered his guest onto the terrace where the huge structure had been hoisted into a vertical position and secured with thin wires by the baffled, well-tipped superintendents of the tower. Side by side with the metal broadcast antenna, it was almost modest, but Mark flicked a switch which sent beams from three concealed spotlights and turned the cross into an illuminated vision. In the center of the vision, there was a gap, half an inch long, an eighth of an inch wide.

"Just as I expected," Dr. Rittenour said.

For the first time, Mark examined his competition—or was she his confederate? She was easily fifty, but her spiritual inquiries had kept her vigorous and she was clearly aware of how attractive she was. Her skin glowed in the reflection. The silk fluttered against her chest, her breasts unconstrained by any variety of elastic cross.

"Really?"

"It was obvious. Last November, the piece of the Omphalos cross was sold to a mysterious, unidentified party, and in April the piece of the Santa Hermina cross was removed from its crypt by undiscovered culprits, as was the Hermitage piece. Yes, I've been watching the gradual disappearance of the pieces of the cross for years. For one with an eye to the sacred, it was clear that they were headed for the same destination. The only piece that was left was Mont St. Scipelli's. That was the key. Wherever it was bound, the rest were to be found, and I rather assumed that they would now be in one piece."

"Elementary, Watson."

"Of course the thing that is truly curious is that although one might hazard an educated guess as to the what of the matter," and she gestured to the giant cross with admiration, "one still wonders about the why."

"I've asked myself that."

"And how have you answered yourself?" She swirled the dregs of wine around the glass and reclined on the terrace's redwood chaise lounge, placing one ankle over the other, toeing a leather sandal to the floor.

"I . . . " He was nervous. "I don't know." Met with silence, he repeated himself. "I just don't know. I suppose there's an emptiness that I'd like filled."

Dr. Rittenour extended one arm to the left.

He was at a loss to echo the moronic language of his books. "It's a need for something greater than myself."

She extended the other arm to the right and remained silent.

"I . . . I never got that at home."

Her voice lower by an octave, the professor purred, "Come to Momma."

•

Words, words, in the beginning were words . . . ecstasy on the page.

From his secret adolescent readings of the sci-fi porn comix that satisfied his imagination as the cheerleaders of White Plains High failed to satisfy his body, Mark had found something cosmically, karmically, he might have said, vital in the notion of words making worlds on paper. Creating something from nothing. Yet even before the disastrous day his vice came to light he had the sense, so clear yet so far from verbalization, that there *was* a prior truth.

Then came the day when his mother discovered his cache, ineffectively hidden under his Sealy Posturepedic mattress. She showed the offending texts to his father, and the man who would later vow to never buy another book turned brick red at the sight of such language. "Filth," the dry cleaner cried when his son returned from school proudly holding forth a sign he had made in wood shop.

It was a rectangle of knotty pine, eight inches wide, eighteen long, notched at the perimeter, bearing upon its unevenly stained surface the chiseled out word *The* followed by the family's surname with an elegant if ungrammatical apostrophe before the pluralizing *s*, and it was set upon a pointed stake.

"They're just. . . . books," he stammered.

The explanation was so insufficient and Mark's father's rage so great. The man's chest expanded barely short of exploding like the primordial Big Bang. Finally, however, as sadly incapable of giving voice to his passion as his own offending offspring, he simply thrust out his arms, and shoved Mark.

Boy and sign toppled backwards, but the sign fell first, and the boy fell upon the sign, the stake of which pierced his temple as it was intended to pierce the quarter acre greensward in front of the suburban ranch.

Mark's mother, absolute cause of his birth, proximate cause of his pain, shrieked and bundled the bleeding child into the family station wagon. She drove at warp speed to the local emergency room, where a sleep-deprived intern stitched him up and left a novice's pucker in the side of his head.

Mark knew what Dr. Rittenour—Judith—meant; that he knew, that he needed. He was sick of answering other people's questions and satisfying other people's spiritual cravings. He wanted his own answers, and if God couldn't give him that perhaps this one of his creatures might.

No further overtures were required. He unbuttoned his shirt, unbuckled his belt, kicked off his shoes. Wearing only briefs, he curled into her arms, surprised for a moment that they were not nailed to a ledge of wood and were capable of embracing him. "Forgive my father," he said, "for he doesn't know what he does."

"Forget him," she murmured, as she reached into her bag and grasped the tiny expensive item between her fingers.

·

He forgot where he was until he felt a pinprick on the temple, most vulnerable point of the body, beside his left eye, in the spot marked by the small indentation from his childhood, the incompetent surgical pucker half an inch long, an eighth of an inch wide.

A second later, the pucker was filled, the searcher's life and vision simultaneously complete. But for that one second, he saw the blinding illumination he had sought for as long as he could remember. The light of eternity flashed, the bite of eternity drew blood, and both of his eyes rolled into his head, and he rolled off the professor, dead as God.

·

Dr. Rittenour sat upright and replaced her shoes. Then she opened the large pocketbook she carried everywhere. She extracted an axe.

Nominated by Gerald Shapiro, Steve Stern, Michael Stephens

THERE GOES THE NOBEL PRIZE . . .

essay by CAROL MUSKE

from GREEN MOUNTAINS REVIEW

I'VE WITNESSED STRANGE THINGS in the twentieth century. I have, for example, watched the figure of the poet change from laureate of nothingness to minor potentate, ruler over various zoned and developed real estates.

W. H. Auden, whom I met in the mid-seventies when I was a young poet, was a laureate of nothingness. He had said, after all, eloquently, that poetry made nothing happen. He had said that suffering occurred while the world went on its indifferent doggy way, and he had downshifted his passionate engagement with leftist politics. Around the time I met him he had just finished translating (with Leif Sjöberg) Dag Hammarskjöld's journal of pensées, which Auden had dubbed *Markings*. He had, in true Auden style, written a pithy introduction in which he dispassionately assessed the character of the Swedish statesman and U.N. leader, whom he admired greatly, but in whom he detected a rather embarrassing and messianic desire to be God.

It was conveyed to Auden that this observation, if retained in the introduction, would not be looked upon kindly by Sweden and further, the Nobel committee would be forced to "reconsider" Auden's suitability for the literature prize. (He had already been "under consideration" a few times. Dag Hammarskjöld had, in fact, written in his private papers that Auden would be a worthy choice for the distinction.)

Despite this discreet editing suggestion, Auden adamantly refused to change his phrasing and mugged, upon the book's publication,

"There goes the Nobel Prize!" Though he was later heard to complain about not being chosen, his complaints were mainly practical—he said he wanted the prize not for prestige's sake but because he wished to buy an organ for the church in the little town of Kirchstetten, Austria, where he made his second home.

I met him a little after this episode. He had translated the work of the Swedish poet, Gunnar Eckelöf and had been invited to talk to a translation seminar in the graduate writing program at Columbia University. I was a friend (at the time) of Daniel Halpern, who had arranged for Auden to visit the seminar. We went down to Auden's dilapidated coldwater flat on the Lower East Side and collected him, then we all rode the subway up to 116th & Broadway.

Auden looked overall like a man who might really have used the Nobel prize, though in fact he was just dressed the way poets used to dress. He wore what looked like very ratty black pajamas, his hair rumpled—and sported run-down carpet slippers with no socks. His fingers and teeth were badly tobacco-stained and he blinked at the sunlight like an owl or a tortoise. I was transfixed. Here was Auden himself! I was stricken with shyness. Auden was very kind to me—it happened that I found it occasionally possible to ask him a question.

In the translation seminar, Auden was amusing and informative. He read his rendering of Eckelöf's *Evening Land* as well as some Icelandic runes. The response of the students was distinctly muted. It was, as I said, the mid '70s. It was a time when students were very politicized, very interested in "liberating" poetry from the house arrest of tradition, of formalism. One got the impression that they would rather have heard Robert Bly ruminating on the Spanish surrealists. But who knew what they wanted? A few students were receptive to Auden, most of them appeared bored. I was appalled, but said nothing. If Auden noticed the coolness of his reception, he did not let on. He told jokes, described himself as "surprisingly bawdy today" and chuckled to himself as he read, smoking and nodding.

I tell this story not for its anecdotal interest—but because I found both the students' reaction—and Auden's—instructive—as instructive as Auden's handling of pressure from On High, in the matter of the Nobel.

The students, clearly, were assuming a posture meant to hint at a politics of protest—and Auden was acting out, (no, *living*!) the role of the poet. That is to say, he was acting with dignity and humility and with a good will and passion clearly generated by his subject, a subject

111

inspiring enough to persuade a poet to overlook almost any personal slight.

Not long after this, Auden moved to Austria, where he died a few years later. He was not a wealthy man at his death, not one routinely "covered" by the media; his funeral was small and plain. The Nobel prize might have guaranteed a more public prestigious funeral ("he became his admirers")—certainly prize money would have "cushioned" his final years or at least bought an organ for the local church.

I have no intention of comparing Auden, his character, style, his self-honor and his honoring of poetry—to life in our own poetry zeitkreig. But forgive me, it's hard to imagine any of us in his shoes (or broken-down carpet slippers) freezing out Caesar with such panache, calmly refusing to be politic, to even consider compromise in a phrase or two. It's hard to imagine any of us tolerating cheerfully such a scornful reception by graduate students.

We all know the great poet-martyrs of our century. Mandelstam's shadow falls like a cloud, a moving shroud, over the post-war decades, and the other names unwind like a litany, Celan, Neruda, Hikmet, Nellie Sachs, Kim Chee. . . . Milosz's words (and Adorno's) on the ruins of culture haunt us.

But since most of us will not wake on the gallows or in a death camp, sentenced for ten lines of accentual syllabics—we might draw a lesson from Auden's unruffled refusal to capitulate to polite intimidating pressure, a pressure we all recognize and have experienced. (Auden, also eschewed crowd favor, when he saw how easy it was to fall into popular demagoguery, as he himself once did in an after-dinner speech.)

There is, of course, polite intimidating pressure everywhere, as there always has been. It is just a question of degree. (There is also less polite pressure, as typified by the NEA struggle for freedom of artistic expression—and this is where the links of connection, in the gradual shift from polite to impolite, grow more illuminating.)

We are in the midst of a fairly heady time for poetry—or the acknowledgement of poetry. We've witnessed a proliferation of lucrative grants, fellowships, cash and publication prizes, goth foundation giveaways and power readings. There are celebrity turns in Rome, Prague and London, there are highly-publicized writers' conferences, there are "genius" grants. It has become cool to support poets and poetry.

Poets are suddenly visible—on public television, on the internet, in the press. And the same process of celebrification that has exploded other disciplines has managed to make poets, if not famous, weirdly marketable. (Is it possible that Emerson's great great granddaughter was photographed for an ad in *Vanity Fair* selling Coach handbags?)

Auden believed that poets should not be entirely visible, that it was necessary for a poet (à la Keats) to lose the self, to be invisible. Outspoken, yes, but not advertised.

In our proliferation of identity politics, identity poems, our debates over the illusion of self, narrative vs. lyric, "subjectless, ego-less" L-A-N-G-U-A-G-E poetry vs. the poems of witness, the poem of memoir-truth, our factionalization and Balkanization—we seem to have bought the franchise, all of us: we are fighting over turf. I'm Somebody, OK—and who are you, pal? And what subtle coercions do we tolerate and bend to? Peer opinion, patronage, institutional good favor, favor of the Academy, of reputation-making critics, of factions. I'm saying that we should consider that our move away from anonymity necessitates an unbuyable self-presence, like Auden's.

Our names seem now not writ in water but in 40 watt lights, not bright enough for Broadway, just shiny enough to attract a few bugs. I recently reviewed a re-issue of Muriel Rukeyser's odd and wonderful *The Life of Poetry*, first published in 1949. In one essay, she talks about "the long preparation of the self to be used"—as if there is an apprenticeship that poets must serve in order to be humble enough to be useful to the art.

What a concept—in our over-exposed times. "The long preparation of the self to be used"—not exposed, exploited, celebrated, defended or promoted, but *used* in the service of poetry.

Recently Larry Levis died and his death has occasioned (as David St. John has eloquently pointed out) perhaps more attention and public scrutiny than he ever elicited while alive. Larry Levis was not a self-promoter, he lived the life of a laureate of nothingness. His work was dazzling—and neglected. But that used to come with poetry's territory. Let the dead bury the dead—and our reputations be established post-Lethe. Auden's life, Rukeyser's and Levis's all stand as lessons—and inspiration—to the rest of us. It's all right to be anonymous, to think of the self as an apprentice and the soul as the final invisible curator of our gifts. Don't hang up on Stockholm, please, but spend the money on the church organ, unless they call with editing advice. Then think of Auden.

Nominated by Green Mountains Review, Ralph Angel, Phil Appleman, Henry Carlile, Joyce Carol Oates, Eugene Stein

PORNOGRAPHY

by ANGELA SHAW

from SENECA REVIEW

Painted, perfect, patient, I couch myself
in lace peignoir. I author the slouching
hours after dusk, bidding the sun go down
over Tucson or Memphis, conjuring love-
rooms from a little perfume, a little blues,
a little bourbon. Every romance opens
at the neckline. Every night a voluptuous
storyline is teasingly unveiled, stocking
by stocking, exquisitely unfastened
at its climax. There are infinite methods
of table setting, of letting backdrop foretell
the spread, the dizzying lick of the graceful
fellatrix. A neatly banked fire is both action
and circumstance. I practice an interior
design,appointing the chamber with chance
reticence: the hush of a thick rug, the space
that embraces the furniture's curves. I rhyme
slipcover with pillow talk, the jaded wallpaper
with my eyes. My body lies to tell the truth,
each gesture disguised as stillness, each over-
wrought pose happening toward aftermath.

114

My past is strapless, hook-less and eye-less.
I freelance, unlacing the vintage syntax
of seduction. My patron sated, I compose
myself—painted, perfect, patient as paper,
falling open like a book to my best parts.

Nominated by Seneca Review

THE BILL COLLECTOR'S VACATION

fiction by PATRICIA HAMPL

from PLOUGHSHARES

ALL WEEK THE HEAT has been killing. Foolish to walk the distance to the credit union even so early in the morning, imagining you can beat the worst of it. Think of the walk back, the pavement baking, not a tree for blocks. *Foolish*—a Kenneth word. *Don't be foolish, Marilyn, take the Volvo.*

This, as so often now, was her cue. The tiny, greased gear of her willfulness downshifted away from him, revving at the barest stroke of his control. Or his contempt. She wasn't free to do the sensible thing—drive the air-conditioned car out of the cool garage to the credit union two miles away. She had to fight. Fight what?

Anyway, it was good to walk. A recent article she had clipped made the point: walking was as good, even for cardiovascular, as jogging. Better, really, less threat to the joints. Kenneth was a runner—he didn't like the word jogger. She had put the clipping on the kitchen corkboard: *Jogging Benefits Questioned*. Not that Kenneth bothered to read the clippings she put up, though he could be annoyed by the sight of grocery coupons pinned there. "What are you wasting time clipping coupons for?" he would say, walking out the back door to the garage. That shrug of disdain as he passed by.

Get to the credit union by eight when it opens, home by nine-thirty, before the real heat of the day: this was her plan. She wasn't due at the bookstore until afternoon. But already the day's new heat was adding

116

itself to the surplus still standing from yesterday. The night had left it all to simmer.

At the credit union, she pulled on the big glass door. It didn't budge. Her eye went to a white rectangle on the glass, above the handle: Weekdays 9 a.m.-4:30 p.m. An added judgment, another cluck of contempt. *Foolish, not to check the hours.*

She turned, was struck by the sun. A man was sitting on the low retaining wall in the shade, apparently having made the same mistake. He held a check and a green deposit slip in a meaty hand. He smiled at her in a way she recognized was harmless. How could you tell that about strangers? Could you? Marilyn trusted her instinct on things like this. Strange, how she bristled at Kenneth, but she still trusted the world for no good reason.

"Plenty of room," the man said. He patted the low wall where he sat, and looked away, toward the state capitol and its immense greensward. She joined him on the retaining wall, ducking out of the sun.

She was annoyed by the hour wait—waste of time. Said so. Wasn't this something new, the nine o'clock opening hour? Were these temporary summer hours? Shouldn't the credit union have sent out notices of any change? "And in this heat," she added. She expected him to meet her on this. But he—beefy, younger than she, dressed in shorts and tee, stomach lazing over his waistband—veered away from the communion of resentment. "I'm on vacation," he said easily, gazing off. "Might as well wait."

Marilyn felt oddly annoyed, as if this fat stranger's contentment subtly betrayed her. *Foolish to be impatient.* She wished she hadn't settled in next to him, but it made no sense to walk back home (plus the question of facing Kenneth), and this was the only shaded place to sit.

A woman in cutoffs, her skimpy yellow hair raked high in a painful-looking ponytail, hurried to the door in flip-flops, her child trailing behind her. She took in the sign, sighed, squinted in the direction of the flower box. No room. Her feet smacked the steps as she rushed back to her car, the child's face impassive as a loan officer at her side.

Several others came by, mostly businessmen in suits too dark, too cruelly heavy, for the day. Sweating figures frowning theatrically at their watches. Each time the plot of discovery and disappointment looked stagier. Always, they walked off, got in their closed cars, drove away. People were becoming cartoons. Only she and the fat man sat there, waiting it out by the retaining wall, electric-blue lobelia rising from the flower boxes behind them.

117

The sharp edges of her annoyance melted, as she sat there regarding other people's irritation. What predictable animals we are. She was going to point this out to the heavy man sitting peacefully to her right. But her observation would seem to him, she sensed, mean-spirited. He wouldn't like it.

How did she know this—that he would be allergic to—to what? Irony? The basic unkindness of reading people, observing them? He would not like judging people. That was it, he wasn't a judger. He was—she hadn't the slightest idea. But how interesting, anyway, to know he wouldn't like a smart observation. You know these things about people. It's the way you size up anyone, quick brush strokes of assessment you hardly know you're making. It's how we make our way through the day, down the street, she supposed. Glancing and judging, feinting to the left, dodging to the right.

She asked what he did for a living.

"I work for the Consolidated Bureaus," he said.

What was that?

A smile, sad smile: "I'm a nasty bill collector."

Was it a hard job?

"Well, only eight to ten percent of the bills sent to me ever get collected. Ever. Believe it. And of all the people I talk to— it's a phone job—only five percent show *any* willingness to work with me on the problem. Can you believe that?" He shook his head in mild wonder.

"Do they admit they owe the money?" Marilyn asked. His earnestness seemed to require the question.

"Sure."

"And?"

"They could care less."

"I suppose it makes you pretty cynical," Marilyn said. God, what a hopeless job.

"You don't trust *anybody,*" he said richly. But his voice gave him away, no edge to it. He was a great unflexed wad of trust. Wasn't cynical, wasn't bruised. He was intact. Rare sight.

She should not believe, however, the people on *Oprah* and *20/20* who told outlandish tales about bill collectors. The part about threats. "There are rules and laws, we can't do any of that stuff," he said, repelled. The very idea he would menace anyone. He shifted slightly, a shiver of disgust.

Imagine being married to such a man. That sweet disgust at his own supposed power, rippling from the center of his soft pudding self—it

118

was reliable, good. Something reassuring about disgust, less aggressive than contempt.

She had gone over this: it was contempt she had to contend with from Kenneth, not just the grit of his practiced will sparking against her worn-out compliance. At first (thirty-six years!—their daughter was a mother twice already) his abruptness had struck her as certainty. Impatient, yes. But the good kind of impatient—eager, ambitious, hungry. Men should be hungry. The growl of love and work, lean and hungry. She used to think that way—men are, women are. Everybody did.

She had been proud, secretly, to recognize that hunger in Kenneth, willing to admit that's what she wanted. A twilight boat ride around the harbor, sponsored by their two Catholic colleges, spring, 1959. Holding a glass of shrimp-colored punch, feeling bold, though she did nothing illicit. Thinking, calculating about him—that was illicit. She shrugged off, in an instant, the domesticated male virtues so prized in Father Sullivan's Attributes of Catholic Marriage class. "Does he give you a champagne feeling of well-being, girls?" the priest rang out to his roomful of putative virgins. A nun, still wearing the Renaissance habit of the Order, sat at the back of the room grading papers, a sardonic eyebrow raised occasionally like a mordant punctuation mark to the old priest's blather. The sins he had in mind were corny, middle-aged fantasies. He warned them about wife-swapping, for God's sake.

The truth was, Kenneth *had* given her a champagne feeling, though not of well-being. Something grainier, like the dry sandiness of real champagne hitting the roof of your mouth. Even the faint sneer on Kenneth's face had not scared her off. Had there been a sneer, even then? She had looked up at his smooth face as he said something— what?—something funny, something a bit unkind, a circle of people around him, crewcuts and candy-colored sweater sets. Whatever he said, it gave her the chance to tilt her face up to him, a kiss-me-angle, laughing, admiring. Oh, she wanted him. The big boat cut the water smoothly, then there was a shift as it turned. Her punch sloshed out of the glass, her hands got sticky. "Better watch that," he said, smiling. Had noticed her. They were married the weekend after graduation, to no one's surprise. They had become one of their campuses' solid "couples" since their sophomore year. Pre-law and el ed. "Great planning, Ken," an uncle whacked him on the back at the wedding, "she'll get you through law school."

119

Which Marilyn had, four years of second grade at Compton Elementary, using birth control without a qualm. *None of their business,* Kenneth said. He led them with amazing nonchalance, away from the crafted certainties of their parochial background. He had no crisis of faith. It wasn't spiritual, not even intellectual. He simply saw that life was elsewhere. He began growing his hair long, not crazy long, just curling over his collar. They marched together downtown to the Federal Building, to protest the draft. But they threw nothing, not rocks, not blood. They did not get arrested. He was *Law Review,* clerked for a state supreme court justice. Good firm, some teaching. Then the children, just two, a girl, then a boy.

By the time the children were in school, Marilyn didn't want to go back to teaching, cramming down a damp sandwich in the staff room choked with smoke, the pent-up aura of captives in the corridors, mayhem roaring from the lunchroom. Motherhood spoiled her. It was orderly—to her surprise. Days alone, doing little things, one after another. Reading books to the children, their small fingers pointing: Train, elephant! Giraffe, giraffe, giraffe!

She opened a bookstore with the mother of another boy in her son's Montessori class. Children's books and educational games. Now the place, Charlotte's Web, was hers. She'd bought out her partner, who had moved to Florida. Business was good, really good. Kenneth was impressed. She had been approached about opening a second store in a mall, books, interactive multimedia products, a whole area devoted to hands-on computers. The computer stations for the new store reminded her of the hi-fi booths of her high-school years, where you could go and listen to a record to see if you wanted to buy it. Sit in the little confession-box-size glass booth, headset clamped on like earmuffs, melting into Johnny Mathis.

She stared off at the green shimmer of the capitol grounds across the avenue from the credit union. Was it Johnny Mathis who had sung "Moon River"? Audrey Hepburn was dead. Marilyn had cried, actually sobbed, alone, looking at the pictures in *People* magazine. My era.

"I was sitting here before you arrived," the bill collector said, as if they had been carrying on a conversation—had they? had she missed something?—"and I was watching that man on the mower on the capitol grounds across the street there, trying to figure out how he runs that thing."

Marilyn looked across at the figure on the mower.

"I've been watching him really close—no hand levers, nothing with his feet. I can't figure it out. He just sits on it, and it goes on its own." Fascinated by the likelihood of magic at work, voice rippling with awe. "Do you see anything?"

"No, I don't," Marilyn said. "He just seems to go."

"That's what I'm thinking," the man said.

This thought seemed to connect him to many other thoughts. There is absolutely no point, for example, he said, in attempting to collect a bill during the full moon: people are *nuts* during the full moon. Ditto during the twelve-year period when he managed a skating rink: he always hired extra security on full moon nights. The kids were nuts then, too. Possessed. More murders on full moon nights, according to the police. More *everything*.

He expressed no irritation at the feckless and sometimes evil ways of the world. Apparently he lived in a state of astonishment.

From the full moon to astrology. He was a Taurus. Again the amazement of it all: most of his family were Gemini or Cancer—he had no *idea* why he was a Taurus. A unbidden mystery boring out of the core of his identity. There was meaning in all this. Believe it.

He also wondered why—as a Capitol Patrol car went by—there were city police and capitol police. Wasn't that a waste of money, an overlap? Marilyn mentioned the existence of the university police, another doubling of duty. Maybe there was a value in having this extra protection in sensitive areas? He thought that over, agreed. "There are lots of chemicals sitting around the university," he said. "Things can blow up."

"The university," he repeated, as if pondering a thesis. It was a place he had come to know well in the last year. Wasn't it incredible, the labyrinth of corridors at University Hospital, the confusion of the place for the non-university person thrust suddenly into that maze? Take himself. He'd gone there every day for months and months. Never figured the place out. Pause. "My brother was a patient there."

They were turning a dark corner, she sensed.

The brother was big in astrology, Tarot, all that. He had come home from California for a family visit, had read their father's cards. He told his brother that the father would be dead before Christmas. But it was himself who was gone before Christmas. Just six months ago. "He read his own cards," the bill collector said, something like reverence in his voice. "The one thing you cannot do is read your own cards. But you can read your own fate in another person's cards. You don't even know it."

Oh yes, the cards had sometimes told him more than he wanted to know, too. He stayed away from the cards now.

He turned abruptly from the occult, steered them toward his *amazing* four-year-old. This boy liked *his* cooking better than his wife's. Why? Because it was spicier. Imagine: a four-year-old who loves spicy food, really spicy, like an adult. Incredible, but true.

So many amazing facts. Flowers can grow out of sheer rock, you saw that a lot along Lake Superior where he, the wife, and the boy were going for the week, as soon as he deposited his check. Or the oddity of sundogs, and the fact that a significant percentage of the population does not believe we ever landed on the moon. Some pretty interesting arguments, you know? His brother had a book on it. Also, he and his brother had once seen a funnel cloud twirling along 61 North. The amazing thing? It looked just the way you always heard they looked: absolutely a funnel, skidding around like a bad fast dancer, touching down, and then, for no reason, up and off again. He leaned back against the flower boxes. Weather was *really* weird.

Not to mention the host of unpaid bills all about us, the carelessness of people. "They say, 'Fuck you,' just like that, and slam the phone down," he said, marveling, not insulted.

Then there's the big one, Big D. The sudden disappearance of blood relatives, their unbelievable dematerialization. You keep seeing people who look just like them. Or rather, you *start* seeing people who look just like them, the backs of heads. You never noticed that before, not till he passed away, was gone. Then he seemed to be everywhere. "My brother was younger than me," he said, "but he goes first. They say, 'Expect the unexpected.' It's easy to forget that." Blue lobelia appeared to sprout from his shoulders where he leaned against the retaining wall.

The day was heating up. The humidity felt intentional, vicious, needling away at the air. It would be another heavy day to live through.

The bill collector wasn't looking at Marilyn. He just gazed out, kept talking, seeing things. Galena, Illinois, used to be located on the banks of the Mississippi River, but no longer is. You see, a river is not a straight line between banks. It's a whole system, and you don't know where it starts or stops, what space it really takes up. They make a big deal about finding the source of the Mississippi. That's dumb. The Indians laughed at that. There *isn't* really a source. It's a big muddle up there. They just choose this stream or that, call it "the source." You don't *know*. What you see is *not* what you got. Nor are you necessarily safe from earthquakes just because you live in the Midwest. Remember that little town in Missouri? Gone. And raisins are not a fruit, not a berry. Raisins are really former grapes, shriveled up—but he bet she knew that one already.

The bill collector's voice wheeled through the heat, his marvels believable and meaningless at once, lovely harmlessnesses making the world work, gears in the great engine carrying us over the rough patches. The grass across the avenue on the capitol greensward had been watered earlier in the morning from jets buried in the ground. Now the green gave off a low weather system, a minute fog just above itself, tiny rainbows evaporating by the minute as the heat burned them into the day.

The man on the riding mower worked the grass like a tidy quarter section of alfalfa, without lever or foot pedal, hands visible on the steering wheel, but no sign of where the energy came from. Something at the knee? Marilyn's eyes shut a quick instant against the disloyal thought. It was too far to see now, anyway. Who knows?

A gray Volvo wagon—their own, she realized—turned the corner. Kenneth coming to get her. He pulled up near the sidewalk, the tires making the watery sound of tires slowing on dry pavement. He leaned across the seat toward the passenger window so she could see him beckoning. His face was filmy behind the gleam of the rolled-up window. *And now you see darkly, but then face to face.* But when, when do you see someone face to face? Not in this life. Was he smiling?—she thought he was smiling. A good smile. Concern there. She could make out a hand,gesturing. He wanted her to be out of the heat. Oh, and safe. He worries. Always has. Sees trouble. It's what he thinks imagination is for—worrying. Remember the first time? "I'll always protect you"—the little patch of movie dialogue, the champagne of well-being, the two of them meeting the length of their pure bodies for the first time, crazy to touch. Some dumb motel on University Avenue, the *l* blanked out on the neon sign. *Star Mote.* Looking for trouble, the sweet, safe kind, a month before the wedding. *I'll always protect you.*

Soon, the big glass door will open. But not yet. Kenneth must wait, just a sec, honey. She must stay here in the shade, the lobelia gushing over the cinder blocks. The fat stranger keeps talking, listing all the unlikely things that happen, that just are. She doesn't move. She will go to the Volvo in a moment, explain it all. But for now, this extra instant, she stays put, here in the killing heat. She wants to look straight ahead at nothing for another minute, wants to keep listening to the bill collector, who, still in mourning, is describing the world as the wonder it must be.

Nominated by Josip Novakovich

ABUNDANCE

by CARL PHILLIPS

from TRIQUARTERLY

Not just the body—be it
as wild loam; as the loom with never a lack
of willing, schooled-enough

hands; or as steady
burning-glass beneath which, smoldering at
last, ah, give up.

But whatever bird, also,
bearing some equally whatever and now
irretrievable small life

where is home. The lip
too, that in its casual meeting with the glass
whose silvered rim

here is faded, here flakes, here
is gone,
meets all the other lips that once knew

and drank from the same glass—
an erotics
of cooled distance, all that history

has been, all that memory
is. . . .
Remember the buck, stepping free

of the dark wood,
of the wood's shadow, as if
just for you? And the antlers, you said simply,

branching like hands or
like trees.
I thought of the branching of mistake when,

presumed over,
forgotten,
on all sides at once it sports a fist

full of blooms.

What you must call the blooms,
call them. Prayers; these willed disclosures—

Nominated by Tri Quarterly, Martha Collins, Rachel Hadas, Ha Jin, Sherod Santos, Lloyd Schwartz

TIMESHARE

fiction by JEFFREY EUGENIDES

from CONJUNCTIONS

M Y FATHER IS SHOWING me around his new motel. I shouldn't call it a motel after everything he's explained to me but I still do. What it is, what it's going to be, my father says, is a timeshare resort. As we walk down the dim hallway (some of the bulbs have burned out), my father informs me of the recent improvements. "We put in a new oceanfront patio," he says. "I had a landscape architect come in, but he wanted to charge me an arm and a leg. So I designed it myself."

Most of the units haven't been renovated yet. The place was a wreck when my father borrowed the money to buy it, and from what my mother tells me, it looks a lot better now. They've repainted, for one thing, and put on a new roof. Each room will have a kitchen installed. At present, however, only a few rooms are occupied. Some units don't even have doors. Walking by, I can see painting tarps and broken air conditioners lying on the floors. Water-stained carpeting curls back from the edges of the rooms. Some walls have holes in them the size of a fist, evidence of the college kids who used to stay here during spring break. My father plans to install new carpeting, and to refuse to rent to students. "Or if I do," he says, "I'll charge a big deposit, like three hundred bucks. And I'll hire a security guard for a couple of weeks. But the idea is to make this place a more upscale kind of place. As far as the college kids go, piss on 'em."

The foreman of this renewal is Buddy. My father found him out on the highway, where day workers line up in the morning. He's a little guy with a red face and makes, for his labor, five dollars an hour.

127

"Wages are a lot lower down here in Florida," my father explains to me. My mother is surprised at how strong Buddy is for his size. Just yesterday, she saw him carrying a stack of cinder blocks to the dumpster. "He's like a little Hercules," she says. We come to the end of the hallway and enter the stairwell. When I take hold of the aluminum banister, it nearly rips out of the wall. Every place in Florida has these same walls.

"What's that smell?" I ask.

Above me, hunched over, my father says nothing, climbing.

"Did you check the land before you bought this place?" I ask. "Maybe it's built over a toxic dump."

"That's Florida," says my mother. "It smells that way down here."

At the top of the stairs, a thin green runner extends down another darkened hallway. As my father leads the way, my mother nudges me, and I see what she's been talking about: he's walking lopsided, compensating for his bad back. She's been after him to see a doctor but he never does. Every so often, his back goes out and he spends a day soaking in the bathtub (the tub in room 308, where my parents are staying temporarily). We pass a maid's cart, loaded with cleaning fluids, mops and wet rags. In an open doorway, the maid stands, looking out, a big black woman in blue jeans and a smock. My father doesn't say anything to her. My mother says hello brightly and the maid nods.

At its middle, the hallway gives onto a small balcony. As soon as we step out, my father announces, "There it is!" I think he means the ocean, which I see for the first time, storm-colored and uplifting, but then it hits me that my father never points out scenery. He's referring to the patio. Red-tiled, with a blue swimming pool, white deck chairs and two palm trees, the patio looks as though it belongs to an actual seaside resort. It's empty but, for the moment, I begin to see the place through my father's eyes—peopled and restored, a going concern. Buddy appears down below, holding a paint can. "Hey, Buddy, " my father calls down, "that tree still looks brown. Have you had it checked?"

"I had the guy out."

"We don't want it to die."

"The guy just came and looked at it."

We look at the tree. The taller palms were too expensive, my father says. "This one's a different variety."

"I like the other kind," I say.

"The royal palms? You like those? Well, then, after we get going, we'll get some."

128

We're quiet for a while, gazing over the patio and the purple sea.

"This place is going to get all fixed up and we're going to make a million dollars!" my mother says.

"Knock on wood," says my father.

Five years ago, my father actually made a million. He'd just turned sixty and, after working all his life as a mortgage banker, went into business for himself. He bought a condominium complex in Fort Lauderdale, resold it and made a big profit. Then he did the same thing in Miami. At that point, he had enough to retire on but he didn't want to. Instead, he bought a new Cadillac and a fifty-foot power boat. He bought a twin engine airplane and learned to fly it. And then he flew around the country, buying real estate, flew to California, to the Bahamas, over the ocean. He was his own boss and his temper improved. Later, the reversals began. One of his developments in North Carolina, a ski resort, went bankrupt. It turned out his partner had embezzled a hundred thousand dollars. My father had to take him to court, which cost more money. Meanwhile, a savings and loan sued my father for selling it mortgages that defaulted. More legal fees piled up. The million dollars ran out fast and, as it began to disappear, my father tried a variety of schemes to get it back. He bought a company that made "manufactured homes." They were like mobile homes, he told me, only more substantial. They were prefabricated, could be plunked down anywhere but, once set up, looked like real houses. In the present economic situation, people needed cheap housing. Manufactured homes were selling like hotcakes.

My father took me to see the first one on its lot. It was Christmas, two years ago, when my parents still had their condominium. We'd just finished opening our presents when my father said that he wanted to take me for a little drive. Soon we were on the highway. We left the part of Florida I knew, the Florida of beaches, high rises and developed communities, and entered a poorer, more rural area. Spanish moss hung from the trees and the unpainted houses were made of wood. The drive took about two hours. Finally, in the distance, we saw the onion bulb of a gas tower with "Ocala" painted on the side. We entered the town, passing rows of neat houses, and then we came to the end and kept on going. "I thought you said it was in Ocala," I said.

"It's a little further out," said my father.

Countryside began again. We drove into it. After about fifteen miles, we came to a dirt road. The road led into an open, grassless field, without any trees. Toward the back, in a muddy area, stood the manufactured house.

It was true it didn't look like a mobile home. Instead of being long and skinny, the house was rectangular, and fairly wide. It came in three or four different pieces which were screwed together, and then a traditional-looking roof was put in place on top. We got out of the car and walked on bricks to get closer. Because the county was just now installing sewer lines out this far, the ground in front of the house—"the yard," my father called it—was dug up. Right in front of the house, three small shrubs had been planted in the mud. My father inspected them, then waved his hand over the field. "This is all going to be filled in with grass," he said. The front door was a foot and a half off the ground. There wasn't a porch yet but there would be. My father opened the door and we went inside. When I shut the door behind me, the wall rattled like a theater set. I knocked on the wall, to see what it was made of, and heard a hollow tinny sound. When I turned around, my father was standing in the middle of the living room, grinning. His right index finger pointed up in the air. "Get a load of this," he said. "This is what they call a 'cathedral ceiling.' Ten feet high. Lotta headroom, boy."

Despite the hard times, nobody bought a manufactured home, and my father, writing off the loss, went on to other things. Soon I began getting incorporation forms from him, naming me vice president of Baron Development Corporation, or the Atlantic Glass Company, or Fidelity Mini-Storage Inc. The profits from these companies, he assured, would one day come to me. The only thing that did come, however, was a man with an artificial leg. My doorbell rang one morning and I buzzed him in. In the next moment, I heard him clumping up the stairs. From above, I could see the blond stubble on his bald head and could hear his labored breathing. I took him for a delivery man. When he got to the top of the stairs, he asked if I was vice president of Duke Development. I said I guessed that I was. He handed me a summons.

It had to do with some legal flap. I lost track after a while. Meanwhile, I learned from my brother that my parents were living off savings, my father's IRA and credit from the banks. Finally, he found this place, Palm Bay Resort, a ruin by the sea, and convinced another savings and loan to lend him the money to get it running again. He'd provide the labor and know-how and, when people started coming, he'd pay off the S & L and the place would be his.

After we look at the patio, my father wants to show me the model. "We've got a nice little model," he says. "Everyone who's seen it has been very favorably impressed." We come down the dark hallway again, down the stairs, and along the first-floor corridor. My father has a master key and lets us in a door marked 103. The hall light doesn't work, so we file in through the dark living room to the bedroom. As soon as my father flips on the light, a strange feeling takes hold of me. I feel as though I've been here before, in this room, and then I realize what it is: the room is my parents' old bedroom. They've moved in the furniture from their old condo: the peacock bedspread, the Chinese dressers and matching headboard, the gold lamps. The furniture, which once filled a much bigger space, looks squeezed together in this small room. "This is all your old stuff," I say.

"Goes nice in here, don't you think?" my father asks.

"What are you using for a bedspread now?"

"We've got twin beds in our unit," my mother says. "This wouldn't have fit anyway. We've just got regular bedspreads now. Like in the other rooms. Hotel supply. They're OK."

"Come and see the living room," my father tells me, and I follow him through the door. After some fumbling, he finds a light that works. The furniture in here is all new and doesn't remind me of anything. A painting of driftwood on the beach hangs on the wall. "How do you like that painting? We got fifty of them from this warehouse. Five bucks a pop. And they're all different. Some have starfish, some seashells. All in a maritime motif. They're signed oil paintings." He walks to the wall and, taking off his glasses, makes out the signature: "Cesar Amarollo! Boy, that's better than Picasso." He turns back to me, smiling, happy about this place.

I'm down here to stay a couple of weeks, maybe even a month. I won't go into why. My father gave me unit 207, right on the ocean. He calls the rooms "units" to differentiate them from the motel rooms they used to be. Mine has a little kitchen. And a balcony. From it, I can see cars driving along the beach, a pretty steady stream. This is the only place in Florida, my father tells me, where you can drive on the beach.

The motel gleams in the sun. Somebody is pounding somewhere. A couple of days ago, my father started offering complimentary suntan lotion to anyone who stays the night. He's advertising this on the marquee out front but, so far, no one has stopped. Only a few families are here right now, mostly old couples. There's one woman in a motorized wheelchair. In the morning, she rides out to the pool and sits, and then her husband appears, a washed-out guy in a bathing suit and flannel shirt. "We don't tan anymore," she tells me. "After a certain age, you just don't tan. Look at Kurt. We've been out here all week and that's all the tan he is." Sometimes, too, Judy, who works in the office, comes out to sunbathe during her lunch hour. My father gives her a free room to stay in, up on the third floor, as part of her salary. She's from Ohio and wears her hair in a long braided ponytail, like a girl in fifth grade.

At night, in her hotel-supply bed, my mother has been having prophetic dreams. She dreamed that the roof sprung a leak two days before it did so. She dreamed that the skinny maid would quit and, next day, the skinny maid did. She dreamed that someone broke his neck diving into the empty swimming pool (instead, the filter broke, and the pool had to be emptied to fix it, which she says counts). She tells me all this by the swimming pool. I'm in it; she's dangling her feet in the water. My mother doesn't know how to swim. The last time I saw her in a bathing suit I was five years old. She's the burning, freckled type, braving the sun in her straw hat only to talk to me, to confess this strange phenomenon. I feel as though she's picking me up after swimming lessons. My throat tastes of chlorine. But then I look down and see the hair on my chest, grotesquely black against my white skin, and I remember that I'm old, too.

Whatever improvements are being made today are being made on the far side of the building. Coming down to the pool, I saw Buddy going into a room, carrying a wrench. Out here, we're alone, and my mother tells me that it's all due to rootlessness. "I wouldn't be dreaming these things if I had a decent house of my own. I'm not some kind of gypsy. It's just all this traipsing around. First we lived in that motel in Hilton Head. Then that condo in Vero. Then that recording studio your father bought, without any windows, which just about killed me. And now this. All my things are in storage. I dream about them, too. My couches, my good dishes, all our old family photos. I dream of them packed away almost every night."

"What happens to them?"

"Nothing. Just that nobody ever comes to get them."

There are a number of medical procedures that my parents are planning to have done when things get better. For some time now, my mother has wanted a face-lift. When my parents were flush, she actually went to a plastic surgeon who took photographs of her face and diagramed her bone structure. It's not a matter of simply pulling the loose skin up, apparently. Certain facial bones need shoring up as well. My mother's upper palate has slowly receded over the years. Her bite has become disaligned. Dental surgery is needed to resurrect the skull over which the skin will be tightened. She had the first of these procedures scheduled about the time my father caught his partner embezzling. In the trouble afterward, she had to put the idea on hold.

My father, too, has put off two operations. The first is disk surgery to help the pain in his lower back. The second is prostate surgery to lessen the blockage to his urethra and increase the flow of his urine. His delay in the latter case is not motivated purely by financial considerations. "They go up there with that Roto-Rooter and it hurts like hell," he told me. "Plus, you can end up incontinent." Instead, he has elected to go to the bathroom fifteen to twenty times a day, no trip being completely satisfying. During the breaks in my mother's prophetic dreams, she hears my father getting up again and again. "Your father's stream isn't exactly magnificent anymore," she told me. "You live with someone, you know."

As for me, I need a new pair of shoes. A sensible pair. A pair suited to the tropics. Stupidly, I wore a pair of old black wingtips down here, the right shoe of which has a hole in the bottom. I need a pair of flip-flops. Every night, when I go out to the bars in my father's Cadillac (the boat is gone, the plane is gone, but we still have the yellow "Florida Special" with the white vinyl top), I pass souvenir shops, their windows crammed with T-shirts, seashells, sunhats, coconuts with painted faces. Every time, I think about stopping to get flip-flops, but I haven't yet.

One morning, I come down to find the office in chaos. Judy, the secretary, is sitting at her desk, chewing the end of her ponytail. "Your father had to fire Buddy," she says. But before she can tell me anything more, one of the guests comes in, complaining about a leak. "It's right over the bed," the man says. "How do you expect me to pay for a room with a leak over the bed? We had to sleep on the floor! I came down to the office last night to get another room but there was no one here."

Just then my father comes in with the tree surgeon. "I thought you told me this type of palm tree was hardy."

"It is."

"Then what's the matter with it?"

133

"It's not in the right kind of soil."

"You never told me to change the soil," my father says, his voice rising.

"It's not only the soil," says the tree surgeon. "Trees are like people. They get sick. I can't tell you why. It might have needed more water."

"We watered it!" my father says, shouting now. "I had the guy water it every goddamn day! And now you tell me it's dead?" The man doesn't reply. My father sees me. "Hey there, buddy!" he says heartily. "Be with you in a minute."

The man with the leak begins explaining his trouble to my father. In the middle, my father stops him. Pointing at the tree surgeon, he says, "Judy, pay this bastard." Then he goes back to listening to the man's story. When the man finishes, my father offers him his money back and a free room for the night.

Ten minutes later, in the car, I learn the outlandish story. My father fired Buddy for drinking on the job. "But wait'll you hear *how* he was drinking," he says. Early that morning, he saw Buddy lying on the floor of unit 106, under the air conditioner. "He was *supposed* to be fixing it. All morning, I kept passing by, and every time I'd see Buddy lying under that air conditioner. I thought to myself, Jeez. But then this god-damn crook of a tree surgeon shows up. And *he* tells me that the god-damn tree he's supposed to be curing is dead, and I forgot all about Buddy. We go out to look at the tree and the guy's giving me all this bullshit—the soil this, the soil that—until finally I tell him I'm going to go call the nursery. So I come back to the office. And I pass 106 again. And there's Buddy still lying on the floor."

When my father got to him, Buddy was resting comfortably on his back, his eyes closed and the air-conditioner coil in his mouth. "I guess that coolant's got alcohol in it," my father said. All Buddy had to do was disconnect the coil, bend it with a pair of pliers and take a drink. This last time he'd sipped too long, however, and had passed out. "I should have known something was up," my father says. "For the past week all he's been doing is fixing the air conditioners."

After calling an ambulance (Buddy remained unconscious as he was carried away), my father called the nursery. They wouldn't refund his money or replace the palm tree. What was more, it had rained during the night and no one had to tell him about leaks. His own roof had leaked in the bathroom. The new roof, which had cost a considerable sum, hadn't been installed properly. At a minimum, someone was go-ing to have to re-tar it. "I need a guy to go up there and lay down some tar along the edges. It's the edges, see, where the water gets in. That way, maybe I can save a couple of bucks." While my father tells me all this, we drive out along A-1-A. It's about ten in the morning by this point and the drifters are scattered along the shoulder, looking for day work. You can spot them by their dark tans. My father passes the first few, his reasons for rejecting them unclear to me at first. Then he spots a white man in his early thirties, wearing green pants and a Disney-world T-shirt. He's standing in the sun, eating a raw cauliflower. My father pulls the Cadillac up alongside him. He touches his electronic console and the passenger window hums open. Outside, the man blinks, trying to adjust his eyes to the car's dark cool interior.

At night, after my parents go to sleep, I drive along the strip into town. Unlike most of the places my parents have wound up, Daytona Beach has a working-class feel. Fewer old people, more bikers. In the bar I've been going to, they have a real live shark. Three feet long, it swims in an aquarium above the stacked bottles. The shark has just enough room in its tank to turn around and swim back the other way. I don't know what effect the lights have on the animal. The dancers wear biki-nis, some of which sparkle like fish scales. They circulate through the gloom like mermaids, as the shark butts its head against the glass.

I've been in here three times already, long enough to know that I look, to the girls, like an art student, that under state law the girls can-not show their breasts and so must glue wing-shaped appliqués over them. I've asked what kind of glue they use ("Elmer's"), how they get it off ("just a little warm water") and what their boyfriends think of it (they don't mind the money). For ten dollars, a girl will take you by the hand, past the other tables where men sit mostly alone, into the back where it's even darker. She'll sit you down on a padded bench and rub against you for the duration of two whole songs. Sometimes, she'll take your hands and will ask, "Don't you know how to dance?"

"I'm dancing," you'll say, even though you're sitting down.

At three in the morning, I drive back, listening to a country and western station to remind myself that I'm far from home. I'm usually drunk by this point but the trip isn't long, a mile at most, an easy cruise past the other waterfront real estate, the big hotels and the smaller ones, the motor lodges with their various themes. One's called Viking Lodge. To check in, you drive under a Norse galley which serves as a carport.

Spring break's more than a month away. Most of the hotels are less than half full. Many have gone out of business, especially those further out from town. The motel next to ours is still open. It has a Polynesian theme. There's a bar under a grass hut by the swimming pool. Our place has a fancier feel. Out front, a white gravel walkway leads up to two miniature orange trees flanking the front door. My father thought it was worth it to spend money on the entrance, seeing as that was people's first impression. Right inside, to the left of the plushly carpeted lobby, is the sales office. Bob McHugh, the salesman, has a blueprint of the resort on the wall, showing available units and timeshare weeks. Right now, though, most people coming in are just looking for a place to spend the night. Generally, they drive into the parking lot at the side of the building and talk to Judy in the business office.

It rained again while I was in the bar. When I drive into our parking lot and get out, I can hear water dripping off the roof of the motel. There's a light burning in Judy's room. I consider going up to knock on her door. Hi, it's the boss's son! While I'm standing there, though, listening to the dripping water and plotting my next move, her light goes off. And, with it, it seems, every light around. My father's timeshare resort plunges into darkness. I reach out to put my hand on the hood of the Cadillac, to reassure myself with its warmth, and, for a moment, try to picture in my mind the way to my room, where the stairs begin, how many floors to climb, how many doors to pass before I get to my room.

"Come on," my father says. "I want to show you something."

He's wearing tennis shorts and has a racquetball racquet in his hand. Last week, Jerry, the current handyman (the one who replaced Buddy didn't show up one morning), finally moved the extra beds and draperies out of the racquetball court. My father had the floor painted and challenged me to a game. But, with the bad ventilation, the humidity made the floor slippery, and we had to quit after four points. My father didn't want to break his hip.

He had Jerry drag an old dehumidifier in from the office and this morning they played a few games.

"How's the floor?" I ask.

"Still a little slippy. That dehumidifier isn't worth a toot."

So it isn't to show me the new, dry racquetball court that my father has come to get me. It's something, his expression tells me, more significant. Leaning to one side (the exercise hasn't helped his back any), he leads me up to the third floor, then up another, smaller stairway which I haven't noticed before. This one leads straight to the roof. When we get to the top, I see that there's another building up here. It's pretty big, like a bunker, but with windows all around.

"You didn't know about this, did you?" my father says. "This is the penthouse. Your mother and I are going to move in up here soon as it's ready."

The penthouse has a red front door and a welcome mat. It sits in the middle of the tarred roof, which extends in every direction. From up here, all the neighboring buildings disappear, leaving only sky and ocean. Beside the penthouse, my father has set up a small hibachi. "We can have a cookout tonight," he says.

Inside, my mother is cleaning the windows. She wears the same yellow rubber gloves as when she used to clean the windows of our house back in the suburbs. Only two rooms in the penthouse are habitable at present. The third has been used as a storeroom and still contains a puzzle of chairs and tables stacked on top of one another. In the main room, a telephone has been installed beside a green vinyl chair. One of the warehouse paintings has been hung on the wall, a still life with seashells and coral.

The sun sets. We have our cookout, sitting in folding chairs on the roof.

"This is going to be nice up here," my mother says. "It's like being right in the middle of the sky."

"What I like," my father says, "is you can't see anybody. Private ocean view, right on the premises. A house this big on the water'd cost you an arm and a leg."

"Soon as we get this place paid off," he continues, "this penthouse will be ours. We can keep it in the family, down through the generations. Whenever you want to come and stay in your very own Florida penthouse, you can."

"Great," I say, and mean it. For the first time, the motel exerts an attraction for me. The unexpected liberation of the roof, the salty decay of the oceanfront, the pleasant absurdity of America, all come together so that I can imagine myself bringing friends and women up to this roof in years to come.

When it's finally dark, we go inside. My parents aren't sleeping up here yet but we don't want to leave. My mother turns on the lamps.

I go over to her and put my hands on her shoulders.

"What did you dream last night?" I ask.

137

She looks at me, into my eyes. While she does this, she's not so much my mother as just a person, with troubles and a sense of humor. "You don't want to know," she says.

I go into the bedroom to check it out. The furniture has that motel look but, on the bureau, my mother has set up a photograph of me and my brothers. There's a mirror on the back of the bathroom door, which is open. In the mirror, I see my father. He's urinating. Or trying to. He's standing in front of the toilet, staring down with a blank look. He's concentrating on some problem I've never had to concentrate on, something I know is coming my way, but I can't imagine what it is. He raises his hand in the air and makes a fist. Then, as though he's been doing it for years, he begins to pound on his stomach, over where his bladder is. He doesn't see me watching. He keeps pounding, his hand making a dull thud. Finally, as though he's heard a signal, he stops. There's a moment of silence before his stream hits the water.

My mother is still in the living room when I come out. Over her head, the seashell painting is crooked, I notice. I think about fixing it, then think the hell with it. I go out onto the roof. It's dark now, but I can hear the ocean. I look down the beach, at the other high-rises lit up, the Hilton, the Ramada. When I go to the roof's edge, I can see the motel next door. Red lights glow in the tropical grass hut bar. Beneath me, and to the side, though, the windows of our own motel are black. I squint down at the patio but can't see anything. The roof still has puddles from last night's storm and, when I step, I feel water gush up my shoe. The hole is getting bigger. I don't stay out long, just long enough to feel the world. When I turn back, I see that my father has come out into the living room again. He's on the phone, arguing with someone, or laughing, and working on my inheritance.

Nominated by Conjunctions

URBAN ANTHROPOLOGY

essay by ALEC WILKINSON

from DOUBLETAKE

THIS IS THE NEW Ravenite Social Club, on Mulberry Street, in the Little Italy section of New York City. Where the bricks are, there used to be storefront windows, and where the screen door is, there was a passageway that led to double doors. The doors had curved brass handles; they were painted a dark, glossy green and had glass on top; and behind the glass were white curtains. There were white curtains also behind the bottom halves of the storefront windows, like a decoration in a funeral parlor, and when you looked in from the street all you could see above them were the upper portions of the walls and part of the ceiling. On a corner of each window were letters in gold script saying, "Members Only."

For seven years, beginning in 1979, I lived across the street from the club, on the fifth floor of 250 Mulberry Street, a tenement. I looked down on the club and on the broad, flat roof of a garage next door. In a corner of the garage was a live poultry market. Over the market's door was a painting on sheet metal of a chicken the size of a sled dog. The name of the market was written in Chinese characters. Chinese women shopped there and old Italian women in black who communicated by means of gestures with the Chinese men in white aprons covered with feathers and blood. The birds were delivered to the market in cages carried on the backs of flatbed trucks. The cages were stacked on top of each other, and each cage held three or four birds. What you saw when you walked through the market's door was a wall of birds, and the backs of the women watching them until they saw the one that they wanted. At the end of the day the Chinese men drew shutters over the windows and a metal gate over the door and left barrels of feathers at the curb. The market kept a rooster that used sometimes to wake me when it was still dark and made me think, in the instant before my mind focused, that I was living on a farm. The squawking and beating of wings I occasionally heard in the middle of the night meant that a rat was loose among them. In winter, snow accumulated on the roof of the garage and lay there for days as unspoiled as snow in a field.

I always said hello to any of the Ravenites I passed on the sidewalk or saw standing in the doorway—it's the way I was raised—but none of them ever said anything to me in response or even acted as if he had heard me. I was never invited into the club either, but from the street, when the doors were open, I could see a bar and an espresso machine—one of those big espresso machines, with brass domes and an eagle with its wings spread, that look like an architect's model of a palace. Across from the bar were tables and chairs and, beyond them, a back room, with a television on a shelf. I lived in the apartment for nearly a year before I learned that the sullen and irritable-looking men who came and went from the club and sat at the tables playing cards with smudges of ash on their foreheads on Ash Wednesday were gangsters.

My apartment had been offered in the paper. Four narrow rooms in a line. By the sink in the kitchen was a bathtub and there was a pull-chain toilet in a closet down the hall. The view from the window by the fire escape was a small cemetery with maple trees that grew taller than the roof of my building. The cemetery was attached to a nineteenth-century church, built of stone, with a row of stained-glass windows along its side. On Palm Sunday the congregation, carrying palm crosses and singing a hymn, came out a door at one end of the church and, following the priest, made a procession down the steps and along the sidewalk and went back in a door on the far end of the church. In the procession one year I saw my building's superintendent and his family of dark-eyed, black-haired boys. He had been a scientist in Lima, Peru, and he lived on the fourth floor in an apartment where all the chairs and the sofa had slipcovers made from clear plastic.

My building belonged to a Buddhist monk in Hong Kong. A woman named Susan held the lease on my apartment. She was a performance artist. The apartment had become available as a result of the response to a piece she had recently given in the living room, called "Why Don't You Come Up and See Me Sometime." She had advertised the piece on posters she taped to walls and light poles around the neighborhood. On the evening of the performance the audience gathered on the sidewalk outside the building—there was no lobby, only a narrow entrance that smelled vaguely of spoiling vegetables: a Chinese vegetable seller rented a refrigerated locker on the first floor. A friend of Susan's brought the audience upstairs. When they walked in the apartment, they saw Susan, a pretty good-looking woman, lying on her side, with her chin in one hand, buck-naked on a slowly turning platform. She had dyed her brown hair jet black, and she had an absent look in her eyes. Several culture hounds from the social club attended and, a few days after, the club extended to Susan an invitation to leave the neighborhood. The invitation was delivered by a functionary who crowbarred the door of her apartment off its hinges one afternoon while Susan was out, and left the rest of the apartment undisturbed. It was not her first strike. She lived alone and had friends come and go at all hours, some of them men, which had led members of the club to conclude that she was a prostitute.

Susan collected three thousand dollars from me for the lease, which was illegal. I thought about taking her to court, but a couple of the stories she had told me about herself had revolved around the pleasures of revenge, and I didn't see any point in finding out if she had been exaggerating.

I had been living in Wellfleet, Massachusetts, on Cape Cod. Susan and I visited the Chinese agent who managed the building, and she told him that she was leaving the city and wanted to turn the apartment over to me, her cousin, and I signed the lease. Then I went back to Cape Cod and loaded my possessions into my car and drove to New York and parked in front of the social club. A man came out as I was carrying a chair and told me to move the car. I assumed I was parked illegally and that he was giving me some friendly, Welcome-Wagon-type advice. I read the parking sign on the light pole and saw that I was legal and said, "Thanks, it's OK." Another man came out of the club and they started arguing. I heard the second man say, "It's all right, it's all right, he's Susan's cousin." I don't know who he heard that from. The man who had told me to move said, "I don't give a fuck who he is." After I finished unloading my car, I drove over to the river and drank some beers and watched the sun go down over New Jersey, and when I came back another car was parked in front of the club. The

141

next morning on my way to breakfast, I saw that the windshield and windows and headlights on the car had been shattered.

The Ravenites kept a Doberman named Duke. During the day Duke paced in front of the club and the garage and at night he slept in the club. A short, fat guy named Mike looked after him. The garage belonged to a trucking company that hauled bananas and pineapples from the Brooklyn docks. Mike's job was to watch the door. This was not a complicated job; trucks came and went from the garage at the rate of about one every other day. Mike spent most of his time in a bentwood chair on the sidewalk outside the garage, or else penned behind a plate-glass window in an office just inside the door. He had wavy, silver hair parted cleanly like a child's and a rolling, splayfooted walk that tipped him from side to side.

Mike's position with the club was obscure. The lowest level of association seemed to be occupied by men in their twenties—mean-looking types with wiry bodies and spiteful, ratty faces. The more prestigious Ravenites arrived at the club in fancy black cars. They left the cars on the sidewalk, and the young men ran out of the garage with sponges and buckets of water and washed the cars while the gangsters were visiting the club. Mike never washed the cars—he was clearly above that—but he never spent much time inside the club, either. Only the broadest assembly of its members seemed to include him. Now and then, taking pains to emphasize his importance, he would say things such as, "Kind of friends I have, you need a job done, they do it. Then they go to Italy for a while."

One day the Doberman was gone. After that, when the club closed at night, an old man stood in the passageway, smoking cigarettes. Occasionally he would take up a position in a doorway somewhere else on the block, and it was spooky to walk down the quiet street in the dark and realize from a shadow you caught sight of from the corner of your eye that someone was watching you.

In addition to Mike, I was acquainted with a dark-haired, round-faced, slightly fleshy, and sinister-looking young man of about thirty named Norman. I often saw Norman behind the bar, and I assumed that he was the Ravenite's bartender.

Norman and Mike had an interest in a flock of pigeons that were kept in a coop on the roof above my apartment. Mike was too heavy to climb the stairs; he said that he hadn't visited the pigeons in years. From his chair he could see them on the occasions when they rose from the roof and wheeled in unison, like a school of fish. For a while after I first moved in, I would hear a knock on the door and I would open it to find Norman holding a plastic bucket. He needed water for the birds, he said. While the bucket was filling in my bathtub, he would look around the apartment and ask what I did for a living. I had to have it explained to me by my neighbor Scott, who lived down the hall, that Norman didn't need water, he was making sure, on behalf of the Ravenites, that I was not a cop. One day I went out and saw Norman standing in the doorway of the social club. He called me over and said, "Look, I know you're a nice guy, you don't want no trouble." I had no idea what he was leading to. I said, "Of course not." He pointed at a geranium in a pot on one of my windowsills and said, "That plant up there, it could come down, you know what I'm saying? It could fall off the ledge when you open the window and hit someone. Or the wind could knock it off. Now if it *did* fall, let it hit a nigger. But I don't think you should have it up there in the first place. Why take the risk?" I took the plant inside.

Scott had lived in the building for forty years, and was familiar to the gangsters; they paid no attention to him. Also, he rarely occupied his apartment. He lived in Hollywood and was a screenwriter. A few years after I arrived, he moved back to New York because he had not found work in Los Angeles for years. His apartment was rent-controlled and cost about a hundred dollars a month. He was a tall, thin, melancholy man with gray hair, a gray beard, and watery eyes. I guess he was about sixty-five. He wrote a movie that John Wayne had starred in toward the end of his career, and he had worked for a while as a writer for a soap opera. He lived on the royalty checks that came every few months from Australia, where the soap opera was being revived. No one he knew could tell him how long it would run or how many checks he would get or when they would stop coming. He drank. I was in his apartment only once, briefly, and what I remember was that there were stacks of newspapers and the paint was peeling from the walls and the ceiling and it was dark. One day he put all the money he had in his pockets and jumped out he window. The cops came upstairs, closed the window, turned over his mattress and the cushions of his sofa, and went through his drawers and the cabinets in the kitchen, looking for a note, I assumed. I said to one of them how difficult suicide calls must be to answer, and he said that he preferred them,

143

because you got to search the apartment before anyone else arrived and any money you found was yours.

During the first year that I lived in the apartment, people would tell me that the Ravenites were the Mafia and I didn't believe them. I thought they looked like people who wished they were in the Mafia but didn't have the nerve or the intelligence or know the right people. For one thing, they seemed easily frightened. Whenever one of them had a dispute with a bicycle messenger or a delivery guy he ran into the club or the garage for a wrench or a tire iron or a piece of lead pipe. Then he came back with three or four friends.

The kids in the neighborhood had the same bullying streak. I often saw boys wearing the blue sweaters and dark ties of the Catholic school around the corner ambush drunks who wandered over from the Bowery. They set upon the frail, raggedy figures like pack dogs and, when they had beaten the drunk to his knees, they ran away.

One morning after I had lived in the apartment for about a year, I learned what had happened to the Doberman and also why the windshield and the windows of the car had been shattered. A story on the front page of the *New York Times* said that the police had managed to hide microphones inside the club. The microphones had been in place only briefly "before they were discovered and ripped out by intended targets of the surveillance." The conversations the police overheard had covered "numerous organized crime activities." Among the Ravenites who were indicted as a result was Norman, who was identified as Norman Dupont, of 32 Monroe Street. He and the others were offered immunity and then of course sent to jail for contempt, since none of them would say anything. Norman was there for a year. He left the flock of pigeons in the care of some high school kids who showed up only occasionally, and most of the pigeons died. Among the organized crime activities disposed of in the conversations was the murder, several months before, of Carmine Galante, the head of the Bonano family. According to the *Times,* he had been killed in a "barrage of shotgun blasts and gunfire" by three men wearing ski masks while he ate lunch in the garden of the Joe and Mary Italian Restaurant, in Brooklyn. *The Encyclopedia of Organized Crime* says that Galante was a "psychopath who was fond of gamesmanship." One of the New York papers published a picture of him in the garden. He was lying on his back with his arms spread, his eyes were closed, and his teeth had clamped shut on a cigar, which stood up like an exclamation point.

The day the story was published, television reporters arrived to film dispatches in front of the club. A group of kids stood around them. Each time a reporter opened his mouth to speak into his microphone, the kids banged trash can lids together like cymbals. Eventually the reporters got back into their cars and drove off, except for one reporter who paid the kids to be quiet.

It turned out that I had parked in front of the social club on the day after the Ravenites had discovered that the police had been parking cars in the space where I had left mine. As a matter of routine, the Ravenites assumed that there were microphones in their clubhouse, so when they had something important to talk about, they went outside. Often they leaned against a car, and in the trunk of the car was a cop who was listening to the gangsters' conversation. Sometimes the gangsters leaned against the light pole, which had a microphone in it.

That the Doberman never woke up from the tranquilizers the police had given him so that they could plant the microphones came out in the court records. The police misjudged the dose they gave the dog and said they felt bad about it.

I often give a copy of the photograph of the Ravenite Social Club to friends as a present. My wife, a photographer, took it one afternoon in the spring just after John Gotti had been acquitted in the last trial that he would win. Gotti had become commander-in-chief of the Gambino family, whose headquarters the Ravenite Club was, by having the former commander killed. By then I no longer lived on Mulberry Street. The club had been renovated because of the microphones and the indictments. The garage had been torn down and replaced by an apartment building. My wife had a studio on the Bowery, and she was walking to the subway when she saw Gotti. She pretended to be a tourist and asked if she could take his picture. She took three. The guy on the right is saying, "Enough." Without looking at her, Gotti said "Don't sell them," something that had not occurred to her. She went to a pay phone and called the *New York Post* and told them she had a picture of Gotti outside the Ravenite Social Club. The man who answered said, "You took it with a long lens, right?" She said no, she had walked right up to him. There was a pause. The man told her to bring the picture right away. He said that the paper had a way of paying her so that no one would know her name. That was when she decided not to publish it.

One night, while I still lived on Mulberry Street, a friend whom I will call Sandy Frazier came to dinner. I made some margaritas, we drank some beer, we drank some wine. Then we decided to walk to the Battery, at the end of the island. I went out the door ahead of him. In a moment I heard someone banging with his fist on the window of the social club and shouting, "Tony. Hey, Tony." I looked over. It was Sandy. Sometimes when I recall this scene I hear a voice in my mind saying, "Farewell, friend." This recollection, though, seems too pointed and self-conscious to me now, and I think I probably made it up later to fill in the parts of my memory that had gone blank from anxiety. What I am sure I remember accurately is thinking, *you should do something to help him,* but at the same time I was unable to stop walking.

Two guys appeared on either side of Sandy. I didn't even see where they had come from; it was as if they had appeared from the air. Sandy stopped banging on the window and said, "Where's Tony?" He had read in the papers that a gangster named Tony was a Ravenite. I think the gangster's full name was Tony "Ducks" Corallo. The two guys looked at each other. They were enough bigger than Sandy that they looked at each other over the top of his head. Sandy said, "Where's Tony? I was supposed to meet him here. Where is he?" One of them said something such as, "Tony tell you he was supposed to meet anyone?" And the other shook his head and said, "He say anything to you?" Sandy was wearing khaki pants and a wool shirt with a plaid pattern. He is from Cleveland. He had short red hair. He said, "Call him up, I'm here. He told me to meet him at the club. It's eleven. I'm here." I could see the two guys thinking of how they could possibly reach Tony. What Sandy needed to do then was say, "All right. All right. Tell him I was here and tell him next time not to be late." He needed to make up a name to leave for Tony and he needed to say, "Fucking Tony." Then he could walk away.

What he did instead was shrug and say something like, "I'm sorry. I don't know what came over me." For a moment, the guys simply looked at him. Then one of them said, slowly, "You fucking rat. Get out of here, you *rat* bastard."

Sandy walked across the street the way people walk in cartoons after they have stuck their fingers in a light socket. I had never come completely to a stop, and now that he was walking toward me I started

146

walking faster to get away from him. I was concerned about how he was, but I also wanted to get off the block without being identified as knowing him.

On the Fourth of July, Norman and Mike and some other Ravenites would fill wheelbarrows with fireworks and dump them in the intersection of Mulberry and Prince, outside my building, and pour gasoline on the pile, and the flames would shoot up and blister the paint on the stoplight. Bottle rockets would rise to my window and throw off sparks and the air would smell like gunpowder. Meanwhile, other Ravenites would light cherry bombs and M-80s and toss them into garbage cans and throw the lids on the cans. The fireworks would rip the seams on the cans and throw the lids into the air and the explosion would rattle the frames of my windows and make my ears ring. It made me feel as if the Fourth of July was an Italian holiday.

One year some friends were having dinner with me and their young son was with us, and the sparks from the bottle rockets coming in the windows and the flashes of light upset him. "The nerves in my skin are hurting," he said.

I called the police. "The Mafia guys at the Ravenite Social Club are setting off fireworks," I said, and the cop said, "There's no such thing as the Mafia."

Nominated by Doubletake

INVISIBLE DREAMS

by TOI DERRICOTTE

from PLOUGHSHARES

"La poésie vit d'insomnie perpétuelle."
—*Rene Char*

There's a sickness in me. During
the night I wake up & it's brought

a stain into my mouth, as if
an ocean has risen & left back

a stink on the rocks of my teeth.
I stink. My mouth is ugly, human

stink. A color like rust
is in me. I can't get rid of it.

It rises after I
brush my teeth, a taste

like iron. In the
night, left like a dream,

a caustic light
washes over the insides of me.

*

What to do with my arms? They
coil out of my body

like snakes; they
branch & spit.

I want to shake myself
until they fall like withered

roots; until
they bend the right way—

until I fit in them,
or they in me.

I have to lay them down as
carefully as an old wedding dress,

I have to fold them
like the arms of someone dead.

The house is quiet; all
night I struggle. All

because of my arms,
which have no peace!

*

I'm a martyr, a girl who's been dead
two thousand years. I turn

on my left side, like one comfortable
after a long, hard death.

The angels look down
tenderly. "She's sleeping," they say

149

& pass me by. But
all night, I am passing

in & out of my body
on my naked feet.

*

I'm awake when I'm sleeping & I'm
sleeping when I'm awake, and no one

knows, not even me, for my eyes
are closed to myself.

I think I am thinking I see
a man beside me, & he thinks

in his sleep that I'm awake
writing. I hear a pen scratch

a paper. There is some idea
I think is clever: I want to

capture myself in a book.

*

I have to make a
place for my body in

my body. I'm like a
dog pawing a blanket

on the floor. I have to
turn & twist myself

like a rag until I
smell myself in myself.

150

I'm sweating; the water is
pouring out of me

like silver. I put my head
in the crook of my arm

like a brilliant moon.

*

The bones of my left foot
are too heavy on the bones

of my right. They
lie still for a little while,

sleeping, but soon they
bruise each other like

angry twins. Then
the bones of my right foot

command the bones of my left
to climb down.

Nominated by Rosellen Brown, Rita Dove, Marilyn Hacker, Ed Ochester, Ruth Stone,
Susan Wheeler

JULY

fiction by BETH CHIMERA

from AGNI

ALICE WAS SPENDING the month as an *au pair* for the Brenkmans, taking care of their two nine-year-old sons from previous marriages, Gabey and Chase, and writing to her convalescent boyfriend Simon. There were four weekends that July, and for each one of them the Brenkmans invited a different couple to the beach house—the Behns, the Twichells, the Crichlows, and the Kaminskys. The couples showed a great deal of interest in Alice, who had just graduated from college that spring. They lent her paperbacks and earrings to wear at dinner, brought her stolen sprays of hydrangea and wrote down the phone numbers of friends in the City with possible job connections or sons and daughters her own age. They engaged her in conversation about her career plans, her love life, her religious beliefs and political opinions, and dispensed borrowed wisdoms which Alice mostly found oppressive—"gather ye rosebuds while ye may," or "youth is wasted on the young," or the worst, from Rilke:

> the highest task of a bond between two people: that each
> should stand guard over the solitude of the other.

Alice would occasionally occupy Gabey and Chase with spelling out words culled from these maxims in brightly colored refrigerator magnets. The letter "N" was defective, and so hung listlessly below "B O D" for most of the month.

The couples often spoke in unison or finished one another's sentences, which irritated Alice. They knew no inhibitions; they discussed

everything openly—medical problems, infidelities, investment strate-
gies. Each couple had shared mannerisms and attitudes and anecdotes
to recount, and each brought a present for the boys and a bottle of
something and stayed two nights. The reason they spent so much time
with Alice was that they couldn't spend it with the Brenkmans, who
were rarely available. The Brenkmans passed most of that summer in
intense private negotiation; they were, in Mrs. Brenkman's words,
"reevaluating their partnership." This required diligence.

Alice's boyfriend Simon was home for the summer, in the suburbs
with his parents, recovering from a nervous episode he had suffered
shortly before graduation. He and Alice had been in the dining hall,
arguing about the Future of the Relationship—she'd been adamant,
implacable, extravagant with ultimatums—when he suffered a break-
down of sorts. She remembered the way his hands began aimlessly to
search the table, to move objects with the jerky rhythm of film run
backward. At the time, she'd thought that he was willfully tuning her
out, and, for one terrible moment, even imagined him to be mimick-
ing her, cruelly, with the rapid workings of his jaw. This last memory,
in particular, haunted and shamed her—perhaps all the more because
she couldn't remember any single, specific word that had passed be-
tween them.

Alice's world was somehow holistically altered since that evening in
the dining hall—as if her personal history had, with that event, entered
its suddenly Technicolor second act. Time seemed to slacken and di-
late. Most mornings, now, she remembered her dreams. Alice felt
guilty about these changes, since it had, in fact, been Simon's episode
and not her own. He had often teased her about living vicariously.

Simon was tall and fair-haired. He was one year younger than Alice,
but had skipped a grade early on. He was Alice's first love, yet when
they weren't fighting, they were, regrettably, a little awkward around
each other. There had been a plan at one time, what seemed a long
time ago now, for a post-graduation, cross-country road trip, just the
two of them alone in Simon's tiny red Festiva. The plan was much dis-
cussed and invested with great significance, the locus of fond projec-
tions and bitter contention, repeatedly canceled and resurrected with
drama and flair. Ever since it had been finally laid to rest in favor of
the health and wisdom of time apart, Alice carried around with her the
sense that in some alternate, phantom reality, the plan persevered.
They were out there, she and Simon, on the open road. She would
think to herself—selecting produce at the mini-market, refilling the

Brenkmans' milk carton bird-feeders, locking up the house at night—
Now we are in Utah. She had difficulty imagining their conversations,
and this pained her. What would they talk about, hour after hour?
Would there be long periods of silence, watching the scenery go by?
Buttes, Joshua Trees.

Alice had been introduced to the Brenkmans at a dinner party given
by Simon's parents the previous summer. Gabey was Mrs. Brenkman's
son from her marriage with Simon's godfather, Phil, and Chase was
Mr. Brenkman's son from his marriage with a paleontologist named
Kiki. The boys were almost inseparable and rarely quarreled. It was
miraculous, almost, the way they got along. Here at the beach they
spent most of their time in a treehouse Mr. Brenkman had built in the
front yard, the nicest one Alice had seen. It had a porthole-style win-
dow, white-washed walls and floors, two old brocade-covered ot-
tomans for seats, and a look-out tower from which one could see the
ocean and the entrance to the private beach. Sometimes when the
boys were otherwise engaged, Alice would climb the rope ladder with
a freezer pop and perch in the tower and watch people enter the
beach. The beach staff was comprised mostly of college kids, but she
never spoke to them. It seemed that the only peer she ever spoke to
was Simon, and felt as if this had been true ever since they'd met two-
and-a-half years before. These days, even they didn't speak, but com-
municated mostly through postcards.

July was bright and fragrant, but the natives unanimously preferred
August. Then, people turned in earlier. Teenagers threw fewer bottles
from the windows of their cars. There were end-of-the-season sales,
and the ocean had lost its chill.

The first Friday afternoon in July, Alice was in the treehouse watch-
ing two pre-teenage girls at the footbath by the umbrella shed tug
gravely at the seats of their bikini bottoms. She watched an older
woman dangle a key in front of a cabana boy's face. She watched a
woman around her own age pass through the gates and out of sight
while a child sat wailing on the pavement.

Gabey climbed the rope ladder and told her, "Cancer is just like
growing, only your body doesn't know when to stop. Think about it.
Cancer is like being too alive."

Gabey disappeared. Alice sat on an ottoman and looked around the
treehouse. On an overturned Fruit-of-the-Month crate was a treasure
map the boys had drawn, pinned fast with a Swiss Army knife stuck

vertically into the wood. Next to each of their names was a red-brown smear where they had sealed some secret pact, like the stains from nosebleeds and gravel scrapes which she soaked out of their clothes at the end of the day. It alarmed her that they should already take a bond so seriously, should so recklessly let blood. Another document, which Alice had not noticed before, was comprised of a series of crossed lines, dots and scribbles, like bedsprings, in green and yellow highlighter. Alice had no access to its intended meaning. She got up and began stacking empty Dixie cups that were scattered over the floor and crumpled her own plastic wrapper into one. She was twenty-two years old. She thought of the French exchange student in high school who asked if Americans ever experienced real love.

Alice climbed down into the yard where the Behns were tossing a beach ball they had brought and waiting for the Brenkmans to emerge from their bedroom. The boys watched from the grass.

"It's just so lovely here," Mrs. Behn said.

"Quite lovely," said Mr. Behn.

"Really, just lovely," Mrs. Behn said.

They were so pale they glowed, opening their arms wide for the ball, and chasing it the length of the lawn each time it got away. What they lacked in talent, they made up for in enthusiasm. They were Buddhists; for four days after they left, the boys insisted that Alice walk around on her knees in the lotus position. Mr. Behn was the Brenkmans' financial advisor in the City, where Mrs. Behn practiced homeopathic pet care out of Alice's father's building.

"You were in my office many, many years ago," Mrs. Behn told Alice, "when you were an itty bitty girl, and you were particularly smitten with this rheumatic tabby, and you looked at your dad and said, 'Father, I must have him.'"

Chase stared at Alice. Alice said, "I'm afraid I don't remember."

"Time flies," Mrs. Behn said, leaping for the beach ball. She squealed, tumbled onto the lawn and quickly sobered. "The cat turned out to have leukemia."

Gabey and Chase were lying prone by the Behns' feet scratching out a floor plan of their future home on the slate walkway. Chase wanted an indoor pool and a network of underground tunnels, Gabey wanted a hallway displaying ancestral family crests and a shooting range.

"A shooting range?" Mrs. Behn asked. "Why would you want a shooting range?"

Alice regarded the intricate maze of icons. Her childhood, all of its allegiances, threatened to blink out like the shrinking point of light on an antique television screen.

"Do you like the beach?" Alice asked the Behns.

"We do," Mr. Behn nodded reverently. "We were just talking with the boys about the importance of proper sun protection."

"Would you like to come with us?" Alice asked.

"They should be down any minute," Mrs. Behn said, gesturing toward the house.

"Any minute now," said Mr. Behn.

"A shooting range is both sportsmanly *and* practical in this day and age," Gabey said.

"Would you like to go to the beach?" Alice asked the boys.

"Later," they said.

Mrs. Brenkman came out the front door, leafing through the morning's mail. She had the sort of face that was negatively defined, composed of large areas of wan, soft blankness. She welcomed her guests with exaggerated gusto, but her eyes were swollen, and her stride seemed off-balance. Alice felt herself blush as Simon's postcard fell into her hands. WISH I WERE THERE, it said on the back of a Magritte reproduction, a blue sky, clouds.

The boys had changed their minds. They had her around the waist now, pulling her toward the walkway, toward the road to the beach, toward the water, where the three of them would float until dinnertime. Beyond the tips of the jetties, men in green slickers dropped huge nets off the sides of boats, and dragged them the length of the beach until Alice could see only their signals flashing at longer and longer intervals. The boys dove and surfaced again and again without words.

* * *

The following weekend, the Twichells arrived. The Behns' beach ball formed a crumpled centerpiece on the coffee table. The Twitchells had the sly lasciviousness of newlyweds. They brought two children of their own, Pauline and Virginia. The four of them had just moved into a converted chapel in Hoboken, New Jersey, which Mr. Twichell, who was an architect, had designed. He explained that the master bedroom, once the apse, retained most of its original stained glass. "It's a Catholic school girl's wet dream," Mrs. Twichell told Alice.

156

A catastrophe had occurred on the drive out—Virginia, six, had left her favorite stuffed animal at a McDonald's off the L.I.E. She hadn't realized this until they were a few minutes from the house and now she stood by the car, crying, refusing to come inside.

Mrs. Twichell told Alice, "She and Lumpy are quite *intimate,* if you know what I mean—you should see the tail on that animal!" Mr. Twichell's brow glistened. He kissed his wife's shoulder before heading out to the car. Pauline, twelve, had brought a walkman and a tape of a female rap star which she played repeatedly all weekend, cocking her elbows and singing along, "Here we go, here we go."

On Saturday, the Brenkmans never came down for lunch. The Twichells had returned from their morning drive with oysters on ice and local corn from a roadside vendor. Pauline stood by the stove with a wine cooler and watched Alice fry burgers for herself and the boys. She said, "When I was a kid, I didn't care about stuffed animals. Virginia's dyslexic, and she's got all these other, like, learning disabilities and stuff. We think she might have had some kind of traumatic experience when she was a baby."

Pauline leaned in confidentially when she said this, glancing sidelong at her sister who stood just outside the screen door clutching the retrieved animal. Pauline wore perfume that smelled of plastic and overripe fruit. Her posture was her mother's, shoulders rounded, hips thrust forward, and when she spoke she dragged her open hand along her throat, her palm coming to rest flat against her collarbone, a woman's gesture. What sensations had pressed on her curveless body, Alice wondered. What did she believe about love? Pauline had been on the phone the night before with someone named Jason. She'd say things to Mrs. Twichell like, "Jason said you should drop me off at Irene's when we get back."

They ate outside on the patio and Mrs. Twichell proved to the skeptical boys that the oysters were actually still alive by squeezing lemon on their gelatinous bodies, causing them to quiver right before everyone's eyes. After the meal, Alice cleared the dishes and everyone picked corn from their teeth and pretended not to listen to the noises that issued from the upstairs windows—a sort of low coaxing and what sounded like choked sobs or sudden, panicked laughter. The Brenkmans hadn't made an appearance all morning; they were busy staking out territories of need, rendering roles fluid. They rarely came downstairs before late afternoon, when they descended upon their guests, weary but ravenous.

The Twichells had brought each of the boys a package of five colored capsules that bloomed in water into sponges shaped like dinosaurs. Ten drinking glasses with ten tiny floating monsters lined the kitchen counter. For the Brenkmans they had brought a small rose-hued shopping bag filled with tissue paper which the girls weren't supposed to touch. The gold sticker on the side said "La Petite Coquette" in a florid script.

"To encourage them to do a little less talking," Mrs. Twichell said.

"Jesus, Mom," Pauline said.

"You know," Mr. Twichell said, "whenever those two start in about 'partners,' I can't help but think of a corporation, or a song-and-dance team."

Mrs. Twichell wagged her finger scoldingly at her husband and patted the seat of his jeans.

Later, everyone went for a stroll along the boardwalk while Gabey and Chase trolled the beach below with Mr. Brenkman's metal detector—a preferred evening past time. They seemed never to tire of pacing the dunes, their shadows long and electric blue beneath the pink street lamps of the overhead walkway, pausing hopefully at each chirp or groan from the machine. They always went home disappointed.

The next day there was a storm-watch in effect. The boys were spending the afternoon with the houseguests at a recently-opened, nearby mall, and Alice went up to the treehouse with a home reference guide to psychiatric disorders borrowed from the Brenkmans' personal library. The sky was dark and the clouds changed quickly, moving past the porthole like stop-motion photography, like a documentary on clouds. Alice wondered if there would be lightning, remembered that she was in a tree, and pulled down the army blanket that curtained the entrance, as if it might shield her. She flipped to "N" in the book's index. *Necrophilia, Needle sharing, Negative thinking, Neuroendocrine side effects.* No *Nervous breakdown.*

She stretched out on the floor, staring up at the tattered underside of an ottoman, and thought of the Donald Duck impression that Simon had amused her with when they first started dating. Alice had at first found it endearing, but she eventually began to worry that he was becoming incapable of expressing affection for her in a natural voice. After a while, the alter-ego was increasingly invoked to incite arguments, or to express irritation. He became derogatory, brusque and sexually aggressive in a way that would have been unthinkable in Simon's own gentle cadences. Alice found herself—despite her misgivings—strangely thrilled by this. It was around the time that she realized she was beginning to enjoy being called demeaning names in a duck voice that Simon stopped using it altogether. Alice climbed the tower and looked out. The gates to the beach were padlocked shut. There was still no rain.

Alice was up late that night. She sat at the desk in her small room off the kitchen and picked through a manila envelope of Simon's postcards. They seemed full of white space interrupted by cryptic, elliptical phrases. A patchwork figure emerged from them, Simon as a composite sketch. What did they tell her? What, after all, did she really know about him? That he ate jumbo shrimp at the airport; that one night in June it was cold enough to see his own breath; that, from his bedroom window, the basketball hoop on his garage door looked as if it were sleeping; that he loved her.

PLEASE, Alice wrote on the back of a soft-focused beach scene, WRITE SOON. But that was all she could think of to say.

*   *   *

The Crichlows came. Mrs. Crichlow had blonde hair to her waist, with which her hands were always occupied, braiding, twisting, smoothing loose, and her fingers were stained with artist's pigments— "from capturing dreams," she told Alice. Mr. Crichlow engaged the boys by debunking pervasive scientific myths, such as the verifiable existence of the atom, or the earth's rotation around the sun. He built aluminum foil models to substantiate his claims.

Mrs. Crichlow had studied "eurythmy" with a Rudolph Steiner group, and was a self-proclaimed "movement analyst." She told Alice that her gestures indicated unresolved sexual issues and an inflexible disposition, though she reassured her that she should nonetheless be capable of leading a contented and productive life. The boys vigorously constructed alternative solar systems. Silver balls littered the carpet.

Alice observed their handiwork. She did not like to think of these little boys questioning the order of the universe.

Later, Chase showed Alice how to use the Brenkmans' computer to send electronic mail. Cheap, instant communication.

I BELIEVE I AM MONOGAMOUS BY NATURE, Alice typed. DO YOU THINK THAT RATIONALITY IS A FORM OF SELF-DELUSION?

159

NURTURE, Simon typed back. NO.

"Let's go into town and get some candy," Gabey said.

The three of them drove to a strip of gift shops and pizza restaurants. All along the narrow streets people walked carelessly, in pale clothes, their arms linked. "Gary!" a girl called from a second story window, "More meat!" It was difficult to find a parking space.

Alice waited in the doorway of the shop while the boys orchestrated much weighing and measuring of Swedish fish and lengths of cherry licorice. It was on the way back to the car that Chase stopped short and crouched down in the middle of the sidewalk. The crowd parted and passed on either side of him. Between his feet was a dead bird.

"Come on," Gabey said.

"Can we bury him?" Chase asked Alice.

"Come on," Gabey said.

It was the first time Alice had seen them disagree. She went back to the confectioner's for a small paper bag and a plastic spoon and handed them to Chase.

"Don't touch it," she said.

Gabey kept walking until he reached the car and leaned there impatiently, eyes squinted against the low sun. Alice watched Chase gently push the corpse to the base of a tree and begin digging with great concentration, a quiet gurgling noise in his throat. She looked from one serious, sunburned face to the other and thought that she could imagine exactly what these two would look like as men.

That evening, Simon called. He'd been leafing through old yearbooks, and had come across his high school biology text.

"Maybe your fidelity isn't a learned phenomenon," Simon said. "Maybe it's a matter of gene fitness, a result of ecological factors, a strategic behavioral alternative subject to strong selection."

Alice stared at the linoleum. "I'm looking forward to getting out of here," she said.

"You know, they've got me on antidepressants now," Simon said. "Some pill with a name like a B-movie alien. Zozax or Zazox." He told her that, actually, the term "nervous breakdown" was a kind of popular catch-all—that it was, in fact, essentially meaningless in psychiatry. He said that, as far as what he had experienced, they were thinking, probably a run-of-the-mill panic attack, fairly common among twenty-somethings in high pressure academic environments. Unless, he said, it was a brief psychotic reaction, in which case a period of depression customarily followed.

Alice blamed herself; Simon protested.

A sound came from above like a table upended.

Alice asked, "So how do you feel now?"

"Pretty good," Simon said, "I mean, I never really appreciated being at home before. Every day now I find something new to appreciate—fabric softener for example."

Alice exhaled sharply.

"You're so impatient with me," Simon said, softly. The boys came downstairs in their pajamas. Soon it would be time to read to them, to plug in their seashell nightlights.

"I'm extremely patient—inhumanly patient," Alice said. "It's just that even your phone call feels like surrealist telegrams."

In the living room, Mrs. Crichlow was folding paper birds for the boys while the Brenkmans changed for dinner. Her voice was a steady chant. The boys listened openmouthed. Alice heard Mr. Crichlow say, "Children are the best. The older I get, the less time I want to spend with adults."

Later that night, when Gabey and Chase had long been in bed, Alice took a shower. The upstairs bathroom she shared with the boys was a treacherous place where Alice felt large and ungainly. Matchbox cars and sharp-limbed plastic animals leapt lemming-style into the tub at her slightest movement. She was scrubbing the sand from her scalp with baby shampoo, thick and elastic as egg whites, when she heard the adults return from their evening out. Their noises were hushed and conspiratorial as they moved beneath her—suppressed giggles, hoarse whispers, a skirmish of silverware and ice cubes. A single set of footfalls mounted the stairs and passed the bathroom door, pausing for a moment by the children's bedroom. Then, through the vent beneath the sink, Alice heard Mrs. Brenkman humming an Eagles tune, a love song, and shuffling along the wooden floorboards of the master bedroom. Alice listened, and let the soapsuds run into her eyes (*No More Tears*, the bottle had promised). Alice hoped that she might be able to slip into the den, to the computer, without being drawn into the party. She wanted to write to Simon about this humming and shuffling in the next room. She felt sure that if she could find the right words, this would be something they could really share, without argument or hesitation. Alice listened until the footfalls passed back down the stairs and

Mrs. Brenkman's voice had moved with the others to the living room. But when she stepped out into the cold salt-air of the hallway, she was startled by Gabey and Chase, who stood flinching at the bathroom's harsh fluorescence. "Alice," Gabey said, "we know it's late, but Mrs. Crichlow told us that Mommy and Daddy may have reached the end of their path together."

"Puh!" Alice expelled, shocked. She led them back to their room, where they all crowded under the covers of Chase's bed and stared at the glow-in-the-dark star stickers that Mr. Brenkman had spent an entire summer accurately mapping out onto the ceiling.

"Mr. Crichlow said that grown-ups lie to children in order to reassure themselves about the ethical order of the universe," Chase told Alice. "Mr. Crichlow said that Santa Claus and multiplication tables and heaven are all just myths that adults made up to make themselves feel better about the actual meaninglessness of human existence. Mr. Crichlow said that the only reason why people have children is vanity."

Gabey said, "Mrs. Crichlow said everyone is always and ultimately alone."

"Mr. and Mrs. Crichlow are not good people," Alice said.

* * *

Several days passed in which Alice had almost no contact with the Brenkmans. They seemed to take their meals haphazardly at different hours, waving through the window to Alice and the boys in the front yard, wandering in to kiss the children goodnight and ask Alice if she needed any money. Once, after an afternoon at the beach, she and the boys returned to find the ice trays filled with orange juice, a toothpick poking up from each cube. Alice began to imagine the Brenkmans, sealed off as they were behind their bedroom door, as a pair of dysfunctional honeymooners. Finally, one evening when Gabey and Chase were playing video games at a neighbor's house, she went upstairs and knocked.

"Hey!" Mr. Brenkman croaked.

Alice felt flustered at having intruded, and snuck silently out to the lawn. She climbed up into the treehouse and looked beyond the rooftops toward the Atlantic. A young man stood alone by the gate, smiling and nodding to no one in particular, his hands raised in the gesture of a saint.

* * *

The Kaminskys' marriage fell into the category commonly re-
ferred to as a May-December union. Mr. Kaminsky was seventy-
five. He was Ukrainian, carried a pocket watch, wore his short,
white hair spiked straight up off his head and wrote essays on his-
torical semantics not intended for publication. He kept on his per-
son at all times a small leather-bound notebook in which he seemed
to jot single word memos at inexplicably chosen moments with a
pencil bearing the logo "Vote Yes for Mental Health!" Mrs. Kamin-
sky watched her husband as he scribbled. She watched him with
fondness and an air of protective concern, such as a mother might
watch a child. Alice thought of the first few months of her rela-
tionship with Simon. She had fallen in love with him quickly and
earnestly, but now she tried to remember what about Simon,
specifically, had inspired this devotion. It was impossible to
recall feelings—only circumstances came back to her. She had just
joined a natural foods cooperative at the time, and had suffered de-
bilitating gas pains throughout much of the semester. The first time
Simon had met Alice's father, he had been wearing a Gay Pride
Week T-shirt which read, front and back: *Don't Assume I'm
Straight / Don't Assume I'm Not,* and Alice's father had offered him
one of his own shirts to change into.

HAVE YOU EVER CONSIDERED HOW ACCIDENTAL IT
IS THAT WE'RE TOGETHER? Alice typed to Simon. They were
on a computer date, testing out the system's simultaneous "chat"
function.

LAST NIGHT'S "DEEP SPACE NINE" WAS ABOUT SOME-
THING LIKE THAT, Simon replied. YOU KNOW, ALL POSSI-
BLE ROMANTIC PERMUTATIONS BEING PERPETUALLY
PLAYED OUT IN OTHER DIMENSIONS.

THE BOYS ARE ONLY ALLOWED TO WATCH PBS, Alice
typed back, hoping now to change the subject.

Mrs. Kaminsky was a petite woman with a sibilant pronunciation
and a serious demeanor. She seemed more genuinely concerned than
the other guests about the Brenkmans' situation—and she ap-
proached it as a question of methodology.

"They're going about this in an absolutely counterproductive man-
ner," Mrs. Kaminsky said, shaking her head. "What they need is de-
tachment, not further enmeshment."

163

"But don't you think that communication is the key to a lasting relationship?" Alice asked.

Mr. Kaminsky wrote something in his notebook.

"Not at all," Mrs. Kaminsky said. "Wasyl and I maintained an in-house detachment for eight full months—we didn't sleep together, we didn't speak. It was the only thing that saved our marriage."

Alice considered this. Maybe connection was neither the means nor the end. She was constantly struggling to connect with Simon, and where had it gotten them? He might have almost traded in his sanity to escape her dream of communion. Maybe separateness was more essential than connection, and maybe the first responsibility of love really was to respect and maintain one another's inescapable aloneness. Alice pondered this, turned it over in her mind. She came to the conclusion that, as a life philosophy, it didn't work for her, and let it go.

Mr. and Mrs. Kaminsky seemed to possess an uncanny ability to guess each other's thoughts with astonishing accuracy. It became the premise of a game, and a seemingly inexhaustible source of delight for the boys, who pivoted back and forth between husband and wife, hissing single-digit numbers, colors, fruits, and names of US presidents wetly into their ears.

"Lavender," Mr. Kaminsky would say, rubbing his temples dramatically.

Chase attempted a look of keen skepticism.

"James . . ." Mrs. Kaminsky would say, "No, Grover Cleveland."

Gabey clasped his hands in ecstasy.

That afternoon, everyone went to the beach except Alice and Mr. Kaminsky, who didn't own bathing trunks.

"I've never been fond of the ocean," Mr. Kaminsky told her. "It's a trait I've learned to forgive in myself."

Earlier that day, in town with his wife, Mr. Kaminsky had bought a child's cardboard kaleidoscope from a souvenir shop. Now he sat by the window with it tilted to his eye, turning it with measured consistency. It made a shushing noise that reminded Alice of sand poured from the boys' sneakers onto the slate walkway.

"It's like magic!" Mr. Kaminsky said, handing the toy to Alice. He had a neat little mustache as white as his hair and wore huarache sandals with his suit pants. "A few plastic beads and a couple of mirrors. Then you look inside and these perfect patterns emerge, like snowflakes, absolutely regular, absolutely whole, no two identical. It's very reassuring, don't you think?"

Before she knew what she was saying, Alice heard herself reply, "Like individuals—melting into one another."

Mr. Kaminsky looked surprised. He said, "The British Marxist thinker Raymond Williams explained that the word *individual,* which is now understood to emphasize a distinction from others, originally meant indivisible, implying a necessary connection."

Alice twisted and twisted the flimsy barrel of the kaleidoscope, felt the tiny pieces tumble under her fingertips. She'd never conversed with a true cultural critic.

"What may seem like a paradox to our contemporary way of thinking," Mr. Kaminsky said, "is actually—when viewed historically—the product of certain developments in scientific, political and economic thought." He was silent for a moment, and then an infinite gentleness came over his voice. "Sometimes when you find a particularly pretty pattern, you want to fix it, you know? But it's nice, in a way, that once you let it go, it's really gone. You'll never get it back exactly the same. Do you know what I mean?"

Alice nodded, and lowered the kaleidoscope to her lap.

"Of course you do," Mr. Kaminsky said kindly.

The kaleidoscope was printed all over with small, simply illustrated sailboats and life preservers and the regularly repeated mantra, "Life's a Beach." Inert against the fabric of her sundress, it seemed to possess an inner life. On Sunday, when Mr. Kaminsky boarded the train with his wife, Alice was sorry to see him go.

* * *

On the last morning of July, Alice helped the boys pack their trunks for a month of sleep-away camp at a Boy Scout reservation in the Blue Ridge mountains. She was trying to explain to Chase why it would be best to leave the high-powered telescope at home, when Gabey sat down on his bed and began to cry.

"I don't want to go," he said, hiccuping through the tears. "Are they gonna make us go even if we don't want to?"

Alice looked down at the pile of underpants she had just folded—miniature Fruit of the Looms, sorted by the name tags which Mrs. Brenkman had ironed onto each waistband before Alice knew her. When she looked up again, Chase had crossed the room, and was now seated next to his stepbrother on the bed, petting his hair slowly like a parent, or a lover.

"We'll have fun," he said in a soft, coaxing tone. "I promise."

Later, Alice made rounds of the house, gathering up the boys' scattered belongings. She was crouched under the front hedges, trying to retrieve a plastic shovel, when the mailman came up the walk.

"I believe this is yours," he said, flourishing a postcard. It depicted a man and woman in a living room: the man seemed to be searching, the woman, visible only from the waist down, stood in the fireplace, her head up the flue. The caption read, "Rebecca and I seemed to be drifting further and further apart." Alice laughed.

"Significant other?" asked the mailman.

"Yes," said Alice.

"Bet he's crazy about you."

A voice from the master bedroom yelled, "I don't give a damn if your mother *was* the president of the PTA!"

The mailman winked.

"We're supposed to go for a family outing this afternoon," Alice said. "Rent some bikes."

"July," said the mailman, "it's rough."

* * *

That night, Alice slept fitfully. She woke periodically to the sounds of cats just outside her window—fighting or mating, she couldn't tell. When she dreamed, it involved couples dancing on the lawn in elaborate, color-coordinated outfits. Fox-trots, lindys, cha-chas. Their movements were deft and swooning. Just before dawn, she rolled out of bed, dressed, and walked out to the front porch, where the screen door glittered with Japanese beetles. She headed for the beach, stopping at a pay phone to call Simon on his private line. The connection was flawed.

"Hi," he said. He seemed wide awake.

"I dreamed about people dancing," she said. "I want to learn how to dance."

There were fragments of other conversations barely audible on the line, and Simon's voice reached her over a sea of static. "When will you be home?" he asked. Alice remembered his embrace like warm, shifting water. She grinned into the receiver.

Nominated by Agni

THE WEATHER THEY WERE WRITTEN IN

by KATHY FAGAN

from CONNECTICUT REVIEW

To start somewhere:
the window, ice, what fire
formed reformed
in frost, and frost itself
an other thing
more private somehow, and
complex, pinioned
like birds' underwings—
an arc and drift
of darkly plumaged peaks.
> In one pane, there's
> a kind of lake lain in
> among them, beveled,
> small, but mostly clear,
> a peephole meant
> to see the cold through—weather
> that would surely
> liquefy your vision
> were you in it,
> weep things off to left
and right. But you
are not—out in it—
nor are you teary,

167

despite a robin, mirrored
in the glass,
who hurls his body at
his body, breathless
after each attempt.
He loves himself,
almost, to death, and who
      can blame him? His eyes
      are lovely, his barrel
      chest . . . ! Look:
      the logic of the male
      cardinal
      in snow is red that makes
      the white bearable;
      a chickadee's dressed
      in birch tree's clothing;
      and sparrow—little splinter,
little ash,
little antic where
am-I-is little
but fat—she is too fat
in fact to fly,
and the sky is, anyhow,
too sharp
to fly through. Settle down
and think now. Didn't
Stevens write, of summer,
           how what's solid
           seems to vaporize,
           denying form
           or definition? And since
           this is the opposite
           of August, couldn't
           smoke in winter prove
           the converse may be
           true? At least, a crow
           has found a pillar
of it—stalled above
a chimney flue—
sure enough to huddle

near: a something
other, separate from,
by which to judge
and warm himself—a staggered
column, woodstove
smoke, that would be nothing
without its circumstance,
         the small flesh
         that needs it.

Nominated by Connecticut Review, Phil Appleman, Linda Bierds, P. Liotta

THE NINTH, IN E MINOR

fiction by FREDERICK BUSCH

from THE GEORGIA REVIEW

THE morning after I drove to his newest town, I met my father for breakfast. He was wearing hunter's camouflage clothing and looked as if he hadn't slept for a couple of nights. He reminded me of one of those militia clowns you see on television news shows, very watchful and radiating a kind of high seriousness about imminent execution by minions of the state.

I knew he had deeper worries than execution. And I was pleased for him that he wore trousers and T-shirt, a soft, wide-brimmed cap, and hip-length jacket that would help him disappear into the stony land-scape of upstate New York. He *needs* the camouflage, I thought, al-though where we stood—in the lobby of the James Fenimore Cooper Inn—he seemed a little out of place among the college kids and com-mercial travelers. The inn advertised itself as The Last of the Great Upstate Taverns. My father looked like The Last of the Great Upstate Guerrilla Fighters. Still, I thought, he's got the gear, and one of these days he will blend right in.

"Hi, Baby," he said. He tried to give me one of the old daddy-to-daughter penetrating stares, but his eyes bounced away from mine, and his glance slid down my nose to my chin, then down the front of my shirt to the oval silver belt buckle I had bought in Santa Fe.

"How are you, Daddy?"

He fired off another stare, but it ricocheted. "I have to tell you," he said, "half of the time I'm flat scared."

His shave was smooth, but he'd missed a couple of whiskers, which looked more gray than black. His face had gone all wrinkled and squinty. He looked like my father's older brother who was shaky and possibly ill and commuting from the farthest suburbs of central mental health. He took his cap off—doffed it, you would have to say. His hair looked soft. You could see how someone would want to reach over and touch it.

"But I don't like to complain," he said.

I got hold of his arm and pulled my way along his brown-and-sand-and-olive-green sleeve until I had his hand, which I held in both of mine. He used enough muscle to keep his arm in that position, but the hand was loose and cool, a kid's.

I asked him, "Do you know what you're scared of?"

He shrugged, and, when he did, I saw a familiar expression inside his tired, frightened face. He made one of those French frowns that suggested not giving a good goddamn, and it pleased me so much, even as it disappeared into his newer face, that I brought his hand up and kissed the backs of his fingers.

"Aw," he said. I thought he was going to cry. I think he thought so too.

"Look," I said, letting go of his hand, "I saw Mommy in New York. That's where I drove up from. We had dinner two days ago. She asked me to remember her to you. She's fine."

He studied my words as if they had formed a complex thought. And then, as if I hadn't said what he was already considering, he asked, "How is she?"

"She's fine. I told you."

"And she asked to be remembered to me."

"Right."

"You're lying, Baby."

"Correct."

"She didn't mention me."

"Oh, she mentioned you."

"Not in a friendly way."

"No."

"She was hostile, then?"

"Hurt, I'd say."

He nodded. "I hate that—I didn't want to hurt anybody," he said. "I just wanted to feel better."

"I know. Do you feel better?"

"Do I look it?"

"Well, with the outfit and all . . . "

171

"This stuff's practical. You can wear it for weeks before you need to wash it. The rain runs off the coat. You don't need to carry a lot of clothing with you."

"Traveling light, then, is how you would describe yourself?"

"Yes," my father said. "I would say I'm traveling light. But you didn't answer me. How do I look?"

I walked past matching club chairs upholstered in maroon-and-aqua challis, and I looked out a window. A crew had taken down an old, broad maple tree. The sidewalk was buried under branches and bark, and a catwalk of plywood led from the street, around the downed tree, and into the inn. The tree was cut into round sections three or four feet across, and a man in a sweated undershirt was using a long-handled splitting maul to break up one of the sections. Behind him stood another man, who wore a yellow hard hat and an orange shirt and a yellow fluorescent safety vest. He held a long chain saw that shook as it idled. A woman wearing a man's old-fashioned undervest, work gloves, and battered boots watched them both. Occasionally, she directed the man with the splitting maul. Her hair beneath her yellow hard hat looked reddish-gold. The one with the chain saw stared at the front of her shirt. She looked up and saw me. She looked at me through her safety goggles for a while and then she smiled. I couldn't help smiling back.

"You look fine," I said. "It's a beautiful spring morning. Let's eat."

In the Natty Bumppo Room, we were served our juice and coffee by a chunky woman with a happy red face. My father ordered waffles, and I remembered how, when I was in elementary school, he heated frozen waffles in the toaster for me and spread on margarine and syrup. I remembered how broad his hands had seemed. Now, they shook as he spread the margarine. One of his camouflage cuffs had picked up some syrup, and he dripped a little as he worked at his meal. I kept sipping the black coffee, which tasted like my conception of a broth made from long-simmered laundry.

"The hardest part," he said, "it drives me nuts. The thing with the checks."

"Sure," I said, watching the margarine and maple syrup coat his lips. "Mommy has to endorse your checks, then she has to deposit them, then she has to draw a bank check, and then she has to figure out where you are so she can send it along. It's complicated."

172

"I'm not making it that way on purpose," he said.

"No. But it's complicated." He looked young enough to have been his son, sometimes, and then, suddenly, he looked more like his father. I understood that the man I had thought of as my father, looking like himself, was no longer available. He was several new selves, and I would have to think of him that way.

"I'm just trying to get better," he said.

"Daddy, do you hear from her?"

He went still. He held himself so that—in his camouflage outfit— he suggested a hunter waiting on something skittish, a wild turkey, say, said to be stupid and shy. "I don't see the point of this," he said. "Why not talk about you? That's what fathers want to hear. About their kids. Why not talk about you?"

"All right," I said. "Me. I went to Santa Fe. I had a show in a gallery in Taos, and then I drove down to Santa Fe and I hung out. I walked on the Santa Fe Trail. It goes along the streets there. I ate too much with too much chili in it, and bought too many pots. Most of the people in the restaurants are important unknown Hollywood celebrities from outside Hollywood."

"Did you sell any pictures?"

"Yes, I did."

"Did you make a lot of money?"

"Some. You want any?"

"Because of how long it takes for your mother to cash my check and send a new one."

"Are you *allowed* to not live at home and still get money from the state?"

"I think you're supposed to stay at home," he said.

"So she's being illegal along with you? To help you out?"

He chewed on the last of his waffle. He nodded.

"Pretty good," I said.

"She's excellent to me."

"Considering," I said. "So how much money could you use?"

"Given the complications of the transmission process," he said.

"Given that," I said. "They sit outside the state office building, the Indians off the pueblos. They hate the people who come, but they all sit there all day long, showing you the silver and the pots all arranged on these beautiful blankets. I bought too much. But I felt embarrassed. One woman with a fly swatter, she kept spanking at the jewelry she was selling. She'd made it. She kept hitting it, and the earrings

173

jumped on the blanket. The rings scattered, and she kept hitting away, pretending she was swatting flies, but she wasn't. She was furious."

"Displacement," my father said.

"It's just a story, Daddy."

"But you told it."

"Yes, but it didn't have a message or anything."

"What did it have?"

"*In situ* Native American displacement, and handmade jewelry. A tourist's usual guilt. Me, on the road, looking around. Me, on my way northeast."

"Did you drive?"

"I did."

"All by yourself?"

"Like you, Daddy?"

"No," he said, fitting his mouth to the trembling cup. "We're both together here, so we aren't alone now."

"No." I heard the splitting maul, and I imagined the concussion up his fingers and along his forearm, up through the shoulder and into the top of the spine. It would make your brain shake, I thought.

"A hundred or two?" he said.

"What? Dollars?"

"Is that too much?"

"No," I said, "I have that."

"Thanks, Baby."

"But do you hear from her, Daddy?"

He slumped. He stared at the syrup on his plate. It looked like a pool of sewage where something had drowned.

He said, "Did I tell you I went to Maine?"

I shook my head and signaled for more coffee. When she brought it, I asked if I could smoke in the Natty Bumppo Room, and she said no. I lit a cigarette and when I was done, and had clicked the lighter shut, she took a deep breath of the smoke I exhaled and she grinned.

"What's in Maine?" I asked him.

"Cabins. Very cheap cabins in a place on the coast that nobody knows about. I met a man in New Hampshire—Portsmouth, New Hampshire? He was on the road, like me. He was a former dentist of some special kind. We were very similar. Taking medication, putting the pieces back together, et cetera. And he told me about these cabins. A little smelly with mildew, a little unglamorous, but cheap, and heated if you need, and near the sea. I really wanted to get to sea."

174

"So you drove there, and what?"

"I slept for most of the week."

"You still need to sleep a lot."

"Always," he said. "Consciousness," he said, "is very hard work."

"So you slept. You ate lobster."

"A lot."

"And what did you do when you weren't sleeping or eating lobsters or driving?"

"I counted girls in Jeeps."

"There are that many?"

"All over New England," he said, raising a cup that shook. "They're blonde, most of them, and they seem very attractive, but I think that's because of the contrast—you know, the elegant, long-legged girl and the stubby, utilitarian vehicle. I found it quite exciting."

"Exciting. Jesus, Daddy, you sound so adolescent. Exciting. Blondes in Jeeps. Well, you're a single man, for the most part. What the hell. Why not. Did you date any?"

"Come on," he said.

"You're not ancient. You could have a date."

"I've had them," he said.

"That's who I was asking you about. Do you hear from her?"

"I'm telling you about the girls in their Jeeps on the coast of Maine, and you keep asking—"

"About the woman you had an affair with who caused you to divorce my mother. Yes."

"That's wrong," he said. "We separated. That's all that I did—I moved away. It was your *mother* sued for divorce."

"I recollect. But you do understand how she felt. There you were, shacking up with a praying mantis from Fort Lee, New Jersey, and not living at home for the better part of two years."

"Do I have to talk about this?"

"Not for *my* two hundred bucks. We're just having an on-the-road visit, and I'm leaving soon enough, and probably you are too."

"I drift around. But that's a little unkind about the money. *And* about the praying mantis thing. Really, to just bring it up."

"Because all you want to do is feel better," I said, lighting another cigarette. By this time, there were several other diners in the Natty Bumppo Room, and one of them was looking over the tops of her gray-tinted lenses to indicate to me her impending death from secondary smoke. *Oh, I'm sorry!* I mouthed to her. I held the cigarette as if I were

175

going to crush it onto my saucer, then I raised it to my mouth and sucked in smoke.

I blew it out as I said to him, "She's the one who led you into your nosedive. She's the reason you crashed in flames when she left you."

"This is not productive for me," he said.

"You're supposed to be productive for *me*," I said. I heard the echo of my voice and, speaking more calmly, I said, "Sorry. I didn't mean to shout. This still fucks me up, though."

"Don't use that kind of language," he said, wiping his eyes.

"No."

"I thought we were going to have a *visit*. A father-and-daughter reunion."

"Well, we are," I said.

"All right. Then tell me about yourself. Tell me what's become of you."

I was working hard to keep his face in focus. He kept looking like somebody else who was related to him, but he was not the him I had known. I was twenty-eight years old, of no fixed abode, and my father, also without his own address, was wearing camouflage clothing in an upstate town a long enough drive from the New York State Thruway to be nothing more than the home of old, rotting trees, a campus in the state's junior college system, and the site of the James Fenimore Cooper Inn.

"What's become of me," I said. "All right. I have two galleries that represent me. One's in Philadelphia and one's in Columbia County, outside New York. I think the owner, who also runs what you would call a big-time gallery on Greene Street, in Manhattan, may be just around the corner from offering me a show in New York City. Which would be very good. I got some attention in Taos, and a lot of New York people were there, along with the usual Hollywood producer-*manqué* people, both has-beens and would-bes, and the editorial stars who hire agents to get their names in the gossip columns. It was very heady for me to be hit on by such upper-echelon minor leaguers."

"When you say *hit on*," he said, "what are you telling me?"

"Exactly what you think. A number of men fancied fucking me."

He let his head droop toward his plate. "That's a terrible way to live," he said. "I'm supposed to be protecting you from that."

"But why start now?"

176

"That's what you came for," he said. "I've been waiting, since you phoned me, to figure out why you would look me up *now*, when you might suspect I'm down on my luck and in unheroic circumstances."

"Unheroic," I said. "But you're wrong. I mean, as far as I *know*, you're wrong. I asked Mommy for your address because I hadn't seen you since I was in graduate school. And you're my father. And I guess I was missing you."

"And because you wanted to tell me the thing about men trying to— you know. Because it would hurt me. And you're angry with me."

"Well, you could say the way you left your wife was a little disappointing to me."

He'd been rubbing at his forehead with the stiffened fingers of his right hand. He stopped, and he looked around his hand, like a kid peeking through a fence, his expression merry and, suddenly, quite demented. Then the merriment left him, and then the craziness, and he looked like a man growing old very quickly. He said, "I have to tell you, the whole thing was disappointing as well."

"You mean, leaving your wife for the great adventure and then being dumped."

"And then being dumped," he said.

"Mommy said you were doing drugs when that happened."

"There was nothing we didn't do except heroin," he said. "If we could have bought it safely, I'd have stuffed it up my nose, shot it into my eyeballs, anything."

"Because of the sex?"

He looked right at me. "The best, the most astonishing. I haven't been able to acknowledge a physical sensation since then. Everything I've felt since then is, I don't know—as if it was *reported*. From a long way away."

"Jesus. *And* you loved her?"

"I've dealt with a therapist who says maybe I didn't. Maybe it was the danger. I seem to act self-destructively, from time to time. I seem to possibly not approve of myself. I seem to need to call it love whether that's what I feel or not. I seem to have conflated sex with love."

"A conflatable sex doll," I said. I snickered. He managed to look hurt. "I'm sorry."

"It doesn't matter much. I'm working on my health. It doesn't have to hurt to hear that kind of laughter. I suppose it's good for me. A kind of practice at coping with difficulties."

"No," I said, "I apologize. It just seemed like a very good damned pun, the conflatable sex doll. I am nobody's spokeswoman for reality. I apologize."

"Tell me how your mother is."

"She's fine. She's living a life. I'd feel uncomfortable if I gave you any details. I think she wants to keep that stuff to herself."

"So she's fine and you've managed to endure the attentions of men with press agents."

"Mostly to evade them, as a matter of fact."

"Mostly?"

"Daddy, if anyone around here's fine, it's me. Nobody has to worry about men, nutrition, the upkeep of my car, or the management of my career. I do my own taxes, I wrote my own will, and I navigate my own cross-country trips."

"Why do you have a will? A legal last will and testament, you're saying? Why?"

"I'm not getting any younger," I said.

"Nonsense. You don't have a family to provide for."

"You know that, do you?"

"You *do*?"

I nodded. I found it difficult to say much.

"What, Baby?"

"A son. His name is Vaughan."

"Vaughan? As in the singer Vaughan Monroe?"

"As in Ralph Vaughan Williams. One of his symphonies was playing when, you know."

"I know nothing," he said. He was pale, and his lips trembled as his hands did, though in a few seconds his mouth calmed down. His fingers didn't.

"He's with Mommy."

"But he lives with you?"

"I'm thinking of living with someone downstate. We would stay together there."

"His father?"

"No. But a man I like. A photographer."

"Criminies," he whispered. "There are all those gaps, all those *facts* I don't know. This is like looking at the family picture album, but most of the pictures aren't in the book. Are you *happy* about this child?"

"Are you happy about me?"

"Sure," he said. "Of course I am."

"Then I'm happy about my boy. Did you really say *criminies*?"

He clasped his hands at the edge of the table, but they upset his breakfast plate. Syrup went into the air, and soggy crumbs, and his stained napkin. The waitress came over to sponge at the mess and remove our dishes. She came back with more coffee and the check.

"Criminies," my father said. "I haven't heard that word for years."

I was counting out money which I slide across the table to him. "I hope this helps," I said, "really."

"I regret needing to accept it," he said. "I regret not seeing you more. I regret your having to leave."

"That's the thing with those family albums, Daddy. People are always leaving them."

"Yes. But I'm a grandfather, right?"

"Yes, you are."

"Could I see him?"

"Ever go downstate?"

"Oh, sure," he said. "I get to plenty of places. I told you, I was all the way up in Maine just a few weeks ago."

"All those girls in Jeeps. I remember. So, sure. Yes. Of course. He's your grandson."

"Big and sloppy like me?"

"His father was a kind of fine-boned man. But he'll have my arms and legs."

"He'll look like a spider monkey."

"You haven't called me a spider monkey for an awfully long time."

"But that's what he looks like? I want to think of him with you."

"And very light brown hair, and a long, delicate neck. And great big paws, like a puppy."

"He'll be tall."

We sat, and maybe we were waiting to find some words. But then my father pulled on his camouflage cap, and tugged at the brim. He was ready, I suppose. I left the dining room and then the inn a couple of steps ahead of him. We stopped outside the front doors and watched the man, now shirtless, as he swung, working his way through a chunk of a hundred and fifty years. Splinters flew, and I heard him grunt as the wedge-shaped maul head landed. The woman in the cotton vest was watching it batter the wood.

I put my arms around his neck and hugged him. I kissed his cheek.

"Baby, when does everybody get together again?"

179

I hugged him again, and then I backed a couple of steps away. I could only shrug.

He said, "I was thinking roughly the same."

I heard the maul. I watched my father zip, then unzip his camouflage hunting coat.

He turned to the woman in the cotton vest and tipped his camouflage cap. She stared at him through her safety goggles.

He was giving a demonstration, I realized. With his helpless, implausible smile, he was showing me his lapsed world of women. He was broken, and he shook with medication, but he dreamed, it was clear, of one more splintered vial of amyl nitrate on the sweaty bedclothes of a praying mantis from Fort Lee, New Jersey. He had confected a ride with a leggy blonde in a black, convertible Jeep on US 1 in Maine. And if the foreman of the forestry crew would talk to him in front of her tired and resentful men, he would chat up that lady and touch, as if by accident, the flesh of her sturdy, tanned arms.

That was why I backed another pace. That was why I turned and went along the duckwalk behind my father, leaving the wreckage of the maple tree and walking toward my car. I wanted to be driving away from him—locked inside with the windows shut and the radio up—before he could tip his cap, and show me his ruined, innocent face, and steal what was left of my life.

Nominated by Georgia Review, David Jauss

JUNK

essay by GORDON CAVENAILE

from EVENT

On the Nod

Like this:

A high wire, on which you swing gracefully, poised in perfect balance. Breath leaves you in long endless drifts, one drift after another until at last you're empty, still swinging. Eiderdown of a sort, sweet eiderdown waits below to wrap you up and send you off to the land of permanent dreamless nods. As you must you fall, balance lost at last, but the spreading cushion below bounces you back to the wire, where you land, softly on ready feet. . . . Eyes flicker open: the wall, the room, your hands quiet on your thighs. It's close, very close, and you're not worried. This one is gentle, this one welcomes rather than terrifies, this is soft-breasted, a womb widening for the great return, moist dark promise of mother spread-eagle on eiderdown, all aglow for her prodigal junky son, for his slow silent crawl back between caressing thighs, to the long-lost zone, back to birth, its annihilation, and before.

Or this:

A small row-boat lost at sea, in which you sit surrounded by an invitingly empty horizon. Breezes stroke you warm beneath clear glareless sunshine and send the boat into an easy rocking drift, nowhere in particular. Unoccupied, you lie down. As you do, water enters the boat from all points. Warm as the breezes, it wraps around you, licking under your clothes while the boat drops away beneath you. You suck slowly at the blue sky, you hold on, but now there's nothing to hold onto, and during the slow drift downward you give up your last breath:

a long seemingly endless exhalation forming great glassy bubbles shot through with receding beams of sunlight. Now darkness, the last bit of breath, the last tiny bubbles you no longer see, and finally, a soft gentle bump as you hit bottom. . . . Eyes flicker open: the wall, the room, your hands quiet on your thighs. It's close, very close. It's in the room with you, behind collapsing eyelids, a slow undulating form with tickling tentacles that carries you upwards through this midnight, this expanding radiance, these breezes still rippling across the ocean's surface and urging you forward, the boat rocking nowhere with you, your long delayed grab for air, the clear glareless sunshine.

A Local Businessman

Jimmy is Vietnamese. He's sculpted and wiry and looks around forty, older than the other delivery dealers, who range between eighteen and twenty-five. He spent a few years in a camp on the border, which is where he got the obscure scrawled tattoos that mark both forearms, and probably where his teeth went bad: they're grey and pockmarked with large cavities. Jimmy's married, he has a child, and he spends his days delivering heroin to a wide variety of customers around the Lower Mainland. The buyer dials his number, leaves a voice message or punches in his number, and within five minutes Jimmy phones back.

'You call?'

'Sure.'

'What you want?'

On a normal night he's at the door in twenty minutes, maybe half an hour. Sometimes he's out in Abbotsford or Surrey, in which case he takes a little longer. He always extends a hand as the door opens, and it's just natural to invite him in. His English still isn't so good, but Jimmy'll take a few minutes to chat anyway. He knows the importance of steady, mature customers—those who have a regular supply of cash and a habit more or less under control, with maybe a bit of room for development—and he honours a sort of unspoken guarantee: If one of his regulars isn't satisfied with a purchase, Jimmy always provides an extra hit, no questions asked. Now and again he'll offer his best customers a free sample of some new supply; when one stops calling, he drops by with a little gift, a little reminder.

Jimmy's been doing business for three years and he's never been stopped by the police, let alone busted. He's so confident that he keeps his papers in a plastic bag on the back seat of his car, in full view. What, after all, do the cops want with him? They can clear him off the street, and achieve zero as far as drug control goes. He knows that, the cops know that, everyone concerned knows that.

So he puts in full busy days that begin around noon: at 1 a.m. he 'closes,' and by that time his wallet is fat with bills, many of them fifties and hundreds. Points go for $30, quarters for $60, and they come in little folded up squares snipped from lottery tickets. The prices are a little steep in today's market but, as Jimmy says, 'This good, best you find.'

That's true only sometimes, but he's reliable and seems like a nice guy, except when he starts to hustle: 'You buy point today and point tomorrow. Why not buy quarter today?'

A good question, unless the buyer is fighting a habit.

'I'm trying to take it easy.'

'You call tomorrow. I make two trips, you spend more money. I have quarter here, fat one for you. Buy two quarters, special price.'

Efforts to explain the logic of buying less—and therefore using less—don't seem to get through to Jimmy. Either he doesn't want to understand, or he still can't handle English in the abstract. Or it might simply be that he's cold-hearted, naturally inclined to profit from the weakness of others. The problem here is that it's never clear if Jimmy understands his product is any different than kitchen knives or quarts of milk. Like the other delivery dealers, Jimmy doesn't use the stuff.

The Product

It's been a dependable devil, so dependable for so long that it's difficult to recall that its reputation originated with specific acts of legislation and a good deal of Christian-based propaganda. Forever, it seems, the very word has had the sinister resonance of what is always and necessarily evil.

Say it out loud: 'HEROIN.'

There he is: the junky—a vague wasted form punctured full of syringe holes and oozing a putrid moral and physical decay.

But consider: The name comes from the German 'heroisch' (itself from the Greek 'heros'), meaning 'powerful,' a sign of the respect physicians once felt for the newly discovered opium derivative. Far more potent than morphine, a shot of heroin gave suffering patients instant release from pain, and doctors new faith in their own effectiveness: not a bad thing by any means. Abscessed teeth, arthritis, consumption, burns, breaks, lacerations—powerful heroin worked a miracle cure on almost all complaints.

First synthesized in 1874, the drug was being used and sold freely by the end of the century. The Bayer Company of Germany advertised it next to aspirin, its other miracle drug: 'Heroin: The sedative for coughs.' Meanwhile, mail-order catalogues and neighbourhood pharmacies continued doing their regular brisk business selling laudanum and various elixirs and cordials and remedies laced with the more traditional narcotic, opium. There were addicts, of course, many of them middle-class women, but if anyone noticed—and they often didn't since narcotic abuse leads more naturally to sleep than violent rages—the users endured no greater disapproval than drunks, and for a simple reason: nobody had said they were any worse.

The American temperance movements of the early 1900s signaled a change in attitude. Alcohol was the main point of attack, but narcotics became a logical secondary target since like alcohol, they provided pleasure and distracted users from less agreeable Christian pursuits. For those used to a legal, steady, and cheap supply of their favourite opiate, 1914 was a significant year. The Harrison Narcotic Act in the U.S. prohibited the sale of non-prescription preparations containing heroin, opium, or morphine, and made possession of these narcotics without a prescription a criminal offense. Under the combined influence of American legislation and a flare-up of racism ignited by reports of the flourishing opium trade in Vancouver's Chinatown, Canadian laws against narcotics became increasingly punitive during the 1920s, culminating in the notably harsh Opium and Narcotic Drug Act of 1929.

These laws north and south of the border redefined narcotic addiction as a vice of criminals, much as prohibition redefined liquor salesmen as gangsters. The new legislation meant only those willing to flout the law could put their hands on a big enough supply to maintain a habit. Without a very compassionate doctor, highly strung Aunt Lil went cold turkey: underworld desperados with the right connections and good business sense began importing and dealing the now highly illegal and highly profitable drug. At the bottom, the now-marginalized junky with nothing to lose and a need bigger than his discretion did what he had to do to stay high.

Biochemistry

Scientists enjoy heroin like a good mystery. The simplicity of the drug hardly seems to account for the profound and perplexing power it exerts. Take opium: isolate the morphine: acetylate two of morphine's hydroxyl groups—now add a syringe, and there you have it.

What's to get so upset about? Why declare war?

Well, unlike its antecedents, junk is lipophilic, lipid soluble, which means it crosses the blood-brain barrier easily, which means the user gets the slow come-on of morphine and the even slower come-on of opium in one solid rush. Shoot it, and we're talking about seconds; smoke it, and in a minute the drug is through the capillaries of the lungs, in the veins again, and headed due north; skin-pop it into a muscle, and the blood cells there soak it up in a couple of minutes; snort it, and the blood-rich mucous membranes in the nose will have it delivered to the hypothalamus in five minutes.

So it hits the brain soon enough. But who needs it? How to account for the drug's legendary ability to rob wills and destroy lives?

This is where even the most fervent anti-drug crusaders should show a little gratitude to junk and its narcotic relatives, maybe even a little respect. This is where the mystery begins unravelling and those watching as it does come to suspect deep secrets.

Imagine a thief of distant origin who enters a house very much like yours. He roams the place at will until he notices a carefully tailored suit lying across a bed. Curious, he tries it on: it's a perfect fit.

Some conclusions can be drawn:

1. The suit fits a resident of the house.
2. The thief bears a close physical resemblance to the resident.
3. The original owner of the suit will have a hard time getting into it while the thief has it on.

So our exogenous interloping opiates come from outside, from another continent, from an odd little flowering plant grown elsewhere. After twenty-five years or so of shooting heroin and morphine into ground up pig brains and decapitating rats blasted on radioactive dope, scientists have determined that, despite their foreign origin, narcotics have a chemical structure which allows them to form tight bonds at specific receptor sites found in animals and humans. It's assumed that the opiate—heroin, morphine, opium, or some derivative therefore—'fits' these receptor sites, which cluster mainly in the

185

brain, like a key fits a lock, a suit its owner. In a sense, foreign narcotics have a destination in the body, a purpose. They are headed to those places where they feel most comfortable.

Questions then surface about the natural residents of these receptor sites, the owners as it were. The suit, let's recall, isn't sitting there just for the thief's use. Postulated, then identified: amino acid chains similar enough to be the basic narcotic morphine to be called endorphins—endogenous morphine—which are produced naturally by the body to kill pain and provide pleasure. When required, endorphins sit on their customized receptor sites, many of them concentrated in the limbic system where sensations of physical pleasure originate. There, they *do things* to the functioning of the neurons, things that make life a little more bearable for the individual under stress or in pain.

Then smack comes along, pounding through the bloodstream to the brain. Indistinguishable from endorphins, welcomed as the body's own, the swarming molecules crowd out the body's natural opiates, lock with confident familiarity onto the opiate receptor sites, and *really* alter neuron behaviour.

Result, by a process that remains somewhat mysterious: a sudden obliteration of all pain and discomfort, an accompanying surge of pure physical pleasure, the breath-stealing euphoria which holds the secret of all narcotic abuse.

You rush. Then you're high.

Either

Like this:

A four-hour orgasm. Stomach flipping with pleasure. Explosion of calm. A halo, glowing. Slow drift into cushioned brain, into insulation. Into nowhere you need to know anything about. Conversion to sainthood, at once. Low, high, exquisite, everything in between. Breath at ease with itself, disappearing. Cancel. Cancel worry. Cancel history. A neutral zone, explore at will. Sweet dreams, beyond which there is nothing. Bed-time wide awake. Mother's back after a long wait. Sigh. The death of outrage, the death of sorrow. Warm. Hip. Kiss off the dirt. A slot in which you sit, inviolable. Order out of chaos. Thought out of need. Perennial as an evergreen. Powdered philosophy. The last frontier of discontent, in the dust behind. Big, but light; broad, but empty. Suspended animation. Pan-global spirit. Euphoria all over the place. Reprieve from that without which. The death of doubt. The death of need. Death, period, and better after all.

The Kids

Nick and Tony don't deliver. They arrange a series of meets on street corners, at bus loops, in parking lots and back alleys that stretch between Chinatown and Metrotown.

You phone. If it's really busy, or they've cashed out for the day, you get a woman's voice: 'You have reached the Cantel Network. The customer you are calling is unavailable at the moment. Please try again later.' If it's moderately busy, you hit a busy signal ten or twenty times in a row before getting through. If it's late or early or you're lucky, a quiet voice answers the first ring:

'Yeah?'

'You guys doing anything?'

Traffic in the background, dull street buzz.

'Who's this?'

'Jeff.'

'Jeff, who?'

'I know Nick.'

'What do you want?'

'Two quarters.'

'Fifth and Clark.'

'How long?'

'Fifteen.'

You go to Fifth and Clark and stand on the corner, any corner. Probably you see a few others standing across the street from you, maybe on the opposite corner. Junkies are easy to recognize, and they fit the stereotype: thin, skin often looking a few days dead, obscure almost to the point of invisibility, with a tendency to lurk. It's a good sign when you see them waiting—like going fishing and seeing birds hovering.

Nick appears, walking down Fifth or maybe up Clark, while Tony watches from across the street, cellular in hand. Nick is Asian, 20, 22 at the oldest, and wears the standard gear of any UBC science undergrad: sweater, loose blue jeans, and runners. His hair is shaved up the sides so that the tinted red mop on top hangs down loose.

Scattered iron fillings in the presence of a magnet, the junkies move in on Nick, who keeps a little tube jammed full of papers in his hand: points for $20, quarters for $40.

'One at a time,' he says, but no junky's yet learned how to control the blaze of instinct hunger sparked by the presence of smack. A semi-circle forms around Nick, bills are out and flapping, the moment has turned urgent. The kids are hot, red-hot, not so much because they're dealing smack, but because of *how* they're dealing it: This is a public scene, visible proof that the cops have failed to contain yet another deadly drug epidemic.

'Back off, one at a time,' Nick says again. That has zero effect, so he grabs at the cash, counting it in a second before he stuffs it into his pocket, squeezing papers out of the tube—twenty, thirty, maybe even forty of them, depending on the crowd. Junkies disperse like tattered bits of paper blown back into oblivion by a sudden wind, and Nick and Tony return the way they came, drop-off done in two minutes, 120 seconds, the heat postponed to another day.

Okay. It's easier to phone Jimmy. No need to move, no standing around in the rain, no flashes of junky paranoia as you imagine the squad cars careening around the corner just as *you* grab your paper: none of that—just have a cup of tea and wait. But these days Nick and Tony are undercutting the delivery dealers. It's a matter of basic economics, the sort that has made McDonald's what it is: Their turnover is greater, the transportation overhead lower, and if you don't mind hanging around on street corners, they're just about as reliable. In fact, for the more traditional junky, the kids are an odd sort of throw-back to the old days, when you got high *only* after a more or less excruciating street-corner wait for the man.

Developing Taste

Who really savoured their first sexual encounter? Some, perhaps. Others were just too overwhelmed by the strangeness of the whole thing to *feel* much. To be enjoyed, after all, pleasure must be recognized as pleasure—and it's difficult to recognize something the first time you run into it.

That's why first-time users generally find heroin something of a let-down, a product that doesn't live up to its reputation. They don't *recognize* the euphoria. At best, they realize 'something's different,' without knowing exactly what. Hard to pin down. After all, if junk acts like a chemical the body naturally produces, it's safe to conclude that the junk high isn't foreign to our physiology. Given a reasonable dose, the first time heroin user finds himself walking and talking normally—it's not alcohol. His mind seems clear, unaffected—nothing as crudely psychoactive as LSD or pot. He's not grinding his teeth down to the gums and he's not crumbling into a stupor in the middle of a cross-walk—not amphetamines, not barbiturates. He's relaxed, calm, not concerned with too much, on a peaceful roll like he's having a good day for a change, and that's about it.

A little disappointing.

The taste for the drug creeps up, as does the taste for most of the finer pleasures in life. The second or third time around the novice starts to recognize the glow in the belly, the almost liquid warmth seeping through his body, a honeyed sort of ecstasy all the more plea-surable for feeling so *natural*. Then it begins: a sort of falling out of favour with normal life. Sensualists realize that once you know how to identify it, the junk rush comes on as deeply and intensely as an or-gasm, and hangs around long enough to turn even the most mundane activity into a pleasure to be savoured. Walking the dog before you get high is never as good as it is after you get high. More meditative users notice that not only does the body feel good, but thoughts flow in a calm, ordered way; personal problems of varying degrees of intensity suddenly appear in reasonable perspective, as small affairs not really worth taking too seriously. Optimism is the order of the day, the sort that springs from complete physical well-being.

Those given to still deeper thought arrive at the understanding that smack poses a philosophical problem: If a single drug can provide ut-ter peace of body and mind, what logic prevents us from making the acquisition of this drug the primary goal of our life?

For your basic garden-variety junky, the answer—if not the ques-tion—is self-evident.

Tolerant and Dependent Rats

Dip a rat's tail into water heated to 52 degrees centigrade. Count the number of seconds until the rat flicks its tail from the water. Make a note of the number. Repeat this process numerous times with differ-ent rats. Establish the time frame within which a normal rat will re-tract its tail from water heated to 52 degrees centigrade.

Select a rat. Shoot it up with a precisely measured amount of morphine. Wait a fixed number of minutes and then dip the rat's tail into water heated to 52 degrees centigrade. Count the seconds until the rat flicks its tail from the water. Make a note of it: calculate the deviation from the normal retraction time. Wait a predetermined number of hours. Shoot the rat up with the same dose of morphine and then dip its tail back into the hot water. Make a note of the number of seconds that pass before the rat flicks its tail from the water. Repeat the process again and again over a number of days. Chart the numbers as dots on a graph: join the dots. Notice that the line descends as the analgesic effects of the morphine dose diminish.

What every junky knows in his body has now been quantified and measured, given visual form: It's called tolerance, the process by which exactly the same becomes measurably less, by which static junk pleasure turns into jumpy, tail-sizzling need, then need into demand, and more into the same.

Now go back to your rat. It's wired to the teeth on precise and regular doses of morphine. A set number of minutes following its last shot of morphine, inject the rat with a precise quantity of naloxone. Carefully observe the sudden withdrawal symptoms brought on by the narcotic antagonist as it shoots to the receptor sites in the brain and knocks the exogenous opiates into oblivion: hypersalivation, shivering, penile erection, ejaculation, ptosis, abdominal contractions, vomiting, teeth grinding, diarrhea, piloerection, abnormal posture, flight, irritability and, over time, weight loss. Group the symptoms together into an overall score for withdrawal intensity, and graph the results of observations taken every six hours over fourteen days. If you want, get another rat. Addict it to an increased dosage of morphine, or a decreased dosage, or if you're so inclined to a different narcotic entirely, like methadone, heroin, demerol, or etorphine. When the rat is utterly strung out, repeat the procedure with naloxone. Graph the results of observations taken every six hours over fourteen days and place them alongside the first graph. Compare.

What every junky knows in his body has now been measured and graded, given visual form: It's called dependence, the ever-intensifying pain that lurks in wait for the addict denied his narcotics, proof of serious disrepair in the local endorphin factory brought on by a steady supply of high-quality foreign imports.

Or

Like this:

Paradise charged to a bad credit card. Scabbing on the nod. What it's like to be three-quarters dead, decaying. The dirtiest little secret in the city. Cardboard veins. Your shit in a vault: Who cares? Your cock in a siphon: Who needs it? Terror is on hold. De-function; zero; skinny scarred arms. Until. Then. Snakes wake up. Mobile bones in back motion. A panic, room 462, Brandiz. Metabolic subversion. Empty craters in the head, phantom aches. When a visit to the graveyard goes bad. The codger dying in your arms, frayed, gasping, nerve-racked. Vaulted shit, the tap turns on; cock leaps awake from a nightmare getting worse by the minute. Exactly what you shouldn't, when you shouldn't. Interest calculated on a lost bill blowing down the street. In your direction.

Economics and Demographics

Small time smack dealing is a growth industry in the Lower Mainland. Cellular phone numbers proliferate. Young dealers go looking for clients. It's conceivably safer and easier to maintain a habit in Vancouver than it has been anywhere in North America since the days before the Harrison Act. A Toronto drug lawyer explained it this way: Heroin headed for the U.S. first arrives in Canada because it's an easier North American entry point than the States. Either 'mules' pack it in on planes and boats from Hong Kong, Bangkok, Vietnam, or the dope arrives stashed deep inside packages of innocent looking consumer goods. Before the stuff goes overland across the border, a certain portion of it is dropped in Canada, more than ever in recent years thanks to the number of Asian immigrants in Canada—and especially in Vancouver—with connections back in the land of poppies.

Add to this the fact that organized crime syndicates are relatively few and far between in this country, and you get a picture of what's happening. Cities and neighbourhoods are not controlled by the Mafia, and local gangs still don't have enough muscle to dictate who sells what to who at what price. Anybody with a line on a quantity of smack is more or less at liberty to sell it as cheaply as he feels he can afford to. The new dealers—generally junk-free, young, Asian, business-minded—need only four things to set up shop:

1. a connection
2. a cellular phone
3. transportation
4. customers

These days, only the last is likely to cause any problem, but for reasons a little more complicated than they at first appear.

Unlike cocaine, heroin has never had much of a social cachet; nobody pulls out a quarter gram of junk for general consumption at an office party. The old demons still hover about the drug. It is evil, corrupting, sinister in its mysterious, relentless power of seduction. Cocaine users laugh, drink, have sex, turn deals; junkies nod out, become asexual, waste away, slip into a sort of inert death-like state—very unappetizing.

Yet heroin use *is* on the increase, and in a strange way the media can be held at least partially responsible for this. The splashy, on-going coverage of the 'killer' smack that's been finding its way into Vancouver in the last few years has acted as a sort of extended free advertisement for dealers. Three demographic groups have paid more than passing interest to this accidental ad campaign.

First are the ex-junkies, straight or on methadone maintenance, who thought they were beyond relapse. Constant reminders that cheap powerful dope is now available on the streets has broken down a lot of resistance. They're lured back to the streets, curious to see if the stories are really true. They are.

There are the younger users, first timers, late teens leaning toward an outlaw existence, kids in leather jackets who drop out of school and go looking for a definitive gesture of contempt for the straight life. Heroin stares at them from the headlines; it provides the gesture; for those with the determination to try it more than once, the drug's flooding calm, its ability to dissolve environmental and financial panic into peaceful oblivion are unexpected bonuses.

Most interesting is a particular subgroup of otherwise respectable baby boomers, successful lawyers, teachers, businessmen, artists, ex-hippies and dopers who made it as far as hard drugs twenty or so years back before the counter-culture turned tedious and they went back to school. Headlines promising junk of astounding quality has stirred up a long-forgotten junk nostalgia, the distant memory of the pure liberating pleasure that has eluded them all these years in the middle of the road. Then an accidental run-in, say, with some old dope buddy still on the streets and they've got a cellular number slotted into their ad-

192

dress book. After a month or two, curiosity gets the better of them. Someone knocks at the door, shakes their hand, drops off a paper of smack that, much like electronic equipment, has gotten better *and* cheaper over the years. An old affair is rekindled.

The problem for the dealers is that as more heroin finds its way into town, as the number of heroin users increases, so does the number of dial-a-fix numbers. It's a curious illustration of the free enterprise system, unregulated competition, borderless markets, a nineties sort of phenomenon. A year and a half ago, Tim, a delivery dealer, sold quarter grams for between $80-$90. Even then he complained about how hard it was to make a living, and eventually gave up his business. He left no gap. At the time of this writing, Nick and Tony are selling quarters for $40. Reeve sells the same for $45, Dave for $50, and Jason— who makes great claims that his shit is close to pure—for $60. Both hardened junky and occasional user are now at liberty to 'shop around.' After all these years, it's a buyer's market.

Puppies

Normal puppies removed from their mothers show obvious signs of separation distress. They whimper and bark, are agitated and lose their appetites. A shot of morphine immediately removes all signs of distress. The puppies stop crying; they grow calm, and eat and drink normally. They are neither groggy nor lethargic, and engage in standard puppy play. They act as they would in the presence of their mother. When an injection of naloxone instantaneously reverses the effects of the morphine, the puppies display sharply intensified symptoms of the initial separation distress. Their cries are doubly intense, as though something even more important than mother had been removed. Sleep is impossible, food rejected; the puppies jump and twist about in their cages, not in play but in pained search of what can't be found.

In the very early stages of the experiment, the appearance of the mother will soothe these exaggerated distress symptoms. With her close by, the puppies resume normal behaviour patterns soon enough. If, however, over the course of several weeks, mother is systematically replaced by regular shots of morphine, things develop differently. High, the puppies go about their business peacefully, as happy alone in a one-dog cage as they are running loose with other puppy playmates.

193

Problems arise when attempts are subsequently made to *trade back* mother for morphine. Denied their drug, the puppies suffer the usual withdrawal symptoms; they whine, leap about, are unable to sleep, refuse food, vomit; their hair stands on end, they get stomach cramps and fill their cages with watery shit. Over time, they all waste away to fur and bones. Given access to mother at this point, the puppies no longer show any measurable response to her; she seems to have no function; if she were a machine, she would be called obsolete.

For the scientists conducting it, this experiment was much more affecting than watching rats jerking their tails out of cups of hot water. And for a change it said something about the mystery of narcotic addiction: Mother comes in different forms.

Nominated by Jewel Mogan

ZEALOUS

by JOSHUA CLOVER

from NEW AMERICAN WRITING

A genie serves a continental breakfast, angel brings the desired—
Broken golden morning, the gabled mnemon called by my keeper
Castle Fifth of May, *a house where all were good,*
Dream into architecture, Adriatic angles and carmine eaves, salt white
Eastern wall holding forth on the copper sea. I came
For the waters, splash splash. Was a charmed thought to
Grow old here, sun *like the trace of the potter's*
Hand on the glazed surface clinging to the copper body
In the sea, a daily letter over coffee beginning Dear
John, Friend: always here the praise-singing, shit-work, *dusting*
  off the
Kingdoms of the world, dawn's *jeunesse dorée* down to the
Last chapter of erotism. Have arrived via no fault of
Mine, as one in turning away from everything else comes
Nonetheless to this deserted, this three-gated house, the sea-broken
  sequence
Of the New World. You will have found this
Page some shaking, lucent years on earth since its music
Quit me. Each of us will appear to the other
Reading right to left as through a looking-glass but spectral,
Shrouded in white paper, bond between us, the world of
Things held in abeyance, the music of my keeper an

Urgent repetition against the eastern wall, *quit me, quit me,*
Very well. A cloud floats by looking exactly like a
Word, a boat looking for all the world like a
Xebec, perhaps this is the Mediterranean? You won't tell me,
You're a ghost, la la la la la la la.

Nominated by Laurie Sheck

THE BURIAL

fiction by STEPHEN DIXON

from CONJUNCTIONS

GOULD'S MOTHER DIES and he makes plans for the funeral. Days before in the hospital when she was still lucid she said she didn't want any funeral-home service. "Too expensive. They charge a fortune to rent a chapel and a little side room and for all their employees to act as ushers and doormen, and it's also so unnecessary. Why should people, if they want to see the whole thing through, come to the chapel and cemetery both? And in addition some even come to the funeral home the night before just to view my cheap casket and pay their respects to you, and I want it to be the cheapest so you don't go broke for a stupid box and I also don't want you opening it once I'm in it. Have it at the cemetery only. Open air and light, even if it's raining, is better than the solemn nonsense and awful recorded organ music of a chapel. A few people I knew saying some brief things about me if they want or just praying to themselves or together from some little prayer book the cemetery could loan you or even staring at their feet or into space if they like, and then drop me in the ground between your father and brother and you go home. If the whole thing takes more than half an hour, starting from the time you get there till you leave, then it's taken too long. People's time shouldn't be wasted for things like that. It's already enough they had to get there." "That's why a funeral home might not be a bad idea, in spite of the expense, if we have to talk about it now," and she said "We do. If you're not going to be the practical one, then I have to, so what were you saying?" "I was saying I could find a home in the city. People wouldn't even have to drive their cars to it, if they lived there and weren't planning on going to the cemetery. They can come by cab or subway or bus, and for some who live on the Upper West Side, where I think the best place is, they can even walk. Then the ones that also want to go to the cemetery can go in my car or someone else's if someone else who comes has one, or even a limo I'll hire if there are that many people coming. I mean, how much can one cost, for the cemetery's not *that* far away, if I remember. The rest will feel they've paid their respects and did their duty and so on by coming to the service or to the funeral home the night before, if they also did that, and they can go back to work or home. But please let's drop the subject," and she said "Who are all these people you're expecting? If you get six, tops, it'll be a lot, or seven, eight, but don't look for a crowd. That's also why the funeral-home service makes no sense. You'll have to get someone to conduct it—a rabbi or some expert in Jewish religious services the home gets for you—and you want him speaking to a practically empty audience? The cemetery; have it all there. And don't let them do anything to my body for it. Just put me in the pine box straight from the hospital, store me for the night someplace—if it's got to be at the funeral home where you buy the casket, then let it be—ship me to the grave site the next day in the cheapest conveyance allowable, and that'll be it. All this is almost a favor I'm asking of you. But since I won't be in any position to argue, do what you want except to cremate me. Even though I'll be gone at the time— *dead*; why not just say it? What else do I expect will happen to me by the end of the week?—the thought of all that fire scares me. If you don't promise you won't cremate me, I swear it will kill me sooner. Worms and bugs and whatever else is underground don't make me feel that much easier, but I just think if there is a soul in your body and it doesn't get completely out of it once you die, it won't survive those terrific temperatures. Besides, I'm leaving you almost no money. I don't have much, that's why, since whatever I had or Dad left me was mostly used up to keep me alive the last few years and for someone to look after me. So why waste what's left plus some of your own on even a simple chapel service when you also have to go through one at the cemetery? I know the burial will also have to cost something. But so would anything you do—cremation; hiring a boat to drop me in the ocean, which by law you can't do—so we know there's a minimum you have to spend on this. I wouldn't even have a rabbi or any kind of burial professional at the grave, since they can set you back a bundle too. Just ask the cemetery to get one of those little old religious guys who hang around the cemetery and who knows the right prayers for the dead, and slip him a twenty to read some passages over me and maybe to point something out for you to read. Or conduct it any way you want on your own, with you or whoever has come there, reading or speaking whatever you want. In the end, what's the difference? And I don't say that to you that way to make a joke. Let's face it, dead is dead, and I know that whatever you say and read and however you say it, even if it comes out fumblingly, is meant well."

He decides to have the body sent to that West Side funeral home, put in the cheapest pine casket they have there and with nothing done to the body, not even washed or reclothed, since once she's in the casket and it's closed nobody's going to see her again, and next morning sent by simple van to the cemetery for a short burial ceremony, though he doesn't know what he's going to do there yet. His wife's cousin and her husband will meet him there, same with his mother's best friend from her street, whose son will drive her and the woman who took care of his mother the last two years. Later that day someone from the funeral home calls him and asks if he wants her marriage bands removed from her finger—she added his father's band to her own when his father died—before she's put in the casket, and he says "Oh God, she never told me what to do about that, and I don't know. She should probably be buried with them, right?" and looks at his wife and points to his own band and she points to her chest and shakes her head she doesn't want them, and the man says "Look, yes or no, because we won't be able to get them off later without, if you'll excuse me, chopping off her finger. And that, unless it was absolutely necessary for some other reason, I'm not allowing any of my workers to do," and he says "Then okay, leave them on. They're hers, whatever that means, and eventually I'd just lose them."

The next day, on the way to the cemetery with his wife and two girls, he blurts out "Damn, just thought of something. I mean I've been thinking and thinking what I'll say at the ceremony after someone reads a couple of prayers, and simply decided to say what comes naturally but to keep it brief. But there's a poem she loved and though she didn't mention it when she talked the other day about everything she wanted and didn't want after she died, except for the wedding bands . . . do you think I made the right decision on that?" and his wife says "Too late, don't even think of it." "But the kids might have wanted them for when they're older," and his youngest daughter says "What?" and his wife says "Nothing, we're not going to talk about it. It'd be totally futile and it wouldn't seem right. What'd you start out to say?" and he says "I remember a couple of years ago when she was very sick and I was called to New York and we thought she was dying . . . we're talking about Grandma, of course," to his girls. "And she said if there's one thing she wanted read at her funeral, but not by a rabbi, she added, it was an Emily Dickinson poem about dying. She gave the title but I can't remember it, though I probably wrote it down then," and his wife says "I don't think hers had official titles. They were all first lines of her poems, weren't they? Either she decided on titling them that way or someone did for her after she died and the poems were found. Wasn't that her?" and his oldest daughter says "Who, Grandma again?" and he says "Emily Dickinson, a poet of the last century, and it was her, I'm sure." "Oh, I know her. We read her in the CTY humanities class I took, but I can't remember any of them now or anything about them except they were all short." "There's one very beautiful one I recall," his wife says, "that starts 'Because I could not stop for death,' and then goes on 'so death stopped for me,' or something," and he says "That's it, her favorite, or one of them. She used to read me them when I was a boy. And for years she kept a copy of all the poems on her night table—there weren't many, or as Fanny said, they were all short. The collected works in one volume, plus the letters, I think, or some of them. I haven't seen the book around in a long time and before that one time in the hospital she hadn't brought up Dickinson in years. It's probably still in her apartment somewhere, or someone borrowed it and never gave it back—it could even have been me—or she just read it till it fell apart. No, I could never have taken it from her; it had been by her bedside for maybe ten years and you don't borrow a book like that, or loan it out. Did she say then that it was at home and I should get it from there? I don't remember. But I have to read that poem at the burial. It might be all I'll read or say, in fact, except that this was one of her favorite poems, maybe her favorite and that Dickinson was her favorite poet, or certainly among her favorites and the only one whose book she had by her bedside so long, if I'm remembering right. And that she used to read them to me and I thought this one appropriate to read today, because of all I've said about it and its contents— the poem's—and so on. Do you remember the rest of the poem?" he says to his wife. "It's short, right? You can write it down for me, or one of the girls can; you can just recite it," and his youngest daughter says "I'll write it down—I've a pad and pen with me," and Fanny says "No, I will; I know her works, or read her, and those first two lines Mommy said I especially remember and won't need her to repeat," and he says

"Either of you, so long as it's written clearly," and his wife says "I only know those two, I'm afraid; and the second's 'He kindly stopped for me.'" "That's right, that's right," he says. "Think, come on, remember; and Josie, get your pen and pad out," and his wife says, "I can't; that's it, a blank. 'Because I could not stop for death' and 'He kindly stopped for me.'" "Then I'll stop in a town on the way—we've time—and buy it at a bookstore if there's one, or an anthology of some sort with that poem in it. It's one of her most popular, so it'd be in one. And every bookstore must have an anthology like that or a collection of her poems, or at a bookstore at a nearby mall where most of them seem to be now," and his wife says "But there could be people waiting for us already. I think even the receptionist in your mother's doctor's office said she was coming. And the funeral-home people with the casket in their van. They all expect you to be the first one there, and for the funeral people, probably for some paperwork to fill out or just sign." "Then this is what. I'll drop you all off. Anything to sign, you do it; you're my wife. If anyone's there or they come, tell them to wait, I'll be back soon. As far as the funeral-van people; well, they can just put the box over the grave, the rest is up to the cemetery. Good thing no rabbi though. If we had one and he was there he wouldn't let me go because he'd probably have a wedding to run to in an hour or another funeral somewhere and he couldn't give us even five minutes more than what we hired him for. I'll go to the nearest store and buy the book. I won't be more than half an hour. If it takes more, I'll drop it. A half hour from the time I leave you might just be when I told everyone the service would start anyway. And tell them I'll keep the ceremony shorter than I had even planned to. *Ceremony, service,* whatever you want to call it; fifteen minutes, if that." "Please don't look for any book," she says. "Why not just talk about the poem, read the first two lines . . . read them twice, three times; they're that good and right for a funeral service. After that, say you don't know the other lines, but what Dickinson's poetry meant to your mother . . . the night table, reading them to you, all that. And how you wanted to read all of this poem; how you almost even started out from the cemetery to get the book at the last minute-" and he says "No, that's all circling around to avoid it, and dishonest—from my part—and lazy, because this is what she wanted. She told me it that first time two years ago and then again about a year later, I just remembered—I think we were in the waiting room of a doctor's office. Didn't say anything about it this last time in the hospital, but she was on drugs and not clear-headed—" and she says "What do you mean? You said she was about as lucid and articulate and well informed as you've seen her recently, using the big words she loved and with you having a long and absorbing personal conversation with her as you haven't had in years," and he says "She was still on medication, and I think a painkiller, and being fed intravenously, and anyway, not clear all the time . . . dozing off, sleeping a lot. Besides"—and she says "I don't know how much to believe you," and he says "Yes, believe me. Besides, maybe she thought I already knew about her poem wish and didn't want to repeat herself. That she didn't want me feeling she thought I had a lousy memory and that she had to say things over and over again for it to sink in. After all, she told me it at least twice before. Listen, you have to see how important this is to me. I don't want to put you and the kids in a bind, but this'll be my last good thing to her, or last chance to do it rather, besides how much it'll help me get through the day. If I can't find the Dickinson collection or that particular poem in an anthology, or one close to it on death or immortality or the ending of life and transmigration of the soul or something, I swear I'll give up after the first store and rush right back."

He drops them off at the burial site. Nobody's there yet, not even the van or the prayer reader he called the cemetery for late yesterday. A secretary in the cemetery office tells him how to get to town and says there are two bookstores there—"Lots of people must read around here, and perhaps there are two stores because the nearest mall is fifteen miles away," and he drives there in five minutes. Both stores are on the main street. The first is really just a used paperback shop, with mostly romances, spy fiction, mass paperbacks of every sort, and the only poetry is religious: St. Augustine is in this section plus several of the same editions of a book of poetry by the pope. The second store has an anthology of twentieth-century American poetry and books of poems by poets like Hardy, Whitman and Blake but no Dickinson. "I know we had one," the salesman says. "The Everyman edition—hardback, complete works, and only eleven dollars—a steal. Ah, it was sold, it says here," looking at the inventory record on the computer screen by the cash register. "Last week, May third. I could order a copy today," and he says "No time; I need it right away." "Try the library; they should have it if Miss Dickinson hasn't been assigned as a class project at one of the local schools," and he says "Great idea, why didn't I think of that?" and at the library down the street he locates a volume of Dickinson poems with the one he wants in it and goes up to the main desk and says "Excuse me, I don't live in this area; I'm not even a resident of New Jersey. But I'd like to borrow this book just for an hour or so," and the librarian says "If you want to sit here and read it, that's fine, but we can't loan a book to a non-New Jersey resident." "Let me explain why I need it," and he does, points out the poem and she says "I'm sorry, I appreciate your reason and offer my condolences, but it's a by-law of our town's library system I'd be breaking if I loaned you the book. In the past we've had every excuse imaginable for loaning books to nonresidents, and if we see a fifth of them returned we call ourselves lucky. Try to imagine what that figure would be if—" and he says "Believe me, I'll return it. I'll drive back here after the burial. You can even call the cemetery—I have the number here—to see if my mother's being buried today," and she says "Whether you're telling the truth or not—" and he says "I *am,*" and she says "Then even though you are telling the truth, which is what I meant to say, it's strictly prohibited to give loaning privileges to people without valid library cards of this town. If they have cards from other New Jersey localities, then that town's library has to request the book for them and it's sent to that library through the state's interexchange system." "Look, I have people waiting at the cemetery for me—the burial service was supposed to start five minutes ago. Not a lot of people—I don't want to lie to you—but my wife and daughters and my wife's cousin and her family from Brooklyn. They drove all the way from there to come to it, and other people—cemetery personnel, etcetera. Again, it was among my mother's favorite poems and to have it read at her funeral was really one of her last wishes. But because I was so distraught at her death yesterday—confused, everything—I forgot, and we didn't—I didn't; I'm the only surviving child—have a regular funeral . . . this is the only ceremony we're having. And when I was driving to the cemetery I suddenly realized—" and she says "I wish I could. What if I photocopied the poem for you?" and he says "I thought of that as a solution. But I want to hold a book—not a Bible, not a prayer book, since she didn't go for that stuff at funerals or really anywhere, but a book of poems—and read from that. Look, I'll leave a deposit. Ten dollars, twenty, and when I return the book I'll donate the money to the library," and she says "This book," turning to the copyright page, "is . . . more than forty years old. In excellent condition for a book that's been circulating that long. Maybe it's the delicacy of the poetry that makes readers handle the book delicately, though I don't want to engage in that kind of glib speculation here. I don't know what it originally cost, nor do I know what this copy is worth now. Fifty dollars perhaps, though more likely five, but around twenty to replace. I'm not a rare book collector, so that's not my point. We simply can't be loaning works to out-of-state residents because they're willing to give money to the library. That policy would mean only the more privileged among you can borrow from us, which wouldn't be the right perception for a library to give." "Okay, okay, I'll try and get the books somewhere else," and starts back to the poetry shelves with it and she says "You can leave it here, sir; I'll restack it," and he says "Nah, I've put you through enough already," and she says "Thank you, then, but please make sure it's in the right classificatory order," and once there he thinks Take the photocopy; better than nothing. Have her copy two or three different Dickinson poems, they're all there in that last Resurrection and something section he just saw . . . No, you want what you said you did and that's a book to read from, not some flimsy photocopy sheet, and this edition particularly because it has a real old book look, and looks around, doesn't seem to be anyone else here but her, and sticks the book inside his pants under the belt. Feels it, it feels secure; he'll take it for the day, return it by mail tomorrow with a donation and his apologies, won't give his name or a return address, of course. Though she can probably find out who he is, if she wants, from the cemetery, for how many burials can there be there at this hour in one day and he gave her enough information to give himself away. But what is she going to do, get the police to arrest him in Baltimore or New York for stealing a book for a day after he sent it back carefully wrapped and in the same condition and with a ten or twenty dollar bill?

Alarm goes off as he's leaving. She's looking at him from behind the main desk. "Oh Christ," he says, "who the hell thought you'd have these books electronically coded in such a small library. Here, take it, will ya," and sets it on a chair by the door and she says "Oh no, mister, you're not getting off as lightly as that. I don't believe your mother-burial story one iota now. And don't think of bolting or I'll follow you outside and take down your license number," and dials her phone and says, "Officer Sonder? Well, anyone then, though he's the one I've dealt with so far for this particular problem. Amy LeClair at the library. I have a man here whom I caught stealing one of our items . . . A book, but a potentially valuable one and I believe he knew it . . . Thank you," and turns to him, and says "He says for you to wait; a police car will be right over," and he says "Call back and tell him I can't; to catch me at the cemetery on Springlake," and she says "Leave now and you'll be in even deeper water. We've lost too many books and documents as it is and this is the only way to stop this kind of petty crime that tallies up for us to grand larceny." What to do? Take the book, read the poem at the burial and then tell everyone what he did and wait for the cops there? Or leave it and go and just hope they don't come after him, or wait for the cops here? Surely they're not going to arrest him. "Do you mind, while I wait, if I call the cemetery to hold up the burial?" and she says "If that is whom you'll call," and he says "Then you dial for me—I have the number right here or get it out of the phonebook," and she says "I'd rather not waste any more of the library's money by using the phone, even for a local call. We have restrictions regarding that too. We're barely surviving, you know. People aren't exactly putting this institution in their wills." "Then will a dollar cover the phone cost?" and she says "I'd also rather not take the money from you. Who knows what that'd imply." Just then a policeman comes in. Gould explains quickly. She says "Nothing for me to add; whatever his reasons for the theft were, he just admitted he was caught walking out with one of our books," and the policeman says to him "Looks like I'll have to write out a summons or even arrest you if Miss LeClair insists I do," and she says "I don't think we have to go that far, but certainly a summons." The policeman starts writing one out. "This means you'll have to appear in a county court in a number of weeks. Unless you check the 'no contest' box on the court notification you get and request to be fined through the mail and the judge accepts it," and he says, "Okay, but please hurry it up. I don't mean to sound disrespectful but there are all those people waiting at the cemetery for me and I still have my mother to bury," and the policeman says "No disrespect meant either, sir, but I can do it much faster with machines at the station house if that's what you want."

Only his wife and children at the cemetery when he gets there, sitting on a bench several plots away; casket's on a few planks above the open grave. "By the time your message got to us," his wife says, "Rebecca and everyone else had left. They all had to be somewhere later this afternoon and didn't know when you'd get back. They were concerned about you, paid their respects to you through me and said a few words of their own to your mother. You'll tell me it all later, all right? Now we should get the cemetery people to help us get the coffin in the ground." "Did you get the poem, Daddy?" his youngest daughter says and he says "Oh, the poem; Jesus, I even forgot to get it photocopied. I could have before but this librarian, you can't believe it, she gave me the option to but I wanted to hold the whole book, this beautiful old hardbound copy of Dickinson's, as if it were a religious book, rather than read from this skimpy transient sheet—" and his wife says "What are you talking about?" and he says "The poem. 'Because I could not stop for Death.' There's a capital D in the death. The prayer guy ever show up?" and she says "He waited awhile, then said he had to go to another grave site, and made some prayers over her casket and left." "So let's do it ourselves, though we'll have to get the cemetery workers to lower the box once we're done. Maybe that's all it should be anyway, since we're the only ones left of her family who are still semisound."

He drives to the office, returns with a cemetery official and two gravediggers in a truck behind him, and standing in front of the grave says "Please, now let the funeral and burial and service and everything else begin. Sally, do you have anything to say?" and she says "Just that we all loved you, Leah, very much. You were always wonderful to be around, wise in your ways, delightful to the girls, and because you're Gould's mother, special to me, and we're profoundly sorry to see you go. Kids?" and the oldest shakes her head and starts crying and the youngest says "No," and then "Yes, I have something. Goodbye, Grandma. I wish I knew you longer and when you were younger, and I feel extra sad for Daddy. And I love you too and am sorry to have you die and be buried." "Thank you, dears," he says. "As for me, if I mention the word love and how I feel I'll blubber all over the place and won't be able to continue. So to end the service, because I've kept everyone here way too long, I'd like to read something—I mean, recite—and very little because it's all I know. I tried to get more but that's another story, Mom, so just two lines of an Emily Dickinson poem you liked so much. 'Because I could not stop for Death' . . . what is it, Sally?" and she says "'He kindly stopped for me.'" "Right. 'Because I could not stop for Death, he kindly stopped for me. Because I could not stop for Death, he kindly stopped for me. Because I could not stop for Death, he kindly stopped for me.' Amen. Now if you gentlemen will lower the coffin, we'll go home."

Nominated by Conjunctions, Eugene Stein

MISSION POEM

by TARIN TOWERS

from 9 x 9 INDUSTRIES BROADSIDE SERIES

When she dreams, she dreams
Of Mission Street, her body a bus (men ride)
Men get on and off, get on and get off.
Her face is as open as a vacant lot,
Walled in and fenced in and empty
Of all but the dirt, the garbage sprinkled
In piles soft enough to curl up in—
But for the broken glass.
Her hands make the shape of a styrofoam cup
Reaching for something to fill it.
Her eyes expand into oceans
Oceans the way they look at night
Cold and wet and black and oh,
They don't stop, they just rush in and out
Like the men from the check cashing shop,
Like the men from the barber shop,
Like the men from the bar,
Like the men from the Triple-Dash-X theatre.
And her mouth, it is something to dance to,
A soft music escaping the dark,
Lips folding and unfolding, teeth seen
(but rarely) as glimmers of hope.

And when she smiles, if she smiles,
You will feel she has snatched a part of you,
You will feel that something is missing,
You will call her a thief, when you call her,
You will marry that mouth in your mind.

Nominated by Conjunctions, Joan Murray, Julia Vinograd

LET'S NOT TALK POLITICS, PLEASE

fiction by JOHN J. CLAYTON

from WITNESS

TOMORROW MORNING or the morning after, Friedman will wake up early to beat the jam on the 405, reach under the night table to finger in the code on the security key pad so he can move through the condo without triggering the alarm and facing an "armed response" from community guards. Tomorrow morning or the morning after, he'll press the button to start the Cookery, and the bread will warm, coffee will brew. He'll take his morning pills and touch his key pad, find the news on his wall screen, start at International and see the riots in London. Friedman has investments in London—rather, the company has investments. He may have to fly over, and flying still gets him nervous, though things are under better control now, and flights accompanied by radar-locking sniffer escort planes. Still, sometimes a surface-to-air missile gets through.

In the underground garage he waves to the guard and beeps his car code, and the tone echoes against the cement. He punches Recall and #1, and waits for the map to come up on the little screen, address printed at the bottom, hits Accept and puts the car into drive, and the voice greets him. "Good morning. Accident on the 190 e-way changes our route for today."

Accept.

Now the weather, a visual scan of car functioning, notice of upcoming maintenance as they head through the gates and checkpoint, wave at the guard, cruise down toward the 230 secondary. It's a fine, clear morning, spring morning, and as Friedman passes community gates, he notices how each community has planted flowering plums and magnolias and cherries to make its show.

And now he's on the 230, now the 502 e-way, and he places the car on beam and sits back to take notes on his key pad, send a couple of messages to colleagues, call his home Cookery to program in the stew he prepared for all-day simmering. A friend's coming by after work. It's lonely, being on company posting for the year. Last night he dreamed about his younger child.

"Exit to the 402 on your right in five hundred yards."

Understood.

He negotiates the car out of e-lane and off towards the exit.

"Accident ahead. No delay."

A minor collision, Guard cars already on the scene to protect against looting or worse. He notices he's heading into the edge of the City, presses *Query.*

"Two-mile detour, expect total delay of seven minutes to destination."

Not bad. *Accept.*

"Troubled neighborhood one thousand yards ahead. Are you secure?"

He checks locks and shields. And now the road roughens; pit holes are to be expected in the City. Other shining cars traverse the streets; he sees a shanty village on the right, and opens his gun compartment just in case, though the People are generally more afraid of Citizens than Citizens are of them. The People—Friedman's even known a couple, two men, one woman, who began in university with him but dropped out, dropped through Citizen Space into the warrens of the City. It's a horror. Half of them end in Security or die of a virus or skin cancer or drug overdoses before they're thirty. It's almost impossible to get back. Oh, you see it on screen, an interview with someone who's made it back, but that's to give everyone else comfort: if someone can, anyone can, so it's their own fault if they don't. But everyone knows better. It's too many to speak about personal fault. And all he can do, all anyone can do, through taxes and donation, is provide funds for clinics, fooderies—warehouses of surplus goods.

At that, it's better than in the old days, ten years ago, when there was no surplus, no food. Then it was better for the animals running wild in the streets of the City; at least the Guards picked up ferals, dogs, cats, coyotes, injected them and disposed of their bodies. But the People—all the People could do was slip through the e-mesh into the hills and gather leavings of the old crops, the old agriculture. They still do that, even now. Or the Crazies set up traps on roads and drop boulders on passing cars and take what they can from the bodies. But the cars are programmed to report automatically, and copters are on the scene so fast that it's become a sport. The numbers of dead or captured outlaws are posted on screen every week.

The People scarcely look at his car as it cruises past. They're dressed well nowadays, in new sneakers and jeans from surplus, all with the same brand imprinted: *s e c o n d s.* Nowhere to wash, so they're still dirty, they still stink. They're building a cooking fire in an empty lot. Strictly forbidden, but they make a fire and keep watch, ready to run. What else can they do? Foods need to be cooked, and they hate to use the City cookeries. Too dangerous—as the official shelters are also too dangerous, are really prisons, everyone knows that. So they live in old-law buildings not yet imploded, or on the streets, burn rubbish, and every couple of minutes he passes another fire, nobody there, the People hiding until the food is cooked.

Citizens used to be afraid—how could the People not hate them?—and drove miles out of their way to avoid these places. No need now. They prey on one another for goods, sex, drugs, stolen e-cards. It's only organized bands of twenty or more, bands grouped into larger "families," the Guards fear. And these are rarely after a Citizen. The bands attack Guard stations to steal guns and disablers. But more, they're after e-codes that let them raid communities, get in, cut communications, get out before Guards or copters can sniff them out. Professionals. The leaders live anonymously in communities or on private estates with electronic perimeters.

Tomorrow morning or the morning after, he passes an empty lot, people sitting in a drug circle—a battery suffuser getting passed. He slows down, others pass him, he's last car in a line. Remember when the People were mostly black or Hispanic, and the Citizens saw them as Other? Now, it's a melting pot, though the phrase is ironic, refers ironically to an old dream. You rarely see an unmixed black or white or Asian among these people. You see brown skins, epicanthic folds at the eyelids, wavy light brown hair. Often beautiful. You see them on big-screen 'Tainments, see them in the Sports—the very few who've come from the City and made it out.

Friedman slows. Up ahead, by overturned polymer barrels left behind by a road crew, a woman lies splattered with blood, flesh torn, a feral cat thrashes out its life beside her. The cat, he sees, must have attacked her in a band of cats; the others took her food or eyes—this one didn't get away. One car after another swings wide around her. He stops, looks around for a possible ambush. In City-Training he was taught: never get out of your vehicle. Keep locks down, shields up, one finger on the Guard-contact alarm button. Go around, back up, even run someone down, do whatever you have to. If there's trouble, call it in. It's Guard business.

Someone must have already called it in.

He's about to call it in and swing wide around her when she stirs, and he can see the pooling of blood beneath her jeans, the hemorrhaging at one of the eyes. There's no trick here. And as a Citizen, he is authorized to assist and take to the hospital anyone injured.

Still keeping watch around him, he takes his remote in hand and gets out. The woman is moaning. She's lost a lot of blood. He doesn't think much of her chances. From the trunk he pulls a blanket and lays it across the back seat, removes his jacket and goes to pick up the woman from the street. "I'll get you to hospital, I'm going to pick you up now." She tries to say something. "Shh, shh." And it's when he has his hands full of her, worried about viruses, annoyed that his shirt is already soaked, glad he keeps an extra shirt in the trunk, that they rush him from the barrels, smash him and the woman to the ground; his remote skitters along the macadam.

"You—strip. We want the suit in good condition. And your e-card."

Getting up to his knees, he's yanked to his feet and he sees there are three of them, now another, and they strip him, leaving him in underclothes. His wrists are taped behind him, his ankles are taped. "I'm a Citizen, don't be a Crazy! They'll get you into the punishment cells, nobody gets away with this. Do you know the judgments for this?"

"What's the car code?" The young man, strong, thick like a wrestler but with the gray skin of so many of the People, holds the remote in his hand.

"You can't get through a checkpoint without a voice print. What's the good? Look—I see your condition, I know what's going on. I want to help. I've always supported the People. But you do this, you're a dead man."

The others laugh. The one with the remote yanks his taped wrists up, higher, and he screams, "All right. 764,257."

"And the e-card?"

"The same. But the voice print, you *know* you can't—"

212

Out of the corner of his eye he sees a board swinging at his head, and is able to jerk away, so when he goes down he's still conscious, but he pretends to be gone, curls into a limp ball the way he was taught in City-Training. Eyes closed, he's lifted and pitched into the back seat; he hears the electric engine hum its high-pitched drone, and it revs down the street and around a corner, and he feels wetness, opens his eyes to see the corners of houses, the upper stories of warehouses, the blood-soaked woman. The car turns another corner, another, doubles back, turns again and slows, and he hears the click of the door and he's rolled out and hits the street and slides over something rough to the curb. He looks up, the car turns the corner and is gone. It's silent. He shakes his head clear. There's blood, but not much of his own, a trickle down his face. His underclothes are ripped. The woman, ten feet away, lies dead. A feral cat has already begun to investigate.

There are no cars here. The tall dead buildings tell him it must be deep inside the City. If he gets the tape off wrists and ankles, he can find a major street and write a message: CALL IN—CITIZEN! Meantime, he can't hobble any distance. He's easy prey. They'll want him for enzymes not available in the City. They'll want his blood for transfusions. Last month there was a report of a Citizen kept tied up for a month and bled regularly by a "People's doctor." Finally, useless, he was allowed to die—was found dead, eyes surgically removed. The blood seller was found by Undercover; under questioning, before he died, he led the Guards to the doctor, who made a political statement before the court. News wasn't permitted to screen the statement, which might have been seen as a precedent, a way to get political messages on screen. But Friedman could have written the statement himself.

Metal's scarce; most polymers won't cut the tape. Keeping his eyes from the woman and the cat, he hobbles to the corner of a burned-out building and uses the rough brick corners to saw the tape. But it's the new "miracle" tape—Friedman wonders where they got it here—and the brick only buckles the edges and makes the tape tighter. His hands are losing circulation. What about glass? He shoulders the door of the gutted apartment building and it gives. Inside, in an open apartment, he works the tape against the shards of glass in a window frame. Slow work but he can sense the tape breaking down.

In the blackened door jamb a tall young man stands watching. Part black, part Indian?—Ari Friedman can't tell. His hair, thick and black, he wears in a band. Around his neck a tight necklace of steel beads.

213

Pack on his back, sleepy, he holds a disabler loosely at his side. "You're one lovely mess. Wait." He unfolds a hunting knife from his pocket; Friedman tries to hobble away. "Please! Please!" He wants to say one of the old prayers, but he can't put a prayer together.

"You're a Citizen. Your skin: sure, a Citizen, for sure. How they trap you? Your car gone? Hey—Take it calm, calm out, I'm cutting the tape. *Comprende?*"

Friedman relaxes and the knife cuts the tape easily enough. The young man puts down his pack and finds a cloth and a bottle of something; he washes the laceration on the forehead. The blood's coming back and Friedman rubs his hands against the tingling.

"Thanks. Thanks. So stupid. If I can convince some driver to call in a report, I'll be okay. And what can they do with a car? They can't dupe the voice print."

"They don't need to. They'll stow the car and program a new voice print. It takes just a little time. You're lucky they didn't kill you. Penalty's the same."

The man was in his early twenties, less than ten years younger than Friedman. He was a big man, like a fullback in old-style football. Already, Friedman was thinking about pulling this man out, out of the City; it was possible, especially if he'd helped a Citizen. And Friedman was grateful enough to stake a man like this, find him training, find him work. "So it was professionals, not Crazies," Ari Friedman says.

"No question. Professionals. That's why you're alive. They'll alter the card electronically, change the holograph. Working for someone from outside the City, with technological access."

"Why *am* I alive? They didn't mind killing a woman. They used her as a decoy. She was ripped apart."

"*She wasn't a Citizen.* But you knew the answer, didn't you. A Citizen gets killed, there be a major investigation. They'd come in here with detection technology, heavy armor. They leave us to one another. It's another form of state terror. We've got to work so hard to stay alive, it keeps us from organizing politically."

"That's paranoid. This isn't a just society—I know that. I hate the division, Citizen, non-Citizen. I can remember when it was introduced—a temporary expedient. Before the Amendment. It's not just. But listen—there's no conspiracy, this isn't fascism; they're trying to handle an immense superfluous population—"

"Superfluous!"

"I don't mean to insult anyone. Isn't that the right word? No work for them. And no education that might get them work, and how can they vote meaningfully without education? I've talked to Representatives who are pained by the whole problem of a superfluous population."

"Pained!"

"You're unusual. You're educated, aren't you? Son of a Citizen? But look around you. And who would dare enter the City to teach? They've even had to give up on fire stations. And where would the e-credits come from? You've got to admit—"

The young man shrugs. He washes Friedman's face with the liquid again. "Need bandaging. That head wound. I've got rags in back."

He sounds apologetic that it's only rags, and that makes Friedman experience instant tenderness for him. "Can you get me to a phone?"

"What phone?" he laughs. "Phone!"

"Can you take me to a main road—I can hold up a sign for help."

"You stand out there, you're prey. *Professionals* don't want to kill a Citizen; there are people in the City couldn't care less. For your blood."

"I'm needed. I've got children . . . in another city."

"I'll get you to a Guard station perimeter. Then you're on your own."

"I'm Ari Friedman . . . What's your name?"

The young man doesn't answer at first. Then laughs. "Call me Ishmael."

"All right. But you don't need to be afraid of me. You can come *in* with me. I can help you get out of the City. I'd like to."

"You *are* naive."

"Let's not talk politics. Please."

"No."

"Listen, I can hear your irony. 'Ishmael.' All I'm saying, I'm expected to report irregular conversations with the People. You know that. I won't of course."

"And you say this isn't fascism?"

"It's a security problem: a lot more People than Citizens. What *should* we do?—I'm sorry, I'm usually the last one to defend—" Ari Friedman sits suddenly, woozy in the head. "A few minutes. I need to rest."

The man goes inside, returns with an open pla-box of soup. Ari drinks out of gratitude and politeness; unheated, the soup is tasteless. Ishmael pulls a notebook and a pen out of his pocket. So quaint. He writes a few minutes, looking up to meet Ari's eyes, then tears off the page and goes out.

It's shock, not hurt, Ari thinks, and he gets himself up. The man returns with running pants and a sweatshirt, both marked *s e c o n d s,* and Friedman puts them on and follows the man out the door.

"We hug the buildings and keep our eyes open." He rubs street soot into Friedman's face. Like the old military camouflage. "All I've got's an old disabler," he says. "But here's something for you." A meter-long pla-board with a spike through one end, it looks medieval. Friedman feels foolish and keeps it at his side as they slip along the side of a street of gutted row housing, roofless, open to the sky like 'Tainment sets. His head throbs only a little. He feels in good hands. It reminds him of trekking the woods with his father, when there were still big woods just north. This man—Ishmael—is younger than he is, but feeling's the same. It's a story for Marjorie and the girls if he can make it through.

Strange—we've done everything we can to avoid adventure. Adventure means risk. Our success has been control. Even vacation-adventures are as risk-free as theme parks, as if the thrill of terror, of crisis, could be distilled from situations of danger and injected directly into the veins.

Now the man huddles against a wall, peers around the corner, gets low like an infantryman in an old film and knees bent, head down, runs across the street, now again, avoiding the diagonal, corner to corner, hugging the walls of a deserted brick school, a warehouse, a street of rubble. He stops, waits for Friedman to catch up.

"Is this really necessary? Ishmael? I can't tell if this is paranoid or realistic. I don't know the rules."

"I'm trying to get you out to a doctor. Otherwise, no way we'd do this until night."

"You live like this?"

"I'm trying to change things. Lots of us."

"Well, we all are. I contribute to the New Cities Movement—"

"I mean *here,* not there. I'm working here. Trying to form safety squads, self-help communities. Till we can stop watching the shadows we can't build anything."

"No one would stop you. Who would stop you?"

"From outside? No. Not yet. But the chaos serves them, I told you. If it gets to the next stage—community organizations—then they'll try. Oh, yes. And thing is, they'll be *right.* We'll be dangerous then."

216

A man and two women cross an empty lot, slip down an alley. Ari follows the man down the next street—sees in the distance a car drive past an intersection. Someone in a hooded sweatshirt stands up in a doorway and waves; Ari follows the man over. Woman takes down her hood. "This a Citizen?"

"Dirt couldn't fool you even at long distance?"

"Hurt, too."

"Doing my best."

"Be careful." And she looks with annoyance, with hostility, at Ari. The woman has ashen skin, blotched. She seems to be carrying twice her actual weight. He thinks: how can people this weak change anything? He thinks about viruses the People carry. Of course, med-insured, he's been inoculated against most extant viruses.

She says to Ishmael, "You're leaving the neighborhood?"

"A couple of miles. I left a note in the usual place. I'm taking him to the Guard station by the old park. That's the best one. Just to the perimeter." She doesn't say anything. "Look," he says. "If he's traced to the City, traced to this neighborhood—think about it . . . Hey, I'll be back."

After this, they walk like soldiers through enemy territory to the e-perimeter, the electronic fence meant to stun or kill anyone crossing, except in cars on the main roads, which can be monitored by camera. Friedman doesn't know what to look out for. He says nothing. He follows. More and more he feels bruised and abraded from the fall from the car. His head throbs.

They see men run in a line down an alley, maybe ten, all in the same sweat suits Friedman and the man are wearing. They move like soldiers, weapons held across their bodies, but most look weak and thin.

Friedman follows the man down an open stairs into a littered cellar.

"They're training," the man says. "I can't be sure what band that is, what community they're part of. Probably just a power-band. You understand the difference?"

"I can imagine." Friedman's panting. He slumps against the cellar wall. "You, you're not sick like some of them. Most of them."

"I was immunized before. There's quite a few of us. We're the hope."

"Why are you here? Child of a Citizen *is* a Citizen."

"Not after a political crime. I gave aid and comfort to escapees."

"How can you live like this?" Friedman holds his hands open, palms up, as if they held a giant specimen he wants them both to look at.

The man shrugs. "*How.*"

"I've read about the concentration camps, how people lived. I've never understood why they bothered."

"It's better than that for us. Most of the time, they leave us alone. And there's fewer children now, so it's not such an agony. Or maybe more of an agony—I don't know. We feel sure it must be something in the food, the sterility, but we have to eat." The man smiles. "You think that's paranoid."

"There *have* been rumors . . . The decline in new births has been noted." Friedman looks away.

The man says, "And you aren't sure that's such a bad thing?"

Friedman can't speak for a while. He thinks of children, his own girls and feels shame. He asks, "Ishmael, why you running this risk for me? You told the woman it was to protect your neighborhood. I don't believe that."

"Then I don't know. I was always a fool."

"I'm sorry, what I said about 'superfluous population.' "

"I worked last month," the man says, "cleaning up along the coast from a spill. They flew us in. And before that, a few months back, after the last China campaign—battle debris, thousands of bodies to burn. Not completely superfluous."

Above, on the street, a band runs by, cutting off the light from the cellar window. Now they're gone.

There's a metallic clang and silence. The man puts a finger to his lips and gestures Friedman *down*. Silently, the man wriggles along the cement floor into a corner, picks up a steel rod and tosses it to the opposite side of the cellar. Now a scene out of 'Tainment, but this terror real—a metal door kicked open, a burst of automatic rounds, old-style machine pistol, and now the man stands and blasts the shadow with his disabler, and a blue lightning fringes the shadow and there's a scream and the figure crumbles.

"Don't touch him—there's still a charge. But let's see if we can get the gun for you." The gun has been flung free; Friedman can see a bluish haze outlining it in the dark. And now the haze dies, and the man picks up the gun. he stands above the figure, still thrashing on the ground. With the handle of the gun he smashes down in the dark, once, again. The body is still thrashing, still fringed with light. "He'll live." He hands Friedman the gun and shows him how to release the safety, loads a new clip of ammunition, puts an extra clip in his backpack. "Let's get out of here."

"Who is he?"

218

The man shakes his head. They're out of the cellar and down the street, a jagged course, street to street, down an alley to another street. Friedman has questions—how can the young man organize anyone amidst this anarchy? How can he still hope? But mostly he thinks about the street, tries to puzzle out their position on a mental map of the City. The park, Ishmael said. How far? Friedman remembers a blank area to the north of the city on maps of the region. Parks—they used to be "public." There was a time, before his own childhood, when children could play in parks alone. Then they became impossibly dangerous, even with police at the call of a beeper. That was many years ago. Now parks keep within community e-perimeters, privately guarded. Safe: you think nothing of sending your child down to the park by himself.

He sees the gray stone wall of a park up ahead, and rising above it, four stories high, a reinforced blockhouse with a high lookout turret. Behind must be the heliport. Surrounding the blockhouse, he knows, are the quarters for the Guards, recreational and exercise facilities, classrooms, for this is how the working poor can get their education. At least their training. It's not a bad posting. It's a lot safer than military bases—the firepower's all on their side.

His friends have always been contemptuous of the Guards. Except for the young career officers of hereditary Citizenship, who quickly move up into the Hierarchy, the Guards are seen as clods, Citizens-by-taxation with doctrinaire attitudes, trained to despise the People. Friedman feels for them; he knows they have nowhere else to go, except marginal jobs, where they can be easily replaced. Fall into useless, stop paying taxes, they can lose their status as Taxed Citizens. Through the Guards they can sometimes rise into hereditary Citizenship.

Now there are fewer standing buildings. The empty lots are filled with rubble and a thick coating of ash or soot. They stop behind a reinforced concrete wall, all that's left of an old school that the Guards blew up to give themselves clear fire lines in case of attack. Like old sculpture, the reinforcing rods twist upward out of lumps of wall. In front of them, past the field of soot, is the old road that rings the park, the low stone wall, an open mine field, mined electronically, then the walls of the compound. The young man pulls from his pack a marking pen and an old movie poster he must have found in some basement. He hands them to Friedman: "Use the back."

Friedman nods. He knows the Guards will read it through their scopes. He writes. *CITIZEN! I NEED HELP!*

"You start back now. I'll wait," Friedman says. "Unless you'll come with me? Ishmael, I'll sign papers, take financial responsibility—"

The young man squeezes his arm. "Thanks. You poor damn Citizen. You think I want to live out there? Got my work here. But I'm glad I could get you out. You be all right now. Give me a couple minutes." He keeps behind the low wall as he takes the machine pistol from Friedman, puts it into his pack. Now, keeping low, he backs away, runs toward the next line of debris.

From the compound a Guard hoverer rises, another, another, shining, pure white against the gray sky. The first darts forward across the road, singing in high electric song. The others stay back, just above Friedman. But the first fires, a silent white beam. The young man doesn't even scream; he's caught in mid-step and drops to the ground, and now Ari Friedman shouts and stands under the hoverers, holding up his sign and gesturing, shouting, "No! No!"

But the first ship has landed, and ash and debris clouds what's happening. Another hovers just above Friedman, then the song changes pitch, lowers as the ship lowers. It never touches down. A door lifts. A helmeted Guard with disabler holstered runs toward him. "This way, Sir!" he shouts over the engine whine. "This way!"

"That man helped me!"

"This way!"

"I'm a Citizen! That man—"

As the Guard takes his arm and leads him to the hoverer, he sees, through the dust, Guards from the other ship stooping over the young man.

In a room at the top of the observation tower, a polymer prefab office, padded, seamless except for window and door, he's handed a hot drink and offered a leather chair. A doctor has already attended to his bruises and lacerations. He's been bandaged, given an anti-bacterial shot, another to help him relax. The officer at the desk, a heavy-set man not in uniform but in Citizen clothes, a man with an educated, pleasant voice, says, "Your car hasn't yet been found, Mr. Friedman."

"It's a company car; it's insured."

"We were expecting you. We got Citizen call-ins about the dead woman, and we went in with investigators and found her body. We didn't have your name, but we had hoped a Citizen might be coming."

"What about the man who got me out? I'd be dead if not for him."

"He's being questioned."

"He'll be released?"

"You called him 'Ishmael.' We picked it up with the voice scanners. That's a false name."

"False. Of *course.* He wouldn't give me his name—it was a joke."

"Wouldn't give you his name? Well, we have his name through voice print and implant. He's being questioned. Were you threatened?"

"Not by him . . . I can give you descriptions of the men who killed the woman and took the car."

"Good. I'll have a specialist work up a compufoto with you. You're lucky to be alive. I'm sure you want to call in to your company soon— of course, they've just been informed—and your family? I understand you're on company posting?"

"This man—Ishmael—he went out of his way—"

"We know all about him. We've got his dossier. You have any idea what he meant, he said *his work was in there?* We monitored that with voice scanners. What work exactly? What is he organizing?"

Political organizing within the city, Friedman knows, is a crime. "He said nothing political. He's working to make a livable community in there."

"That's just what we understood, Mr. Friedman. But he lost his citizenship for political crimes. Did he tell you that?"

"He told me . . . But he said nothing treasonous to me." There is a long pause, a long, long, conscious silence. Friedman understands the silence. "I'm sure not," the officer says. "Or you would have told us. Isn't that right? Still—we know from his dossier, he's dangerous. We think he wanted to use you somehow . . ."

"He saved my life. He saved a Citizen."

"We can understand your gratitude . . . He'll be released. You can watch, Mr. Friedman." The officer presses a button and gives instructions. The young man, pack on his back, staggers out of the compound. Ari waves, and the man waves back and crosses the perimeter road, starts through the rubble into the City.

And suddenly he's simply not there. All Friedman can hear is a slight hiss, he sees a white flame flare up, and then nothing. Soot, black ash.

"That was a dangerous man, Mr. Friedman. Much more so than the men who killed that woman."

Friedman stares at the empty ground. Even the backpack is gone. He's trembling, and the trembling seems as if it's happening to a separate body. He can't stop it. *Dangerous.* Not theft and murder; those are routine. It must be the organizing. And so Ishmael must be right. He slumps back into the leather easy chair, still shaking. "Dangerous? He was certainly a *strange* man," Ari Friedman says. "Nothing actually treasonous," he goes on. "But he spoke—crazy talk—about links to people in Citizen space. Hints, that's all. He spoke about Guards, *at this station,* but he didn't want me to understand . . . " Friedman closes his eyes. "I'm tired. I'm tired."

"We'll get you back, Mr. Friedman, as soon as we've got those compufotos. We've found that Citizens are often loyal to their captors for a while. Nothing to be concerned about. I'm very glad you finally remembered what he said. *This* station, he said?"

Ari pretends to fall into sleep. He feels good, having lied. Let them turn their own station upside down, let them suspect one another, devour one another. He's found new loyalties.

Friedman will wake up early next morning to beat the jam on the 405, reach under the night table to finger in the code on the security key pad. He'll press the button to start the Cookery. He wonders how he'll be able to reach Ishmael's friends. He isn't a brave man. He wonders: maybe there are Citizens who have contact with the People, maybe there's an active movement—how would he know? He knows now he can't trust news on the wall screen, knows all his assumptions have to be rethought. It makes him angry, angry, though it's absurd, angry at Ishmael, the responsibility Ishmael has made him face. *This isn't a bad life,* he says. He thinks about seeing Marjorie, Danielle, Lisa on screen last night. *Not a bad life.*

Ari touches his key pad, finds the news on his wall screen. he asks for *local* and fast-forwards through the celebrations of local economic successes, capture of a professional electrocuted at a perimeter, until he sees the Guard station, tower rising out of the compound. "Last night the Park station was thoroughly examined upon reports of treasonous political activity. A cache of arms, clearly meant for illegal revolutionary groups within the City, was found in trash barrels inside this storeroom." A small room is shown. "Computer disks have been confiscated. Three Guards are being interrogated . . ."

Ari stops breathing. He has inadvertently exposed them by his lie? Ishmael's comrades? Is that why Ishmael chose this particular Guard station? Or was the news story concocted for other purposes. He knows he can't know.

How, he wonders, sitting in front of his cooling bread, how can he find his way back?

Nominated by Witness

THE MOST RESPONSIBLE GIRL

essay by EMILY FOX GORDON

from BOULEVARD

I: The Rose Court

She was the most responsible girl, the leader of our dormitory floor, and twice monthly we all trooped into the room she shared with two high-status roommates. I remember her, sitting in her Lanz nightgown at the end of her neatly made bed, with its colorful afghan, hand-embroidered throw pillows and pyramid of stuffed animals. Her hair was rolled up on giant-sized orange juice cans—that produced the full, sleek effect we were all after in the early sixties—and she managed to paint her toenails, chin balanced on one knee, while listening judiciously to both sides of disputes about runaway rumors or food left on the radiator to attract ants. The girls arranged themselves on the floor around her bed in a fan formation, the most favored in the rank nearest to her.

I was least responsible, or close to it, and least favored. I stood by the door. Sometimes another outsider would join me, and we would lean together smirking and giggling subversively. These companions came and went; nobody was as steadily incorrigible as I. Often I would arrive at a meeting to find my latest co-conspirator re-absorbed by the group, sitting somewhere in the outer ranks, casting guilt glances at me over her shoulder.

My behavior was beneath the notice of the responsible girl and her auditors, but I caught scathing looks from the Dorm Advisor. This was our Drama teacher Virginia, a failed actress and singer in her early forties. She kept a baleful black and white neutered tomcat named Booey and she was full of campy mannerisms—double-takes, facetious gasps of horror, derisive snorts. She wore her hennaed hair in a beehive and plucked and re-drew her eyebrows into tufted peaks. She was one of those odd adults who rattles around for years before settling down to discover the pleasure of engineering and enforcing adolescent hierarchies. She acted as a kind of palace guard, and her allegiance to some particular girl signaled that girl's ascendancy as unmistakably as white smoke hanging over the Vatican. I hated her, and she hated me back with a shocking directness. It was Virginia who got me thrown out. She caught my roommates and me drinking Chianti and ginger ale on the roof, identified me as the ringleader and persuaded the directors of the school that I was too immature to benefit from the experience that the school had to offer.

What did it take to be most responsible girl? This is a question I've pondered for years. Not looks or wit or academic superiority. Any marked distinction which might help a girl's chances in the world of men, or in the mixed world of men and women, actually tended to work against her candidacy. While never ugly or unattractive, the most responsible girl was often rather plain and solid, but with good bone structure. She was a high-average student, quiet and even tempered. More frequently than would seem likely, she had a small physical defect—a slight limp or a noticeable but non-disfiguring birthmark—or some mild chronic illness like asthma.

The most responsible girl often rose up out of a discarded carapace of shyness; she had been, for example, the wardrobe mistress for the school play rather than the lead, the recording secretary or treasurer of the student government rather than the president. But her developmental pace was as regular as a healthy pulse; by the time she reached her junior year she had begun to show new poise and a quiet confidence. She was the tortoise, confounding all the upstart hares; the wattage of her glow grew steadily. Around this time, she often acquired her first boyfriend, a big, earnest masculine one, a muscular-Christianity type, not quite handsome but nearer to the male ideal than the most responsible girl was to the female. He and the m.r.g. walked together hand in hand, giving off a powerful musk of responsible ardor. I remember sensing this as I watched the two of them, hit in the solar plexus with my first apprehension of what married sex might be like, in all its hairy maturity.

The m.r.g. was surrounded by a kind of rose court of the pretty and the witty. This most inner circle was the place allotted to girls with natural gifts. When the m.r.g. had a fight with her boyfriend they clustered around her as she sprawled on her bed weeping, and their celebration of her grief gave it a special gravity.

Now we had to credit Virginia with an eye for spotting dramatic potential; suddenly the m.r.g. was transformed, a new creature with a vastly expanded emotional range. Her hollow-eyed pallor became her; now we could feel the depth of her female authority. She was Medealike in the haggish glory of her rage and sorrow. A hush hung over the second floor; the m.r.g.'s attendants scurried up and down the back stairs, carrying trays of tea and chocolate pudding up from the kitchen, ordinarily out of bounds between meals but opened up on this occasion by special arrangement with Virginia.

I felt a faint dismay, a sense of disillusionment. Was all love imperfect, even the love between these two paragons? And I was deeply shocked when I learned, some months after the fact, that the most serious of these fights—I can still remember the sobs of the m.r.g. and the shouts of Virginia—was the consequence of the betrayal of a member of the inner circle; she was caught by Virginia in the alley of pines behind the dormitory necking with the m.r.g.'s boyfriend. They were both stripped to the waist when she discovered them, according to the report I heard. Virginia marched them back to the school, prodding the reprobates in the smalls of their backs with a stick.

For the m.r.g., female society was bedrock. However perfidious men might turn out to be, women could always be trusted, at least once the traitors had been weeded out of the garden. She and the girls surrounding her took refuge in a pre-feminist female solidarity. The group provided a soft place for retreat from the pre-feminist gender wars, and it offered an alternative view—somewhat more broad-based and democratic than the erotic wishes of the boys—of ideal and desirable female traits. The ordinary-looking girl who knew what to do with her hair, or how to dress, who had a sense of style and groomed herself immaculately, was closer to this ideal than was, for example, one particular friend of mine, a good-looking slob with an air of fey distraction and a need for solitude. A great emphasis was placed on communitarian virtues—reliability, organization, maturity, a willingness to subordinate one's desires to the interests of the group.

Sometimes I speculate about the m.r.g. from a Darwinian perspective; perhaps she and her court represented a check, a refining influence, on the indiscriminate operations of natural selection at work behind simple male lust, the hard-wired tropism of males toward females with clear skin and large breasts and a ratio of .7 between the measurements of their hips and waists—all very rough indicators of health and superior genetic endowment. Too rough, too dismissive of the moral and the social; so the girls got together and created an m.r.g., an intelligent young woman built to the specifications of responsible motherhood and civic participation, and offered her to the male camp as a sensible alternative to the sweet-smelling decoy-flower females for whom they clamored.

The m.r.g. was more the locus of the group's feelings and values than its leader, more emblematic than active. But she was also more than raw material for the construction of a cult object; she had real authority, grounded in a finely tuned sense of psychic proprioception. She knew at all times exactly where she was in the complex terrain of social interaction, just how the various parts of her social being were poisoned, and how far into the imaginative worlds of other people they extended. This is an aptitude which blossoms with developmental maturity. I've shown so little of it myself that I have to wonder whether I lack it the way some people lack a spleen or whether I lack it because I never fully grew up. Even now, the world makes sense to me mostly as something to look out on; once entered into it I'm vulnerable to a panicky sense of dislocation, floundering without coordinates as faces move past me and horizons loom and disappear. It's this deficit, I suppose, that explains my style of friendship, which is nearly always predicated on a shared sense of exclusion, and on shared conspiratorial sniping. "Come my dear, let us abuse the company!": This invitation, offered to Becky Sharp by her outrageous aunt in *Vanity Fair,* has always delighted me.

I was certainly a slow and uneven developer. I arrived at boarding school—a progressive coeducational one in the Berkshires—dazed with anxiety and homesickness. At thirteen I was really still a little girl; I needed reminding to bathe and pick up after myself. This my roommates did, bluntly and effectively. They wadded up the dirty clothes I'd left strewn around the room and threw them over the balcony into the empty swimming pool. They locked me in the bathroom with a box of tampons until I could learn to use them. It's hard for me to say, from the distance of thirty-five years, whether this treatment was damaging or just the right rough remedy for my backwardness.

227

I soon discovered that I had one social card to play, a quick wit and a willingness to put it to whatever unkind use might win me friends. I became the Dorothy Parker of the smoking porch, or so I saw myself, blowing rings and drawling witticisms. I gravitated toward the boys, who always gave me plenty of commissions for limericks and imitations. Among the boys I found, some solid, if necessarily partial, friendships. Early on I became a kind of mascot figure, a tagalong treated with alternating affection and contempt.

At the end of my freshman year I was taken aside by one of the graduating seniors, a charismatic boy named Dutch with floppy blond hair and an elegant aquiline nose. I had been in love with him for some weeks, and when he beckoned me to follow him into the woods I did so with knees shaking.

We walked some distance, following a trail of muddy tire tracks through a forest of maple saplings just coming into yellow-green leaf, arriving finally at the door of a little abandoned shack, half hidden in underbrush. I recognized this as the legendary place the older boys called "the house," passed each spring from one senior boy to his chosen successor, a hideout where rumor had it six-packs of beer were consumed and sex acts performed. I felt a little frightened, though even then I was in touch enough with reality to think it unlikely that Dutch had designs on my pudgy, barely pubescent person. He gestured me into the shack, which was cold, dusty and tidy, neatly fitted out with surplus classroom chairs and a military-style cot.

I also recognized a small mosaic coffee table on which Virginia had displayed ceramic ballerinas, a photographic portrait of Booey and a montage of snapshots of herself mugging with a series of most responsible girls. It had stood against a wall in the short hallway outside her suite of rooms. She inspected the dorm the morning it was discovered missing; flanked by two henchwomen from the inner circle, she swept through the rooms and closets of likely suspects.

The shrine had been neatly reassembled in a corner of the shack, all the objects placed in their original positions, though by now of course the ballerina statuettes were headless, the photographs of Virginia and the m.r.g.s were vandalized with devils' horns, supernumerary breasts, and crudely drawn pubic bushes, and the silver frame from which the smoldering eyes of Booey looked out had been pitted with BB shot.

"Yours," Dutch said, waving to indicate the shack and all its contents. "I bequeath it to you." I was the first girl, and the first nonsenior, to receive this honor, and while I was sensible of it, I was also obscurely disappointed.

By the following fall I had matured a bit, and while my chances for acceptance by the m.r.g. and her court remained as remote as ever, I found my roommates more inclined to tolerate me. They, in turn, had rounded another developmental bend far ahead of me and become cautiously disinhibited, though still far less naughty than I was. I remember this school year, when I turned fifteen, as my happiest in adolescence. It was the year I began to do well in my classes, the year my roommates taught me to take care of my hair and clothes, the year I found a confidant in my kind, elderly French teacher, a man who treated me with a delicate respect when we met for our weekly talks.

It was also the year I began to get myself into male-pattern trouble. My ostensibly docile roommates were often just as guilty of misdeeds as I, but they lacked my flair for getting caught. At our last meeting, after I had been expelled, my French teacher rose from his chair, bent over from the waist and kissed me on the forehead, a light, dry kiss like a blessing.

That year I contracted passionate crushes on a series of boys, mostly the older ones. Around these boys I spun intense, near-hallucinatory fantasies: in the earliest ones I was often a nurse, flying to my beloved as he lay wounded on the golf course, crouching to attend him as bullets whizzed over my head. (Wounded how? By some shadowy "opposition group," whatever that meant. Why the golf course? Because I saw one in the distance every time I looked out my window.) The elements of the fantasy were makeshift and arbitrary. What mattered was the flow at the center of my imagination, the oceanic pull of feeling as I lowered my cheek to his chest, the lingering of the sensation as I tore myself away from him, his cries of gratitude to me, the failed rescuer, ringing in my ears.

Later, my fantasies took the form of imagined dialogues in which I confronted and challenged the beloved. I took as my text Jane Eyre's address to Rochester at the foot of the great chestnut tree:

> Do you think, because I am poor, obscure, plain and little,
> I am soulless and heartless? You think wrong!—I have as
> much soul as you,—and full as much heart.

I was, of course, not able even in imagination to chivvy the object of my fantasy with an eloquence like Jane's, but I did my best to imitate her brave, tremulous dignity. And I ended with an attempt at the same transcendent claim to essential equality, my own paraphrase, after which the beloved rewarded me by taking me into his arms, just as Rochester gathered up Jane:

> I am not talking to you now through the medium of custom, conventionalities, or even of mortal flesh:—it is my spirit that addresses your spirit; just as if both had passed through the grave, and we stood at God's feet, equal,—as we are!

How this thrilled me! I have to admit that it still does. It remains my paradigm for relations between men and women. The dyad! How much I prefer it to the group. In my heart I believe that the presence of more than two introduces a tragic warp into the world. From a developmental point of view, no opinion could be more retrograde, but I can defend it by pointing out that, on one account at least, God agrees with me.

I was sent to a new school after my expulsion. There, I began to develop the rudiments of a sexual style. A certain kind of male, I could now see, responded to a boldly frontal approach, a challenging, slightly teasing manner. I learned that it was possible to walk up to certain boys and simply engage with them. Never, of course, with a directly sexual intent; my innocence protected me from even conceiving the notion. My longings were unfocused and the erotic was hidden behind a hundred lyrical veils.

Often, this technique misfired, but sometimes, to my delight and surprise, it worked! I had found a way to run out, briefly, from under the cover of androgyny, to feel, just for a few moments, quite dangerously feminine. How satisfying it was to walk through the halls of my new school, deep in conversation with some boy, and to catch in the periphery of my vision the stupefied stares of girls who had been trying to snag him for months. It was not so much the envy of the very pretty girls that gave me this visceral and vindictive pleasure; I knew myself to be out of their league entirely, and felt a little ashamed at my apparent presumption. (When I look at pictures of my seventeen-year-old self I'm chagrined to realize that I was more adequate than I thought. I was almost pretty, or would have been if only I had known myself better.) What really gratified me were the looks I got from the girls I had identified as m.r.g. types, the mature girls, the *womanly* girls. I had confounded them by innocently and fearlessly crossing the zone that divided me from men, the territory that Virginia and the m.r.g. would have you believe was strewn with hazards, and only to be attempted if you could be sure that the company of women stood waiting to succor you when you staggered back across the border into home territory.

II: Anna

Five years ago I embarked on a promising new friendship. I had just moved, with my husband and daughter, to a new city. After my daughter started school I began to make tentative moves toward establishing a life in this new place. I audited a course at the university where my husband had taken a teaching position and met a few people, one of whom introduced me to this interesting woman—I'll call her Anna—who, like me, was married to a faculty member, had literary leanings and felt alienated by the academic establishment. My husband and I were both charmed by her; she had a touchy rectitude, a bluestocking intensity and an endearing vulnerability. She seemed available to friendship—still open, still thinking, still, like me, on the outside of things, peering in. I find it's not easy to make friends in middle age; so many of my contemporaries seem closed and completed.

Anna served as my guide to the people in the academic and writing communities to which she belonged and I aspired. What's so and so like, I'd ask, and, after some protestations and shows of evasive tact, Anna would blurt out her opinion of that person, whom she almost invariably viewed as arrogant, rude, self-involved and treacherous, or as the innocent dupe of others with these qualities. And there was always an illustrative anecdote.

An example: Anna belonged to a university women's group, ostensibly leaderless but actually run by a politically powerful group of women in the English department. To her, Anna, they had delegated all the clerical work, all the typing, copying and note-taking, because, as she noted bitterly, they assumed that her time was less valuable than theirs. I laughed sympathetically and made some observation about the cultural contradictions of feminism—or any *ism,* I was quick to add. I also said something about the ironies of groups with utopian agendas and dystopian dynamics. Anna's reaction—I barely registered this at the time—was rather veiled. She went opaque for a moment,

231

but I interpreted this as a welling up of her incompletely discharged anger.

I too knew about the maddening condescension of the credentialed toward those they took to be their inferiors. I felt indignant on Anna's behalf. I also assumed—wrongly as it turned out, and perhaps this was a symptom of my continuing failure of psychic proprioception—that I was free in this new friendship to express my opinions, even those that ran against the conventional grain.

For example: as Anna and her husband sat with my husband and me in our living room one evening, finishing our coffee, the conversation turned to the Senate hearings on the confirmation of Clarence Thomas which were then in progress. I was in a convivial mood, feeling comfortable with these new friends, feeling the wine I'd drunk at dinner. We seemed on the brink of a real intimacy, and so I gathered the nerve to express my real feelings about this contretemps, something I would have known better than to try in the company of most academics. I remarked—laughingly—that while I considered Clarence Thomas an inadequate nominee for the Supreme Court, I thought Anita Hill's (an m.r.g., by the way, if ever I saw one) protestations of horror and Long Dong Silver and the other indignities were ludicrous and transparently trumped-up, and I went on to say further that this new strand in feminism, this new sanctimony, this soppy protectiveness of female innocence—well, I said, it was pernicious indeed. In response to Anna's husband's polite inquiry about how I would feel if the Coke can with the pubic hair on it were brandished in my face, I said, Just fine! Wouldn't bother me a bit. I've had worse waved at me. I went so far as to invoke the name of Camille Paglia before I began to realize that my guests had gone cold on me, and that it was time to change the subject.

As we all stood at the doorway, some minutes later, saying goodnight, I pressed into Anna's hands the manuscript of a novel I had just completed. Anna had offered to read it and I gave it to her with the hope that we could recover from the small chill I had felt on our friendship that night.

Three long weeks later—days pass with a gluey slowness when you're waiting for reaction to a manuscript—I broke down and called Anna. She answered the phone after six rings, out of breath and apologetic. She and her husband, she explained, had been putting in some plants. Her voice was cheerful. We talked for a few moments about the gardening she'd been doing. As she spoke I went blank—gardening is terra incognita for me—but I pictured Anna, standing in the shade of the screen porch, her hair pulled back under a bandanna, wiping the sweat of Indian summer from her forehead with the back of her wrist as she talked on the cellular phone. Her husband was barely visible to the eye of my imagination, viewed in diminished perspective at the bottom of their property, his gray head lit by late afternoon sun, bending over a wheelbarrow like a figure in a Diego Rivera painting.

"So," I said, "did you get a chance to read the novel?" I was prepared to hear that she hadn't yet; Anna taught at a local community college and the preciousness of her leisure time was a persistent theme in her conversation. "I did," said Anna, with a bell-like forthrightness. A silence followed.

"I thought there was a lot of good technique," she began. I made some registering noise. "A lot of good writing. Of course, as a whole it's a deeply misogynistic novel."

"What?" I said.

"I said it's deeply misogynistic."

My novel, originally titled *The Mall Walker*, concerns an academic couple with a small child. The wife of the couple, Miranda Blau, is a passive detached personality. Now that her daughter is in day care she finds herself at loose ends; she makes a few gestures toward finding a part time job and drifts into a kind of half-life, watching reruns of "Marcus Welby M.D." on television and wandering through shopping malls like an anomic ghost. She is surrounded by charged-up, goal-directed female exemplars—it's a comic novel and I'll grant that they are portrayed paradoxically—but the prospect of imitating them leaves Miranda more languid than ever. I had intended her as a sort of female Oblovmov; I wanted her stillness to serve as a surface on which reflections of the comic and chaotic world around her might play. Her ruminations, her internal dialogue, represented the best of whatever wisdom I had managed to acquire. For Miranda, I hardly need to mention, read me. "Misogynistic?" I said.

I've had years now to replay that conversation, to erase the spluttering and the lame rejoinders, to fill my incredulous silences with wit and sense. But now I can't separate what was said from what I wish had been said. I do remember clearly how the conversation ended. I put myself in the wrong by shouting an obscenity and slamming down the phone.

That was the end of my friendship with Anna, and my anger and remorse caused me acute pain for three months. I tortured my husband

233

with my moodiness; he was patient, willing to engage in marathon sessions of ventilation and consolation, quite ready to agree with me that Anna's stand on artistic solidarity with other women was rigid and unreasonable, especially in light of her complaints about the group of university feminists who had misused her. But why did she send such conflicting signals? He had no idea, he said.

I was continually prying the incident apart, as if by disassembling it I could disarm its power to hurt me. I should have seen it coming. I said, and my husband concurred. I went on to anatomize all the hints and foreshadowings that should have warned me. Soon I was talking to myself, and my tired husband was nodding dully. At the end of these talks, when it seemed that his sympathy had only exacerbated my agitation, he repeated his observation that, in spite of her charm, Anna carried a large chip on her shoulder and was not very rational. What more was there to say? He shrugged and left the room.

What more? I was irritated at my husband for pitching the whole mess into the miscellaneous bin. I wanted to push on the incident until it yielded some insight. What I couldn't convey to my husband was the peculiar quality of the shock Anna had given me. She was like a grimly cheerful physician producing, with a flourish, the giant wriggling tapeworm that had been causing a multitude of obscure and apparently unrelated symptoms: here's the culprit! As long as I protested the injustice of Anna's accusation. I was sparing myself a confrontation with the real source of my pain. This was the rearing up, after years of semi-dormancy, of the loneliness, the sense of anomaly in myself, that I felt when I walked into a dorm meeting to see some erstwhile friend's back, now one in a circlet of female backs ringing the bed of the m.r.g. My hard-won middle-aged equanimity, my years of steadying wife-and-motherhood, my place in the world of adults; all this dropped away. At some point in the phone conversation with Anna I had been hit by a wave of recognition and the shock of sudden exposure. I heard her calling me something worse than misogynist; I received her words as confirmation of my fear that I was an unnatural woman.

III: A Male-Identified Mutant

At this juncture, I'll admit that my identification with men runs deep. While I recognize and acknowledge the historical fact of the oppression of women, I don't have much firsthand feel for the rancor against patriarchy that informs the movement.

234

And in fact, some expressions of that rancor make me rancorous in return. I bridle, for example, at the casual offering of anti-male slurs as conversational gambits by women I have only just met. I take umbrage at the notion that women cannot or should not find guidance in male mentors. Indignation leaps into my throat when I hear it said that women cannot be expected to identify with male protagonists in literature, or worse, when I read, as I did a few years ago, that all men are to be considered potential rapists, and that sexual intercourse between married partners (the dyad! the dyad!) is always, in its essence, rape. I've come to feel that same visceral, reactive response in defense of men that many women feel when they spring to the defense of other women. Just as homosexuals were once described, in tones of veiled horror, as pathological creatures directing sexual passion wrongly, so I too could be seen as a sort of invert. But in my case it is the passion of anger that has been attached to the wrong object. Living as I do, in an Age of Indignation it hasn't been possible for me to stay in the closet.

How is it that my experience has been so different from that of other women—particularly those many feminists who have documented their transformation from dupes of the patriarchy to participants in a group rebellion against it? I can get closer to the source of my contrarian impulse by acknowledging that my childhood was nonstandard. I grew up encouraged by my talented and unhappy mother to express a masculine side she suppressed in herself.

I was butch to my older sister's femme; she wore pinafores and braids while my mother cut my hair in a bowl and dressed me in overalls. I was never encouraged to put any stock in my appearance or to dream of marriage and children; instead I was urged to roam and play freely, and to read. My mother was advanced in many ways; quiche appeared on our table fifteen years ahead of the world-historical schedule, and I was raised in a scrupulously non-sexist manner.

I grew up pained by the absence of just those influences which so many feminist accounts recall as noxious and stifling. I wondered what was wrong with me, that my mother pressed the bauble of femininity into my sister's hand, but kept it hidden from me. Never mind about that, she seemed to be saying, hastily concealing the glittering thing behind her back. You wouldn't be interested. You were meant for better things.

But I couldn't help noticing that she cultivated her own femininity, that she enjoyed clothes, that she flirted, that she became semi-anorexic in her determination to stay slender. And the non-sexual side

235

of her femininity was perhaps even more important to her; how hard she worked to make her cooking and housekeeping seem effortless and offhand! How important to her, much as she dismissed it as the mere performance of an animal function, was the fact of her motherhood.

What I assumed was fundamental and unquestioned in the lives of other girls was problematic in mine. It was only quite late, after I had provided myself with a secure substructure of marriage and motherhood, that I was able to turn my energies to writing, the vocation my mother had foreseen for me.

Over the years I've assembled an adequate stock of conventionally feminine experiences. Those boys, for example, who responded to my frontal approach usually did so only temporarily, and soon enough I was complaining, just like other women, about the common male syndrome of emotional withdrawal after the fact of intimacy. I've given birth, and suffered the ordinary maternal pangs of love and worry. I'm a veteran of a long, struggling, and ultimately successful marriage. Still, even now, in the presence of women whose womanliness runs deep, I often feel like an overgrown child, a shy, sad monster—dim, clumsy, incompetent, but somehow, in some transcendent but useless way, superior.

I grew up with a blustery contempt for all things feminine and a secret longing for them. My exclusion from the m.r.g.'s rose court was defensively self-imposed, but no less painful for that.

My mother sent me out as a proto-feminist scout into a future which she trusted to catch up with her enlightened notion. I wandered for years in what seemed to me a wilderness. Feminism, when it came along, should have rescued and vindicated me, but instead it has left me more isolated, I think, than I would have been without it. Here at last was the cavalry, rumbling at full gallop—but in the wrong direction! Here I remain years later, still apart, still watching as they thunder by.

IV: Shama's World

As I observed earlier, I'm a slow developer. A few years ago it began to dawn on me that fear of anomaly in the self is as common as the condition itself is rare.

When I first read V. S. Naipaul's novel, A *House for Mr. Biswas*, I encountered a passage in which the protagonist, Mohun Biswas, ruminates about his pregnant wife Shama and the matriarchal family structure which surrounds her. What Shama wants is

> . . . to be taken through every stage, to fulfill every func-
> tion, to have her share of the established emotions: joy at a
> birth or marriage, distress during illness and hardship, grief
> at a death. Life, to be full, had to be this established pattern
> of sensation. Grief and joy, both equally awaited, were one.
> For Shama and her sisters and women like them, ambition,
> if the word could be used, was a series of negatives; not to
> be unmarried, not to be childless, not to be an undutiful
> daughter, sister, wife, mother, widow.

This passage hit me with the force of revelation. For me, it was a kind of Rosetta stone, a means by which I could translate my language into the language of others.

Instantly, I knew it to be true, not only of Shama and her sisters, but also of me. Given a feminist quarter-turn, updated and purged of language which assumes any connection with men, it applies to nearly every woman I know. We understand this fear, this negative impera-tive—"not to be . . . not to be." It predates feminism, but the matriar-chal movement that feminism has become exploits it, threatening to unwoman anyone who dares to lay claim to any but the prescribed nar-rative of the rejection of patriarchy followed by identification with the group, any but "this established pattern of sensation."

The m.r.g. wept, surrounded by her sisterly court. I was left feeling sick and spiteful, full of an insupportable envy because I knew that just as I would never feel the fullness of the m.r.g.'s satisfaction, so I would never feel the fullness of her misery. Her groans were everywoman's, echoed by a chorus. They had a roundedness, a primal dignity. To wail while cradled and celebrated; this was surely a good kind of pain. Like the agony of childbirth, it laid a claim on universality. My hurts, on the other hand, were private. I felt them as stinging reminders of my own anomalousness, and I hid them.

Naipaul draws a comic and horrific portrait of a matriarchal ex-tended family. The daughters of Mrs. Tulsi, the widowed matriarch-in-chief, all live together in a compound, bringing up one another's children in true "villager" style. They support and protect one another, and they also make each other quite miserable. Shama, for example, feels compelled to beat her children brutally in order to save face before her sisters, and her marriage to the hapless Mohun Biswas is continually undermined by their mockery. The group makes a cult object of the eldest sister in a way that instantly reminded me of the m.r.g.; all compete to wait on her and to attend to her numerous ailments. The sisters hold one another hostage through shame. It is the fear of exclusion from the mainstream of feminine experience that motivates them. Above all else, they fear the charge of unwomanliness.

Naipaul reminds us that female solidarity is often found in enclaves of poverty and backwardness like the West Indian Hindu colony where Mohun Biswas and his family live, societies where women live in subjugation, where their choices are few and their power indirect. This is the natural milieu of matriarchy. The system of values matriarchy enshrines—the celebration of competitive self-sacrifice, of a militant relatedness to others, of a gestural "macha" defiance in the face of male domination—all this develops where and when patriarchy is most oppressive. It occurs to me that this kind of "strong" woman is not always, or even usually, a free woman.

V: Two by Two

What went on in their minds, those girls in the third and second and even the first ranks as they sat listening to the m.r.g.? And the m.r.g. for that matter; what was her subjective state? Is it possible that some or all of them were feeling, or at least suppressing, something like what I was feeling, some degree of that sense of anomalous isolation?

Their backs told a story of creaturely fealty; seen from that angle they were as charming as a school of dolphins swimming in formation. But what did they look like from the m.r.g.'s vantage point? She was the only one with a privileged view of all their faces, individual and vulnerable, tipped up into her gaze like bowls awaiting the distribution of oatmeal.

How could I have failed to perceive that the m.r.g.'s anguish, even when the others pressed around her like a poultice, came from a lack of exactly what the group could never give her—that is, intimacy and mutuality? How wearisome the group must have seemed to her then, what a burden. She must have felt herself to be a singular creature indeed, like the great turtle on whose back some mythologies have placed the world. Where, she must have asked herself, is a mate fit for me?

238

Groups have no mind; only in dyadic relationships can I, or anyone, be known, or know another. Only in friendship—and particularly in the long combative friendship that has been my marriage—have I been able to free myself of the feeling of anomalousness that I've harped on so obsessively here.

Which is not to say that my marriage has been unproblematic. Over the course of the first fifteen of its twenty five years, through a protracted, sometimes agonized process of (here I pause to consider a sequence of possible words—confrontation? negotiation? encounter?—only to reject them all as euphemistic) fighting, my husband and I each formed full, separate selves.

All my life I had been itching for a good fair fight and my husband was the man to give it to me. He has been a formidable adversary, lucid and dogged, with an extraordinary capacity for sustained feistiness. For me, these purely personal wars have been the only ones to end in peace. Better a battle with a single antagonist, even a resourceful scrapper like my husband, than a hopeless struggle to preserve myself in the face of the grossly numerical superiority of the group, an entity which can only subsume.

Here at last, inside my marriage, I've been able to express, and eventually to temper and control, the aggressive, masculine side of my nature. Here I was able to be—and to become—my unwomanly self, without shame. How many other women have had some variant of this experience?

Meanwhile, as we fought, I sensed the presence of an invisible panel of feminist judges suspended in the air of the kitchen or the bedroom which was the scene of the engagement. (Every woman carries them in her head. Surely it was this same manifestation which hovered translucently before Anna as she spoke into the cellular phone on that warm autumn afternoon, renouncing and denouncing me and all my works.) Any impulse I felt toward compromise or capitulation set these white-wigged apparitions to frowning and shaking their heads in concert. They exhorted me to bravery; they reminded me of my duty to myself, and I obeyed. But always, at exactly the moment when the battle grew most heated, they took sudden alarm. "Leave him!" they shrieked, and fled. Now? I wanted to ask. Just when we were starting to get somewhere?

It seemed the terms of engagement had changed, and that to remain in any relation to my husband at all, even a belligerent one, was to admit defeat. This demand to sever bonds was a call to honor, and one it hurt me to refuse. I accused myself of weakness.

The cognitive dissonance I endured! I was angry at my husband, who was quite capable of being pigheaded without being cast in the role of a pig. I was angry at the spectral judges, because I had never invited them to preside in my consciousness, and I was angry at myself, for allowing an ideology I viewed with such ambivalence to colonize me against my will. I was angry most of all at the complexity of the situation, because I had to grant that sometimes women *do* need some sense of solidarity, some back-up, in order to negotiate their part of the great collective bargain being transacted between the sexes. I have to acknowledge that I need it too, but only a little bolstering—something a friend might offer—not the great unbalancing blast of wind that has blown marriages apart in such great numbers.

Patriarchy died when marriage broke its connection with the extended family. Deprived of an intergenerational conduit, it could no longer perpetuate itself. I believe that much of social history of the last fifty years can best be understood as a competitive scramble to reconfigure society after this profound alteration. Has anyone noticed that marriage has changed? The hierarchical role-bound form which found its origins in the division of labor has now been replaced by the companionate egalitarian dyad.

Surely we are witnessing the continuation of Tocqueville's "irresistible revolution, advancing century by century over every obstacle and even now going forward amid the ruins it has itself created." The Tocquevillean juggernaut has plowed through our society, leveling inequalities and leaving flattened in its wake all the complicated foliage of social organization, the shadowy places of refuge. Only marriage seems to have adapted and survived, transformed by the equalizing process that destroyed so much else.

The insides of marriages have always been obscure, but in earlier days one could presuppose a certain uniformity in their furnishings. A good marriage was tranquil and fecund, supportive of the male partner. The extended family had its means of penetration and inspection; at least one front parlor had to be kept neat and dusted.

Marriages like my mother's were semi-private accommodations, but marriages like my own are radically private. While intact, they are sealed against the outside world; any penetration tends to destroy them. When prompted to view my marriage from the outside—from

240

the perspective of the feminist judges—I find that I can't see into it at all. Or, rather, I can, but only through a sort of pinhole which gives me a distorted, leering view, like the reflection of a kitchen seen in the shiny surface of a toaster. Only when restored to my place inside it can I remember the realms of solace that my marriage contains, the real proportions of our shared space.

By now it has been amply demonstrated that children can be raised outside of marriage—some even say successfully—and that families need not rest on a marital foundation. Marriage can no longer claim the begetting and raising of children as its primary reason for being. But if not that, then what is marriage for? Why does marriage remain?

It remains to provide the simplest and most essential of psychic shelters, a sort of human lean-to inside which truth can be told and selfhood can unfurl. In the desert of mass society it provides the patches of shade necessary for the cultivation of shared private worlds.

Marriage is a mutuality reservation: as such it is absolutely necessary, but from another point of view it seems dangerously inutile. When marriages have broken free of extended families, what becomes of the lonely children who hang unsupported from these mysteriously self-contained unions? And when the breach between married couples and the families which engendered them cuts off the transmission of cultural norms, how are children to be socialized? And for that matter, aren't marriages themselves impoverished by an absence of the limitations and expectations once imposed on them by extended families? How dearly bought are freedom and equality!

Socially problematic or not, the new kind of marriage exactly suits the new kind of woman that my mother raised me to be. Sometimes I feel a faint nostalgia, not particularly for the extended family—I hardly knew such a thing—but for the lively community of faculty wives that surrounded my mother, for the slow-growing friendships of affinity and shared interest that flourished among them and no longer seem possible in an age of ideology. But I find I can't sustain this prelapsarian mooniness for long. I know I could never accept the terms of my mother's marriage, relatively enlightened though it was. Here at last is my feminism. For just this moment I seem to be sitting with the others, not standing by the door grousing. But as I've said, it's the next step I can't seem to take, the baptismal immersion in the group, the terrifying loss of self.

Marriage has been a kind of salvation for me, and for many others, I feel sure, including some of those feminists who regard it with official suspicion. But it can't be salvific in any more general way. Unlike individuals and families, dyads cannot be added up to make a society. If anything, the insular privacy of marriage works against social cohesiveness. More and more, marriage becomes a purely human good.

The gap between the human and the social continues to widen. I've taken a contrarian pride in staying on my side of the divide, watching from a distance as the others file in and arrange themselves in rows. Marriage has confirmed me in that old habit of withdrawal.

But even now I sometimes imagine what it might be like to walk across the space that separates me from the others, to sit down and take my place among them. Would I feel a sense of homecoming, a gratifying internal collapse?

My husband and I look out at the world together from within the protection of our marriage. Year by year we feel further removed, so much so that recently we've begun to imagine ourselves as colonists reconnoitering the landscape of a lighted planet, parched by the unmediated heat of an ideological sun. Our module is self-contained and highly maneuverable; it can skim the blasted surface or withdraw to a perspective of high, hovering detachment. Our removal sometimes leaves us feeling a little cramped, but also dizzyingly free. We carry our own atmosphere. Our craft is ingeniously designed and stocked with nearly everything we need.

Nominated by Boulevard, Rosellen Brown, Robert Phillips

CARPE DIEM: TIME PIECE

by MARILYN KRYSL

from WARSCAPE WITH LOVERS (Cleveland State University Poetry Center)

In the next seat the young man from Bangalore sleeps,
or so it seems. I dream, toss, lean—
do I?—into his shoulder. Or say his shoulder
slides—does it?—against mine. A woman reads
the *Times* across the aisle, and Big Spender sun
puts money on the Pacific. My breast, that heap

of wheat Solomon sang. Bangalore's heaped
hand, my breast a hill where swallows sleep
as though they've drunk some sweet elixir. Sun
burnishes the sea, I close my eyes, lean
into his long fingers. Listen, I've read
The Song. Eyes closed, it's like that. His shoulder,

armored, gleams: a buckler's brass. My shoulder
stakes the linen tent. Now conjure heap
of my belly, thicket of hair. (Later I'll read
Mary Oliver.) Years before I'd slept
with someone blind, my body braille. We lean
into our book. The text reads us. The sun

looks sideways at the sighing sea. The sun
looks on, our hands mouths. My hand shoulders
forward, looking for antelope, a leaning
slope. Cunning hunter, crossing the heaped
savannah of his lap. Afterward, sleep
is milky sweet. I've read Duras, I've read

Huang O, Rabindranath Tagore, I've read
the Tao, and David Bohm. Each day the sun
lays down its ultimatum. Be: don't sleep
away this blazing gift, your life. His shoulder,
my eyes, his eyes: we look our fill. That heap
of sea is called a swell. It's not who leans

on whom, not gender, not power. I've always leaned
toward earth, air, water. Fire. I read
the body's scripture, freely chose. A heap
of wheat, in scripture, is poetry. The sun
strokes the sea every day, and the slope of a shoulder
is lyric braille. A stewardess (she'd slept,

leaning on the steward's shoulder) brings us heaps
of rice. The woman sleeps beneath her *Times*.
Bangalore's work is watches. The sun reads braille.

Nominated by Brigit Kelly

STUPID GIRL

fiction by LOUIS BERNEY

from STORY

No ONE EVER DIES AT Disneyland, at least that's what she'd heard, so even though it was obvious the old dude's heart was history— when the ride ended he was sagging in his safety harness like he weighed a thousand pounds, his eyes rolled back to the milky whites—paramedics loaded his body onto a stretcher, clipped an oxygen mask to his face, and whisked him safely off park property. Where, she supposed, Disney authorities would finally release his soul and allow the emergency room attendant at Anaheim Memorial to check him out.

Snow White, who'd been strapped in with the dead man, clawed her way out of the bobsled, ripping one of her pleated, mutton-leg sleeves in the process. She stumbled to the nearest trash can. Even on the best of days? The swoops and dips of the Matterhorn always made her feel like pitching. And today was most definitely *not* the best of days. The old dude they'd paired her with for an in-action publicity shot was some high-roller insurance tycoon from Houston. Potbelly, pink piggy eyes, cigar smoke, and Old Spice. When she first gave him her hand to shake, he held it a little longer, got it a little moister, than was really necessary.

No *way,* she'd thought, am I getting on that bobsled with you.

But then she'd felt sad, like somebody had jabbed her heart with a fork. Here she was, only nineteen years old and always she looked at life as something about to sneak up on her and pounce. Maybe this old dude was a nice old man, a dad and granddad who gave the kids dollar bills and root beer barrels whenever they stopped by. Maybe?

Smiling at the insurance tycoon smiling back at her, Snow White (Suzanne Elizabeth Bailey when she was off the clock) had made up her mind, as she did periodically, to screw past experience and try thinking the best of people. To be less jaded in the hope that the world, somehow—she tried not to think too much about this logic—might therefore turn out nicer.

That, and she really really needed the extra money she'd get for the job, you betcha.

Hunched over a trash can trimmed with glitter-paint fairy dust, Suzanne wondered now if it was possible for a girl to die of chronic dumb judgment. Right before he kicked, right after the bobsled shot into the last fast curve, the insurance tycoon had hooked a fat pimply arm around her shoulder and—smack!—grabbed a handful of boob.

She'd seen too many people dead or dying (her dad, her first stepmother, a grandmother, a boyfriend sheared from his Yamaha by the kingpin of a jackknifed semi) to feel anything but sympathy for the man; she wasn't pissed off, only tired. And glad to be off the Matterhorn, somewhere she could puke in peace.

When she finished doing that, she felt better, though not by much. She had three hours left on her shift, and nights in August were almost as hot as the days; her scalp smoldered inside the black, bow-topped wig.

Her own hair was dirty blonde. Brown eyes, a gap between her two front teeth. Very embarrassing, those claw-hammer teeth of hers, but when she scored the TV series they'd been part of her so-called charm; the producers had even written a clause into her contract. After that, well—the fact of the matter was that stepfathers, and the boyfriends of ex-wives of former stepfathers, didn't invest hundreds of orthodonto-dollars in little girls to whom they were barely connected.

With the back of her hand she swiped at the black mascara sweating spider legs down her cheeks. Worse than the heat or the heaves was the thought that they'd never use 8 × 10s of a corpse. They'd probably still pay her, she considered, but then again what if they didn't?

She kicked the side of the trash can. That money, whenever it finally came, she'd already promised to her stepsister, who'd been waiting two months for her June rent. The stepsister, really just the ex-wife of one of Suzanne's half brothers, wouldn't believe what had happened on the Matterhorn. She'd conclude that Suzanne had snorted away the cash, even though Suzanne had been moderately clean for almost a year and absolutely so since the Fourth of July, since the day after the Fourth of July. A fight would erupt, Tita would call her an ungrateful coke-head tramp—this from a woman who considered crystal meth one of the four basic food groups—and then Suzanne would end up sleeping in her friend Robert's van, if she was lucky.

The thought of all that was too much to bear on an emptied stomach. She glanced around. At the foot of the Matterhorn, security was busy trying to hustle everyone along to Mr. Toad's Wild Ride. Her own lead, a guy in charge of shadowing her through the park, in case she dehydrated and collapsed in costume and traumatized some moron kid who'd think Snow White was dead, was searching for her in exactly the wrong direction.

She dodged a pair of eight-year-old autograph piranhas and slipped into the Skyway to Tomorrowland, a timber and cake-frosting facade that was supposed to look like a Swiss chalet. Taped yodeling. The greeter, a skinny blonde kid in lederhosen, passed her through, and a heartbeat later she was in one of the buckets that coasted on cables, forty feet above the asphalt surface of the park.

It was cooler up there, and quieter. No shrieking kids, no hydraulic spitting of the rides, no dink-dink-tinkle of "It's a small world, after all," piped through speakers hidden in the bushes. From inside her bodice, from the elastic edge of her jog-bra, she plucked a match and a joint. She slouched in her seat so that, from the ground, the only thing you could see above the wall of the gondola was her polka-dot bow. Not that she gave a shit if she got fired. But if she was caught getting baked on the Skyway, the jarheads from security might search her locker and find the rest of the Chocolate Tide she had stashed there. And that would mean another three months of court-ordered treatment, another ninety-day twelve-step recover drill.

"God grant me the serenity to blah blah blah."

Please. But she was golden up here, as long as she slouched. No worries. *Hakuna* fucking *matata*.

She lit the joint and blew out the match with a smudge of gray breath. She took a good, deep rip, pulled the smoke up and over her heart like a goose-down quilt, pulled and pulled until her brain was tucked in as well.

Every time was like the first sweet time. She'd been nine. Her TV dad, now a born-again bass player for a Christian rock group, had

247

turned her on to bong hits between takes of an episode about cheating. Should little Cathy (that was the character Suzanne had played, little Cathy raised in the station house by a band of kooky firemen), should she copy her best friend's test answers? She had, of course, and they'd been nabbed by the teacher, of course, and there'd been some important lessons, of course, to be learned right after the commercial break.

The lessons? Little Cathy learned the importance of personal integrity, etc.; little Suzanne learned that weed was good and good weed turned your lips to liquid rubber. They'd had to tape the last scene three times, because she'd sounded like she was speaking Chinese.

Suzanne closed her eyes, smiled her first sincere one of the day, and enjoyed the slosh of blood in her veins as the gondola rocked along above the canals of Storybook Land.

The show hadn't set the world on fire, but for two seasons and a half, at least, she'd had a manager, a theatrical agent, a commercial agent, a tutor, an acting coach. She had a woman who was in charge, as far as she could tell, of nothing else but slathering her up with sunscreen every time she even thought about going outside.

After the show was canceled, when she was eleven, Steven Spielberg didn't exactly come knocking. So she did the school thing for a few years, then worked a delightful array of bad jobs and worse jobs—Baskin-Robbins, JCPenney's, a cocktail place on Hollywood. About a year ago she landed the part-time Disney gig, where the money wasn't much, but steady.

"I beg your pardon!" someone shouted, loud. "Pardon me!"

She sighed. Was that too much to ask, she wondered, four minutes of peace without some asshole father, down below, throwing a hissy fit because Minnie Mouse hadn't signed his kid's book yet?

"I BEG YOUR PARDON!"

Something stung her on the arm and she swatted it. Another something, hard and small, pinged off the metal wall of the gondola; she heard it fall to the floor.

Startled, she sat up, leaned forward, patted the floor with the palms of her hands. After a minute she found it, pinched it, sniffed it: a chocolate-covered raisin.

A chocolate-covered raisin?

She peeked over the lip of her gondola. In the gondola directly behind her stood a big black man.

248

Really black and *really* big. Three hundred and fifty pounds if he was an ounce, butt as broad as a love seat. He wore a short-sleeved dress shirt, striped tie, and glasses with dark plastic frames.

"PARDON ME!" he roared. He stamped his foot and whipped another Raisinet at her. Another one. "Snow White does not smoke!" he roared. "PLEASE EXTINGUISH THAT AT ONCE!"

Oh, she thought, my fucking God. She flicked her roach away and bonked her head on the plastic seat when she ducked back behind the wall of the gondola. She sat there for a minute, stunned, wondering what in the *fuck* her Chocolate Tide had been dusted with. Because she was tripping, wasn't she? What other explanation could there possibly be?

Very cautiously she took another peek at the gondola behind her, but it was still there, *he* was still there. He'd stopped roaring and stomping and winging Raisinets, but he kept glaring at her. There was another guy in the gondola, a white guy about half his size. She could hear the crackle of cussing as he tried to yank the monster dude back to his seat.

Her own bucket swung into the wheelhouse. Suzanne hitched her skirt over her knees, crouched next to the hatch, tried to think, to *think*. If the big black guy called security on her, she was fucked. That stupid weed: she swore to herself she'd never do another drug for as long as she lived. And what if he decided not to bother with security at all and came tearing after her himself? He could probably twist her head off like you'd twist the cap off a bottle. She thought she was going to have a heart attack.

"Welcome to Tomorrowland," the attendant said. When he popped her door open, she jumped to the ground and didn't look back. The cast member locker room was behind Aladdin's Oasis, so she blew across the Central Plaza and made for Adventureland. She started to relax, a little, when she hit the bridge, but then she was blindsided by a Dopey, who must have spotted her from the Castle Forecourt. He grabbed her around the waist and tried to waltz her back to a group of giggling Japanese tourists.

"Fucker," she hissed. She shoved him away and he went reeling backward. His big, molded-plastic dwarf head hit the bridge railing like a bomb, with a colossal hollow boom that scattered the birds from the trees. Everyone turned to see what had happened, and in that instant she shimmied through the crowd, over the bridge, shimmied safe and sound through the bamboo portcullis hung with bunches of plastic bananas.

He'd had this game, her dad, that he liked to play with her when he was drunk or stoned or whatever. Which, in other words, was most of the time. He'd come home and open the front door and pretend she was invisible.

"Suzanne, girl, where are you?" he'd cry. "I can't see you!"

"Daddy!" she'd holler. "Right here!" She'd pound her fists against his legs.

"Suzanne!"

"Daddy!"

He'd trip over her, stumble, knock her gently down to the shag with him, tickle her until she could barely breathe, until her laughter was just weak, wet, happy squeaks.

"Suzanne! Where are you darlin?"

Well, when he wasn't drunk or stoned, lifting her over his head like a surfboard and tickling her down to the grass and threatening to surf her heinie all the way to Australia, then she really was invisible to him. Sobriety, she would have to conclude, was a general concept highly overrated.

She always seemed to think about her dad late at night, when it was time to go home. She'd been only five years old when he died, and yet her memories of him were sharper than yesterday's. Particles of dust churning in a shaft of July light. The texture and taste of American cheese slices, the crinkle of the cellophane wrapper. American cheese was his favorite snack, and sometimes he'd flip squares to her like fish to a seal.

Marvin punched her card—1:03 A.M.—and motioned her through the gate with a flick of his *Sports Illustrated.* She slid her time card up under the sun visor. It was 1:03 A.M. and her day from hell was officially over.

She turned off the AC, which was worthless anyway. Her hand, she noticed, was trembling, and no wonder. One dead man on the Matterhorn; one giant psycho; forty dollars worth of perfectly good Chocolate Tide flushed down the toilet. A cool, fishy breeze had managed to work its way inland, and there wasn't much smog; what smog there was even seemed kind of romantic, made the stars down along the horizon look fuzzy and soft.

Not another car in sight, either direction, but the light stayed red. She wasn't in any particular hurry, come to think of it. Right turn, left turn, straight? The apartment in West Hollywood was out of the question, of course, because of the wicked stepsister and the rent money

250

Suzanne didn't have; Robert's van was a possibility, if it hadn't been impounded since she last talked to him, but it was a *van* for God's sake, decorated with yellow tennis balls he'd cut in half and glued to the walls. The thought of a night alone in there (Robert worked the dog shift till dawn) was just too lonely, too depressing, for words.

That song by Garbage was on the radio again, "Stupid Girl," her own personal anthem. The light changed and Suzanne eased off the clutch, whispered a short prayer of the please-God-please variety. The engine fluttered for a second, but her Rabbit rolled out of the employee lot and onto the street without conking again.

"Thank you, God," she murmured, just in case. You never know, right?

She turned . . . left. Why not? Ahead of her were the guest lots, empty now, three motels, every window dark and curtains drawn, the Pick-N-Pay, another motel, and an abandoned Church of the Holy Pentecost. On the wall of the church there was a faded picture of a child riding an escalator up to heaven, up out of a tangle of pale yellow flames. Suzanne wondered if there was a down escalator too, if there was a food court in heaven, a Nordstrom's, and (drowsy, floating in that weird in-between, that trippy frappe of asleep and awake and Garbage on the radio) she almost didn't see the car with its hood up and engine smoking; she almost didn't see the man who stepped out to flag her down.

Reflex, she tapped the brakes, gave the wheel a jerk. That was a mistake, she realized, even before she'd done it. Her little Rabbit was pretty single-minded when it came to following instructions; you could turn, or stop, but not really both at the same time. The car stalled, blew a big sweet breath of gasoline at her, and rolled into the parking lot of the Holy Pentecost.

Fuck, Suzanne mused. Fuck. Fuck. She cranked the ignition, just for the fun of it. Nothing.

The guy tapped on her window. She glanced up at him—he was unshaven, about forty years old, with blue bloodshot eyes and a stringy ponytail. Perfect: just the sort of drifter you'd want to encounter late at night, in an abandoned Orange County parking lot. She tried the ignition again.

"Hey," he said through the glass, "could you give us a lift to a gas station?"

Us? she wondered, just as (Did she need this shit? Did she really need this shit?) rumbling up into the puddle of yellow streetlight came the big black maniac from the Skyway.

251

"Charlie," he said, "you didn't let me finish explaining my theory about Critter Country." He saw her. "Show White!"

Suzanne gave up on the *fucking* ignition and reached for her purse. She found the can, pushed open her door, stepped out of the car. The drifter back off a few steps.

"Leave me alone!" Suzanne screamed. She shook the can hard so that they would hear the rattle of the aerosol bead. "Leave me alone! I've got Mace! Why do you keep bothering me?"

"Wait!" the drifter said. "Shit!"

"Don't move!"

"Shit! I won't!"

"Don't move! *Both* of you!"

"Take it easy!" the drifter yelled. "Christ Almighty!"

"I swear to God I'm going to mace you both if you don't leave me the *fuck* alone!"

"What the fuck is your problem?" He edged away, palms up.

"What the fuck is my *problem?* What the fuck is *my* problem?"

"I know *you!*" the big maniac said suddenly, excited. He rumbled closer.

"Shit, Walter!" the drifter said. He dropped to one knee on the broken asphalt and covered his face with his hands.

"Leave me *alone!*" Suzanne screamed. She stared up, up, up the slope of the big guy. It was impossible, how huge he was. "Get the fuck *back!*"

He studied her face intently, one long, surprisingly slender finger pressed against the bridge of his glasses. He lifted his chin and lowered it very slowly.

"Come on down and meet some friends of mine," he began to sing—to *sing*—in a frail little wisp of a voice that couldn't possibly come out of a monster bod like that, "meet some friends of mine, down at engine house, engine house number nine."

The drifter friend had hunched down into himself, his hands still wrapped around his face. "Walter, goddamnit," he warned softly. "Get *back.*"

Suzanne couldn't help but snort. "You *remember* that?"

"You lived with your dad who was a fireman," the big guy said, "and a Dalmation named Lazy."

"Nobody remembers that," Suzanne said. "It was only on two seasons and a half."

"Sunday nights on the Disney Channel. The plotting was somewhat derivative, but the acting was superb. You reminded me of a young Haley Mills. Suzanne Bailey."

Somewhere, not far away, a dog barked, paused to hack something up, then started barking again; across the street, razor wire coiled down off the dead Best Western sign like a strand of Christmas tree tinsel.

"Listen," Suzanne said, "if you guys are star-stalkers? I'm guessing you could do better. I know a girl who played a girl in *Forrest Gump,* if you want her number. One of the minor hippies. My career is currently on hiatus."

"Don't lose heart," the big guy said. "Look at Walt Disney, for example. *Pinocchio,* when it was first released, was a financial disaster. My name is Walter. This is my friend Charlie. I'm sorry we acted so impetuously on the Skyway, but you shouldn't smoke cigarettes when you're in costume. You really shouldn't smoke at all, you know."

"Could you put that down, please?" the drifter said, peeking through his fingers. "I have some really bad tear-gas memories."

Suzanne shrugged, snorted again. "Just Aqua Net." She flashed them her best spokesmodel smile, dazzling and insincere, swept spokesmodel fingers across the can's label, then pitched it up onto the roof of the Church of the Holy Pentecost. "And it's empty," she said. "Story of my life."

The white drifter guy slowly unfolded from his crouch, groaned, and stretched out flat on his back.

"It must be very exciting," the black guy said, "to be a cast member at Disneyland. Would you like to know what I think is the only negative aspect of Disneyland?"

"The stupid shows?" said his friend. He had his arms flung out and looked as if he'd been dropped there from a helicopter. "The right-wing patriotism and corporate butt-licking? The colorful audio-animatronic Third World peasants?"

"The only negative aspect," he continued cheerfully, "is that eventually you have to *leave.* Not so at Walt Disney World in Florida. When you go home for the night, you can take the monorail to the Polynesian Resort and wake up in the morning to a stunning view of the castle." He straightened his glasses. "Suzanne," he said, "what would you consider the ten most indelible moments in Disney animated history?"

"Jesus Christ," the drifter muttered.

"Indelible?"

"Memorable," the big guy said. He bounced on his toes and Suzanne wouldn't have been surprised if he'd soared off suddenly like a helium-filled cartoon parade balloon.

"No offense?" she said. "But are you like some sort of fanatical Disney freak?"

"The proper appellation," the drifter said, in what she had to admit was a pretty dead-on imitation of his friend, "is Disney enthusiast."

"Of course one must include the final scenes of both *Snow White* and *Pinocchio*," the big guy went on, "but I'd argue the final sequence of *Cinderella* is just as rich with possibilities."

She shrugged. "Never seen it," she said, and you'd have thought from the horrified look on his face that she'd suggested he go in for a rectal swab. "I liked *The Lion King*."

"*The Lion King?*" He chuckled.

The drifter guy sat up, rubbed his thumb along his bottom lip, contemplated the torn toe of his Chuck Taylor high-top. He wore rings on all the fingers of his right hand, even the thumb. "What show did you say you were in?" he asked.

"*Engine House Number Nine*," the black guy said. "Oh, she was superb, Charlie. Suzanne had the sort of elusive Disney star quality one doesn't see much of anymore. A young Haley Mills."

"You know," he said, rubbing his bottom lip, hooking a hank of hair behind his ear, "I might have an idea. I might have just stumbled across the opportunity of a lifetime."

Suzanne leaned back against her Rabbit. She took off her Dodgers cap and raked fingers through her hair. For a moment she pretended there was someone, out there, who was tracking her progress across the wide, white face of a clock, in a cheerful kitchen, someone who was sipping coffee and watching a *Cheers* rerun and expecting her home at such and such a time, on the dot, and would be worried if she was a minute late.

"What?" she asked, before she could stop herself.

"Picture this," Charlie said. He set his coffee cup down on the counter and gazed up at the ceiling, at the fluorescent tubes lisping and fluttering there. He was telling her how famous and rich it was going to make her, this opportunity of a lifetime, how she'd get soap operas and sitcoms and all the parts Alicia Silverstone turned down, how she'd have a condo in Malibu with room for as many dogs as she wanted.

They were at the International House of Pancakes, a couple of miles from the park and across the street from the gas station where she'd driven them. 2 A.M. They'd offered to buy her breakfast, and she'd agreed. Why not? She hadn't had anything to eat since her shift break at four, and then only a bagel with hummus. She knew she shouldn't trust the two of them, but she had to keep reminding herself. Not once had either one of them brushed against her boob or tried to slide an arm around her shoulders. She hadn't caught them, not once, looking at her with the subtle, acquisitive, half-lidded lizard stare she was used to. They might be dangerous—she wasn't *that* naive—but at least, she reasoned, they would be dangerous in original ways.

Charlie made a fist and pressed it against his ear. She realized the rings on his fingers weren't rings at all, but tattoos. A black-ink circle of vines and tiny thorns tooled around each finger, just beneath the second knuckle.

"Hello?" he said, fist still pressed to his ear.

"What?" she asked.

He shushed her. "I've got a call. Hello? This is Pepsi. Who was that blonde girl I saw on the tube last night? Suzanne Bailey? Get her in here. We want her for our Super Bowl spot."

"Please," she told him. "National commercials are impossible. There are a million girls for the smallest part."

"You're not a million girls," he said. "It's all about exposure. Once they see you, they'll have to have you."

She finished her eggs and noticed that Walter, perched on a stool that had disappeared beneath him, was leafing very slowly, very seriously, through a coffee-table book on the art of *Pinocchio*. He was humming softly to himself, a tune she recognized after a second—"Hi-diddle-de-dee, an actor's life for me." She propped her elbows on the counter, lit a cigarette, and smoked through a faint smile. For a minute it seemed the most normal thing in the world, to be sitting here at the International House of Pancakes, two o'clock in the morning, with a long-haired drifter and a giant black Disney enthusiast, considering a proposal for your own abduction. She tapped ash into her coffee saucer and turned to Charlie.

"And what makes you think you're the best possible applicants for this position?" she asked. "Do you have references? What would you say are your three greatest strengths as a kidnapper?"

He stared at her very intently. His eyes were blue, with shifting shadows inside, like light at the bottom of a swimming pool. She wanted to ask him about the significance of the thorn tattoos, but figured it was none of her business. "Just keep an open mind," he said. "It's very simple. It's so simple that absolutely nothing can even possibly go wrong. We fake a kidnapping, we send a ransom note, we collect the money."

"The money?" she laughed. "From who? I hate to rain on your parade, but there's no one in the continental United States who would pay to get me back. There's no one in the continental United States, actually, who'd even notice I'd been kidnapped, which let me tell you is a really pleasant thought to consider." The roof of her mouth itched and she wished she had some snow, some good old snow, just a taste.

"Disney will," he said. He had a narrow angular shape to his face, like a wedge, and a way of leaning a little bit forward all the time, as if he was always in the middle of squeezing through a tight place. "They don't give a shit about you *now*, I know. But once the word gets out that Snow White has been *kidnapped*—do you know what kind of media coverage that will get? What's Disney going to do then, when every evening over Tom Brokaw's shoulder there's a blue box with your picture: Day 17—the Snow White Crisis. They'll pay a million dollars. Two million. That's ashtray change for a company like that. And you'll be famous. Suzanne Bailey. Ten minutes after it's all over you'll be curled up on a sofa across from Barbara Walters, telling the tale of how you survived your terrifying ordeal."

"In Florida, you see, Walt learned anticipated urban development," Walter said. He reached across Charlie and touched her wrist. "He bought up forty square miles of virgin orange grove. At Walt Disney World in Florida, you can avoid the real world altogether."

Charlie snorted, but Suzanne had to admit that she wasn't particularly pro-reality herself. There was something to be said for clean streets and plenty of toilet paper and no cockroaches sifting through the Grape-Nuts and no neighbors above who, seriously, once dragged a goat up the stairs for some sort of Santeria thing. Once in a while, riding in the Electrical Parade, she'd stare so hard at some girl's smiling face that she'd fall into it; she'd daydream herself down into a life that seemed so happy (she wasn't dumb enough to think it actually was) she'd stop pelting the crowd with posies.

"Forget it," she told Charlie. "You've got to be kidding. Do I look that stupid and pathetic that I'd go for something like that? Tell me, OK, because if I do? I might as well kill myself right now."

"We'll be the ones who rescue you," he said. "Picture this. An old abandoned warehouse. A couple of guys driving along and a flat tire, or a belt goes flapping, and then through the flap of the fan belt they hear a muffled cry for help."

"Forget it," she said.

"We'll make the place look like the Manson family's been living there. Empty water jugs, cookie wrappers, duct tape with your blonde hairs stuck to it. Our two heroes creep inside and there she is, Suzanne Bailey. The nation rejoices."

"You're whacked," she said. She watched the line-cook scrape grease off the grill with a plastic spatula. "No way. Don't you think they're going to know it's a scam?"

"How?" he demanded. Those spooky blue eyes—it was a good thing, she supposed, her head wasn't made of flammable materials. "Who's going to call Snow White a liar, after her ordeal, this sweet weepy-eyed Disney Channel blonde girl? It's foolproof."

"No," she said. "Forget it."

No.

No.

And then, finally:

"OK."

She sighed a smoky sigh that could have been the last long sigh on earth, winding out to the outer eternal reaches of the universe. *OK.*

"Hey, Suzanne," Charlie said, "I know it's a crazy thing I'm asking you to do, but—"

"I've done crazier," she said with a shrug, which shut him up, a miracle. "Believe it or not."

Believe it or not. The fact of the matter made her want to giggle and cry at the same time, so she just lit another cigarette and watched the shreds of tobacco redden, crumble.

"*The Lion King,*" Walter said, out of the blue, "is certainly a *secondary* classic. But one would be hard pressed to rank it in the same group as *Cinderella.*"

She lay with her head tilted back, so that when she opened her eyes she stared up at the torn cloth ceiling and the tuft of stripped copper wires where the overhead light should have been. She'd always meant to get it fixed. Charlie was driving, just his fingertips on the wheel because the plastic was so hot; Walter was in the backseat, humming "Whistle While You Work," and flipping through the pages of his *Pinnochio* book. Every time he shifted on his monster haunches she thought they'd had a blow-out.

She'd been dozing. The sun had finally rolled over the horizon, like an egg off a table, but it was still hot. A hundred and twenty degrees, Charlie said, and he was probably exaggerating only a little. She thought her nostrils were going to melt every time she tried to inhale.

"I hate the fucking desert," she said. The heat made the macadam squiggle. "Hate it, hate it, hate it."

Charlie concentrated on the road ahead, didn't answer. He was convinced the desert was the place to go. He'd already figured out a place to hole up—the abandoned silver mines high in the hills above the Colorado River, just across the border into Arizona. He'd been there years ago, though she wasn't exactly clear why. It was critical they get off the beaten track, he said, and those old, high-desert silver mines were as far off the beaten track as you could get.

"It'll be like hiding on the moon," he'd said. "The whole world could be looking for you, the whole world could be holding hands and looking for you, and they'd never find you out here."

She counted the cigar-stub stumps of organ-pipe cactus, watched the telephone lines, barbed with desert birds, go spinning past. Charlie was prepared—she'd give him that much. He had details worked out that she wouldn't have thought of in a million years. The photos, for example; he was going to take pictures of her to go with the ransom note, once they got to the hideout. He was high if he really thought the scam was foolproof, but there was a chance they could pull it off. Stranger shit had happened. When the police questioned her afterwards? She'd be the fucking ice queen; she wouldn't give a fucking inch. "Three Asian men . . . bound and gagged . . . frightened for her life." Et cetera. She'd stick to her story and they could hammer at her morning and night, for all the good it would do them.

She reached over and touched one of Charlie's tattoos, traced the curve of thorns with the tip of her finger. "Are they religious?" she asked him.

He glanced at her, blinked. "What?"

"Are they supposed to be religious?" She was thinking of the crucifix her grandmother had hung on the wall above her bed the summer

Suzanne had stayed there, the foot-long Jesus carved from dark, oily wood, the crown of thorns. He was one buff Jesus, she remembered, all knotted muscles and tendons and just the skimpiest scrap of loin cloth, which she'd actually peeked under once.

Charlie thought about the question. "Yeah," he said finally.

"Hey," she said. "How did you and Mr. Disney back there end up together?"

Charlie was staring hard at the road again, looking for the turn-off. "Shit," he said. "Don't ask."

Greasewood spurs, a few clumps of prickly pear, dry shallow washes scored east to west across the desert floor. Along the highway shoulder there were occasional smears of blood, pin-feathers, single scattered reptile scales that caught the light and blinked like sequins.

Maybe it was the dusk, the soft toasted orange of it, or maybe it was the half a lude Charlie had scored for her back at a gas station in Twenty-Nine Palms, to show his good faith, but for the moment she felt rosy as hell; she was so hopeful her heart felt pinched, like a green olive squeezed until out comes shooting an exclamation point pimento. This was the absolute last time, she promised herself, she'd do something this nutty.

They were off the state highway now and onto a dirt road that branched out from it. After a few minutes Charlie turned off and angled across the desert floor, toward the mesas, stumps listing like guttered candles in the mess of their own wax.

"I thought we were going to cross the river first," she said.

He checked the gas gauge, gave it a thump with his knuckle. She turned to watch their dust, drifting off toward the empty road, and noticed that Walter, in the backseat, was weeping. Very quietly, with just the slightest pucker of his lips, the slightest shiver to his shoulders. There was a spot of wet shine on each dark cheek.

Charlie glanced into the rearview mirror. "Shut up," he told Walter softly. "Shut up, goddamnit."

Suzanne turned back around, stretched out her legs and kicked her feet up onto the dashboard. "What's wrong with *him*?" she asked Charlie.

He flipped on the headlights, gave her a wink.

"Almost there," he said.

Nominated by Story

259

VANDALS, HORSES

by ALAN MICHAEL PARKER

from THE ANTIOCH REVIEW

The vandals are dreaming, wolves are dreaming,
The horses are staked to their deaths.

In the poem of the vandals dreaming
A word bites through a lip,

Drawing blood (The poem is in ruins.)
The vandals dream their arms unseen,

Dream themselves buried in the belly
Of the birthing mare, as a foal is

Torn to life. (The poem is banal
As the barn is bloody.)

And you and I, and you and I, we steal
Each other's blankets, wrap ourselves

In darkness, wind, in anything
The night will let us, to feel safe.

Do you feel safe? (Soft,
the vandals sleep). Because a word

Is a dream of its meaning, you and I
Must dream the vandals dreaming:

Soft, the horses nicker in the barn.
(Soft, our poem begins as vandals dream.)

Nominated by Michael Heffernan, Andrew Hudgins, Cleopatra Mathis, Campbell McGrath

TEA AT THE HOUSE

fiction by MEG WOLITZER

from PLOUGHSHARES

I WAS BORN ON THE GROUNDS of the Mount Mohonk Hospital for the Insane, where my father was Chief of Psychiatry, and because of this I grew accustomed to the sounds of misery before I went to sleep at night. I would lie in bed upstairs in my family's house, which was situated one hundred yards from the main building, and after lights out, I would hear shrieking and weeping as though animals were being slaughtered. No, no, it was nothing like that, my father assured me, coming into the bedroom. These patients were in psychic anguish, he said, and no one was laying a hand on them.

Now it has been nearly fifty years since I lived there, and while the hospital still exists, its nurses now wear street clothes, the bars have been sandblasted off all its windows, and "Insane" has long been extinguished from its name. But back when I lived on the grounds of the hospital with my father and mother, the gates were padlocked at dusk by an aging groundskeeper, and those nighttime shrieks echoed through the surrounding hills, frightening the locals and waking the deer.

"Is anyone being beaten?" I asked my father before bed.

"No one is being beaten," he answered.

"Is anyone being whipped?"

"No one is being whipped."

"Slapped?"

"No one is being slapped."

'Throttled?"

"Where did you learn *that* word?" asked my father. And so it went, this bedtime ritual, and though many of the patients stayed up weeping and howling throughout the long night, I was able to sleep the fluent sleep of children. To the patients, this place was a hospital, a prison, but to me it was home.

It was my father who decided that I would become a doctor. He had read in one of his medical journals that an unprecedented number of girls were entering the field of medicine, and there were even photographs accompanying the article, as if anyone needed proof: a fleet of bulky young women in white coats and harlequin glasses, standing behind an autoclave. The idea of me, a seven-year old girl who pasted pictures of iceboxes and hairstyles into scrapbooks, eventually transforming into one of these women, seemed a reach. But my mother had been told she could bear no more children. This meant there would never be a son, so one morning my father walked into my room, sighed, then stretched the jaws of a stethoscope around my neck. For a brief moment, thinking it was jewelry, I picked up the silver disk at the bottom and held it between my fingers like a religious medal. My father tried to smile encouragingly, for this was clearly a big moment for him, a rite of passage. His stethoscope and his trays of equipment and his vast library with titles such as *The Hysterical Female* and *Sexual Normality and Abnormality: Twelve Case Studies*—all of this would be turned over to me at some appropriate point in my life.

By the time I grew up, most of the authors were long dead, as were their tormented patients. Even the publishing houses—with names like Pingry & Seagrove, Burroway Bros., Smollet and Sons—no longer existed. The entire world, as I knew it then, no longer existed, but seemed to have been snuffed out like some ancient star. Back when my father decided I would become a doctor, the Depression had settled in over the whole country. Nurses had been "let go," as my father said, and I pictured packs of women in white scattering across the lawn, their fluted cupcake-paper nurses' caps sent sailing. Week after week, families yanked seriously ill patients out of the hospital. A schizophrenic man might be shipped off to distant cousins in Iowa or Nebraska, doomed to spend his days with an American Gothic couple who had agreed, for a fee, to take in this peculiar relative who never spoke. The farm couple would stare in perplexity at their boarder and wonder what in the world to do with him: sit him down on a thresher and put him to work? Wrap his hands around the swollen udders of a cow? Or just let him sit on the porch and rock? Other patients were pulled out of the hospital and deposited on the streets of New York City, which swallowed them effortlessly. Many of these men and women drank themselves sick or froze during the long winter.

A small, elite population remained at Mount Mohonk throughout the Depression, and these patients were my father's bread and butter. They were an unlikely assortment of men and women whose families had secret, inexplicable reservoirs of money, and who seemed untouched by dark times. Here was the nucleus of unassailably rich America: shrewd bankers who could afford to keep unbalanced, yammering wives confined to the mountaintop for as long as it took. And sometimes it took forever.

Over the years, seeing the same faces in the windows of the hospital, the same figures in soft robes lumbering down the gravel footpath, I became comforted by how little anything changed. The faces were as familiar as those of relatives seen year after year at holiday dinners. There was Harry Beeman, a financier who had jumped from his fifteenth-floor office in the Bankers' Equity Building, only to bounce twice on the striped tarp of the building's awning, crushing several ribs and both legs. Now he limped through the halls of Mount Mohonk with a copy of *The Financial Times* in front of his face, muttering about figures as though any of it still mattered to him. There was Mildred Vell, a society matron with milky cataracts and a delusion about being Eleanor Roosevelt, which none of the nurses really minded, because it made Mildred a great help on the ward, always volunteering for some project or other. The core group of patients never grew worse, never seemed to get better, and never asked when they could leave. The world wasn't going to open up for these people; it stayed stubbornly shut, an aperture that let in no outside light.

The same was true, in a way, for my family. We seemed separated from the world, at least the world as it revealed itself through the large rosewood radio that sat in the living room. The Depression touched the edges of our lives, fraying them, certainly, but leaving everyone intact. What I did learn about the world came largely from a source that had been available to me for years, but which I had never thought to consult. One morning, when I was twelve years old, with my mother in the kitchen downstairs and my father at the hospital across the lawn, I entered my father's study, mounted a rolling ladder that was attached to the floor-to-ceiling bookshelves, and brought down the copy of *Sexual Normality and Abnormality: Twelve Case Studies*.

What did I know about these matters? All morning I sat with the book heavy in my lap, struggling to make out the tiny type-face. I sat with legs crossed, chewing a piece of hair, shocked but caught up in the tide of words and their meanings. All winter my father kept the thermostat in his study at fifty-eight degrees, and I imagined that the temperature had to be kept so low or else the books might self-destruct. It was as though I were holding the original Gutenberg Bible in my hands, and that this room served as some special emergency vacuum in case of fire or apocalypse. But even if there was an apocalypse, these words would float over the wreckage of the world, so deep were they embedded in me, so deep already at twelve.

And all my father had done was drape a stethoscope around my neck. But somehow he had crowned me some twisted version of Miss America: Miss Toilet Mouth, Miss Disgusting Secrets, *Little* Miss Disgusting Secrets. I could hardly get through the week without dipping into my new fund of knowledge. Images scrolled by in pornographic frescoes, and I realized that I could have become rich in the playground of my day school, had I sold my classified information. Any single page torn from *Sexual Normality and Abnormality: Twelve Case Studies* would have fetched a good price at school, and since the volume was over five hundred pages long, my father would never have known the difference. But I couldn't tear anything out of that book; it would have been like ripping "Letters to the Romans" out of the Gutenberg Bible. Entire sections stayed in my mind, eventually memorized as thoroughly as the Pledge of Allegiance.

"Miss H.," began the case study on p. 348, "was born in a rural home in Norway to illiterate parents. Because she did not attend school, but instead worked the fields alongside her brothers, she had no official medical records. It was not until many years later, when she was working as a cook in the village of S— and was subsequently hospitalized for acute appendicitis at the regional clinic in that village, that physicians discovered the truth about Miss H. She was a rarity, a true hermaphrodite, equipped with both phallus and vagina, the former being no bigger than a pea pod, and the latter being equally undeveloped. The doctors at the clinic in S— allowed a small group of visiting medical students to view their patient's deformity, and she was thusly paid a wage to appear regularly at lectures at the medical college in nearby O——. Miss H.'s life, while spent alone, proved far more satisfying than the lives of other such individuals, many of whom attempt to join in sexual relations, and who find their advances rebuffed, often by a horrified individual who has just realized the True Nature of this creature.

Sometimes, the hermaphrodite can find a peaceful home among the denizens of a carny troupe or travelling sideshow."[1]

The story of Miss H. was as riveting as it was appalling; I could imagine the woman's wide Nordic face, and even, if I tried hard enough, her collision of sex organs. Sometimes I would forego the text entirely and just read the index, my finger skittering along the stunning list of words. Every body part was in this list, and every perverse activity; nothing was excluded. All the shameful words from the school bathroom walls were here, printed neatly on heavy-bond paper, not gouged into plaster by a twelve-year-old's erratic penknife. No janitor had tried to paint over them, to refinish the surface with some virginal gloss. No, these words were *actually meant to be understood.*

So this was my future, this world where people with contorted minds and bodies coupled blindly in assorted ways. I couldn't bear to believe it, yet I knew it was true. I knew it because of my parents, could see it in their eyes and their easy posture when they were together. My father was always touching my mother; there was rarely a moment when they were in the same room and their limbs did not lightly connect. Since my mother could not conceive, what they did in their bedroom was done for the pleasure of it. They were a good fit, my father with his red mustache and rimless glasses and thick arms, my mother with her black hair swept off her neck with a silver comb.

They had met and fallen in love one summer when both of their families were staying at a bungalow colony in the Catskills called Lustig's. My father, David Welner, was a young medical student at the time, which gave him a certain clout. Whenever anyone approached him that summer, he would cheerfully agree to listen to a litany of complaints, to inspect what someone called, under his breath, a "suspicious" mole. In reality, he had no clinical experience yet; at City College's medical school, his class was still enmeshed in the fundamentals of biology and chemistry, spending afternoons drawing diagrams of the Krebs Cycle, or becoming familiar with the respiratory systems of fish. When he lifted the ribbed undershirt of a sixty-year-old man on vacation and peered at a dark brown disk the size of a quarter, he was simply using a combination of common sense and bits of knowledge he had gathered from the weekly "Ask Dr. Colin Sylvester" columns in *The New York Herald.* But he charmed everyone, and no one was worse off for his diagnosis.

[1]Dr. Lucian Hargreaves, *Sexual Normality and Abnormality: Twelve Case Studies* (New York: Eppler and Keeney, 1919).

"Avoid the sun like the plague, Mrs. Kimmel," he told a woman with parchment skin. "Get some rest," he told a nervous young newlywed husband. All around the colony, men and women followed David Welner's instructions, lying in the shade for naps, swigging plenty of fresh water, eating roughage. Everyone was happy, mosquitoes dotted the surface of the lake, the summer slowly unrolled.

Toward the end of the season, my parents became engaged. My father had been chosen to judge the bungalow colony's annual beauty pageant. Of the twelve Brooklyn and Bronx girls who paraded along the dock, making their way across the scarred planks in their stiletto heels, my mother was the one he chose, hands down. At eighteen, Justine Fogel was tall, with a head of jet hair and high, impressive breasts. She was planning on studying voice in Manhattan in September. A neighbor knew of a vocal coach named Oskar Mennen who would instruct her once a week for a low fee. His slogan was "If *you've* got a sliding scale, I've got one, too."

But my mother never went to see Oskar Mennen. Instead, she married David Welner shortly after Labor Day, and the couple moved to a tenement apartment on Chrystie Street in Lower Manhattan. During the day, my father went to classes and my mother sat at home practicing scales; at night they cooked a plain dinner on their stove and went to bed. Sometimes in the middle of the night, he woke up and sat in the living room studying; she could see a tiny yellow bulb burning in the living room, and his silhouette curved in concentration under the light.

Slowly, my father became noticed in his classes. One day he attracted the attention of a visiting professor of psychiatry named Fox Mendelson, and over the years the two men kept up a correspondence. Later, when my father was looking for a position, Mendelson recommended him to the board of trustees at a private hospital called Mount Mohonk. The job paid poorly, but my father was willing. He was a Jew, and had noticed a distinct strain of anti-Semitism among psychiatrists, despite the fact that their god was a Jew himself. In the hospitals and clinics of New York City, he encountered psychiatrists with names like Warner Graves and Loren St. John, men with silver-threaded hair and deep, uninflected voices and degrees from Amherst and Harvard. What my father had going for himself was wit, dexterity, and the ability to leap from bed at four in the morning and subdue a schizophrenic who was smacking a nurse over the head with a cast-iron bedpan. He was handsome and didn't seem too ambitious, and he raised interesting points during grand rounds. At age thirty-two, he became the youngest chief psychiatrist in the brief and undistinguished history of Mount Mohonk Hospital for the Insane.

He and my mother inhabited the large house across the lawn from the hospital, taking as their bedroom the room that overlooked the road out front. It was almost possible for them to lie in their four-poster and imagine that they lived in a normal home, on a real street, like any other young couple. But at night, when the howling started, they remembered.

My father was a hit with the nurses and orderlies. He strode the shining halls of the hospital as though he had been running the place since birth. Even his memos were praised. ("Re: hospital gowns. It has come to my attention that the dung-colored gowns worn by our patients are perhaps no good for morale. Might we find something with a bit more dash—perhaps peach or sky-blue?")

My mother fell quickly, but less gracefully, into her role as the chief psychiatrist's wife. Before the Depression, her job largely entailed standing in the middle of her kitchen, conferring with a mute Negro hospital cook about upcoming dinner parties at the house. She would wave her pale hands vaguely, opening drawers and pointing to spoons and knives, saying, "Now, there are the spoons. Oh, and the knives." She was hesitant in this role; no one had ever waited on her before except her grandmother, who used to section her grapefruit for her with a serrated knife. But that was different. That was family. This was help. *Help;* the word itself was so strong, something you would call out when you were drowning. Her whole life seemed unrecognizable.

They were aimless, both of my parents, rolling around in this huge house together, anxious to populate the rooms with children. By the time I was born, they were ready, tired of seeing only mentally ill people, eager for an infant's simple and understandable cry. But when the obstetrician told my mother that she could bear no more children, my father let his only daughter into his life in a way that no one, not even his wife, had been allowed.

Every few months he took me on a whirlwind tour of the hospital: the dining room, which smelled perennially of fried flounder, the Occupational Therapy room, where dead-eyed patients pressed images of dogs and presidents onto copper sheeting, the solarium, the visitors' lounge. We breezed past doors with doctors' names stenciled onto the grain, and past doors with signs that read WARNING: ELECTRICITY IN USE. These doors were always shut, and I longed to see what electricity looked like when it was "in use." And I also longed to see where the patients actually lived, where they showered and dressed and bathed. But the wards themselves, with their heavy doors with chicken wire laced into the glass, were off-limits. I was allowed to see hospital life only from a distance, watching as patients slogged through the halls in their dung-colored gowns and flannel robes. I often stood staring at them, and once I made prolonged eye contact with an obese man whose face was blue with stubble, until I was whisked off into the nurses' lounge, where big band music emanated from the radio and I was given a handful of sourballs by a trio of fussing women. And then the tour was over.

Although I was allowed into the hospital only at my father's invitation, I was free to explore the grounds whenever I liked. With the sun sinking and the air aromatic with pine and earth and Salisbury steak, the whole place smelled like a summer camp. One day, at the rear entrance of the building, I saw delivery men unloading drums of institutional disinfectant. As they rolled them up a ramp and into the service entrance, I could read the words "Whispering Pines," and even though the name referred to nothing more than a rancid fluid that would be swabbed across the floors and walls at dawn, it sounded like a perfect alias for the hospital, the ideal name for a splendid summer camp.

Whispering Pines, I whispered to myself as I stepped into the thicket that continued until the edges of the grounds, where it was held back by the iron fence. Vines flourished along that fence, wound around the spokes like a cat winding around a human leg. Just as the patients often seemed to want out, so did the vegetation. Everything grew frantically at the farthest reaches of the property. The most tangible signs of the times could be found there, at the edges of the land, where nobody had bothered to prune or clip or chop away at the excess. Sometimes a group of patients would sit on Adirondack chairs on the lawn, taking in a chilly hour of sun, and sometimes a nurse would take a patient on a supervised stroll, but only along the circular path closest to the hospital, and never into the woods. The woods were mine, at least for a while.

The summer I turned fourteen, my father implemented a program he called "Tea at the House." This involved inviting a promising patient to join him and my mother for afternoon tea in our living room. The patient was always someone at least a little bit appealing, someone who wouldn't make any sudden moves. Someone very close to

269

health, who needed a bit of encouragement to topple him or her completely onto the other side.

The first person invited to Tea at the House was a woman named Grace Allenby, a young mother who had had a nervous breakdown and was unable to complete any action, even dressing herself in the morning, without dissolving into hysterical, gulping sobs. At the hospital she had made a slow but admirable recovery. She came to tea on Friday before her husband was to bring her home, and I sat watching at the top of the stairs. Both Mrs. Allenby and my mother were lovely-looking and uncertain, like the deer that occasionally made a wrong turn in the woods and wound up stunned and confused and frightened on the hospital lawn. The women shyly traded recipes, while my father sat between them, nodding with benevolence.

"What you want to do is *this*," Mrs. Allenby kept saying, and as she spoke, she blinked rapidly, as if to remove a speck from her eye. "You take an egg and you beat it very hard in a bowl with a whisk. Then what you want to do is *this* . . ." The living room smelled strong of Oolong tea, my father's favorite. He liked it because it was the closest thing to drinking pipe tobacco.

I eavesdropped on several Teas at the House over the year, and I came to understand that mental patients could be divided into two groups: those who wore their affliction outright like a bold political stance, and those who hid it so actively that that became their trademark, grinning until their teeth might splinter, wanting so badly to hold themselves together.

Warren Keyes was of the second variety. He was a nineteen-year-old Harvard undergraduate who had tried to kill himself in his dormitory room eight months earlier, and who was close to leaving Mount Mohonk to return to school. Over dinner, my parents discussed this boy, who would be coming to Tea at the House the following day. "He's young," my father said, "and good-looking, in that Harvard way."

Warren Keyes registered in my mind in that moment, was locked into place even before I had met him. Here was a Harvard man. That went over well with my father, who often fantasized about a privileged upbringing, complete with long walks along the Charles River and various racquet sports. And it went over well with me, too, for even before I met Warren Keyes, I had sculpted his features and his limbs into some crude rendering of attractiveness.

The next afternoon at four o'clock, Warren sat in the living room gripping the fragile handle of a teacup. He had trooped across the lawn with a squat nurse, who now sat in the foyer, dulling knitting like Madame Defarge. I knew that he had been invited to the house as a reward for getting well, but casting a critical, fourteen-year-old eye on him from the top of the stairs, even I could see that he was not well.

"Warren plans on returning to Harvard next semester," my father said. My mother hummed a response. "Leverett House, isn't it?" my father went on, he who had studied at City College, yet who knew the names of all the houses at Harvard. He, who had ascended to Chief of Psychiatry at Mount Mohonk and yet who was, irrevocably, a Jew.

"No, Adams House," said Warren. His voice was relaxed, although his cup jitterbugged in its saucer.

Conversation pushed on about Harvard in general, football season, and New England weather. My mother didn't add much, and my father kept plying Warren with questions, which he politely, if wearily, answered. At the end of the hour, Warren Keyes looked exhausted. I imagined that he would go back to his hospital bed and sleep for thirty-six hours straight, regaining his strength.

Breaking his own tradition but questioned by no one, Dr. Welner invited Warren Keyes back for a second Tea at the House, and then a third. On his fourth tea, he was unaccompanied by the dour-faced nurse. Instead, he made a solo flight across the lawn, his coattails floating out behind him. That afternoon, I had been strategically sitting on the porch doing my homework before taking a walk in the woods. My hair was sloppily bound up behind my head with elastic, and there was ink on my fingers, for I had not yet mastered the fountain pen. But even so, Warren Keyes climbed onto the porch and gave me a good hard look. Although it was not the first time I had seen Warren Keyes, it was the first time he saw me. "I'm the daughter," I said. He nodded. "They're inside," I told him, inclining my head toward the screen door. Deep in the house, the tea kettle shrilled.

"Do you like tea?" Warren asked. It was the kind of question that my father's colleagues often asked me when they came to dinner: well-meaning and uninteresting probings from people who had no idea of what to say to children, yet somehow, maddeningly, meant to be answered.

"I like it okay," I said.

"Your mother makes good tea," Warren said. "It's Chinese, you know."

I slid off the railing. "I have to go," I said.

His eyes widened slightly. "Where are you going?" he asked.

And for some reason, I told him. I told him where I went every afternoon; I practically drew him a treasure map with an X. Later, I sat in the woods reading *The Red Badge of Courage*, and suddenly there was a parting of branches. Warren Keyes came through, stooped and stumbling in. He had in his hand a familiar folded linen napkin with scalloped edges. He squatted down beside me, this handsome, ruined Harvard sophomore, and he opened the napkin, which contained three golden circles: my mother's Belgian butter cookies. I took them silently, and ate them just as silently, while Warren watched.

"So what's it like to live here?" he asked.

What it was like, I thought, was like anything else. Like going to the day school seven miles away. Like owning arms. I shrugged. How I wanted to ask him a similar question. What was it like to live *there*, inside a hospital for the insane? What was it like to be insane? Was it like a long and particularly vivid nightmare? Did you know you were insane? Did you long to crawl out of your body? Did you actually see things—shapes and animals and flames dancing across the walls of your room at night? But I couldn't bring myself to ask him anything at all. Light was draining from the patch of woods, and suddenly Warrren said, "May I ask you something?"

"Yes," I said.

"Could I maybe touch you?" the boy asked.

I nodded solemnly, really believing, in that moment, that he was referring to my hand, or my arm. He wanted to touch me to see if I was real, the way, years earlier, I myself had surreptitiously touched the bloodless face of my cousin's beloved china doll. He wanted to touch me in order to have the experience of touching someone who wasn't insane—someone who had a normal life and lived with her parents in a real house without bars on the windows. He wanted to touch me to see what I was like.

Warren came closer, sliding across the dirt floor to where I sat with my book. "I won't hurt you," he said.

"I know," I said. When his hand came down on one of my breasts, those recent arrivals, I could not have been more shocked. I did not know how to stop this, and I felt at once hurled out of my own realm and into his. "Now wait," I said, but his hands were already moving freely above my clothes. He seemed not to have heard me. He sat in front of me, touching my breasts, my neck, my shoulders, and in fact he wasn't hurting me. So what was I upset about? I didn't know what to call it, this thing he was doing, this casual exploration. It was his face

272

that frightened me—the intense and worshipful expression on his features, as though he were kneeling and lighting candles. His mouth hung open, his eyes were focused.

"I'm not hurting you," he kept repeating. "I'm not hurting you."

And all I could answer was, "No. You're not."

I closed my eyes so I wouldn't have to see his face. I closed them as if to block out a strong sunlight. I felt myself grow dizzy, but I thought it would be worse if I fainted, because who knew what would happen then? When I came to, I could never be sure of what had taken place. So I made myself stay conscious, and I felt each motion he made, the starfish movements of his fingers as they slipped beneath my blouse and headed downward. I knew the names of all the parts he was touching, and in my panic I recited them under my breath. His hands toured a living index from the back of my father's book, and as they did, I summoned up all the words I knew. But what good did it do me to know these things, to know what they meant when I couldn't even *manage* them?

He moved against me as if in a trance, and I felt like a wall, something for others to rub against; I was a cat-scratching post, a solid block. I felt his large hand inside my underwear, so out of place, so wrong. The elastic waistband with its row of rosettes was pulled taut against his knuckles. Just that morning I had chosen the underwear from a drawer, where it lay with the others, ironed, white, floral, and touched only by me and by Estella, who did our family's laundry. No one else was meant to touch it. Warren's hand was trapped inside, like an animal that had run into a tent and was now caught. It seemed there against its will, if that were possible, if hands had a will of their own.

Now one of Warren's fingers was separating itself from the others and pushing into me, sliding up into my body. I felt a shiver of pain, and then something that wasn't pain at all, but surprise. I sat straight up, and started to cry. His big finger which had held on to my mother's teacup, which probably wore a Harvard ring sometimes, which had a flat fingernail that he trimmed in his cubicle in the hospital for the insane, if they let him have nail scissors, was deeply embedded in me, like something drilled into the ground to test for water or crude oil. Like a machine, a spike, testing the earth for vibrations or for moisture. The finger felt all these things, but I felt nothing.

After some endless time, Warren Keyes made a small sound like a lamb bleating or a hinge groaning open, and I knew that it was over. I sank back onto the surface of leaves, my body returning to itself: small, flexible, a skater's body, while Warren turned away from me, wiping his face and the front of his trousers with my mother's napkin.

In a gentle, quaking voice, he told me it was better if we left the woods separately and, of course, if I told no one about what had happened. "There's nothing to tell, anyway," he added. "I didn't hurt you." And it was true; he hadn't hurt me.

I left first, walking slowly with a book in hand as though nothing had happened, like a dreamy teenage girl leaving an afternoon of reading, but when I reached the edge of the woods, where the lawn began, I broke into a run toward the lights of my parents' house. Inside, I walked straight up the stairs, claiming I was ill and didn't want dinner. My mother pressed a cool hand to my forehead, but I shrugged it off. There would be no more touching today; even the back of a familiar hand, prospecting for fever, was too much.

That night, before going to sleep, I pushed up the window by the bed and poked my head out. From the hospital across the lawn, I heard the familiar crying and baying, and without thinking, I opened my mouth and softly joined the chorus. The sound came naturally, and I hung out that window in the warm spring night, howling quietly in a low, effortless voice, as though I had been doing it since I was born, as though it was natural to my species.

Weeks passed, and I noticed my shift in feeling almost as though I were charting the progress of a bruise, watching it go from black to blue to brown to yellow, until finally it was only a smudge, a small trace memory. I didn't understand whether what had happened was something that Warren Keyes had actually wanted to have happen, or whether he had been unable to stop himself because he was, as the name of the hospital announced, insane. Should I have felt furious, or should I have felt compassion, as my father would have? I was lost, not knowing, and after a while it became too late to ask anyone. Time separated me from the memory, and other things rose to replace it—real things, much more important than a young man touching a girl in the woods of a mental hospital in the mountains of New York State.

Arching over everything was the war in Europe. It had come into our lives through the rosewood cabinet that my father kept in the living room beneath a Winslow Homer print, and now during dinner parties, when the meal was through, my father and his colleagues gathered around it. The maid moved through the rooms emptying ashtrays, while the doctors' wives sat quietly, sipping brandy and looking concerned, and the men out-shouted the broadcast with a running commentary of their own. They argued about invasions and strategies, and I was confused. How much would the war in Europe affect any of us? After all, the Depression had touched only the edges of our lives. The hospital had far fewer patients and a much smaller staff than it once had, but it still stayed intact, a neutral duchy in the middle of a rapidly dividing world. I decided that a war on another continent could not really touch anybody here, not these psychiatrists with their identical little mustaches, or these wives who sat listening to the barbershop quartet of male voices around them, or even me. For a while I was actually able to sustain this feeling; for a while I hung suspended in it.

But then eventually we were in the war, too; *we,* my father had said, and the word referred to some of the hospital's staff. Dr. Rogovin, Dr. Sammler, young Dr. Herd, and several of the orderlies had all enlisted. Nurses, too, left that winter to work for the Red Cross. Whispering Pines had actually gone to war.

Then one night at dinner late that January, my father slipped a letter from his breast pocket. It was written on Harvard stationery. "You remember Warren Keyes," my father said to my mother. "That Harvard boy." When I heard this my hand sent a butter knife involuntarily crashing against a glass. After the chime subsided, my father began to read the letter aloud:

> Dear Dr. Welner,
> I hope you still remember me. You helped me a great deal not too long ago, and after leaving the hospital I returned to school where I gave my attention to Classics and found great pleasure in my work. Last year I took first prize here for my translations of Catullus. I wanted to let you know that I have enlisted in the Navy, and, despite my psychiatric record, have been accepted. Before I go overseas, I thought I should write you a short note to thank you for everything you have done. My regards to your wife.
> Respectfully,
> Warren Keyes

I sat very still at the table while my father finished reading. As he held the page up toward the light, I could see the silhouette of a small, perfect crimson seal shining through.

Nominated by Joyce Carol Oates

AUTUMNAL

by MARK IRWIN

from DENVER QUARTERLY

The saffron-colored leaves are cresting into their moment. It's
the impinging lateness of things that's scary. Rusting,
rushing leaves now astonish, omitting what
they began to say. I saw people standing
in a circle on a hill, and the youthfulness of bodies
slowly began to separate toward soul. Perhaps forgetfulness
is a way of cleansing the fear. I saw a woman
with yellow hands and red lips weave
through the circle. She spoke but one word and they
loved her. Their names were leaves in no
hurry. Her lips were the world's cherry. They said
"Stop," then "Go faster," while the grapes' purpling scent
pierced the air and each brick of the old house
seemed an impossible slowly melting hour. I saw
the kite in the air. "The wind must be greater than the weight
of the string and its body." —Clouds. Sun illumined
their marrow. The slow furiousness of leaves
blew at our feet. "Give it some string," he said, "and feel
how strong the pull." The man carried the kite
home. The leaves are nothing but words. How wonderful
it is to be here. And because we are not gone, still we are early.

Nominated by John Drury, David St. John, Bin Ramke

BODYSURFING

fiction by RICHARD BURGIN

from WITNESS

THERE WAS A RUSTLING, then Lee saw it, fat and gray and big-eyed with an orange crown as it slid across the path. They were going to have the last laugh—the iguanas—that was for sure. There were so many of them Costa Rica was going to be their world some day. The path ended and the boogey board banged against his knee. He swore out loud as he began walking down the road. It was madness, sheer madness to have rented the board. He knew that within two minutes, he knew that when he reached the first wave. There was the wave and his body and nothing ever should come between them, that alone should be pure. Sheer lunacy to think otherwise. He looked at it— baby blue with a dangling wrist strap like an umbilical cord, this "boogey board" with its silly name—it was idiocy in its purest form to let it ruin his rides, bang about in the wind and hit his knee. Why had he done it, why? It was because he'd remembered his wife saying that they were so much fun. Years ago she'd said that, he had a distant memory of it. It was that and the surfboard morons who were taking over the ocean, crowding him out of his space. He'd let them intimidate him, let them infantilize him into thinking he should maybe get some kind of board of his own, so when he left the beach and saw it in the store he'd rented it on an impulse.

It was the same store that was in front of him now, the Palm Store, a combination travel agency and gift shop run by a good-looking man and his wife with a yellow-haired kid who didn't look like either of them, particularly not the man. So he would return it now, eleven minutes after he took it. Of course he wouldn't ask for his money back. He would take responsibility. They would wonder why, perhaps ask him why, but he wouldn't let himself worry about it. He was about to lose his job in two weeks, to be transferred to a lower job in the bank in a different city, to be screwed over like that at his age, and with his mother at death's door too, no, he wasn't going to worry about returning a boogey board to a store that looked like it was made out of cards, with its pathetically corny painting of a sun sinking below the waves, a store that rented surfboards and goggles and boogey boards and tickets for turtle tours!

He went inside The Palm Store. A tall good-looking blond man, a surfboardoron, perhaps two inches taller than he was, perhaps a dozen years younger, perhaps with fourteen better defined muscles than he had, had finished talking to the owner and was fingering a surfboard as Lee placed the boogey board beside it. He is going to ask me how I liked the boogey board, Lee thought, he is going to try to have a conversation with me. The blond man turned toward Lee. He is from California, Lee thought. "How did it ride?" the blond man said.

"How did it ride: *It* didn't ride at all. I didn't have any use for it."

"Surf too strong today?"

"Board too superfluous today, or any day."

"OK. I hear you."

Lee was struck by how straight the surfer's teeth were, which perhaps accounted for the extraordinary hang-time of his smile.

"I don't like anything to come between me and the wave, me and the water. I think that relationship ought to stay pure. Today I violated that relationship, I'm sorry to say. Today I let myself be conquered by a product and I corrupted that relationship."

The blond man's smile vanished and Lee felt vindicated.

"I don't think I get what you mean."

"These boards," Lee said, indicating the blond man's surfboard with his gesture, "they're just another way people've found to make money off the water. They're about buying and selling, that's all."

The blond man showed a second smile, a quizzical but still friendly one. "I guess I don't see it that way," he said.

"Really? How do you see it, then?"

"They're just a piece of equipment for a sport, they're just a means to an end. Like you can't play baseball without a bat or football without a ball, can you?"

278

Lee felt an adrenaline rush. Apparently the man really wanted to discuss this. "There was a time when you could play sports without buying things," Lee said. "To me, the more a sport costs the less its value. The more it's about buying these accessories, the more of a fetish it becomes instead of a sport. By the way, I hope I didn't desecrate the flag, so to speak, with my remarks about surfboards. I know you guys get sensitive about that."

"No, man, I don't mind. I just never met anyone who thinks like you. It's kind of interesting, really."

Lee felt flattered in spite of himself. Ridiculous to feel that in this situation, though he did for a moment, and thought he should soften himself. Besides he was beginning to get an idea and he needed time to figure it all out. Just before he spoke he made a point of looking at the surfer's eyes.

"And by the way I know whereof I speak," Lee said. "I'm a banker. You can't be much more of a whore than that. My whole life is buying and selling. I'm in middle management at Citibank. Need I say more? Or I soon will be. I was actually at a somewhat higher level of management but that's like bragging about being in a higher circle of hell, isn't it? But at least on my vacation I want to stay pure when I'm in the water. I said to my secretary, 'I don't care what kind of hotel you get me (and she got me Le Jardin del Eden, the most expensive one in Tamarindo), but I insist on big, world-class waves. I want you to research that for me.' Well, the waves here are certainly world class and they deserve the best from me."

Lee looked at the man closely, who in turn appeared to be concentrating intensely on what he said. "So, I'm on my way now. I'm going to have my twilight drink, and again, I hope I haven't offended you at all."

"No way, I enjoyed talking with you. You're the first American I've spoken to in three days. I don't speak Spanish so I've practically been talking to myself since I've been here."

Lee looked at him closely once more, wondering if he were gay or just needy, or perhaps one of those friendly, New Age types. He had decided something important, something definitive in the waves yesterday, but this young man might make it even better. Besides he was a surfer and that would make him the cherry on the sundae and his possible gayness would never enter into it.

"I've enjoyed it too," Lee said. "Hey, you know the restaurant, Zullymar?"

279

"Sure."

"That's where I'm going for my drink. Why don't you join me and have one on the bank?"

The blond man laughed and extending his hand, said, "Sure. My name's Andy."

"I'm Lee Bank or should I say Le Bank, and we all know what shape banks are in."

Lee turned and walked out of the store and Andy followed after him laughing.

"Is Bank really your last name?"

"I'm sometimes known as Lee Bastard or when I'm in Paris as Le Bastard. But we are far from Paris now, aren't we?"

Lee looked straight ahead as they walked down the dirt road and seemed unaware that Andy was walking beside him. It was not much of a road, Lee thought, full of holes and rocks and puddles so they could have, should have left it alone and not put up so many toy-like stores. Laughable really how small they were—the little shack that probably doubled as someone's home—with the giant sign saying Nachos and Ice Cream, a sign that was half as big as the shack. Pathetic really, the hut beside it called Jungle Bus that advertised Killer Burger and Munchies. If it rose a couple of inches, the puddle on the road in front could swallow it.

Zullymar was on the other side of the road, facing the Jungle Bus on one side and the beach on the other. It was a big (by Tamarindo standards) open-air restaurant and bar filled with surfers, the same crowd that forced him off his path two days in a row in the water and actually made him yearn for a lifeguard to patrol things. A wall mural that clashed with the red floor depicted a pink pelican, circling over some anchored boats and a small island beyond that—the approximate scene outside. Across the street at another bar, a man was playing the marimba with two little boys.

Lee and Andy sat down at a table facing the water and looked briefly at the half-filled room. As soon as they focused on each other Lee said, "You'll want a beer, won't you? Isn't that the drink you guys favor?" He had a tight semi-sarcastic smile and Andy smiled back.

"You surfers, you surf wizards. You don't want to drink anything too hard, anything that might put you at risk when you go out on your boards again."

"I'm done surfing for the day and I drink lots of things. No routine."

"Fine, dos Mai tais," Lee said to the waiter.

The incredulous smile reappeared on Andy's face. Lee was going to say something to try to get rid of it but Andy spoke first.

"You've got some negative feelings toward surfers, don't you?"

Lee shrugged. "What did they do to you, man?" Andy said, half-laughing, his hand absently caressing his board for a moment, Lee noticed, as if he really thought the goddamn thing was alive. "Did they run into you once or something?"

"No, that would never happen, though they have crowded me out more than once here in Tamarindo, kept me from where I wanted to go, but believe me I stick to my own path. I don't mingle. I am not only on a different path from them, I'm in a different world."

"But what's so different about your world?"

"Night and day, Andy. Night and day."

"Why, what do you do? You bodysurf, right? I respect that. So I get up on a board and you bodysurf. Have you ever surfed?"

"I do surf."

"I mean with a board."

"Years ago when I was actually young."

"So what do you have against it?"

The drinks came. Andy took a big swallow while Lee let his sit.

"It's about buying and selling again. Kids see it on TV in ads and think 'that's it.' Then they make movies about it and create a surfing tour and sell all this equipment, all these fetishes and the young guys think 'if I do this I'll be a man, if I do this I'll get some first-class pussy. It will all happen if I can just buy the right board.'"

Andy was laughing now. He was not an easy man to offend, Lee concluded, as he sipped his drink.

"I'm not agreeing with you, by the way," Andy said. "I just think what you're saying is funny and interesting in a way."

"Of course you think that surfboarding is the greater sport, the greater challenge, don't you? After all, you stand up, you are Homo Erectus, whereas I am still on all fours. You go out further to sea whereas I am nearer the shore. You walk on water like Jesus Christ whereas I only ride with it like a fish. And then when gravity must eventually bring you down you take the deeper, more heroic fall. You think all those things, don't you?"

"I just enjoy surfing. I haven't thought it out like that really. And like I say, I respect what you do."

"I wonder if you know what I do. Because there are a number of bodysurfers out there—it isn't just me—and very few of them know

281

when or how to jump, and once they do jump how to go with the wave. They almost always start too late."

"I probably wouldn't know, man," Andy said. "Isn't that the way it is with everything? We don't really understand the other person's thing or point of view."

"Dos Mai tais," Lee said, catching the waiter's attention, although he had not yet made significant progress on his first drink.

"So, now tell me your story, Andy. What brings you to glorious Tamarindo?"

Andy looked flustered, ran his fingers twice through his longish blond hair. He could be Kato Kaelin's younger brother, Lee thought.

"I just came here to surf."

"From whence did you come then?"

"Santa Cruz, in California."

Lee smiled tightly again. "This is your vacation then. You came to Tamarindo directly on your vacation?"

"Not exactly. I was in Monteverde first. I went to Costa Rica directly, but I went to Monteverde first, you know, in the mountains."

"Then you are a mountain man, too."

Andy lowered his head a little. Lee couldn't tell if he were burying his smile or giving birth to a new one. In Tamarindo smiles were the iguanas on every surfer's face. Lee distrusted smiles in general because he had discovered that if you believed in them a time would come when that belief would hurt you. He remembered he had once been very moved by his wife's smile.

"So how were the mountains?" he finally said.

"Some bad stuff happened there, so I came here earlier than I expected."

"I'm sorry to learn that. What exactly was the bad stuff?"

The waiter came with the new drinks and Andy took a big swallow as the waiter took his first glass, while Lee carefully placed his second glass next to his first (which was still almost three-quarters full) as if he were positioning two bowling pins.

"The woman I was with went bad on me. She met a dude on the tour we took in the cloud forest. He was older than me, around your age I guess, and he had a lot more money than me, you know, I was never very good at making money. I just help run a little Xerox store. But this rich guy was a businessman, a big businessman, though he was in the same hotel as us, only he was in some luxury suite. Anyway, she told me she was sorry, she said she didn't plan it that way, that it was a one-in-a-million thing, but she thought he was the man for her and she was going to go with him for the rest of her vacation and beyond. So . . ."

"So what could you do?"

"Just got drunk. Woke up alone the next morning and got in my Suzuki and came down here 'cause they said this was where the surf was, and they didn't lie about that. The last couple of days I took it out in the waves, six, seven hours a day and just flushed that bitch right out. It hurt though, I'll tell you. So when you talk about money corrupting things I really hear you."

"And when you talk about women being bitches I hear you. I lost my sense of smell from a woman once."

"How'd that happen?" Andy's incredulous smile had sneaked back, Lee noted, as if it were taking a curtain call.

"I discovered my female friend had cheated on me and I got extremely ill in an odd way. I developed a sinus condition that's never really gone away. I think it was my ex-wife who did me wrong, though it might have been someone else before her. Over the years people tend to blur together, don't they? Anyway I have very little to do with women now. The only woman in my life besides Mother Sea is my secretary and she's far too valuable to bother having sex with. I am completely dependent on her. It was she who arranged this trip for me. Of course I'll lose her when I'm transferred to my next job but that's the way it is with women, we always lose them. They were put here on earth so we would know what losing is. Even when we have them we lose them—did you ever think about that?"

"What do you mean?"

"We watch them lose their looks, their charm, their ability to have children, their sex. We lose our mothers, too, and then our wives become our mothers and we lose them again. We lose our mothers a second time."

"But men age too," Andy said.

"But we don't notice it as much since we don't desire men, do we? Anyway, you don't have to worry about all this now. It'll be years before you'll have to realize this."

"I realize it, I realize some of it now."

"Then you might consider giving them up as I have. You can get a greater high than the orgasm from bodysurfing, at least you can the way I bodysurf."

Andy looked away morosely. Lee waited a minute. There was a rustling sound in the restaurant as if the waiters were really iguanas. Lee couldn't stand hearing it so he spoke. "Thinking about her?"

"Yah."

"How long were you two an item?"

"Just a couple of months but . . ."

"Impact can be made in a couple of months. Impact can be made in a minute if we allow it to happen. I understand."

"Yah, I thought this one would work out. I had hopes . . ."

"Ah, hopes," Lee said, gesturing vaguely toward the sea. "Listen, I have an idea for you, a proposal to make you . It does not involve 'hope' but something better. It involves a challenge."

"Go on."

"Something very special happened to me yesterday. Do you know that inlet that separates our beach from the other one, the one that goes straight to the mountains?"

"Yes."

"Have you ever been on that other beach?"

"No. No one surfs over there so I just assumed there wasn't much there."

"That's precisely the point. The beach goes on for miles but because there's no access from the road, because there is a thick jungle of trees to walk through and no other way to reach it unless you swim across the inlet, there is almost no one there. Well, yesterday I swam across that inlet. It was sunset, a little earlier than now and the swim wasn't easy but I found the beach deserted and astonishingly beautiful. There were no footprints on the sand, just swerving lines of hermit crabs and the twisted branches from trees. I don't think there were even any butterflies, it wasn't civilized enough for them. It was like being on the moon or on a new planet. The waves were enormous and there was no one around to get in my way. My path was totally clear. Why don't you go there with me now and bodysurf with me? Leave your board at your hotel room and just go there with me now. I know you've only known me thirty minutes or whatever it's been. I know it's getting dark and it's a little dangerous."

"It's not that dangerous. I could do that."

"Fine, marvelous. Here, why don't you have my other drink, I haven't touched it, and I'll finish my first one and then we'll go out together and meet the waves with our bodies alone. I promise you it will be extraordinary."

"Yah, OK," Andy said, looking Lee straight in the eye. "I'll go with you. I'm open to it."

They finished their drinks quickly and Lee paid the bill. The moment he put the money in the waiter's hand he saw the sun slip below the water. Some people were watching it in the restaurant and beyond them others watched from the beach. It was an understandable ritual, Lee thought. It had been advertised, like a Citibank card, and people needed to see the promise delivered. In her condominium in Florida, his mother was probably watching it too from her wheelchair, perhaps with one of her nurses. She more than anyone believed in advertised beauty. All her life she believed in Jackie Kennedy and Marilyn Monroe and Marlon Brando and Holiday Inns and sunsets. It would not do any good to tell her the deeper beauty came after the sunset, came with the night when the whole world slid below water. She had never listened to him. They should have switched positions. She should have worked for Citibank and he should have been the cripple. He might have done well in a chair . . .

There were only occasional street lamps outside but he could see the night was thick with moths. They were not talking now, so he could hear another iguana slide past in front of him. Then he decided it wouldn't have mattered if they were talking, he would have heard it anyway. In Tamarindo every sound on earth was an iguana, you could only escape them in the water.

"There's your hotel," Lee said, pointing to the Diria, barely bigger than the travel agency it seemed. "Why don't you drop your board off here. You won't be needing it. It'll only get in the way."

"OK," Andy said softly. He walked off in the dark and Lee waited in the road, thinking he should have told him 'go put your dick away there too. That's what your board really is. You won't be needing it where we're going. There aren't any dicks in the ocean, not in the night ocean.'

Andy came back. Lee had never really considered that he wouldn't.

"Let's go," Lee said. There were about fifty yards of road before they reached the path that led to the beach. It will be a bakery of iguanas, Lee thought, but they would be left in their ovens.

The deep orange of the sky had passed. It was now a dark purple and silver, tinged with spots of fading pink. There were not many people on the beach and most of them were leaving. Except for the white of the waves, the ocean was dark.

285

"It gets dark quickly," Andy said.

"Drops like a plank," Lee said. He is very young, Lee thought, and his fear is showing. Lee thought of himself as a thousand years old. This will be good for him. He needs to put on a hundred years. Then he didn't think about him anymore.

They walked the length of the beach toward the inlet. Andy was talking about the girl who had dumped him, whose name was Dawn.

"Forget the girl," Lee said. "Drown her in the ocean."

When they reached the inlet the sky was nearly black. There were lots of stars out and three-quarters of a moon.

"I was hoping it'd be low tide so we could walk across," Andy said.

"We can swim it," Lee said. He threw the towel he'd been carrying into the sky and the black swallowed it.

"What did you just do?"

"I threw my towel away. I won't be needing it. It's a hotel towel."

"Yah, you told me about your hotel. Very impressive. It's supposed to be the best hotel in Tamarindo." There was sarcasm, even a trace of contempt in Andy's voice that stung Lee for a second.

"The hotel can drop dead, " Lee said as he walked into the water. He was surprised again by how wide the inlet was but he didn't feel tired this time while he was swimming. He could hear Andy breathing heavily, almost gasping, as he swam beside him and thought for a moment that he shouldn't have let him drink three Mai tais.

"Stop racing," he said, nearly yelling. "Stop trying to beat me. It's not a race. You have to pace yourself."

Andy slowed down the rest of the way. When they reached the shore of the deserted beach there were only a few slivers of sky that weren't black.

"I wish it were lighter, man," Andy said.

"Why?"

"I can't see the things you said would be here. I can't see the things you promised."

"Yes, you can. Look harder."

"I can barely see in front of myself."

"I can look at anything and see the beauty in it. Especially the dark."

"Tell me what I was supposed to see here again, and walk slower, will you. I can barely keep up with you."

"Twisted tree branches and hermit crab lines," Lee said.

Lee walked briskly, saying nothing for the next few minutes. Andy ran after him, stumbling occasionally, trying to keep up with him or at least keep him in sight, feeling like he did when he was a child trying to keep up with his father's longer, relentless stride.

"Come on, we're going in the water. It's time to face the black water now."

Lee walked toward the ocean in fast imperious strides like a fixated scoutmaster.

"Slow down, will you? Why are you racing?" Andy said and then repeated himself, yelling this time because the ocean was so loud he felt he wasn't being heard.

Lee kept walking into the water without changing his speed, the big blustery businessman from the fancy hotel who had to know it all, who had to take what he wanted when he wanted it. Why had he listened to him, why had he come with him to this crazy beach? He was chasing after him in the water now while his legs felt like rubber. The water was up to his knees and he knew something was wrong, had known it for some time.

"Lee," he yelled. "Lee. Lee Bastard."

A few seconds before he'd seen him fifteen yards ahead, propelling himself forward, not even ducking for the waves but somehow willing himself forward like a man walking into a wall, into the earth, until the water covered him. Andy heard himself scream. It might have been "Lee," it might have been "help." His legs wouldn't move at first and when they could he knew he wouldn't move them because he'd already known Lee wanted to be witnessed while he disappeared by a sucker like himself, just as Dawn did, and one of those humiliations was enough. Lee Legend gets back at a surfer. "Lee," he screamed, "Lee Bastard," knowing he would see and hear nothing now except the constant roar in the black and his own sickly voice boomeranging back at him like spit in the wind because the bastard had wanted it this way.

Nominated by Elizabeth Inness-Brown, Josip Novakovich

TWO JOURNEYS

essay by PHILIP LEVINE

from MICHIGAN QUARTERLY REVIEW

Is what follows a fiction by Balzac? It would seem unlikely, for there is no one standing out in the dark on a rain-swept night as a carriage pulled by six gray horses splashes down the Boulevard Raspail on the way to the apartment of that singularly beautiful woman, Madame La Pointe, although it does involve a beautiful and singularly gifted woman. Is it a fiction at all? That is a harder question to deal with. If Norman Mailer had written it and its central character were a novelist living in Brooklyn, the author of an astonishingly successful first book called *the Naked and the Dead,* a man deeply immersed in an ongoing depiction of the CIA, he would describe it as a fiction, and he would most likely name the central character Norman Mailer. One of my central characters is named Philip Levine, he is a poet from Detroit, he lives mainly in Fresno, California, where he has an awful job teaching too many courses in freshman comp at the local college, and on this particular summer day he is traveling with two fellow poets by train to give a reading almost no one will attend. It is twenty years ago, he is in his fiftieth year, as I was then, and though I cannot call it a fiction, I will begin now to fictionalize this tale.

I will say the local railway has a reputation for first-rate service, they are never more than a few minutes late even in the worst weather, and on this day the weather is a delight; blue sky with a few puffy clouds overhead as the poets head for the provincial town where their reading, though almost entirely unadvertised, will become the event of that summer's cultural history, a history that will never be written except for the present effort, which since it may be a fiction may not be a history at all. Shall I say that the events I am about to recount are as true

288

as an old man's memory allows them to be? No, that would not be true, for I am about to give the other two poets fictional names and disguise them so as to protect them. Protect them from what or from whom? Neither does anything to be ashamed of; indeed both behave with marvelous integrity. I will protect them from me, that untrustworthy poet who might alchemize them into former production line workers or assemblers of universal joints and thus ennoble them to a degree that would appall both them and you. I will remain Philip Levine, 49 years old, six months from my seventh book of poetry, *The Names of the Lost,* and my first terrible reviews by that great friend to poetry, the *New York Times.* The other two poets I will give fictional names. The man, just approaching middle age, is slender, taller than I, and though still in his thirties his hair is beginning to go gray, but he is far more youthful and youthful-looking than I, and unlike me he dresses with good taste. His name, Gabriel Sienna. The woman is even younger; she is fair-haired, delicately constructed, and in the soft light falling into our car very beautiful—I shall call her Elaine Langer— though she cannot be much over thirty her poems have already begun to attract enormous attention.

I am pleased to be here with these two who I am beginning to like far more than I expected. Sienna, I had heard was something of a dandy and a political conservative, but for the past several days I have observed him treating working class people—waiters, maids, cab drivers, cops, train conductors—with a grace and regard that I immediately recognized was part of his democratic nature. Elaine had been a mystery to me. I had met her only twice before when we'd read together in New York City and Iowa, and both times she had insisted on referring to me as the star. To me a star was Marlon Brando or Willie Mays, so I had assumed—incorrectly—that she was either ditzy or sucking up to me in the hope I might advance her career, but it was now clear to me that she was not so stupid as to think I was endowed to advance anyone's career, even my own. In the few days we'd been traveling together it had become clear that she was neither ditzy nor a careerist: she was simply a shy woman. That she had not the least interest in me or Sienna as sexual or romantic beings was clear from the moment we'd assembled in the capital, for she was mad about a very handsome, stylishly dressed young man who sat sleeping across the aisle from the three of us, perhaps exhausted by the previous night.

To our mutual delight Sienna and I had discovered that before this trip we had both been rereading *The Prelude* by Wordsworth and finding it both awesome and inspiring. For me this was largely unexpected, for I had not read the entire poem since my undergraduate days when my professor had forced a class of a dozen students to race through it in less than a week and to keep our eyes open for the key passages which might indicate its deeper themes. Rereading the poem in my own sweet time I discovered the majesty of passage after passage, which reaffirmed my belief in this art I seemed to be giving my life to. Elaine broke in at one point to express her astonishment that two active poets would spend so much of their summers on so dated a text and would both feel the experience had fueled their own work. She was not in the least critical. To the contrary; she was utterly charmed and vowed that when these readings were over and she was home she would sit down with Wordsworth and Keats (who had been the topic of the previous day's train conversation) and discover for herself these treasures. Here the fiction or the history or the poem—for as Edwin Muir has reminded us, "the poet's first allegiance is to imaginative truth" and "if he is to serve mankind that is the only way he can do it"—grows crucial, for one of us, Sienna or I, asks where she had received her education in poetry. (For the purposes of this "history" I will invent a university and place it in Peoria, the University of Ambition, famous for its dedication to the arts, often referred to as "the Athens of Central Illinois.") Elaine answers, "U of A," and Sienna then inquires if she had not been obliged to read the great Romantics. At this point tears well up in her eyes, and it is clear that some memory just come upon her is devastatingly painful. The three of us are silent for several minutes.

Elaine wipes her eyes with the back of her hand; she does not cry. She begins a slow explanation: she had gone to the university with the express purpose of becoming a poet. She was some years older than the other entering students having done "other things" after finishing high school, and one of the other things was to try to become a writer on her own, chiefly a writer of poetry. She knew no one in her New Jersey town who wrote poetry so she had to go it alone and discover what she could. In the local library and in New York City bookstores she happened upon three kindred spirits: Louise Bogan, James Wright, and Theodore Roethke, but she was sure there were many others and hence her enrollment at U of A. Her entrance scores were good enough to allow her into poetry writing and a "period course" in the Romantic poets, courses usually reserved for juniors and seniors. "So you've read Keats and Wordsworth," I say, "and you've been sit-

ting here for two days listening to us mis-describe their great poems."
Once again I had it wrong. While they were still on Blake and what her
teacher termed "the Pre-Romantic poets," he had asked her to visit his
office so that they might discuss her Blake paper. And she laughs, her
face full of lively animation as well as sorrow. They never got to her pa-
per. Tweedy Professor X put down his unlighted pipe and launched
into a spiel about the evils of nursing an unacted desire, both his and
hers, for he was quite sure they felt *that way* about each other. The
lust of the goat, he assured her, is the bounty of God and one law for
the lion and ox is oppression (he didn't say which one he was); he
placed a long-fingered hairless hand on her knee. "Long fingered and
hairless," she repeats, "I will remember that hand for as long as I live."
She felt the sweat leap from her pores, and for a moment she thought
she would faint. "What did you do?" asks Sienna. "I just got out of
there." She dropped the course.

Elaine goes on to explain that it was actually more serious than it
sounded in the telling, for she began for the first time in her life to
doubt the value of poetry, to doubt the whole enterprise. This of
course was noticed by her poetry-writing instructor, a short, balding
man much impressed with his own wit and vitality. He required the
students to turn in poems written according to strict formal demands.
He had lavishly praised her first two attempts, ten heroic couplets and
a Petrarchan sonnet, which were followed by no villanelle, no pan-
toum, no narrative in blank verse. Professor Y, or Mac, as he insisted
his students call him, asked Elaine to stay after class on their sixth
meeting. When the other students departed, he closed the classroom
door, turned suddenly toward her, and literally shouted, "What the
fuck is going on?" He began a long rap on the theme of her special gifts
and his generosity in allowing her into the class in the first place. Be-
fore she could begin to describe her own problem, he launched into a
tirade on the need for these beginners to follow the proper path, the
path their elders had followed, the path that had produced such giants
as Nemerov and Justice. She tried to assure him that her situation had
nothing to do with the ongoing quarrels over formalism and free verse.
"You have the talent to become a published poet within a year, and I
have the clout to see you are published. I've done it for others." And
then he began to rattle off the poets he'd "made," a word he used be-
fore each woman's name. His hands were short and plump; they
looked as though they'd never picked up anything heavier than a
check, and he placed one on her shoulder and began to slide it down

toward her left breast when she rose and called him a "fat pig." She dropped out of the university that afternoon. "I'd had such hopes for the place," she says and goes on to describe her bus ride to Chicago, her confusing hours there, wondering if she'd done the right thing, and then the even longer lonely trip back to New Jersey. She spent the year as an office worker for a textbook publisher in New York City commuting from her parents' place.

"When did you get back to poetry?" Sienna asks. Within a month or so she realized she could not let herself be scarred by those two creeps; poetry was something she had to write, if only for herself. "It's a long story," she says, "but I had the good fortune to discover through a course at the 92nd Street Y a true mentor, also a man, but one who cared about me as a person as well as my work." Her lover, Daniel, has awakened across the aisle and is stretching himself. The train is drawing through the green suburbs of our destination; we pass tennis courts, most of them in use, a small white church, and then enter a darkened tunnel only to emerge into the terminal. We rise and that conversation comes to an end forever as Daniel struggles with the two huge suitcases loaded with the clothes, makeup, and tchotchkes of this small and determined woman.

Is the fiction you've just heard true? If Aristotle in the *Poetics* is right then it is truer than history, or to quote Edwin Muir again, it is "a symbolic stage on which the drama of human life can play itself out." Let me ask a more essential question: Is it of any use? Does it contain any nuggets of wisdom you can take with you on the long voyage toward a life in poetry, or if you would prefer, a life without poetry? Poetry itself we know is of use. How do we know such a thing, stated so finally by me as a fact that might sit beside such assertions as "all men are mortal," or "Michael Jordan wears Nikes"? I could answer as Keats would have, that I have tested it on my pulse and felt that pulse surge—a fact—and I knew that I was alive to a degree rare in my experience. Or as the contemporary poet Jane Cooper has written, "Poetry can be *useful* in providing us with a theater of total human responses." Cooper was in the process of defining the essential qualities of that very essential poet Muriel Rukeyser, who herself wrote in her book *The Life of Poetry*, "The making of a poem is the type of act which releases aggression. Since it is released appropriately, it is creation." If your nature is totally pragmatic you might demand to know if Marvell's "To His Coy Mistress," when heard by his beloved—for surely he intoned it to her in his rich baritone—caused her to become so much less coy that she rewarded his advances. A question I, of course, can't answer, but if Rukeyser is right, and I believe she is, it hardly matters, for the poem itself was an act of creation the rest of us have had joy in for centuries. If that other act of creation never transpired it may have mattered enormously to Andrew Marvell or perhaps not at all, for the poem may merely have been that symbolic stage Muir referred to.

Before I get back to the three poets in the provincial terminal waiting impatiently on wooden benches for the promised host to collect them—and Daniel, the lover, as well—and escort them to their hotel and there complete arrangements for that night's dinner and reading, I have something of a parable to share with you, one that deals with a life with poetry and a life without poetry. At age eighteen when I found the poetry in English of the last century and a half, Stephen Crane first, then Eliot, Auden, Spender, Wilfred Owen, Dylan Thomas, Yeats, Hardy, Stevens, Frost, Dickinson, Whitman, and finally Williams—I thought that without these words life would be a pale thing. I took Williams' famous words from "Asphodel, that Greeny Flower" very seriously and recited them to any innocent victim I could corner: "It is difficult / to get the news from poems / yet men die miserably every day / for lack / of what is found there." I took them to be about me and everyone else. To the credit of my patient students, many of whom went on to become poets while others opted for careers in law, medicine, wine making, journalism, organic farming, housewifery, and the military, when I stated and restated the absolute need of poetry in every life, no one laughed in my face or contradicted me.

Fortunately not everyone was so docile. At a poetry conference in Bisbee, Arizona, about a dozen years ago I went into my usual rant about the essential need for poetry in each life. No one in the audience blinked, but on the panel with me was that wonderful and very wise poet Robert Duncan who after hearing me out gently corrected me. He reminded me that we are not all alike: what turns some of us on bores others to death. He asked me if that indeed had not been my experience. Indeed it had been, I agreed, for at one time I had hoped that all productions of Wagner's operas be staged underwater, music which Mark Twain had once remarked was not as bad as it sounded. From then on I stopped badgering my students and friends and any other captive audiences. After listening to Duncan I came to believe that the teacher's function was not to force an art down the throats of his students but rather to help them find the art that thrilled their hearts.

Now for the parable. It bears some resemblance to the "history" or fiction of the three poets journeying to their reading, though there is one difference: it is composed of nothing but facts. It involves a poet journeying to a reading, a lone poet, one of the very same three, Levine, now a bit older, a bit tougher having survived a number of bad reviews, but not so tough that passing over the island of Manhattan where he will spend the weekend with his oldest son and then read for a small mob at the 92nd Street Y, he does not feel his secret heart swell with excitement, his pulse quicken, his breath surge as though he had just heard Galway Kinnell recite one of those magical passages from his great poem "The Avenue Bearing the Initial of Christ into the New World." So excited and perhaps foolish is he at that moment that he turns to the man seated next to him and says something profound, like "Isn't that amazing!" The man, a large, besuited fellow who has had his head stuck in a huge tome depicting some of the world's longest bridges, leans across Levine's lap to have a look and says, "My." A conversation ensues. The large man, it turns out, is headed for a conference on the uses of reinforced concrete. It will convene on Monday, at noon, in a large hotel that is part of the complex known as Dulles Airport. He had planned to change planes at La Guardia and fly directly to Dulles although this is Saturday afternoon, and he could just as easily spend two nights in New York City, for he is on an expense account. Levine calms the fellow's fears regarding the dangers of the city and assures him that if he stays away from the wrong neighborhoods he'll be just as safe as he'd be in Indianapolis where he works and lives. What could he do in New York? he wonders aloud. Almost anything, Levine replies. What are you interested in? No response. Does he like painting? The museums are among the best in the world. Painting is OK. How about theater or movies? A tepid response. Levine tried food, for every sort of ethnic food is available. Well, the fellow has to watch his weight, and he jabs a thick forefinger into his barely pouching waist and goes on to describe this incredible exercise regimen, though he avoids lifting weights for that can give you a false sense of power. Levine runs through dance, jazz, classical music, rock—which it turns out gives the fellow terrible headaches—; just walking the streets of what is probably the world's most energetic city can be a heady experience. The cement maven sits impassively. Levine offers to share a cab in from La Guardia and direct him to a nice hotel. After a long silence the poet says, I think it's probably best if you get to Dulles as quickly as possible.

So while I believe Duncan was right and since receiving his tactful remarks on my position regarding the situation of poetry in the world, I have never again browbeaten those who do not respond to it, write it, care if it exists at all. I have come to believe that something must be there to, as Jane Cooper so aptly put it, "provide us with a theater of total human responses." My seatmate on that flight into La Guardia is the perfect example of someone who lacks that theater, who seems to have no idea such a thing could exist. An educated man with a degree in engineering from Purdue, he must once or twice in his life have attended to a poem and barely noticed it as it flew by him on its way to glory. In my description of our conversation I left out one detail which occurred near its end; out of some growing distaste for the man as well as to determine the degree to which he had stopped being a total person, I added that Manhattan was full of the sexiest people I had ever seen, both men and women, and their styles of walking, talking, dress, made it clear just what treasures they possessed. For all he seemed to care I might have been describing varieties of apples. I went on: "You just see them on the streets in midtown or in the Village or Soho at all hours, bodies and faces the likes of which never filled the streets of the Midwest." His only response was, "I am married," which suggested to me not his moral rectitude—which may have been wonderfully intact—but his total lack of curiosity as to how people have been behaving for the last few thousand years.

I have at times considered a world totally without music and reacted with a horror so absolute that I immediately knew it was the art that fired my heart and blood like no other even though I have no talent for it. Thanks to the discoveries of Thomas Edison I have it even without New York City. Indeed in Fresno, where I have lived longer than anywhere else, I have it each morning when I waken to the mockingbirds doing their thing from high in the Atlas cedar that grows in my front yard. But the art I have pursued for better or worse for over fifty years is poetry, and I have found it an enterprise worthy of a human life, and I haven't the least notion if anything I have written will in the hearts of others outlive me. Why, you might well ask, with that knowledge do I call it an enterprise worthy of a human life? Because I have been part of something far larger than myself: I have been part of the attempt to verbalize as precisely as possible what it has meant to live through the great depression, the horrors of World War II, the fiasco of anti-communism, the long, painful failed struggle for racial justice, and wind up in old age in a country gone to ruin through the greed of capitalism with a technology that can take us to the moon while our streets are stained by the lives of the poor and the homeless, the present world of Microsoft, unfettered pollution, the epidemic of murderous drugs, and the economic policies of Ronald Reagan. I have been part of the generation of Adrienne Rich, John Ashbery, Galway Kinnell, W. S. Merwin, Robert Creeley, Anthony Hecht, Denise Levertov, Etheridge Knight, Sylvia Plath, Allen Ginsberg, Gary Snyder: we have done our best to capture the century in verse. We have told America, and the rest of the world should it care to listen, what it's been like living through this age. We have been useful.

What has become of the three poets just arrived in the provincial town of X, justly famous for its great cathedral and its filthy brown river that drags slowly through the town? With Daniel the two men grow restless and begin to pace the gradually emptying train station while Elaine sits composedly staring off into the dusty building at nothing in particular. At last the emissary arrives with two taxis in tow, thank heavens for no single taxi can handle all the luggage Elaine has loaded upon the shoulders of her young lover as well as the three poets and their host. She, the emissary, is breathless and apologetic, and her apologies are quickly accepted, for the poets have learned they in fact have hotel rooms, plans for dinner, and an almost totally unannounced reading to give that night. The emissary, Catherine, who prefers to be called Cate, is both a younger and more attractive woman than those usually strapped with these functions; today she seems flustered and more than a little overwhelmed by her duties. Even before we reach the hotel we are warned that it is not top-notch as the local arts council is strapped for cash and also that due to a screwup by some hireling of the council the only advertising for the event consists of small posters placed "in just the important places" that very Saturday morning by Cate herself. "To have great poetry you need great audiences," Whitman had written, but I learned that night what I had suspected for years, that for once at least good father Walt was wrong.

After being deposited in our mediocre digs—one room with two single beds for Sienna and me, bath down the hall—we are free for some hours to walk the almost deserted town, inspect the massive local cathedral, and gaze longingly into the sluggish river a dozen local boys find suitable for a dip. We return to our room in time to shower and dress in the expected jackets and ties and meet with Elaine and

Daniel in the tiny chairless lobby where a waiting Cate leads us a few blocks to a modest restaurant. The meal begins with something I still believe the waitress called sorghum soup and goes rapidly downhill from there. Cate keeps reminding us not to expect a crowd. No, there will be no books available for signing and sale; no one at the arts council knew how to go about obtaining them. When we arrive on foot at the community house at which we will read there is no audience at all besides the three young men arranging the lights and moving some of the furniture out of the way, for in fact we will be reading on the set of a Pinter play that will have its first performance the following week. We wait in silence until fifteen minutes past the assigned hour, but no one arrives. I ask the lighting technicians to stay and along with Cate to become our audience, and two agree to do so; the third has made arrangements for the evening but promises to return as soon as possible with his girlfriend. I read first after introducing myself, for Cate has confessed she has no idea who we are, what we have published if anything, and what our work might be about. I read as well as I have ever read, finding unusual strength in my voice and aiming my words toward my two fellow poets who have heard me for several nights in a row but never before seemed so alert to what I was reading. Elaine reads next after a short introduction by me; it is by far the best reading I have ever heard her give. She is usually nervous to the point of being almost inaudible, directing her attention not to her listeners but rather to an invisible audience riding ten or twelve feet above the actual one, but this night she looks directly into my eyes. I hear the fullness of her language, the delicacy of her rhythms, and the startling freshness of her tropes as I've never heard them before. She introduces the poems with only their titles and launches them into the utter silence of the room in a strong alto voice. Sienna comes next. He begins with no wisecracks or small talk but instead goes into a long and extraordinarily moving elegy to his father which he follows with three short lyric poems; this is far more daring and powerful work than he is known for. When he finishes, the six of us—Elaine, Daniel, Cate, the two technicians, and me—rise and applaud this stunning presentation and its creator. Before we can leave for drinks at the local watering hole "on the arts council," the third technician returns with his stunningly attractive friend in tow, and they are assured they have missed something astonishing. I suggest that each of us poets read one poem for these two, and to my surprise my fellow poets are equally enthusiastic. The magic is still there.

297

What startled me most and what I recall most clearly from that night was my sudden and overwhelming discovery of Elaine's poetry. For the first time I was truly getting it. Even in the theater of my mind, alone with the poem on the page, I had not attended to it with the intensity and passion it demanded. I had been reading her work as a series of bright moves, of smart decisions, I had been hearing harmonious phrases and lines moving gracefully from one to another, careful pacing and lovely ploys that brought the poems to a satisfying closure. That night I heard a unique human voice calling out from the deepest roots of its nature, calling out to be heard by what was deepest and most human in me. I was hearing poetry. We here in America have been practicing this art for hundreds of years almost without an audience for the single reason that we must in exactly the way a born dancer must respond to the music. That night Elaine had an audience—I know that as well as I know anything—and though it may have been only an audience of one, the act was complete, for one human being had reached across the immense gulf our education has taught us exists between each of us, had reached across that gulf through the magic of her language to remind me I was human.

Let me return to a question I asked earlier as a way of avoiding the question of the truth of this narrative: what use is this story? I think it contains two extraordinary truths about a life in poetry. The first is that we as poets (and no doubt also as people) need each other. As a boy first composing poetry at age thirteen I truly believed that some day I would be addressing the world. I was perfectly able to wait for that day, for the composing itself was such a delicious experience. Even at eighteen when I began my second career as a poet—my first was quite short, lasting less than three years and fortunately producing nothing that is extant—I thought that what I wrote in both prose and verse would have an enormous influence on the way my fellow citizens behaved toward themselves and each other. I had every reason to believe this, for the writers I was reading, especially the fiction writers (Dreiser, Dos Passos, Chekhov, Dostoyevsky, Balzac, Sherwood Anderson) were creating a me I had not known could exist. Within a year I would read Keats's letters, for me the most extraordinary document on what it means to be a poet, and again become someone else. Through the agency of his letter to his brother George on the world as the *Vale of Soul Making* I felt myself becoming a religious person. In the letter he asks George, and because the letter has been preserved those of us who will follow, what the use of a world like ours is and goes on to define that use. "There may be intelligences or sparks of divinity in millions," he writes, "but they are not Souls till they acquire identities, till each one is personally itself." And how will this happen? "How, but by the medium of a world like this?" In order to clarify what he only dimly perceives he put it "in the most homely form possible," and he goes on to tell George and us that the world is the horn book from which each intelligence learns to read, that is, to become what it is capable of becoming, a singular identity, a soul; without the education our experience of *this* world can give us we remain less than a soul, merely a potential. It is an extraordinary vision for a twenty-three year old man to coin to account for human suffering, which Keats knew full well as an apprentice surgeon working in a London hospital, but then Keats was one of the most extraordinary twenty-three year olds who ever lived. As the oldest of four siblings and with both parents long dead, Keats was deprived of what most of us take for granted, an adolescence. He had to become a man at a very early age; he had even to nurse his younger brother Tom through the final stages of TB to his death at eighteen. When he asked after the use of a world like ours he knew that world in its glory—his poems attest to that—and in its savagery. If Keats is right, the experience of this world can school each one of us into becoming a soul, and of course literature is part of the experience the world gives us. That night of the reading with an audience of no more than eight and no less than one, Elaine revived a human soul.

A genius such as Rimbaud or Dickinson or Blake can go it alone. There are those among us who are so gifted and so furiously and originally motivated that nothing can stop them from becoming poets except themselves. The rest of us need each other; we need to know this largely ignored art is still cherished and useful to others, and we need each other's counsel and encouragement to stay on course. (I suspect many of you have learned this or you wouldn't be at a place like this.) In my thirty-something years of teaching I've seen it over and over: one truly gifted and generous aspiring poet can excite an entire class and direct them to a poetry they did not know they possessed. In the fall of '61 a psychology major trying his hand at writing in my first poetry writing class rose in the back of the room and asked if he might offer a poem to the class. Thinking no harm could come from this I let him recite a piece he had not yet written down. It began thusly:

If a broken-down roan in a fenced-in-field had only two
   legs would it be a man?
If a spotted dog wearing a napkin had one leg would it be
   a Republican?
If a man had common sense would the governor make
   him pick clover for the next two thousand years?
In my last incarnation I looked for the perfect apple and
   so walked from Albany to Sacramento
And chain-smoked the entire way.
My health is better for it so don't believe anything you
   read.

His name was Charles Moulton, and he was a genuine Fresno surre-
alist. To say the class never quite recovered from the experience is an
understatement. Moulton had managed in a few minutes to fire the
imaginations of twenty young and not so young poets who suddenly
understood it was open house and that whatever the brain concocted
was material for poetry. A few years later it was an entering freshman,
Larry Levis, who wrote, "He numbed himself to photographs / of
farmers swatting flames off their faces. / He lived at least / as well as a
cold rat, // waiting for his number to come up." Yes, even the draft was
material for poetry; Larry's classmates began to write utterly surpris-
ing poems that struggled with the agony and humor of coming to age
or middle age in their brutal Central Valley towns. Two years later it
was the lyricism of David St. John, also a freshman, that did the trick;
later the sardonic anger of Sherley Williams and Gary Soto. It's amaz-
ing how far we can go with each other's help. The myth is that we must
remain solitary and write out of the sources of our deepest woundings.
Keats describes something totally different in another letter: "When-
ever I find myself growing vaporish I rouse myself, wash and put on a
clean shirt, brush my hair and clothes, tie my shoestrings neatly, and
in fact adonize as if I were going out—then all clean and comfortable
I sit down to write. This I find the greatest relief." He prepares him-
self for company—for he loved the fellowship of men and women—
and invites his muse in. The truth is we form a family with all the poets,
living or dead, or we go nowhere.

   The second truth I also learned from Elaine. The impulse, the drive,
if you will, to write poetry is incredibly powerful. In spite of the worst
efforts of two terrible men disguised as teachers, Elaine had only
briefly been sidetracked. This young woman who at less than a hun-

dred pounds and, as her early photographs attest, of a delicate beauty and, as I learned through the contact of some weeks, of a delicate emotional constitution contained an unkillable need to create true poetry, to build that "theater of total human responses." Each of us no doubt takes a differing and private route to this art (or in some cases away from it); those of us who need it, who see it as essential to our spiritual survival, will overcome the discouragements of an indifferent society and a corrupted literary world. We will do this simply because we have to. Why is this true? I believe the need to write poetry (and I assume prose fiction) is exactly the need as Plato defines it to love, that is, to possess the halved soul's complement, to be whole. The sense of completeness that writing at our best gives is comparable to nothing else in my experience, but that is no doubt because I have no gift for music and can draw nothing that resembles anything. I don't see poetry as chief among the arts nor writing as chief among human vocations. Rather I see imaginative writing as one among many useful pursuits. Not long ago I heard the great tenor saxophonist Sonny Rollins say of his life in music, "Everybody has something to do in this world." Being able to play the music he loves he found a blessing. Being able to play it with Gillespie, Hawkins, Max Roach, Clifford Brown, and Coltrane he found a blessing far beyond his early hopes. From what I know of Rollins's life—and I know a lot—like Elaine nothing could stop him.

Of course when Rollins said each of us has something to do he meant something useful. In his case it was the making of music, and if you don't know why music is useful then there's nothing I can do to help you. And how useful is poetry? Let me go to one of the great writers of the century for a little help. In his essay "Why the Novel Matters," D. H. Lawrence writes, "As a man alive you may have a shot at your enemy. But as a ghastly simulacrum of life you may be firing bombs into men who are neither your friends or enemies, but things you are dead to: Which is criminal when the things happen to be alive." For Lawrence it is in the novel that we learn exactly what a man or woman alive is; by reading novels. "You can develop an instinct for life, if you will, instead of a theory of right and wrong, good and bad." The only three great novels Lawrence names in the essay are the Bible, Homer, and Shakespeare. He calls these "the supreme old novels," but as any reader knows, two are poetry and the other when it is at its most eloquent is also poetry. I don't have to lecture you on how completely contemporary life can deaden us to what is alive; you have all

301

experienced it enough for me not to add an ounce to your burden. "The grass withereth, the flower fadeth, but the Word of the Lord shall stand forever," quotes Lawrence and goes on to claim, "That's the kind of stuff we've drugged ourselves with," for the truth is the grass comes back, the flower dies and gives birth to new buds, but "the Word of the Lord, being man-uttered and a mere vibration on the ether, becomes staler and staler, more and more boring till at last we turn a deaf ear and it ceases to exist." But truly imaginative writing can bring us back to the living presence of the grass, to the fields that feed us, to the cities we live in and the nature of the men and women among whom we live.

> Tenderly will I use you curling grass,
> It may be you transpire from the breasts of young men,
> It may be if I had known them I would have loved them,
> It may be you are from old people, or from offspring
>   taken soon out of their mother's laps,
> And here you are the mothers' laps.

> This grass is very dark to be from the white heads of old
>   mothers,
> Darker than the colorless beards of old men,
> Dark to come from under the faint red roofs of mouths.

In fact the greatest of our poets can make us come alive to the world in all its richness to a degree we scarcely believe.

I confess I not only find poetry useful these days, I find it absolutely necessary. I am presently living in one of the most complex, turbulent, disturbing, unfathomable communities in the world: New York City. Even my twenty-six years in industrial Detroit failed to prepare me for this. But through the work of its poets—Whitman, Hart Crane, García Lorca, and Galway Kinnell—I have come not only to a degree of peace with all the tumult, I have also become so comprehending of its presence that at times I can see its ordinary diurnal street life as the arena of the sublime and the sacred:

> It is night, and raining. You look down
> Toward Houston in the rain, the living streets,
> Where instants of transcendence
> Drift in oceans of loathing and fear, like lanternfishes,

302

or phosphorous flashings in the sea, or the feverish light
Skin is said to give off when the swimmer drowns at night.

From the blind gut Pitt to the East River of Fishes
The Avenue cobbles a swath through the discolored air,
A roadway of refuse from the teeming shores and ghettos
And the Caribbean Paradise, into the new ghetto and new
    paradise,
This God-forsaken Avenue bearing the initial of Christ
Through the haste and carelessness of the ages,
The sea standing in heaps, which keeps on collapsing,
Where the drowned suffer a C-change,
And remain the common poor.

Through the magic of language I live my daily life in Kinnell's City of God without God; that's how useful poetry can be.

What became of our three poets after their triumphant, scarcely attended reading? Their host, Cate, walked them to the local pub and there stood them to a drink on the arts council, and then they stood her to one on their meager stipends. The place was noisy with Saturday night celebrants, and so the poetry party came to a rather abrupt ending. The poets went off on foot to the shabby digs, at least two of them with the intention of sleeping. Elaine and Daniel may have had more serious work to do, for as Rilke reminds us those who make love do a very essential work. Exhausted, Sienna seemed to fall off before his head hit the pillow. Levine was too wired from the reading, and for more than an hour he sat on his bed writing in his journal that day's events without knowing that some day, perhaps today, he would find them useful. Finally he too grew weary and turned out the light and welcomed the darkness. Perhaps he slept. In any case all three poets rose the next morning from soiled beds to hurry off by cab to the station for still another voyage to still another tiny audience.

Let me close with a final cautionary tale. Some years ago I received a letter from a very dear man who also wrote poetry, had in fact published several books though none recently and altogether only a fragment of what he had written. To put it bluntly he was and is what the world might call "a failed poet" though he is a gifted writer. He is both unlucky and without any clout in what I will call the "church temporal" of poetry, that world of ass-kissing and favor-trading that brings so much useless work to acclaim. He had decided that even without a

303

publisher he would put together his complete poems, and he did so under covers supplied by Kinko's. His letter was a response to this event, a dignified and touching letter which described his own emotions as he beheld this utterly unique volume. But he used one phrase that by now even he would regard as suspect; he wrote "now the granary is full." He sat for some weeks with this volume finding its presence less and less satisfying and finally sent it off to a university press. Knowing the speed with which any press deals with poetry he grew restless and uncharacteristically crabby. He told me later he put his household into a state of anxiety it had not known for over thirty years, since the coming of children. The cure for these ills was his own and obvious: his need to be a useful person could not be quieted, so complete poems or not he went back to the day by day undramatic work of trying to make poems. This man knew, as all of us who write poetry know, that if the work is worthy eventually it will find its readers. It may take more years than we have, as it did in the case of Dickinson and Kit Smart, but our job is the work of creation and as such it never ends.

I'm frequently asked, especially by students, how I got into poetry and what kept me going. I always tell the truth: once when I was very young I heard a knock at the door; I was home alone and so I answered. There was a man in a bowler hat who asked if Philip Levine were home. "Yes," I said, "I am he." (Even then I was a stickler for grammar.) "My name is Tom Eliot," he said, "though you may know me as T. S. Eliot. I've come to tell you that American poetry needs you." What he was doing in a lower-middle class neighborhood in Detroit, a Jewish neighborhood no less, I wasn't sure, but as our only Poet Nobelist could I refuse him? You don't believe that and you shouldn't. No one asked me to try to become a poet; it's what I chose to do and it's what I choose to continue to do, and if it takes me nowhere I have no one to thank except myself.

Nominated by Michigan Quarterly Review, David Baker,
Christopher Buckley, Timothy Geiger, Richard Jackson

ONCE A SHOOT
OF HEAVEN

by BECKIAN FRITZ GOLDBERG

from FIELD

Even when you see through the lies, the lies they
fed you as a child, you
believe some it, still, when you drift
from thinking. When the air's true and simple
like a sheet you've laundered for as long

as you can remember, and your mother before you. There was an
    end,
and a beginning, and love, wrong and right and
someone who loved the world and someone who did not
and someone who made the moon and the moon that just was.
Always.

Now there's a white disappearing brow at the edge of September,
    usual stars.
        A siren sets off a dog.
        A car radio flies down the road.
        In between the acacias tick, tick in a lightness not yet wind.

The early bird is asleep,
        The world still isn't safe for democracy.

There was a mother and a father and a child and an hour
and exactly so many minutes, and left and right,

and people who ascended like doves and people
who slept in the earth, and apples that could make you strong
and sugar that could make you weak, and people who burned.

And tonight you still talk to someone who is not there, not
    yourself—crazy promises, little pleas, momentary

thanksgivings. This no one who has never been there is like the cat
    who only went away they said

to live and raise a family in the Christenson's barn. So there was the
    one who went on living forever and the one you realized could not
    live forever.

Here there's the sound of a neighbor dragging his trash cans down
    the driveway to the curb. No one on this street sleeps.
        The crickets are poor not lucky.
        The ear might as well be gold.

Nominated by Melissa Pritchard

VALOR

fiction by RICHARD BAUSCH

from STORY

AFTER IT WAS ALL OVER, Aldenburg heard himself say that he had never considered himself the sort of man who was good in an emergency, or was particularly endowed with courage. The truth was that, if anything, he had always believed quite the opposite. The truth of it hurt, too, but there it was. Problems in his private life made him low and he'd had no gumption for doing anything to change, and he knew it, way down, where you couldn't mask things with rationalization, or diversion, or bravado—or booze, either. In fact. he would not have been in a position to perform any heroics if he had not spent the night sitting in the bar at whose very door the accident happened.

The bar was called Sam's. At night, the neon Budweiser sign in the window was the only light at that end of the street. Aldenburg had simply stayed on past closing, and sobered up playing blackjack for pennies with Mo Smith, the owner, a nice gentleman who had lost a son in the Gulf War and was lonely and had insomnia, and didn't mind company.

It had been such a miserable winter—gray, bone-cold days, black starless nights, ice storms one after another, and a wind blowing across the face of the world like desolation itself. They talked about this a little, and about the monstrosities all around. Monstrosity was Smitty's word; he used it in almost every context, to mean, vaguely, that thing he couldn't quickly name or understand. "Bring me that—monstrosity over there will you?" he'd say, meaning a pitcher of water. Or he would say, "Reagan's presidency was a monstrosity," and sometimes it

307

was as though he meant it all in the same way. Smitty especially liked to talk about the end of the world. He was perpetually finding indications of the decline of everything, everywhere he looked. It was all a monstrosity. Aldenburg liked listening to him, and if on occasion he grew a little tired of the dire predictions, he simply tuned him out. This night he let him talk without attending to it much. He had been struggling to make ends meet and to solve complications in his marriage, feeling depressed a lot of the time because the marriage had once been happy, and trying to work through it all, though here he was, acting bad, evidently past working to solve anything much—staying out late, giving his wife something to think about.

The present trouble had mostly to do with his brother-in-law, Cal, who had come back from the great victory in the gulf needing a cane to walk. Cal was living with them now, and the victory didn't mean much. He was as bitter as it was possible to be. He had been wounded in an explosion in Riyadh—the two men with him were killed instantly—less than a week before the end of hostilities, and he'd suffered through three different surgical procedures and eleven months of therapy in a military hospital in Washington. Much of his left knee was gone, and part of his left foot and ankle, and the therapy hadn't helped him much. He would need the cane for the rest of his life. He wasn't even twenty-five and he walked like a man in his eighties, bent over the cane, dragging the bad leg.

Aldenburg's wife, Eva, couldn't stand it, the sound of it—the fact of it. And while Aldenburg thought Cal should be going out and looking for some kind of job, Eva seemed to think nothing should be asked of him at all. Aldenburg felt almost superfluous in his own house. He was past forty and looked it. He had a bad back and flat feet, and the money he made selling shoes wasn't enough to support three adults, not to mention Cal's friends who kept coming around: mostly pals from high school, where he had been the star quarterback. Cal's fiancée, Diane, ran a small beauty parlor in town, and had just bought a place that she was having refinished; so she was over a lot, too. There seemed never anywhere to go in the house and be alone. And lately Eva had started making innuendoes to these people about her difficult marriage—fourteen childless years with Aldenburg. As if the fact that there were no children was anyone's fault.

God only knew what she found to say when he wasn't around to hear it.

308

Toward the end of the long night, Smitty said, "Of course a man doesn't spend this much time in a saloon if there's a happy home to return to."

Aldenburg caught just enough of the sentence to know he was the subject. He said, "Smitty, sometimes I look around myself and I swear I don't know how I got here."

"I thought you walked over," Smitty said.

They laughed.

Sometime after three in the morning, he had made coffee, and they had switched to that. Black and strong, to counter the effects of the night's indulgence, as Smitty called it. He had broken an old rule and consumed a lot of the whiskey himself. It was getting harder and harder to be alone, he said.

Aldenburg understood it.

"Damn monstrosity didn't last long enough to make any heroes below the level of general," Smitty said. "My son was a hero."

"That's true," said Aldenburg. "But take somebody like my brother-in-law. Here's a guy standing on a corner looking at the sights, and this oil burner goes off. You know? Guy standing in the street with a couple of other boys from the motor pool, talking football, and whoosh. Just a dumb accident."

"I don't guess it matters much how you get it," Smitty said, shaking his head. His son had been shot through the heart.

"I'm sorry, man," Aldenburg told him.

"Hell," said Smitty, rubbing the back of his neck, and then looking away.

Light had come to the windows. On the polished table between them was a metal ashtray stuffed to overflowing with the cigarettes they had smoked.

"What day is this, anyway?" Smitty asked.

"Friday. I've got to be at work at eleven. Sales meeting. I won't sleep at all."

"Ought to go on in back and try for a little, anyway."

Aldenburg looked at him. "When do you ever sleep?"

"Noddings-off in the evenings," Smitty said. "Never much more than that."

"I feel like all hell," Aldenburg told him. "My liver hurts. I think it's my liver."

"Go on back and take a little nap."

"I'll feel worse if I do."

They heard voices, car doors slamming. Smitty said, "Uh, listen, I invited some of the boys from the factory to stop by for eggs and coffee." He went to open the door, moving slow, as if his bones ached. The curve of his spine was visible through the back of his shirt. He was only fifty-three.

Aldenburg stayed in the booth, with the playing cards lying there before him, and the full ashtray. He lighted a cigarette, blew the smoke at the ceiling, wishing that he'd gone on home now. Brad and Billy Pardee came in, with Ed Crewly. They all wore their hunting jackets, and were carrying gear, looking ruddy and healthy from the cold. Brad was four years older than Billy, but they might have been twins, with their blue-black hair and identical flat noses, their white, white teeth. Ed Crewly was once the end who received Cal's long passes in the high-school games, a tall, skinny type with long lean arms and legs—gangly looking, but graceful when he got moving. He was among the ones who kept coming to the house now that Cal was back from the war. Aldenburg, returning in the late evenings from the store, would find them all in his living room, watching a basketball game or one of the sitcoms—every chair occupied, and beer and potato chips and a plate of cheeses laid out for them, as though this were all still the party celebrating the hero's homecoming.

He never had the nerve to say anything about it. An occasional hint to his wife, who wasn't hearing any hints.

Brad was bragging now about how he and Billy and Ed had called in sick for the day. They were planning a drive up into the mountains to shoot at birds. Billy turned to Aldenburg sitting in the booth.

"Hey, Gabriel," he said. "You're early, ain't you?"

"Yep," Aldenburg glanced at Smitty, whose face showed no reaction.

"Have a seat at the bar, guys," Smitty said. "I'll put the bacon on. Help yourselves to the coffee."

"I was over at your place last night," said Crewly. "Didn't see you."

"Didn't get in till late, there, Ed."

"I think I'd like to start the day with a beer," said Brad.

"Me, too," his brother put in. The weekend was ahead of them, and they were feeling expansive.

Smitty put the beers down on the bar.

"I didn't leave your place till pretty late," Ed Crewly said to Aldenburg. "Eva figured you were down here."

"I was here last night, Ed. That's true."

310

"Stayed late, huh." Crewly had a dour, down-turning kind of face, and a long nose. His skin was dark red, the color of baked clay.

Aldenburg shook his head, smoking the cigarette.

"I bet Gabriel's been here all night," Billy Pardee said.

"The whole night," Aldenburg said, not looking at them.

"Damn, Gabriel," Brad Pardee said. "What're you paying rent for, anyway?"

Aldenburg looked at him. "I'm paying it for my wife, my brother-in-law, and all their friends."

Billy put his beer down and shook one hand, as if he had touched something hot. "Whoo-ee," he said. "I think he told you. I'd say somebody's been told the harsh truth. I'd say I smell smoke."

Aldenburg watched them, wishing he had gone before they arrived. It had been plain inertia that kept him there.

"Wife trouble," Smitty said. He was leaning against the doorframe, so he could attend to the bacon, and he held a cigarette between his thumb and index finger, like a cigar. The smoke curled up past his face, and one eye was closed against it. The odd thing about Smitty was that whenever these other men were around, nothing of the kindness of the real man came through; something about their casual hardness affected him, and he seemed to preside over it all, like an observer, a scientist—interested without being involved. The others performed for him; they tried to outdo each other in front of him.

"Hey, Gabriel," Brad Pardee said. "Come on, You really spend the night here?"

Billy said, "You going to work today, Gabriel? I need some boots."

He held his empty coffee mug up, as if to toast them. "We sell boots, all right."

"What're you drinking there, Gabriel?"

"It's all gone," said Aldenburg. "Whatever it was."

"You look bad, man. You look bleary-eyed and real bad." Billy turned to the others. "Don't he look bad?"

They were having fun with it, as he could have predicted they would. He put his cigarette out and lighted another. Because Ed Crewly was in Aldenburg's house a lot, they all knew things, and perhaps they didn't have much respect for him—though they meant no harm, either. The whole thing was good-natured enough. When he got up, slow, crossed the room to the bar and poured himself a whiskey, they reacted as though it were a stunt, whistling and clapping their hands. He saw that Smitty had gone into the kitchen and was sorry for it, wanting the older man as an audience, for some reason.

They watched him drink the whiskey for a little time—it was almost respect—and then they had forgotten about him. Smitty brought their breakfasts, and they scarfed that up, and a few minutes later they were going out the door, all energy and laughs. Like boys out of school.

They weren't gone five minutes when the accident happened.

He had walked back to the bar to pour himself another whiskey, having decided that whatever badness this would bring, including the loss of his job, was all right with him. He was crossing the space of the open door, holding the whiskey, and motion there drew his attention. He saw a school bus entering slowly from the left, bright morning sun on the orange-yellow metal of it, and in the instant he looked at the reflected brightness, the bus was struck broadside by a long white speeding car, a Cadillac. The Cadillac seemed to come from nowhere, a flying missile, and it caved in the side of the bus with a terrible, crunching, glass-breaking sound. Aldenburg dropped the glass of whiskey, and bolted out into the cold, moving through it with the whiskey swimming behind his eyes. In no time, he had come to the little water-trickling place between the Cadillac's crushed front grill and the door of the bus, which must have flown open with the collision. A young woman lay on her back partway onto the street, her arms flung out as though she had taken a leap from her seat behind the wheel. There was something so wrong about a lovely woman lying in the road like that, and Aldenburg found himself lifting her, bending, not really thinking, bracing himself, supporting her across his legs, his arms under her shoulders. It was hard to keep from falling backward himself. Somehow he had lifted her up, where she had been thrown, and on the metal step before his eyes, a little boy lay along her calves, one arm over her ankles, unconscious, blood in his dark hair, something quivering in the nerves of his neck and shoulders. There was a crying, a screeching. Aldenburg held the woman, and tried to take a step, to gather himself. She looked at him, upside down, but did not seem to see him.

"Take it easy," he heard himself say.

The boy was still now. The screaming went on in another part of the bus. Was it screams? Something was giving off a terrible high whine. He looked at the woman and thought, absurdly, of the whiskey he had drunk, his breath.

312

She moaned, "Is everyone all right?" But she didn't seem to be speaking to him.

He lifted slightly, and she said, "Don't."

But she wasn't breathing. He could feel the difference. Her weight was too much. He put one leg back, and then shifted away from the bus, and the full weight of her came down on him. Her feet clattered on the crumpled step, slipping from under the boy's arm, and dropped with a dead smack to the pavement. And then he was carrying her, dragging her. He took one lurching stride, and another, and finally he got her lying on her back in the road. The surface was cold, and damp, and he took his coat off, folded it and laid it under her head, then re-membered about keeping the feet elevated, for shock. Carefully he let her head down, and put the folded coat under her ankles. It was as though there were nothing else and no one else but this woman and himself, in slow time. And she was not breathing.

"She's gone," a voice said from somewhere.

It was Smitty. He moved toward the bus, but then shrank back, limping. Something had gone out of him at the knees. "Fire," he said. "Jesus, I think it's gonna go."

Aldenburg placed his hands, gently, on the woman's chest. He was afraid the bones might be broken there. He put the slightest pressure on her, but then thought better of it, and leaned down to breathe into her mouth. Again, he was aware of his breath, and felt as though this was wrong; he was invading her privacy somehow. He hesitated, but then he went on blowing into her mouth. It only took a few breaths to get her started on her own. She gasped, looked into his face and seemed to want to scream. But she was breathing. "You're hurt," Aldenburg told her. "It's gonna be okay."

"The children," she said. "Four—"

"Can you breathe all right?" he said.

"Oh, what happened?" She started to cry.

"Don't move," he told her. "Don't try to move."

"No," she said.

He stood. There were sirens now, far off, and he had a cruel little moment of realizing they were probably for some other accident, in another part of the city. He saw Smitty's face and understood, at some wordless level below thought, that he was in charge, that this moment was somehow his alone, and was beautifully separate from everything his life had been before. He yelled at Smitty. "Call the res-cue squad."

313

Smitty said, "It's gonna blow up," and moved to the doorway of the bar and in.

Aldenburg stepped into the space between the Cadillac, with its hissing radiator, and its spilled fluids, and the bus, where the boy lay in a spreading pool of blood, in the open door. A man was standing there with his hand out, as though he were afraid to touch anything. "Fire," the man said. He had a bruise on his forehead, and seemed dazed. Aldenburg realized that this was the driver of the Cadillac. He smelled alcohol on him.

"Get out of the way," he said.

From inside the bus, there was a scream. It was screaming. He saw a child at one of the windows, the small face cut and bleeding. He got into the doorway and looked at the boy's face, this one's face. The eyes were closed. The boy appeared to be asleep.

"Son?" Aldenburg said. "Can you hear me?"

Nothing. But he was breathing. Aldenburg took his shirt off and put it where the blood was flowing, and the boy opened his eyes.

"Hey," Aldenburg said.

The eyes stared.

"You ever see an uglier face in your life?" It was something he always said to other people's children when they looked at him. He pulled the boy out, away from the flames.

"Where do you hurt?"

"All over."

The sirens grew louder. The boy began to cry. He said, "Scared." Blood lined his mouth.

The seat behind the steering wheel was on fire. The whole bus was on fire. The smoke drifted skyward. There were flames licking along the spilled fuel on the road. He carried the boy a few yards along the street, and the sirens seemed to be getting louder, coming closer. Time had stopped, though. He was the only thing moving in it. He was all life, bright with energy. The sounds went away, and he got inside the bus again, crawling along the floor. The inside was nearly too hot to touch. Heat and smoke took his breath from him, and made him dizzy. There were other children on the floor between the seats and under the seats, a tangle of arms and legs. Somehow, one by one in the slow intensity of the burning, he got them all out and away. There was no room for thinking and deciding. He kept going back, and finally there was no one else on the bus. He had emptied it out, and the seat panels burned slow. The ambulances and rescue people had begun to arrive.

314

It was done.

They had got the flames under control, though smoke still furled up into the gray sky, and Aldenburg felt no sense of having got to the end of it. It had felt as though it took all day, and yet it seemed only a few seconds in duration, too—the same continuous action, starting with letting the little glass of whiskey drop to the floor in Smitty's and bolting out the door. . . .

Afterward, he sat on the curb, near the young woman, the driver, where the paramedics had moved her to work over her. He had one leg out, the other knee up, and he was resting his arm on that knee, the pose of a man satisfied with his labor. He was aware that people were staring at him.

"I know you're not supposed to move them," he said to the paramedics. "But under the circumstances."

No one answered. They were busy with the injured, as they should be. He sat there and watched them, and watched the bus continue to smoke. They had covered it with some sort of foam. He saw that there were blisters on the backs of his hands, and dark places, where the fire and ash had marked him. At one point, the young woman looked at him and blinked. He smiled, waved at her. It was absurd, and he felt the absurdity almost at once. "I'm sorry," he said.

But he was not sorry. He felt no sorrow. He came to his feet, and two men from the television station were upon him, wanting to talk, wanting to know what he had been thinking as he risked his own life to save these children, and the driver, all of whom certainly would've died in the fumes, or been burned to death. It was true. It came to Aldenburg that it was all true. The charred bus sat there, blackened; you could smell the acrid hulk of it. Firemen were still spraying it, and police officers were keeping the gathering crowd at a safe distance. More ambulances were arriving, and they had begun to take the injured away. He thought he saw one or two stretchers with sheets over them, the dead. How many dead? He asked. He stood there looking into the face of a stranger in a blazer and a red tie. "How many?"

"No deaths," the face said. "Not yet, anyway. It's going to be touch and go for some of them."

"The driver?"

"She's in the worst shape."

"She stopped breathing. I got her breathing again."

"They've got her on support. Vital signs are improving. Looks like she'll make it."

There were two television trucks, and everyone wanted to speak to him. Smitty had told them how he'd risked the explosion and fire. Him, Gabriel Aldenburg. Yes, Aldenburg said in answer to their questions. It's Gabriel. Spelled exactly like the angel, sir. Yes. Aldenburg. Aldenburg. He spelled it out for them. A shoe salesman. Yes. How did I happen to be here. Well I was—

They were standing there holding their microphones toward him; the cameras were rolling.

Yes?

"Well, I was—I was in there," he said, pointing to Smitty's doorway. "I stopped in early for some breakfast."

Some people behind the television men were writing in pads.

"No," he said. "Wait a minute. That's a lie."

They all were looking at him now.

"Keep it rolling," one of the television men said.

"I spent the night in there. I've spent a lot of nights in there, lately."

Silence, Just the sound of the fire engines idling, and then another ambulance pulled off, sending its wail up to the blackened sky of the city.

"Things aren't so good at home," he said. And then he was telling all of it—the bad feelings in his house, the steady discouragements he had been contending with. He was telling them all how he had never considered himself a man with much gumption. He heard himself use the word.

The men with the pads had stopped writing. The television men were simply staring at him.

"I'm sorry," he told them. "It didn't feel right lying to you."

No one said anything for what seemed a very long time.

"Well," he said. "I guess that's all." He looked beyond the microphones and the cameras, at the crowd gathering on that end of the street—he saw Smitty, who nodded, and then the television men started in again—wanting to know what he felt when he entered the burning bus. Did he think about the risk to his own life?

"It wasn't burning that bad," he told them. "Really. It was just smoke."

"Have they told you who was driving the Cadillac?" one of them asked.

"No, sir,"

"Wilson Bolin, the television news guy."

Aldenburg wasn't familiar with the name. "Was he hurt?"

"Minor cuts and bruises."

"That's good." He had the odd sense of speaking into a vacuum, the words going off into blank air. Voices came at him from the swirl of faces. He felt dizzy, and now they were moving him to another part of the street. A doctor took his blood pressure, and someone else, a woman, began applying some stinging liquid to his cheek. "Mild," she said to the doctor. "It's mostly smudges."

"Look, am I done here?" Aldenburg asked.

No. Others approached. They took his name. They wanted to know everything about him—what he did for a living, where he came from, his family. He told them everything they wanted to know. He sat in the backseat of a car and answered questions, telling everything again, and he wondered how things might be for a television newsman who caused a terrible accident while driving drunk at seven o'clock in the morning. He said he felt some kinship with Mr. Bolin, and he saw that two women among those several people listening to him exchanged a look of amusement.

"Look, it's not like I'm some kid or something," he said sullenly. "I'm not here for your enjoyment or for laughs. I did a good thing today. Something not everyone would do—not many would do."

Finally, he went with some other people to the back of a television truck and answered more questions. He told the exact truth, as best he understood it, because it was impossible not to.

"Why do you think you did it?" a man asked.

"Maybe it was because I'd been drinking all night."

"You don't mean that."

"I've been pretty unhappy," Aldenburg told him. "Maybe I just felt like I didn't have anything to lose." There was a liberating something in talking about it like this, being free to say things out. It was as though his soul were lifting inside him; a weight that had been holding it down had been carried skyward in the smoke of the burning bus. He was definite and clear inside.

"It was an act of terrific courage, sir."

"Maybe. I don't know. If it wasn't me, it might've been somebody else." He touched the man's shoulder, experiencing a wave of generosity and affection toward him.

He took off work, and went home. The day was going to be sunny and bright. He felt the stir of an old optimism, a sense he had once possessed, as a younger man, of all the gorgeous possibilities in life, as it was when he and Eva had first been married and he had walked home from his first fulltime job, at the factory, a married man, pleased with the way life was going, wondering what he and Eva might find to do in the evening, happy in the anticipation of deciding together. He walked quickly, and as he approached the house he looked at its sun-reflecting windows and was happy. It had been a long time since he had felt so light of heart.

His brother-in-law was on the sofa in the living room, with magazines scattered all around him. Cal liked the pictures in *Life* and the articles in *Sport*. He collected them; he had old issues going all the way back to 1950. Since he had come back from the gulf, Eva had been driving around to the antique stores in the area, and a few of the estate auctions, looking to get more of them for him, but without much luck.

"What happened to you?" he said as Aldenburg entered. "Where've you been?"

"Where've *you* been today, old buddy?" Aldenburg asked him. "Been out at all?"

"Right. I ran the mile. What's got into you, anyway? Why're you so cocky of all sudden?"

"No job interviews, huh?"

"You know what you can do with it, Gabriel."

"Just wondering."

"Aren't you spunky. What happened to your face?"

He stepped to the mirror over the mantel. It surprised him to see the same face, there. He wiped at a soot-colored smear on his jaw. "Damn."

"You get in a fight or something?"

"Right," Aldenburg said. "I'm a rough character."

Cal's fiancée, Diane, appeared in the archway from the dining room. "Oh," she said. "You're home."

"Where's Eva?" Aldenburg said to Cal. Then he looked at Diane—short red hair, a boy's cut, freckles, green eyes. The face of someone who was accustomed to getting her way. Gazing at her, Aldenburg felt a rush of confidence in his ability to divine secrets; he was aware of a fresh sensitivity to the hidden side of people, a new, bright bloom in himself, of intuition. It was clear that she wanted to be far away from here. He would not be surprised to find that she was about to back out of her engagement to Cal.

318

"Where were *you* all night?" she said. "As if I didn't know."

"To the mountaintop," Aldenburg told her. "I've been breathing rarefied air."

"Gabriel," she said. "You're funny."

"You sure you want to go through with marrying Cal, here?"

"Don't be mean."

"What the hell?" Cal said, gazing at him. "You got a problem, Gabriel, maybe you should just say it out."

"No problem in the world on this particular day," Aldenburg told him.

"Something's going on. What is it?"

Aldenburg ignored him, and went calling through the house for his wife. Eva was in the bedroom, sitting at her dressing table putting makeup on. "Keep it up," she said. "You'll lose your job."

"They wanted me to take the day off," he said. "Fact is, they were proud to give it to me."

She turned and looked at him. "What is it?"

"You see something?"

"Okay."

"Well, do you?"

She turned back to the mirror. "Gabriel, I don't have time for games."

"This is serious."

She said nothing, concentrating on what she was doing.

"Did you hear me?"

After a pause, she said, "I heard you."

"Well?"

Now she looked at him. "Gabriel, what in the world?"

"Want to watch some TV?" he said.

"What're you talking about. Look at you. Did you get in a fight or something?"

"I had a rough night," he said.

"I can see that."

"Look into my eyes."

Diane came to the doorway of the room. "Cal and I are going over to my place for a while. I think we'll stay over there tonight."

"What a good idea," Aldenburg said.

Diane smiled, then walked away.

Eva sat staring at him.

"Look into my eyes, really." He stood close.

319

"Gabriel," she said. "You smell like a distillery. You're drunk."

"No," he said. "I'm not drunk. You know what happened?"

"You've been drinking at this hour of the morning."

"Listen to me."

She stared. He had stepped back from her. "Well?" she said.

"I saved human lives today." He felt the truth of it move in him, and for the first time paused and looked at it reasonably in his mind. He smiled at her.

"What," she said.

"You haven't heard me," he told her. "Did you hear what I said?"

"Gabriel," Eva said. "I've been thinking. Once again, I had all night to think. I've done a lot of thinking, Gabriel."

He waited.

"Quit smiling like that. This isn't easy." She gathered her breath. "I'm just going to say this straight out. Okay?"

"Okay," he said.

"I'm—I'm splitting."

He looked at her hands, at the mirror with her back and shoulders in it, at the floor, with their shadows on it from the bright windows.

"Diane has room for me in her house. And I can look for a place of my own from there. After she and Cal are married—"

Aldenburg waited.

His wife said, "It's a decision I should've made a long time ago.

"I don't understand," he said.

"Haven't you been listening?"

"Haven't *you?*" he said. "Did you hear what I just told you?"

"Oh, come *on,* Gabriel. This is serious."

"I'm telling you it *happened,*" he shouted.

"Gabriel—" she began.

He went back to the living room, where Cal and Diane were sitting on his couch. Diane had turned the television on—a game show. They did not look at him when he came in. They knew what had been talked about, and they were feeling the awkwardness of it. He went to the door and looked out at the street. The sun was gone. There were heavy dark folds of clouds to the east. He turned. "I thought you were going over to your house," he said to Diane. He could barely control his voice.

"We are. As soon as Cal finishes this show."

"Why don't you go now?"

"Why don't you worry about your own problems?"

"Get out," Aldenburg said. "Both of you."

Cal stood and reached for his cane. Aldenburg turned the TV off and waited by the door as they came past him. "Look, if it makes any difference," Cal said, "I argued against it."

Aldenburg nodded, but said nothing.

When they had gone he returned to the bedroom, where Eva had lain down. He sat on his side of the bed. He was abruptly very tired, and lightheaded.

"Do you want to tell me about it?" she said.

He said, "Would it matter?"

"Gabriel, what did you think was happening here—"

He came to his feet, removed his shirt. He felt the scorched places on his arms. Everything ached. He walked into the bathroom and washed his face and hands. Then he brushed his teeth. In the room, Eva lay very still.

"I'm not asleep," she said. "I'm going out in a minute."

He had a mental image of himself coming home with the news of what he had done, as if it were some prize. What people would see on TV this evening, if they saw anything, would be Aldenburg telling about how unhappy life was at home. No, they would edit that out. The thought made him laugh.

"What," she said. "I don't see anything funny about this."

He shook his head, trying to get his breath.

"Gabriel? What's funny."

"Nothing," he managed. "Forget it. Really. It's too ridiculous to mention."

He lay down. For a time they were quiet.

"We'll both be better off," she said. "You'll see."

He closed his eyes, and tried to recover the sense of importance he had felt, scrabbling across the floor of the burning school bus. He had been without sleep for so long. His wife's voice seemed to come from a great distance.

"It's for the best," she said. "If you really think about it, you'll see I'm right."

Abruptly, he felt a tremendous rush of anxiety. A deep fright at her calmness, her obvious determination. He was wide awake. When he got up to turn the little portable television on, she gave forth a small startled cry. He went through the channels.

"What're you doing?" she murmured. "Haven't you heard any-thing?"

"Listen," he told her. "Be quiet. I want you to see something."

"Gabriel."

"Wait." He heard the tremor in his own voice. "Dammit Eva. Please. Just one minute. It'll be on here in a minute. One minute, okay? What's one goddamn minute?" He kept turning the channels, none of which were news—it was all cartoons and network morning shows. "Where is it," he said. "Where the hell is it."

"Gabriel, stop this," said his wife. "You're scaring me."

"Scaring you?" he said. "Scaring you? Wait a minute. Just look what it shows. I promise you it'll make you glad."

"Look, it can't make any difference." She began to cry.

"You wait," he told her. "It made all the difference."

"No, look—stop—"

He grasped her by the arms above the elbow. It seemed so terribly wrong of her to take this away from him, too. "Look," he said, "I want you to *see* who you married. I want you to *know* who provides for you and your goddamn hero brother." When he realized that he was shaking her, holding too tight, he let go, and she sat there, crying, her hands clasped oddly at her neck.

"I can't—" she got out. "Gabriel—"

"Eva," he said. "I didn't mean—look, I'm, sorry. Hey, I'm—I'm the good guy, honey. Really. You won't believe it."

"Okay." She nodded. He saw fear in her eyes.

"I just hoped you'd get to see this one thing," he said, sitting next to her, wanting to fix this somehow, this new trouble. But then he saw how far away from him she had gone. He felt quite wrong, almost ridiculous. It came to him with a strange heat in his face and neck that he was going to have to go on being who he was. He stood, and the ache in his bones made him wince. He turned the television off. She was still sniffling, sitting there watching him.

"What?" she said. It was almost a challenge.

He couldn't find the breath to answer her. He reached over and touched her shoulder, very gently, so that she would know that whatever she might say or do, she had nothing to fear from him.

Nominated by Story, Mark Halliday, David Jauss, Joyce Carol Oates, Ellen Wilbur

INVOCATION

by MARILYN HACKER

from THE PARIS REVIEW

This is for Elsa, also known as Liz,
an ample-bosomed gospel singer: five
discrete malignancies in one full breast.
This is for auburn Jacqueline, who is
celebrating fifty years alive,
one since she finished chemotherapy
with fireworks on the fifteenth of July.
This is for June, whose words are lean and mean
as she is, elucidating our protest.
This is for Lucille, who shines a wide
beam for us with her dark cadences.
This is for long-limbed Maxine, astride
a horse like conscience. This is for Aline
who taught her lover to caress the scar.
This is for Eve, who thought of AZT
while hopeful poisons pumped into a vein.
This is for Nanette in the Midwest.
This is for Alicia, shaking back dark hair,
dancing one-breasted with the Sabbath bride.
This is for Judy on a mountainside,
plunging her gloved hand in a glistening hive,

Hilda, Patricia, Gaylord, Emilienne,
Tania, Eunice: this is for everyone
who marks the distance on a calendar
from what's each year less likely to "recur."
Our saved-for-now lives are life sentences
—which we prefer to the alternative.

Nominated by Philip Appleman, David Baker, Maureen Seaton

BAD BOY NUMBER SEVENTEEN

fiction by LUCIA PERILLO

from NEW ENGLAND REVIEW

YOU DON'T HAVE TO TELL ME about bad boys. I've seen bad boys coming and going. Coming they walk with their shoulders back like they've got a raw egg tucked inside each armpit, and they let their legs lead them. Going, you can count on the fact that their butts will cast no shadow on those lean long legs. In fact you can't be a bad boy if you're one of those guys shaped in the rear like a leather mail sack; you're automatically disqualified. That's just the way it is. I didn't make up the rules.

Bad boys make up for slender means by wearing their Levis tight enough to make it look like the billfold has a hard time sliding in. And bad boys make up for the fact that they're usually kind of stupid by not saying much. This is important. This is a bad boy litmus test. The last thing you want is a bad boy with a big mouth; you might as well invite a wild elephant home for dinner.

See, for years I have done some serious looking, up close and from a distance, at them hawking before the Burgermaster's drive-up place-your-order box or jimmying the pinball machine at King Solomon's Reef. Yeah, yeah: King Solomon had a mine, he didn't have a reef, but ours is a coastal town and the natives get claustrophobic inside any bar that doesn't have a nautical theme. Why it matters I don't know, because inside is always dim—so you can't see that really the only decorating theme is duct tape, which holds together the awful stuffed fish on the walls and the puckered vinyl in the booths, and even some of the more expensive and infrequently-sampled bottles of liquor that no one has the heart to throw away because of something picayunish as broken glass.

But out of all the low-rent dumps in town, this is probably the best laboratory for the study of bad boys, from the wannabes with their ballcaps and Aerosmith T-shirts to the shy bloodhounds who rest their elbows on the bar and silently massage their dewlaps. Inside every genuine bad boy there's a brooding Schopenhauer, a chronic melancholy that he nurses like a sourball in his cheek. He can see the whole arc of his life—from the uphill curve that is his freedom to the downhill slope that is his doom. And a bad boy without this flaring sense of precognition is just a loser, plain and simple. Like one night in The Reef there's this guy sitting on a barstool, checking me out over his shoulder from time to time? The fact that he's missing part of one finger shrouds him with the kind of mystery that ought to make him a contender, were this aura not counteracted by his jeans' riding so low they expose a length of his crack that's about equal to what's missing from his hand. Which knocks him out of the running, especially when a few boilermakers later he erupts in my direction with something about letting him know whenever I'm ready to have him take me outside to his Chevy where he's going to—his phrasing—*eat me out.*

I'm sitting in the booth with my sister Louisa, who giggles. "Don't giggle," I tell her. "What that guy said to us wasn't funny." Even though she's my older sister, since she's got Down's syndrome I have to explain everything.

"I think he's funny," she said in that woofy voice of hers. "I think he's cute. I think that boy wants to be my boyfriend." This is the kind of thing Louisa'll say that drives a stake of abject terror into my mother's heart. Lately Mom's been talking about getting Louisa's tubes tied, a plan I could condone on pragmatic grounds but against which I've nonetheless felt compelled to launch a few squeaks of protest. Louisa's been living with Mom ever since she got kicked out of the group home for repeated makeup theft, and even though Louisa's relatively self-sufficient—she can ride the bus, she has a job assembling calendars and pens—my mother feels that Louisa is both her millstone and her mission; until Louisa's fate is sewn up my mother won't rest easy in her old age. I mean, Louisa needs a baby about as badly as she needs a scholarship to M.I.T., but then another part of me says, who are we to go monkeying around with Louisa's body? And who am I to say that

Louisa shouldn't go outside to the missing finger's car—which I'm guessing is a Nova, black or gold, mid-seventies, needs a whole new exhaust—and let him take her on a rapturous spin around the block? Why should Louisa be barred from these transient joys that the rest of us got to purge from our systems in high school? I even feel squeamish about bringing Louisa into the bar, like someone's going to call Child Protective Services on me, though Louisa's well past thirty. When the bartender checks our IDs she lingers for a long time with Louisa's, her eyes ping-ponging between the mug shot and Louisa's face.

After a few minutes of scrutiny the bartender slides her ID across the table. "What does she want?" the bartender asks me.

One thing Louisa's figured out recently is what-to-do-when-people-refuse-to-speak-to-you routine. "Beer!" she pipes angrily.

"You want me to bring her a light beer?"

"St. Paulie Girl," Louisa insists. Where she gets this from I didn't know. *St. Paulie Girl.* Meanwhile the bartender's still looking at me for consensus.

"Hey I'm her older sister, not her mother. Give her what she wants. She's not the one driving." And I order a St. Paulie Girl for myself too, just so Louisa won't get paranoid that she's done something weird.

Anyway, the bartender vindicates herself later, by taking care of Finger when he makes his suggestion about taking me outside. Or maybe this is ego talking, my thinking that Finger was bird-dogging me and not my sister, who is after all not a bad looking woman, especially with her new perm and stylish John Lennon frames. I guess the bartender decides to step in as Louisa's protectress since she thinks I'm being too lax about that job. Bartender says something to Finger underneath her breath, something threatening enough to make his eyes go wide. Then to soothe him she takes a bunch of change from the till and drops it in the jukebox, one of the fancy new breed that play CDs. This does the trick: the bar falls silent while the lead guitar knifes its way through the intro. Then, with the grace and synchronicity of ballerinas, all the bad boys start playing air guitar by strumming the folds of skin around their navels. Finger tilts woozily over his glass, and not too long after the song ends he's got his arms folded on the bar with his head nested inside, whistling the strange birdcalls of sleep.

"Look," Louisa says elbowing me. "That funny boy is sleeping."

"I told you he's not funny. He's a jerk."

"Yeah," she says, bobbing her head. Often I find myself wishing Louisa did not agree so enthusiastically with everything I say. It forces

327

me to police myself all the time, and this policeman speaks in a voice I recognize as belonging to my mother, who'll say (like in defense of turning off Louisa's plumbing) *I wish you would start considering your sister's future more seriously. All I'm trying to do is set things up so that Louisa will be less of a burden to you when the day comes that neither I nor your father are around.* My mother always gives the words *your father* an extra jab. He has a new wife who lives with him in a house overlooking the Tacoma Narrows and the bridge that replaced the one they call Galloping Gertie because it turned into jell-o on a particularly windy day. My mother, on the other hand, is stuck living with Louisa in a trailer, though she becomes offended when I refer to it as such. "It's a *mobile home*", she insists huffily. "And it's got everything that anybody else's house has, except that I don't have to mow a lot of grass. *And* I've got the pool and the clubhouse. I notice you don't mind coming down off your high horse whenever you want to use my pool." As you can tell, it's a sore subject—that my mother's stuck with a clubhouse whose lone asset is a machine dispensing last year's Ho-Hos, and a pool that can barely accommodate a decent cannonball, while my father's got Galloping Gertie and the whole of Puget Sound right in his living room window. My mother thought she could salve her pride by hiring a decorator, whose handiwork ended up making the trailer look like the set of a late-night TV talk show, which must remind Louisa all the more about how her life has paled ever since she had to leave the group home, where she could tussle her girlfriends on the battered furniture every night, like attending summer camp forever. Louisa is simply too big for my mother's place—not that she's fat or anything, but her high spirits make her seem loud and clumsy. And my mother takes them as evidence of Louisa's naiveté and thinks we must band together to instruct her in the ways of evil.

"Look, Louisa," I say, watching Finger's drool run from his downhill cheek. "You've really got to start looking out for yourself. There's a lot of boys out there who are not nice boys."

Her face darkens. "Like the boys who yell at me at the bus stop. Mommy says they aren't nice."

'No, they're not nice. You know what I call them? Creeps." And then I ask her, "What did Mom tell you to do about them?"

Louisa answers ambivalently, and I can tell that despite their terrors the bus stop boys still glitter. "Mommy said just ignore them. She said

328

for me to pretend their voices were like the wind." This she demonstrates by blowing our cocktail napkins off the table.

"Good-bye creeps!" Louisa whooshes.

I mentioned that I've observed bad boys up close, but now let me confess that I haven't always proved to be the shrewdest judge of human nature. Most of my run-ins with bad boys have turned out . . . well bad. In my freshman year of high school I encountered Bad Boy Number One, who had me doing his pre-algebra problems half the night while he worked out the science of break and entering. Number Two was old enough to drive a car, and this romance (with the car more than the boy per se) left me with a greenstick fracture of my collarbone. Number Six was the one who suckered me into co-signing the loan on his brand new Mustang—how this story ends you don't need me to say—and Number Eight was the proud owner of a set-yourself-up-in-the-creative-and-lucrative-world-of-tattooing-with-EZ-monthly-payments kit, which he'd ordered from the back of a comic book. Pretty soon I figured out what you have by now no doubt concluded: Number Eight had loser written all over him. But this was not before I'd let him go to work on my left arm, inking a rattlesnake whose tail was rooted inside my elbow. It was supposed to be a little snake, but Number Eight had not yet mastered his craft, and the tail came out blotched and broken. Which compelled Number Eight to keep on keeping on, running the snake down the length of my arm, zig-zagging its sausagey shape so that he could get the most practice in. There was no way I could shut him off without leaving a lopped-off reptile on my arm, and by the time he got to my wrist, I have to admit the snake was starting to look pretty good, and the head—which he ran onto the back of my hand, too large for the rest of its body by half—was a masterpiece, complete with fangs and tongue and all the scales' fine reticulations.

Number Eight OD'ed on a speedball when the snake was just about complete but for the eyesockets that he hadn't gotten around to filling, which was about the same time I realized that putting a snake's head on your hand means that you have chosen an idiosyncratic road to head down in life, unless you plan to wear little white gloves all the time like Mr. Peanut. The snake gives you a hundred demerits in all but a few select kinds of job interviews; they finally took me in at the boat shop, where a tattooed woman is not considered all that strange. Boat people have a tendency to give what other people might consider sluttishness a wide berth. There aren't really any sluts in the boat world, the way there aren't really sluts at the Handy Rental, or working in Accounts Payable at Ralph's Kustom Kar Kustomizing, maybe because these industries top-heavy with bad boys are willing to extend women a quid pro quo of retroactive grace.

Of course the tattoo was what convinced my mother I had finally gone around the bend: ever since, she's been afraid I have an unsettling influence on Louisa. Her preference would be for the two of us not to be left alone, but she waffles on this because I am Louisa's most obvious (and cheapest) chaperon. When my mother wanted to go on a cruise, for instance, she had no choice but to ask me to come live at the trailer for those two weeks. As always, Louisa is thrilled at my presence—she knows when I come to stay we will turn the radio up full blast and eat all kinds of disgusting takeout foods and launch ourselves into a cleaning frenzy to get the greasy pizza boxes into a dumpster just minutes before my mother walks back through the door.

So I'm staying there on a drizzly Sunday, when what Louisa wants to do is see a movie. We commit the ultimate naughtiness by spreading the newspaper on the white carpet, and after Louisa scrutinizes the movie ads she lets her finger stab down on one called "Primal Reflex," which stars Hollywood's latest flavor-of-the month in some pretty steamy scenes. Junctures like these are where my mother's voice cuts in, and I point out the comedies instead.

Louisa's mind is made up. "I want to see this girl do the hula-hula," she says. In the advertisement, Latest Flavor's got a hibiscus flower pinned behind one ear, her face framed in the cross hairs of some anonymous gun.

"It's not a hula movie," I explain. "You're thinking of like Annette Funicello."

"No, I'm thinking of *her*." Louisa trots into her room to retrieve a movie magazine that's got a picture of Flavor wearing a lei and a thong bikini, bodysurfing off the coast of Waikiki.

"Toldja," Louisa says.

With Louisa, you can never go into the obvious, the *this thing had nothing to do with anything, oh my dearest darling one*. Louisa's brain moves like a jackrabbit, and when she's threatened she uses the jackrabbit's zig-zag to escape. Like after she makes her point, Louisa immediately launches elaborate preparations for the movie, which mostly revolve around finding this folding plastic rainhat that my mother brought home as a souvenir from her last trip to Greece. *All*

330

you brought her's a goddamn rainhat from the hotel? I complained, which made my mother snipe about how Louisa wouldn't know the difference. And it irked me to realize later that my mother had been right, because the rainhat became one of Louisa's prize possessions. She wears it proudly as we board the bus downtown, which I suggest in order to make the trip seem like more of an adventure. Or maybe I'm subconsciously stalling so we'll have to catch the 3:15 show instead, which is "101 Dalmatians." No luck: we get there right on time, and during the movie I hear Louisa giggle whenever the woman appears naked on screen. Of course we don't get to see the men naked, and for once I'm grateful for Hollywood's injustices.

Afterwards Louisa gives the movie two thumbs up and can't wait to boogie—*I want a happy beer,* she says. I suspect she's thinking of the boy on the stool again but is afraid he's off-limits as a topic of conversation. Luckily, he's not there when we get back to The Reef, just a few blocks from the theater, where I give Louisa five dollars in quarters for the jukebox. This makes her so excited that I'm almost afraid I've done some permanent damage to her health. She punches in "Jesus is Just All Right with Me," by the Doobie Brothers, comes back to the table knowing all the words, which surprises me because I've never heard Louisa say anything about Jesus. Mom sometimes drags her to the Church of the Parted Waters, a Baptist outfit Mom joined because of its zeal for coffee clatches and potlucks, though often she returns home with her own dishes barely touched. I think the Baptists are afraid my mother's hexed: why else would she have given birth to a Down's kid when she was only in her twenties, the other one don't even mention—they've all heard about the snake. I also suspect Mom's main interest in the church is that she thinks it'll dignify the ugly rituals of cruising men. She's sailing to Nassau with the Baptists as we speak, because I didn't have the heart to tell what any woman with two working eyeballs should be able to see: that Church of the Parted Waters is a magnet for losers. And I mean the capital-L Losers—we're talking bankruptcy and thorazine. Personally I think she's got better odds of scoring heroin among them than a husband.

But I should talk. I'm not even going to tell you about Bad Boys Nine through Sixteen, though my not mentioning them doesn't mean they're not etched permanently in my brain along with all the ways I behaved shamelessly in their presence. They're printed with such big block letters that when the next one walks into The Reef—and I know he's the next one, don't ask how I know—the word rolls up my throat

and into my mouth without the slightest calculation. *Seventeen.*
Straightaway that culprit gland starts spewing acid in my gut and
cranking down the ratchets in my chest.

See, when you meet a boy like Seventeen he sticks like a nasty bout
of flu: a few days ago at work, he was the one I'd shown a half-dozen
used boats we had sitting on the lot. I trailed behind him so I could
make a careful study of his hips, and now, as he's walking in, I get the
full-on view: black T-shirt with a breast pocket, breast pocket with a
cigarette pack, cigarette pack a quarter full and crumpled. Right away
he recognizes me and sits down to give me an update, something like
*Yesterday I decided on the Bayliner and went over and gave Milty
some money down. What I liked about the Bayliner was that it came
stocked with this Mercury outboard that you could tear down with
both eyes closed and one arm tied behind your back.*

I say, *Let's see if the gasoline smell's still on your hand.* No, just kid-
ding, I don't say that—the last thing a bad boy needs is a woman who's
off-kilter, though that's what he'll end up with 99.9 percent of the time.
"You got a good buy," I say. And something like: "We haven't even had
that Bayliner for a week." The reason I have a hard time tracking what
we say is because Louisa's sitting beside me, still crooning; in fact by
now she's got her eyes closed and is belting out "Jesus is Just All Right
with Me" at the top of her lungs. In a place like The Reef a woman
singing won't turn anybody's head, at least not until she starts a fist-
fight. But when Louisa finally opens her eyes and sees Seventeen, her
face flushes as dark as an eggplant.

"Keep singing," he says. "You sing good."

Louisa's afraid he might be teasing, "Naw . . ." she demurs. But he
says, "No, really, I like this song. And when it comes on the radio I can
never understand the words because the guy mumbles. But you don't
mumble. Shoot, you sing better than he does."

This must be one of the famous moments in Louisa's life. She trem-
bles but retains enough composure to keep singing, and after the
song's over Seventeen applauds and volunteers to buy us all another
round. Reading the label on Louisa's bottle, he whistles.

"You sure got expensive taste, sister." It's a word Louisa grabs onto
joyfully.

"I'm her big sister," she announces, elbowing me. "I get to boss her
around."

"I bet you do," he says. The beer comes; he and I pass the time de-
bating the various merits of the Mercury versus the Evinrude out-

board while Louisa beams in and out of the conversation. When he goes to the can, Louisa leans toward me and says, "I think this one will be my boyfriend."

"Oh, yeah? How can you tell?"

"I think he's nice to me."

It's my mother talking again when I hear myself say, "You don't know the first thing about that boy," which makes Louisa silent, sulky, tracing out letters in her spilt beer.

Finally she says, "Even though you're my sister, you know what?" And she goes on to answer without looking at me: "You don't always know everything."

The three of us leave The Reef buzzed and giddy from what has been a very happy hour, Louisa with the dopey rainhat accordioned on her head and almost swooning when Seventeen volunteers to tie the plastic flaps in an awkward bow beneath her chin. We're walking to Seventeen's pickup so he can give us a ride home, Louisa hanging on his arm, and though it doesn't seem physically possible her happiness escalates by yet another order of magnitude when she sees what's bounding in the truckbed: some kind of animal resembling a cross between a mountain goat and a Saint Bernard and an old upholstered chair.

"That's my dog Red," says Number Seventeen. "I bet he's glad to see us."

"He's white!" Louisa declares. "How come you call him Red?"

"Well I'm glad to see that someone's on her toes around here. But I'm afraid I can only explain by telling you a story that you've got to promise me won't make you cry." As he shoves and scruffs the dog, who's chained to an old tire plus its rim, he tells us how he paid four hundred dollars for a purebred he was going to use for hunting ducks " . . . and I ended up with this thing. Now does this look anything like a golden retriever to you?"

No! No! we shout half-drunkenly. And again when he starts to drive us home—*No! No!*—Louisa and I riding in the back with an old canvas tarp pulled up to our chins. The truck is just a dented riceburner with two bucket seats, and when we all wouldn't fit inside I watched Louisa wrestle with her loyalties: she wanted to pat the dog, she wanted to stick with her sister, she wanted to ride up front with the boy who's as glamorous to her as any movie star. In the end that made two against one and Louisa got in back with the dog and me.

"Take us to see the boat!" I holler into the open driver's window. But Seventeen hollers back about how he hasn't picked it up yet.

Instead he takes us to see where he's going to keep it berthed, as we drive through the beautiful monotony of northwest summer—the sky a metal color that we can't see through and the air warm and misting just enough that we can feel it on our faces. We head down the bayshore road with the water on our left shoulders and the mountains on our right, and suddenly through tall firs the late sun spikes in shafts so deeply yellow they are almost opaque. Northhope Harbor cuts into the point ten miles from town, where the Sound picks up current and breaks into chop, and it's there that Seventeen pulls up in the gravel parking lot and crunches around the truckbed, shouldering a six-pack he's pulled from behind the seat. "It's shit beer, ladies," he says as he climbs in. "But it's all I got."

Louisa's getting wasted, way past the two-beer limit that I usually nail her to. But today I say oh what the hell: she is happy, she is happier than I've ever seen her. The boy is lying underneath the tarp between us, and the dog is nosing the folds of her rainhat—until he discovers skin and starts making big slurps up and down her face.

Here's the last thing I know about bad boys: most bad boys are lousy lays. Going into it you have to understand they're not the kind of guys who'll care whether or not you come. That part of the equation goes right over their head, the whole idea of female orgasm reminding them of high school math class and having to solve for X. What they do best is look out for themselves, which means popping a beer or falling asleep or—and perhaps this is the epitome of bad boy post-coital tristesse—turning on the television and (if stars are aligned in their favor) discovering a replay of the Indy 500, the cars going round and round and round.

This is how the world is starting to look when we finish the last of Seventeen's beer, dusk settling on the water, which seems to whirl in a slow eddy that spins the boats and ricochets the early stars. After Seventeen takes us out for cheeseburgers and doesn't even squawk when Louisa uses about forty of those little packs of ketchup, ripping them open with her teeth and shooting the contents in jags that scribble her with red, the three of us end up, where else, at my mother's trailer, where Louisa, despite her happiness or maybe sated with it, falls on the sofa and commences snoring like a man. In my mother's bedroom Seventeen says, *now you gotta let me see the rest of that snake* and

334

when I roll up my sleeve he starts to improvise his murmurs . . . *let's see if you got any other secret pitchers.* . . .and I show him it all to prove there's no more pictures.

Let me say flat-out that, despite these promising overtures, Seventeen's lovemaking is not a memorable event. The beer makes his athleticism sloppy, and when he touches me he's wide on all his marks. I know I should say *our* lovemaking, but with bad boys the woman is not held accountable once she's tilted off the upright. And that's not laziness but a female way of lending grace: you've got to give these boys control of one thing when everything else about their lives is veering off its course, the one thing they think is most important, the one thing they think'll turn them into men.

What I'm trying to explain is why I'm not crestfallen in the morning when I discover Number Seventeen gone. Only for a moment does his vanishing even come as a surprise, until I remember that sometime during his examination of my marked and unmarked skin he told me that he'd have to be at a roofing job by six. In fact when I first wake up I think I'm lying in a strange motel until I realize that it's just my mother's bedroom with its Johnny Carson drapes. And just like in a cheap motel there's this loud thump-crashing coming from the other rooms, where I find Louisa romping with Seventeen's beast, who's still chained to the tire that he's dragging across my mother's formerly white rug. Already they've broken one wing off the wingback chair, and now he puts his paw right through a sofa cushion as though he were stepping in a bucket. Hanging from his teeth the dog's got some kind of translucent seaweed, which I finally recognize as Louisa's rainhat.

"What's going on here?" I scream.

Obviously she's confused that I could be angry on such a joyful morning. "I think that boy left this nice dog for me." And damned if she's not right: on the counter there's a note that reads *Didn't want to tell you I am married, etc. Wife has allergies and wanted me to put the dog down yesterday, so maybe it was Red's good luck that I ran into you and your sister, who seems like she could use a hound like him.* Spelling is not Seventeen's best subject; actually the note reads, "I am marred, ect." *I am marred?* Christ, I slap myself when I finally get it. I should have known he was married. Said his mother was dead and yet that T-shirt reeked of laundry soap.

I crumple the note and ask Louisa why these fucking things are always happening to me.

335

"What's the matter?" Louisa's still confused. "I love this dog." She drapes her body along its length and squeezes the dog's ribs, which makes its mouth flop open with a big pink tongue I swear could break your heart, as the dog spreads its legs and lays a yellow stream onto the rug.

Too late for either of us to go to work, we call in sick, lie on the sofa moaning and holding blocks of frozen peas to our heads while Red laps from the toilet. "I have a *hangover*," Louisa chants, savoring the word like it's a million bucks. Before noon the toilet's dry and Red is hankering for out, so we make bologna sandwiches and carry them down the street to the vacant lot. First I have to take a hacksaw to his chain to cut the tire free, and until we get there Louisa uses one of her plastic jumpropes as a leash, on the end of which he strains and wheezes— *Hold on boy,* Louisa bellows. As soon as Red's untied he's bolting across the meadow like a streak, the late summer flowers still in bloom but what does the dog care as he tramples them underfoot, every now and then glancing over his shoulder to tease Louisa into hot pursuit. I watch them leaping fair-haired in the weeds, both too big for this world, both too big to be concealed.

Nominated by New England Review, Dorothy Barresi, Ron Tanner

HISTORIES OF BODIES

by MARIKO NAGAI

from NEW LETTERS

for J.R.
Be ahead of all partings.
—Rainer Maria Rilke

I.

That's how we can distinguish a man from a woman, or from
    ourselves: only in
a moment of embrace. Judgment on bodies has already passed,
    they say we are
like any other, cock is a breast, balls another pair that
    swings like hands
of a clock. Our stories have no listener, our stories are like
    any other.
We misunderstood each other, our bodies the only proof of intimacy,
    a repetition
of bodies coming together as we move on top or under each other,
we fill each other with ourselves in the moment of embrace, an imago
stretching its wings out, two bodies connected by embrace.

II.

"Hush," you say, "I love your body," "I get hard only for you," "I am
    yours only."

You say that sex is another word for how we leave the body, or, how,
    like the Whirling
Dervishes, we seek the eternal in the embrace, in the moment of
    unveiling
the white so much like a butterfly, or our selves. You hold your cock,
    your release
comes like a magician releasing the doves. They land on my
    stomach, they stay there until they dry like scabs over wounds.

I love you: "Love is another way to say how unoriginal we are," or,
    "You and I are separated
by a word, a mere word." Love is a division, it is a barrier that makes
    us what we are,
another word for how repetition becomes the way we part from each
    other, over
and over again, Love is another way of saying, *Your face in this light
    is how I want to remember*
you, a face only a few steps away from death; this is when I like you
    best.

III.

You call it *shoah,* the unrepeatable. Here's a picture: soldiers
    burning books.
Another picture: soldiers dragging an old man who held the Torah
    as if it were
his child, or God. Let us move thirty years ahead: here's a picture of
    students burning
books, another of students pushing an old man clutching the Classics.
The faces of these boys are so many years before any partings they
    can understand,
their bodies taut with how little years they have. Pictures are
    repeatable, so are events.
God loves innocence and children, but two are not the same.
I say that the holocaust is an image of bodies ahead of all partings.
The souls have already forgotten the rib cages, the backbones that
    protrude like a broken
violin. A picture: bodies after bodies thrown into a ditch. The only
    thing

338

separating a man from a woman is by how their sacks are carelessly
    placed:
here is a man, his balls have shriveled to the size of a large pea;
    there, a woman,
where her breasts once were, two broken pendulums that no longer
    tell time hang. *I want*
to say, the shaved heads tell all: holocaust is the debasement of
    bodies,
where bodies turn into grotesque universality. In this picture, a
    woman lies
on top of two men, their mouths open as if almost a kiss, an embrace.

IV.

The proof is the body, not in words: you lie on your stomach, slowly
    rocking yourself
to sleep as if the bed is another body you can ease yourself into. I lie
next to you, my thighs slightly open like a window, or a door,
    anyone can look
in, even you. But we have stopped our movements already. In this
    early morning, words are bodies
heaped up high, each body imprinted with past, they are
    remembrance. But we have already turned
our eyes inward, we do not hear. Each come-cry hides in the cave
    of the mouth,
stays inside of us like doves in a magician's pockets, waiting for the
    signal they've been trained to recognize.

Nominated by New Letters

IN THE MIDST OF SISTERS

essay by JANE McCAFFERTY

from WITNESS

THE Little Sisters of the Poor took care of my grandmother for the last fifteen years of her life, in a Delaware nursing home named for Jean Jugan, a woman from Brittany who founded this order of nuns over 150 years ago. Jean Jugan was a young French woman who once saw an old, blind and semi-paralyzed woman trying to survive on the streets. It was a winter night in Saint-Servan, and Jugan, who had long been sharing her meager salary, her food, and much of her spare time with the people of the streets, took the old woman, Anne Chauvin, in her arms, carried her home and placed her in her own bed. This kind of charity was as radical then as it is today in America.

Soon Jean Jugan was taking care of many women, and other young women were helping her. The Congregation of the Little Sisters of the Poor was born, and now, in 250 homes in thirty countries, these women care for old people who find themselves penniless and alone near the end of their lives, as my grandmother had been for many years.

My family supported my grandmother as best they could, and she lived with us until she was seventy, but finally her bouts of severe depression and extraordinary dependency became too much for family members to contend with. I had just moved to Pittsburgh then, and wanted her to come live with me. Perhaps this would have been a disaster, like my mother said, but I was never given a chance to find out. After a few attempts at assisted living, The Little Sisters took her in.

She lived there, for those fifteen years, in that immaculate nursing home that had no smell at all—not the typical odor of decay and neglect that so many nursing facilities have, nor the heavy pine scent that often lingers in the air as a cover-up—and she died there, in a room with a long window cut into the wall, letting in the light.

Her death was described as "beautiful" by her two daughters, because of the quality of care she received while she lay dying that month. I spoke to my mother long distance each day to check on my grandmother, and what surprised me was how consistently peaceful, even joyful my mother sounded. "It's this place," she'd say. "It's the sisters. They're contagious."

I know well how to discern from my mother's voice the various emotional states she visits or tries not to visit; she has struggled all her life with manic depression, and as her daughter, I can't help but listen carefully to how tone imbues her language. The voice in which she spoke as my grandmother faced death was unique for her. At least I'd never heard it before. It was a voice without an edge, but with great strength at its center. It had the character of depth, tenderness, and solidity, and somehow struck me as her "real" voice, the one I'd unknowingly missed all my life. Gone was the desperate sound of someone trying with all her notable energy to be, as she would say, "upbeat." Gone was the raw, loud laughter whose source was the urgent need to erase silence that might allow for reflection. In its place this past summer, there in the Jean Jugan home, was laughter from her gut, enriched by a mysterious peace.

"You sound good," I kept saying, in wonder. And I'd want to hang on the phone for as long as she'd let me.

What I wanted to hear was the simple story of my mother's day, told to me in this new voice. "S. and I got here about eight in the morning, as usual. I brought donuts for us and the nuns. These nuns have sweet tooths like you wouldn't believe. And Gram's responsive today. She smiled a few times. You have to talk into her ear. She doesn't open her eyes much but she knows we're always here. And the nuns, I can't even begin to describe them." (But she could.) "Sister Bernadette, she used to be a model, she's six-foot-one and she's a riot. She goes around singing. Not just hymns."

"She used to be a model? And now she's a nun?"

"She's gorgeous. And she's a riot. And then Sister Thomas, she's a talented artist. She's a regular Monet. And the way they treat Gram . . ."

341

"They sound great."

I had been taught by nuns all my life—Saint Joseph's nuns in black and white habits. As a very small child I admired them; I even had a nun doll. She had a stiff, plastic, flat-chested body, a benign, pretty face, glassy blue eyes, and a black and white habit exactly like the Saint Joe's nuns I knew. You could pull a string on her back, and she'd say, "Judge not, that ye be not judged."

But after fourth grade, my friends and I stopped appreciating nuns (except for the Flying Nun, the Singing Nun, and our own fat, sneakered Recess Nun). Nor did it seem anyone held them in high esteem. They were seen by most people as vaguely pathetic—women who couldn't get men. When I announced I wanted to be a nun in third grade, my mother looked stricken and told me I'd grow out of it—even though she was a devout Catholic. The sexism of society in the Sixties and Seventies, and more pointedly of the Catholic church, had much to do with this. Priests were the respected "fathers." Girls referred to "cute" priests as "Father What-a-Waste." Boys never had such a name for nuns. Nuns were asexual, repressed, lonely. Many were "bullies." Some of this was sometimes true. But nobody told me how to see nuns as independent women who were, in part, rejecting the constricting roles of wife and mother and mate that society deemed "normal," not to mention the role of consumer. And certainly nobody paid much attention to the Little Sisters of the Poor.

"You just have to see all this," my mother said. "When are you coming?"

Nine months pregnant, I made the trip, not primarily to "see all this" though I was curious, but rather to say good-bye to a grandmother I had adored as a child. She had always been there—first across the street in my cousin's house, and later in our own house. She had ten grandchildren, but had singled me out as her secret favorite, no doubt because I was clearly the most devoted to her, the most visibly enamored.

She was not "grandmotherly." She had no apron, no kitchen with cookies baking, no softness, no gray hair in a bun. She was tall and angular with dyed hair the color of which she named "San Fernando red" for reasons nobody knew, and black cat-eyed glasses enlarging her already large blue eyes. She had an Irish Catholic shame of the body deep in her bones, so that when she hugged you, a space was left in between that was never filled. She would pat you on the back, almost apologizing for her lack of warmth. She had enormous wit—even a

342

child could sense this, though her jokes were not for children. And she was vain: her hair, nails, polyester blouses and slacks were always impeccable, as was her tiny green apartment where I loved to sleep beside her on her pull-out couch, the satin pillow cases one of her few real luxuries.

Perhaps on the surface it's a mystery as to why I loved her with such intensity. For children are usually drawn to warmth, to adults who can warmly love them back, adults who can enfold them when tears fall, whose rooms are comfortably cluttered. I suspect it was partly her coolness and distance that seemed an oasis of safety in a childhood that was shaped by parents too visibly struggling with personal demons. And then later, when I wasn't so interested in safety, I admired her *story,* the one I knew from my mother and from photographs.

She had what I considered a good heart. She'd fallen in love and married a Russian Jew in the late 1930s, the near equivalent of an interracial marriage today. She had grown up in a strict Catholic family, and now she was raising children in Wilmington, Delaware's Christ Our King parish where the priest regularly reminded her daughters that their father would burn in hell if they didn't convert him, and where some of the neighbors forbade their own children from playing with the "half-Jews down the street." "To hell with them," she'd say. "We don't need their kind."

In old photographs her head is cocked to the side and she's not smiling. She's often smoking. I recognized in her face the expression of the quintessential outsider.

Her marriage ended in divorce after fourteen years—rare in the Forties—and then my grandfather took off for California, and my grandmother was left to raise her daughters, who were twelve and thirteen, alone. My mother's stories all suggest she was not particularly cut out for motherhood. For example, when my mother and her sister would come home from school, they would find my grandmother stretched out on a bed upstairs, "playing dead." They would shake her and shout to her and perhaps out of a truly desperate need for solitude, she'd simply pretend she was dead. I chose to hear the black humor in the story, not the cruel pathology. I loved my grandmother even more when I heard stories like this, and there were many.

Yet what I'm interested in here is not the love I once held for her, but rather what became of the love.

Somehow in my late twenties I stopped visiting her more than once or twice a year. I had the excuse of living five hours away, but that wasn't the real problem. I stopped visiting because she was willfully disengaging herself from life. She didn't talk much when you visited her, and it was a strain to try to fill her in on my life because I couldn't feel her listening. What I could usually count on back then was a smile, some light in her watery blue eyes, some laughter when I made a joke. Eventually, even those signs disappeared, and a kind of bitterness seemed present in her face. And when I looked in her eyes I thought I saw anger. Or was I imagining it?

I never asked her.

When I did make those infrequent, obligatory visits in my late twenties, I was always struck as I stood in the doorway by the image of her lying on her bed, hands folded on her stomach, eyes closed to her spotless room that was like a monk's, her few choice possessions on the table by the bed. The sadness I felt was always complicated, and eventually nearly replaced with impatience and disappointment that she was wasting precious life, that she was retreating so entirely from this world.

But there are two visits I remember well before this impatience—which I recognize now as a hardening of the heart—took hold.

One takes place before she lived with the Little Sisters. I am in my early twenties, and I take a bus up from college to visit her in her apartment, which is located in a kind of communal high-rise for "seniors." It's lunchtime, and I find the dining room, and walk among the chattering old people, most of them gathered at large round tables, until I spot my grandmother clear across the room at a deuce table by the curtained window where she is seated with a small woman older than herself. I rush toward her, filled with more emotion than I know, so that when I reach her and bend down to kiss her cheek I'm crying. It's the sight of her in a place filled with people who know nothing about her that moves me—these people who could never understand her, who know nothing of her history, who believe she is simply Mary, the woman who doesn't talk much, the woman who closes her door. And it's something else too, something in her posture that looks like submission, an obedience to circumstance, a pure powerlessness.

And yet I cherish this memory, because her face lit up when she saw me; she was not yet angry, not bitter. She loved me with what I then imagined was unconditional love, and I loved her back with what I then would have sworn was unconditional love.

The other visit I find myself remembering takes place years later, after I am married. It's a hot summer day, and I'm alone and bound for Rehoboth Beach to see an old friend, and again I surprise my grandmother, who now is settled in the Jean Jugan home. I leave the hot day and walk through the cool, clean halls to find her room, then stand in her doorway and look at her lying on her bed with my black-and-white wedding picture framed and standing on the table beside her. The room is in shadow, and because there are so few possessions, my own face framed beside my sleeping grandmother takes on an almost eerie life of its own. I feel the power of the room's loneliness surrounding the image of me in a veil, and though I haven't visited in half a year, I don't initially feel guilt. Love obliterates guilt for the time being.

But when she opens her eyes to find me sitting beside her on the bed with tears in my own eyes, her face hardens. "Why the tears?" she asks. And I'm torn between the power of my own feeling for her and the realization that my tears seem to her like a sentimental display. "Why the tears?" she says again. "I just miss you," I say. To which she says nothing. I try to stop my tears. Her eyes grow vague. I *did* miss her.

But she was right to mistrust the presence of my emotion. For if I really missed *her* and not the idea of her, the memory of her, why didn't I visit more often? Send cards? Flowers? Something? Unconditional love it wasn't.

Wasn't she interesting enough now?

She was getting old, but without the grace we all hope will accompany those we love, and eventually ourselves. She wasn't getting old in an "interesting" way. She wasn't sitting back and telling me wonderful stories, or asking me to tell stories of my own. And I judged her for it, and felt threatened by it, and abandoned by what I thought of as her decision to detach from this life. I told myself that my visits didn't matter to her anyhow.

Many of the subsequent visits felt almost loveless to me. Or rather, whatever love was there was weighted with something unspoken that seemed almost a presence in the room. Perhaps in the place of old, reliable love was her anger—which I don't think she was even conscious of—and my unvoiced (even to myself) disappointment that she hadn't managed to be stronger as she'd aged.

As she lay in what would be her deathbed, my mother and aunt left me alone in the room with her. They had just given me her rosary beads—the only possession she really cared about. I clenched these in my hands, but it was not an easy gift to receive.

345

Her breathing was shallow and labored. Her face was beautiful—smooth and white, nearly unlined. Her long white hair was also beautiful. I had never seen her hair this way; she'd gone to beauty parlors to get her hair "done" all her life. (There was even a beauty parlor in the Jean Jugan home.) I touched her hair; white silk. I did not cry because she seemed so peaceful, and because she was so utterly unlike herself that it was almost as if I were visiting a stranger. They told me I could speak loudly into her ear and that she would answer me. "Gram, I love you!" I tried. She didn't respond. "Are you comfortable?" I nearly shouted. No answer.

So I sat there, my hand on her hand, and tried without success to say a prayer for her. I was unable to locate any center in my self that would allow for the depth that precedes any kind of real prayer. I felt dispersed—a part of me not willing to be present there.

Afterwards, her favorite nun came into the room. She spoke to my grandmother in a normal tone, without putting her mouth anywhere near her ear. "How are you, Mary? Are you comfortable?" The nun was small, with a kind, serious face.

"Sister. Fine. Fine," she managed. The words were strained, and unclear, but there they were. A smile on her lips. "How are you, Sister?" she managed.

I understood then that whatever I had or hadn't done for my grandmother, I wouldn't be forgiven.

I stayed and watched the nun brush her hair, and turn her over onto her side with the help of another nun. My mother and aunt returned to the room and spoke to me about the wonder of the nuns.

How they brush her hair twice a day. They bathe her. They rub her feet. They change her gown—beautiful gowns—every day. They put a little make-up on her cheeks, because they know appearance had always been important to her. They turn her in her bed every two hours. They give her morphine when she's in pain. Her room is scrubbed and polished every day. It *shines*. They bring flowers. They hold her hand and talk to her, always using her name. "Mary, how are you, love," they say. Two or three sit by the bed and pray all night long, keeping watch in case her "time should draw near."

These were the nuns who had cared for her for fifteen years. This was unconditional love. Unsentimental love. The love that stays with you when you change. The love that moved my grandmother to speak as she was dying.

346

I saw the nuns in action. The certainty of their hands and bodies as they went about the task of giving comfort. But what I found most compelling were their vivid faces.

Their eyes had a kind of clarity and focus, a kind of intention, that was utterly humbling to witness. And at the core of this intention was concentrated joy. No denying it. It wasn't delusion. It wasn't simple self-forgetting, though that was there too. It was happiness, pure and steady. The happiness of the spirit that must come from deep faith. The happiness that fueled the love they felt for the aged people they served. That made the place feel so *real*—so devoid of artifice.

I watched them and remembered working in a nursing home when I was twenty, trying to teach a poetry-writing workshop to people in their eighties and nineties, a job I loved. But in that American nursing home, you could barely breathe without wanting to gag. Most of the underpaid nurses and nurses' aides looked haggard, resentful. The residents cried out from their beds and wheelchairs and because the place was understaffed, nobody came. Nobody came to change their diapers, to hold their hand, to feed them, to assure them they were not alone. They were alone. It was the more typical American nursing home, a kind of nightmare, really.

One of the Little Sisters told me that there are many stories of how people die, but a common thread emerges: the desire deep in the heart of every person to *live* until the very last moment, a willingness to continue an existence which may seem impoverished, sorrowful, painful, *on condition* that one knows oneself to be esteemed and loved, and assured that everything possible will be done to alleviate suffering. "That's what always strikes me. Their *passion* to live if they're loved," she said.

I think of my grandmother's last moment. She died with her favorite nun nearby, and her two daughters, all of them singing a hymn in her dark room where the moon shone in the window at four in the morning, her face as happy as my mother had ever seen it.

I will probably never grasp the mysterious depth of the faith that fuels the Little Sisters. But I'll think of it often, and I'll see all the loves of my life now in relation to their kind of love, which finally, is work, joyful work.

Nominated by Witness, Jim Daniels

PRAYER

by GRACE SCHULMAN

from **POETRY**

For Agha Shahid Ali

Yom Kippur: wearing a bride's dress bought in Jerusalem,
I peer through swamp reeds, my thought in Jerusalem.

Velvet on grass. Odd, but I learned young to keep this day
just as I can, if not as I ought, in Jerusalem.

Like sleep or love, prayer may surprise the woman
who laughs by a stream, or the child distraught in Jerusalem.

My Arab dress has blue-green-yellow threads
the shades of mosaics hand-wrought in Jerusalem

Jews, Muslims, prize, like the blue-yellow Dome of the Rock;
like strung beads-and-cloves said to ward off the drought in
   Jerusalem.

Both savor things that grow wild—coreopsis in April,
the rose that buds late, like an afterthought, in Jerusalem.

While car-bombs flared, an Arab poet translated
Hebrew verses whose flame caught in Jerusalem.

And you, Shahid, sail Judah Halevi's sea as I,
on Ghalib's, course like an Argonaut in Jerusalem.

Stone lions pace the Sultan's gate while almonds bloom
into images, Hebrew and Arabic, wrought in Jerusalem.

No words, no metaphors, for knives that gore flesh
on streets where the people have fought in Jerusalem.

As this spider weaves a web in silence,
may Hebrew and Arabic be woven taut in Jerusalem.

Here at the bay, I see my face in the shallows
and plumb for the true self our Abraham sought in Jerusalem.

Open the gates to rainbow-colored words
of outlanders, their sounds untaught in Jerusalem.

My name is Grace, Chana in Hebrew—and in Arabic.
May its meaning, "God's love," at last be taught in Jerusalem.

Nominated by Witness, Marianne Boruch, Carl Dennis, Stuart Dybek,
Marilyn Hacker, Sherod Santos, Arthur Smith

CYBERMORPHIC BEAT-UP GET-DOWN SUBTERRANEAN HOMESICK REALITY-SANDWICH BLUES

fiction by LANCE OLSEN

from ANYONE IS POSSIBLE (Red Hen Press)

I'M A, LIKE, POET. Mona. Mona Sausalito. I write lyrics for my boyfriend's band, Plato's Deathmetal Tumors. Plato's Deathmetal Tumors kicks butt. It's one of the best Neogoth bands in Seattle. My boyfriend's name is Mosh. Mosh shaved his head and tattooed it with rad circuitry patterns. He plays wicked cool lead and sings like Steve Tyler on amphetamines. Only that's not his real name. His real name is Marvin Goldstein. But so. Like I say, I'm a poet. I write about human sacrifices, cannibalism, vampires, and stuff. Mosh loves my work. He says we're all going to be famous some day. Only right now we're not, which bites, 'cuz I've been writing for like almost ten months. These things take time, I guess. Except we need some, like, cash to get by from week to week? Which is why Mosh one day says take the job at Escort à la Mode. Why not? I say. Which I guess kind of brings me to my story.

See, I'm cruising Capitol Hill in one of the company's black BMWs when my car-phone rings. Escort à la Mode's a real high-class operation. Escortette's services go for $750 an hour. We usually work with foreign business types. Japs and ragheads mostly. Politicians, too. With twenty-four hours' notice, we can also supply bogus daughters, brothers, and sons. You name it. Except there's absolutely nothing kinky here. We don't even kiss the clients. No way. Handshakes max. Take them out, show them the town, eat at a nice restaurant, listen to them yak, take them to a club, watch them try to dance, take them home. Period. We're tour guides, like. Our goal is to make people feel interesting. Therma Payne—she's my boss—Therma says our job is to "give good consort." Therma's a scream.

But so. Like I say, my car-phone rings. I answer. Dispatcher gives me an address, real chi-chi bookstore called Hard Covers down by the fish market. My client's supposed to be this big-deal writer guy who's reading there. Poet. Supposed to've been famous back in the like Pleistocene Error or something. Worth bazillions. So important I never even heard of him. But, hey. It's work.

Now I'm not being like unmodest or anything, okay? But I happen to be fricking gorgeous. No shit. My skin's real white. I dye my hair, which is short and spiked, shoe-polish black, then streak it with these little wisps of pink. Which picks up my Lancôme Corvette-red lipstick and long Estée Lauder Too-Good-To-Be-Natural black lashes. When I talk with a client, I'll keep my eyes open real wide so I always look Winona-Ryder-surprised by what he's saying. I'm 5'2", and when I wear my Number Four black-knit body-dress and glossy black Mouche army boots I become every middle-aged man's bad-little-girl wetdream. So I don't just *walk* in to Hard Covers, okay? I kinda, what, *sashay*. Yea. That's it. *Sashay*. I've never been there before, and I'm frankly pretty fucking impressed. Place is just *humongous*. More a warehouse than a bookstore. Except that it's all mahogany and bronze and dense carpeting. Health-food bar. Expresso counter. Dweeb with bat-wing ears playing muzak at the baby grand. Area off on the side with a podium and loads of chairs for the reading. Which is already filling. Standing room only. People are real excited. And books. God. Books. Enough books to make you instantly anxious you'll never read them all, no way, no matter how hard you try, so you might as well not.

I'm right on time. So I ask the guy at the register for the famous rich poet. He points to the storeroom. Warming up, he says. So I go on back and knock, only no one answers. I knock again. Nada. My meter's running, and I figure I might as well earn my paycheck, so I try the knob. Door's unlocked. I open it, stick my head in, say hi. It's pretty dark, all shadows and book cartons, and the room stretches on forever, and I'm already getting bored, so I enter and close the door behind me. When my eyes adjust a little, I make out a dim light way off in a distant corner. I start weaving toward it through the rows and rows of cartons. As I get closer, I can hear these voices. They sound kind of funny. Worried, like. Real fast and low. And then I see them. I see the whole thing.

Maybe five or six guys in gray business suits and ties, real like FBI or something, are huddling over this jumble on the floor. At first I don't understand what I'm looking at. Then I make out the portable gurney. And this torso on it, just this torso, naked and fleshy pink in a Barbie-doll sort of way, rib cage big as a cow's, biggest fucking belly you ever saw. Out of it are sticking these skinny white flabby legs, between them this amazingly small little purple dick and two hairy marbles. Only, thing is, the chest isn't a real chest. There's a panel in it. And the panel's open. And one of the guys is tinkering with some wiring in there. And another is rummaging through a wooden crate, coming up with an arm, plugging it into the torso, while a third guy, who's been balancing a second arm over his shoulder like a rifle or something, swings it down and locks it into place.

I may be a poet, okay, but I'm not a fucking liar or anything. I'm just telling you what I saw. Believe it or not. Go ahead. Frankly, I don't give a shit. But I'm telling you, I'm standing there, hypnotized like, not sure whether to run or wet myself, when this fourth guy reaches into the crate and comes up with, I kid you not, the *head*. I swear. I fucking swear. A *head*. The thing is so gross. Pudgy. Bushy. Gray-haired. And with these eyes. With these sort of glazed *eyes* that're looking up into the darkness where the ceiling should've been. I could spew rice just thinking about it.

Anyway, after a pretty long time fidgeting with the stuff in the chest, they prop the torso into a sitting position and start attaching the head. It's not an easy job. They fiddle and curse, and once one of them slips with a screwdriver and punctures the thing's left cheek. Only they take some flesh-toned silicon putty junk and fill up the hole, which works just fine. And the third guy reaches into his breast pocket and produces these wire-rimmed glasses, which he slips into place on the thing's face, and then they stand back, arms folded, admiring their work and all, and then the first guy reaches behind the thing's neck and pushes what must've been the ON/OFF button.

Those eyes roll down and snap into focus. Head swivels side to side. Mouth opens and closes its fatty lips, testing. And then, shit, it begins *talking*. It begins fucking *talking*. *I'm with you in Rockland. I'm wuh-wuh-wuh-with you . . . But my agent. What sort of agent is that? What could she have been thinking? Have you seen those sales figures? A stone should have better figures than that! I'm wuh-with you in the nightmare of trade paperbacks, sudden flash of bad PR, suffering the outrageousness of weak blurbs and failing shares. Where is the break-through book? Where the advance? Share with me the vanity of the unsolicited manuscript! Show me the madman bum of a publicist! Movie rights! Warranties! Indemnities! I am the twelve-percent roy-alty! I am the first five-thousand copies! I am the retail and the whole-sale, the overhead and the option clause!*

Give me the bottom line! Give me the tax break! Give me a reason to collect my rough drafts in the antennae crown of commerce! Oh, mental, mental, mental hardcover! Oh, incomplete clause! Oh, hope-less abandon of the unfulfilled contract! I am wuh-wuh-wuh-with you . . . I am wuh-wuh-wuh-with you in Rockland . . . I am . . .

"Oh, shit," says the first guy.

"Balls," says the second.

The body is a prosthesis for the mind! the famous rich poet says.

"We should've let him go," says the third guy.

"When his ticker stopped," says the first.

"When his liver quit," says the second.

"One thing," says the fourth. "Nanotech sure ain't what it's cracked up to be."

"You got that right," says the third.

Thirty thousand books in 1998 alone, the famous rich poet says, *but they couldn't afford it. Tangier, Venice, Amsterdam. What were they thinking? Wall Street is holy! The New York Stock Exchange is holy! The cosmic clause is holy! I'm wuh-wuh-wuh . . . I'm wuh-wuh-wuh . . . wuh-wuh-wuh . . .*

"Turn him off," says the fifth one.

Pale greenish foam begins forming on the famous rich poet's lips, dribbling down his chin, spattering on his hairless chest.

"Yeah, well," says the second.

"Guess we got some tightening to do," says the third, reaching be-hind the thing's neck.

But just as he pressed that button, just for a fraction of an instant, the stare of the famous rich poet fell on me as I tried scrunching out of sight behind a wall of boxes. Our eyes met. His looked like those of a wrongly convicted murderer maybe like one second before the executioner throws the switch that'll send a quadrillion volts or something zizzing through his system. In them was this mixture of disillusionment, dismay, fear, and uninterrupted sorrow. I froze. He stretched his foam-filled mouth as wide as it would go, ready to bellow, ready to howl. Except the juice failed. His mouth slowly closed again. His eyes rolled back up inside his head.

And me? I said fuck this. Fuck the books, fuck the suits, fuck Escort à la Mode, fuck the withered old pathetic shit. This whole thing's *way* too fricking rich for *my* blood.

And so I turned and walked.

Nominated by Janice Eidus, Ray Federman, Thomas E. Kennedy

O EVE

by ROSEMARY C. HILDEBRANDT

from ARTWORD QUARTERLY

O EVE. That rubricose ball is no apple. Plump fist rubbing rubbing rubbing a supple imposter of polish and deceit against plush robustious bosom, is it so then?—This is a heart too easily made a blush pulp glissando of red joy—too easily abandoned to the bric-a-brac of green desire and conceit—a soul, listing listing listing in this captious garden passage of bright wait and balm. Closeted in sun lace dresses of moral, unruffled blue days, does will o' the wisp grace collapse?— There, there in the volitional black winch of sweaty grasp, willing eclipse and savor. O Eve. See the purplish cloud capes dripping dripping dripping naked, profligate seedlings. Wince, now, at history's lush precept. How everyone smiles when the shiny haired girl brings the glass bowl of perfumed fruit.

Nominated by Artword Quarterl

FAITHLESS

fiction by JOYCE CAROL OATES

from THE KENYON REVIEW

1.

THE last time my mother Cornelia Nissenbaum and her sister Constance saw their mother was the day before she vanished from their lives forever, April 11, 1923.

It was a rainy-misty morning. They'd been searching for their mother because something was wrong in the household; she hadn't come downstairs to prepare breakfast so there wasn't anything for them except what their father gave them, glutinous oatmeal from the previous morning hastily reheated on the stove sticking to the bottom of the pan and tasting of scorch. Their father had seemed strange to them, smiling but not-seeing in that way of his like Reverend Dieckman too fierce in his pulpit Sunday mornings, intoning the Word of God. His eyes were threaded with blood and his face was still pale from the winter but flushed, mottled. In those days he was a handsome man but stern-looking and severe. Gray-grizzled side-whiskers and a spade-shaped beard, coarse and grizzled too with gray, but thick springy-sleek black hair brushed back from his forehead in a crest. The sisters were fearful of their father without their mother to mediate among them, it was as if none of them knew who they were without her.

Connie chewed her lip and worked up her nerve to ask where was Momma? and their father said, hitching up his suspenders, on his way outside, "Your mother's where you'll find her."

The sisters watched their father cross the mud-puddled yard to where a crew of hired men was waiting in the doorway of the big barn. It was rye-planting season and always in spring in the Chautauqua Valley there was worry about rain: too much rain and the seed would be washed away or rot in the soil before it could sprout. My mother Cornelia would grow to adulthood thinking how blessings and curses fell from the sky with equal authority, like hard-pelting rain. There was God, who set the world in motion, and who intervened sometimes in the affairs of men, for reasons no one could know. If you lived on a farm there was weather, always weather, every morning was weather and every evening at sundown calculating the next day's, the sky's moods meant too much. Always casting your glance upward, outward, your heart set to quicken.

That morning. The sisters would never forget that morning. We knew something was wrong, we thought Momma was sick. The night before having heard—what, exactly? Voices. Voices mixed with dreams, and the wind. On that farm, at the brink of a ten-mile descent to the Chautauqua River, it was always windy—on the worst days the wind could literally suck your breath away!—like a ghost, a goblin. An invisible being pushing up close beside you, sometimes even inside the house, even in your bed, pushing his mouth (or muzzle) to yours and sucking out the breath.

Connie thought Nelia was silly, a silly-baby, to believe such. She was eight years old and skeptical-minded. Yet maybe she believed it, too? Like to scare herself, the way you could almost tickle yourself, with such wild thoughts.

Connie, who was always famished, and after that morning would be famished for years, sat at the oilcloth-covered table and ate the oatmeal her father had spooned out for her, devoured it, scorch-clots and all, her head of fair-frizzy braids lowered and her jaws working quickly. Oatmeal sweetened with top-milk on the very edge of turning sour, and coarse brown sugar. Nelia, who was fretting, wasn't able to swallow down more than a spoon or two of hers so Connie devoured that, too. She would remember that part of the oatmeal was hot enough to burn her tongue and other parts were icebox-cold. She would remember that it was all delicious.

The girls washed their dishes in the cold-water sink and let the oatmeal pan soak in scummy soapsuds. It was time for Connie to leave for school but both knew she could not go, not today. She could not leave to walk two miles to the school with that feeling *something is wrong,* nor could she leave her little sister behind. Though when Nelia snuffled and wiped her nose on both her hands Connie cuffed her on the shoulder and scolded, "Piggy-*piggy.*"

357

This, a habit of their mother's when they did something that was only mildly disgusting.

Connie led the way upstairs to the big bedroom at the front of the house that was Momma and Pappa's room and that they were forbidden to enter unless specifically invited; for instance if the door was open and Momma was cleaning inside, changing bedclothes so she'd call out *Come in, girls!* smiling in her happy mood so it was all right and they would not be scolded. *Come in, give me a hand,* which turned into a game shaking out sheets, fluffing out pillowcases to stuff heavy goosefeather pillows inside, Momma and Connie and Nelia laughing together. But this morning the door was shut. There was no sound of Momma inside. Connie dared to turn the doorknob, push the door open slowly, and they saw, yes, to their surprise there was their mother lying on top of the unmade bed, partly dressed, wrapped in an afghan. My God, it was scary to see Momma like that, lying down at such an hour of the morning! Momma, who was so brisk and capable and who routed them out of bed if they lingered, Momma with little patience for Connie's lazy-tricks as she called them or for Nelia's sniffles, tummyaches, and baby-fears.

"Momma?"—Connie's voice was cracked.

"Mom-ma?"—Nelia whimpered.

Their mother groaned and flung an arm across one of the pillows lying crooked beside her. She was breathing hard, like a winded horse, her chest rising and falling so you could see it and her head was flung back on a pillow and she'd placed a wetted cloth across her eyes masklike so half her face was hidden. Her dark-blond hair was disheveled, unplaited, coarse and lustreless as a horse's mane, unwashed for days. That rich rank smell of Momma's hair when it needed washing. You remember such smells, the sisters would say, some of them not-so-nice smells, all your life. And the smell in their parents' forbidden room of—was it talcum powder, sweaty armpits, a sourish-sweet fragrance of bedclothes that no matter how frequently laundered with detergent and bleach were never truly fresh. A smell of bodies. Adult bodies. Yeasty, stale. Pappa's tobacco (he rolled his own crude paper cigarettes, he chewed tobacco in a thick tarry-black wad) and Pappa's hair oil and that special smell of Pappa's shoes, the black Sunday shoes always kept polished. (His workboots, etc., he kept downstairs in the closed-in porch by the rear door called the "entry.") In the step-in closet by the bed, behind an unhemmed length of chintz, was a blue-

358

speckled porcelain chamberpot with a detachable lid and a rim that curled neatly under, like a lip.

The sisters had their own chamberpot—their potty, as it was called. There was no indoor plumbing in John Nissenbaum's farmhouse as in any farmhouse in the Chautauqua Valley well into the 1930s and in poorer homes well into the 1940s, and even beyond. One hundred yards behind the house, beyond the silo, was the outhouse, the latrine, the "privy." But you would not want to make that trip in cold weather or in rain or in the pitch-black of night, not if you could help it.

Of course, the smell of urine and a fainter smell of excrement must have been everywhere, the sisters conceded, years later. As adults, reminiscing. But it was masked by the barnyard smell, probably. Nothing worse than pig manure, after all!

At least, we weren't *pigs*.

Anyway, there was Momma, on the bed. The bed that was so high from the floor you had to raise a knee to slide up on it, and grab on to whatever you could. And the horsehair mattress, so hard and ungiving. The cloth over Momma's eyes she hadn't removed and beside Momma in the rumpled bedclothes her Bible. Face down. Pages bent. That Bible her mother-in-law Grandma Nissenbaum had given her for a wedding present, seeing she hadn't one of her own. It was smaller than the heavy black family Bible and it was made of limp ivory-leather covers and had onionskin pages the girls were allowed to examine but not to turn without Momma's supervision; the Bible that would disappear with Gretel Nissenbaum, forever.

The girls begged, whimpered. "Momma? Momma, are you sick?"

At first there was no answer. Just Momma's breath coming quick and hard and uneven. And her olive-pale skin oily with heat like fever. Her legs were tangled in the afghan, her hair was strewn across the pillow. They saw the glint of Momma's gold cross on a thin gold chain around her neck, almost lost in her hair. (Not only a cross but a locket, too: when Momma opened it there was, inside, a tiny strand of silver hair once belonging to a woman the sisters had never known, Momma's own grandmother she'd loved so when she was a little girl.) And there were Momma's breasts, almost exposed!—heavy, lush, beautiful almost spilling out of a white eyelet slip, rounded like sacs holding warm liquid, and the nipples dark and big as eyes. You weren't supposed to stare at any part of a person's body but how could you help it?—especially Connie who was fascinated by such, guessing how one day she'd inhabit a body like Momma's. Years ago she'd peeked at her mother's big milk-swollen breasts when Nelia was still nursing, jealous, awed. Nelia was now five years old and could not herself recall nursing at all; would come one day to believe, stubborn and disdainful, that she had never nursed, had only been bottle-fed.

At last Momma snatched the cloth off her face. "You! Damn you! What do you want?" She stared at the girls as if, clutching hands and gaping at her, they were strangers. Her right eye was bruised and swollen and there were raw red marks on her forehead and first Nelia then Connie began to cry and Momma said, "Constance, why aren't you in school? Why can't you let me alone? God help me—always 'Momma'—'Momma'—'Momma.'" Connie whimpered, "Momma, did you hurt yourself?" and Nelia moaned, sucking a corner of the afghan like a deranged baby and Momma ignored the question, as Momma often ignored questions she thought nosy, none of your business; her hand lifted as if she meant to slap them but then fell wearily, as if this had happened many times before, this exchange, this emotion, and it was her fate that it would happen many times again. A close sweet-stale blood-odor lifted from Momma's lower body, out of the folds of the soiled afghan, that odor neither of the little girls could have identified except in retrospect, in adolescence at last detecting it in themselves: shamed, discomforted, the secret of their bodies at what was called, invariably in embarrassed undertones, *that certain time of the month.*

So: Gretel Nissenbaum, at the time she disappeared from her husband's house, was having her period.

Did that mean something, or nothing?

Nothing, Cornelia would say sharply.

Yes, Constance would insist, it meant our mother was *not* pregnant. She wasn't running away with any lover because of *that.*

That morning, what confusion in the Nissenbaum household! However the sisters would later speak of the encounter in the big bedroom, what their mother had said to them, how she'd looked and behaved, it had not been precisely that way, of course. Because how can you speak of confusion, where are the words for it? How to express in adult language the wild fibrillation of children's minds, two child-minds beating against each other like moths, how to know what had truly happened and what was only imagined! Connie would swear that their mother's eye looked like a nasty dark-rotted egg, so swollen, but she could not say which eye it was, right or left; Nelia, shrinking from look-

360

ing at her mother's bruised face, wanting only to burrow against her, to hide and be comforted, would come in time to doubt that she'd seen a *hurt eye* at all; or whether she'd been led to believe she saw it because Connie, who was so bossy, claimed she had.

Connie would remember their mother's words, Momma's rising desperate voice, "Don't touch me—I'm afraid! I might be going somewhere but I'm not ready—oh God, I'm so afraid!"—and on and on, saying she was going away, she was afraid, and Connie trying to ask where? where was she going? and Momma beating at the bedclothes with her fists. Nelia would remember being hurt at the way Momma yanked the spittle-soaked corner of the afghan out of her mouth, so roughly! Not Momma but *bad-Momma, witch-Momma* who scared her.

But then Momma relented, exasperated. "Oh come on, you damn little babies! Of course 'Momma' loves you."

Eager then as starving kittens the sisters scrambled up onto the high, hard bed, whimpering, snuggling into Momma's arms, her damp snarled hair, those breasts. Connie and Nelia burrowing, crying themselves to sleep like nursing babies, Momma drew the afghan over the three of them as if to shield them. That morning of April 11, 1923.

And next morning, early, before dawn. The sisters would be awakened by their father's shouts, "Gretel? Gretel!"

2.

. . . never spoke of her after the first few weeks. After the first shock. We learned to pray for her and to forgive her and to forget her. We didn't miss her. So Mother said, in her calm judicious voice. A voice that held no blame.

But Aunt Connie would take me aside. The older, wiser sister. *It's true we never spoke of Momma when any grownups were near, that was forbidden. But, God! we missed her every hour of every day all the time we lived on that farm.*

I was Cornelia's daughter but it was Aunt Connie I trusted.

No one in the Chautauqua Valley knew where John Nissenbaum's young wife Gretel had fled, but all knew, or had an opinion of, why she'd gone.

Faithless, she was. A *faithless woman.* Had she not *run away with a man: abandoned her children.* She was twenty-seven years old and too young for John Nissenbaum and she wasn't a Ransomville girl, her people lived sixty miles away in Chautauqua Falls. Here was a wife who'd committed *adultery,* was an *adulteress.* (Some might say a *tramp,* a *whore,* a *slut.*) Reverend Dieckman, the Lutheran minister, would preach amazing sermons in her wake. For miles through the valley and for years well into the 1940s there would be scandalized talk of Gretel Nissenbaum: a woman who left her faithful Christian husband and her two little girls with no warning! no provocation! disappearing in the middle of a night taking with her only a single suitcase and, as every woman who ever spoke of the episode liked to say, licking her lips, *the clothes on her back.*

(Aunt Connie said she'd grown up imagining she had actually seen her mother, as in a dream, walking stealthily up the long drive to the road, a bundle of clothes, like laundry, slung across her back. Children are so damned impressionable, Aunt Connie would say, laughing wryly.)

For a long time after their mother disappeared, and no word came from her, or of her, so far as the sisters knew, Connie couldn't seem to help herself teasing Nelia saying "Mommy's coming home!"—for a birthday of Nelia's, or Christmas, or Easter. How many times Connie thrilled with wickedness deceiving her baby sister and silly-baby that she was, Nelia believed.

And how Connie would laugh, laugh at her.

Well, it *was* funny. Wasn't it?

Another trick of Connie's: poking Nelia awake in the night when the wind was rattling the windows, moaning in the chimney like a trapped animal. Saying excitedly, *Momma is outside the window, listen! Momma is a ghost trying to get* YOU!

Sometimes Nelia screamed so, Connie had to straddle her chest and press a pillow over her face to muffle her. If they'd wakened Pappa with such nonsense there'd sure have been hell to pay.

Once, I might have been twelve, I asked if my grandfather had spanked or beaten them.

Aunt Connie, sitting in our living room on the high-backed mauve-brocade chair that was always hers when she came to visit, ignored me. Nor did Mother seem to hear. Aunt Connie lit one of her Chesterfields with a fussy flourish of her pink-frosted nails and took a deep satisfied puff and said, as if it were a thought only now slipping into her head, and like all such thoughts deserving of utterance, "I was noticing the other day, on TV, how brattish and idiotic children are, and we're supposed to think they're cute. Pappa wasn't the kind to tolerate children carrying on for a single minute." She paused, again inhaling deeply. "None of the men were, back there."

Mother nodded slowly, frowning. These conversations with my aunt seemed always to give her pain, an actual ache behind the eyes, yet she could no more resist them than Aunt Connie. She said, wiping at her eyes, "Pappa was a man of pride. After she left us as much as before."

"Hmmm!" Aunt Connie made her high humming nasal sound that meant she had something crucial to add, but did not want to appear pushy. "Well—maybe more, Nelia. More pride. After." She spoke insinuatingly, with a smile and a glance toward me.

Like an actress who has strayed from her lines, Mother quickly amended, "Yes, of course. Because a weaker man would have succumbed to—shame and despair—"

Aunt Connie nodded briskly. "—might have cursed God—"

"—turned to drink—"

"—so many of 'em *did*, back there—"

"—but not Pappa. He had the gift of faith."

Aunt Connie nodded sagely. Yet still with that strange almost-teasing smile.

"Oh, indeed, Pappa did. That was his gift to us, Nelia, wasn't it?—his faith."

Mother was smiling her tight-lipped smile, her gaze lowered. I knew that, when Aunt Connie left, she would go upstairs to lie down, she would take two aspirins and draw the blinds, and put a damp cold cloth over her eyes and lie down and try to sleep. In her softening middle-aged face, the hue of putty, a young girl's face shone rapt with fear. "Oh yes! His faith."

Aunt Connie laughed heartily. Laugh, laugh. Dimples nicking her cheeks and a wink in my direction.

Years later, numbly sorting through Mother's belongings after her death, I would discover, in a lavender-scented envelope in a bureau drawer, a single strand of dry, ash-colored hair. On the envelope, in faded purple ink *Beloved Father John Allard Nissenbaum 1872-1957*.

3.

By his own account, John Nissenbaum, the wronged husband, had not had the slightest suspicion that his strong-willed young wife had been discontent, restless. Certainly not that she'd had a secret lover! So many local women would have dearly wished to change places with her, he'd been given to know when he was courting her. His male vanity, and his Nissenbaum vanity, and what you might call common sense suggested otherwise.

For the Nissenbaums were a well-regarded family in the Chautauqua Valley. Among the lot of them they must have owned thousands of acres of prime farmland.

In the weeks, months, and eventually years that followed the scandalous departure, John Nissenbaum, who was by nature, like most of the male Nissenbaums, reticent to the point of arrogance, and fiercely private, came to make his story—*his side of it*—known. As the sisters themselves gathered (for their father never spoke of their mother to them after the first several days following the shock), this was not a single coherent history but one that had to be pieced together like a giant quilt made of a myriad of fabric-scraps.

He did allow that Gretel had been missing her family, an older sister with whom she'd been especially close, and cousins and girlfriends she'd gone to high school with in Chautauqua Falls; he understood that the two-hundred-acre farm was a lonely place for her, their next-door neighbors miles away, and the village of Ransomville seven miles. (Trips beyond Ransomville were rare.) He knew, or supposed he knew, that his wife had harbored what his mother and sisters called *wild imaginings,* even after nine years of marriage, farm life, and children: she had asked several times to be allowed to play the organ at church, but had been refused; she reminisced often wistfully and perhaps reproachfully of long-ago visits to Port Oriskany, Buffalo, and Chicago, before she'd gotten married at the age of eighteen to a man fourteen years her senior . . . in Chicago she'd seen stage plays and musicals, the sensational dancers Irene and Vernon Castle in Irving Berlin's *Watch Your Step.* It wasn't just Gretel wanting to take over the organ at Sunday services (and replacing the elderly male organist whose playing, she said, sounded like a cat in heat), it was her general attitude toward Reverend Dieckman and his wife. She resented having to invite them to an elaborate Sunday dinner every few weeks, as the Nissenbaums insisted; she allowed her eyes to roam the congregation during Dieckman's sermons, and stifled yawns behind her gloved hand; she woke in the middle of the night, she said, wanting to argue about damnation, hell, the very concept of grace. To the minister's astonished face she declared herself "not able to *fully accept* the teachings of the Lutheran Church."

If there were other more intimate issues between Gretel and John Nissenbaum, or another factor in Gretel's emotional life, of course no one spoke of it at the time.

Though it was hinted—possibly more than hinted?—that John Nissenbaum was disappointed with only daughters. Naturally he wanted sons, to help him with the ceaseless work of the farm; sons to whom he could leave the considerable property, just as his married brothers had sons.

What was generally known was: John woke in the pitch-dark an hour before dawn of that April day, to discover that Gretel was gone from their bed. Gone from the house? He searched for her, called her name, with growing alarm, disbelief. "Gretel? Gret-el!" He looked in all the upstairs rooms of the house including the bedroom where his sleep-dazed, frightened daughters were huddled together in their bed; he looked in all the downstairs rooms, even the damp, dirt-floor cellar into which he descended with a lantern. "Gretel? Where are you?" Dawn came dull, porous and damp, and with a coat yanked on in haste over his night clothes, and his bare feet jammed into rubber boots, he began a frantic yet methodical search of the farm's outbuildings—the privy, the cow barn and the adjoining stable, the hay barn and the corn-crib where rats rustled at his approach. In none of these save perhaps the privy was it likely that Gretel might be found, still John continued his search with growing panic, not knowing what else to do. From the house his now terrified daughters observed him moving from building to building, a tall, rigid, jerkily moving figure with hands cupped to his mouth shouting, "Gretel! Gret-el! Do you hear me! Where are you! Gret-el!" The man's deep, raw voice pulsing like a metronome, ringing clear, profound, and, to his daughters' ears, as terrible as if the very sky had cracked open and God himself was shouting.

(What did such little girls, eight and five, know of God—in fact, as Aunt Connie would afterward recount, quite a bit. There was Reverend Dieckman's baritone impersonation of the God of the Old Testament, the expulsion from the Garden, the devastating retort to Job, the spectacular burning bush where fire itself cried *HERE I AM!*—such had already been imprinted irrevocably upon their imaginations.)

Only later that morning—but this was a confused, anguished account—did John discover that Gretel's suitcase was missing from the closet. And there were garments conspicuously missing from the clothes rack. And Gretel's bureau drawers had been hastily ransacked—underwear, stockings were gone. And her favorite pieces of jewelry, of which she was childishly vain, were gone from her cedarwood box; gone, too, her heirloom, faded-cameo hairbrush, comb and mirror set. And her Bible.

What a joke, how people would chuckle over it—Gretel Nissenbaum taking her Bible with her!

Wherever in hell the woman went.

And was there no farewell note, after nine years of marriage?—John Nissenbaum claimed he'd looked everywhere, and found nothing. Not a word of explanation, not a word of regret even to her little girls. *For that alone we expelled her from our hearts.*

During this confused time while their father was searching and calling their mother's name, the sisters hugged each other in a state of numbness beyond shock, terror. Their father seemed at times to be rushing toward them with the eye-bulging blindness of a runaway horse—they hurried out of his path. He did not see them except to order them out of his way, not to trouble him now. From the rear entry door they watched as he hitched his team of horses to his buggy and set out shuddering for Ransomville along the winter-rutted Post Road, leaving the girls behind, erasing them from his mind. As he would tell afterward, in rueful self-disgust, with the air of an enlightened sinner, he'd actually believed he would overtake Gretel on the road—convinced she'd be there, hiking on the grassy shoulder, carrying her suitcase. Gretel was a wiry-nervous woman, stronger than she appeared, with no fear of physical exertion. A woman capable of anything!

John Nissenbaum had the idea that Gretel had set out for Ransomville, seven miles away, there to catch the mid-morning train to Chautauqua Falls, another sixty miles south. It was his confused belief that they must have had a disagreement, else Gretel would not have left; he did not recall any disagreement in fact, but Gretel was after all an *emotional woman, a highly strung woman;* she'd insisted upon visiting the Hausers, her family, despite his wishes, was that it?—she was lonely for them, or lonely for something. She was angry they hadn't visited Chautauqua Falls for Easter, hadn't seen her family since Christmas. Was that it? *We were never enough for her. Why were we never enough for her?*

But in Ransomville, in the cinderblock Chautauqua & Buffalo depot, there was no sign of Gretel, nor had the lone clerk seen her.

"This woman would be about my height," John Nissenbaum said, in his formal, slightly haughty way. "She'd be carrying a suitcase, her feet would maybe be muddy. Her boots."

The clerk shook his head slowly. "No sir, nobody looking like that."

"A woman by herself. A—" a hesitation, a look of pain, "—good-looking woman, young. A kind of a, a way about her—a way of—" another pause, "—making herself known."

"Sorry," the clerk said. "The 8:20 just came through, and no woman bought a ticket."

It happened then that John Nissenbaum was observed, stark-eyed, stiff-springy black hair in tufts like quills, for the better part of that morning, April 12, 1923, wandering up one side of Ransomville's single main street, and down the other. Hatless, in farm overalls and boots but wearing a suit coat—sombre, gunmetal-gray, of "good" wool—buttoned crooked across his narrow muscular torso. Disheveled and ravaged with the grief of a betrayed husband too raw at this time for manly pride to intervene, pathetic some said as a kicked dog, yet eager too, eager as a puppy he made inquiries at Meldron's Dry Goods, at Elkin & Sons Grocers, at the First Niagara Trust, at the law office of Rowe & Nissenbaum (this Nissenbaum, a young cousin of John's), even in the Five & Dime where the salesgirls would giggle in his wake. He wandered at last into the Ransomville Hotel, into the gloomy public room where the proprietor's wife was sweeping sawdust-strewn floorboards. "Sorry, sir, we don't open till noon," the woman said, thinking he was a drunk, dazed and swaying-like on his feet, then she looked more closely at him: not knowing his first name (for John Nissenbaum was not one to patronize local taverns) but recognizing his features. For it was said the male Nissenbaums were either born looking alike, or came in time to look alike. "Mr. Nissenbaum? Is something wrong?" In a beat of stymied silence Nissenbaum blinked at her, trying to smile, groping for a hat to remove but finding none, murmuring, "No ma'am, I'm sure not. It's a misunderstanding, I believe. I'm supposed to meet Mrs. Nissenbaum somewhere here. My wife."

Shortly after Gretel Nissenbaum's disappearance there emerged, from numerous sources, from all points of the compass, certain tales of the woman. How rude she'd been, more than once, to the Dieckmans!—to many in the Lutheran congregation! A *bad wife. Unnatural mother.* It was said she'd left her husband and children in the past, running back to her family in Chautauqua Falls, or was in Port Oriskany;

367

and poor John Nissenbaum having to fetch her home again. (This was untrue, though in time, even to Constance and Cornelia, it would come to seem true. As an elderly woman Cornelia would swear she remembered "both times" her mother ran off.) A shameless hussy, a tramp who *had an eye* for men. *Had the hots* for men. *Anything in pants.* Or was she *stuck-up, snobby.* Marrying into the Nissenbaum family, a man almost old enough to be her father, no mystery there! Worse yet she could be sharp-tongued, profane. Heard to utter such words as *damn, goddamn, hell.* Yes and *horseballs, bullshit.* Standing with her hands on her hips fixing her eyes on you, that loud laugh. And showing her teeth that were too big for her mouth. She was *too smart for her own good*, that's for sure. She was *scheming, faithless.* Everybody knew she flirted with her husband's hired hands, she did a hell of a lot more than flirt with them, ask around. Sure she had a *boyfriend, a lover.* Sure she was an *adultress.* Hadn't she run off with a man? She'd run off and where was she to go, where was a woman to go, except *run off with a man?* Whoever he was.

In fact, he's been sighted: a tower operator for the Chautauqua & Buffalo railroad, big red-headed guy living in Shaheen, twelve miles away. Or was he a carpet sweeper salesman, squirrely little guy with a mustache and a smooth way of talking, who passed through the valley every few months but, after April 12, 1923, was never seen there again.

Another, more attractive rumor was that Gretel Nissenbaum's lover was a thirty-year-old Navy officer stationed at Port Oriskany. He'd been transferred to a base in North Carolina, or was it Pensacola, Florida, and Gretel had no choice but run away with him, she loved him so. *And three months pregnant with his child.*

There could have been no romance in the terrible possibility that Gretel Nissenbaum had fled on foot, alone, not to her family but simply to escape from her life; in what exigency of need, what despondency of spirit, no name might be given it by any who have not experienced it.

But, in any case, where had she *gone*?

Where? Disappeared. Over the edge of the world. To Chicago, maybe. Or that base in North Carolina, or Florida.
We forgave, we forgot. We didn't miss her.

The things Gretel Nissenbaum left behind in the haste of her departure.

Several dresses, hats. A shabby cloth coat. Rubberized "galoshes" and boots. Undergarments, mended stockings. Knitted gloves. In the parlor of John Nissenbaum's house, in cut-glass vases, bright yellow daffodils she'd made from crepe paper; hand-painted fans, tea cups; books she'd brought with her from home—*A Golden Treasury of Verse*, Mark Twain's *Joan of Arc*, Fitzgerald's *This Side of Paradise*, missing its jacket cover. Tattered programs for musical shows, stacks of popular piano music from the days Gretel had played in her childhood home. (There was no piano in Nissenbaum's house, Nissenbaum had no interest in music.)

These meager items, and some others, Nissenbaum unceremoniously dumped into cardboard boxes fifteen days after Gretel disappeared, taking them to the Lutheran church, for the "needy fund"; without inquiring if the Hausers might have wanted anything, or whether his daughters might have wished to be given some momentos of their mother.

Spite? Not John Nissenbaum. He was a proud man even in his public humiliation. It was the Lord's work he was thinking of. Not mere *human vanity*, at all.

That spring and summer Reverend Dieckman gave a series of grim, threatening, passionate sermons from the pulpit of the First Lutheran Church of Ransomville. It was obvious why, what the subject of the sermons was. The congregation was thrilled.

Reverend Dieckman, whom Connie and Nelia feared, as much for his fierce smiles as his stern, glowering expression, was a short, bulky man with a dull-gleaming dome of a head, eyes like ice water. Years later when they saw a photograph of him, inches shorter than his wife, they laughed in nervous astonishment—was that the man who'd intimidated them so? Before whom even John Nissenbaum stood grave and downgazing.

Yet: that ringing, vibrating voice of the God of Moses, the God of the Old Testament, you could not shut out of consciousness even hours, days later. Years later. Pressing your hands against your ears and shutting your eyes tight, tight.

"'Unto the WOMAN He said, I will GREATLY MULTIPLY thy sorrow and thy conception; IN SORROW shalt thou bring forth children: and thy desire shall be to THY HUSBAND, and he shall RULE OVER THEE. And unto Adam He said, Because thou hast harkened unto the voice of THY WIFE, and has eaten of THE TREE, of which I commanded thee, saying, THOU SHALT NOT EAT OF IT: cursed is the ground for thy sake; in sorrow shall thou eat of it all the days of thy life: THORNS ALSO AND THISTLES shall it bring forth to thee; and thou shalt eat the herb of the field; in the SWEAT OF THY FACE shalt thou eat bread, till thou return to the ground; for out of it thou wast taken: for DUST THOU ART, and UNTO DUST SHALT THOU RETURN.'" Reverend Dieckman paused to catch breath like a man running uphill. Greasy patches gleamed on his solid face like coins. Slowly his ice-eyes searched the rows of worshipers until as if by chance they came to rest on the upturned yet cowering faces of John Nissenbaum's daughters, who sat in the family pew, directly in front of the pulpit in the fifth row, between their rigid-backed father in his clothes somber as mourning and their Grandmother Nissenbaum also in clothes somber as mourning though badly round-shouldered, with a perceptible hump, this cheerless dutiful grandmother who had come to live with them now that their mother was gone.

(Their other grandparents, the Hausers, who lived in Chautauqua Falls and whom they'd loved, the sisters would never see again. It was forbidden even to speak of these people, *Gretel's people.* The Hausers were to blame somehow for Gretel's desertion. Though they claimed, would always claim, they knew nothing of what she'd done and in fact feared something had happened to her. But the Hausers were a forbidden subject. Only after Constance and Cornelia were grown, no longer living in their father's house, did they see their Hauser cousins; but still, as Cornelia confessed, she felt guilty about it. Father would have been so hurt and furious if he'd known. *Consorting with the enemy* he would deem it. *Betrayal.*)

In Sunday school, Mrs. Dieckman took special pains with little Constance and little Cornelia. They were regarded with misty-eyed pity, like child-lepers. Fattish little Constance prone to fits of giggling, and hollow-eyed little Cornelia prone to sniffles, melancholy. Both girls had chafed, reddened faces and hands because their Grandmother Nissenbaum scrubbed them so, with strong gray soap, never less than twice a day. Cornelia's dun-colored hair was strangely thin. When the other children trooped out of the Sunday school room, Mrs. Dieckman kept the sisters behind, to pray with them. She was very concerned about them, she said. She and Reverend Dieckman prayed for them constantly. Had their mother contacted them, since leaving? Had their been any . . . hint of what their mother was planning to do? Any strangers visiting the farm? Any . . . unusual incidents? The sisters stared blankly at Mrs. Dieckman. She frowned at their ignorance, or its semblance. Dabbed at her watery eyes and sighed as if the world's weight had settled on her shoulders. She said half-chiding, "You should know, children, it's for a reason that your mother left you. It's God's will. God's plan. He is testing you, children. You are special in His eyes. Many of us have been special in His eyes and have emerged stronger for it, and not weaker." There was a breathy pause. The sisters were invited to contemplate how Mrs. Dieckman with her soft-wattled face, her stout-corseted body and fattish legs encased in opaque support hose, was a stronger and not a weaker person, by God's special plan. "You will learn to be stronger than girls with mothers, Constance and Cornelia—" (these words *girls with mothers* enunciated oddly, contemptuously). "You are already learning: feel God's strength coursing through you!" Mrs. Dieckman seized the girls' hands, squeezing so quick and hard that Connie burst into frightened giggles and Nelia shrieked as if she'd been burnt, and almost wet her panties.

Nelia acquired pride, then. Instead of being ashamed, publicly humiliated (at the one-room country schoolhouse, for instance: where certain of the other children were ruthless), she could be proud, like her father. *God had a special feeling for me. God cared about me. Jesus Christ, His only son, was cruelly tested, too. And exalted. You can bear any hurt and degradation. Thistles and thorns. The flaming sword, the cherubims guarding the garden.*

Mere *girls with mothers,* how could they know?

4.

Of course, Connie and Nelia had heard their parents quarreling. In the weeks, months before their mother disappeared. In fact, all their lives. Had they been queried, had they had the language, they might have said *This is what is done, a man, a woman—isn't it?*

Connie, who was three years older than Nelia, knew much that Nelia would not ever know. Not words exactly, these quarrels, and of a tone different from their father shouting out instructions to his farm hands. Not words but an eruption of voices. Ringing through the floorboards if the quarrel came from downstairs. Reverberating in the windowpanes where wind thinly whistled. In bed, Connie would hug Nelia tight, pretending Nelia was Momma. Or Connie was herself Momma. If you shut your eyes tight enough. If you shut your ears.

371

Always after the voices there came silence. If you wait. Once, crouched at the foot of the stairs it was Connie?—or Nelia?—gazing upward astonished as Momma descended the stairs swaying like a drunk woman, her left hand groping against the railing, face dead-white and a bright crimson rosebud in the corner of her mouth glistening as she wiped, wiped furiously at it. And quick-walking in that way of his that made the house vibrate, heavy-heeled behind her, descending from the top of the stairs a man whose face she could not see. Fiery, and blinding. God in the burning bush. God in thunder. *Bitch! Get back up here! If I have to come get you, if you won't be a woman, a wife!*

It was a fact the sisters learned, young: if you wait long enough, run away and hide your eyes, shut your ears, there comes a silence vast and rolling and empty as the sky.

There was a mystery of the letters my mother and Aunt Connie would speak of, though never exactly discuss in my presence, into the last year of my mother's life.

Which of them first noticed, they couldn't agree. Or when it began, exactly—no earlier than the fall, 1923. It would happen that Pappa went to fetch the mail, which he rarely did, and then only on Saturdays; and, returning, along the quarter-mile lane, he would be observed (by accident? the girls weren't spying) with an opened letter in his hand, reading; or was it a postcard; walking with uncharacteristic slowness, this man whose step was invariably brisk and impatient. Connie recalled he'd sometimes slip into the stable to continue reading, Pappa had a liking for the stable which was for him a private place where he'd chew tobacco, spit into the hay, run his calloused hands along a horse's flanks, think his own thoughts. Other times, carrying whatever it was, letter, postcard, the rarity of an item of personal mail, he'd return to the kitchen and his place at the table. There the girls would find him (by accident, they *were not* spying) drinking coffee laced with top-milk and sugar, rolling one of his clumsy cigarettes. And Connie would be the one to inquire, "Was there any mail, Pappa?" keeping her voice low, unexcited. And Pappa would shrug and say, "Nothing." On the table where he'd dropped them indifferently might be a few bills, advertising flyers, the *Chautauqua Valley Weekly Gazette*. Nelia never inquired about the mail at such times because she would not have trusted her voice. But, young as ten, Connie could be pushy, reckless. "Isn't there a letter, Pappa? What *is* that, Pappa, in your pocket?"

And Pappa would say calmly, staring her full in the face, "When your father says *nothing*, girl, he means *nothing*."

Sometimes his hands shook, fussing with the pouch of Bugler and the stained cigarette-roller.

Since the shame of losing his wife, and everybody knowing the circumstances, John Nissenbaum had aged shockingly. His face was creased, his skin reddened and cracked, finely stippled with what would be diagnosed (when finally he went to a doctor) as skin cancer. His eyes, pouched in wrinkled lids like a turtle's, were often vague, restless. Even in church, in a row close to Reverend Dieckman's pulpit, he had a look of wandering off. In what he called his earlier life he'd been a rough, physical man, intelligent but quicktempered; now he tired easily, could not keep up with his hired men whom he more and more mistrusted. His beard, once so trim and shapely, grew ragged and uneven and was entirely gray-grizzled, like cobwebs. And his breath—it smelled of tobacco juice, wet, rank, sickish, rotted.

Once, seeing the edge of the letter in Pappa's pocket, Connie bit her lip and said, "It's from *her*, isn't it!"

Pappa said, still calmly, "I said it's *nothing*, girl. From *nobody*."

Never in their father's presence did either of the sisters allude to their missing mother except as *her, she*.

Later when they searched for the letter, even for its envelope, of course they found nothing. Pappa had burned it in the stove probably. Or torn it into shreds, tossed into the garbage. Still, the sisters risked their father's wrath by daring to look in his bedroom (the stalesmelling room he'd moved to, downstairs at the rear of the house) when he was out; even, desperate, knowing it was hopeless, poking through fresh-dumped garbage. (Like all farm families of their day, the Nissenbaums dumped raw garbage down a hillside, in the area of the outhouse.) Once Connie scrambled across fly-buzzing mounds of garbage holding her nose, stooping to snatch up—what? A card advertising a fertilizer sale, that had looked like a picture postcard.

"Are you crazy?" Nelia cried. "I hate you!"

Connie turned to scream at her, eyes brimming tears. "Go to hell, horse's ass, I hate *you!*"

Both wanted to believe, or did in fact believe, that their mother was not writing to their father but to them. But they would never know.

For years, as the letters came at long intervals, arriving only when their father fetched the mail, they would not know.

This might have been a further element of mystery: why the letters, arriving so infrequently, arrived only when their father got the mail. Why, when Connie, or Nelia, or Loraine (John's younger sister, who'd come to live with them) got the mail, there would never be one of the mysterious letters. *Only when Pappa got the mail.*

After my mother's death in 1981, when I spoke more openly to my Aunt Connie, I asked why they hadn't been suspicious, just a little. Aunt Connie lifted her penciled eyebrows, blinked at me as if I'd uttered something obscene—"Suspicious? Why?" Not once did the girls (who were in fact intelligent girls, Nelia a straight-A student in the high school in town) calculate the odds: how the presumed letter from their mother could possibly arrive only on those days (Saturdays) when their father got the mail; one day out of six mail-days, yet never any day except that particular day (Saturday). But as Aunt Connie said, shrugging, it just seemed that that was how it was—they would never have conceived of even the possibility of any situation in which the odds wouldn't have been against them, and in favor of Pappa.

This question I could never ask, even of my aunt: *You never suspected, either of you, that possibly he'd murdered her? That that was where Gretel Nissenbaum had disappeared: into the grave.*

5.

The farmhouse was already old when I was first brought to visit it: summers, in the 1950s. Part red brick so weathered as to seem without color and part rotted wood, with a steep shingled roof, high ceilings, and spooky corners; a perpetual odor of woodsmoke, kerosene, mildew, time. A perpetual draft passed through the house from the rear, which faced north, opening out onto a long incline of acres, miles, dropping to the Chautauqua River ten miles away like an aerial scene in a movie. I remember the old wash room, the machine with a hand-wringer; a door to the cellar in the floor of that room, with a thick metal ring as a handle. Outside the house, too, was another door, horizontal and not vertical. The thought of what lay beyond those doors, the dark, stone-smelling cellar where rats scurried, filled me with a childish terror.

374

I remember Grandfather Nissenbaum as always old. A lean, sinewy, virtually mute old man. His finely cracked, venous-glazed skin, red-stained as if with earth; narrow rheumy eyes whose pupils seemed, like the pupils of goats, horizontal black slats. How they scared me! Deafness had made Grandfather remote and strangely imperial, like an old almost-forgotten king. The crown of his head was shinily bald and a fringe of coarse hair bleached to the color of ash grew at the sides and back. Where once, my mother lamented, he'd been careful in his dress, especially on Sundays, for church-going, he now wore filth-stained overalls and in all months save summer long gray-flannel underwear straggling at his cuffs like a loose, second skin. His breath stank of tobacco juice and rotted teeth, the knuckles of both his hands were grotesquely swollen. My heart beat quickly and erratically in his presence. "Don't be silly," Mother whispered nervously, pushing me toward the old man, "—your grandfather *loves you.*" But I knew he did not. Never did he call me by my name, Bethany, but only "girl" as if he hadn't troubled to learn my name.

When Mother showed me photographs of the man she called Pappa, some of these scissored in half, to excise my missing grandmother, I stared, and could not believe he'd once been so handsome! Like a film actor of some bygone time. "You see," Mother said, incensed, as if the two of us had been quarreling, "—this is who John Nissenbaum really *is.*"

I grew up never really knowing Grandfather, and I certainly didn't love him. He was never "Grandpa" to me. Visits to Ransomville were sporadic, sometimes canceled at the last minute. Mother would be excited, hopeful, apprehensive—then, who knows why, the visit would be canceled, she'd be tearful, upset, yet relieved. Now, I can guess that Mother and her family weren't fully welcomed by my grandfather; he was a lonely and embittered old man, but still proud—he'd never forgiven her for leaving home, after high school, just like her sister Connie; going to the teachers' college at Elmira instead of marrying a local man worthy of working and eventually inheriting the Nissenbaum farm. By the time I was born, in 1951, the acreage was being sold off; by the time Grandfather Nissenbaum died, in 1972, in a nursing home in Yewville, the two-hundred acres had been reduced to a humiliating seven acres, now the property of strangers.

In the hilly cemetery behind the First Lutheran Church of Ransomville, New York, there is a still-shiny black granite marker at the edge of rows of Nissenbaum markers, *JOHN ALLARD NISSENBAUM*

1872-1957. Chiseled into the stone is *How long shall I be with you? How long shall I suffer you?* Such angry words of Jesus Christ's! I wondered who had chosen them—not Constance or Cornelia, surely. It must have been John Nissenbaum himself.

Already as a girl of eleven, twelve, I was pushy and curious, asking my mother about my missing grandmother. *Look, Mother, for God's sake where did she go? Didn't anybody try to find her?* Mother's replies were vague, evasive. As if rehearsed. That sweet-resolute stoic smile. Cheerful resignation, Christian forgiveness. For thirty-five years she taught high school English in the Rochester public schools, and especially after my father left us, and she became a single, divorced woman, the manner came easily to her of brisk classroom authority, that pretense of the skilled teacher of weighing others' opinions thoughtfully before reiterating one's own.

My father, an education administrator, left us when I was fourteen, to remarry. I was furious, heartbroken. Dazed. *Why? How could he betray us?* But Mother maintained her Christian fortitude, her air of subtly wounded pride. *This is what people will do, Bethany. Turn against you, turn faithless. You might as well learn, young.*

Yet I pushed. Up to the very end of her life, when Mother was so ill. You'd judge me harsh, heartless—people did. But for God's sake I wanted to know: what happened to my Grandmother Nissenbaum, why did nobody seem to care she'd gone away? Were the letters my mother and Connie swore their father received authentic, or had he been playing a trick of some kind? And if it had been a trick, what was its purpose? *Just tell me the truth for once, Mother. The truth about anything.* I'm forty-four years old, I still want to know.

But Mother, the intrepid schoolteacher, the good-Christian, was impenetrable. Inscrutable as her Pappa. Capable of summing up her entire childhood *back there* (this was how she and Aunt Connie spoke of Ransomville, their pasts: *back there*) by claiming that such *hurts* are God's will, God's plan for each of us. A test of our faith. A test of our inner strength. I said, disgusted, what if you don't believe in God, what are you left with then?—and Mother said matter-of-factly, "You're left with yourself, of course, your inner strength. Isn't that enough?"

That final time we spoke of this. I lost patience, I must have pushed Mother too far. In a sharp, stinging voice, a voice I'd never heard from her before, she said, "Bethany, what do you want me to tell you? About my mother?—my father? Do you imagine I ever knew them? Either of them? My mother left Connie and me when we were little girls, left us with *him*, wasn't that her choice? Her selfishness? Why should anyone have gone looking for her? She was trash, she was *faithless*. We learned to forgive, and to forget. Your aunt tells you a different story, I know, but it's a lie—*I* was the one who was hurt, *I* was the youngest. Your heart can be broken only once—you'll learn! Our lives were busy, busy like the lives of grown women today, women who have to work, women who don't have time to moan and groan over their hurt feelings, you can't know how Connie and I worked on that farm, in that house, like grown women when we were girls. Father tried to stop both of us going to school beyond eighth grade—imagine! We had to walk two miles to get a ride with a neighbor, to get to the high school in Ransomville; there weren't school buses in those days. Everything you've had you've taken for granted and wanted more, but we weren't like that. We hadn't money for the right school clothes, all our textbooks were used, but we went to high school. I was the only 'farm girl'—that's exactly what I was known as, even by my teachers—in my class to take math, biology, physics, Latin. I was memorizing Latin declensions milking cows at five in the morning, winter mornings. I was laughed at, Nelia Nissenbaum was *laughable*. But I accepted it. All that mattered was that I win a scholarship to a teachers' college so I could escape the country, and I did win a scholarship and I never returned to Ransomville to live. Yes, I loved Pappa—I still love him. I loved the farm, too. You can't not love any place that's taken so much from you. But I had my own life, I had my teaching jobs, I had my faith, my belief in God, I had my destiny. I even got married—that was extra, unexpected. I've worked for everything I ever got and I never had time to look back, to feel sorry for myself. Why then should I think about *her*?—why do you torment me about *her*? A woman who abandoned me when I was five years old! In 1923! I made my peace with the past, just like Connie in her different way. We're happy women, we've been spared a lifetime of bitterness. *That* was God's gift to us."

Mother paused, breathing quickly. There was in her face the elation of one who has said too much, that can never be retracted; I was stunned into silence. She plunged on, now contemptuously, "What are you always wanting me to admit, Bethany? That you know something I don't know? What is your generation always pushing for, from ours? Isn't it enough we gave birth to you, indulged you, must we be sacrificed to you, too? What do you want us to tell you—that life is cruel

377

and purposeless? That there is no loving God, and never was, only accident? Is that what you want to hear, from your mother? That I married your father because he was a weak man, a man I couldn't feel much for, who wouldn't, when it came time, hurt me?"

And then there was silence. We stared at each other. Mother in her glisten of fury, daughter Bethany so shocked she could not speak. Never again would I think of my mother in the old way.

What mother never knew: In April 1983, two years after her death, a creek that runs through the old Nissenbaum property flooded its banks, and several hundred feet of red clayey soil collapsed overnight into the creek bed, as in an earthquake. And in the raw, exposed earth there was discovered a human skeleton, decades old but virtually intact. It had been apparently buried, less than a mile behind the Nissenbaum farmhouse.

There had never been anything so newsworthy—so sensational—in the history of Chautauqua County.

State forensic investigators determined that the skeleton had belonged to a woman, apparently killed by numerous blows to the head (a hammer, or a blunt edge of an ax) that shattered her skull like a melon. Dumped into the grave with her was what appeared to have been a suitcase, now rotted, its contents—clothes, shoes, underwear, gloves—scarcely recognizable from the earth surrounding it. There were a few pieces of jewelry and, still entwined around the skeleton's neck, a tarnished-gold cross on a chain. Most of the woman's clothing had long ago rotted away and almost unrecognizable too was a book— a leatherbound Bible?—close beside her. About the partly detached, fragile wrist and ankle bones were loops of rusted baling wire that had fallen loose, coiled in the moist red clay like miniature sleeping snakes.

Nominated by Richard Burgin, Jane Hirshfield, Jewel Mogan, Robert Phillips

BEFORE THE BEGINNING: MAYBE GOD AND A SILK FLOWER CONCUBINE PERHAPS

by PATTIANN ROGERS

from THE HUDSON REVIEW

The white sky is exactly the same white
stone as the white marble of the transparent
earth, and the moon with its clear white
swallow makes of its belly of rock neither
absence nor presence.

The stars are not syllables yet enunciated
by his potential white tongue, its vestigial
lick a line that might break eventually,
a horizon curving enough to pronounce
at last, *my love.*

The locked and frigid porcelain barrens
and hollows of the descending black plain
are a pattern of gardens only to any single
blind eye blinking, just as a possible stroke
of worm, deaf with whiteness, might hear
a lace bud of silk meridians spinning
and unraveling simultaneously on the vacuous
beds of the placeless firmament.

An atheist might believe in the seductive
motion turning beneath the transparent gown
covering invisibly the non-existent bones
and petals of no other. Thus the holy blossom,
spread like the snow impression of a missing
angel, doubts the deep-looped vacancy
of her own being into which god, in creation,
must assuredly come.

Is it possible there might be silver seeds
placed deep between those legs opening
like a parting of fog to reveal the plunging salt
of a frothy sea? But god digresses, dreaming
himself a ghost, with neither clamor nor ecstasy,
into inertia, his name being farther
than ever from time.

Static on the unendurably boring white
sheet of his own plane, he must think hard
toward that focus of conception when he can rise
shuddering, descending and erupting into the beauty
and fragrance of their own making together—
those flowering orange-scarlet layers and sun-
shocking blue heavens of, suddenly, one another.

Nominated by Rick Bass, Walter Pavlic, Jane Hirshfield

DIRECT MALE

fiction by RISA MICKENBERG

from **THE BAFFLER**

A private message to a special friend.

Dear Annie Byrne:

This is a private invitation sent to you alone. I hope you'll accept my proposal. But even if you decide not to, I want to send you a gift. . . . **ABSOLUTELY FREE.**

Yes. A 4 $\frac{1}{4}$″ × 4 $\frac{3}{4}$″ table-top calculator (battery included) - with a wide display screen and large keys will be delivered right to your door. You can't buy this fabulous calculator at any store in **New York.** But it can be yours . . . without any obligation . . . simply by saying you'd like to have it!

Why I'm Writing To You

The list from which I selected your name indicates that you are a single, 34-year-old woman who earns $90,575, is concerned with fashion and health, has a cursory knowledge of politics, a bit of a Barney's addiction and a penchant for a certain discreet sex toy mail order catalog.

I like your profile.

I want you to marry me and as a FREE GIFT to you, Annie, you will receive the **marvelous table top calculator.**

How can I make such an incredible offer?

As Customer Service Representative for the Omni American Card, I see millions of interesting women in our database, but none whose spending habits and psychographic profile excite me the way yours do.

I'm confident that you will enjoy my sense of humor. My endearing mannerisms. My dog. **My full head of blonde hair.** You'll get it all when you marry me by **September 16, 1996.**

I'm sure you'll be delighted and intrigued by every little thing I do, Annie. Won't you accept this free calculator and be my wife?

Sincerely,
Richie Glickman
Customer Service Representative
Omni American Card

P.S. This **FREE GIFT** offer expires after August 16, 1996. I urge you to return it today.

* * *

OBITUARY
ANNIE BYRNE DIES, ALONE AND NEVER MARRIED, AT THE AGE OF 75.

Dear Miss Byrne:

A fictitious obituary? Perhaps.

But when it comes to finding a husband, the facts are grim:
   * There are over 250,000 single women in New York City
      Murphy Brown ratings are at an all-time high.
      This town is crawling with competition.
   * 30% of the men deemed "eligible" by most surveys are actually prisoners. And fewer than ⅓ of those prisoners are serving sentences for white-collar crimes.

*Pretty much <u>everyone who's really fun is gay.</u>

The fact is, <u>there just aren't that many good men out there.</u>

HOW MANY MORE NIGHTS CAN YOU SIT AT HOME ALONE WATCHING MARY TYLER MOORE ON NICK AT NIGHT AND EATING MOO SHU VEGETABLES?

You can't do it anymore, **Annie**, can you?

That's why I'm writing to you—to ask you to marry me. Please affix the YES sticker to the attached card and send the enclosed envelope with your answer today.

A legal marriage with me will protect you from the stigma of being a lonely old maid 24 hours a day, 7 days a week, anywhere in the world.

What is peace of mind like that worth these days?

Please marry me, Annie, before another gray hair appears on your head. **I've extended this unbelievable offer until October 15, 1996.** Mail your response today. Thank you.

Sincerely Yours,
Richie Glickman
Customer Service Representative
Omni American Card

* * *

Dear Ms Byrne:
Recently, I invited you to be my bride. My reason was clear. As a highly valued female cardmember, you <u>deserve</u> to join the select group of women who enter into matrimony. Being married to me instantly identifies you as someone special. You'll enjoy a new degree of respect and attention from waitresses who formerly sneered, "Table for one?" at you or acted sympathetic which was even worse. You'll be instantly upgraded at hotels across the United States

and around the world. You'll even be invited to more dinner parties.

The portfolio of benefits offered to you by marrying me will noticeably augment those you currently enjoy and will enhance the way you lead your life.

Complimentary Companion Tickets to My Parents' Home in Minneapolis, Minnesota Every Thanksgiving

With married life comes the joy of an extended family. "Mom" and "Dad" Glickman will welcome you every Thanksgiving with a home cooked meal, including yams, turkey and traditional stuffing, all with no salt added.

A Night Table For Your Side Of The Bed

You will be entitled to a walnut night table to fill with photograph albums, bedtime reading and maybe even, God willing, baby books.

Safe Sex

You'll receive a signed certificate, suitable for framing, from a qualified medical practitioner, ensuring that I am free from all sexually transmittable diseases—*a valuable thing to know in this day and age.*

It's O.K., I Was Up.®, My Exclusive 24-Hour Listening Service

Whether you have a bad dream, or you're lying awake seething with rage over the way I leave my socks on the living room floor, or you're up at 4 a.m. convincing yourself you have cancer, you can wake me up and I'll listen. Really listen. You've earned this recognition and now I believe you should be wearing the ring that signifies your value: my wedding ring.

Sincerely,
Richie Glickman

Customer Service Representative
Omni American Card
    P.S. If you have already responded to my offer, please excuse this reminder letter. I just wanted to be sure you were aware of this very special offer.

*   *   *

Dear Miss Byrne:

Just what the hell were you doing spending $156 at **The Odeon** and $128 for tickets to *Rent* last Thursday?

Never mind how I know.

I hope you haven't started dating. I've enclosed a brochure on the risks of rape, disease, attack and scam artistry. It's just plain stupid.

I want you. I want to marry you. <u>I know we're perfect for each other.</u>

<u>It's not too late to respond.</u>

Look. Meet me.

Let me help resolve whatever it is that's keeping you away. Simply bring this letter to my apartment at 190 Waverly Place #4B and redeem it for a FREE DINNER AT LA GRENOUILLE **worth well over $156**, you may rest assured.
Don't spend another night, or another cent, with some cheapskate loser you picked up God Knows Where.

Come over now and I'll never mention this little date of yours ever again, I swear.

Do we have a deal?

I look forward to seeing you.

385

Sincerely,
Richie Glickman
Customer Service Representative
Omni American Card

* * *

DID I DO SOMETHING WRONG?

Dear Annie:

I haven't received your response.
I've sent you several notices, asking for your hand in marriage but I haven't received your answer.
Please take the time to fill out the response card and mail it back today. At this point, we'll be lucky if we can find a halfway decent place for the reception.

Cordially,
Richie Glickman
Customer Service Representative
Omni American Card

* * *

Dear Miss Byrne:

You've moved!

It's a busy time. New apartment, lots of unpacking to do, a bunch of light switches to figure out, a whole new life. You were probably too busy to send a simple change of address, right?

Don't apologize.
It's fine.

Chances are, when the craziness dies down and you're lying in that empty apartment, surrounded by empty boxes and wads of packing tape, you'll wish you had someone—at least to help you reach those high shelves.

This is just a reminder that wherever you go, in every state and in 52 countries, whenever you need me, I am here. I can find you and be there in twelve hours.

Whether you need medical attention, a cash advance or you're finally ready to make a commitment that will provide you with the love, honor and respect you deserve, I'll always be here. 24 hours a day. A phone call away. Whenever you're ready. I will find you.

I look forward to hearing from you.

Sincerely,
Richie Glickman
Customer Service Representative
Omni American Card

Nominated by The Baffler

LIKE GOD

by LYNN EMANUEL

from BOSTON REVIEW

You hover above the page staring
down on a small town. By its roads
some scenery loafs in a hammock of
sleepy prose and here is a mongrel
loping and here is a train pulling into
a station in three long sentences and
here are the people in galoshes waiting.
But you know this story and it is not
about those travelers and their galoshes,
but about your life, so, like a diver
climbing over the side of a boat and
down into the ocean, you climb, sentence
by sentence, into this story on this page.

You have been expecting yourself
as the woman who purrs by in a dress
by Patou, and a porter manacled to
the luggage, and a matron bulky as
the *Britannia,* and there, haunting
her ankles like a piece of ectoplasm
that barks is, once again, that small
white dog from chapter twenty.
These are your fellow travelers and
you become part of their logjam of
images of hats and umbrellas and
Vuitton luggage, you are a face

behind or inside these faces, a
heartbeat in the volley of these
heartbeats, as you choose, out of all
the passengers, the journey of a man
with a mustache scented faintly with
Prince Albert. "He must be a secret
sensualist," you think and your awareness
drifts to his trench coat, worn, softened,
and flabby, a coat with a lobotomy, just
as the train arrives at a destination.

No, you would prefer another stop
in a later chapter where the climate is
affable and sleek. But most of
the passengers are disembarking, and
you did not choose to be in the story
of the white dress. You did not choose
the story of the matron whose bosom
is like the prow of a ship and who is
launched toward lunch at The Hotel Pierre,
or even the story of the dog-on-a-leash,
even though this is now your story:
the story of the man-who-had-to-
take-the-train and walk the dark road
described hurriedly by someone
sitting at the cafe so you could discover it,
although you knew all along it
would be there, you, who have been hovering
above this page, holding the book in
your hands, like God, reading.

Nominated by Jennifer Atkinson, Philip Booth, Gary Fincke, William Matthews

THE FIRST ANNUAL PERFORMANCE ART FESTIVAL AT THE SLAUGHTER ROCK BATTLEFIELD

fiction by THOMAS M. DISCH

from THE HUDSON REVIEW

As they drove up along the Delaware, Professor Hatch would keep pointing out objects of interest, mostly having to do with nature. K.C. had no use for nature. He'd had more than enough of it growing up in West Virginia, and the nature here seemed pretty much the same as the nature there, except for the river, and the fact that things weren't as level here so the road had to keep switching directions as it wound around the hills. Otherwise, you saw the usual stuff—trees, tall weeds along the road, some big rocks behind the weeds. According to Professor Hatch there were no towns for miles, just a few scattered convenience stores and filling stations. All the rest was nature.

"Funding," said K.C., lighting another cigarillo from the butt of the last one, "that's been my big problem. I could be doing *incredible* things if I didn't have to be thinking about funding all of the fucking time!"

Professor Hatch nodded sympathetically. "I know," she said. "It's the same here. It's the same everywhere."

"For instance," K.C. went on. "With the blood. I don't use *real* blood in what I do. Human blood, I mean. I buy the blood I use from a slaughterhouse, and I keep it refrigerated. It's *safe*! But then I go to this nowhere museum in Omaha or somewhere like that and, just because Ron Athney was there a couple months earlier and someone got a little blood on them . . . I mean, hey! is that my fault? I told them Athney uses his own blood, I use *animal* blood. Do animals have AIDS? So, suddenly I'm not part of their festival, and they want the money back on my air ticket."

"I've had the same sort of thing happen to me," said Professor Hatch, swerving to avoid a road kill.

K.C. swiveled round to see what they'd missed. Raccoon. When he was in the driver's seat K.C. generally tried to connect with the road kill by way of putting his signature on the highway.

"I've had *worse*," Professor Hatch went on. "I've had the police put chains across the doors of a church to keep my dance troupe from going in."

"No shit," K.C. sympathized. "Blood?"

"No, just nudity. In nineteen-eighty-seven! I can tell you I was depressed for a long time after that. And Alison—she's the co-director of the Festival but at that time she was my dance partner—Alison, was traumatized. This lawyer, some official, I don't know, was reading this legal nonsense, and then four policemen started *tearing down our posters*! There were photographers from the newspaper, Alison was in tears, and I myself was frantic. They were destroying my whole life! I will tell you—*that* is the meaning of censorship. When two women cannot dance inside a Unitarian church!"

K.C. tried to imagine Professor Hatch nude, but he couldn't even imagine her with a first name. She wasn't a Miss, or a Mrs., or even a Ms. And he knew better than to ask where she was a Professor, or what she was a Professor of. She liked to talk but she wasn't interested in answering questions, unless they were the kind to keep her moving smoothly along her own private highway.

"This Alison, was she much younger than you back then?"

He'd thought it was a neutral question, but the Professor gave him a dirty look. "She was as much younger than me then as she is now. She was not a minor, if that's what you mean."

"No problem. I just meant they will always use that as a pretext if they can. I know from personal experience: I discovered that I wanted to be a performance artist when I was sixteen, so you could say I was a prodigy. I was working with this group called Early Death. We were more of a rock group really. Anyhow they wouldn't let *us* perform in this club in North Carolina because I was underage."

"North Carolina: that's Jesse Helms, isn't it?"

"I guess so. The blood was a problem there, too. Anyhow, like you say, it's all censorship."

Professor Hatch piloted them through a green tunnel of scenery that veered away from the river to the right. The conversation had fired her up to cruising speed, where she could drive along without feeling she had to keep talking. There was an alert, birdish glint in her eye, and the cords in her neck were stretched tight in a way that K.C. associated with being wired to just the right degree.

He smoked, she drove, the road unrolled in front of them, and then the first sign appeared for Slaughter Rock Battlefield. "There it is!" Professor Hatch said, hitting the brakes. The van skidded past the historical plaque, but she reversed until they were right alongside it.

The plaque said:

SLAUGHTER ROCK BATTLEFIELD

In this area on August 15, 1780, was fought one of the bloodiest battles of the Revolutionary War. Over 120 militiamen were ambushed and savagely slaughtered by a party of 27 Tories and 60 Iroquois Indians.

"You wouldn't think," said K.C., "that they'd want to advertise what happened—being beat by about half their own number of Indians."

"There's two ways to look at it," said Professor Hatch, as the van lurched off the shoulder and back onto the highway. "You can see it as our militia suffering a sorry defeat—or as the Iroquois enjoying a spectacular victory. The park ground has become very popular with Native Americans. They come from all over the state. But of course that doesn't make for a large overall annual attendance. I've picnicked there on summer weekends when *no one* visited the park all afternoon. As though it weren't *there*. When I made out the applications grant for the Festival, I pointed out that here was one of the finest

392

recreational resources of Sullivan County going completely unused. They were spending thousands of dollars maintaining this hidden treasure, with its wonderful natural amphitheater that no one ever performed in. What a waste! But also, how typical. For there is practically *no* art in Sullivan County. Of course, for me, and a few friends, that's been a kind of blessing in disguise. You see, New York State's grants programs for the arts are organized county by county. So, if you live in Manhattan, forget it! You could be Judy Chicago herself and you wouldn't get a nickel."

"Judy Chicago?" K.C. asked.

Professor Hatch smiled a Buddhalike smile. "Judy Chicago is the Pablo Picasso of the twentieth century."

K.C. knew he was being condescended to, but he didn't mind. The Slaughter Rock Performance Arts Festival was offering him an honorarium of $250 for his gig, plus bus fare. Plus, most importantly, a chance to be able to show what he could do as a solo artist instead of as part of Early Death. There were critics coming all the way from New York City to see the show—two busloads of them, according to Professor Hatch, who was the driving force behind the Festival. The woman definitely knew her way around the performance art world, so it made sense to suck up to her and listen to what she had to say like she was some kind of guru.

"Sorry," he said, "I didn't mean to interrupt. You were saying about how New York works things county by county."

"Yes. So, it stands to reason, doesn't it, that the counties with the fewest artists will offer the best opportunities? Over the years I've received grants as a choreographer in Allegheny County, and for my poetry in Oswego County. But it was opening the Slaughter Rock Gallery that's been the real godsend, since when you're an institution you can keep reapplying every year. Of course, I still have to do the outreach work, bringing the art to the local communities. There's no escaping that. And it makes sense: it's the people who are paying for our grants with their tax dollars, so it's only fair that there should be something we give back to the communities."

K.C. couldn't resist: "But I thought you said, when we were driving away from the bus station, that we were leaving civilization and that there weren't any real towns up this way."

"There are no towns—but there are communities. What do you think Sullivan County's biggest industry is?"

"I don't know. Timber?"

393

"It *used* to be tourism. But that was forty years ago. No, corrections is the big employer here."

"Corrections?"

"Actually, adult warehousing of all sorts. There is a federal prison, and three good-sized state prisons—the biggest of them just for teenagers. Plus all sorts and sizes of halfway houses and rehabs tucked away here and there. Including one you may have heard of—Utopia, Incorporated."

"No shit, that's *here*? One of the guys in Early Death got sent there. The last I heard he was still locked up. So what do you do at these places? You go inside the prisons and do your performances there?" In the nude, he was wondering.

"No, much better than that. We offer workshops. In dance. In quilting and poetry. In all the creative arts. It's been a marvelously successful program. There is a genuine *hunger* for the arts among those who have been denied their freedom."

"Believe it," K.C. agreed. "A hunger for *anything*. I know, I been there."

"You were? You didn't mention that on your application." There was something taunting and maternal in her tone of voice that K.C. could relate to.

"I served time in a state home," he said, "around when other kids would be serving their time in sixth or seventh grade. So those records are sealed under court orders. But you want to know what I *did*, right? The basic charge was arson and destruction of property."

"Plus ça change," the Professor said, possibly thinking he wouldn't know what she meant.

"You're right," he agreed. *"Plus c'est la même chose*. In terms of the performance art. Though I don't think that would serve as any kind of extenuating circumstance with the family court. For them torching a building is a crime, not an esthetic decision."

"That is the outlook," observed Professor Hatch primly, "of all but a very few. What thin partitions, as they say."

She'd stumped him with that one, as she had with her Judy Detroit, but he wasn't vain about asking to have things explained. How else do you get an education unless you suck up to people who know things you don't? "Okay," he said, "I give up. *What* thin partitions?"

"Dryden," she said. "His *Achitophel*: 'A fiery soul, which working out its way, / Fretted the pigmy body to decay.' Then, a few lines later: 'Great wits are sure to madness near allied, / And thin partitions do their bounds divide.'"

K.C.'s first reaction was to cop a resentment. He was sensitive to re-marks about his height relative to anyone else's, and "pigmy body" had to be figured as a slap in the face. But this was not the moment to score one for the home team, so, filing away the slight for future reference, K.C. concentrated on his party manners. "I guess that's like saying ge-nius is right next door to madness." And then, by way of putting a pol-ish on the apple: "Thin partitions: I'll remember that."

Half a cigarillo later, and up a long series of switchbacks, they came to the gate of the Slaughter Rock Battlefield Memorial Park—a pair of four-foot-high pillars of unmortared fieldstone, each bearing an heraldic shield of painted plywood. On the right-hand shield a toma-hawk, on the left a musket. Professor Hatch drummed her fingers on the steering wheel while an attendant uniformed in urban camo low-ered the chain that barred access to the inner drive. As they passed through the gate, the guard saluted Professor Hatch, a real spit-and-polish heel-clicking salute, which she accepted as carelessly as any five-star general.

After a further steep climb, the road split in two. To the left was Parking, to the right Picnic Grounds. They hung right, passing through another pair of dwarf fieldstone pillars to draw up beside a large Win-nebago parked in front of a row of portable toilets. The side of the Winnebago was lettered "Slaughter Rock Gallery — Preserving Sulli-van County's Artistic Heritage." Beyond the toilets, scattered among high, thick-boled pines, were some dozen heavy-duty picnic tables and brick barbecues.

At one of the farther tables a small tribe of Mohawks was enjoying a lunch of Kentucky Fried Chicken and keg beer. The Indians waved at Professor Hatch, and she waved back.

"They're not the genuine article, of course," she said. "They're our re-enactors."

"I figured," said K.C.

"There was never any problem getting the young people to volun-teer for the Festival once they heard that we'd be re-creating the events of Slaughter Rock. Of course everyone wanted to be on Thayendanegea's side, and not a militiaman."

"No surprise there. Who wouldn't rather dress up like it's Hal-loween—feathers and war paint and all that? And then, like you said, the Indians were the winners. That bunch over there sure started early."

"We should get started ourselves," said Professor Hatch, unlatching her seat belt and stepping out of the van. "Or at least I should. I'm going to have to leave you here with Alison, while I deal with some of the others. Meanwhile, if we could get your equipment unloaded. . . . "

Professor Hatch opened the rear of the van with a remote, and then stepping away from the van, out of K.C.'s hearing, started talking into a cellular phone.

K.C.'s first concern was for the trunk that Liberty and Justice had been traveling in the whole long way from Camden, New Jersey. They'd never traveled such a distance confined in such a small space, and K.C. had been worried that they might get baked or would suffocate from being stowed at the back end of the luggage compartment on the underside of the bus. He'd wanted to open the trunk back in New York City, when he was changing from Greyhound to Trailways, but there hadn't been time. And when he got out at the crossroad where Professor Hatch was waiting, there wasn't time again. She seemed the kind of person who's always in a hurry, plus she probably was a herpetophobe. Lots of times people will tell you how they think snakes are so cool, the ideal pets and all that, but then you introduce them to Liberty and Justice and they'll go into shock.

They were both dead. He could tell without touching them. Any other time they'd spent some hours in the trunk, being bumped around, they would be hyperactive as soon as the top came off their case. Like as not, one of them would be curled up in position to attack, or might even take a lunge at him, forgetting about the steel mesh or just not giving a fuck. Not this time. They were dead.

K.C. did not believe in stuffing his feelings. When he felt something he expressed it. Any very intense or sudden pain took the form of a scream that started as a low growling, then took a yodel-like two-octave leap into a "Fuck this shit!" of high-octane primal rage. Even in grade school his tantrums had been legendary, but two years of professional experience with Early Death had perfected his native ability, and K.C.'s scream of grief for his two dead rattlesnakes transfixed everyone in hearing distance. Professor Hatch froze. A fat woman, who turned out to be the Professor's dancing partner, Alison, bounded out the door of the Winnebago. The imitation Indians sprinted across the picnic area, zigzagging between the tables, alarmed and excited.

With an instinct for the grand manner, K.C. took up Liberty in one hand and Justice in the other and lifted them over his head and screamed a second, even more artful howl—not as loud but shriller and wonderfully drawn out, with a quaver in it that would stop anyone who heard it in his or her tracks, like a baby's utmost scream. People are hard-wired to respond to that particular sound the way sprinkler systems respond to a fire.

It was Alison who took charge. She was a large, bottom-heavy woman, each thigh the size of an average torso, and she used her weight as a badge of authority. She marched forward, thigh by thigh, and took hold of the limp bodies of the snakes. "No more of this nonsense," Alison told K.C. "Let go."

He let her take the snakes from him and then, grateful as a musician might be for a good segue, went limp himself. Down on his knees with a silent wince of pain as the gravel ground at his kneecaps, then a fetal curl forward so that he could hide his face in his cupped hands and wait for the tears, if any, to begin. He thought of his own naked corpse, with all his friends and family gathered round (a trick he'd learned taking acting lessons at the community college in South Jersey), feeling guilty and regretful. Sure enough, the thought of his own tragic waste, so young and so talented and so thin, released the tears. Not a flood exactly but enough so that when he lifted his head they were there to be seen by the ring of spectators—all wearing Mohawks and war paint and looking amazed.

"Hey, K.C." said the most elaborately authentic of the Indians, "get a grip, man."

"Jethro? Death Row Jethro?"

Jethro opened his arms invitingly, and, after K.C. had got back on his feet, they performed a solemn male embrace, jeans apart, arms wrapped tight around each other's shoulders.

"It's been awhile," Jethro said, disengaging and taking a step backward, "since anybody called me *that*. Here I'm just John." But he grinned in a way that assured K.C. that that was just a lie he had to tell for the sake of Professor Hatch and all the other Indians. This was the familiar wolfish grin of the lyricist and lead singer of Early Death's only song to hit the charts, "Homicidal Maniac."

K.C. wiped away his genuine tears with the cuff of his shirt. "You look a whole lot healthier, man. Compared to two years ago."

"It's holistic," explained Jethro. "You can't deal with just the symptoms alone, like in Western medicine, you have to treat the whole man. Plus, I've been eating a lot of food."

Jethro stroked the area of his thin, jutting chin where his goat used to be. Without the beard and with his irregularly shaped cranium exposed by the Mohawk, Jethro's face seemed even more like a skull than when he'd been Early Death's lead guitar. The weight he'd put on hadn't altered his basic persona, he was still a living reminder that all men are mortal, some more than others.

"I'm sorry about the snakes," Jethro commiserated, laying thin, fluent fingers on K.C.'s shoulder. "But that doesn't mean you'll be left out of the show. Where there's a problem there's also a solution. Remember when we were in Winston-Salem and the amps got busted up by those rednecks? Wha'd we do? We used those car alarms for back-up and we had a big success. Right? Am I right?"

"Yeah," K.C. conceded sullenly. He didn't like surrendering the drama inherent in his grief for Liberty and Justice, which he probably could have milked for more sympathy, particularly from Professor Hatch and her buddy Alison, who were the impresarios. On the other hand, maybe it wouldn't be such a good idea to come across as too unstrung. Jethro's instincts were right, even if he did sound like he was whistling some limpdick tune by Oscar and Hammerstein: When you walk through deep shit, keep your bootstraps dry, and don't be afraid of the dorks.

In any case, K.C. had a short emotional attention span, and after a primal scream had given his insides a good reaming-out he was usually ready to move on to new feelings. Liberty and Justice were gone now, no changing that, and he'd expressed his grief in a suitable way. Walk on, walk on, like the song says. The whole idea of performance art, as K.C. had come to understand it as a mature artist, was to deliver a gut punch, then step back, go somewhere else where for a while you might seem to be boring, and then when they weren't expecting it, Wham, a kick to the groin. Shock treatment. That was how a good horror movie worked, or a stand-up comic. Make 'em laugh, make 'em barf, keep 'em guessing.

So after being formally introduced to Alison (who was the strict sort of feminist who didn't shake hands with men but just looked at the hand being offered and nodded her head) and to the other Iroquois from Utopia, Incorporated—Keno, Duster, Winthrop, Lou, and Marlene—K.C. settled down with his old pal for a session of lateral thinking. At first Jethro's inspirations were all in the direction of nudity, which was no surprise. Jethro had a big dick, and he'd always been the first to drop his pants at any Early Death concert. And it had worked, since it is a gross-out for everyone, and an inspiration for those who can identify, to see someone so cadaverous also so well-endowed.

K.C. had a hard time diverting Jethro to alternate veins of inspiration, but he persisted. "We got to think of something that will work

398

with that flagpole. The snakes may be out of the act now, but I still got all these ropes and pulleys and the harness. They're a major investment, I can't just scrap them."

"Okay, okay. We're looking at a flagpole. We're looking at *you* being raised *up* the flagpole."

"Upside-down," K.C. reminded him.

"Right. Up the flagpole, upside-down. Plus, you're in handcuffs?"

"Yeah, but they're gimmicked. I can get them off when I need to."

"I got it!" said Jethro. "What's the most natural thing to send up a flagpole? A flag! We'll burn a fucking flag."

"You think?"

"I know."

"We tried that once at the end of our gig in Durham. It didn't go down so well there, if you remember. Freddy lost two teeth."

"But that was North Carolina, this is New York. We've got two buses of critics coming up from the City, and those dudes will have *no* problem with burning a flag. They're liberals up here, they get off on that kind of thing. It's like you'd be exercising your First Amendment, or the Second, whichever. And it would fit right in with the re-enactments. Better than the snakes would have, if you think about it. Here's a battle that the Indians *won*. This was their land before there was any flags or flagpoles, just fucking trees. And the Professor is very big on the Native American angle, so she'll dig the idea of setting the flag on fire, I can guarantee, besides which it'll give us Mohawks something to do besides scalping our victims. We got a whole lot of Mohawks in the show. Basically, everyone who isn't doing guard duty at the gate is wearing war paint."

"Your whole rehab?" K.C. marveled.

"All of them in the *show*," Jethro qualified. "Some of them opted out. So they're back at Utopia or decorating the grounds here as fallen heroes. Anyhow, in terms of putting *you* in the line of fire, Old Glory is as good as snakes any time. I like that: the line of *fire*?"

"Yeah yeah, I get it."

"And while the flag is being raised to where you're up there hanging by your heels, we can have Duster play a tape of 'The Star-Spangled Banner.' The Hendrix version. Well?"

"Lemme think about it." K.C. took the last cigarillo from his pack and snapped a wooden match alight with his thumbnail. But instead of lighting the cigarillo he just stared at the quivering yellow flame as it crept up the matchstick toward his fingers. When the heat got too intense, he dropped the match.

"Okay," he said, having thought it over, "I think it'll work. Let's go talk to the Professor."

It was Freddy Beale, Early Death's drummer and resident psychic, who'd originally got K.C. involved with the Tarot. The first time Freddy had read the cards for K.C. he'd told him to pick a card from the deck to be his Significator, and K.C. had picked The Hanged Man. Freddy had objected to his choosing a card from the Major Arcana, but K.C. had never had any doubt in his mind that The Hanged Man had to be his Significator, because his first childhood memory was of his dad dangling him upside-down from a pedestrian bridge while the traffic whizzed by on the highway below. What he was being punished for K.C. couldn't remember, and later his dad would insist that nothing like that had ever happened, that K.C. was either remembering a dream or else making it up. But the physical details were as clear now as though he'd seen it happen on a wide screen with Dolby sound: the perspective lines coming to a V at the upside-down horizon, and the cars hurtling toward him and disappearing with a whoosh and then a semi, sounding its horn like a blast from the last trumpet. Most of all he remembered the way it felt—not at all scary, like his dad had probably intended, but thrilling, like a ferris wheel. Years later, outside St. Louis, riding the big ferris wheel overlooking the Mississippi, K.C. had tried to recapture that sensation by hanging from the safety bar by his knees, trapeze-style, but before he could start spacing out on the visuals, the operator of the ferris wheel had freaked and K.C.'s death-defying ride had wound up in the amusement park's security office, which is not an ideal environment when you're peaking on acid.

This now was the best that upside-down had ever been, thanks in part to the equipment, which was designed for a balanced distribution of weight and minimum chafing, but mostly on account of the view. The flagpole he'd been raised to the top of was thirty feet high and situated at almost the highest point of the amphitheater, with a view in one direction of the tiers of stone benches where the audience would be sitting, and in the other direction across the whole actual battlefield, which was enormous. "Field," however, was not exactly the right term for it, since what K.C. could see was a steep downward vista of trees and rocks and suicidal plummets. From where K.C. was slung in the suspension harness he could see across the leafy treetops to the

400

actual Slaughter Rock the place was named for, which had been decorated by the re-enactors with various dead bodies—very realistically done up, at least from this distance—representing the Yankee militiamen the Iroquois had slaughtered. If he squinted, he could see one corpse that looked like it had been genuinely scalped. Professor Hatch's FX people deserved high points for that one.

Those old Iroquois had been into savagery, no doubt about it. According to Professor Hatch's friend, Alison, who was some kind of expert about the Revolutionary War and Native American torture techniques, the major casualties of the battle had all taken place right underneath that one long ledge of reddish-black rock. As the militiamen had been wounded in different other parts of the mountainside they'd been brought there for medical attention, and then, when everyone else who could had escaped, the Indians had found the field hospital and the 74 wounded men. And that was how the place had got its name of Slaughter Rock. As Alison had pointed out, history isn't always just a lot of names and dates.

Though K.C. was not one to pay much attention to nature and the weather and all such as that, he had to give credit where it was due, and this was shaping up into one beautiful day with big old clouds sailing by underfoot and a wind that kept swinging him round in unexpected ways. He started writing lyrics in his head, which was something he only did when he was in a special mental space. This one looked like it might be a haiku, though he didn't bother counting the syllables the way he would have had to do if he was a formalist-type poet.

Real is the crowd in the bleachers

his haiku began. Then, after one or two false steps, it continued

No less real the clouds
Sailing by my combat boots.

Strictly speaking, the first line wasn't true. There was no crowd in the bleachers at this point, just Jethro and a few other fake Iroquois who were doing Tai Chi exercises on the topmost stone ledges of the amphitheater, so that their half-naked bodies were silhouetted against blue sky and billowing clouds.

Freddy had tried to get K.C. interested in Tai Chi, but for some reason it hadn't clicked. Where was Freddy now? he wondered. The last

401

he'd heard Freddy had been in a shelter for battered women in Biloxi, having finally got himself transsexualized and then married to exactly the wrong guy. Talk about karma. Anyhow, he, or she, was probably still alive, which was one better than Gordon, who'd played rhythm guitar for Early Death—and Russian roulette, once too often. Right on the stage of the 4-H Club Building at the Linnet County Fair. *Those* fans had sure got more than they'd bargained for. And now all those screams and excitement were just so much nostalgia like the snows of yesteryear.

At first it had seemed an amazing coincidence to bump into Jethro this far away from the scenes of their old crimes. But there are no coincidences in real life, there's only networking. Jethro had explained to K.C., while he was being fitted into the suspension harness, how it was all his doing, Jethro's, that K.C. had been contacted to be one of the major acts at the First Annual Performance Art Festival at the Slaughter Rock Battlefield. How Professor Hatch had been skeptical at first but finally caved in when Jethro had explained about K.C.'s act with Liberty and Justice. Never mind that the act had never in fact been performed before a paying audience: it *was* a great idea, even on paper, and Jethro had even been able to dig up a copy of the application to the National Endowment for the Arts that he'd helped K.C. write up just before he, Jethro, had been shipped off to Utopia, Incorporated. Professor Hatch had expressed a respectful admiration but it was her friend Alison, according to Jethro, who had gone bananas. "Darlene," she had said (that being the Professor's Christian name), "we have got to get this boy here. He sounds archetypal." Alison, according to Jethro, was the real decision-maker. Professor Hatch, for all her greater visibility (Alison tended to stay inside the Winnebago), was only following orders most of the time. According to Jethro.

So here K.C. was, by Fate's decree, and Alison's, hanging upside-down from the highest flagpole in Sullivan County in the State of New York, waiting for fame's lightning to strike. K.C. had always known that he was destined to be a celebrity artist on a par with Karen Finley or David Wojnarowicz, transgressing the boundaries, destroying old categories, bringing down the house. It was what his whole life had been pointing toward since even before the accident, so-called, with the kittens in the laundromat when he was only four years old. Back in France there was Rimbaud, and now there was K.C., and who could say for sure which of them would make a bigger dent on the human psyche in the long run? K.C. was bound for glory: he could feel it in the very fillings of his teeth.

A sudden gust of wind twisted K.C. around (his harness had a swivel bolt) so that he was, once again, facing toward Slaughter Rock—and there at long last, on the woodland path leading to the amphitheater, were the critics, off their buses and being herded along by Professor Hatch, who was identifiable even at this distance by her peculiar hairstyle, which looked like a large gray doughnut on top of her head. The critics had stopped to admire the re-enactors, who were brandishing their spears and tomahawks and executing and re-executing the wounded militiamen. The spectacle was given a muted, ballet-like solemnity by the way Alison had choreographed the scene to resemble the clockwork motions of elves in a department store window at Christmastime. Behind and to the sides of the cluster of critics were guards in urban camo, like the one who'd greeted Professor Hatch at the entrance to the park ground.

The wind shifted and K.C. swiveled round so that he could no longer see Slaughter Rock and the arriving critics. His right shoulder struck the flagpole, but he managed to twist his cranium out of harm's way. At just that moment his earphones staticked into life. "K.C., can you hear me? This is Alison."

"Hey, Alison, finally. We've got problems."

"K.C.? K.C., can you hear me? Oh dear. I can see you, with my binoculars, moving your lips. But the sound isn't coming through."

"Come on, don't *do* this to me. I know you can—"

"There's always some glitch, isn't there," Alison went on in a tone of imperturbable sweetness. "Well, we'll muddle through. The show is about to get on the road, and I don't think you could be any more nervous that I am at this point. The things we do for art!"

K.C.'s mike, in the shape of a miniature cobra, was positioned right to the side of his mouth. He did not believe that it wasn't working, but on the chance he *wasn't* being lied to he spoke into the mike with the exaggerated clarity that he'd had to use when he was taking classes to become a TV anchorman, as though his crisp pronunciation might magic away the technical problems. "Alison, we have a problem here. My good buddy Jethro has decided to play some kind of practical joke. These cuffs he's put on me are not the cuffs I supplied him with. There's no spring, and I cannot get my hands loose. Can you hear this?"

"You're trying to say something, aren't you? But it isn't getting through. The artist's eternal plight!"

403

"Fuck," said K.C. feelingly.

"I can *hear* Darlene perfectly—she's telling our visitors all about the events leading up to Slaughter Rock, from the perspective of the Iroquois *women*—and I can *see* you, but not vice versa. I would like to be able to fix your mike, but there isn't time now to lower you and do that and get you back up there again, and you do make such a startling first impression. I'm chattering, aren't I? I always get like this before the curtain goes up. Don't you? I call it The Moment. It's not exactly stage *fright*, more a feeling that something unique and terribly important is about to happen. As though—Wait a moment, I'm getting something from Darlene."

The earphones went dead for a while, and K.C. tried to do the same with his thoughts. He was beginning to intuit that something was not right. It wasn't just that Alison seemed flakey. The world is full of flakes, that is a given. But what K.C. was picking up was that the Festival was not the simple scam he'd been expecting, not just an opportunity to give the NEA-funded finger once again to the bourgeoisie, which is to say, to the people who have to pay for their tickets. The organizers of the Festival seemed to have a more ambitious agenda.

Why, for instance, was Jethro, on the top tier of the stone bleachers, firing imaginary bullets in K.C.'s direction from what looked like it might be a real rifle? Jethro would mime taking aim and then, mouthing a *pow*! inaudible at this distance, he'd jerk the barrel upward. K.C. began to reappraise their relationship. Jethro was a fellow artist, true, and in an ideal world there should be honor among thieves. But Jethro might well be harboring a grudge toward K.C. with respect to how he'd been admitted in to Utopia, Incorporated, under a court-mandated order that allowed him to be detoxed in lieu of serving hard time. The last time K.C. had seen his old friend, on the night he'd freaked, Jethro had been exercising his right to bear arms, and his *Pow!s* then had had real bullets attached, which were aimed at real people, K.C. included. Sometimes cops are the only solution, but even otherwise rational felons tend to hold a grudge against those who pursue that solution.

A while back, Jethro as part of his ongoing recovery had E-mailed a note to K.C., apologizing for the bullet holes and offering amends, but what if that letter, so sincere and full of honest feeling, did not represent Jethro's final thinking on the matter? What if he was looking for a payback? And what if these new friends of his had agreed, for their own flakey reasons, to help him get even?

404

Alison came back on line. "It's me again," she said brightly, "and everything is all right, no need to worry. One of our guests was making problems. He wanted to go back to the bus. Which is not exactly possible at this point. But Darlene has things under control. It was the critic from the *Voice*, and we can't very well let *him* miss the show, can we? Good Lord! Especially since the *Times* never showed. Wouldn't you know. After all the promises! Critics!

"Do you know what our major expense had been for this whole event? Catering! I'm not kidding. Each of the buses had to have two cases of champagne. Et cetera. But if we hadn't laid out the money and chartered the buses and *groveled*, there wouldn't be anyone here but us chickens. For a New York critic even Brooklyn is terra incognita, and that has been the story of my life! But not any longer. Somebody has got to draw the line. This far, no farther, stop. Life isn't long enough. Literally."

Alison stopped talking but K.C. could still hear her wheezing breath over his earphones. She sounded like a car that had flooded its engine and couldn't get started.

While Alison was still stomping on the gas pedal, so to speak, the critics began to file into the amphitheater. One of the critics began to make a stink when the guards—who were now serving as ushers—insisted that she had to sit in the area reserved for the press, in the middle of the second and third tiers. She wanted to know why she couldn't sit up in the top tier, since there was no one else in the amphitheater. Unless you counted Jethro, who had finished with his imaginary target practice and settled down into lotus posture, eyes closed, chanting his mantra, which was *Hare Kali, Kali Hare!*

The sound of the argument was drowned out by the opening squawk of the amps and then Hendrix's "Star-Spangled Banner." A procession of local grade-schoolers appeared from out of nowhere, dressed up as little Pilgrim Fathers and Mothers, in cocked hats and bonnets, and trying to sing along with the National Anthem.

Hendrix was faded to allow Alison's much amplified whispery soprano to announce, "From the Benjamin Tusten Elementary School in Fort Tusten, New York, won't you please welcome The Thirteen Colonies."

The critics dutifully applauded as the thirteen children came to attention in front of them. There's nothing like having kids on stage for making an audience settle down and behave, unless it's dogs or horses. The critic who'd wanted to sit higher up had plunked down where she

405

belonged and was paying a bemused, condescending attention to The Thirteen Colonies, who had marched up single file into the bleachers to surround the critics in a loose oval.

Alison began a dramatic reading of Robert Frost's "Mending Wall." "Something there is that doesn't love a wall," etc. As the poem was read, the guards erected, with astonishing rapidity, a real wall of spiraling razor-wire between the children and the critics. As the progress of the wall's construction passed one of the children, he or she would hold aloft a miniature version of Old Glory and announce which of the original thirteen colonies he or she represented. Only little Delaware muffed her line.

"Well, there they are, Darlene," said Alison, unamplified, over the earphones. "Our captive audience. Didn't I tell you?"

"You're right, they just sat there for it," said Professor Hatch. "Amazing."

"It's what they're trained to do, isn't it? No critic will admit to being fazed, or shocked, or disconcerted by anything they might be made to witness. Besides, with that ring of darling children around them, waving flags, and Robert Frost to boot. . . . "

"Which, I must say, you read very well, my dear."

"Thank you. It's a poem I've always loved. I do wish those children could have stayed on for the finale, though."

"Now, we've discussed all that before. *Some* entertainments really are not suitable for the young. In any case, our thirteen darling little colonies are back on their school bus, which must be somewhere along Route 97 by now. And believe me, *cara mia*, they will never forget this night. It will live with them forever."

"Forever is such a lovely word," Alison whispered. "Forever and a day!"

This was followed by a sound that K.C., if he'd heard it over the radio, would have interpreted as a kiss. Did they know he was listening? Would it have mattered?

"K.C., are you still there?" Alison asked, reading his mind. "Oh, I know—what choice do you *have*? But you mustn't think I mean to tease you. I actually have a great deal of respect for your physical courage. That's something I lack entirely. Your friend Jethro says that you are like the boy in the fairy tale who simply could not feel fear, or even embarrassment. I'm just the opposite. Sometimes I simply can't bear to be *looked* at, even by Darlene. So you can imagine what a breakthrough it was for me, with two left feet and ten thumbs, to become a dancer. Every performance I felt I was about to commit suicide. Well, and here we are now, doing just that! So to speak.

"Have you ever had a major medical problem, K.C.? Are you, for instance, HIV-positive?"

K.C. shook his head no.

"No?" She must have been watching from inside the Winnebago, which stood like a dam across the path leading from the parking lot to the amphitheater. "Jethro didn't think you would be. He said you'd get a lobotomy sooner than have sex. The reason I ask is not that I have any anxiety against dealing with Persons with AIDS. It's because it's so hard to explain what I've been through to someone who's never been there. Have you ever heard of Crohn's disease? Not c-r-o-n-e, but C-r-o-h-n. It's what I've got. A medical condition not very well understood. The walls of the intestine thicken, and that can lead to fistulas and abscesses, and that can result in peritonitis. Which is fatal. There's no certain cure. A surgeon may remove one section of the bowel, and then it recurs somewhere else. So . . . What is one to do? That's what I've had to ask myself. Submit to surgery? That's like telling a woman that since she *must* be raped she might as well relax and enjoy it. I don't think that is a rational solution to the problem. In fact, I don't think rationality itself is a solution. Western medicine treats symptoms, so the essential problem, which is spiritual, remains unsolved. So what *is* the solution? Art! Think about it, K.C. Art."

There was some actual art happening, meanwhile, in the amphitheater, in the form of an old-fashioned square dance, the kind when the men wore little white wigs and the women had big dresses. Apparently, the Festival's budget didn't have room for anything but the most notional wigs and ball gowns, but imagination made up for the lack of funding. The "dancers"—two men and two women—were strapped into wheelchairs and they were being do-si-do-ed and allemanded at high speed by eight of the Iroquois, while, in combination with some jingly super-loud harpsichord music, Professor Hatch spelled out the significance of the event.

"Before the Europeans came to these shores," she boomed out over the amplified harpsichord, "there were no walls. No amber fields of chemically fertilized grain. The dances of the Native Americans were shamanic rituals that united the dancer and her goddess, not geometric diagrams designed to subdue and deform the bodies of women. For the Europeans who came here in their *Niñas* and *Pintas* and *Mayflowers* this entire continent was one vast woman, whom they

407

would bind with treaties and title deeds and claims of ownership—and then . . . rape!"

At this cue, the four wheelchairs were equipped with old-fashioned muskets that were supported on tripods connecting to the seats and armrests, so that each weapon would be aiming in the same basic direction as the chair on which it was mounted. The music changed from a square dance to a fife-and-drum version of "Yankee Doodle," and Professor Hatch read the verses of that song at a death-march tempo in her throatiest, most menacing tone of voice, deconstructively repeating some of the phrases, such as "keep it up" and "went to town." To this accompaniment the four miniature armored vehicles converged on the front row of the amphitheater, then tilted back so that the muskets were aimed directly at the critics enclosed within the circle of razor-wire.

K.C. had once attended a performance in Louisville of *The Cencis*, a tragedy by the great French schizophrenic Antonin Artaud. At the very beginning of the play, two actors dressed up as soldiers had emptied their bladders into a plastic bucket at the side of the stage. For the remaining four hours of the drama that bucket just sat there, but everyone knew what was going to happen with what was in that bucket before the play was over, just the way you know when you see a gun in Act One that it will be fired before the last curtain.

The difference between the bucket back in Louisville and the muskets here and now was that there was no four-hour wait. Not even four minutes. "Yankee Doodle" came to an end—Professor Hatch was screaming "And with the girls be handy! And with the girls be handy!"—and without anyone having to pull a trigger (they must have been detonated by remote control) the muskets discharged, and the critics went into a state of panic. The muskets had sprayed them with pellets of colored chalk, which, exploding on impact, had turned them into instant living bunting. This was how Indians of India celebrated the holiday of Diwali, as Professor Hatch was trying to explain, but K.C. seemed to be the only one there paying any attention to her text.

One of the women in the critics' enclosure, her clothes and hair red from the chalk, tried to tunnel under the ring of spiraling razor-wire. The wire could not get a purchase on the motorcycle jacket she was wearing, but it did snag into her hair and her blue jeans, despite which she kept crawling forward with her face pressed against the ground until she'd managed to break free of the wire. Then she headed in the direction of the Winnebago and, presumably, the exit. No one set out in pursuit. The Iroquois stood beside the wheelchairs they'd been pushing, and the uniformed guards posted along the upper tier of seats remained where they were, as did the critics, who didn't have that much choice in the matter, after all. Everyone watched as the escaping critic rounded the Winnebago and ran out of sight. Only K.C., from his privileged point of view, saw what happened next, as Duster tackled her to the ground, and Jethro ran her through with a bayonet and then in true Native American style took off her scalp.

"If everyone would kindly return to his or her seat," said Professor Hatch in a schoolmarmish tone of voice, "the performance will continue."

The critics had not actually *left* their seats (with the one significant exception, whose body was being dragged to the parking lot by Duster), but they'd heard their colleague's screams of protest and of pain and taken them to heart. K.C. wondered if it had begun to dawn on them that they'd been cast as extras in a homemade horror movie. (He assumed that someone was putting all this on videotape.) For that matter, when had *he* copped to the fact? Not till he'd actually seen Jethro scalping the lady behind the Winnebago, really. And yet there was that other scalpee laid out beside Slaughter Rock, which it now seemed safe to assume was not the work of set decorators but a genuine dead body. Whose? Probably someone connected with Utopia, Incorporated—one of the counselors so-called. There was enough free-floating ill will at any rehab to provide the psychic energy necessary for systematic mayhem. Rehabs aren't that much different from prisons, except for the way in a rehab they try and make you say how much you love Big Brother.

"We'll be raising the flag shortly," Alison confided to K.C. over the earphones, "but before we do, I wanted you to know how pleased I am that you've been able to be part of the Festival, K.C. In just a short time you've become very special to me. You have the gift of basic trust, as I do. I've always known that Someone or Something is looking after me. Some call it a Higher Power. Others believe in angels. Darlene has been both to me, especially since the diagnosis. *She* was always the one, before that, who had such crushing depressions. She was the one that had to be rushed to the emergency ward to have her stomach pumped. And my role was the pillar of strength. I'd tell her, 'Darlene, your day will come. Your work *will* be recognized. You mustn't give up now, on the brink of success. Don't turn your anger inwards: *use* it!' Oh dear, our time is so limited, and there's so much to express, to

409

explain, to celebrate! But Jethro and Duster are giving me signals. It's that time."

"The Star-Spangled Banner" kicked in at once, but at a very low volume, as though you were a teenager again listening to forbidden music in your bedroom late at night. Jethro and Duster emerged from behind the Winnebago with a flag the size of a bedsheet. As Jethro and K.C. had mapped it out, the flag had been stiffened at both ends by bamboo rods so that it wouldn't flap around as it was hoisted up the flagpole by the pulley system knotted into K.C.'s braided ponytail. At the base of the pole, they sprayed the flag with gasoline syphoned from the Winnebago's tank, and then, once it had been raised to where the whole length of the flag was lofted up and on display, Jethro flicked his Bic and Duster started hauling on the cord of the pulley.

K.C. knew he was in a desperate situation, but he had had time to think about how best to employ his limited resources. With his hands securely cuffed behind his back (and he had scraped his wrists down to the basic hamburger putting that "securely" to the test), there was no way he would be able to get to the knife inside his belt buckle for some quick assistance. Which ruled out his being able to cut through the pulley's cord or the hank of hair that held it in place. An alternative remained—sit-ups.

K.C. had always wanted washboard abs, and he never finished up any workout without fifty sit-ups on a steep incline. Not full inversion sit-ups, but the principle was the same. He had time for one good try. He turned his head sideways and tightened his gut muscles so his body bent pretzel-wise.

God helped: the double cord of the pulley was hanging down across the front of his ear. With a further twist of his head, he was able to clamp his teeth on both cords, at which point he slowly eased back from his sit-up so that he was hanging back in his original Tarot-inspired position. Directly underneath him, Duster was tugging at the cord of the pulley, each tug a little more vigorous and threatening to the integrity of K.C.'s molars. The burning flag had reached its full First Amendment glory, and K.C. could feel the heat and smell the reek of gasoline.

Duster, who was obviously the kind of person with a low threshold of frustration, gave one final furious jerk to the cord, cracking one of K.C.'s molars but at the same time bringing the burning flag down on himself in a billowing bright extravaganza that could not have been more dramatically satisfying if it had been planned, though K.C.

410

doubted that any of the assembled critics were making such reckonings at this point, for they were being squirted with some flammable fluid by the uniformed guards, who had gathered round the critics at full battalion strength.

"K.C., that was *sensational*! We haven't that much time left to talk, but if you *do* survive, Darlene and I have made tapes that explain everything. The rejections we've encountered as artists over the years. The critical sneers. The assessments of peer panels who never came to a single performance. Basically, it's so simple. I don't understand why no one has thought to do it before. If one is ready to take a big enough risk, and to make real sacrifices, finally, the Establishment can't stop an artist from achieving immortality. Jethro understood that from the first, and so did Darlene in her way. Well, I'm getting signals again. It's closing time."

The charges buried beneath the benches of the critics' enclosure were detonated first, and the critics, guards, the wheelchair square-dancing team, and all superfluous Mohawks were united in a single, kerosene-laced sphere of flame that dissolved all differences between actors and audience, text and context.

The Winnebago went next in a blast that would not have looked meager even in a *Die Hard* sequel.

So was K.C. alone left to tell the tale? In which case what was he looking at in terms of fees from the tabloids, appearances on talk shows, book royalties, and, why not, a TV docudrama? Maybe he might even get to play himself! But no, he had to be realistic. He was too short for a leading role. His best hope was to share credit on the script. Even so, the whole basket of unhatched eggs had to amount to more than a million.

Perhaps it was unseemly to be focused on his performing career at such a moment, with the other victims of the tragedy dismembered by the explosion and still in flames all about the amphitheater, but K.C. had never had strong feelings about other people than himself. In that, according to many of the authorities on the subject, he was not unlike other major artists past and present from Andy Warhol to William Burroughs.

His basket of eggs was not yet out of jeopardy, however, not while Jethro was still alive and, potentially, kicking. The electric motor that powered the winch that had lifted K.C. to the top of the flagpole began to whir, and K.C. found himself descending, a little too quickly for comfort, toward ground level. But a concussion was not what Jethro had in mind, for he braked K.C.'s descent some three feet above the flagstones. K.C. found himself staring into Jethro's beaded loincloth and thinking he was about to be the victim of the most elaborate rape in human history. But that wasn't what Jethro had in mind either, for he started the motor again and raised K.C. up another three feet so that they were eye to eye.

When someone is crazy, or very spaced, the best way to deal with him, according to all the police shows that K.C. had seen on TV, is to pretend he is rational. So that's what he tried to do. "So, what are your plans now, Jethro? I suppose you'll escape through the woods, just like the guys who survived the original battle here."

"I hadn't made any plans actually."

"Oh, come on. You expect me to believe this was all improvisation?"

"I mean, no plans for afterwards. I was supposed to be in the Winnebago with Alison and the Professor. There weren't going to be any survivors. It was going to be like Jim Jones down in South America."

"Well, maybe Fate's decided we're supposed to be survivors. It wouldn't be the first time."

"Fate, huh," said Jethro.

There is something about having an upside-down conversation that is very disconcerting. The other person's eyes are where the mouth should be and they blink in the wrong direction, while the motions that the face makes as it speaks—the lips exposing and concealing the teeth, the glimpses of tongue, the lifting and lowering of the jaw— begin to have the hyper-fleshy look of a Giger alien. Add a Mohawk and war paint and features as naturally Giger-like as Jethro's and the total effect can induce a first-rate sense of alienation or, as they say in the theater, *Entfremdungseffekt*.

"You shouldn't push your luck, Jethro. Even if there aren't any next-door neighbors that close by, there's bound to be some kind of official reaction to those explosions. I wouldn't linger backstage."

"So I should go hide in the woods? Live on berries and mushrooms?"

"If they think you died in the Winnebago, they won't start a manhunt."

"And why would they think that?"

"Cause I could say I saw you go in there right before it blew up."

"And why would you say that?" Upside-down and with the war paint it was hard to know if the expression on Jethro's face was a sneer or a frown of indecision.

"Cause it makes a better story. When it's made for TV. At the end of a story like this you want all the bad guys dead."

412

"So I'm one of the bad guys, am I?"

The look on Jethro's inverted face was definitely a sneer, and K.C. began to see light at the end of the tunnel.

"You've always been one of the bad guys," K.C. assured him. "One of the worst."

Jethro nodded. "I could take one of the buses the critics came in."

"No," said K.C. "If you do that, they'll know there's someone to look for. What you've got to do is wash that stuff off your face and change into some regular clothes and toss what you're wearing now into the Winnebago while it's still blazing. Then disappear."

"And leave you to be a witness?"

"Right. But hoist me back up to the top, so I'm hanging up there when the cops get here. It shouldn't be much of a wait."

"I *could* just use your head for a football."

"You could, but if you do that, know what the result will be? When they make the movie about all this, it'll be Susan Sarandon and Geena Davis who are the stars. Whereas, if it's based on *my* version of events, it'll be a movie featuring Death Row Jethro—the first genuine mass murderer ever to be funded by the N.E.A. Is that reason enough?"

Jethro nodded. The basket of eggs was saved.

Later, hanging from the top of the flagpole, enjoying the scents of the night breeze, K.C. continued casting the movie in his imagination.

Nominated by Melissa Malouf

SAD SONG

by LAURA KASISCHKE

from **THE KENYON REVIEW**

There are women
carrying torches
coming toward us. Their

eyes are accidents. The kind
that happen on the highway
in the middle of the night. The kind

we glimpse as we drive by. A flare
in snow, a metal cage
with ruined tigers in it. We
look away, and then we're home. There

are hundreds of women marching forward, carrying
torches like a burning orchard. They're
coming for us, and everything's on fire. Even

the torpedo boats. Even the starfish creeping along
the ocean floor in families, in

the utterly deaf and dumb. Here

they come: You
open your mouth and I
see the word *bye*
float out, like
a jeweled wasp with

a golden Y around her neck. Those
wasps have made
an elaborate nest in the attic, in

my trunk of party dresses: All
that buzzing about you, all
that frantic dancing

like a barbed breeze in my hair. I

lift the lid of that trunk
for the first time in years. Stale

carnations and yellow lace. All
the invitations I didn't take
turned to female dust. *I'll*

always love you, I say, and you
wince a bit like Zeus
who didn't know he had

an armored woman in his head. Those

women wait
with their torches on the porch, but when
I step outside to take
my own flaming place, they

turn suddenly to stone, like
all the marble madonnas, trapped
and standing
on Saturday

at the empty art museum. Their

long medieval shadows drape the floor like
loose blue cloaks: Look

carefully under the veil
of one of those—the one
who has been waiting at his tomb
for seven hundred years. If
you hold your breath you'll see she's
grieving

with a sly, white smile. Perhaps

that one's only posing
as a stone. Maybe
she's just as alive

as the garden hose, coiled
and breathing in the dank

dark of the garden shed. Perhaps

she's held her stone breath
a long, long time. The way
some moths, fearing nets, will

fold their wings in half
and seem to the untrained eye to be

just a few more brown and withered leaves

clinging to the tree. But

they're not: if

you sing a sad song loud enough, the boys
on those torpedo boats
can hear you under the sea.

Nominated by Pinckney Benedict, James Harms, Tony Hoagland

THE SEVEN SISTERS

essay by AURELIE SHEEHAN

from THE AMERICAN VOICE

> The Pleiades is a relatively young cluster of stars enshrouded in gas and dust. To the unaided eye, the Pleiades consists of six faint stars. Binoculars reveal many more, and a telescope shows that there are hundreds of stars in the cluster. Of these, nine are named: the seven sisters and their two parents. These were called the "sailing stars," for early Greek seamen would set sail only when they were visible; at other times storms were too likely.
> —*Audubon Society Field Guide to the Night Sky*

IF YOU LOOK SLIGHTLY AWAY, the Seven Sisters seem brighter—they start disappearing if you stare. The murmur of women in my life is like that, veiled but returning like tricky stars. It started with a pale girl who furtively picked her nose behind her Reading For Understanding flashcard and lately included my vet and a married woman in love with a ski racer. When I point toward these lights, what am I pointing toward?

Alcyone was twelve years old and her parents were old and Italian. It was a strange house because the grandmother lived there, and she wore black and had gray hair swirled in a bun and was always lurking and murmuring with a thick accent. She knit my doll Maggie a poncho with white, red and black stripes. This was nothing my mother would do—Mom wasn't into church, sewing, baking or mink coats. In fact, my mom was a Feminist. Once I wore her pendant to school, a raised fist in the middle of the circle and cross, which depicts the female (as opposed, and I mean fucking opposed, to the circle and arrow—arrow headed off to the nearest bar). I had my own poncho too, it was Afghan, or made out of llama fur. Alcyone and I got our hands on a 50-cent booklet on witchcraft and, making use of my earth-tone poncho, we caused a stir at reading hour—all the little boys and girls thought we were about to cast spells. Plucking a lock of Lucy's long uncombed hair. Stealing Albert's pencil. The principal called our parents and we had to give up the little book. But it was all part of a grander plan, for we lived wholly in our imaginations. Our giant, bespectacled math teacher, Mr. O'Mara, would appear, looming over us in the library where we hunched behind the last bookshelf, cross-legged, giggling and gulping and picking our noses over some story about princesses and knights, the props for which were the felt shapes we cut out for our semi-legitimate art project. We were freaks. She was a year older than me and well-versed in *The Hobbit* and anything medieval. Her starter-sperm must have been weakened by a few too many gin-and-tonics, or the egg may have cracked and crusted over, because she was frail and underdeveloped. Her hair was thinner than my antique doll Elizabeth's; it was reddish and curly around her shoulders and never grew. You could see her scalp. Her head was hot, knobby, vulnerable as an infant's. She wore tight-fitting pilled "bodysuits"— those shirts that snap at the crotch. Her body was crustacean, a turtle shell in the shape of a girl. Her skin was pale and freckled, her long fingers were thin, her teeth were scattered here and there like stumps in a red bog. She had a funny grin, but if she was pissed or proud, she would hold her mouth shut as if holding a tiny live bird right behind her lips, and her eyes would get lidded and obscure. She tiptoed around in highwaters and ballerina slippers. She was my best friend. Her imagination kicked ass.

Besides playing with your basic dolls and running around the yard as Lancelot and Merlin, we had the lives, loves and adventures of our tinfoil queens. I don't remember how it began, who invented them—she probably did. You take some tinfoil. Make a little ball, smaller than a marble, then place it in the middle of a bigger sheet. Wrap it around, twist a neck, rip the top edge into two long arms, squeeze a waist, shape the bottom gently into a full, swirly skirt, rub this in circles on a tabletop until the queen is flat-bottomed and will stand on her own. Then you make some hair out of black thread and glue it on (a topknot with loose strands underneath) and create clothes with scraps of fabric from Alcyone's grandmother—capes, robes, banquet outfits tied with ribbons and lace. Our queens would meet and do the things queens do, talk about their lives (invariably they were orphans or besieged by ominous suitors), and once they went on a boat ride down the river. It was gloriously sunny and the boat was a green waxed cardboard fruit container. When it overturned, the queens lost their entire traveling wardrobes. We'd make new queens if, for instance, a neck became weak and wobbly, or an arm tore off.

I spent the night at Alcyone's and she sang "I Could Have Danced All Night" and she sang "I'm Going to Wash That Man Right Out of My Hair." She had a beautiful voice (I had no faith in my own). We lay in her attic bedroom on twin beds and in the dark she sang, and I was impressed she could remember all the words, for one thing. She had this whole other world—musicals, Italian grandmothers, the frailty that made her seem one step away from the grave. She sang her own campy " 'Enry 'Iggins." There was always this recognition that I was healthy and robust and normal in a way she wasn't. She would look at me furtively. She would gallop away as Lancelot. One game we played brought this all to bear, it was an Evil Queen/Poor Girl scenario. I think we played it more than once, but I remember when she was the Evil Queen and I came up the stairs as the Poor Girl and threw myself at her mercy. She was wearing a bedspread-cape and a crown. Her face had that pissed/proud expression, only there was something new behind it, an imperial *fuck you*. She would forgive me, take me in, if I did something for her. It required undressing and laying beside her under the blanket of her cape. The wool was thick, and we didn't look directly at each other, but I held her in my arms, and I saw her nipples, little pink hats raised above the white flat skin of her chest, and she was looking at my breasts, slight swells but swells nonetheless, and further down. "You have hair," she said. I had left her, left the knights and the tinfoil queens and even the Evil Queen. I had abandoned her to her body and to her fate.

Merope had been the victim of a Satan worshiping cult, sadly enough. She was stolen away from her parents and returned only after unspeakably evil acts had been performed on her, rituals she could now just barely recollect. It was Merope who let me know there was a satanic underground network across the country. We were in her car on our way back from Seattle to Santa Fe. It was sunny and sweet and summery out, and I was behind the wheel. She told me about the cult, and then she said she had to stop speaking and could I please respect that and perhaps just keep driving, meanwhile she put on a tape, The Violent Femmes. The window magnified the sun, the heat, and Merope locked the door and put her head down on my leg and her long, grasshopper arm was bent and her guitar-playing hand rested on the seat.

Merope was in a band, or anyway she had been, it was called Chaos, I think, or Alien Fuckface. The bass guitarist and the drummer had moved to Seattle, and so we had gone there for a reunion. Merope was the lead singer and guitarist and I had known her for two weeks. I was housesitting an adobe on San Miguel Canyon Drive in Santa Fe, and a friend brought her over one afternoon. Merope was wearing men's shorts and a loose striped t-shirt, Keds, and a black leather motorcycle jacket. Her legs were scrawny and delicately blondly furred. Her hair was short, brown and blond both, it stuck up here and there, and she had a muted, hurt, beautiful little boy's face and her eyes were the color of water. But it was her arms I noticed when she took off her jacket. They were long and jangly, tendons like guitar strings, feminine but not soft. We were in the kitchen and she was upset. She said that as a child she had been abused and that something around it was "coming up for her" just then. She stood in the doorway between the kitchen and the living room and I was cutting up vegetables for dinner, my birthday dinner, and I had spent most of my life being efficient and on top of things and cutting up peppers, mushrooms, tomatoes and onions into unified little piles of one cup each. Cool, I thought: Deep Sadness. That week I started talking to her on the phone, or really, listening. She was breaking up with her girlfriend—kind of. They were fighting. Actually punching each other is what I heard later from our mutual friend who was trying to steer me clear of Merope. Merope was in AA and Sex Addicts-A (SA?). And NA and Incest-A. Merope said she had a crush on me but that it was sort of against her religion to act on it, not because she was with the other girl, but because flirting and affairs and sexual attraction and all that was a danger zone for her, something that had to do with back in the old days when she would get bombed and pick up people at parties and bring them home and get laid and then start again the next night with someone else. I nodded, impressed by her current self-control. I had a phone-sex relationship going with this guy who, in person, pawed me unrelentingly, said naughty things, always had a hard-on and a girlfriend waiting for him at some coffee shop. He liked to talk about raping me. There was another guy who was bisexual and darned proud of it too, an actor who acted so furiously that spittle spit across the room when he embodied a part, and he had a wife or girlfriend and they had a child and he laid

420

claim to being in love with me, for what reason I don't fucking know, but anyhow. I wanted Merope. When we were in the car and she brushed her hand against my leg, I became rigid and giddy. It was hard to desire a woman because I didn't know how to picture it. I didn't have a good fantasy going, except for kissing and unzipping jeans—but then what? Wouldn't it be boring for everyone if I rubbed her breasts, I mean, it would be boring to rub my own breasts. I wanted to be shown.

But not the way she did show me. First of all, we hadn't kissed or touched in a dead-on romantic way all the way to Seattle, there was just this flirting going on. Then we got to the rainy-day hovel on top of a hill where the six-foot hulking drummer with a bandana around her forehead and a power-bra and workboots and a waitress-on-the-night-shift or even tougher (definite night-shift but maybe in the mines) demeanor, lived with the bass guitarist—long red hair, puffed as a gingerbread cookie, Doc Martens strapped tight around bare white legs, thrift store dress, job at the packing plant. Almost immediately we went for a drive with the redhead cookie and that's when Merope put her hand on my leg proprietorially. I felt warm and cuddly inside, and also fucking used. *Use me, fuck me, make me write bad checks*—that's what my friend Leo used to say. I became an insta-lesbian. I became Merope's. I was hers all week. I lost my lipstick. No one else around there used lipstick. It was Chanel. I was a tropical bird on display. Merope and I slept on a mattress in the living room, and the drummer and bassist went into their bedroom and closed the door. "Well, Merope," I said, as we lay in the pale stripes of the streetlight. I was wearing a nightgown. She wore a t-shirt and boxers. Her eyes twinkled, her face like a pear or a beautiful triangle or a flower of planes and shadows, and her lips were closed and darkly fragile and shadowed, a half-pillow away from my mouth. Our knees were so close. She said, "Kiss me like we are falling asleep." So I leaned over and put my mouth to hers and our tongues touched and mingled, and I sat up a little more and I felt driven, motivated. And then she pulled her face away and chastised me. She said, "That's kissing to stay awake."

I fell asleep with this conundrum in my head, and I dreamed that my grandmother died. The next day I was nauseous and filled with anxiety. In the grocery store, the yahoos stared at Merope and I wanted to protect her and I suddenly became political. *You're staring at her, motherfucker? Who do you think you are, you bastion of bullshit, you fucking stupid Dorito-stuffed fleck of smallminded America?* In the basement studio, listening to the punk music, I heard, most of all, the lilt of her voice, the questions and answers there, the magical childhood walk she took with each note. She went high and low, and there she was, arm like a grasshopper. In the car on the way home, while she slept, Merope's hand lay on the seat, half-curled, half-open. I placed mine around it tentatively, afraid that to touch her was to hurt her.

It was Thanksgiving weekend, and I took the bus from New York City to Vermont to visit Celaeno and her husband and her child. I knew she was having an affair with the neighbor, but I didn't know he'd join us at the dinner table, and I didn't know Celaeno's brother would leave me a note on my bed the first night I was there that said, *Come on in and get it*. Before the wedding two years earlier, the husband had told me that he wanted to make Celaeno happy: his goal was to protect and support her. When Celaeno and I were fourteen and thirteen, I had bought a pair of sapphire earrings and, with a needle and a cork and some ice, pierced a second hole in my right ear. She was supposed to pierce hers too and wear one of the studs but she never did, so when she got married I gave her the second blue earring, something old, something blue, and in a sense something borrowed and something new, too. It was sixteen years after I had pierced the third hole, and Celaeno and I sat on the bed after her husband had gone to sleep, after we had peered at her baby boy sleeping in the crib, and after I had tucked away the invitation from her brother. We sat in our nightclothes, leaning on the wall, facing each other. Her eyes were blazing and she said, "I've never felt this way before. What should I do?"

I had liked Celaeno from the day she showed up in my backyard: tall, high-rise ponytail, braces. She gave me a critical assessment and a knock-down smile. I had just moved to town. I wore a back brace and had gone to a Montessori school where we had gardens and caterpillars, learned Latin, Greek, algebra and how to wipe down a table. Celaeno and I both had dapple-gray horses and we began riding together, racing our ponies full-tilt down dirt roads, laughing as the animals nipped at each other and sparks flew off their horseshoes. When eighth grade started, I knew nothing of how to get by in a clique. The girls surrounded me in the hall and asked me if I thought I was pretty. "Yes," I said (wrong answer). I wore a floppy red reversible hat and yellow clogs—far from the prevailing code of brown or blue corduroys and pastel sweaters and turtlenecks. Celaeno lost friends because of our alliance, and we spent afternoons crying over hot dogs with cheddar cheese and ketchup and bowls of fudge ripple ice cream about how hateful everyone was, including our parents. We sat on her bed, the same one her father chased her under with a belt. We looked out the window, the same one she let her little cat Winna out of to play on the roof before her parents made her get rid of it. We began to find ourselves extremely amusing. When she got pleurisy, we said *I had a pleurisy attack last night* in a funny voice, and then shrieked. We acted out the groaning parts of Donna Summer's "Love to Love You Baby" as if we had been punched in the stomach; I'd lurch around like a tin-man in my brace, and we'd stare bug-eyed at each other until we burst out laughing. She loved her Pekinese, Tammy, and we constructed a language stemming from the way she talked to that dog. It became so-phisticated enough so that we could have entire conversations and anyone listening would have no idea what we were talking about. Our word for love was *sib,* as in *sib su,* I love you. We thought this language would be useful if we were ever picked up by the police, which we were once for trespassing (they found us hiding behind the shower curtain in an abandoned mansion, we said we had followed a lost kitten through a broken window, the cops gave us sodas down at the station). One day we skipped study hall. It was a wet spring afternoon and we cut across the wide, mushy fields of Nimrod Farm (later turned into a housing complex). The plums and Seven-Up we bought at the town center tasted great and the whole day was sublime, one of our favorite new words. The next day, the assistant principal took us out of class separately for questioning, and we tricked him with the same, un-rehearsed story.

I spent many nights at Celaeno's house, in her bed, even before we came to use the laxity of her parents to suit ourselves—smoking pot, drinking, staying out late. Her bedroom changed three times because her parents initiated that many moves in five years, for no particular reason, before her father snorted away everything they owned and they sold the his-and-her Porsches, and she stopped getting stuffed animals with $100 bills in their ears and Gucci purses for Christmas. We lay together in the dark and talked. The outlines of everything in the room got more defined, we understood each other and it was safe there and fun, and eventually the silences would get long between sentences, and then we'd be asleep and separate again. We never touched. I remember her eyes staring at me before we turned off the light—visionary, vulnerable. The poetry Celaeno wrote was scary and sharp and she stopped writing at some point, just stopped. But in those days we were writing poems and showing them to each other, reading each

423

other's journals and cutting each other's hair. The guys we had crushes on were the grist for conversation, the purported subject. Is there a line that makes sex more intimate than secrets? The boys pulling on Marlboros, slouching around the periphery in jeans made velvety by gasoline spills, were the ones we kissed; for each other, we had words, laughter, sadness. I remember her folding laundry the morning I came in crying from a kind of fucked-up sex scam that had gone on the night before. I remember the crestfallen, tender look she had as she put down a t-shirt.

Sitting on the bed with Celaeno late that November night, it was obvious her marriage was already over, that there was no answer I could give her. Our connection had lasted all those years. It was thin as thread. As she spoke, her robe had fallen slightly off her shoulder, and I saw and tried to keep my eyes off her breast, nipple hardened. With everything else going on, with the electric sex in the air, with all the brothers and neighbors and husbands and everyone else, I could have reached out and touched her breast. I knew its shape well, as if I had already cupped it in my hand. This was the girl who had hid under the bed to get away from a belt, who had whooped with laughter at her own illness. She'd sit between her neighbor and her husband at the cruel Thanksgiving dinner table, she'd have the neighbor's child but for a long while he'd refuse to marry her, the teacher would call from daycare about her first child's behavior, she'd cart her dog and two cats off to the animal shelter herself because she could no longer care for them. The gasoline-stained boys had become men. Celaeno and I succeeded in loving each other for a time, but the specter of what worried her years before had solidified and I had done, could do, nothing to stop it from happening. Except not reach for her breast. Except write once in awhile, like I write my demented grandmother.

Maia, in my language, means *taken away*. She bicycled up my driveway on a summer evening in cut-off denim overalls and sat cross-legged on the kitchen floor of my trailer in Wyoming while I cut up onions, mushrooms and garlic for spaghetti. We leapt into our life stories. She told me about playing the guitar for spare francs on rues and boulevards and stealing a whole chicken from an open market even though her Parisian flat had no oven. She told me about the long-ago death of her best friend in Cambridge, a girl from France. At dinner, Maia laughed loudly. She had this lust for life that was hard to get around, impossible not to respond to. She'd been a bicycle messenger in New York City and a madcap drinker and now she was sober and lived in Oakland, and her father was a violin maker and a drunk, and her mother was an actress and a dry drunk. She'd gotten into a prestigious writing program by lying. Before she ate, Maia took digestive pills—but she hardly seemed sick, and I was sweaty in the armpits and giggly with our complicity, our instant camaraderie. That summer we bicycled past the barking dogs and I told her of the crush I had on a man who was so shy you had to lean in to hear him talk, and she told me about Sarah, and at the bar she drank O'Doulls and I drank Budweiser and we enjoyed each other and the peach pie and the sagebrush and the sky and we took it for granted and then I left for France. She wrote me the funniest letter in history, which I read on the Mediterranean shore, hooting between throngs of gold-decked, bare-breasted beauty slaves, and a few months later she returned to Wyoming, this time as a writer-in-residence at the colony where I worked. When I met her at the airport, she was wearing green Levis and a workshirt and sunglasses and cowboy boots, and she looked jaunty and tough and sexy, but she was walking with a cane, and her words came out resigned and tremulous. In the car, she leaned her head against the window and closed her eyes.

For the next few weeks, I'd stop by her studio after work and we'd boil water for tea and sit on either side of her desk, feet up, and talk about writing and love and travel. We used the tea bags twice, three times, and sometimes while she was talking, right before or after we put the light on against the furtive twilight, her eyelids trembled, her head jerked slightly to the side, she'd smile with resistance and endurance—and then the current passed through her body and she'd resume what she was saying. Finally I needed to ask, needed to find out, and she told me all about lupus and how there were two kinds and one was degenerative and ultimately fatal and I asked which she had and she said, "Well, that kind."

It wasn't until I discovered she was having an affair with someone else that my feelings shot out of the realm of the platonic. "But didn't you feel it last summer?" she asked. "And then you fell for that boy." We squinted at each other in the spring sunlight, sitting on the porch, this sexual attraction between us. A preplanned experiment in bed with a female friend in college had been uninspired—I should have known that it's not the meat or even necessarily the motion but emotion that takes hold of a person and explodes an ordinary day. Maia and I were on a plateau where we saw what decisions we might have made, what we might even have in the future—but right then she went back to her affair and I went back to my boyfriend, and together we drank all the tea in China.

We went through another box or two of Irish Breakfast and Cinnamon Stick in the cowboy-town hotel where she stayed for two weeks after her residency ended. The Mansion House hadn't been renovated since some ancient time when guests had hat boxes and polka-dotted rain caps. Maia's room had twin beds and pink vinyl headboards and above them these clever lamps masquerading as paintings, bulbs illuminating Degas-ripoff ballerinas. In the curve of a turret were two armless, brocade chairs and a table, and we'd sit there or lay one each on the beds, golden evening light slanting in, and we'd flirt, the most energizing session of which was when she told me how fluid the boundaries were between female bodies while making love, how fused they could become in feeling. "Really?" I asked, imagination making my cheeks red. I blew her a kiss behind my boyfriend's back, and I brushed and braided her hair. Her body was off-limits because of our other attachments, but I don't think it was just that. She gave me a belt buckle and I gave her a little perfume bottle from France. These hard, small things were neat and easy to understand; they don't come apart in your hands.

Maia applied for disability. She took a hundred and one tests and some of them over and over again because the labyrinthine application process has rules and tricks that could drive the healthiest, most organized and patient among us to drink and disorder. No one could diagnose her. She spent full days waiting in clinics, hospitals and social security offices. She got prescriptions for the wrong drugs, spun around into new symptoms, was berated in hospital corridors for "faking" seizures, tied to beds, given unnecessary, repetitive and invasive procedures, treated like a total fucking loser, required to explain to a revolving contingent of neophyte interns her decade-long history with this, reduced time and again to tears, and generally forgotten by the public health system of this country, not to mention her own family and friends. The night of her spinal tap, I lay in my bed in a stupid little town. She was suffering; I was a thousand miles away. The color had drained from the hills.

Maia is tired of, among other things, making friends feel better about their impotence and their alarm. Her girlfriend is her helpmate, drags her around on a bathroom rug when she cannot feel her legs, talks her through a night when the pain of blood vessels exploding

426

leaves her sightless. Maia's poetry is filled with connections only the most delicate brain neurons can make. She says, "I'd like to go back to France someday." But right now her body is bloated up from Prednisone, her skin has a yellow cast, and she's taken to staying indoors. She says, "I've bought the darkest pair of sunglasses I can find."

Love is unrelenting, like the return of spring to the cold hills. Sprouts, buds, color sweeping the land, lambs and calves and sparrows and a gurgle to the creeks and gullies. Consummation of desire has a different beauty than winter, the chill of remove and dormancy. But do you think better in the cold? In any case, Taygete was pure and white, thin and sharp as a winter night, and loving her was like whittling myself down to a pencil point.

I was waist-deep into a relationship with a man, and it occurred to me that perhaps I could have sex with a *woman* and still be technically faithful. Taygete was marked as a genius by our graduate school professor, a charm box of flirtation, exuberance and creative charge. Since she was a lesbian, his respect for her work couldn't be anything but honest. She was bone thin and wore plain clothes: wool skirts, spinster shoes, drab sweaters, no jewelry, no makeup. Her face was hard to explain—it was that of a chameleon, a serpent, a sprite. She was always frowning, head bowed, smoking a cigarette. She was having deep thoughts, so far as I could tell. I was new to New York City and felt more like a bus passenger than an intellectual. When I asked her to sign a collection of experimental fiction that included her story (a linguistic topiary made with the characters from a board game, a literary spread like the hotel and garden in *Last Year at Marienbad*), she said no. I read her careful, unprecedented stories five times to overcome my bafflement. I fumbled in conversation, stammered compliments. One day I got a message from her on my machine speaking about a story of mine, about liking it. We began having dinner and coffee dates, and at times I was comfortable, but just as often I felt like myself at a cumbersome twelve, pirouetting across a room of younger, smaller, lithe ballerinas. I also felt lucky, like I was learning something. She sat across from me in a cafe one winter afternoon, an elbow on the marble tabletop, cigarette in hand, head cocked, and spoke of Henry James. She had just finished *The Beast in the Jungle*. The story hid its answer from the reader in plain view, she said, just as the beast was always in plain view, too plain for Marcher to see. The tragedy of it as described by Taygete struck deep in the cool din of the restaurant, seemed inevitable, rhapsodic and beautiful. Her understanding was personal, private, and when I bought my copy of the book, I plunged past the cheapness of the paper and the dumb cover and read the story meticulously, to see what she had seen.

Taygete's childhood had a bit of madness in it. This was part of her darkness, her ongoing grief. When she wrote, she smoked, and when she was done she hated what she had written, again and again. One night when I called, she had just seen a TV documentary in which a man in a car in a field was burned almost entirely and put in the hospital where his burns were scraped down to the bloody core every day—as soon as scabs formed they were peeled away. The fire had blinded him, and he spoke to the camera from his hospital bed. His story affected Taygete more than she could explain. I remained at a resolute distance and comforted her pathetically, unusefully. I wanted to stand by *her* hospital bed and feed her poppyseed cake and chocolate cake and lemon cake, forkful upon forkful, and open the blinds and let sun in and bring tulips and make her happy.

She moved to California and started dating her ex-girlfriend. She quit smoking and began running and when she came back to visit, we met for coffee one afternoon at Dante Cafe in the Village, and she told me she had stopped writing because smoking and writing were inextricably linked for her, and that she was, for now, choosing life. She seemed healthy. She was tan, braless, smiling. Her girlfriend was a writer, just then having much success. I knew nothing of their relationship really, but it was disturbing to think of Taygete smilingly looking on at her girlfriend's achievements when surely Taygete was the genius among us, she was the brilliant one. I understood her reason for discontinuing her work, and I hoped also that someday she would go back to it, and she did. We met up a year or two later in San Francisco. She sported a page-boy-revisited haircut, wore platform shoes and silver-sheen bellbottoms and a gray slinky top. She worked at an *au courant* magazine and was making herself generally indispensable there. We had a conversation about the professor who had originally turned my attention her way. She said, "You can't expect from people what they aren't able to give, you just have to love them for who they are." "Yes, of course," I stammered. She was five feet away in the sunny park, but she could have been on another planet. Her apartment with the same girlfriend had burned a month before. It was her lunch hour. She wouldn't write letters (snail mail). What did we have left, what was there to expect from her? She had never known my love, although maybe she guessed it. Adoration only goes so far, it's not warm enough.

My star women all need their own biographies, their own laced-up volumes, and it is just the gazer's perspective that brings them together in this hazy mash, bright points light years from one another and set in motion each with her own fitful breath. About men and women, a friend posed it like this: who's in the circle? Whose secrets do I reveal, and who do I leave out of my life? With Electra my allegiance got murky. When we held hands we were balanced between friendship and passion—playing, and in our play was the disappointment of pale fire.

She touched her finger to the back of my neck and said she couldn't resist. I had just cut my hair, and for her touch alone it was worth hacking off the foot and a half of insecurity or sexuality, depending on how you look at it (all my boyfriends had insisted I keep it long). We lived for a few days with this delight in the air, *attraction and acknowledgement* she called it. She had thick, bluntly-cut blond hair, a tan, athletic body. She asked me to guess what animal she was. Lion? Yes. She was interested in a man at the time, too, whom we concluded was a heron. There was also her husband—I'd meet him later. During those first early fall nights, it was warm enough to sit around a picnic table with candles and citronella torches, drink cheap Scotch and tell stories, and she leaned her leg on mine and gazed at the man she'd sleep with that night. For a month she'd dream of us three, and I too would gather an attraction for this fellow, and then let it fall again from my fingers like feathers. Because I was 32 and still had not copped a major feel with a woman (not counting my drunken grope in college), and continued to be curious about what Maia meant by bodies without owners, orgasms with no borders, I considered having sex with Electra. When she was leaving town, we sat on a bench and locked hands and my leg lay on top of hers and we felt each other's skin and said nothing in particular. Her eyes and her mouth asked for more than they gave. They said *kiss me.* Her hand was small in mine, like a child's, and what would it be like to kiss her tiny mouth, to hold her tiny head? When I bent toward her, I felt like a bull in a china shop, an older sister.

We talked on the phone for hours and our friendship became a balm in the night. When she came back for a visit, I cooked her a pheasant I had dropped from the sky and we tucked the stray shot onto the side of the plate and drank wine and talked about sex, sex in general, and you know it is hard to talk about that without getting hot, and I don't know why we started talking about it, why it came up that particular night. We lingered on the couch, legs intertwined, time passing into the decision of where to sleep. In bed we lay together like two soft birds, limbs like folded wings, careful and lightly touching arms, a hip—nothing further. Her body was warm and (surprise) feminine. I wanted to snuggle up to, touch, this breathy thing beside me. I didn't want to fuck her, exactly, but if she had leaned up on one elbow and guided me to a next step, I probably would have gone there. My years-previous musing about whether I could have sex with a woman and still be "faithful" to a man wasn't relevant now. But that she was married and totally into this other guy did put a damper on things, made intimacy seem on the chancy side. This was part of why Electra and I fell asleep dry not wet in our white feathery nest.

Still, sleeping curled into each other was something of a revolution. I bounced around the house the next morning. We had done nothing really—held each other, kissed a bit—but even this was forbidden. We had placed our two female bodies close enough to be aware of affection, physicality, shape. It wasn't sexual so much as romantic. A month later, I saw her again when I had a layover in her city. I'd had a fantasy of taking Electra into a toilet stall and seducing her in the silence of noise, the stainless steel echo chamber of the airport rest room. I thought it was clever and interesting that we'd be able to go innocently into the ladies room together. When I got off the plane, she greeted me with the intoxication of love, but it wasn't for me: she was thinking about a man she had met recently whom she was even *more* in love with than the other guy and whose plane was also getting in that hour. She paged him, and as we ate a baguette and jam in the fake French airport cafe, we waited for him to show up. Her mind was on him, and my little plot fell asunder.

The Seven Sisters are radiant in their gauzy outfits, flirting and teasing in the night. Asterope, the earthy one, was my vet. I brought my cat to her when he had been sitting under my desk dull-eyed and lethargic, his long gray fur flattened against his back. She ran a few tests, and later in the afternoon we talked in the echoing white room, my fingers between the bars of the cat's second-tier cage. She explained it all to me: kidneys, medicine, cause, chance of survival. In New York, my vet had been perfunctory at best, and I had always left his office with little money and less confidence. Asterope had a no-frills approach, and she didn't make light of my feelings for the cat. He got well. A couple of months later, I stopped by the animal hospital and asked if I could come in once a week to see what was going on there and help out where I could. She said sure.

I went mostly on Saturday mornings. We got our bearings over hot chocolate and coffee and Coke and sometimes pastries. Asterope and her assistant joked easily, and I chimed in here and there. Pretty soon, we'd go back to the attached barn and take care of a horse with a barbed wire gash, a bull with a penis rubbed raw from sagebrush and too inflamed to retract. Asterope mixed molasses with a white powdered antibiotic then forced a syringe filled with the gooey substance into the horse's mouth. The animal opened his jaws like a pair of legs stuck in a tight skirt, licking and swallowing and nodding his head up and down. We chased the bull into the chute—a clanging banging cage that held him by the neck and squeezed his body upright—and Asterope washed his infection with sudsy water. She took another syringe and squirted the cleansing solution up into his sheath,wiping away yeasty chunks of stuff. You've got to realize, I'm from Connecticut. I'm from New York. I hail cabs, file my nails and can't change a tire. I stood in the cold room and watched Asterope in total, unprecedented awe. Another time she stuck a huge vibrating dildo into a bull's rectum and turned it on, stimulating him until his corkscrew-shaped penis emerged and shot sperm into a little cup (she needed a sperm count). I held up a drugged horse's head as she sewed together a ten-inch wound on his chest. She sat on a bucket and made two rows of small, even stitches—hooking and looping together the wet, membranous inner layer first, then the shaven skin. I lay my hand on the velvety shoulder of a tiny "Parvo puppy" while she injected water under his skin, vainly attempting to rehydrate the squeaking, doomed animal. A man dropped off a thin orange cat, giving Asterope instructions to kill it. Asterope gave the cat a shot and after it died, she took a pair of shears, cut open its belly and took out a lump of cancer cauliflowered to the size of a child's fist. Then she put the whole mess in a plastic garbage bag to be brought to the dump. She was in her worst mood one morning when for three days she'd been caring for a friend's horse and it wasn't getting any better. Sometimes she'd kind of flirt with me—but she flirted that way with everyone. She was my age and she'd grown up in this town. If she were a lesbian (a question I felt prurient even considering), it was probably necessary she keep that

431

under wraps in this town of 3,500 Republican ranchers where she was building a vet practice. She told me she loved and never would leave her hometown.

She had short hair, a stocky, capable body, and green eyes. Her face was etched with no easy answers and no absolutes and only herself to blame in life and death situations. She said when she got home at the end of the day, she didn't want to read about more pain and misery (on the page I was always fanning emotions into Frankenstein-life, and for me bisexuality was a diversion). By noon on Saturdays, she had spayed, x-rayed, inoculated, sewn-up or diagnosed a dozen cats, dogs, cows, bulls and horses, and I had wiped down the examination table once or twice, sprayed water under the chute to clean up the cow shit and blood and pus—but more often I just followed her around ready to be helpful but not really doing much except staying out of the way and falling in love.

I screwed up the courage to invite her skiing, and she led me on a marathon cross-country trek in which I tried to maintain a casual, *sportif* image while nearly dying of exhaustion. We went to a bar and she drank two beers for each one of mine, and she showed me how to hit the pool ball low, high or center for various effects, more or less beyond me. We agreed on mothers but disagreed on wolves. She always drove. I was constantly in the position of knowing nothing, learning, inquiring. It was right around the time when I was going to somehow tell her I had this crush on her when she began giving me the cold shoulder. She was putting together the chain-link sections for a new kennel and berating herself for shoddy work and I said, "It looks like you know what you're doing," and she said, "You're easy to fool." Walking around behind her, I began to feel more and more like a damp-palmed nerd following a cheerleader, and I could no longer tell if I really was staying out of the way, or if she'd prefer I weren't there at all. Politely, stiffly, I thanked her for my ten months of Saturdays at the animal hospital and bowed out of her world.

A few weeks later, I saw Asterope again. My boss's dog Jenny had ping-pong sized cancer balls on her foot and was having seizures and generally wasn't long for this world. She was a sweet-tempered, wise-eyed, sly, playful pit bull. Rachel wanted her to die at home, so she paid Asterope to drive out the twenty miles. She had painted Jenny's name in blue on a river stone. Her sister had cut wildflowers. Asterope arrived at the appointed hour with a little blue nylon bag. A neighbor was on the far end of the lawn, digging the hole for the grave with a skidloader. You could hear the groan and whir of the machine in the summer air. We all started walking toward that noise at the edge of the creek. Rachel and her sister walked on ahead, and so did I, and then there was Jenny, limping along behind us. I think Rachel was too grief-stricken to look back. Jenny was meandering on the grass, sniffing here and there, barely filled with the momentum to go forward. Out of impatience or empathy, Asterope picked up the dog and carried her the rest of the distance. In the shadow of the machine, near the rich brown hole and the little clutch of flowers and the pretty headstone, Asterope unzipped her bag and took out the cyanide, and the dog lay in front of her, panting, slack-skinned. Asterope gave the injection in the leg. She waited, we all waited, and then Jenny lay her head down. Under the roar of the skidloader, Asterope listened for Jenny's heart.

Nominated by Barbara Selfridge, Marie S. Williams

THE CUP

by KATRINA ROBERTS

from HOW LATE DESIRE LOOKS (Gibbs-Smith) and BOSTON BOOK REVIEW

Pleased to consider the cup. On a high-up shelf it stands, waiting to be fingered. Finders keepers. It's its simplicity, to envy. This configuration of complicity with air, and arms enact handles to tilt it. Roundelay for a sip and care beneath it, cantankerous baby. Upholds the light in holes, holding in liquid minutia as though a sister. Or twinned slippers hushing carpet stairs; four hands with glasses, crown glass with milk and a nipple knob in it.

*

Cucurbit for the spilly pieces. Pleased to consider the cup. Precisely why it matters most emphatically. Usufruct of quantities of unknown property. By which method of doing. If saucers—a dado below in difference. Or blue, for example. Teethed with crenels like castle turrets, yes.

*

What I want is to hand around it, insideways often. It hurts less to know its absence is natural. Pleased to consider. The cup lobs lookingly like honey.

*

So, abandon hope. Of course, it's most natural to want it intact; the crack from lip to base faces south and south. Smooth lazy susan whirls and twirls so. But, if it basks in perfection, call it cul-de-sac. Call it caved-in-cup, spinning—unpleased to consider the consequences of indabbing fingers, which lose their gloves—minus the digit-mask, like some anemone from the sea.

Enemy is the pace. In which manner of thinking. Space to curl into it. So pleased! Drink up. To consider most lovingly intonations of re-fusal, drains your energy. Gully dint is coming. Bees don't squeeze from honeycomb fumes. Out back the hat-hive-house stands, pleased to squat in sun—most roundly. Only to have itself to consider.

*

Enclosed spaces with borders not to be crossed—jimpson fences. So that's why the bell stings. Orchestrated petals reek havoc in the shade of night. Sweet and sour pork. Pleased to be sure to lock all doors, to hit the light. Casuistry says this is the way the gentlemen ride—hippety, then, but, oh—from toe to heel the campanile shifts, suffering contrecoup. An elegant silence darkened by sidelighting.

In the cup she puts five things. Today the tides, some crumbs, a lu-nar key. The wolf of Gubbio leaves five teeth, a bloody kiss by her neg-ligee. Put them in, and then. . . . So what of laughter bouncing within? Intaglioed complaints brim her blown-glass goblet. What he cups in his hands is neither, nor water.

*

Slip on his hands, the cup grows. Soft underneath, it will harden. *Cunning,* She says, *touch.* She says: *Massage and mass . . . sage . . . message . . . mess and age . . .* and the cup grows most pleasingly. *Don't touch,* she says—*much, to consider.*

—*for Robert Antoni*

Nominated by Michael Waters

435

BLOWING SHADES

fiction by STUART DYBEK

from ONTARIO REVIEW

LIKE A BOY WITH A KITE.

One he's labored over all afternoon, fashioned from sticks, news-paper, tape, and bakery string. A tail of rags.

Running bareheaded down an empty beach, trailing a tail of foot-prints through wet sand, shorebirds scattering before him.

How effortlessly the birds mount air, soaring off sideways on gusts of sea breeze, crying out from on high, while the kite stubbornly re-fuses to rise.

Wind whooshes over foaming water. Despite the drag of the kite he runs harder, faster. If he were a kite, he'd be up there, though it's no longer a day for launching a kite—even a store-bought kite from Japan made of silk the shade of women's underclothes, let alone a kite of sticks and newspaper. Maybe that's why the kite won't rise; it knows flying could tear it to shreds.

Only when the boy acknowledges defeat, slows to a half-hearted jog and turns at a cross angle to the wind, does the kite sail off sideways on a gust, twisting crazily, barely holding together, but climbing, tug-ging at the ball of string the boy can't unravel fast enough.

He pays it out over the ocean. Stands at the shoreline, squinting up as if it has just occurred to him to read the print on the newspaper the kite is made of, but the words are too far away.

Too late for words. The kite is barely recognizable, a speck above the horizon; and is it merely to see what will happen next, or to set it free, that without warning he lets go?

Or a bird, wingbeats flailing for a hold on air.

Futility strips it of grace. When it falls clumsily to earth, the boy gently gathers it up again.

"Try, please," he whispers and tosses it back into the air.

Again the bird flaps and falls, weaker for its failed attempt, and the boy gathers it up, gently folds in its wings, and more violently this time tosses it up.

The bird crashes helplessly as if it has forgotten that it ever defied gravity.

"I'm sorry, I didn't mean to hurt you," the boy insists.

How beautiful the bird appears, iridescent like a woman's slip in the gleam of an afternoon in which sun beats drawn shades to bronze.

He traces the curve of its nape. He's never seen a bird like this before, never before been allowed to stroke his fingertips along such smoothness, to touch a life so different from his own, to hold an inhabitant of air, that mysterious sphere about which the boy can only dream. He feels its rapid heartbeat. Its body heat intensifies in his hands, and suddenly he's afraid the heat is blood. But his hands are dry. He doesn't know exactly where he's inflicted the wound.

He's never shot anything with the pellet gun but empty cans and factory windows. True, he's shot at birds—sparrows on wires, starlings in the trees, pigeons on the girders under railroad bridges—but never hit them. He's either a naturally bad shot or his nerve fails at the last instant so that the pellet whizzes harmlessly into the sky or ricochets with a ringing spark off the girders while a flock of pigeons beats from an underpass and swoops away.

He's always missed before, perhaps, because that's what his heart demands. Now, he could argue that, though he pulled the trigger, hitting this bird was the merest chance—an accident.

He could argue that, but to who? Who's here besides the two of them?

Look what he's done.

What difference does the truth make now?

"Like a boy," she said, as if more to herself.

Then she leaned from the bed and released the shade.

Perhaps the pullcord accidentally slipped from her fingers. The shade, gleaming like a sheet of bronze, shot up, and blinding daylight blazed across the bare mattress slicing the bed in two.

Heat streamed into the room; pigeons launched from the ledge as if a shot had been fired.

She was on her feet, knocking over the chair, kicking through the clothes strewn beside the bed, and pulling on her slip.

A slip she sometimes didn't remove. But today, before they'd exchanged a word, she'd stripped off her clothes, no longer shy about the sag of her breasts. Maybe it was simply too close—still air before a summer storm—to lie beside him in the slip. Nonetheless she'd worn it beneath her sundress. She knew he liked her in it from how he drove her into the mattress kissing her throat like he was crazy for her, her shoulder straps slipping down, a breast popped over the lacy bodice, while the silk rode up her jittering legs so that the V of her dark bush showed like a flash of panties.

"Haven't I been good to you?" she asked, softly. "Haven't we been happy up here in our own little world? Who is it?—a girl, no doubt more your age. Or have you found another lonely woman? There are so many of us."

He shook his head: *it's not like that,* he wanted to tell her, to say, as he'd rehearsed it, *I'm getting in with you over my head.*

That sounded stupid now. Looking at her standing in her slip against the shade-drawn window at the foot of the bed, her eyes too full of hurt for his to meet, he choked up. The choice was between total silence or rising to hold her. He sat naked on the mattress, paralyzed; she released another shade with a violent yank, clearly on purpose this time, so that it clattered up, and light obliterated the foot of the bed.

"So," she said in that soft voice, unsettling after the racket of the shade, "you thought maybe we'd fuck goodbye."

She let another shade fly as if releasing a kite.

Sparrows on the wire, starlings in the basswood trees that lined the curb and threw the network of their branches across the shades—city-wise birds—beat their wings and flew away. It might have been someone shooting.

"What happened?" she asked gently—too gently—the way he'd told her it was once when she asked him why he'd whisper *no no no* while she came down on him. *Too sweet,* he'd tried to explain to her then, *so gentle it aches.*

I never wanted it to go this far, he wanted to say, *never wanted to hurt you.*

"I showed a little feeling and scared you away," she said, answering her own question as she paced, bare feet slapping the floorboards, moving from window to window, tripping the drawn shades the way an executioner might trip the lever on a gallows.

438

"I'm a fool. You really were too young for me."

The shades rattled up and the fierce light that obliterated the mattress bleached her skin from bronze to a white that made it seem like she was fading. Before his eyes, their room, secret in the sunbeaten shadows of drawn shades, was revealed for what it was: an unrented apartment with a few sticks of shoddy furniture.

And when she'd reduced it to that, she stood dressing before him one last time, against an open window that looked out on a blur.

"You opened me up, and then just let go. Like a boy—confused, callow, and cruel."

Blocks away the spooked birds resettled on other sills and wires, and the crab apple trees in a little park.

"My pretty boy," she said, and stepped out, quietly shutting the door.

After a while he rose, pulled the shades on the windows down, lay back on the bed, closed his eyes, spit into his hand. But it was impossible to touch himself with her sweetness.

The braided hoops at the end of pullcords began to sway like miniature nooses. A tingle of grit on the panes against which the shades nervously rustle. A whoosh of coolness. The shades lift and float back. Hypnotically. Billowy, translucent like a slip through which summer light outlines the shadow of a woman's body. Until, seized by a sudden gust, the shades crash like paper cymbals and tread air on the edge of tearing apart. They want to fly in this room that once seemed perfectly ordered in its bareness—bed, mirror, chair. Chair on which to drape discarded clothes; mirror in which to watch his hands cupping her breasts.

While on the other side of the door, the girl who spied all summer, drawn by the forbidden sounds of her mother's lovemaking, strains to listen. Now that she no longer has to hate and envy her mother, she's free. Free to concentrate on her own crush on the guy from Frost's Service Station. That's what's stenciled on the back of his coveralls, the tan pair he wears partially unbuttoned over a smooth, bare chest. *Carlo* stitched in green over the pocket. Baby's what her mother called him, behind the closed door, sometimes sighing it over and over. She's never heard her mother say the real name of the nameless young man with the dark, dreamy kind of eyes she's seen on holy cards of saints. St. Francis eyes, or St. Sebastian nailed down by arrows but gazing up at heaven. Her saint's alone in there. Why won't he come out, she wonders. This

439

time she won't run and hide. Is he weeping, perhaps, like her mother, or has he merely fallen asleep?

She holds her breath to listen harder, but all she can hear is the thrash of shades blowing in an echoey room.

Nominated by Ontario Review

EARTHLY LIGHT

by MARCIA SOUTHWICK

from DENVER QUARTERLY

Miracle seekers bring offerings of money, candy, and teddy bears
to the glass-topped coffin bearing the body of Miguel Angel,
a one year old who died thirty years ago of meningitis
and is dressed in the tiny soccer uniform of Argentina's champion
    team,
the Boca Juniors. If we need to believe in something, why not
believe in heaven, where the Safri Boys Band in fluorescent clothes
play reggae, as saints with portable vacuums strapped to their waists
suck up dust from the purple silk curtains, and on scaffolds drag
six-foot-long feather dusters across the plaster cornices—all
in preparation for tourists to help pay for the gazillion-dollar
restoration project. Heaven's a tear-down. Frankly I prefer
earthly light, bands of moss and water-washed stones.
I like the way this laceleaf pours over the retaining wall,
echoing the pond's waterfall. The good news is that peregrine falcons,
wearing tiny satellite transmitters, can be tracked all the way
    from Alaska
to Argentina. The bad news is we'll soon be watching Disney's
version of David shooting Goliath with a slingshot. And the Japanese
have beaten us to the microcar, as tiny as a grain of rice, complete
with 25 parts, including headlights and hubcaps. It can travel
up and down a matchstick. Every 12 weeks a new aquatic microbe
swims into San Francisco Bay. Now there are sponges, sea squirts,
and microscopic protozoa from Japan. The Chinese Mitten Crab
walks its hairy claws right into houses in Germany! The good news is
I grew up between a hardware store and a lumberyard. Back then,

if anybody had proposed painting the front door hot pink
and the exterior purple, to show off the orange trumpet roses,
we'd have laughed. If anybody had proposed buying Gucci loafers
with the signature horse bit, we'd have laughed. We wouldn't have
    laughed
at the bronze statue of B. B. King, holding Lucille, his guitar.
But we *definitely* would have laughed if anybody had said, "Did you
    know
that from our country estate windows, you can see the Pyrénées?"

Nominated by David Lehman, Sandra McPherson, David Lehman, James Reiss, Authur Sze

MR. AGREEABLE

fiction by KIRK NESSET

from FICTION

WHEN YOUR WIFE SAYS she's leaving you do not object. You don't even let her know you're insulted—you've already foreseen the foreseeable, quaint as it sounds, and the business no longer shocks you. Politely, agreeably, you tell her to do as she pleases, watching the suitcases open and fill. You tell her to call when she can. Does she need any money? She says you shouldn't be so agreeable. You nod. You tend to agree.

In a world so rife with contention, why disagree? Some people you know—neighbors, in-laws, people you work with—home in on discord like heat-seeking missiles. They blast great holes in their lives, thriving on willful, blood-boiling chaos. This is not you—agreeable, peaceable you. Ready-made hardened opinion, you feel, goes quite against nature. It defies this earth we breathe and traverse on, which is fluid, they say, and constantly shifting, alive at the core.

Last year, before this business began, you saw your daughter committed. Foreseeable, foreseen. Your daughter, who wasn't ever quite "there" in the first place, thinks she's a cipher, that she is turning into the wind. Better that, of course, than a cave girl out of Ms. What's-her-name's novels, those books your daughter drank in to enter prehistory. When you visit you don't debate her absent identity. You agree to the terms. You offer your fatherly best as it were, fresh-shaved, patient, mildly heroic, compact and trim if a bit frayed at the edges; no need to let her know you're depressed. You bring her the weight of your affable nature, your humor, your unswerving desire to accept and agree, along with a snack of some kind, some candy, a bag of almonds or unsalted peanuts.

443

The visits increase once her mother is gone. Three, say or four times a week. The house has grown strange, to be truthful, and you like to get out. Your once-agreeable furnishings, the sofas and tables you decided to keep, have taken on auras, gray hazy outlines, which tend to unsettle. The bedroom exudes a disagreeable air. You hang around late at the office, rearranging your files; you visit your daughter. You sit in cafés on the weekends skimming the paper, thinking, deciding which movie to see. At night you awaken sitting upright in bed, discussing strange things with your curtains.

One Sunday, at an outdoor café, a man sits down at your table. He's thirty years younger than you, wide-shouldered, black-haired, buck-toothed. A fading tattoo on his hand. You come here a lot, he declares—he says he's seen you before. You do, you agree; he probably has. You're fond of the scones, you tell him. You glance at the crumbs on your plate.

Your agreeability, alas, makes you the ideal listener. People seem to sense this right off. You have a compassionate face, a kind face, you have heard. Like a beacon, your face pulls people in, strangers out of accord with good fortune, survivors and talkers, victims of the ship-wreck of living.

The man has led a colorful life, as they say. He is funny, almost. You hear of his days as a kid in a much larger city, of all the hitch-hiking he did, how for years he zigzagged the country, shacking up here, camping out there, he and a spotted castrated dog, a dog with one eye and one ear, a dog he called Lucky. You hear about his most recent romance.

He entertains, you have to admit. His problems, so vivid and real, draw you away from your invented anxieties. You lean back and listen, agreeably nodding, sipping your tea. The ideal listener.

So I blow into town, he says, fully into his story. I go up to the apartment and open the door, and guess what?

You raise your eyebrows in question, unable to guess.

My girlfriend's in there with Eddy, he says, this guy from downstairs.

Delicacy forbids you to ask what were they doing, what did he see. You wipe your mouth with your napkin. You look at your watch. The story's growing less and less pleasant; you're afraid for the girl; you don't really like speaking with strangers. You take a few bills from your wallet and lay them down on the table.

He asks if you're leaving, teeth extending out past his lip. You tell him your daughter is waiting. You've had a nice chat. He asks you

444

which way you're headed. You tell him. He says he's going that way. You need to hear the rest of the story.

Down the block by your car he says to hand over your billfold. The billfold, he says. You feel the nudge of the gun at your kidney.

You are no crime-drama hero. You hand over the billfold, agreeing in full to his terms. He opens the wallet and scowls. You've never carried much cash on your person. Move up the street, he says—removing your bank card from its niche in the leather, tucking the gun in his pocket—we'll stop at the bank. You move up the sidewalk. Nervous, giddy, you ask what became of his girlfriend.

I forgave her, he says, hands in his pockets. Then she skipped out.

He slides your card in the slot at the bank. You stand side by side. He asks for your PIN, which you promptly reveal. He taps in the code.

Silence. The street seems strangely deserted. You ask if he's found a new girlfriend.

Shut up, he says. He stuffs the cash in his pocket. Story's over.

Half-joking, you ask if he'd mind if you kept the receipt.

Shut up, I said, he exclaims.

You begin to say that you're sorry—you don't quite shut up in time—and then the hand is out of the pocket, there's a blur of tattoo and you're down on your knees in the flowerbed, there among nasturtiums and lupine and poppies, reeling from the shock of the blow.

Don't be so shit-eating nice, he says, his shadow looming over like Neanderthal Man's. He says you remind him of Eddy, that two-faced adulterous creep. Lay flat on the ground now, he tells you. Don't move for five minutes. Down, if you ever want to get up.

You lie in the dirt on your belly, no hero, purely compliant. In a while you touch your scalp where he hit you, fearing there's blood; there isn't. You're lucky. The soil, barky and damp, clings to your fingers and hair. Your eyelashes brush against flowers—poppies, you think. Petals as vibrant as holiday pumpkins.

How long is five minutes?

People step up to get money. You hear them push in their cards and tap on the keyboard. You feel the individual discomfort, the dismay they endure to see such a sight, outlandish, right here out in the open, a man flung down on the ground in broad daylight, mashing the orange and blue flowers.

It seems you've been here forever. You've been here in dreams, you believe, in piecemeal visions—even this was foreseen in a way, if not quite clearly foreseeable. You should get up, you suppose, but you feel

445

fine where you are. Sprawling, face in the black fragrant mulch, burrowing, digging in with your fingers, digging in like the wind. You press into the earth. The street grows quiet again. Ear to the ground, you hear plates trembling beneath you, weighty, incomprehensibly huge, aching with age and repeated collision, compelled by what is to agree and agree and agree.

Nominated by Melissa Malouf

EYE SHADOWS

by JUDITH TAYLOR

from MARLBORO REVIEW

All aristocratic men wore makeup at the court of Louis Quinze.
The seducer Lovelace looked foppish but was lethal.
Since then, men's cosmetics have taken a precipitous fall.
Now he's ill-tempered as she struggles with her mascara.
In the moonlight, no one wears makeup, and if there's blush left on
     her face, it's blanched out.
She sits on him, and he's her rocking horse, familiar, steady, silver.

Nominated by Stephen Dunn, Carol Muske, James Reiss

THE ORDER OF THINGS

fiction by NANCY RICHARD

from SHENANDOAH

THE BIGLER girl had known it would happen again, so she was not alarmed when she emerged from Touchet's Grocery to find her mother had scaled the Chinese tallow tree behind the store. For a woman of her size, the girl observed, her mother was uncommonly graceful. And quick. When the girl called out, her mother settled in on one substantial branch before she answered. She may have been picking up the thread of an old conversation.

"It's the only real escape," she said, addressing some invisible listener, "from the rising waters of time's bitter flood."

Yeats again, the girl thought. Yeats and the hospital.

Old Mr. Touchet, whose breath already sang of whiskey, clutched the girl's arm. "I'm not responsible," he insisted, "if something happens. If your mama falls." He seemed overcome by the sight of Myrtle Bigler in his tree and returned almost immediately to his store. "I don't have no insurance for that," he announced from behind his screen door. "Only if it falls on my store in a hurricane. Nothing else."

If a small crowd had formed behind her, the girl scarcely heard their voices or the gravel beneath their feet as they gathered, milled about and left. Soon a stout, fair young man appeared and remained alongside her as if this were his custom.

The sun was getting hot, and though Myrtle Bigler usually descended her perch within a couple of hours, her daughter knew there could be no rushing things.

Because for a time neither said anything, the girl merely watched her mother and listened to his breathing, a labored wheezing she could not ignore because he stood so close. She had seen him before, cleaning the

448

store windows, pushing a broom, the whistle from his lungs a solemn accompaniment to his monotone humming. Soon he left her side and within moments returned, carrying two chairs. He set them in the shade of the Chinese tallow, directed her to one of them, and sat beside her.

"Your mama, I hear she does this often."

"Often enough," the girl said. Her mother had long ceased to pay attention to anything below. She might have dozed off.

He withdrew a handkerchief from a back pocket and wiped his forehead and upper lip, then the back of his neck. His wheezing had climbed in pitch.

"You don't have to sit here," the girl said. "Sometimes she takes an hour, sometimes all day. She'll come down when she's ready. Don't you have something else to do?"

The sun had climbed from behind the tree so it now glared without relief from nearly overhead. The girl wished she'd brought a hat. Her mother looked down at last and waved but said nothing.

"You want me to go get the priest?" The young man seemed to think she would welcome his idea for the ultimate solution it was.

"Why? Does he have a ladder?" The girl wondered why he thought a priest could talk her mother out of a tree. Or perhaps he feared she might jump and therefore be in need of some final words.

"I don't think so. But Father Mike, he makes things seem not so bad. Like in confession, he says 'Okey doke' when you finish. Your sins, they don't sound so bad when he says that. I can go get him if you want."

The girl tried to imagine her mother talking to a priest: *Sometimes,* her mother might say to him, *everything, everyone gets too close. I can't see the order of things.*

Okey doke, the priest would say.

"No," she said. "Thanks just the same."

They sat in silence while the girl regarded her mother, who stirred little except to swing her crossed ankles. So the girl sat and waited, the young man beside her, until just past dark, when Myrtle Bigler descended the tree.

That night her mother slept fitfully, the girl not at all. She drank coffee to stay awake, in order that she might watch and listen. She was watching when the sun crept into their dark kitchen, when her mother's breathing slowed to the comforting rhythm of sleep. Early on Monday morning the girl walked into Catalpa, and from the telephone at Touchet's Grocery, called the state mental hospital again. Then she bought their bus tickets.

449

Two days later, the girl woke before dawn to find her mother had already packed her bag.

"How many times is this?" She stood in the kitchen, facing the window where the sun announced itself every morning.

"I'm not sure," the girl said. "Six or seven, maybe?"

Her mother's gaze had not left the east horizon. "Oh, it must be more than that," she murmured. "I could remember that many." She ran water into the sink, let it run over her finger, turned it off. "We don't have to leave before sunrise, do we?"

"No," the girl said. "We have plenty of time."

Her mother turned finally to look at her. "Good," she said. "I want to watch the sun come up. I don't want it to happen behind my back. Not today."

In Touchet's Grocery, from behind the array of Daily Special signs, they watched for the bus. Her mother was checking the contents of her bag for the third time, though there was little to pack. She owned few clothes, a single pair of shoes which she wore for the occasion— *You never know what's on the floor of a bus*—her collection of Yeats's poetry—*Maud Gonne was crazy, too, but she was beautiful so nobody cared*—a half dozen prescription bottles.

"Is it still Wednesday?"

The girl nodded. As she had seven names, arranged alphabetically, her mother kept track of them according to the days of the week. Myrtle had named her daughter after women she'd known in state hospitals. The drugs steal away parts of your memory, she explained to her daughter: the names hold them fast.

"There's something important I meant to say, Hattie," her mother went on, "and I'm telling you this so you'll know." She seemed to have been distracted by the clutter in her bag. She moved her hairbrush to the opposite side, checked the cap on her shampoo, and repositioned the Yeats. The front cover was missing. The girl had recovered it from a box of discards on the parish bookmobile, where the librarian had seen her but had pretended not to.

"What, Mama? What should I know?" She secured the latches on her mother's bag and checked the pocket of her dress for her own return ticket.

"Every time it starts," her mother said, without moving, "I think this time I won't let it. This time I'll hold on and I won't worry you. It is as if someone had rearranged the furniture in a familiar room and then turned the lights off. It is all disarray."

450

The girl saw the bus approach, took her mother's arm, and led her toward the grocery's exit. "I know, Mama," she said. "Let's go; we'll miss the bus."

For the next several weeks, or maybe it would be months, the girl would live alone, but she didn't mind; she had a fireplace, a cistern, a big washtub on her back porch. A couple of days a week she sold her produce from a roadside stand along the parish highway. On Friday nights she wrote a letter to her mother. On Saturdays she walked to Catalpa.

One Saturday morning in midsummer, instead of Mr. Touchet, the young man met her at the back door of the grocery. His gaze was clear and direct as a child's.

His name was Claude Joseph Doiron, he said. She could call him T-Boy. He stood in the doorway and stared at her.

"My vegetables," the girl said, "I bring them every Saturday. For the rent. When it's paid I get cash."

"I knew that," he said. "I'm the Saturday manager now. I knew that."

She crossed the store and made her way toward the annex where the Touchets ran the town's post office. He followed and stepped behind the counter. The girl was suddenly conscious of her mass of tangled hair, her bare feet, the size of her hands. "Any Bigler mail? And a stamp, please."

He shuffled through the stack of General Delivery. "Your name is Grace?"

"This week," she said, and took the envelope. Her mother had run through her names alphabetically, week by week; with her last letter she'd begun again with Alma.

"What you mean this week? Your name, it's going to be something else next week?"

"I have seven," she said, "seven names."

"Like the days of the week," he said, "and like that poem about Monday's child has a fair face and one of them works hard for a living." He studied her patiently, while from deep in his chest came a thin, high whistling, like a small mournful bird's.

"Yes, something like that," the girl said.

She pushed the wheelbarrow, which held her few purchases, from the back of the store around to the front and onto the shoulder of the highway. Though she avoided turning around, she knew he was watching.

"I never knew nobody with so many names," he called and, "You come every Saturday?"

451

At home she read the letter:

July 30

Dear Grace,

Old Mrs. Guidroz is back, the one whose dead child visits her dreams now and then. So's the boy with the scarred wrists. The routine hasn't changed. They won't let me read past ten, though sometimes I think the fire in my head is enough light to read by. I miss our vegetables; such curious food for a healthcare facility.

They tell me it's been nine weeks, but I always lose time in here. There's nothing to make one day any different from any other, except when somebody checks in or out. They tell me I will get used to these drugs, that soon I will be able to tell one day from another, one memory from another.

I have dreams, but I can't remember them. They wake me up, and they're gone. A kind of hit and run. What's left is all "testy delirium and dull decrepitude." How could Yeats have known? Did he get those words from poor Maud Gonne?

Your mother

The following week the young man appeared at her roadside stand. One morning he bought tomatoes and peppers. The next, all her eggplants. How did she manage to carry all this? he wanted to know. Could he give her a ride home? he asked.

The Bigler girl said, "I have a wheelbarrow," and, "No, thanks."

That Friday night the sky was violet, the moon a broad Cheshire grin. The girl sat on her front porch in the dark and watched the rabbits move about in the moonlight. When they scattered suddenly into the overgrown pasture, she looked up to see him walking toward her, at the far edge of the darkness, following his moonshadow. She went inside and from her window saw him stop at the edge of the blackness that was the woods and stand just beyond the fenceline, where the posts listed north and south, silvery in the moonlight. The rabbits had disappeared; she pictured them huddled and watchful among the thistles, waiting.

He carried a shovel. With one hand he withdrew something from a pocket in his trousers, stooped, placed it on the ground, and began to dig. One spadeful, two. Then he took the object, dropped it into the hole and buried it. When he'd tamped the dirt into place with the back of the shovel, he turned and made his plodding way across the light-bathed pasture toward the railroad tracks.

She waited until he was gone, until the midnight freight had chuffed its way past, toward the river crossing and Baton Rouge, and she could see only the glow of the lantern that hung at the door of the caboose. Then she retrieved her own shovel from beneath the back porch and unearthed the thing he'd buried. It was a small black crucifix which trailed an inch or so of fragile silver chain. She dropped it into the pocket of her dress. *There's plenty of strangeness in the world, Mary-Margaret,* her mother might say on a Friday. *Pay it no mind.*

The next morning she took her produce to town as usual. He met her at the back door and collected her fine green and red peppers and a basket of zucchini. The girl ignored his stares and questions, picked up her letter and left.

August 6

Dear Hattie,

They think I'm making fine progress. Beginning to Co-operate is how they put it. They have found a combination of drugs that let me see past breakfast and I must be giving the right answers in Group. As many times as I've done this, you'd think I'd have got the hang of it by now.

A new patient arrived yesterday, an old man here to dry out. Mr. Badeaux. He's gone blind, and his daughter thinks he's Not Taking It Well. I asked her how she thought he was supposed to take it. She said I shouldn't be so hostile. A person can take only so much, she said. I said yes, I could certainly understand that, the "stir and tumult of defeated dreams" and all. She warned Mr. Badeaux he should watch who he spends time with. She whispered, but I heard.

M.

The next week the young man pulled up to the Bigler girl's stand and bought all the okra. "Your hair," he said, "in the sun it's three different colors. You knew that?"

She said, "You'll want some tomatoes to cook with the okra."

Late that night, as the girl drew water from the cistern and filled the washtub on her back porch, the train announced itself in the distance.

The whistle sounded in Maringouin, and the light on the engine came into sight at the mill. She thought about Claude Joseph Doiron. He stared at her, as if whatever she might say was exactly what he'd hoped to hear, even if she never answered his questions. He was slow and fat and he wheezed. But he didn't look at her in the way she had come to expect: *Poor girl her mama's a little funny, calls her a different name every day, it's no wonder she's shy.* And he saw colors in her hair.

That night there was no moon, and in the blackness that cloaked her garden, the pasture, the woods, it was easy to believe herself alone in the world. The lantern she'd set on the porch cast shadows that danced to the nightmusic she loved: the hum of treefrogs and cicadas, the clacking of the eastbound freight. She imagined she could hear the bayou lapping at its banks, the slap of a gar's tail on its surface, but soon the girl heard what she knew to be the young man's voice. Claude Joseph Doiron stood out there in the darkness, singing to her: "Grace, sweet Grace."

She went to the end of her porch. "What do you want?" she called into the night. "Why are you here?"

Soon she heard a rustling and the movement of large, heavy feet. His voice came from just beyond the glow of her lantern. "Don't be mad," he said. "It's not safe, being by yourself all the way out here. I just wanted to check up on you."

She held the lantern high and squinted but couldn't see him. "I'm just fine, I never asked you to come out here and check up on me. Please go away," she said. "I'm fine."

"You sure are pretty," he said.

She was already awake when the sun's first light found her kitchen. She went out into the garden and picked fat, red Creoles, rinsed and dried each one and set the baskets into the wheelbarrow. Pushing past the house, she spotted a small mound of dirt directly before her front porch. This time her shovel found a small creased card bearing the image of a saint. "Saint Jude," the printing on the back said, "patron saint of lost causes."

She walked alongside the highway. The sun on the back of her head was already hot, the nape of her neck damp beneath her hair. When she accompanied her mother to town on Saturdays, they talked. Sometimes it was about important things, like why the eggplants were stunted this year. Sometimes it was about other things, like why Mrs. Touchet had a moustache, why Mr. Touchet smelled like whiskey at

454

seven in the morning. She wished for her mother, wondered when she might be well enough to read this in a letter. What does it mean, Mama, what?

It's just more strangeness, her mother might say, or, *Hospitals don't have room for all the strangeness there is, Alma. Pay it no mind. On a Monday or any other day.*

When Touchet's Grocery appeared, the girl turned her wheelbarrow and headed back home. It didn't have to be Saturday, she thought. She could take her produce any day. On Friday morning. Or Tuesday. He couldn't work all the time; she would find out when he was off, and she would never have to see him again. The next morning when she went out onto her front porch with a cup of coffee, she found a letter from her mother stuck into the frame of the screen door.

August 13

Dear Katherine,

    I'm making you a present in Art Therapy. I have painted some dreadful pictures, but my pottery isn't too bad. Comes from working in the mud, I guess. I've already messed up two of them, but this one looks like the potter was both awake and sober. Which Mr. Badeaux is now, though he says being blind hasn't much to recommend it, being sober, less. Says he liked it better when the edges of things felt the way they were beginning to look.

    That's white flies on the eggplant. Tell Mr. Touchet you need the Thiodan. Regards from Mr. B. and me,

Your loving mama

On Monday the girl walked toward town and got close enough to Touchet's to see his truck in the parking lot. On Tuesday his truck was not there, so she delivered her produce and hurried home, where she filled her wheelbarrow again and set up her roadside stand. She was prepared to ignore him when he came by, but he did not. On Friday night she sat and watched for him from her front porch. She fell asleep there and woke with the sun. Later, between her garden and back porch she unearthed from a long narrow trench a palm leaf. It was brittle, and when she brushed a finger across the tip, it drew blood. Sunday morning another letter appeared on her front door.

Dear Mary-Margaret,

I read Mr. Badeaux the paper every morning, front to back, even the classified. What people buy and sell, what they find and lose. What they're willing to give to get it back. Evenings I read him Yeats. Why shouldn't an old man be mad, he said over his eggs this morning. Why not, when the end never lives up to the beginning? You got no quarrel from me, I said.

Are you talking about that retarded boy? What do you mean he's burying things around the house?

Don't let the okra get woody.

Your soon to be sprung,

loving mother

The rain began on Sunday night, loud and violent at first, and then by Monday afternoon, slow and steady. Except for odd lapses at dawn and dusk each day, the rain continued all week. The girl lifted tomatoes from the sodden ground, straightened bean poles, rebanked two rows that had begun to wash away. A leak in the kitchen got worse and she set her washtub beneath it. At night she lay awake and imagined her little house an ark. The bayou would flood, she would wake and find herself floating over the railroad tracks, down the highway all the way to the Basin, and out to sea. Every pot in her kitchen was full of vegetables, the refrigerator and its tiny freezer were both full of vegetables, and she knew how to fish. No one would visit. No one to bury strange things in her yard. No one to look at her with pure delight, whether she answered his questions or not.

I am not like my mother, she thought, listening to the rain. *My mother would like this.*

Before she was fully awake on Sunday morning she heard his truck, then his step on her porch. When she'd dressed and reached her front door, a letter waited.

August 23

Dear Sophie,

Mr. Badeaux died yesterday. I was reading to him from the Merchandise for Sale: Appliances, and before I could get to "Excellent condition, make offer," he took one deep breath—I thought it was a sigh—laid his hand on my arm,

456

and didn't breathe again. I picked up a poem he liked and kept on reading, just in case he was still listening. Then an aide showed up and asked couldn't I tell he was dead? I said I thought some of us took our leave slower than others, and I wanted him to have some company. I wouldn't be surprised if this didn't set me back some.

Be careful with that man. There's patients here who talk like that. Colors in your hair. Really.

Yours in experience,
Mama

Over the next three days there were more and longer spells when there was no rain and she was able to patch the hole in the roof. She was shelling peas on her front porch at midday on Wednesday when his truck crested the railroad tracks. The girl crept through her garden, her shoulders brushing okra leaves, and stepped behind the oak tree to watch the truck bounce across the rutted fields. She grabbed hold of the lowest limb, swung one leg over and then the other, and made her way to the place where she'd seen her mother sit.

From the tree the girl watched him step from the truck and onto her porch. He disappeared from view for a moment, and when he reappeared he hopped from the porch and headed through her garden, his blue and yellow plaid shirt a moving patch of light among the cornstalks. When he emerged from the garden he hesitated briefly and then strode toward her tree.

"Grace," he called.

She imagined herself part of the tree, quiet and still enough for a bird to trust.

Presently he began to wave.

I should have known, she thought, I am too large to hide anywhere. Now he will go away, he will think I am like my mother, and he will leave me alone.

He moved a step closer and she could now discern his face. It was a face, the girl realized, that never anticipated disappointment. No doubt he had been the brunt of rejection. But he seemed not to expect it.

"It's because of my mother, isn't it? You think I'm just like her, and so of course I would be sitting in a tree."

"There's a saint used to climb trees."

"I don't think my mother's a saint."

457

"You never know," he said.

"Who was she, the one who climbed trees?"

"Christina," he said. "Saint Christina the Astonishing. She climbed mountains and cathedrals, too."

The girl imagined her mother perched atop St. Basil's, another bus ride to the hospital. "Why did *she* do it? The saint."

"She could smell people's sins, so she climbed things. To get away from the smell of sin."

"Not much to recommend it," she said. "Being a saint."

"That depends," he said, "on who you get close to." He stepped forward a little and moved from the sunlight into the shade. "A letter from your mama came this morning. Maybe it's important." He drew the envelope from his shirt pocket and held it up.

"You didn't have to do that," she said, taking the letter. "I can get my own mail. Is that all you came for?" She opened the envelope and read.

August 30

Dear Theresa,

Come on the 6th. I'm going to be sprung, as they think I've learned some Coping Skills. They still talk like that.

Ma

"I don't mean to criticize," he said, "but sometimes you can be a little rude. How's your mama?"

"Just because you ask a question doesn't mean I have to answer it. If it was any of your business how my mama was, I'd tell you."

"For her letter to come in the middle of the week, I figure either she's better, or she's worse. Tell her hey for me. If you feel like it."

"She gets out on Saturday," the girl said. "She's fine."

"Your figs," he remarked, "they ripe. You don't pick them, the birds will."

"Where does your mother think you are when you're here? Late at night, hanging around in Mr. Touchet's pasture."

"I'm thirty years old," he said. "I told my mama, I said, I'm thirty, Mama, and I got my driver's license and I have me a friend and I'm going to go visit when I want."

"What'd she say?"

"'*Mon Dieu*,' she said, 'it must be a girl. You be careful, Claude Joseph. Don't matter how old you are, you can't be too careful about

458

things like that.'" He turned and gazed briefly in the direction of her house. "What you did with everything?"

"With what?"

"The things I buried. They're blessed articles. You can't throw them away. You have to burn them or bury them. I put them here so your mama, she'd get better. And to keep you safe."

"They're in the house," she said. "I was going to give them back to you. We're fine. We don't need you to bury things for us."

"I know," he sighed. "You don't need nobody to do nothing for you. I know why you don't come on Saturday no more. I told my mama you were mad at me. She says I been too pushy. Women don't like that, she said. So I won't come back. I won't bother you no more."

From her spot in the tree the girl saw him now as part of the landscape she knew: the tiny shotgun house, the garden, the pasture where the rabbits lived. The day had brightened with his arrival, but now he turned to go, and she became aware he carried the brightness with him.

"Wait," she called, "you're right about the figs."

"I brought some buckets," he offered. "They in my truck."

Later she watched the truck top the railroad crossing and disappear over the other side. She went round to each window in her house and tried to examine her reflection, but there was too much light. That evening she filled her washtub early and stared into the surface of the water. She saw a round, dark face framed by too much hair that gave off no color at all. I don't know what he wants, she thought. What does he want?

On the following Saturday the girl woke to humming and dressed quickly. It was not yet dawn, but T-Boy Doiron was already there, sitting on her porch. He was eating biscuits from a brown paper sack. He wiped his hands on his trouser legs and removed a letter from his shirt pocket. "It's a letter from your mama. It came yesterday." There were crumbs around his mouth and down the front of his shirt. "How come you look like that when you just woke up?"

"Like what?"

He stood and wiped his mouth with the back of his hand. "Like you didn't just wake up."

"My hair," she said. "What about the colors? What three colors is it?"

"Come stand in the sun," he directed. She joined him in the patch of light which had found her porch through a clearing in the trees. He took into his hands a broad fan of her hair and splayed it out into the early light. "Red," he whispered, "and copper. And gold. I never saw

459

hair like this." Then suddenly he'd leaned into it and closed his eyes. "And it smells like the earth," he added.

She thought about the smell of her garden, humus and peat and fertilizer. Insecticide. "What does that mean?" she demanded. "I wash it every night."

"No, like the earth. Like what grows: sweet olive, magnolias, lantana. Like that."

He smelled of fresh-baked bread and after shave. The cowlick on the crown of his head stuck straight up. She took the bag he offered and inhaled its warm goodness.

"My mama, she made these for us. I tried not to eat too many."

There were two left. "Come into the kitchen," she said. "I'll make some coffee." Facing her kitchen window they watched the sun clear the treetops and illumine the wet pasture. "She gets out today. I'm taking a bus to go get her."

"I'll meet you at Touchet's tonight," he declared, "when you get off the bus. I know you can find your way home even in the dark. I just want to. You don't want that other biscuit?"

She handed him the bag, and when she noticed he wasn't drinking his coffee, she added more sugar and milk. "Is this how it will be?"

"Yes," he said, "if you want."

She said, "My mother wasn't always unhappy. But she's always been . . . different. You mustn't ever get a funny look when she does something odd."

He shrugged. "I can't say what's odd. Everytime you turn around in this town, somebody's doing something I wouldn't do. It's not for me to say."

His coffee was untouched. She poured it into a glass, added still more milk and sugar and handed it to him. "I eat vegetable sandwiches," she said, "and we hardly ever wear shoes and in the morning my hair is pretty knotty."

"I think you're perfect," he said, and drank the entire glass of coffee milk. He set the glass onto the ring where his cup had been and cleared his throat. "When it's like this I think people get married. If they want."

"I don't know how this is." She studied his hand, which lay between them on her table. She thought about touching him but didn't. "I don't know how it is to be married."

"Neither me," he said, "but if we get married you have to be Catholic. Are you Catholic?"

460

She cleared the table and took their things to the sink. "I don't know. I don't know what I am."

"If you were Catholic," he said, "you would know."

"Maybe I was and I forgot." She ran water into his glass and watched it fill, murky as summer fog.

"No," he said, "that's not something you forget. If you're Catholic, you know it. All the time."

She rinsed the glass twice more until the water ran clear, picked up her bag and moved to the door. "We'll see," she said.

"About getting married?" The bird in his chest was singing.

She thought about her mother, who was no help sometimes, when her daughter's pain got absorbed into her own. But there were more times when her mother could gaze down over the surface of things and see the pattern and make sense of it. It's what comes of sitting in trees, she'd said.

T-Boy Doiron cleared his throat again. "About being Catholic?"

She pulled the front door shut behind them. "About anything," she said. "About everything. We'll see."

He said, "I'll talk to Father Mike."

She said, "Okey doke."

At Touchet's he refused to leave until her bus had arrived and she had boarded and the bus had made its way toward the river. She found a window seat and opened her mother's letter.

September 3

Dear Alma,

I packed this morning and intend to live out of my suitcase till you arrive. Last night they admitted a girl they put in the bed next to mine. When the night nurse found her under the bed for the third time she tied her in and sedated her. How do you hold on, daughter, looking after me and "my own great gloom"? The goddess had her ugly blacksmith. Choose who you will, and I will keep my mouth shut. I will try to hold tight and work our garden. I do not think I can stay out of trees.

Do you mean marriage?

Take a fast bus. The food here is beginning to look okay.

Good dreams (which I am now having),

Mama

461

The girl gazed through her own reflection in the bus window, down at the Mississippi. As a teenager who had come here from other cities and from across other rivers, she'd thought it wide as the earth itself, broad and strong and brown, something which would separate the two of them from the very world. Now she was crossing a river that seemed not so wide. To get her mother and bring her home. To fill grocery sacks with sad paintings and misshapen pottery.

There is a man, she'd written her mother. He is slow and he wheezes, but he thinks I'm beautiful. He sees no strangeness he cannot love. He thinks he wants to tell his mother, though I am sure she knows. Just as you would know. And when you are home, you will hear him come at midnight on Fridays and stand in the moonlight when there is a moon, and in the utter darkness when there is not, and sing to me: "Grace, sweet Grace." Like that was my real name.

Nominated by Shenandoah, Carolyn Kizer

MEDITATION ON AN APHORISM BY WALLACE STEVENS: "A POEM IS A PHEASANT"

essay by JEFFREY HARRISON

from THE GETTYSBURG REVIEW

THIS ENIGMATIC STATEMENT STANDS all by itself, without explanation, in Wallace Stevens's collection of aphorisms, titled "Adagia." Four pages later the metaphor resurfaces in expanded form, becoming "Poetry is a pheasant disappearing in the brush"—which, by being more specific, dispels some of the mystery of the earlier aphorism. But before poetry (or a poem) is a pheasant disappearing in the brush, it is a pheasant, period.

Not a phoenix, rising out of its own ashes. Not the fire-fangled golden bird of "Of Mere Being." Not even a peacock, which is too fancy, too merely decorative. The peacock, in fact, is a member of the same biological family as the pheasant. So is the smaller, plainer quail, which whistles spontaneously at the end of "Sunday Morning." But a poem is not a quail or a peacock; it is something in between, in terms of size and adornment: a pheasant.

A pheasant is a quail raised to an exquisite plane, or a peacock brought into agreement with reality.

Not long ago I found one dead in the road, not a poem but a pheasant, blood and guts spilling from "the pressure of reality," but the rest of it still beautiful: the red, wattled face; the shiny green head and white neck-ring; the long, barred tail-feathers that looked as if they would make good quill pens; the soft, russet, imbricated feathers of its breast, exquisitely patterned and tinged with a violet iridescence.

All species of pheasant are native to Asia. The one that we know on this continent, the ring-necked pheasant, is derived from the English pheasant, itself imported from the Black Sea area, and several Chinese and Japanese varieties. This exotic hybrid from several far-off lands is like a creature from the worlds of mythology, folklore, and dreams—essentially a product of the imagination, "the faculty by which we import the unreal into what is real."

But the pheasant is real, one of the "particulars of reality" that, for Stevens, a poem must be composed of. Its habitat is farmlands, meadows, pastures, even the outskirts of cities—which is to say, not far from our own lives. It feeds on berries, seeds, buds, and leaves, spending its days pecking around in the *real*. "The imagination," said Stevens, "loses vitality as it ceases to adhere to what is real." As it happens, the pheasant is a bird that spends most of its time on the ground, flying only rarely.

So the pheasant partakes of two worlds, the real and the imaginary, and, like poetry, enacts "an interdependence of the imagination and reality as equals."

Stevens describes two linguistic poles: "an asceticism tending to kill language by stripping words of all association and a hedonism tending to kill language by dissipating their sense in a multiplicity of associations." The first is a pheasant with all its feathers plucked out, while the second is a pheasant with the plumage of peacocks, birds of paradise, quetzals, parrots, and macaws stuck into its body feather by feather. Fancy, yes, but also bleeding to death. A fiction that is not credible.

If the poem is a pheasant, the pheasant is also a poem, an element of the "physical poetry" in which we live. Like poetry, the pheasant "enhances the sense of reality, heightens it, intensifies it." It may even lead to the creation of a poem. "The poets who most urgently search the world for the sanctions of life, for that which makes life so prodigiously worth living, may find their solutions in a duck on a pond or in the wind on a winter night." Or in a pheasant disappearing in the brush.

The pheasant is capable of flight, though it rarely flies. It will fly if we startle it. Then it startles us, as a good poem does.

Nor does the pheasant fly very high or very far—only as high and far as is necessary, as will suffice. And yet it achieves a credible elevation slightly higher than the ground, perhaps even "a momentary existence on an exquisite plane," which it also offers to us. For a moment, we may attain "a degree of perception at which what is real and what is imagined are one: a state of clairvoyant observation."

Have I gone too far? No matter: the pheasant has already landed, the imagination has been brought back into agreement with reality. Something has happened to us, but we aren't sure what. In any case, it is safe to say we have had an experience. "To read a poem should be an experience, like experiencing an act."

So: an exotic yet real bird; colored by the imagination but part of our world; unseen until it suddenly takes flight with a shudder of wings (startling us like a poem with "the freshness or vividness of life"), flies a short distance, then runs again on the ground with tough legs into the brush.

The pheasant's disappearance reflects the evanescence of beauty, which is true even of the beauty of a poem: we flush out its surprises as we read, but can't hold onto them, though some part of them has entered us. Put another way, the quality of disappearance will always be a part of poetry, and of pheasants.

Nor can the pheasant's meaning be captured. "Poetry must resist the intelligence almost successfully." Who cares what it means, anyway? "When we find in poetry that which gives us a momentary existence on an exquisite plane, is it necessary to ask the meaning of the poem?"

A poem whose meaning is completely clear has no mystery and is a dead poem. Think of a pheasant shot by Audubon, its body pierced with wires to give it the illusion of life.

The brush is as real as it gets, a briary tangle of reality. And yet, after the pheasant disappears in the brush, we have to imagine it again, so in that sense it is disappearing into the imagination. Anything we make of it there is based on the real pheasant but will, in turn, alter our perception of the world around us, as a poem does.

And the dead pheasant? It was still warm when I picked it up, its neck limp. I placed it in the tall grass by the side of the road and walked to my car. Then I went back and pulled the longest feather from its tail.

Nominated by Wally Lamb

LOS ANGELES,
THE ANGELS

by JAMES HARMS

from POETRY NORTHWEST

Doves love a dying palm. They nestle in the loud fronds. They hum
and shiver. The way days end here: no click; no door sealing in the
  light.
The way dusk enters the room and embitters it; the way
the paint absorbs its shadows, the skin absorbing stares.

I hear you and I hate it. I hate hearing your voice in the leaves
as I sand down the bureau; I drag out the furniture, drag it out
onto the driveway but still, *How have you come so far
without belief?* I rake the yard to muffle your voice.

Evening is slithering toward me, and behind it, believe me,
the cold. Night is a chance to see the stars as they were
when Greeks in their shifts and leather slippers, their
gruesome beards sandy and caked with salt—before turning
toward each other to sleep—listened, terrified, to the laughter
breaking with the waves, the slim sheet of water drawing close.

And their dreams were worn as singlets in the next day's race,
the cloth of sleep sewn into waking, the long day of sleep.
Because they knew, as I have chosen not to—each turn at the wheel
a chance to drive my purchases and children to a clear spot
on the hillside—they knew what we would become: old thieves
in beaten-up cars, idling at the signals, skin going bad in the sun.

Night is a wind blowing away the light, which streaks and burns
on its way west. Night is an empty lung, and here's the moon:
the armoire mounts a broken dresser; the lawn grows plastic chairs.
How can I forgive you? How have you come so far? I rake
the dark shards from the grass, your voice in pieces, *so far, belief.*

Nominated by Ralph Angel, Pinckney Benedict, Gary Fincke, Laura Kasischke,
William Matthews, Ann Townsend, David Wojahn

FLOWER CHILDREN

fiction by MAXINE SWANN

from PLOUGHSHARES

They're free to run anywhere they like whenever they like, so they do. The land falls away from their small house on the hill along a prickly path; there's a dirt road, a pasture where the steer are kept, swamps, a gully, groves of fruit trees, and then the creek from whose far bank a wooded mountain surges—they climb it. At the top, they step out to catch their breaths in the light. The mountain gives way into fields as far as their eyes can see—alfalfa, soybean, corn, wheat. They aren't sure where their own land stops and someone else's begins, but it doesn't matter, they're told. It doesn't matter! Go where you please!

They spend their whole lives in trees, young apple trees and old tired ones, red oaks, walnuts, the dogwood when it flowers in May. They hold leaves up to the light and peer through them. They close their eyes and press their faces into showers of leaves and wait for that feeling of darkness to come and make their whole bodies stir. They discover locust shells, tree frogs, a gypsy moth's cocoon. Now they know what that sound is in the night when the tree frogs sing out at the tops of their lungs. In the fields, they collect groundhog bones. They make desert piles and bless them with flowers and leaves. They wish they could be plants and lie very still near the ground all night and in the morning be covered with tears of dew. They wish they could be Robin Hood, Indians. In the summer, they rub mud all over their bodies and sit out in the sun to let it dry. When it dries, they stand up slowly like old men and women with wrinkled skin and walk stiff-limbed through the trees towards the creek.

Their parents don't care what they do. They're the luckiest children alive! They run out naked in storms. They go riding on ponies with the boys up the road who're on perpetual suspension from school. They take baths with their father, five bodies in one tub. In the pasture, they stretch out flat on their backs and wait for the buzzards to come. When the buzzards start circling, they lie very still, breathless with fear, and imagine what it would be like to be eaten alive. That one's diving! they say, and they leap to their feet. No, we're alive! We're alive!

The children all sleep in one room. Their parents built the house themselves, four rooms and four stories high, one small room on top of the next. With their first child, a girl, they lived out in a tent in the yard beneath the apple trees. In the children's room, there are three beds. The girls sleep together and the youngest boy in a wooden crib which their mother made. A toilet stands out in the open near the stairwell. Their parents sleep on the highest floor underneath the eaves in a room with skylights and silver-papered walls. In the living room, a swing hangs in the center from the ceiling. There's a woodstove to one side with a bathtub beside it; both the bathtub and the stove stand on lion's feet. There are bookshelves all along the walls and an atlas, too, which the children pore through, and a set of encyclopedias from which they copy fish. The kitchen, the lowest room, is built into a hill. The floor is made of dirt and gravel, and the stone walls are damp. Blacksnakes come in sometimes to shed their skins. When the children aren't outside, they spend most of their time here; they play with the stones on the floor, making pyramids or round piles and then knocking them down. There's a showerhouse outside down a steep, narrow path and a round stone well in the woods behind.

There's nowhere to hide in the house, no cellars or closets, so the children go outside to do that, too. They spend hours standing waist-high in the creek. They watch the crayfish have battles and tear off each other's claws. They catch the weak ones later, off-guard and from behind, as they crouch in the dark under shelves of stone. And they catch minnows, too, and salamanders with the soft skin of frogs, and they try to catch snakes, although they're never quite sure that they really want to. It maddens them how the water changes things before their eyes, turning the minnows into darting chips of green light and making the dirty stones on the bottom shine. Once they found a snapping turtle frozen in the ice, and their father cut it out with an axe to make soup. The children dunk their heads under and breathe out bubbles. They keep their heads down as long as they can. They like how their hair looks underneath the water, the way it spreads out around their faces

469

in wavering fans. And their voices sound different, too, like the voices of strange people from a foreign place. They put their heads down and carry on conversations, they scream and laugh, testing out these strange voices that bloom from their mouths and then swell outwards, endlessly, like no other sound they have ever heard.

The children get stung by nettles, ants, poison ivy, poison oak, and bees. They go out into the swamp and come back, their whole heads crawling with ticks and burrs. They pick each other's scalps outside the house, then lay the ticks on a ledge and grind their bodies to dust with a pointed stone.

They watch the pigs get butchered and the chickens killed. They learn that people have teeth inside their heads. One evening, their father takes his shirt off and lies out on the kitchen table to show them where their organs are. He moves his hand over the freckled skin, cupping different places—heart, stomach, lung, lung, kidneys, gall bladder, liver here. And suddenly they want to know what's inside everything, so they tear apart everything they find, flowers, pods, bugs, shells, seeds, they shred up the whole yard in search of something; and they want to know about everything they see or can't see, frost and earthworms, and who will decide when it rains, and are there ghosts and are there fairies, and how many drops and how many stars, and although they kill things themselves, they want to know why anything dies and where the dead go and where they were waiting before they were born. In the hazelnut grove? Behind the goathouse? And how did they know when it was time to come?

Their parents are delighted by the snowlady they build with huge breasts and a penis and rock-necklace hair. Their parents are delighted by these children in every way, these children who will be like no children ever were. In this house with their children, they'll create a new world—that has no relation to the world they have known—in which nothing is lied about, whispered about, and nothing is ever concealed. There will be no petty lessons for these children about how a fork is held or a hand shaken or what is best to be said and what shouldn't be spoken of or seen. Nor will these children's minds be restricted to sets and subsets of rules, rules for children, about when to be quiet or go to bed, the causes and effects of various punishments which increase in gravity on a gradated scale. No, not these children! These children will be different. They'll learn only the large things. Here in this house, the world will be revealed in a fresh, new light, and this light will fall over everything. Even those shady forbidden zones through which

470

they themselves wandered as children, panicked and alone, these, too, will be illuminated—their children will walk through with torches held high! Yes, everything should be spoken of in this house, everything, and everything seen.

*   *   *

Their father holds them on his lap when he's going to the bathroom, he lights his farts with matches on the stairs, he likes to talk about shit and examine each shit he takes, its texture and smell, and the children's shits, too, he has theories about shit that unwind for hours—he has theories about everything. He has a study in the toolshed near the house where he sits for hours and is visited regularly by ideas, which he comes in to explain to their mother and the children. When their mother's busy or not listening, he explains them to the children or to only one child in a language that they don't understand, but certain words or combinations of words bore themselves into their brains, where they will remain, but the children don't know this yet, ringing in their ears for the rest of their lives—repression, Nixon, wind power, nuclear power, Vietnam, fecal patterns, sea thermal energy, civil rights. And one day these words will bear all sorts of meaning, but now they mean nothing to the children—they live the lives of ghosts, outlines with no form, wandering inside their minds. The children listen attentively. They nod, nod, nod.

Their parents grow pot in the garden, which they keep under the kitchen sink in a large tin. When the baby-sitter comes, their mother shows her where it is. The baby-sitter plays with the children, a game where you turn the music up very loud, Waylon Jennings, "The Outlaws," and run around the living room leaping from the couch to the chairs to the swing, trying never to touch the floor. She shows them the tattoo between her legs, a bright rose with thorns, and then she calls up all her friends. When the children come down later to get juice in the kitchen, they see ten naked bodies through a cloud of smoke sitting around the table, playing cards. The children are invited, but they'd rather not play.

Their parents take them to protests in different cities and to concerts sometimes. The children wear T-shirts and hold posters and then the whole crowd lets off balloons. Their parents have peach parties and invite all their friends. There's music, dancing, skinny-dipping in the creek. Everyone takes off their clothes and rubs peach flesh all over each other's skin. The children are free to join in, but they don't feel like it. They sit in a row on the hill in all their clothes. But they memorize the sizes of the breasts and the shapes of the penises of all their parents' friends and discuss this later amongst themselves.

One day, at the end of winter, a woman begins to come to their house. She has gray eyes and a huge mound of wheat-colored hair. She laughs quickly, showing small white teeth. From certain angles, she looks ugly, but from others she seems very nice. She comes in the mornings and picks things in the garden. She's there again at dinner, at birthdays. She brings presents. She arrives dressed as a rabbit for Easter in a bright yellow pajama suit. She's very kind to their mother and chatters to her for hours in the kitchen as they cook. Their father goes away on weekends with her; he spends the night at her house. Sometimes he takes the children with him to see her. She lives in a gray house by the river that's much larger than the children's house. She has six Siamese cats. She has a piano and many records and piles of soft clay for the children to play with, but they don't want to. They go outside and stand by the concrete frog pond near the road. Algae covers it like a hairy, green blanket. They stare down, trying to spot frogs. They chuck rocks in, candy, pennies, or whatever else they can find.

In the gray spring mornings, there's a man either coming or going from their mother's room. He leaves the door open. Did you hear them? I heard them. Did you see them? Yes. But they don't talk about it. They no longer talk about things amongst themselves. But they answer their father's questions when he asks.

And here again they nod. When their father has gone away for good and then comes back to visit or takes them out on trips in his car and tells them about the women he's been with, how they make love, what he prefers or doesn't like, gestures or movements of the arms, neck, or legs described in the most detailed terms—And what do they think? And what would they suggest? When a woman stands with a cigarette between her breasts at the end of the bed and you suddenly lose all hope—And he talks about their mother, too, the way she makes love. He'd much rather talk to them than to anyone else. These children, they're amazing! They rise to all occasions, stoop carefully to any sorrow—and their minds! Their minds are wide open and flow with no stops, like damless streams. And the children nod also when one of their mother's boyfriends comes by to see her—she's not there— they're often heartbroken, occasionally drunk, they want to talk about her. The children stand with them underneath the trees. They can't

472

see for the sun in their eyes, but they look up, anyway, and nod, smile politely, nod.

The children play with their mother's boyfriends out in the snow. They go to school. They're sure they'll never learn to read. They stare at the letters. They lose all hope. They worry that they don't know the Lord's Prayer. They realize that they don't know God or anything about him, so they ask the other children shy questions in the schoolyard and receive answers that baffle them, and then God fills their minds like a guest who's moved in, but keeps his distance, and worries them to distraction at night when they're alone. They imagine they hear his movements through the house, his footsteps and the rustling of his clothes. They grow frightened for their parents, who seem to have learned nothing about God's laws. They feel that they should warn them, but they don't know how. They become convinced one night that their mother is a robber. They hear her creeping through the house alone, lifting and rattling things.

At school, they learn to read and spell. They learn penmanship and multiplication. They're surprised at first by all the rules, but then they learn them too quickly and observe them all carefully. They learn not to swear. They get prizes for obedience, for following the rules down to the last detail. They're delighted by these rules, these arbitrary lines that regulate behavior and mark off forbidden things, and they examine them closely and exhaust their teachers with questions about the mechanical functioning and the hidden intricacies of these beings, the rules: If at naptime, you're very quiet with your eyes shut tight and your arms and legs so still you barely breathe, but really you're not sleeping, underneath your arms and beneath your eyelids you're wide awake and thinking very hard about how to be still, but you get the prize anyway for sleeping because you were the stillest child in the room, but actually that's wrong, you shouldn't get the prize or should you, because the prize is really for sleeping and not being still, or is it also for being still . . . ?

When the other children in the schoolyard are whispering themselves into wild confusion about their bodies and sex and babies being born, these children stay quiet and stand to one side. They're mortified by what they know and have seen. They're sure that if they mention one word, the other children will go home and tell their parents who will tell their teachers who will be horrified and disgusted and push them away. But they also think they should be punished. They should be shaken, beaten, for what they've seen. These children don't touch themselves. They grow hesitant with worry. At home, they wander out into the yard alone and stand there at a terrible loss. One day, when the teacher calls on them, they're no longer able to speak. But then they speak again a few days later, although now and then they'll have periods in their lives when their voices disappear utterly or else become very thin and quavering like ghosts or old people lost in their throats.

But the children love to read. They suddenly discover the use of all these books in the house and turn the living room into a lending library. Each book has a card and a due date and is stamped when it's borrowed or returned. They play card games and backgammon. They go over to friends' houses and learn about junk food and how to watch TV. But mostly they read. They read about anything, love stories, the lives of inventors and famous Indians, blights that affect hybrid plants. They try to read books they can't read at all and skip words and whole paragraphs and sit like this for hours lost in a stunning blur.

They take violin lessons at school and piano lessons and then stop one day when their hands begin to shake so badly they can no longer hold to the keys. What is wrong? Nothing! They get dressed up in costumes and put on plays. They're kings and queens. They're witches. They put on a whole production of *The Wizard of Oz*. They play detectives with identity cards and go searching for the kittens who have just been born in some dark, hidden place on their land. They store away money to give to their father when he comes. They spend whole afternoons at the edge of the yard waiting for him to come. They don't understand why their father behaves so strangely now, why he sleeps in their mother's bed when she's gone in the afternoon and then gets up and slinks around the house, like a criminal, chuckling, especially when she's angry and has told him to leave. They don't know why their father seems laughed at now and unloved, why he needs money from them to drive home in his car, why he seems to need something from them that they cannot give him—everything—but they'll try to give him—everything—whatever it is he needs, they'll try to do this as hard as they can.

Their father comes and waits for their mother in the house. He comes and takes them away on trips in his car. They go to quarries, where they line up and leap off cliffs. They go looking for caves up in the hills in Virginia. There are bears here, he tells them, but if you ever come face to face with one, just swear your heart out and he'll run. He takes them to dances in the city where only old people go. Don't they

474

know how to fox-trot? Don't they know how to waltz? They sit at tables and order sodas, waiting for their turn to be picked up and whirled around by him. Or they watch him going around to other tables, greeting husbands and inviting their wives, women much older than his mother, to dance. These women have blue or white hair. They either get up laughing or refuse. He comes back to the children to report how they were—like dancing with milk, he says, or water, or molasses. He takes them to see the pro-wrestling championship match. He takes them up north for a week to meditate inside a hotel with a guru from Bombay. He takes them running down the up-escalators in stores and up Totem Mountain at night in a storm. He talks his head off. He gets speeding tickets left and right. He holds them on his lap when he's driving and between his legs when they ski. When he begins to fall asleep at the wheel, they rack their brains, trying to think of ways to keep him awake. They rub his shoulders and pull his hair. They sing rounds. They ask him questions to try to make him talk. They do interviews in the back seat, saying things they know will amuse him. And when their efforts are exhausted, he tells them that the only way he'll ever stay awake is if they insult him in the cruelest way they can. He says their mother is the only person who can do this really well. He tells them that they have to say mean things about her, about her boyfriends and lovers and what they do, or about how much she hates him, thinks he's stupid, an asshole, a failure, how much she doesn't want him around. And so they do. They force themselves to invent insults or say things that are terrible but true. And as they speak, they feel their mouths turn chalky and their stomachs begin to harden as if with each word they had swallowed a stone. But he seems delighted. He laughs and encourages them, turning around in his seat to look at their faces, his eyes now completely off the road.

He wants them to meet everyone he knows. They show up on people's doorsteps with him in the middle of the day or late at night. He can hardly contain himself. These are my kids! he says. They're smarter than anyone I know, and ten times smarter than me! Do you have any idea what it's like when your kids turn out smarter than you?! He teaches them how to play bridge and to ski backwards. At dinner with him, you have to eat with your eyes closed. When you go through a stoplight, you have to hold on to your balls. But the girls? Oh yes, the girls—well, just improvise! He's experiencing flatulence, withdrawal from wheat. He's on a new diet that will ruthlessly clean out his bowels. There are turkeys and assholes everywhere in the world. Do they know this? Do they know? But he himself is probably the biggest ass-hole here. Still, women find him handsome—they do! They actually do! And funny. But he *is* funny, he actually is, not witty but funny, they don't realize this because they see him all the time, they're used to it, but other people—like that waitress! Did they see that waitress? She was laughing so hard she could barely see straight! Do they know how you get to be a waitress? Big breasts. But he himself is not a breast man. Think of Mom—he calls their mother Mom—she has no breasts at all! But her taste in men is mind-boggling. Don't they think? Mind-boggling! Think about it too long, and you'll lose your mind. Why do they think she picks these guys? What is it? And why are women al-most always so much smarter than men? And more dignified? Dignity for men is a completely lost cause! And why does anyone have kids, anyway? Come on, why?! Because they like you? Because they laugh at you? No! Because they're fun! Exactly! They're fun!

*   *   *

Around the house there are briar patches with berries and thorns. There are gnarled apple trees with puckered gray skins. The windows are all open—the wasps are flying in. The clothes on the line are jump-ing like children with no heads but hysterical limbs. Who will drown the fresh new kitties? Who will chain-saw the trees and cut the fire-wood in winter and haul that firewood in? Who will do away with all these animals, or tend them, or sell them, kill them one by one? Who will say to her in the evening that it all means nothing, that tomorrow will be different, that the heart gets tired after all? And where are the children? When will they come home? She has burnt all her diaries. She has told the man in the barn to go away. Who will remind her again that the heart has its own misunderstandings? And the heart often loses its way and can be found hours later wandering down passage-ways with unexplained bruises on its skin. On the roof, there was a child standing one day years ago, his arms waving free, but one foot turned inward, weakly—When will it be evening? When will it be night? The tree frogs are beginning to sing. She has seen the way their toes clutch at the bark. Some of them are spotted, and their hearts beat madly against the skin of their throats. There may be a storm. It may rain. That cloud there looks dark—but no, it's a wisp of burnt paper, too thin. In the woods above, there's a house that burnt down to the ground, but then a grove of lilac bushes burst up from the char. A wind is coming up. There are dark purple clouds now. There are red-coned sumacs hovering along the edge of the drive. Poisonous raw, but fine for tea. The leaves on the apple trees are all turning blue. The sunflowers in the garden are quivering, heads bowed—empty of seed now. And the heart gets watered and recovers itself. There is hope, everywhere there's hope. Light approaches from the back. Between the dry, gnarled branches, it's impossible to see. There are the first few drops. There are the oak trees shuddering. There's a flicker of bright gray, the underside of one leaf. There was once a child standing at the edge of the yard at a terrible loss. Did she know this? Yes. The children! (They have her arms, his ears, his voice, his smell, her soft features, her movements of the hand and head, her stiffness, his confusion, his humor, her ambition, his daring, his eyelids, their failure, their hope, their freckled skin—)

Nominated by Maxine Kumin, Caroline Langston, Jewel Mogan, Joyce Carol Oates, Robert Schirmer, Eugene Stein

SEWING WITHOUT MOTHER: A *ZUIHITSU*

by KIMIKO HAHN

from TRIQUARTERLY

As with tending a newborn, the days pass slowly, the months quickly. With each new season we all, even the littlest, recognize what Mother has missed when she died over a year ago and what we see through our loss. Even the bamboo shoots that father digs up with the girls and parboils for us to take home. Mother has suggested it and now we eat them thinking—how tender, how tender.

I think of famous writers such as Bashō, Ki no Tsurayuki, Issa, Sei Shōnagon—Kamo no Chōmei's bubbles we read about in *bungo* class with Professor Varley, read even the annotations in Japanese. A decade ago. I am returning to the work now to see how they wrote diaries and miscellaneous entries. Particularly Issa's *Oraga haru*.

The elation and detail in Issa's book—even watching his wife count their daughter's flea bites as she's nursing—then his grief with the same attention. The reader's engagement.

Yes, I walk past a certain frame shop near the children's school just to see the proprietress who resembles Mother. Her hair covers her cheeks as she leans over an Utamaro print. Like an Utamaro print.

The Issa journal becomes an anthology as he jots down other poems on grief.

478

I sometimes think my many years in graduate school were a waste, especially since I can no longer read Japanese with ease. And because the renowned scholar with whom I wished to study didn't really give a shit about me. But recently, in thinking about the women who have been influential in my life, I remembered the professor who chose me as a research assistant for work on censorship in postwar Japan. I scoured the library and annotated dozens of books for her bibliography. I recall her unsettling intellect.

In Iowa City I baby-sat for my writing instructor who lived down the alley. In her bedroom I noticed several bottles of perfume and tested them at a local shop. One was "green" and not too expensive. I wear it still.

Eighteen months after losing Mother in a violent car accident our lives have spun on. Still, even in our apartment we hear the related terror as boys shout the brands of crack they're peddling.

Over a year now and I can travel and unpack my nightshirt, toothbrush and manuscript. I can stand at a hotel window and watch pedestrians flee a thundershower they thought would not cross their commute. Waves of rain flood the street. Traffic lights change for no one. Music videos block the hum of the building and the fact of strangers in the next room.

In July we have the dog "put down." Four months later our first parakeet dies within a day.

Miyako tells me Grandmother's death is her fault. I do not understand what she does not understand.

Reiko asks Ted if the universe goes on forever. He says it does. She comments that it must be very big and now it's bigger because grandma is there.

Miyako acts badly at Dad's house. I realize she cannot bear the absence of Mother sewing potholders, piecing together a puzzle, rolling out biscuit dough.

In a remote Southeast Asian society people view sudden death as an honor—that the goddess who gave them life, needing their assistance,

479

summoned their presence. The deceased enjoy a modest sainthood for a period of seven weeks, a number closely associated with harvesting. I make up these rituals.

The entries in a typical Japanese journal are nature-oriented, a convention. The frost, maple, cherries. All exhibit what lies at a tangent to language. I think of the sound of straw under Basho's head as he turned in his sleep.

The change of season brought fresh grief, it's true, but in the second year I think: a year ago it was only a few months , or a year ago we were buying this birthday cake without her.

There are still several of her suits in Father's hall closet. I keep promising to go through them but know I won't any time soon.

I imagine leaving our two-bedroom rent-stabilized apartment that transported me through a first marriage, divorce, romances, a second marriage, two pregnancies and births. Mother's death. Waking for the phone at 2 A.M. for this news that would change our lives forever.

Earlene says the roots of one's behavior will not change, but one's relationship to it can be modified. Even radically. But what happens when a party to that behavior is missing?

Sometimes I become annoyed with Mother's inabilities—the jealous streak I wasn't aware of but inherited, absorbed from her silence. Her shutting off instead of confronting.

A student said that if Genji is symbolically searching for his dead mother he must have felt abandoned as a child. That the parents' departure indicates this to the child.

I watch the aerobic instructor talk with her mother. Both wear unitards.

After a vigorous workout I lock the lavatory door and weep as if from physical fatigue.

If only I could read the texts again—but even my dictionary usage is rusty. Wish I could navigate the reference books. Wish I could read the annotations with ease. Wish I could read the *kanji* without counting the number of strokes in the radical.

As Father describes her jealousy he describes a powerful emotion I never witnessed in her but wish I had. Any strong emotion.

Reclamation for the married ones may mean the spouse will become more "Mother." For my Father, that he will seek relationships with women. But for the children, who will provide them with the many missing pieces? Will they live with more loss than the adults? Will they grieve forever?

The taste of *daikon*.

I see a book on Tibetan thought regarding reincarnation. I am tempted to purchase it. Perhaps there are a certain number of souls that circulate. Perhaps she is an infant, now learning to speak. To touch a mirror. A child with her own mother.

What did she think of herself?

I make up myths to comfort myself, give myself rites I do not possess.

I want Father to continue grieving as an expression of my own pain and to pay for his arrogance toward Mother. Interrupting her. Telling her she was wrong. Correcting her. Dismissing her opinion. Poking fun at her. Silencing her. All this unresolved for the daughter. But he knows all this.

Sipping a beer he keeps me company while I cook. Corrects me with "kitchen tips."

Are our lives spiraling around if we retrieve our annoyances with one another? If we can take the risk?

We still haven't decided where to place her ashes, cannot think of a single place she might have liked. Maui still comes to mind. Or some body of water.

Did Ted and I begin the process of "resolution" when we viewed her body? Said goodbye to the body no longer "hers." To believe she was dead.

481

How did we explain her death to ourselves? On one level an "accident." But a part of me believes the Japanese superstition that she was a substitute death for a loved one. She subverted fate.

A friend with two little boys tells us the older one wants to kiss her romantically. I tell her my daughter also wants to kiss me romantically.

Are the boys in Lee's kindergarten class so raucous because they perceive her as Other? As the one whom they are not like?

Reiko is especially tired this evening. She cries hysterically as Ted walks out of the room. After twenty minutes I go in and ask, What's wrong? *Daddy took me into the kitchen but there is a red bucket. Then he carried me into my room but there are red letters on the circus poster, and the book he chose has a girl with a red dress. And my elephant was red and I'll never see it again.*

When she falls asleep where does she go?

The girls believe Mother is *somewhere.* Even after one asks what I think and I give my cloud-sun-wind version, they still believe she is somewhere waiting for them, looking like she did when we saw her two days before the crash when we waved goodbye from the car and she turned to go back into the warm house.

The poet reading before me is slender. I am not as delicate and beckoning. My body is curvier partly from type, partly from a few extra pounds. Mother was slender but for a very round abdomen. Fibroids? I disliked her stomach. Yet, here is mine. As I recall her she was probably thirty-eight.

Several people told me I will speak to her.

She loved to speak Italian. It must have been a cord to her years in Rome when everything was shiny and exquisite. And I was part of that time.

I am pleased with the girls' manners. *Yes, please. Fine, thank you.*

482

Ueda defines *zuihitsu* as "stray notes, expressing random thoughts in a casual manner. . . . [Though some] do show a semblance of logical structure." I am attracted to this feeling of *semblance.*[1]

We finally find a co-op we like and the bank will approve. The building is a brownstone but white, not brown. We have a garden with a pink dogwood. We will watch it from the bedroom.

I have an envelope of seeds Mother marked *marigolds.*

Ki no Tsurayuki saw the pebbles and recalled his daughter playing in the sand.

I feel I think of her more since she died but it isn't true. It's how I think of her.

Father says "the pillow book" is always of an erotic nature but I can't find a citation to that effect. I can't even find a reference to its origin, which I think was a little drawer in a box-like "pillow." Keene calls this form a *zuihitsu* in the introduction to his translation of *Tsurezuregusa.* *Zuihitsu:* free-flowing brush.

In both Sei Shōnagon's and Kenkō's work, the pieces are more discreet than my own, which are often a cross between a journal entry and a sketch. I like the flow in my own structure but I also like the gemlike quality of the so-called "essays."

A fan with the mother-of-pearl fallen out.

When I fly on an airplane I wear her jade snow pea as a talisman—and possible means of identification.

Miya's best friend, who has seen a number of classmates leave the city, vows she will be the next one to move *so I can break someone's heart.*

I am still not sure how to wind the bobbin of mother's machine—I'll need to wait for Tomie to return from Japan. I hope she will remember. Then I hope this antique will work.

1. Makoto Ueda, "The Taxonomy of Sequence," in Earl Miner, ed., *Principles of Classical Japanese Literature* (Princeton University Press, 1985), p. 90.

To teach a course on the diary: Sei Shōnagon, Kenkō, Bashō, Anais Nin, Samuel Pepys, Alaskan woman, Anne Frank, Thoreau.

Why the diary? The immediacy of the record—the spontaneity. Also the artifice in the face of publication.

To teach them how to thread a needle, stitch and knot it.

A box of white buttons.

Reiko says she wants to die when I die.

Keene: "The formlessness of the *zuihitsu* did not impede enjoyment by readers; indeed, they took pleasure not only in moving from one to another of the great variety of subjects treated but in tracing subtle links joining the successive episodes."[2]

Even my "stories" utilize the *zuihitsu* antistructure.

I hear a toddler left with a sitter cry out: *mommy, mommy*. An echo in my ribcage.

If Ted turns away from me in bed I feel my body disappear until all that's left is one thought, trying to turn abandonment into sleep.

Every day I want to call Mother. Especially since Dad has returned from his various trips. He tells me not an hour goes by that he doesn't think *of that woman*. Mother.

Ted asked what I want from my relationship with Dad—but is that something I can even articulate? Perhaps I need to try.

Since Mother died I have no one to whom I can really brag about the girls—who will now take pleasure in their small accomplishments.

The seminar is nearly halfway through *Genji*. They will be surprised when he dies before the book's end.

2. Donald Keene, *Essays in Idleness: The Tsurezuregusa of Kenkō* (Columbia University Press, 1967), p. xvi.

The black cherry blossoms.

A boy about eleven kicks me as I exit a bus and I turn and shout at him. He shouts back and before I realize it, I've grabbed him by the jacket and pulled him off the bus stairwell. I'm tired of taking shit.

I am tired of taking shit.

He sees a red kimono and thinks of her.

I am suddenly struck by the intense interest mother had in reading Nin's diaries—I attributed it, at the time, to their offbeat quality and short entries. I never considered the way they were written, that is, as a means to recreate one's experiences. That she must have needed this kind of healing. I will look at the books differently now. I need to call Dad to get them.

Can't seem to reach Dad. The phone rings at least ten times.

I never knew about Mother's intense jealousies. Her fabrications— just as I would fabricate jealousies in order to feel miserable. In order to feel.

Finally roast a turkey myself. Timid cook though I am, I alter the stuffing to suit my taste: add chestnuts, apples and a tsp. of curry.

A chartreuse circle skirt Mother had pinned for hemming was draped on a chair when I arrived after the accident. It has hung on a chair in my bedroom now eighteen months. Forever. Not a long time at all.

Blanket, arrowhead, cloud filling, herringbone, wheat-ear, Holbein, overcast, star filling, Vandyke, fly, fern, fishbone—

Miya wants to make sense of the loss so the world can make sense.

How to define ambition for oneself, apart from one's parents? Can a girl really use her father as a model?

I've given the girls potholder looms—the metal kind I had. I actually couldn't wait till they were old enough because I had enjoyed them. As usual Reiko needs more attention; for Miyako it is a solitary activity.

Mother, Rei's feet are narrow and long like Ted's.

Nominated by Reginald Gibbons, Ha Jin

THE OLD MORGUE

essay by FRANCINE PROSE

from THE THREEPENNY REVIEW

MY FATHER was a pathologist. For most of his professional career—that is, for all of my early life—he worked in the autopsy rooms and laboratories of the Bellevue Hospital Mortuary.

The Old Morgue, people call it now. And whenever the Old Morgue is mentioned, a passionate nostalgia shines (a little crazily) in the eyes of those who still remember the beautiful gloomy brick building (built near the turn of the century by McKim, Mead and White) that's been replaced by the "new" Bellevue's glass and steel.

The Old Morgue had stone staircases, wrought iron railings, tiled floors, dark halls, and the atmosphere of an antiquarian medical establishment—part torture chamber, part charnel house, part research laboratory—so brilliantly captured in David Lynch's film version of *The Elephant Man*. In my memory, the Old Morgue evokes those shadowy group portraits of distinguished scientists performing anatomical dissections, arranged with formal ceremony around a flayed cadaver painted with the esthetic high gloss of Dutch Master *nature morte*.

The autopsy room was enormous—cavernous, people say—with twenty foot ceilings, windows reaching from roof to floor, and, high above, a skylight that cast sheets of dusty light onto the doctors, the assistants, the students gathered round the gleaming chrome tables. For all the disturbing tools of the trade—the hoses, scalpels, saws, the scales for weighing organs—the room had the classical elegance of an old-fashioned hotel lobby in which the dead might rest for a while until their rooms were ready.

486

The morgue was my father's office—where he went every day to work. It was where my mother took me after ballet lessons so he could drive us home to Brooklyn. On school holidays, I dressed up so he could show me off to his colleagues and then find me a quiet corner of his lab where I could read until lunch. I liked going with him to his job. I never thought much about the beauty of the Old Morgue, or its strangeness, or the strangeness of growing up in a household in which dinner-table conversation concerned the most fascinating cases that had come down for autopsy that day.

Most everyone's childhood seems normal to them, and everyone's childhood marks them. Like army brats, like diplomats' kids, like the offspring of Holocaust survivors and (so I'm told) suicides, the children of pathologists recognize each other. Two of my friends are pathologist's daughters; we speak a common language. Last week, confessing to one that I'd binged on some fast-food fried chicken, I complained—disgustedly, unthinkingly—that the layer of fat beneath the skin was "just like every goddamn autopsy you've ever seen." She laughed, and then said, "I hope you know not to say things like that to most people."

This fall, at a dinner party in Manhattan, I met a writer, a woman whose mother worked with my father; both were pathologists at Bellevue. As the other guests put down their forks and looked on, faintly appalled, we reminisced nostalgically about growing up in the Old Morgue. We discussed our shared fascination with the morgue employees known as dieners. German for "servants," the word had always made us think of Dr. Frankenstein's trusty helper, Igor. Though they were usually busy with the physical work of the autopsy room—sawing through the breast bone and skull, sometimes making the Y-shaped incision—the dieners knew the best stories (accounts of the more peculiar cases that had come into their provenance) and took time to tell them, like fairy tales, to the two little girls waiting for their parents to finish work and take them home.

We talked about how you always knew you were getting close to the morgue when you heard the keening, asthmatic whine of the dieners' electric saws . . . And for just a moment, that high-pitched buzz seemed more immediate and more real than the genteel clink of silver as the other guests bravely returned to their meals.

FORENSIC AND clinical pathologists are said to be different breeds. Articulate and extroverted, the forensic scientist (who deals with suspicious, violent, or accidental death) is drawn to popping flash bulbs and adversarial courtroom situations, while the stereotypical pathologist (whose patients are more likely to have died of organic disease) is an eccentric loner without the minimal social skills to interact with the living. But until 1961, when the New York City Medical Examiner's Office traded the Victorian gloom of Bellevue for its own faux-Bauhaus quarters on 30th Street and First Avenue, the forensic pathologist shared the Old Morgue with clinical pathologists, like my father.

Indeed, the history of pathology at Bellevue is inseparable from that of the Medical Examiner's office, established in 1917. (Previously, the city coroner was rarely a physician, which is still not a job requirement in many areas of the country, where the county coroner may be a mortician or a moonlighting tow-truck driver.) Pathologists reverentially recite the names of the first ME's—Norris, Gonzales, Helpern—like a royal line of succession dating back to the era when the morgue was known as the deadhouse.

The Old Morgue had no air-conditioning. From the safe distance of decades, my father's former colleagues take pride in having braved working conditions that no one would stand for today. No young pathologist would consider doing those long postmortems in the stifling summer heat, when the smell of the autopsy room, barely cloaked by disinfectant, permeated the whole building: you took it home in your clothes.

The doctors at the morgue worked hard: long hours for little pay, often for the loftiest and most idealistic of reasons. "More than any other specialty, pathologists teach other doctors," says Marvin Kuschner, who left Bellevue to become dean of SUNY-Stony Brook Medical School. "And my generation was inspired by *Arrowsmith,* by *The Microbe Hunters.* We all wanted to save the world and find the cure for cancer." Pathologists have a broader knowledge of the science of medicine than their counterparts in other fields; they know who the good diagnosticians are, which surgeons make fatal mistakes.

No one becomes a pathologist for the money. Most have comparatively low-paying university appointments, and though it's possible to supplement an academic salary with a high-volume business reading slides of biopsies and cervical Pap smears, still the sum is a fraction of the income of the surgeon or orthopedist. Medical examiners—city or state employees—receive even lower salaries, for which they are obliged to contend with unsympathetic reporters and merciless political pressure: the unscientific angendae of the government and the police. One way you can tell an honest ME, they say, is that he's probably been fired. And no one goes into the field for the glory: pathologists don't tend to have grateful patients passing around their business cards at Park Avenue dinner parties.

Pathologists speak unashamedly of their work as a vocation, a calling, and—with tender care and respect—of their patients, the dead. ("We have to learn to talk to our patients as much as an internist must talk to living patients," says Michael Baden, the outspoken former New York City Medical Examiner now serving as Director of the Forensic Unit of the New York State Police. "A dead person can't tell us where it hurts. But we can figure it out.")

And yet for all the seriousness with which the doctors took their work, the Old Morgue was an oddly jolly place, with its camaraderie, its in-jokes, its characters and legends. Everyone knew the story of the Irish politician whose body was left by the dieners on a table overnight; by morning his nose had been devoured by roaches or rats. The problem was solved when an artistic doctor fashioned a new nose of putty—tinted green to match the skin color produced by the dead man's cirrhotic liver. But the embalming process blanched the skin, leaving the deceased with a green nose at his open-casket Irish wake.

I remember hearing about the dapper pathologist who did autopsies in an elegant suit with a cornflower in his lapel and who scrawled obscenities on the walls and blackboards. About the doctor with the eerie booming laugh who had his mother-in-law exhumed to prove that his wife had poisoned her—and was doing the same to him. The withdrawn medical examiner who played handball against his office walls at midnight; the pathologist who taught his students these precious home truths: "Burial is just long-term storage" and "Maggots are your friends." (In fact, human DNA and evidence of drug use can be obtained from maggots who have skeletonized a corpse.) The doctor who procured human brains for medical students and committed suicide when this service he'd provided gratis was exposed by the press.

After autopsy, the organs of the deceased are put in a bag and sewn up inside the corpse; still, one hears rumors about souvenir-taking. Officially, JFK's brain is missing, though Baden, who examined the Kennedy autopsy findings for the Congressional Select Committee on Assassinations, has an elaborate theory positing that Robert Kennedy safeguarded the tissue removed from his brother's body and restored it to the coffin just before burial. Trotsky's brain has never been found, while Einstein's surfaced in Illinois in the possession of a former Princeton neuropathologist planning to write a paper on the physiology of genius.

One Bellevue veteran recounts meeting, on the street, a colleague who opened a package wrapped in newspaper and showed him a human heart. My friend's pathologist-father brought home a heart in a Kentucky Fried Chicken bucket and dumped it into the bathroom sink for an impromptu anatomy lesson. Another friend was nearly dismissed from her Upper East Side private girls' school when her fellow students found, in her locker, a foetus that her mother had given her to bring to biology class.

My father never brought keepsakes from the morgue home to us. And yet he—readily, eagerly—took me along to the morgue. When I was fourteen, during the summer between my freshman and sophomore years of high school, he got me a summer job as an assistant in a chemistry lab next door to the autopsy room.

Only lately, as the mother of teenagers near the age that I was then, have I begun to wonder: *What in the world was he thinking?* Most likely, it seemed perfectly normal to employ his daughter in the family business. (Recently, his best friend told me that he'd got his son a summer job driving the truck that picked up bodies for the Long Island Medical Examiner.)

THE OLD MORGUE was definitely hardball. It had a heavily macho ambiance, a gum-chewing, cigar-smoking rough and tumble. "There were certain ragged edges to the performance," admits one veteran.

"Bellevue fostered a great brotherhood," says Renate Dische, a pediatric pathologist. "People who worked there have a mutual bond. It was a tough environment. The first week I got there, it was summer, hot as blazes. And there was terrific excitement: they'd found a body in a steamer trunk. It was like the good old days in the 1920s! Everyone was running around, taking pictures of the trunk open, the trunk closed. Inside was this plug-ugly guy curled up in foetal position. Some loan shark who had lent money to a poor artist."

I don't imagine that my father worried much about exposing me to the teeming activity of a workplace in which twenty autopsies might be going at once, far more in cases of disaster. (I remember him working through the night after two planes collided over downtown Brooklyn.) Nor do I think he was greatly concerned about any psychic damage that might result from my intimate acquaintance with mortuary life.

But what about the real dangers? "I always felt there was TB on the *staircases* at Bellevue," says Renate Dische. "And the staff was careless about tuberculosis. So quite a few doctors came down with TB and had to go to sanitariums." (On vacation in the Adirondacks, my father took us to see the former TB hospital at Saranac Lake, a marvelously creepy cluster of buildings surrounded by porches on which the sick were dosed with sunlight and fresh air.)

Hepatitis was also a problem, as were the flies which swarmed in whenever the tall windows were opened to relieve the stifling heat— flies so fat and preoccupied that, one doctor recalls, "you could take a scalpel and cut right through them as they ate off the bodies." Then there was the oppressive odor that permeated everything. People warned me: Wait till they bring in a floater, a body that's been in the water. I couldn't imagine anything worse than the normal smell, but on the day a floater came in, I knew at once what had happened—and that I'd been correctly warned.

In the basement was an embalming school, and beneath that the tunnels through which bodies were transported; the tunnels were home to packs of wild cats installed to control the rat population and to an underground mini-society of the homeless, even then. Upstairs, the quotidian routines of the mortuary were regulated by disgruntled city employees like the elevator operator who punished impatient interns by stopping the car between floors and making them jump or climb; when he died, the staff attended his autopsy to make sure he was really dead.

I don't believe my father had any particular pedagogical or philosophical interest in exposing me to the harsh fact of death. Nor was he careless about my safety; he was, if anything, overprotective. I think he believed the slim risk was worth it because he was fervently hoping—as he continued to hope long after I'd published several novels—that I would be drawn to his profession, that I would become a doctor.

In fact, I enjoyed my job in the lab, mostly washing glassware. I liked my boss, a biochemist who hoped to prove experimentally, by analyzing the urine of schizophrenics, that a percentage of the patients in the Psychiatric Building across 29th Street (in those years before drug therapy, one could hear the inmates screaming day and night) were suffering from porphyria, the kidney ailment with symptoms mimicking insanity that plays a crucial role in Alan Bennett's play, *The Madness of George III*. I liked the research staff who'd accompanied my

491

boss from the Midwest—a crew of friendly, conservative lesbians who wore rings with dollar signs as visible symbols of their faith in the beliefs of Ayn Rand.

For the first week or so I avoided looking into the autopsy room, though the door was always open, and I had to pass it many times daily. Then one day I stopped in the doorway. I stood there and made myself watch. I don't remember exactly why. I felt that it was time. One of the women in my lab had told me a story about some first-year medical students who had toured the mortuary and gone out and thrown up on the sidewalk. I must have wanted to prove to myself that I was tougher than that.

The first time was terrifying. I felt as if the act of looking were like the act of wading into a rough icy sea. Tentatively, I glanced at the feet, the tag attached to the toe, then up the leg with as much relation to flesh as wax fruit to a pear. By now I knew that it was a man, an old man, though his scalp was pulled down like a veil over his face. The flaps of skin folded back from the central incision reminded me of a jacket flung open in the suffocating heat . . .

It all seemed absolutely strange and at the same time utterly normal. Since then I have looked at photos of murder and disaster victims, and I can say with certainty that this was entirely different. How exposed and surprised the dead always look to be strewn about like rag dolls, causing us the gnawing suspicion that they wouldn't want us looking—such pictures always strike me as vaguely pornographic. But the old man on the steel table was an eternity beyond all that. There was no titillation in watching, no sense of the forbidden. In the harsh artificial light that supplemented what leaked in through the dusty windows, it looked so calm and otherworldly that what I felt was like an enchantment.

No doubt the spell would have been broken—I might have been really scared—if someone had chased me away. But that summer no one paid any attention to the young girl who stopped from time to time to watch from the doorway. (I don't remember ever seeing my father do a postmortem, though I always sought out his familiar comforting face.) It was as if I'd taken on the doctors' competent matter-of-factness. Unlike them, though, I hadn't forgotten how this might appear to the outside world, and I took every chance to boast to my friends about the gruelsome tableaux I was seeing. (I should say that the more disturbing autopsies—on badly decomposed corpses or on children—were done in a hidden back room.)

Unless you knew what the doctors were looking for, the procedures took on a certain sameness, and finally what engaged me more than the painstakingly thorough postmortems were the stories I was hearing about the morgue's most notorious cases: the gangland bosses, the high-society dead, the briefly and lastingly famous.

The chief diener, Betty Forman, knew the details of every murder that had come through the ME's office. A former Gibson girl, Betty—even in late middle age—still showed unmistakable flashes of glossy, robust blonde beauty. I was fascinated by her: How had she lost one eye? How had she gone from the vaudeville stage to a career as a Bellevue diener?

Those were questions I couldn't ask. But I could inquire about the horrors Betty had seen in her line of work. Doctors have told me that Betty taught them lots they hadn't known—for example, the fact that female suicides were nearly always menstruating. One pathologist recalls how Betty tried to help him with his apartment-hunting. She'd call him and say, "Quick! There's a place in the Village! The tenant's just come in. There'll be a bullet hole in the couch—but that won't matter much!"

I remember Betty mentioning a scandalous case in which a political boss was found to have killed his ingenue mistress and stuffed her body into the trunk of his car. I tried to fake comprehension, but it soon became clear: I'd never heard of this scandal from decades before I was born. I can still see Betty looking at me with polite incredulous wonder, as if I'd just confessed to never having heard of Abraham Lincoln.

I REMEMBER my father telling us—this was in 1981—that Bellevue was beginning to see some very peculiar cases: men whose immune systems appeared to have shut down. Even more strangely, a number of these patients were Orthodox Jews, who had never told their families that they were gay, and certainly not about the impressive numbers of sexual partners they'd had in the previous decade. Once more, my father began staying late at the hospital or going into work on weekends when he got a call saying that one of these patients had come down for a postmortem.

Later, when the riddle was solved, some of the younger pathologists became reluctant to do autopsies on people who'd died of AIDS. I can still see the expression on my father's face—at once bellicose, lofty, and righteous, a look one might find on the faces of bronze generals

493

in military monuments—as he rehearsed the speech he intended to give those little shits. They were doctors, trained physicians. They had taken an oath to treat the sick, to help the living and the dead without discrimination.

"We did those early AIDS cases before we knew what we were doing," recalls Marvin Kuschner. "Guys were coming in with Kaposi's and pneumocystis pneumonia. I was always contemptuous of people who were afraid to do autopsies. I was brought up to believe you just did them. There were times when I was up to my elbows in tuberculosis pus. But there was—and there is now—a certain reluctance to do AIDS cases. And it's a pity, because those postmortems are a gold mine for pathologists. Those patients have so many things wrong with them."

In fact, says Baden, "no forensic pathologist has ever gotten AIDS in the normal course of work. It is a potential problem for pathologists, who, statistically, cut themselves once in every six autopsies. Fortunately, you need to come in contact with a lot of the AIDS virus to get infected. Just a little bit of hepatitis virus will make you sick—but it takes a lot of HIV."

ONLY A YEAR or so after my father shamed his staff into treating the AIDs dead with the respect that is still so often denied the living, he experienced severe chest pains and checked himself into the hospital, where he was found to have suffered a coronary—a minor problem, as it turned out, compared to the malignant lung tumor discovered, unexpectedly, on a routine chest X-ray. Twenty years had passed since my father gave up cigarettes, but he'd replaced them with a pipe, on which he constantly inhaled.

I've always thought that, in his final illness, my father got less-than-optimum medical care. Physicians (and I am not speaking of pathologists so much as the profession as a whole) do in fact have a complex relation to death. His colleagues and friends—now his doctors—could barely handle the fact that one of their own was at risk. It brought the idea of death too close to home, and their pain and misery were palpable. After it had become obvious that his tumor had metastasized, one of his doctors—a friend—suggested that his problem might be an exotic parasite. Had he recently traveled to an underdeveloped country?

My father had to handle it for them and, really, for us all. As a pathologist, he knew what sort of tumor he had, how serious it was. But he died with courage and grace: a fact that, I think, had less to do with his autopsy experience than with who he was. He was most

494

concerned, as always, with sparing his family pain. One of the last times he left the apartment in which he died was to buy me a new computer because he worried that my vintage CPM drive would soon become outmoded.

In the last weeks of his life he became intermittently disoriented. The most obsessive of these delusions was that he was late for work—that, at any minute, he would go downstairs and get a cab, and travel across town to Bellevue, to his old office, his lab.

Nominated by Threepenny Review, Rachel Hadas, Josip Novakovich, C. E. Poverman, Sigrid Nunez

MIS-SAYINGS

fiction by MARY KURYLA

from THE GREENSBORO REVIEW

CHIP SAYS, "Ballet is how you say it. Say it," he says.

"Belly," I say.

He says, "That's your stomach."

"Belly?" I say.

"Ballet," he says.

How I say what I say in his language I will get right sometime. There are no words with *rrr* to stutter my tongue like in Russian. They called it a defect, that I could not get the *rrr* to roll out my tongue—I and others like me. Leave Russia to come up with a sound many Jews can't make.

Dancer is what I wrote in the classified ad. Did I say what kind of dancer? It wouldn't matter—Chip says, "Ballet is how you dance there."

That I dance caught his taste for thumb-tip nipples, no boob, all the fat a toe dancer can spare. "I can get to that live thing inside a woman," Chip says, "when her boobs are small."

The big size of my boobs, you notice them first, before my face. In my picture, they were there. I am the third girl Chip has sent for after meeting through a picture. Of the girls before, Chip says, "You can't get it right from a picture."

Possible getting it right is not all we are after.

The classified ad Chip wrote said conveyor, import/export, foreign goods. I am his import. But it's the Russia in me—this is what is foreign.

Chip takes out Chinese when I line my cook pots on his stove. Not a pot in the kitchen when I arrived, mine under my arm, many pots of many shapes in a box that had pressed into my side since I took the plane out of Russia. I brought these pots believing that enough pots in a kitchen can make a home, but Chip's never tasted my cooking.

The doorbell rings, and Chip goes fast to the door, faster than I can. "Hey, hey, man," he says, opening the door only enough to get only himself out to the corridor.

When Chip comes back in, he is counting money but he hano cartons of food. The first few times I asked where was the takeout Chinese.

"I'll show you," Chip said.

Show is how Chip tells. We met, really, at the airport where he showed himself by pointing to himself, said "Chip, Chip," then he took my hand in his very big hand and made a fist to say we are together now. Straight to the grocery aisles after that. Tap-tap on the butcher's glass, Chip nodding his head with long hair at the layers of local meat, nodding until I did, too. Bananas he balanced on his palm while the other hand ran over rounder fruits. Did I see what all there was?

His apartment, my new home, got a quick show. I stayed on in the bathroom—for the size of it—even after he shut off the light. The size of rooms swells in dark mirrors. Chip had more to show: a show was on TV of two men and a woman, the man on the rear, spanking her. I sat down and watched skin on the woman's thigh ripple with each slap, and I was happy. Chip thought to show me all the things I could now have in America—but of all the things I had gone without, sex was not one of them. I laughed at this, making Chip smile. Then I got the shirt over my head and saw his face fall at the size of them. I took his head to them, anyway. His hand came up and covered my mouth. He said, "You okay?" Under Chip's hand I was still laughing, thinking of all he could show me.

"It's Chip," he said, "not cheap."

"I know," I said, but what I wanted to say was two languages stumble through my head, both fools.

Chip worked on how I said things. "TV is a tool," he said. We watched in bed, Chinese cartons tossed in the sheets. In such remains we did sex, him coming in from behind. "Man, you learned to fuck in the old, old country," Chip said.

"What of the girls before me?" I said.

"I want arms," he said, "arms that hold."

"Didn't the girls' arms hold?" I said.

"They weren't long enough," Chip said, opening my arm up, "they weren't ballet dancer's arms."

Chip's arms are long enough. They hold me longer and they hold more of me than other arms ever have. Hours, days in Chip's hold let me go to black waters that rise beneath my feet, shoelessly hanging off railings. Mother lays a cloth by the sea, and we eat hard-boiled eggs with salt until the waters build up and blacken. Then I run, her hand up my arm, back to where it's safe on the railings. Where mother promises black waters don't dare touch your soles. Watch the course of the baby's carriage cutting ridges in mounted snow; and my brother in it, so small. The carriage goes nicely on skis. One push too hard and down he'd go. Nooooo. This is milk Mother carries for her own mother; milk whitening a glass cupped against the pull and go of the street rail. Milk one day she will allow me to carry. Until then I watch to see if it spills on Mother's skirt. They watch, too—the other men riders. Mother is so pretty, and this is why they watch; but she says they watch the Gypsies like that, too.

Carried, I am carried over to these rememberings by Chip, my conveyor.

I laugh, nervous again of this place—Chip's place—where all is new, his country so new even the trees are older than anyone's memory of them. And nervous of this language, too, where there is no *rrr* to stutter my tongue; and if there were, would anyone listen for it?

What Chip needed and what I needed, we got in bed. We did not get out, unless doorbells called.

I have waited for a time when Chip goes away for longer than the short time he takes out in the corridor, and longer than it takes to take out Chinese. The things to pack can't be hurried. I had less in Russia than now, and it took me years to get out.

It is true I could stay in Chip's hold and only see what he wants to show. What he doesn't want to show he keeps behind the door, in the corridor. It would not be so hard not to see. It is not so hard for Chip. When he hears I danced, he sees only the ballet, a handkerchief-lace body propped up and spun again and again. But it is because I danced that I smell past closed doors into corridors where Chip stands in corners with this or that guy who stinks like he will come open if he doesn't get some of what Chip sells in his vein, in his nose, in his gut. It is because I danced a kind of dance I can never show to Chip that I do know. I know that I did not come this long way from a Russia, where business is done mostly in the dark, to an America where dark business has just moved out to the corridor.

Start with my pots. They stack back into their box, and I think, maybe if I had cooked for Chip. I think maybe I must think about me, about how I will need money. A city like this, some streets cost just to walk down. I think now I am not so different than the girls before me—so what if he says I have arms that hold—I'm just another that Chip imported but did not marry. So maybe I will have to do my dance again.

The doorbell rings. My suitcase is filled but still open.

Ring-ring.

"Wait," I call, guessing that on the other side of the door is just one who buys from Chip in the corridor.

I open the door, wider than Chip does. Why hide dark business in the corridor anymore—it was me Chip was hiding it from. A man is there, a boy-man who has braided his beard and likes eating too much. He sees them first, my boobs of course, then my face. "Chip's not here," I say.

He says, "That true?"

"Do you see him?" I say and I let him look right in.

He doesn't look. He comes in close to me and pulls a scissors out of his pants. Such scissors children use to carve pictures. He tilts them up at me. I step back into the apartment. "Come in," I say. "But put those away."

He follows me into the apartment that does have souvenirs from other countries, but what you notice is the X of the Southern flag Chip says covers cracks left by earthquakes.

I see that the scissors are put away before I tell the—call him a boy—to please sit down. I start loading my last bag, with shoes.

He sits on the couch, placing jumpy hands first on his knees, then on the table. "Going on a trip?" he asks.

I say, "I am coming from one."

He says, "I hate coming home."

"It's only home if that's what you left," I say. Zip up the bag, then snap close the suitcase.

"You're packing," he says. "Chip doesn't know, does he?"

"What does Chip know?" I say.

He laughs, looks around. His leg is jumping now so he slaps a thigh. "It's Chip," he says, "but maybe it's better how you say it."

I laugh. "Thank you," I say.

"Where's the can?" he says.

I look around, think, What can?

499

This he has no patience for. Through the bedroom he goes on legs jigging loose in loose trousers. He's into the bathroom. Bottles and pills make sounds of hitting the sink, then floor, the mirrored door hitting shut.

Pills fill the boy's hands when he comes back. He sits down on the couch, and pills drop into the rug. Down I go on my knees, picking red and yellow out from between threads, dropping the pills back into his palm. His eyes are on them again. I look down and understand. From where he sits, my boobs are something.

"They for real?" he asks.

"What is 'for real,'" I say.

His face asks, Is she simple? "They a part of you," he says, "or the doctor rig them up?"

"Chip says, 'No matter how warm it gets, women's nipples stay cool,'" I say. "Maybe only the nipples are for real." How Chip says things doesn't always sound right but this is what I like. From the first time we held each other, he said our bodies fit together like bark fits to a tree.

"Who is the tree," I said, "and who is the bark?"

"You are my tree," he said, "my tender, tender tree."

The boy comes from the kitchen with a bottle of juice. He looks at my suitcase. "What're you waiting for?" he says. "Hoping Chip'll show up and stop you?"

I smile. This boy may know some things. "I need a plan," I say.

He lays the pills out on the table, grouped by colors and size, this army. "Start with a map," he says.

Whose map? Chip said not to lose him in the immigration building and when I lost him, I looked at a map on a wall, arrows pointing up and down floors to arrows pointing to exits. A map is not the same from language to language. Pushing up on me to read the map were more Russians, other Russians, also confused with maps, shouting their language that makes my hands sweat. The map told me where I was, but I knew where I was—I was lost without Chip.

The boy begins to put Chip's medicines onto his tongue, one pill at a time, following with a swallow of drink. The hand holding the bottle is shaking so he can't get his lips tight on the rim. Fluid works into the weave of his beard. He sets down the bottle.

"What's the accent?" he says.

"I am from Russia," I say.

"Like those guys in the park who cheat at dominoes?" he says.

"Do they speak with an accent?" I say.

500

"Who doesn't speak English with an accent," he says, this American says.

I say, "It's how Jews speak Russian that makes us alike."

"How do you speak Russian?" he says.

"With an accent," I say. "Do you see?"

He shrugs and goes back to the pills. Sealed beneath foil is a flu cure. These tablets are not easily available. He pulls out his scissors to cut the foil, but no such luck with puncturing what bubbles the pill. Shit scissors.

He looks back at me. "You speak English with an accent. You speak Russian with an accent." He says, "Where don't you speak with an accent?"

I knock on my skull.

"Words," he says.

That was good. We have become familiar. I have no more to hide. He is willing to see. The boy sets aside the flu pills. Enough is enough. He sits back in the couch, looks at his hands.

"Where'd he go?" he says.

"To buy tickets," I say. "A Russian ballet is in town."

"Chip buys tickets to ballets?" he says.

"He hoped I would get him in free," I say. "I dance," I say.

"You're no ballerina," he says.

"Well, I know a dance," I say. I lift my box and pick up my suitcase and bags.

"Let me help you," the boy says.

"No, thank you," I say.

I step around him, going toward the door. From behind, he puts his hands on my hands that hold my things. One of his hands holds the scissors. I try to pull away, but he doesn't let go, and the scissors gathers my skin between its blades.

"Thank you," I say and let go. The box drops to the floor and a lid to a pot shoots out.

"Do you know what kind of dancer I am?" I say.

"I can guess," he says.

"I'll show you," I say. "I'll show you now."

The boy takes the suitcase and bags to the couch and sits down next to them. He puts the scissors on the table and waits for what I will do next.

What I do is better done with music, layers of air, some crowd. This boy, he doesn't even smoke. Maybe the pills washing into his blood will create atmosphere.

Take a time, go inside. There, in my skull. Start the movement on the outside.

The body remembers. My hands push down on my stomach, fabric spreading fingers wide. Between the hips they go. Hot, hot, to the seat of myself. One foot on the table, skirt slips away to thigh. Arch back, there's the shirt flapping, opening to skin. Take away the bra now, the thing that hates to let boobs go. Fucking hooks. Can't get them . . .

My audience is up, on his feet.

This show must go on!

Yes, yes! No hiding now.

His scissors cold-mouth my skin, gumming at the bra strap. I laugh and allow the pill swallower to dig and twist my boobs free from Russian machining.

The bra is cut. Shake, and the straps knock down around my arms, and the bra swings from my wrist to the floor. Dance now and sing the song, the one that turns young cheeks red. Sing:

I was a little dressmaker.
I stitched a wavy pattern.
But now I am an actress
And I've become a slattern.

I look at the boy a little to see of he likes my song and to see how my dance works on him.

He looks back at me—but kindly.

Could be the pills have taken measure of what is sad and sick in a life and dissolved a dose into his soul. He picks up my shirt and brings it around me in a warm and wrapping motion. I can stop the dance now but I don't want to. The truth was not so hard to show, after all, and I can dance and dance for it. Secretive smiling like a drunk, the boy seems to know this, too. Finally, I sit beside him to find my breath, but he has already gone sleepy with pills. I look at this boy, thankful for his audience, but wishing it was Chip I did the dance for.

Chip said import/export. He didn't say what of. He didn't have to. Behind doors, exchanges in corridors, soon Russia is not so foreign. Only with Chip it's worse—with him, I must pronounce ballet.

It's not what you say, but how. Was it how I said what I said that gave the idea?

Dancer.

Conveyor.

Words, they go to the surface, coating with alikeness. Finding the exception in one from the next, this is the place where what we say can make room for what we really are.

Say, I am a Russian. What kind?

With an accent. What kind?

Sure, a Russian accent when I talk to America, but how is it called an accent in Russia, where I never spoke in any other tongue? Is it how I say it or how it sounds, this accent, this scent of outsider that leaves its scent on every language that I speak? Every language except what would be my own—Mother's tongue, blood tongue—a language that I will never know and so can never speak.

Could I make for Chip a place to say what he really is? Say, a man. What kind of man? Good, bad, new, old—newly bad, maybe but never old enough. Hearing accents is an art very much older than the first memory an American has of trees.

What kind of boobs? Large boobs.

Chip likes them small.

Still they are boobs. The nipples are cool, no matter the size, cool against his naked chest that fits so well to mine when I am in his hold. When I am in his hold, the black waters rise and the baby carriage cuts ridges and the milk whitens glass—in his hold, my first memories speak without accent.

I should leave my pots. Chip must learn cooking, to stop taking out.

Possible I will stay a little longer and cook him a meal something hot and teasing on the tongue. Chip could have a taste for it, after all.

Nominated by Tom Filer, Sandra Tsing Loh

FROM *ROSARY*

by BARBARA TRAN

from PLOUGHSHARES

Do I begin at the here and now,
or does the story start
with the first time
my mother took the wheel—
the first woman to drive
in a country where men
are afraid to walk?

My mother's story begins
when the steam rises.
It ends when it's ready.
Taste it. Does it need more salt?

Heat

Today, at sixty-seven, she stands at the stove at work. The heat over-
comes her. She thinks she is standing at the shore. The stream is like
a warm breeze being carried out to sea. My mother hears the seagulls
circling above. She feels the sun on her skin and admires the reflec-
tion on all the shining fish bodies. Her father's men have been col-
lecting the nets for days now, laying the fish out for fermenting. The
gull with the pure white underside swoops toward the fish farthest
away, lands on an overturned boat, its sides beaten and worn, its bot-
tom sunburned like a toddler's face after her first day of work in the
rice fields. Beside the boat, a palm hut, where the fishermen hang

their shirts, and where their wives change when it's time for a break from the scooping and jarring, when their black pants become hot as the sand itself. And then the laughter starts, and the women's bodies uncurl from their stooped positions, their pointed hats falling back, the men treading anxiously in the water as they imagine a ribbon pulling gently at each soft chin.

Bait

Through the eye, my grandfather threads the rusty hook, forces it back through the body of the fish. The tail curves around as if frozen mid-leap. The seagulls never leave. The smell of fish always in the air. To-day, the old man will give them nothing. It is his daughter he is thinking of. My mother is fourteen and beginning to turn heads. Her father thinks she will like the seagull with the pure white underside. He watches the birds, daring one another to come closer. He watches the younger ones in their confusion. The swoop and retreat. He has not fed them for days. Minutes go by, and he thinks the boats will come in soon, scattering the gulls. The year of the Snake is only days away. He would buy his daughter a dove, but she likes the wind. With a quick swoop, a gull grabs the fish in its beak. The old man raps the line around his roughened hands, braces himself for the tug, as the line grows more taut. And suddenly the bird jerks in the sky, wings extended as if it's been shot.

Cage

Easter lilies spill from her thin arms. The flowers and her gloves equally as spotless. This is how it began. My mother would never forget the seagull with the hook through its bill. Often she would recall how wrong the imagination could go. All she had been thinking about was the pure white of its underside. Not the high-pitched cry of a child being separated from all it knows. The best part was seeing it finally take to its wings again. It was still in the cage that her father had built, but she could pretend it had its freedom. It could fly higher than she could reach.

Downpour

She knew it was coming by the way the glass jars shook in the darkness, the occasional flash of lightning, crawling the walls like quick lizards.

A rain so heavy, things would be hammered into the earth. She thought of all the glass jars resting on their shelves, all the hours the men spent, blowing these cylinders for the *nuoc mam* they made from the anchovies they caught, and then, the few drinking glasses they made for themselves on the side when her father wasn't watching. After the rain, the broken pieces would once again have to be melted down and mixed together. And here, her father lay in bed, smoking away the profits. With each breath in, the fishing boats moved farther and farther away. With each breath out, more jars needed to be made, sold. Her father couldn't even hear the thunder. The lightning, warm flashes on his lids, like the sun when he was trying to nap in the afternoon. He thought the glass-blowers earned him a puff on his pipe with each puff on theirs. He should reap the rewards of being an old man, of owning his own fishery. But with each breath, his daughter grows more impossibly beautiful. He knows he will not be able to keep her long.

Safe

The three sisters watch her lean over as they sip their tea, as they try to keep up the conversation, try not to alert her that they are watching as she uncovers the safe, piles the bars of gold to the side, and pulls out the sack of bills, grabbing two bundles and putting the rest back. She covers the safe with the red cloth as before, bowing to the picture of her grandmother. The women think of their brother in Saigon, playing poker in his white jacket, his slicked back hair. They think of the young girls he has loved, the ones he has impregnated, they think of all the angry parents they have faced. Then they think of him married, married to Tran Thi Marie, driving her father's Mercedes; they remember her grandfather and his plot full of banana trees and fruit drying in the sun; they have seen her father's fishing fleet. They think of all the delicious meals they will enjoy when they visit their brother. Marie is a gorgeous woman. They will tell their mother.

Faith

For years, my grandfather thought he could keep my mother by his side. She seemed content with her prayers and fasting. But he didn't know about the couple that sat before her at Mass that Sunday morning. She had noticed them, the man sitting next to the woman as if she were any other. But then, the stolen glances, the passing of a prayer book, the spreading of goose bumps, from the neck down the arms, the woman crossing herself.

The first time my father saw my mother, she was driving the barren countryside of Bien Ho. How vain, he thought to himself: wearing Easter lilies in her hair. What he didn't know was that they actually were Easter lilies, she was on her way to Mass. She wore them year-round to remind herself that Jesus was always risen—if you kept Him alive in your life.

Proof

They were married before her father knew it,
her father smoking opium in the bright sun.
All he could remember
was the white jacket, the black tie,
the boat rocking, the boys reaching,
dragging the net.
The net full of fish.
The fish drying in the sun.
The seagulls swarming like men
honing in on the scent.
The slow peeling of an orange.
Smoke coming from his pipe.
The juice squirting.
The spewing out of pits.
And then, she was packing.

Prayer

My grandfather had always had three women in the kitchen, someone continuously preparing something. Fresh bread, hot banana pudding, sweet rice with coconut. And now his daughter was leaving, and the women were selecting china for her to take. He wondered how this happened. She was the last of his daughters, and he had spoiled her, hoping to keep her for himself. For years, he spent his days, from the moment he woke until the sun began its slow dive into the water, submerged, working the fishing nets, his skin puckered like a mango left in the sun too long. And here, his daughter would still need to watch the gills heave up and down, the gasping at the small mouth. Still, she'd need to chop the head off, blood running down the sides of the cutting board, her hands covered with scales. For years, he tried to keep her hands from coming in contact with anything but the food she ate and the money she counted. Now they would be roasted daily over a fire.

He wondered how crowded her new home would be, how long she would have to live with her in-laws, how such a small child would bear a child. He knew she would find it difficult to breathe in the smog-filled streets of Saigon. He closed the trunk for her, knelt down beside her, pressed a bar of gold into her palm. He wanted her to write as often as possible. She nodded. She wanted to stay, to hold her father's hand, to watch the fishing boats come in, to listen to the seagulls like hungry beggars outside.

Hope

It all began with her driving the barren country roads, barren because the men were too fearful to walk them. Knife blade to the neck, my mother still refused to hand over the pearls her father gave her for her first Christmas as a teen, as a target for unmarried men. Really, what she hoped they wouldn't find was the pearl rosary her mother left behind. She felt the blade bite deeper into her neck: the same place her husband would often bite her the first year they were married, the last year she would think of love as something shared between two people.

After the first child, she would think of duty and responsibility and mirrors. She cared for herself and so, her child. Love remained between her and God. Husbands were meant to be fathers, children to be married off. Her mother's rosary was proof she agreed. The cross was melded from her wedding ring. It was crooked from being slammed in the door as she ran from her husband. One day my mother would hide the same beads beneath her pillow, as if to ward her own husband away, as if after seven children, he might somehow stop.

Hunger

In Saigon, a daughter on each hip, she began to wonder where the rice was going. Leaving one child home sucking her thumb, the other hold-

508

ing her empty belly, my mother hailed a taxi. In front of the cathedral, the pink nails in the car ahead crept across the man's neck, and she recognized both. This was, after all, the man who woke her body. Before him, she knew only the ache of chopping and carrying, of balancing heavy loads. Now there was a different kind of pull, like the sea, and after it, a different kind of heavy load, filling her belly. Of course, she followed him.

*   *   *

Balance

On the way back from the market each day, the pole teeters across her back, a pot on either side. The one on the right, emptied of its *pho;* the one on the left, full of dirty bowls and the leftover dishwater she was too impatient to drain. Cuong skips ahead, his short hair bouncing with each step. She quickens and grabs her youngest son's ear, twisting it, not because he is getting too far ahead, or because he is daydreaming, but because she can't. Her husband gone with the two oldest children, my mother still has four. He lives in a duplex in Manhattan; she sells *pho* for ten cents a bowl and needs someone to hold. Cuong is getting too big, with his slingshots and firecrackers, his patched eye from Tet. Each day she drags my grandmother's bed a little closer to hers, brings a mirror along with dinner to her mother's bedside.

Measure

My mother's recipes are not even close to precise. Everything is in approximate proportion. One portion of *nuoc mam* to three of water and one of vinegar, some lime, a big pour of sugar. Maybe some more. This is in opposition to her determination to keep my father. With this, she was painfully methodical.

When she got off the plane, rosary wound around her left hand, her right dragging Cuong along, did she think about the child growing inside her? I was not yet growing inside her, but she knew I would be soon. She knew also that there was a child growing inside some other woman's womb, and that it would be born first, and that her husband

509

would be there. Still, she had four children in tow, all of whom would cry out "Ba!" on cue. They had had enough rice with *canh* for dinner. Now they were in the United States of America, with all its independence and escalators, its planes, trains, and fast ways of getting away. They weren't letting go.

Epilogue

Brush stroke number 49
and her hair shines like a black cat's.
She can think of nothing
but the days when she wore her hair
above her shoulders, moved her hips
like a boy. And still the men
couldn't help but look. Now
there are so many things
to fit into the frying pan:
the daughter with the red
lingerie rolled inside her dirty
school uniform, the son
with the twisted jaw
and the constant longing
for a cold beer, the husband
she chased in taxicabs,
holding her extended belly
only to finally say, *Please,*
take me home. At seventeen,
my mother counted her Hail Marys
on the little white beads
of her rosary. Now she counts them off
on the heads of her seven children,
counting herself as eight,
and her husband,
as one and ten.

Nominated by Joan Murray

GIRLS LIKE YOU

fiction by JENNIFER MOSES

from ONTARIO REVIEW

THIS YOUR SECOND BABY? New White Lady say. She make a pursed-up face like she taste something bad. Pink lipstick lips all squished together like some worm. It say on your transcript that this your second baby.

Yeah white ho', what of it? Onlies I don't say that. Don't say nothin. They hates that, when you don't say nothin. It say fuck-all on my transcript. Ain't no transcript say I got no baby. First White Lady gone tell her. First White Lady even uglier than new White Lady: teeth all yellowish, dent down her forehead like she hit with a truck, big butt and no tits. Titless Wonder I called her.

Full name?

But I just gives her more nothin. Say on my transcript full name.

Okay, Retha, she say. You want to play dumb, play dumb. Your life.

Fuck right 'bout that, bitch.

Only I got a piece of paper here from the School Board say it my job to educate you while you pregnant. Would you like to see it?

All I like to see is Oprah. On any minute. Momma and Jancine (that my baby girl) sitting in the front room right now warmin' up to watch. Peoples gets on say the stupidest thing. And old Oprah sleek and fat like a hog and rich too, but still no man wants her. I like to know why? Maybe she secretly like the womens? Still, I like to get on the Oprah show, say: Where I come froms, the momma do it in fronts of the childruns, see? Dat way we knows how to give good pussy. See old Oprah's mouth drop open. Hear her talkin' all that feelings shit.

That a good one.

New White Lady snort, wrinkle up her nose. Say: Says on your transcript you in the seventh.

Read real good, don't you?

Say on your transcript you fifteen years old. How come you still in the seventh?

You know everything, bitch, so you tell me. Only again I don't say that. I don't say nothin. Let her guess.

Okay, she say after a little bit more time pass. Now I can hear the TV real good: the Oprah song has come on, and the clapping from the audience. Shit! So hot in this kitchen, feel like I stuck in somebody's bad breath. New White Lady sweating, too. Only she actin' like she *pretending* she ain't sweating. Like it beneath her.

Whole lot of no talkin going on here. Sure wish I had a Coke and a slice.

You think you the first pregnant teenager I ever taught? New White lady finally say. (You leave 'em be long enough, they always start blubbering.) You think you so tough? You think at fifteen you seen everything?

Ooh my, but she worked up now. Face red. Forehead shiny. Ugly old gray-yellow hair frizzing. Probably dried up inside, that why she so mean. No juice left. That what happens when you git old.

Fine, Retha, we'll just sit here for an hour while you think about it. Then tomorrow I want a paper on the subject.

That when I git mad. Bad enough bein' bossed at school from that snot-nosed Liver Lips (real name Ms. Milton). Bad enough sittin' through Algebra with that fat-assed Ms. Gireaux (I calls her Miss Girdle). But this my kitchen; this my house; this my baby.

You got a booger hangin out, I finally say.

What?

A big gooby one. Hangin out your nose.

New White lady swipe at her nose with the back of her hand, then reach down to her pocketbook, lookin' for a tissue. Then she wipe her nose, real careful like. Tissue all wadded up, like it used before. Some of these people, their hygienic care ain't too good.

I big so no ones mess with me too much, not anymore. Didn't no one at school knows I had a baby growin' insides me. Just kept puttin' on them big old shirts, and no one can tells the difference. I knew, though. Your monthlies stop, mean something going down. (Not like Jancine, that my baby girl. When I pregnant with Jancine,

I too little to know anything. How I know I pregnant? Now I experienced.) Ain't no one at school gonna mess with me nohows. Then one days it so hot and in the middle of Social Studies class teacher droning on and on, she won't never shut up, that Liver Lips, and then she looks right at me and she say: Miss LaMonte? Are you with us today?

No, I am a clone of Miss LaMonte, you blind?

Class crack up at that one. But Liver Lips, she just go on.

Perhaps then you can tell us where Miss LaMonte went? Perhaps she's on Mars?

She a Martian, yeah. She come down zap your butt.

(No liver-lipped Ms. Milton gonna get the best of me. She think she better than the rest us niggers. Talkin' all the times about when she was All-Honors at Southern. Right down the road, she always saying. Historical black school, she say. Who care?)

Do you have your book today, Miss LaMonte? Or did you perhaps leave it on Mars?

(All those little kids lookin' at me. Cause I kind of a hero to them, being so much bigger. Liver Lips with her tight-wrapped hair put me in mind of aluminum foil. I could take her down in ten seconds flat.)

Book here, I say.

Perhaps, then, you could tell us what system of government we have here in the United States of America?

Fuck the United States of America. This ain't no United States of America. This here Baton Rouge. Woman think I can't read a map.

So I says: the answer is—and then I say the first thing that comes to mind—Ain't nobody, ain't *nobody*, can beat our low everyday prices!

Oooh. Kids falling out laughin'. Liver Lips face turnin' Coca-Cola colored, looking like she about to start blubbering.

But then I gets to feelin' woozy-like, like my head fill with bubbles, then my throat fill up too, then I hot down the back of my neck and nex' thing I know I wakin' up all them boogery pimple-face kids lookin' down at me and Liver Lips herself holdin' up my head.

Takes me down to school nurse. School nurse dumb as they come. School nurse takes my temperature, like I got fever. Makes me breathe in and out. Ask me all kind of dumb-butted questions: have breakfast? What you eat? (I eat four Chips Ahoy.) Stupid cow finally says, You pregnant again girl? Two days later I out of school again, back in the Special Program for Girls Like You.

513

First White Lady was always asking stupid questions. Where you from? she say. Dumb bitch. Where I from? Ain't she sitting in my house? North Twelve Street, Baton Rouge, Louisiana. No, she say, I mean, where your *people* from? What part of the country? What part Africa?

What I want to know about Africa? Africa where they got all thems voo-doo peoples dying of AIDS, not just the homos and whores but the women and children too. Africa where they got all that dying, and I mean every day. She think I stupid? She think I don't know my World Events?

What part of the South? Did your ancestors work the plantations? It's your history, it might be interesting to find out.

Yo Momma. Where great-great-great-great-grandmammy born? She come over on the Mayflower? So I just looked at First White Lady like she some ghost all covered with slobbery-spit.

(First White Lady kept wanting to know who Jancine daddy is. But I never would tell. She kept shaking her head. Only twelve years old, she say. That a tragedy.)

Truth is, I didn't really knows I got a baby inside me first time it happen, with Jancine, until Miss Caesar who live next door ask me. Then she tell my momma. Then the shit really hit the fan.

Who the daddy? First White Lady say. Then she nag me to go see some Jew lady social worker she know.

How this happen? Tell me, she say.

Momma said she be right back, but she didn't come right back. She gone all day. She missed Oprah, missed Price Is Right, missed Fresh Prince. Me and Oline (that my sister) went and got us some Super Fry chicken for dinner, ate it right there. Momma gone when we get back to the house. Her boyfriend there, waitin on her. Watching TV. Man send Oline out to get mo' chickens. That when he do it to me.

Man put his ding-dong in you, white slime squirt out, you can get pregnant, everybody know that. I always big girl, even at twelve I got big titties, almost as big as Momma's, and big hips, so I not sure what is what, monthlies or no monthlies. What you doing to me? But man say hush gal this ain't nothin to worry 'bout. Man say: quiet little bitch, I ain't gonna hurt you none, I your friend. I love you, why I want hurt you? Man smelled bad, too, like something rotten. Like rotten fruit. Then man say: yo momma like it like this. Man say: apple don't fall far from the tree. Man say: you a woman now.

514

Momma real mad when Principal call her that first time. What you done do girl? You shame me? Face turning all kinds of purple. Me and her, we gotta sit in those real slimy chairs they got in Principal's office, back of our legs sticking to the cushion, while Principal tell Momma about the Special Program for Girls Like You.

Say: School Board increase Special Needs Funding. Say: School Board sending Special-Train teachers right to your Place of Residence.

Later Momma and the man yellin' then POP, Momma down. Man gone. Momma rubbing her cheek and crying over that man like he some superhero. Ugly man with sour smell, color of eggplant. I only twenny-eight years old don't I have no right 'round here? Ain't I got a right to have me a life? She in her bed, cryin' all night 'cause that rotten-fruit smellin' nigger gone and me and Oline have to say hush now, Momma, it get better. (Oline bring her two pieces ice in a towel for her cheek and a bottle of Budweiser.)

Cryin' and yellin' that she didn't raise no girl to be no ho'. Then Miss Caesar who live next door come runnin' over say: You blind? Everyone know that man no good.

And *that* how I get Jancine.

I almosts feels sorry for New White Lady. She try, I say that for her. Drives up every day three o'clock sharp in that Chevrolet minivan, color of a blue popsicle. She got her windows rolled up, her doors locked. Air conditioning going full blast. Looks right and left. Then walks right up to the front porch, calls through the screen. Retha? Retha? It me. Mrs. Warton. (I call her Mrs. Wart. Oline calls her Mrs. Fart.)

Baby kicking? she say.

Drinking nuff milk? Eating right? Sleeping?

She put the ends of her thumbs together and the rest of her fingers go straight up and she say B go this way and D go this way just like a bed. Her hands suppose to be the bed. The silent E make the vowel say it name, she say. What she think I am, two years old?

She say she got a daughter jus' my age and two sons too. Name Elizabeth and Joe Jr. and Chuck, like up-chuck. She say Elizabeth want to be a nurse when she grow up. What you wan' be, she say? You smart, she say. You smarter than you think.

Every day she come I think she ain't gon come no more. She come all the ways from Bocage or the Country Club Louisiana or some fancy do-daw place with swimming pools in every backyard barbecue pits family room with giant color remote control TV and them built-in bars and wall-to-wall carpeting so soft you feel like yo' feet are melting so what she know about me? One day I gon git myself a Cadillac or a Lincoln Town Car and I jus' gon cruise on by old Mrs. Wart's house and say hello.

Last time when I pregnant with Jancine my tits got real big but they didn't droop none. Now they big and droopy-like. Couple mean kids callin' me Great Fruit but I come back on 'em kick 'em in the nuts they don't call me no Great Fruit no more. What them little kids with their little doinkers hanging between their legs know 'bout no sex? Girls getting all worked up about doin' the thang-thing but ain't no great thing once you does it. First it hurt then maybe you git to liking it some but then it all over jes like that anyways, and you panties wet all day long just from the slime going drip drip drip out your pussy. Boys wanting it bad and if you hangin' with the main man you gots to do what he say and my man say, What you 'fraid of Retha, ain't you my woman? You no baby no more you fourteen years old, and, he feeling me all over, feeling my titties and my butt and his hand up my pants and I caint barely see Family Matters but it a dumb one anyways I seen it before. We gets to doin' it, know what I say? His name Scooter. His real name somethin' else but everyone call him Scooter. I seen him around. All the girls knows him. Then one day he come up to me he say: Who you? Looking me over all slow. I say: I Janet Jackson, want my autograph? Soon we laughing. Then we doin' it. At school people sure enough looks up to me 'cause I hanging with the man got the stuff. Got him the look. Got him the CDs. Got him the car. We all over in that car and he good-looking too. Don't smell like no rotten-fruit man. Don't smell like no dead thing. Scooter got a fine, clean, fresh smell, cause he clean all over. Clean inside and out. Shower three time a day. Wash that car till it shine. Yes ma'am and no ma'am to his Maw Maw who he lives with. The lady work cleaning in the Hilton. Don't take no drugs either. Don't smoke no smokes. New pair sneakers every other week he say he don't like things old and scuffed-up none. He sweet to Jancine too. He take her and me drivin' up the river past all them stinking refineries past all them sugar cane fields and the paper plant rotten egg smell coming out of it and he jus' laughin'. Say he ain't gonna work no paper plant. Say he ain't gonna be no garbage man or no janitor or gardener. Say he goin' places, and he is.

I feel like some somebody now. I sure does.

Come home Momma sucking on that can of Budweiser. Oline goin' up and down the street on that fancy new bicycle with the Pocahontas wheels, her little-girl-butt tight and high in the air. Gotta keep an eye on Momma now when she in these mean mood sucking on Budweiser and no man about she say she off men for good! She and Miss Caesar from next door talking late at night and Miss Caesar shaking her old head (she so old nothin' left but bone) saying You give yourselves a while, honey, you ain't the first woman gonna make it by herself. But Momma gettin' meaner and meaner one day she throws all my new clothes that Scooter done buys me out the closet calling me ho' this and ho' that. Another day Jancine and I in bed sleeping she start whapping me with the back of her hairbrush. Why she go do that for? I sock her, she crumple down. I in deep shit now but what she got go bust my butt with her hairbrush? So I say goodbye I don't need you gonna go where I wanted. But over North Street Maw Maw says No teenage slut staying 'round here with no crying baby. So now I got no place to go but Scooter say it okay, you come back when the old lady go to work. She work late shift. And that just what I did. And that very night we do it in her bed and he just laugh and laugh.

That was the happy time.

New White lady got some of the dog-ugliest clothes I ever seen. Shoes like them nurses wear, rubber wavy soles. Glasses make her look like a frog. Hair like a dirty gray mop. And them legs: ugly blue veins stickin' out of them. She don't even notice. She tell me she got a degree in Education and another in Social Work. Like she some kind of genius.

You can trust me, Retha, she say. I just give her the look. She don't even blink.

You wants to go back to school, you got to keep plugging away, she say. Give me a book. Book 'bout nigger talking to God. Turn into lesbo at end and make these clothes. Lady nigger wrote it, her picture on the back. I hates that book, I tell New White Lady. Book called Color Purple. What Color Purple? Ain't bout no *purple*. What kind of dumb-ass title. Should be called: Nigger Git Fucked By Step-Daddy Turn Dyke.

How it make you *feel?* she say. Just like on Oprah. Wants to know my feelings.

Make me good and angry. Make me want to throw that there book into the toilet. Nigger lady wrote it, but wouldn't never happen that way. Girl never would git rich makin' no clothes, doing the thang-thang with women, rubbin' their pussies together, make me sick.

517

She give me another book. This one called Bluest Eye. She say, What you think? I don't tell her it make me cry.

When Jancine come thought I on fire. Hurt like I never done hurt before. Hot pain in my spine. Water rushin' between my legs. Who the daddy who the daddy? Nurse want to know. But I tells, then what? Then Momma come kill me for sure. Who the daddy? This chile ain't old enough for no baby, she barely out of diapers. Twelve years old, ain't that a damn shame. Where her momma? (It Oline call 911 'cause Momma cold out on the bed). Hospital nice, though. Where they put me after Jancine got born, prettiest room I ever saw, with pink curtains and flowery wallpaper. Could have stayed there forever. Chocolate and vanilla ice cream. All I got to do is ring a button on my bed nurse come give me a Coke. But they make me leave. Then Jancine she up scream-ing all night, and me bleeding out my privates, and Momma saying she too young to be nobody's grandmother. It gonna hurt again, I guess. Time coming. I try not to think about it too much, all that hot pain.

But the thing hurt most of all was when Scooter, he start takin' up with this bitch calls herself Raven. Cow mo' like it. One them girl-cows always mooing after him. Tell me I a slut and a whore. Then I kicked out of school and no ones talks to me no more. I in the Program for Girls Like You. Then those neighborhood boys whispering; Great Fruit. But I fix them. At home, Momma doing nothing but sucking on that beer bottle, gittin' fat. Oline growing her own pair titties. Jancine crying. New White Lady giving me books to read, but I don't tell no-body about them, they mine. New White Lady be gone soon, too. I al-most glad when Scooter done git hisself killed.

Nominated by Ontario Review, Philip Booth, H.E. Francis, Joyce Carol Oates

MONOLOGUE OF THE FALCONER'S WIFE

by COLETTE INEZ

from CONNECTICUT REVIEW

As was my duty, I oversaw the carting in of birds
to taste in broths and cunning pies.
What does the falcon owe to the falconer?
Diversions, my lord, and uses for your hand and eye,

that you may watch blood spurt and confess
to the priest your love of the kill.
And I knew what the falconer owed to the falcon.
Jesses strapped to its leg, a leash, a solid block,

a covering to slip off just before flight.
Spoils of the kill, hearts of quail, pheasant necks.
These I have split with your kin and curs
slavering at tables piled with glistening meat and bones,

knowing you to plant your priapus in every arse
that sits at court, into sheep should they dance the quadrille
for you. Lord, I would sail home to my clan and sup on eels,
and boiled cod. Send a falcon as solace for grief

at a barren daughter's return, and tell the priest
who prodded me to speak of our marriage bed,
say to him I am released
from that vassalage.

Nominated by Joan Murray, Pamela Stewart

ERNIE'S ARK

fiction by MONICA WOOD

from GLIMMER TRAIN STORIES

E RNIE WAS AN ANGRY MAN. He felt his anger as something apart from him, like an urn of water balanced on his head, a precarious weight that affected his gait, the set of his shoulders, his willingness to move through a crowd. He was angry at the melon-faced CEO from New York City who had closed a paper mill all the way up in Maine—a decision made, Ernie was sure, in that fancy restaurant atop the World Trade Center where Ernie had taken his wife, Marie, for their forty-second wedding anniversary last May, another season, another life. Every Thursday as he stood in line at Manpower Services to wait for his unemployment check he thought of that jelly-assed CEO whose name he could never manage—McKay or McCoy or some such—yucking it up at a table decked to the nines in bleached linen and phony silver, figuring out all the ways he could cut a man off at the knees two years before retirement.

Oh, yes, he was angry. At the deadbeats, and no-accounts who stood in line with him, the Davis boy who couldn't look a man in the eye, the Shelton girl with hair dyed so bright you could light a match on her ponytail. There were others in line—pipefitters and tinsmiths and machine tenders booted out of the mill like diseased dogs—but he couldn't bear to look at them, so he reserved his livid stare for the people in line who least resembled himself.

And he was angry at the kids from Broad Street who cut through his yard on their dirt bikes day after day, leaving moats of mud through the flowery back lawn Marie had sprinkled a season ago with Meadow-in-a-Can. And he was angry with the police department, who didn't give a hoot about Marie's wrecked grass. He'd even tried City Hall, where an overpaid blowhard, whose uncle had worked beside Ernie for ten years on the Number Five, had all but laughed in his face.

When he arrived at the hospital after collecting his weekly check, Marie was being bathed by a teenaged orderly. He had seen his wife in all manner of undress during their forty-two years together, yet it filled him with shame to see the yellow hospital sponge applied to her diminishing body by a uniformed kid who was younger than their youngest grandchild. He went to the lobby to wait, picking up a newspaper from among the litter of magazines.

It was some sort of college paper, filled with mean political comics and smug picture captions fashioned to embarass the President, but it had a separate section on the arts, Marie's favorite subject. She had dozens of coffee-table books stowed in her sewing room, and their house was filled with framed prints of strange objects—melted watches and spent shoelaces and sad, deserted diners—that he never liked but had nonetheless come to think of as old friends. In forty-two years he had never known her to miss a Community Concert or an exhibit at the library, and every Sunday of their married life Ernie had brought in the paper, laid it on the kitchen table, and fished out the arts section to put next to Marie's coffee cup.

The college paper was printed on dirty newsprint—paper from out of state, he surmised. He scanned the cheap, see-through pages, fixing on an announcement for an installation competition, whatever that was. The winning entry would be displayed to the public at the university. Pictured was last year's winner, a tangle of pipes and sheet metal that looked as if somebody had hauled a miniature version of the Number Five machine out of the mill, twisted it into a thousand ugly pieces, then left it to weather through five hundred hailstorms. Not that it would matter now if somebody did. *The Burden of Life,* this installation was called, by an artist who most likely hadn't yet moved out of his parents' house. He thought Marie would like it, though—she had always been a woman who understood people's intentions—so he removed the picture with his jackknife and tucked it into his shirt pocket and faltered his way back up the hall and into her room, where she was sitting up, weak and clean.

"Can you feature this?" he asked, showing her the clipping.

She smiled. *"The Burden of Life?"*

"He should've called it *The Burden of My Big Head.*"

She laughed, and he was glad, and his day took the tiniest turn. "Philistine," she said. "You always were such a philistine, Ernie." She often referred to him in the past tense, as if he were the one departing.

That night he hung the clipping on the refrigerator before taking Pumpkin Pie, Marie's dottering Yorkshire terrier, for its evening walk. He often waited until nightfall for this walk, so mortified was he to drag this silly-named pushbroom of an animal at the end of a thin red leash. The dog walked with prissy little steps on pinkish feet that resembled ballerina slippers. He had observed so many men just like himself over the years, men in retirement walking wee, quivery dogs over the streets of their neighborhood, a wrinkled plastic bag in their free hand; they might as well have been holding a sign above their heads: Widower.

The night was eerie and silent, this end of town strangely naked without the belching smokestacks of Atlantic Pulp & Paper curling up from the valley, an upward, omnipresent cloud rising like a smoke signal, an offering to God. Cancer City, a news reporter once called this place, but gone now was the steam, the smoke, the rising cloud, the heaps and heaps of wood stacked in the railyard, even the smell—the smell of money, Ernie called it—all gone. Every few weeks there was word of negotiation—another fancy-restaurant meeting between McCoy's boys and Atlantic's alleged union—but Ernie held little hope of recovering the bulk of his pension. *For Sale* signs were popping up even in this neighborhood of old people. The city, once drenched with ordinary hopes and good money, was beginning to furl like an autumn leaf.

As he turned up his walk he caught the kids from Broad Street crashing again through his property, this time roaring away so fast he could hear a faint shudder from the backyard trees. "Sonsabitches!" he hollered, shaking his fist like the mean old man in the movies. He stampeded into the backyard, where Marie's two apple trees, brittle and untrained, sprouted from the earth in such rootlike twists that they seemed to have been planted upside down. He scanned the weedy lawn, dotted with hopeful clumps of Marie's wildflowers and the first of the fallen leaves, and saw blown down everywhere, spindly parts of branches scattered like bodies on a battlefield. Planted when their son was born, the trees had never yielded a single decent apple, and now they were being systematically mutilated by a pack of ill-bred boys. He picked up a branch and a few sticks, and by the time he reached his kitchen he was weeping, pounding his fist on the table, cursing a God who would let a woman like Marie, a big-boned girl who was sweetness itself, wither beneath the death-white sheets of Maine Medical, twelve long miles from home.

He sat in the kitchen deep into evening. The dog curled up on Marie's chair and snored. He remembered Marie's laughter from the afternoon and tried to harness it, hear it anew, make it last. The sticks lay sprawled and messy on the table in front of him, their leaves stalled halfway between greenery and dust. All of a sudden—and, oh, it was sweet!—Ernie had an artistic inspiration. He stood up with the shock of it, for he was not an artistic man. The sticks, put together at just the right angle, resembled the hull of a boat. He turned them one way, then another, admiring his idea, wishing Marie were here to witness it.

Snapping on the floodlights, he jaunted into the backyard to collect the remaining sticks, hauling them into the house a bouquet at a time. He took the clipping down from the fridge and studied the photograph, trying to get a sense of scale and size. Gathering the sticks, he descended the stairs to the cellar, where he spent most of the night twining sticks and branches with electrical wire. The dog sat at attention, its wet eyes fixed on Ernie's work. By morning the installation was finished. It was the most beautiful thing Ernie had ever seen.

The university was only four blocks from the hospital, but Ernie had trouble navigating the maze of one-way roads on campus, and found the art department only by following the directions of a frightening girl whose tender lips had been pierced with small gold rings. By the time he entered the office of the university art department, he was sweating, hugging his beautiful boat to his chest.

"Excuse me?" said a young man at the desk. This one had a ring through each eyebrow.

"My installation," Ernie said, placing it on the desk. "For the competition." He presented the newspaper clipping like an admission ticket.

"Uh, I don't think so."

"Am I early?" Ernie asked, feeling foolish. The deadline was six weeks away; he hadn't the foggiest idea how these things were supposed to go.

"This isn't an installation," the boy said, flickering his gaze over the boat. "It's—well, I don't know what it is, but it's not an installation."

"It's a boat," Ernie said. "A boat filled with leaves."

"Are you in Elderhostel?" the boy asked. "They're upstairs, fifth floor."

"I want to enter the contest," Ernie said. And by God, he did; he had never won so much as a cake raffle in his life, and didn't like one bit the pileup of things he appeared to be losing.

"I like your boat," said a girl stacking books in a corner. "But he's right, it's not an installation." She spread her arms and smiled. "Installations are big."

Ernie turned to face her, a freckled redhead. She reminded him of his granddaughter, who was somewhere in Oregon sharing her medicine cabinet with an unemployed piano player. "Let me see," the girl said, plucking the clipping from his hand. "Oh, okay. You're talking about the Corthell Competition. This is more of a professional thing."

"Professional?"

"I myself wouldn't *dream* of entering, okay?" offered the boy, who rocked backed in his chair, arms folded like a CEO's. "All the entries come through this office, and most of them are awesome. Museum quality." He made a small, self-congratulating gesture with his hand. "We see the entries even before the judges do."

"One of my professors won last year," the girl said, pointing out the window. "See?"

Ernie looked. There it was, huge in real life—nearly as big as the actual Number Five, in fact, a heap of junk flung without a thought into the middle of a campus lawn. It did indeed look like a Burden.

"You couldn't tell from the picture," Ernie said, reddening. "In the picture it looked like some sort of tabletop size. Something you might put on top of your TV."

The girl smiled. Ernie could gather her whole face without stumbling over a single gold hoop. He took this as a good sign, and asked, "Let's say I did make something of size. How would I get it over here? Do you do pickups, something of that nature?"

She laughed, but not unkindly. "You don't actually build it unless you win. What you do is write up a proposal with some sketches. Then, if you win, you build it right here, on site." She shrugged. "The *process* is the whole entire idea of the installation, okay? The whole entire community learns from witnessing the *process*."

In this office, where "process" was clearly the most important word in the English language, not counting "okay," Ernie felt suddenly small. "Is that so," he said, wondering who learned what from the heap of tin Professor Life-Burden had processed onto the lawn.

"Oh, wait, one year a guy *did* build off site," said the boy, ever eager to correct the world's misperceptions. "Remember that guy?"

"Yeah," the girl said. She turned to Ernie brightly. "One year a guy put his whole installation together at his studio and sent photographs. He didn't win, but the winner got pneumonia or something and couldn't follow through, and this guy was runner-up, so he trucked it here in a U-Haul."

"It was a totem," the boy said solemnly. "With a whole mess of wire things sticking out of it."

"I was a freshman," the girl said by way of an explanation Ernie couldn't begin to fathom. He missed Marie intensely, as if she were already gone.

Ernie peered through the window, hunting for the totem. "Kappa Delts trashed it last Homecoming," the girl said, "These animals have no respect for art." She handed back the clipping. "So, anyway, that really wasn't so stupid after all, what you said."

"Well," said the boy, "good luck, okay?"

As Ernie bumbled out the door, the girl called after him, "It's a nice boat, though. I like it."

At the hospital he set the boat on Marie's window sill, explaining his morning. "Oh, Ernie," Marie crooned. "You old—you old surprise, you."

"They wouldn't take it," he said. "It's not big enough. You have to write the thing up, and make sketches and whatnot."

"So why don't you?"

"Why don't I what?"

"Make sketches and whatnot."

"Hah! I'd make it for real. Nobody does anything real anymore. I'd pack it into the back of my truck and haul it there myself. A guy did that once."

"Then make it for real."

"I don't have enough branches."

"Then use something else."

"I just might."

"Then do it." She was smiling madly now, fully engaged in their old, intimate arguing, and her eyes made bright blue sparks from her papery face. He knew her well, he realized, and saw what she was thinking: Ernie, there is some life left after everything seems to be gone. Really, there is. And that he could see this, just a little, and that she could see him seeing it, buoyed him. He thought he might even detect some pink fading into her cheeks.

He stayed through lunch, and was set to stay for supper until Marie remembered her dog and made him go home. As he turned from her bed, she said, "Wait. I want my ark." She lifted her finger to the window sill, where the boat glistened in the cheesy city light. And he saw that she was right: it *was* an ark, high and round and jammed with hope. He placed it in her arms and left it there, hoping it might sweeten her dreams.

When he reached his driveway he found fresh tire tracks rutted by an afternoon rain, running in a rude diagonal from the back of the house across the front yard. He sat in the truck for a few minutes, counting the seconds of his rage, watching the dog's jangly shadow in the dining-room window. He counted to two hundred, checked his watch, then hauled himself out to fetch the dog. He set the dog on the seat next to him—in a better life it would have been a Doberman named Rex—and gave it a kiss on its wiry head. "That's from her," he said, and then drove straight to the lumberyard.

Ernie figured that Noah himself was a man of the soil and probably didn't know spit about boatbuilding. In fact, Ernie's experience in general (forty years of tending machinery, fixing industrial pipe the size of tree trunks, assembling Christmas toys for his sons and then his grandchildren, remodeling bathrooms, and building bird boxes and planters and a sunporch to please Marie) probably had Noah's beat in about a dozen ways. He figured he had the will and enough good tools to make a stab at a decent ark, and in a week's time had most of a hull completed beneath a makeshift staging. It was not a hull he would care to float, but he thought of it as a decent artistic representation of a hull; and even more important, it was big enough to qualify as an installation, if he had the guidelines right. He covered the hull with the bargain-priced tongue-and-groove boards he picked up at the lumberyard, four footers left over from people who'd wanted eights. He worked from sunup to noon, then drove to the hospital to give Marie a progress report. Often he turned on the floodlights in the evenings and worked till midnight or one. Working in the open air, without the iron skull of the mill over his head, made him feel like a newly sprung prisoner. He let the dog patter around and around the growing apparition, and sometimes he even chuckled at the animal's apparent capacity for wonder. The hateful boys from Broad Street loitered with their bikes at the back of the yard, and as the thing grew in size they more often than not opted for the long way 'round.

At eleven o'clock on the second day of the second week, a middle-aged man pulled up in a city car. He ambled down the walk and along the side yard, a clipboard and notebook clutched under one arm. The dog cowered at the base of one of the trees, its dime-sized eyes blackened with fear.

"You Mr. Ernest Whitten?" the man asked Ernie.

Ernie put down his hammer and climbed down from the deck by way of a gangplank that he had constructed in a late night fit of creativity.

"I'm Dan Little, from the city," the man said, extending his hand.

"Well," Ernie said, astonished. He pumped the man's hand. "It's about time." He looked at the bike tracks, which had healed over for the most part, dried into faint, innocent-looking scars from two weeks of fine weather. "Not that it matters now." Ernie said. "They don't even come through much anymore."

Mr. Little consulted his notebook. "I don't follow," he said.

"Aren't you here about those hoodlums tearing up my wife's yard?"

"I'm from code enforcement."

"Pardon?"

Mr. Little squinted up at the ark. "You need a building permit for this, Mr. Whitten. Plus the city has a twenty-five foot setback requirement for any new buildings.

Ernie twisted his face into disbelief an expression that felt uncomfortably familiar; lately the entire world astonished him.

"The lot's only fifty feet wide as it is," he protested.

"I realize that, Mr. Whitten," Mr. Little shrugged apologetically. "I'm afraid you're going to have to take it down."

Ernie tipped back his cap to scratch his head. "It isn't a building. It's an installation."

"Say what?"

"An installation. I'm hauling it up to the college when I'm done. Figure I'll have to rent a flatbed or something. It's a little bigger than I counted on."

Mr. Little began to look nervous. "I'm sorry, Mr. Whitten, I still don't follow." He kept glancing back at the car.

"It's an ark," Ernie said enunciating, although he could see how the ark might be mistaken for a building at this stage. Especially if you weren't really looking, which this man clearly wasn't. "It's an ark," Ernie repeated.

Mr. Little's face took a heavy downward turn. "You're not zoned for boatbuilding," he sighed, writing something on the official-pink papers attached to his clipboard.

Ernie glanced at the car. In the driver's seat had appeared a pony-sized yellow Labrador retriever, its quivering nose faced dead forward as if it were planning to set that sucker into gear and take off into the wild blue yonder.

"That your dog?" Ernie asked.

Mr. Little nodded.

"Nice dog," Ernie said.

"This one's yours, I take it?" Mr. Little pointed at Marie's dog, who had scuttled out from the tree and hidden behind Ernie's pants leg.

"My wife's," Ernie told him. "She's in the hospital."

"I'm sorry to hear that," Mr. Little said. "I'm sure she'll be on the mend in no time."

"Doesn't look like it," Ernie said, wondering why he didn't just storm the hospital gates, do something sweeping and biblical, stomp through those clean corridors and defy doctor's orders and pick her up with his bare hands and bring her home.

Mr. Little scooched down and made clicky sounds at Marie's dog, who nosed out from behind Ernie's leg to investigate.

"What's his name?" he asked.

"It's, well, it's Pumpkin Pie. My wife named him."

"That's Junie," Mr. Little said, nudging his chin toward the car. "I bought her the day I got divorced, ten years ago. She's a helluva lot more faithful than my wife ever was."

"I never had problems like that," Ernie said.

Mr. Little got to his feet and shook his head at Ernie's ark. "Listen, about this, this—"

"Ark," Ernie said.

"You're going to have do something, Mr. Whitten. At the very least, you'll have to go down to City Hall, get a building permit, and then follow the regulations. Just don't tell them it's a boat. Call it a storage shed or something."

Ernie tipped back his cap again. "I don't suppose it's regulation to cart your dog all over kingdom come on city time."

"Usually she sleeps in the back," Mr. Little said sheepishly.

"I'll tell you what," Ernie said. "You leave my ark alone and I'll keep shut about the dog."

Mr. Little looked sad. "Listen," he said, "people can do what they want as far as I care. But you've got neighbors out here complaining about the floodlights and the noise."

Ernie looked around, half expecting to see the dirt-bike gang sniggering behind their fists someplace out back. But all he saw were *For Sale* signs yellowing from disuse, and the sagging rooftops of his neighbors' houses, their shades drawn against the new, clean-air smell of unemployment.

Mr. Little ripped a sheet off his clipboard and handed it to Ernie. "Look, just consider this a real friendly warning, would you? And just for the record, I hate my job, but I haven't been at it long enough to quit."

Ernie watched him amble back to the car and say something to the dog, who gave her master a walloping with her broad pink tongue. He watched them go, remembering suddenly that he'd seen Mr. Little before, somewhere in the mill—the bleachery maybe, or strolling in the dim recesses near the Number Eight, his face flushed and shiny under his yellow hardhat, clipboard at the ready. Now here he was, harassing senior citizens on behalf of the city. His dog probably provided him with the only scrap of self-respect he could ferret out in a typical day.

Ernie ran a hand over the rough surface of his ark, remembering that Noah's undertaking had been a result of God's despair. God was sorry he'd messed with any of it, the birds of the air and beasts of the forest and especially the two-legged creatures who insisted on lying and cheating and killing their own brothers. Still, God had found one man, one man and his family, worth saving, and therefore had deemed a pair of everything else worth saving, too. "Come on, dog," he said. "We're going to get your mother."

As happened so often, in so many small, miraculous ways in their forty-two years together, Marie had out-thought him. When he got to her room she was fully dressed, her overnight bag perched primly next to her on the bone-white bed, the ark cradled into her lap and tipped on its side. "Ernie," she said, stretching her arms straight out. "Take me home."

He bore her home at twenty-five miles an hour, aware of how every pock in the road rose up to meet her fragile, flesh-wanting spine. He eased her out of the car and carried her over their threshold. He filled all the bird feeders along the sunporch out back, and carried her over to survey the ark. These were her two requests.

By morning she looked better. The weather—the warmest fall on record—held. He propped her on a chaise lounge on the sunporch in the brand-new flannel robe their son's wife had sent from California, then wrapped her in a blanket, so that she looked like a benevolent pod person from a solar system where warmth and decency ruled. The dog nestled in her lap, eyes half-closed in ecstasy.

He propped her there so she could watch him work—her third request. And work he did, feeling the way he had when they were first dating and he would remove his shirt to burrow elaborately into the tangled guts of his forest green 1950 Pontiac. He forgot that he was building the ark for the contest, and how much he wanted to win, and his rage fell like dead leaves from his body as he felt the sunshiny presence of Marie watching him work. He moved one of Marie's feeders to the deck of the ark because she wanted him to know the tame and chittery company of chickadees. The sun shone and shone; the yard did not succumb to the dun colors of fall; the tracks left by the dirt bikes resembled nothing more ominous than the faintest prints left by dancing birds. Ernie unloaded some more lumber, a stack of roofing shingles, a small door. He had three weeks till deadline, and in this strange, blessed season, he meant to make it.

Marie got better. She sat up, padded around the house a little, ate real food. Several times a day he caught a sharp squeak floating down from the sunporch as she conversed with one of her girlfriends, or with her sister down from Lewiston, or with their son over the phone, or with the visiting nurse. He would look up, see her translucent white hand raised toward him—*It's nothing, Ernie, just go back to whatever you were doing*—and recognize the sound after the fact as a strand of her old laughter, high and ecstatic and small town, like her old self.

"It happens," the nurse told him when he waylaid her on the front walk. "They get a burst of energy toward the end sometimes."

He didn't like this nurse, the way she called Marie "they." He thought of adding her to the list of people and things he'd grown so accustomed to railing against, but because his rage was gone there was no place to put her. He returned to the ark, climbed onto the deck, and began to nail the last shingles to the shallow pitch of the roof. Marie's voice floated out again, and he looked up again, and her hand rose again, and he nodded again, hoping she could see his smiling, his damp collar, the handsome knot of his forearm. He was wearing the clothes he wore to work back when he was working, a grass-colored gabardine shirt and pants—his "greens," Marie called them. In some awful way he recognized this as one of the happiest times of his life; he was brimming with industry and connected to nothing but this one woman, this one patch of earth. When it was time for Marie's lunch he climbed down from the deck and wiped his hands over his work pants. Mr. Little was standing a few feet away, a camera raised to his face. "What's this?" Ernie asked.

Mr. Little lowered the camera. "For our records."

Ernie thought on this for a moment. "I'm willing to venture there's nothing like this in your records."

"Not so far," Mr. Little said. He ducked once, twice, as a pair of chickadees flitted over his head. "Your wife is home, I see."

Ernie glanced over at the sunporch, where Marie lay heavily swaddled on her chaise lounge, watching them curiously. He waved at her, and waited many moments as she struggled to free her hand from the blankets and wave back.

"As long as you've got that camera," Ernie said, "I wonder if you wouldn't do us a favor."

"I'm going to have to fine you, Mr. Whitten. I'm sorry."

"I need a picture of my ark," Ernie said. "Would you do us that favor? All you have to do is snap one extra."

Mr. Little looked around uncertainly. "Sure, all right."

"I'm sending it in to a contest."

"I bet you win."

Ernie nodded. "I bet I do."

Mr. Little helped Ernie dismantle the staging, such as it was, and soon the ark stood alone in the sun, as round and full-skirted as a giant hen nestled on the grass. The chickadees, momentarily spooked by the rattle of staging, were back again. Two of them. A pair, Ernie hoped. "Could I borrow your dog?" he asked Mr. Little, whose eyebrows shot up in a question. "Just for a minute," Ernie explained. "For the picture. We get my wife's dog over here and bingo, I got animals two by two. Two birds, two dogs. What else would God need?"

Mr. Little whistled at the city car and out jumped Junie, thundering through the open window, her back end wagging back and forth with her tail. Marie was up now, too, hobbling down the porch stairs, Pumpkin Pie trotting ahead of her, beelining toward Junie's yellow tail. As the dogs sniffed each other, Ernie loped across the grass to help Marie navigate the bumpy spots. "Didn't come to me before now," he told her, "but these dogs are just the ticket." He gentled her over the uneven grass and introduced her to Mr. Little.

"This fellow's donated his dog to the occasion."

Marie held hard to Ernie's arm. She offered her free hand to the pink-tongued Junie and cooed at her. Mr. Little seemed pleased, and didn't hesitate a second when Ernie asked him to lead the dogs up the plank and order them to sit. They did. Then Ernie gathered Marie into his arms—she weighed nothing, his big-boned girl all gone to feathers—and struggled up the plank, next to the dogs. He set Marie on her feet and snugged his arm around her. "Wait till the birds light," he cautioned. Mr. Little waited, then lifted the camera. Everybody smiled.

In the wintry months that followed, Ernie consoled himself with the thought that his ark did not win because he had misunderstood the guidelines, or that he had neglected to name his ark, or that he had no experience putting into words that which could not be put into words. He liked to imagine the panel of judges frowning in confusion over his written material and then halting in awe at the snapshot—holding it up, their faces all riveted at once. He liked especially to imagine the youngsters in the art office, the redheaded girl and the boy with rings, their lives just beginning. Perhaps they felt a brief shudder, a silvery glimpse of the rest of their lives as they removed the snapshot from the envelope. Perhaps they took enough time to see it all—birds lighting on a gunwale, dogs posed on a plank, and a man and woman standing in front of a little door, she in her bathrobe and he in his greens, waiting for rain.

Nominated by Glimmer Train Stories

LIES

by MARTHA COLLINS

from FIELD

Anyone can get it wrong, laying low
when she ought to lie, but is it a lie
for her to say she laid him when we know
he wouldn't lie still long enough to let
her do it? A good lay is not a song,
not anymore; a good lie is something
else: lyrics, lines, what if you say *dear sister*
when you have no sister, what if you say *guns*
when you saw no guns, though you know
they're there? *She laid down her arms; she lay
down, her arms by her sides.* If we don't know,
do we lie if we say? If we don't say, do we lie
down on the job? To arms! in any case,
dear friends. If we must lie, let's not lie around.

Nominated by Lloyd Schwartz

PEACE PLAN: MEDITATION ON THE 9 STAGES OF "PEACEMAKING" AS TRIBUTE TO SENATOR CLAIBORNE PELL: 1997

by MICHAEL S. HARPER

from GREEN MOUNTAINS REVIEW

[define problem; you and me against the problem; shared concerns v. what you don't share; work on what is doable; work on listening skills; have a peace plan; work on forgiveness, purify your heart.]

The *Trident*, in nightmare,
sits on the ocean floor;
the canopy of education
(as an active verb)
is sometimes schizophrenic;
its lessons lost in reflex
of the congressional record,
behind the iron and rice curtains

you wonder
what language the French spoke
in pronouncing Dien Bien Phu,
what part of our menu
still Hungarian goulash,
on what government menu
Kiev appears, or Riga
or the Asian side of the Bosphorus;

A Pell poem should have a panel
in the Civic square
it should hold a pelican
who dines, always alone,
in the cemetery pyres
of the Revolutionary War Black Regiment
which is near his neighborhood;

it might strive, in perfect diction,
for clarity on the issues of sport;
at every hospital dance and shuffling
move to the whistles of the territory
bands; it is didactic in its rhythms
and it tells the truth;
I have sat in the waters of foggy
bottom, tape-recorder going,
adjudicating individual grants,
and seen a henchmen in the changeover
enjoy the joblessness of secretaries
who have worked freely on overtime;

I have appeared to the public
late Saturdays
slightly afraid of the punster
who has marked our regional
comings and goings
in the transfer of op-ed
and logarithm
and seen this calculus
reduced to novel synod
or tabernacle
and personal justification;

I have seen your principle
in the gait and habit
or staff, gallery, protocol:

it is a difficult peace plan:
prayer/service/non-violence.

You are strong in the broken places;
we *could* win a war or an earthquake
if we embraced, in close quarters,
ethical teachings the only answer
to a violent culture
(in *Trident*, in nightmare)

might protect even the aquifers,
conifers; our seas are idea rich
as plankton; as honest as pantomime

and we will find the intuitive organ—
the heart, and find the peace organ

and not let the year 2000
be compass alone
but compassion;
and know victims
understand violence best

and cultivate the peace gene:
the conflict resolution by example
of Claiborne Pell.

read at the First Annual PELL AWARD For Excellence in The Arts, January 9, 1997

Nominated by Green Mountains Review, Rita Dove, Reginald Gibbons

DESCENDING

fiction by MARK WISNIEWSKI

from THE GETTYSBURG REVIEW

THERE ARE THOUSANDS OF would-be novelists in Manhattan, most of them lacking talent outright, a portion of this majority blessed with the inkling that they need assistance, a few from this portion affluent enough to pay someone like me to raise their manuscripts toward publishable quality. Without me, my clients write barely disguised autobiographies rife with passive voice verbs, run-on sentences, and forced usages of the word *shards*. With me, they think they have a chance. I know that all of them vie for a shred of chance regardless, because the bottom line these days is that, thanks to the personal computer, more people write books than read them.

I am trying to ignore this nineties form of illiteracy as I walk down Central Park West, completing an appointment with the two-hundred-pound editor-in-chief of a commercially successful women's pornographic magazine. Minutes earlier, in a pub beside one of four thriving coffee houses just off 68th and Columbus, we discussed my suggestions for her latest work of, as she put it, "erotica," and she is now, as we walk, telling me of her "contact" with a member of the cast of *Gilligan's Island,* and of the fact that he has designed for her an "intense" exercise program that has tripled her appetite for sex. I nod, and she continues talking, about how she, as a result of her position at the commercially successful women's pornographic magazine, has seen "more penises than a Times Square whore," and that, as a result, the only thing that stimulates her sexually of late is intellectual conversation. She falls silent for three strides, I slightly ahead of her, she significantly out of breath, and I wish that her exercise program were more intense—because I need to relieve myself of the lager I gulped before we discussed her wording of the policeman's orgasm on page ten. I surge ahead, to beat traffic just released by a green light, and she grabs my left triceps, stopping me, squeezing me, telling me, between breaths, "I saved your life."

"Thank you," I say. Had I been alone, I tell myself, I'd have made it across easily. She does not let go of me until the signal we're facing turns green, and we walk on, again abreast, she resuming our conversation, referring to either male or female genitalia in every other sentence until I finally glean subtext: she is suggesting I lead us to my apartment to have sex.

Can't do, I think. I just want to get home to my bathroom. I endure two blocks of monologue about her expertise in assisting "the male multiple orgasm"—the phenomenon itself news to me—and then we finally reach Columbus Circle, where, trusting she'll take Central Park South to her apartment on Madison Avenue, I slow down to prepare for goodbyes.

"Why are you stopping?" she asks. I point east and she says, "No. I'll walk you home and cab to my place whenever."

"Whatever," I say. No way, I think. I can't let her know where I *live*.

For the record, I am not turned off by her girth. In fact, Florida, my former and only serious girlfriend, with whom I shared no small amount of pleasure, outweighed the Editor-in-Chief by the heft of a large bag of dog chow. It's just that the Editor-in-Chief, to be blunt, bugs me, probably because she enjoys significant remuneration, publication, and celebrity on account of her position while I, unknown author of twelve unpublished novels, edit her work at a dollar a page to afford rent.

"I've got to find an ATM machine," I say, and *I* head east on Central Park South, my need to urinate reaching a density I've never felt, not even in kindergarten, enough to make me grimace. I shout over my shoulder, "Are you coming?"

"I guess," she says, catching up. "Listen," she says, again winded. "I just remembered I have an appointment right now. But on Thursday? I'm going to the Romance Writers' Ball. If you'd go, I could introduce you to people who'd publish your novels."

I stop walking to make sure I've heard right. Facing a hansom cab's horse's ass, I ask, "Are you serious?"

"Sure. If you'd wear a tux. You'd be my date."

This, I think, is how books get in print. I cross my legs to assist my kidneys, then assess the Editor-in-Chief's eyes, which, set back in her head and seemingly the size of champagne grapes, could, I fear, spark my libido more than all of her mention of genitalia—if she aimed them directly at mine. They are, instead, following the buttocks of a Fabio look-alike rollerblading toward Seventh Avenue. I consider my tenth novel, the one I *know* is good, then say, "I'll call you."

She grabs my wrist and tickles it. "Then I'll see you?"

I begin walking backwards toward Columbus Circle, then running toward relief. "I'll call you," I shout over my shoulder.

HALF AN HOUR LATER, preparing to meet my last client of the evening—brightening my expression, stiffening my hunched musculature, and clearing my throat—I ride an elevator up a six-story building in Hell's Kitchen. The car is humid, slow, and dank smelling, like gray mop water, the building itself one of those former warehouses liberally rezoned and parcelled out in the eighties, where many of the occupants are now subleasing on the sly and scared to report illegally hiked rent. The avocado green walls to my left, as I step onto the sixth floor, were, at one time, pink; those on the right are mustard yellow and marred with footprints; the spouts of the sprinkler system are painted over so thickly they can't possibly work.

The first door I pass says WOMEN. Bathrooms down the hall, I think. Honest people suffering for their art. Then I see 611. I knock once and inadvertently open the door. "Whip her!" I hear: a woman's voice full of grit and frustration, a voice somewhat like mine when I line-edit the Editor-in-Chief's fiction while my next novel sits in my head. "Manuscript Doctor?" the gritty voice shouts.

"Yes?" I say.

I am not proud of this name. I adopted it only because the day before I had calling cards made, when I owed two months' rent and therefore *had* to charm the Editor-in-Chief over the phone in order to secure her as a client, she advised me to distinguish myself with a "creative title." And in that advice—and my hesitancy to follow it—lay a hint of the difference between us: she believes literary success is attained by manipulating social contacts, I that writers truly succeed in the solitude of revising their own sentences.

"Get in here," the gritty voice says.

I step in and see trumped-up suffering for art: a water-stained thirteen-foot ceiling over a dusty white-washed hardwood floor, and, sandwiched between, a conglomeration of secondhand materialism that reminds me of the garage of my flea-market-obsessed grandfather. The apartment itself, perhaps intended as office space, is the length and width of a railroad car, and it smells like sandalwood incense, cigarette smoke, and brie. Three rusty chains toggle bolted to the ceiling suspend a silenced portable television aimed at a red-headed woman, perhaps fifty-five years old, lying on a mattress. "Hang on," she says, facing the screen. I guess she is watching pornography, but that might be because I've just seen the Editor-in-Chief, and in any case, given the trajectory of the television, I can't be certain what she's watching unless I lie on the mattress beside her. I like the redhead—she is taut and magnetic, and comparing her to myself makes me feel successful, young, and adjusted—but not enough to risk having sex with her.

"You're Jerry?" I ask.

"Jerry!" she yells. Her eyes are the color of vanilla, and beneath make-up she's overdone, to hide the sprinkling of freckles across the bridge of her nose, her face retains childish cuteness. She appears to be wearing a Wonderbra. "Jerry," she says, "is probably napping in the bathroom." She focusses behind me, so I turn and see, standing in the doorway, a sizeable, elderly, pear-shaped man—sloping narrow shoulders measuring across less than half the width of his hips—wearing a Yankees cap, a yellow and purple silk kerchief knotted around his neck, a faded red Izod sports shirt like the one Florida bought me in 1985, stone-washed relaxed-fit jeans, and no shoes or socks. What strikes hard enough for me to lower my glance to the doorknob, though, is the fact that the left side of his face is disfigured, as if a section of his jawbone has been removed.

"Jerry?" I ask as I complete, I realize, an obvious double take.

He nods, then pulls a notepad from his back pocket.

"Jerry can't speak," the redhead says, and Jerry sidles to my left and elbows my forearm, writing on the pad with a pencil the length of his forefinger. He tears off the sheet and hands it to me, his cursive large, looping, and uncertain, almost juvenile: *Manuscript Dr.?*

"Yes," I say, and he blinks at me, and I nod—as if he can't hear. We shake hands, his large and enveloping: the hand, I think, of a dockworker or home builder, although its skin is loose and smooth. "My pleasure," I say. He smiles and nods, exaggerating both expressions, I figure, to avoid having to write small talk.

"Should we tell him?" the redhead asks with an undertone at the impatience I feel when a client forgets to pay me up front. Tell who what?

541

I wonder, and Jerry writes more, then tears off the sheet, walks past me, and hands it to the woman. As she reads, her lips move so slowly I can't read them. She crumples the sheet and tosses it into a bushel basket full of assorted nuts and bolts. "Jerry," she says, "is a superb writer."

"I'm sure he is," I say. They always, I think, try to sell themselves. I offer the line I've used too much for it to be true: "I don't deal with people unless they have talent."

"You're not listening," she says. "Jerry's the *best*. He's written the novel of the century, if you know what I mean."

"I do, Ma'am. And I can probably provide the polishing it needs to get published."

Jerry clears his throat as the redhead sighs. "It's already published, Honey," she tells me. "You've read it in high school. Everyone has. It's made Jerry so famous he has to hide."

Uh-huh, I think. This man, in this Izod, is the Great One.

To be clear here, I don't actually think the words "the Great One"; I use the phrase now, as I write this, because the Editor-in-Chief mentioned that her attorney advised her that all writers, even journalists, refrain from using actual names.

"His name's not really Jerry," the redhead says. "You know what I'm saying?"

I nod, and Jerry—or the Great One—begins scribbling on his pad. He crosses a *t*, then taps the tip of his pencil under his message: "*Don't mind Joyce. She likes to tell stories.*"

I consider reading this aloud, reconsider, then smile, and he reciprocates, and the stiffness of his smile, conveying faint discomfort, jars me into believing that he, rather than she, is being fictitious here. After all, I remind myself, the Great One *did,* according to recent literary history, choose to avoid public exposure, presumably to keep intact his personhood, and by now that personhood has doubtlessly aged. The speechlessness and the problem with the left side of his face can be explained, I imagine, by cancer surgery, as well as the possibility that he, without the pressure of exposure—without the agents, the public relations gurus, the managers, the plastic surgeons—decided, perhaps for health reasons, against reconstruction. I am about to speak to him as if I am not affected by these possibilities—that is, begin my canned spiel on my array of services as Manuscript Doctor—when the lights in the apartment flicker.

"Shit," Joyce says.

Then the lights go out altogether. I hear traffic outside, but nothing in the apartment, no refrigerator hum, no sound from the television: we have not only lost light, we've lost power.

And the loss, the darkened doorway tells me, has cost the whole building.

"Find a candle, Jerry," Joyce says, and to make sense of what I have seen, heard, and smelled here, I theorize that the Great One has allowed this apartment to deconstruct in order to construct a setting for his next novel, and befriended Joyce for the sake of creating an edgy female character—and, in the process, fallen in love.

Theory aside, his ability to inhale sounds troubled as he opens what sounds like a steel bureau drawer to the left of the door. He is obeying the command to find the candle, it seems, and the troubled inhaling sounds not unlike the wheezing of someone recovering from strangulation, and I am bombarded, as I listen to it and his rifling through silverware, with thoughts about my forthcoming decision regarding the Romance Writers' Ball. I think about this decision as one does any life crisis—quickly and simply, yet struck by all of its complexity and horror—and the wheezing falls silent.

"Jerry?" Joyce says. "Are you all right?"

I picture the Great One rolling his eyes at the obviousness of his inability to answer. Then I fear what Joyce might be fearing: that he is down the hall resuming his nap in the bathroom, or supine, for whatever reason, at our feet. I reach to stop myself from pitching forward after a sudden failure of my own balance, perhaps anxiety-induced, and the heel of my palm presses the knot of his scarf, my fingers confirming that half of his jawbone is gone.

"Sorry," I say, retracting my hand.

"For what?" Joyce asks, now behind me.

"I'm talking to Jerry," I say. "I, uh, touched him."

"For God's sake, we need a candle."

Fingernails tickle my back. I hear more rifling.

"Where did you put the candle, Jerry?" Joyce says, now near the steel drawer, and something squeaks at the far end of the room: the quick rise of a large, room-darkening shade. Nightfall has captured Manhattan, so the window allows in just enough indirect orange streetlight to silhouette the Great One's head, neck and shoulders. His left shoulder, I see now, is not merely sloped; it is gone, like the phantomed half of jawbone, and he is walking toward the window—did the shade, I wonder, rise by itself?—stepping over cardboard cartons and flea-market whatnot, and climbing onto the windowsill using a wobbly silver radiator as a step. Then he's up there, on the sill, tiptoe, facing the pane, keeping himself from pitching backward by spreading his arms to grab both sides of the window frame with his fingertips.

A Christ figure, I think.

"Changing the fuse won't help, Jerry," Joyce says.

The Great One sidesteps toward the left side of the frame.

"Jerry," Joyce says. "Did you hear me?"

The Great One offers two exaggerated nods, then reaches toward the ceiling.

"Stand behind him," Joyce tells me. "So he doesn't fall backwards."

Or forwards, I think. Walking toward the Great One, I trip over the bushelbasket and land on the mattress. It smells like witch hazel. The Great One glances at me over his missing shoulder. "I'm okay," I say, and I stand, the step behind him, and reach over my own head, hands spread the width of his flat buttocks, fingers poised either to catch him or grab his belt loop.

"I'm telling you, Jerry," Joyce says. "A new fuse won't help an iota."

The Great One's breathing hisses until, without turning around, he gives Joyce the finger. I have to admit I agree with her—what good is a fuse when the whole building is powerless?—but I admire his spunk in this round of the battle of sexes. He pulls down the shade, lets it rise, pulls it down, lets it rise. He removes his notepad from his shirt pocket and the pencil from behind his ear, then writes slowly, his balance wavering but working, his toes large and clawlike. He tears the message off the pad and lowers it toward my face. *The shade is broken. Get me a fork.*

"What," Joyce says.

"He wants a fork," I say.

"You don't change a fuse with a fork."

"He says the shade's broken," I say, although in my experience, a broken shade is a victory for planned obsolescence.

"Don't mind the shade, Jerry," Joyce says. "The shade hardly matters with the lights out at night."

The Great One shoots a look at me and snaps his fingers twice, and I walk, avoiding the bushelbasket, to the steel bureau drawer.

"Don't give him a fork," Joyce says.

I clear my throat. "He said he wanted it."

"You can't do whatever he wants just because he is who he is."

He *is* the Great One, I tell myself. You are actually in the man's presence. I grope in the drawer until I find a fork, then walk it back to his hand. His breathing is fine. "The faster he fixes the shade," I tell Joyce, "the faster he'll fix the lighting."

The Great One unhooks the shade, then uses a space between fork tines as a wrench on the tiny silver rectangle on the end of the shade's dowel, cranking it counterclockwise.

"I think I smell smoke," Joyce says—and she's right. And it's not from cigarettes, either. It smells like the exhaust of a campfire, and it's growing stronger, more palpable. The Great One must smell it, I decide, and the fact that he keeps cranking the fork handle calms me: this is the man who, in all situations, knows what he's doing. And if he is indeed the Great One, I don't want to be the wuss who says "fire."

Then I remember the sprinkler system's painted-over spouts, and my own breathing begins to feel taxed.

"And these are nonsmoking hallways," Joyce says.

"Is that right," I say.

The Great One continues to crank.

"I'm going downstairs," Joyce says. "To see where it's coming from."

I feel compelled to answer her, but then, given her silence, I gather she's left. The Great One's silence has taught me a lesson: bitching by one's partner is best addressed quickly, then ignored.

He hangs the shade and pulls it down, returning us to absolute darkness. "Fixed," I say as he steps to the floor, and the shade, on its own accord, rises an inch. "Dammit," I say. I wonder if speaking for the Great One is causing me to feel what he feels.

"We're not going to burn," Joyce's voice says from the doorway. A veneer of streetlight hangs over the mattress. "Zevon said smoke descends, so if there is a fire, it's coming from the roof. Which means we won't have a problem getting out."

Smoke *descends*? I think. "Who's Zevon?"

"Our super. He lives in the basement. I saw him on the stairs."

"He just checked the roof?"

"I don't know."

I cough. "Don't you think someone should check it?"

"Let me ask you something, Mr. Manuscript Doctor. You live in the city?"

"Yes."

"And you never smelled smoke in your building?"

545

"Not like this."

"Then you haven't lived here long enough."

The plane of streetlight illuminates the Great One's grimace. He is apparently sitting on the mattress and, given several grunts and the aim of his eyes, putting on socks or shoes. He gestures his notepad toward my hand. I take it and use the light to read: *"Let's get out of here."*

"What," Joyce says.

"He's leaving," I say.

"If you think there's a fire, Jerry," she says, "take your manuscript."

I trust, given my experience with clients, that he'll heed her advice. I hear the door creak. I grope for the doorway, find it without touching Joyce, then follow the squeaking of sneakers down the hall. "Jerry?" Joyce's voice calls from behind us.

The squeaking leads me down a smoke-filled staircase. Wooden, I realize as I descend. Finally I see more orange light: the ground floor. Then we're out, standing on the sidewalk, the Great One and I. He sports red and black Air Jordans.

"You didn't bring your manuscript?" I ask.

He pulls his notepad from his front pocket and writes. *"I just wanted to breathe."*

"Oh," I say.

"And I'm not talking about the smoke, either."

"You don't think there's a fire?"

He shakes his head, and I nod to show I understand, unintentionally suggesting that I agree, and he leads me across the street, where we stand, facing his building, beside a grocery store brightened by a sidewalk display of lemons, tomatoes, pomegranates, ugly fruit, cactus pears, and red and white grapes. No champagne grapes, I think. I picture myself dancing cheek-to-cheek with the Editor-in-Chief at the Romance Writers' Ball. I hear a siren, growing closer, apparently a fire engine's. Wanting to tell Joyce that I know sirens are as meaningless as distant gunshots, I study the Great One's building and notice that enlarged headshots of personalities I'm probably supposed to recognize, one to a window, line the second floor: a photography studio.

Then a fire engine rounds the corner and stops at the Great One's building. Firemen armed with extinguishers, hatchets, axes, and bags of sunflower seeds lope toward its door. One of them pushes a button to buzz up as the Great One writes on his pad: *"A precaution."*

"A precaution," I say aloud. I believe I am feeling what the Great One feels, a sense of calm salted conservatively with panic. I wonder

546

if this burgeoning skill of mine—the ability to put into words what others are feeling rather than coerce them into believing what I think—is the key to today's literary success. "Listen," I say. I tell myself I'm diverting the Great One's thoughts from the firemen. "You want me to look at your manuscript. And I will. But I think I know who you are, and I'm hoping you can answer a question."

The Great One flashes the okay sign.

"Aside from all the stuff about structuring plots and sentences, how does one write to make it big?"

He smirks and hunkers down on his pad. *"Please everyone."*

"But everyone says writers *can't* please everyone."

"I did."

"But that was a different era," I say. "I mean, everything is different now, don't you think?"

"If so, I am finished."

So am I, I think. Because I've spent my writing life trying to revive the spirit of the Great One's work.

"One more question," I say. "If you don't mind?"

"Shoot."

"What do you think about sleeping with editors?"

The Great One raises one finger, acknowledging, I am sure, that his answer will be worth both my wait and his effort. He writes hard, blinking repeatedly, then hands over the notepad.

"Doing that doesn't make you a writer. Just a whore."

A headshot in a second floor window explodes, glass raining onto the sidewalk across the street, a hatchet retracted from the punctured blown-up nose, smoke twisting out and rising past the third, fourth, and fifth floors, past the window on the sixth floor without a drawn shade, behind which a television hangs from three chains.

"Joyce better get out of there," I say.

The Great One writes: *"There's a fire escape in back."*

"Good," I say.

The Great One nods.

I ask, "What was on your television, anyway?"

"Cable Horseracing."

Another headshot explodes, this one female, and then they are exploding from left to right in lock-step fashion: male, female, male, female, axes popping through smiles like stuck-out metallic tongues. This is serious, I almost say, but the escaping smoke tapers. The axes begin shattering third floor windows. My glance at the Great One, who

547

is watching his window, assures me that he, unlike Zevon, knows that heat and smoke rise, and that he's picturing Joyce dashing through his dark hallway while his manuscript sits.

"Excuse me," I tell him.

I walk past the fire engine, head for the Great One's building, and a fireman yells, "*Numb*skull. Where are you going?"

"I've got to get something," I say. "Before it burns."

"It's burning."

"What if it's still there?"

"It's burning. You might as well phone your insurance."

"I can't run up and check?"

"You run up and I lose my job. So you're not running up." He lifts an industrial-size crowbar. "Got it?"

I nod and walk back to the Great One. We stand, side by side, wordless, watching the smoke blacken—until a hand squeezes my triceps. Joyce, I think, and I turn and see the Editor-in-Chief flanking my left as closely as the Great One is my right.

"Hey there," she says. "What's up?"

"A tragedy," I say.

"It's just a fire, Home Boy," she says, and *that* bugs me.

"Did you follow me here?" I ask.

She pins back her shoulders. "Yeah."

"How?"

"They're called cabs."

"You actually got in a cab and said 'follow that guy.' "

"What, is that a crime?"

I turn toward the fire. "It's kind of like stalking."

"Do you want me in handcuffs now? Or later?"

The Great One is dotting an *i*. He hands his notepad to me, and I read it as the Editor-in-Chief does: *"This is your woman?"*

"I wouldn't put it that way," I say. "She's an editor."

The Editor-in-Chief elbows me. "What's with the notepad?"

The Great One faces her, then draws a fingertip across his throat.

"Who *is* this guy?" the Editor-in-Chief asks me.

Another fire truck rounds the corner. "Ask him politely," I say, "and he might tell you."

"Why? He's obviously a sexist simpleton."

The Great One and I exchange glances. He shrugs. Then his window explodes—without the help of an axe. Inside his apartment, the tip of a flame stretches high enough for us to see yellow. His breathing grows troubled, then vexed. He has not made a copy of his manuscript, I am sure, and he is picturing the pages singeing, and his words might have pleased Everyone enough to change everything. I feel sorry for Everyone, and for him. I feel ashamed that I considered getting published by servicing the Editor-in-Chief—because her connection with Everyone is probably null. My only contact with Everyone, I realize, is when I am hungry and on line at the A & P, when I resent being nicked by elbows on sidewalks, when I am wasted, worn, and burned by the lottery—when I crave something priceless and brilliant from someone who demands neither subservience nor pay.

"Well," the Editor-in-Chief says. "You up for the ball?"

I clear my throat. "I just remembered. I've got to stay home that night to write."

Her eyes engage mine. They do, as I feared, ignite something inside me. "Screw you, too," she says, and she walks toward a policeman across the street.

"I bet she tries to seduce him," I tell the Great One, and I begin babbling about the impossibility of pleasing *anyone* these days, using fragments and run-ons that make, I fear, neither sense nor a favorable impression. I babble anyway, for the sake, I realize, of the babbling, and then I try to explain that, these days, in this decade, almost all writing, editing, publishing, and love-making does nothing but add to the discord that separates Everyone from everyone else. Noticing that the Great One's breathing has silenced, I turn and see his pencil finish a message: *"I know what you mean."*

"Do you really?"

He nods, sits on the curb, and watches his building burn. Then he reclines, legs fair game for pizza delivery bicycles, spine flat against sidewalk concrete dotted black by discarded gum, eyes shut, palms down, one atop the other, on his chest.

"Careful," I shout at a passerby, though I'm hoping for a response from the Great One.

His eyes remain shut. He can't, I tell myself, handle the discord.

"Jerry?" I try.

Someone taps my shoulder: Joyce, a piece of ugly fruit in each hand, as if weighing them. "He's napping," she says. "He does this wherever he feels."

The Editor-in-Chief, I notice, is returning. "Is he okay?" she asks.

"He's felt better," I say.

"I took CPR at the gym," she says. "If anyone here knows what she's doing, it's me." She plants her feet on either side of the Great One's chest, then crouches, buttocks touching his abdomen, then resting on it.

"Can you believe what I have to put up with?" Joyce says.

"You're smothering him," I tell the Editor-in-Chief.

"I'm helping him," she says.

"I don't think so," I say. "He doesn't need CPR. It's a *breathing* thing, for Christ's sake."

She places her palms on his chest and shoves. "It's his heart."

I set my palms on the side of her arm and shove harder. She doesn't budge—she's that heavy—so I push again, using my forearms and shoulders and the balls of my feet against concrete, and she lets go of his shoulders and rolls off of him. She is lying beside him, pulling down her skirt and straining her neck to sit up, but I don't see her rise: I am on my knees, beside the Great One, pinching his nose and grabbing his jowls and lowering the remains of his jawbone. Then I'm descending, hoping his eyes open before our lips touch. Then we are sharing his muteness. His mouth still holds warmth, and I exhale into it, and my palm feels my breath raise his chest. I won't have to do this more than twice, I think, and I inhale, tasting garlic, halitosis, and cinnamon. I hear glass pelt the sidewalk across the street. I try not to hear the Editor-in-Chief, who is shouting at me with instructions. One more time, I tell myself, and I'll hear that troubled breathing. Everything will be exactly the way it was.

Nominated by Caroline Langston, Clarence Major

BLUE KASHMIR, '74

by CAROL MUSKE

from AMERICAN POETRY REVIEW

L.A. spring, our boulevard of flowering jaca-
randa. Twelve trees: Ophelia's delirium. The
color the clapper makes inside the bell, the bell's
explosion twelve times into addled violet. I see

the equal signs, but no two things on this
earth are the same. The symbol of wings that
follows me is the real maker of equations:
blue rain and my dogs panting beside me.

See. That's my dark Expressionist painting the first
extraneous cross: dying Christ as just an element of
landscape, like *blue:* the hare's throat, the contusion
of clouds, backlit, and the varying mountain sky. Count

the intrusion of a dog's bark. Trout-fishing in Kashmir,
I followed my guide faithfully, a child into white water.
He pointed deep, deeper into the Himalayas. *There*
was China. Dressed as a boy, I didn't know how to paint

my own naivete: everything in my gaze faithful, true as a dog's.
August 15th. Lower Wangat. Below us the Jhelum was flooding
into Srinigar. Consequences, dark as blood mixed with cerulean,
the color in the skull as the head dips underwater. The beggar's

"long gone" cry like the floating arias of the peddlers, little boat-
sleighs criss-crossing Dal Lake, loaded with gold and bones stolen
from Tibetan temples. The hotel-houseboats capsized, but not
every one. Woe is the woman who walks in blue, it's her ecstasy,

she cannot see it. At the Oberoi, the Hindu Female
Doctor I'd placed in the book of strong women pulled me aside,
veiled, hissing. *They will kill me.* I stepped into the whitewater.
The dogs look back at me, race the wave-colored hill. She un-

dressed the Moslem women, which was forbidden. Eyes turned
sideways above the veil, then a downward glance. She saw that
they required the cautery blade, biopsy. He pointed out a trout.
Dun-flash. She had to find the soft places where the tumors hid,

behind breastbone or ovary. On the wall, sunlight:
her bone chart, twenty blue vials of penicillin.
She was the first unsteady step into the secular,
into expression. An element in the landscape: rain

pencilling itself on the glass as they stepped free
of their veils, naked: breasts, buttocks. The neigh-
bor's bucket seats overflow with blue wings, trees'
sex. The women stood, ecstatic, keeping their arms

straight, perpendicular to the floor. Equal sign,
I don't know how anyone could change sex so ex-
peditiously. I wore jeans, my hair under a cap.
He must have opted to look the other way, away

from the waves. The men accosted her in the street,
shouted how she'd defiled their wives. *Help me.*
Her eyes. He taught me how to thread on the fly, cast.
The tree holds out its arms: falling blossoms.

I begged off. Eyes, eyes, the color of the dogs, crosses.

Nominated by Ralph Angel, Philip Appleman, Henry Carlile, Joyce Carol Oates

SPECIAL MENTION

(The editors also wish to mention the following important works published by small presses last year. Listing is in no particular order.)

POETRY

Augury—Lynne McMahon (The Kenyon Review)
Position of Strength—Alane Rollings (TriQuarterly)
One Is the Hardest Ice—Cal Bedient (Volt)
Arcady (10)—Donald Revell (New American Writing)
Ring Out, Wild Bells—James Reiss (New Letters)
Report from the Interior, A Swan Song—Erin Mouré (Denver Quarterly)
Island Life—Mark Levine (Fine Madness)
The Rose Maker's Fever—Peter Richards (Colorado Review)
El Compadre, Again—Cecilia Woloch (Cahuenga Press)
The Black Jacket—Henri Cole (New England Review)
The Sorrow Pageant—Rodney Jones (Southern Review)
Thunderstruck—Allen Grossman (Boston Review)
Threads, End of Another Day—Michael Chitwood (Doubletake)
The Last Photograph of My Sister—Sherod Santos (Yale Review)
The Calligraphy Shop—Ben Downing (The Paris Review)
Testimony—Yusef Komunyakaa (Brilliant Corners)
The Greeks—Linda McCarriston (TriQuarterly)
nahna aldulvdi gesvi of that wanting which is—Diane Glancy (Xcp cross cultural poetics)
The Lone Pedestrian—May Swenson (The American Voice)
ode—Douglas A. Powell (Volt)
Prayer—Dorianne Laux (BOA)
Nocturne: Joshua Tree—Timothy Liu (Gettysburg Review)

Black Stone on Top of Nothing—Philip Levine (Poetry)
Hecuba Mourns—Marilyn Nelson (The Southern Review)
Heaven is Just Another Country—Jamie Jacinto (Kearny St. Workshop)
Skinnydipping with William Wordsworth—Maxine Kumin (Hudson Review)
When the Grain is Golden and the Wind is Chilly . . . —Nick Carbo (Synaesthetic)
The Frame—Elizabeth Spires (Partisan Review)
Collateral Damage—John Balaban (Copper Canyon Press)
Mardi Gras Masks—Preston Merchant (New England Review)

ESSAYS

Oakland, Jack London and Me—Eric Miles Williamson (Chattahoochee Review)
Henry James—Mona Simpson (Conjunctions)
Bad Eyes—Erin McGraw (Gettysburg Review)
Inherited Holocaust Memory And the Ethics of Ventriloquism—Lori Hope Lefkovitz (The Kenyon Review)
Consequences of Darwinism—Marilynne Robinson (Salmagundi)
Mixed American Pak . . . Lisa McCloud (Xcp)
Emily Dickinson: The Heft of Cathedral Tunes—Daniel Hoffman (Hudson Review)
Critical Disobedience: Nine Ways of Looking At a Poem—David Baker (The Gettysburg Review)
Ferality and Strange Good Fortune: Notes of Writing and Teaching—David Wojahn (Shenandoah)
The Milosz File—Mark Rudman (The Kenyon Review)
Tradition and the General Dumbing-Down—Lucia Perillo (Michigan Quarterly Review)
Economy, Its Fragrance—Anne Carson (The Threepenny Review)
Traces of Light: The Paradoxes of Narrative Painting and Pictorial Fiction—Alan Cheuse (Antioch Review)
In the Shadow of Memory—Floyd Skloot (Southwest Review)
Silence—Scott Russell Sanders (Witness)
The Uncertainty Principle—Robert Cohen (Boulevard)
Jinx—Robin Hemley (Prairie Schooner)
The Barn—Suzanne Whedon (Massachusetts Review)

After the War—Tessa Dratt (Northeast Corridor)

FICTION

The Rain in Kilrush—Michael Collins (TriQuarterly)
Dead Man's Fuel—Mike McCormack (Conjunctions)
Midrash—Sandell Morse (New England Review)
Jesse—Lex Williford (Glimmer Train Stories)
Among the Azores—David W. Lavender (Georgia Review)
Seven Stories for All the Animals—George Clark (White Pine Press)
The Marriage—Elizabeth Kemper (Story Quarterly)
The End—Josip Novakovich (New Letters)
The Weekend Girl—Marie Sheppard Williams (Alaska Quarterly)
The Oboist—Anne Miano (Missouri Review)
What Exactly About the Word NO Don't You Understand?—Ron
    Carlson (Red Rock Review)
Chauffeur's Song—Peter LaSalle (Press)
Captain Midnight and the Code of the West—Steve Heller (South
    Dakota Review)
Aliens of Affection—Padgett Powell (Paris Review)
Marrying Jerry—Margaret Benbow (Wisconsin Fiction: Transactions)
Spaniards On the Sea—Catherine Scherer (Another Chicago Maga-
    zine)
Young Lion Across The Water—Thomas E. Kennedy (Prism Interna-
    tional)
The Woman From New York—Ha Jin (Boston Book Review)
Kol Nidre—Garth Wolkoff (Indiana Review)
In The Small World of A Warehouse—David Newman (Fuel)
Whatever's Out There—D. R. MacDonald (Southwest Review)
A Friend of Mine—Wendell Berry (Kenyon Review)
Starlings—Kent Nelson (Gettysburg Review)
Oregon—Jessica Treadway (Boston Book Review)
Mercy—Jean Thompson (American Short Fiction)
My Gun—Tess Gallagher (Kenyon Review)
Pinch Hitter—Robert Cohen (Tikkun)
Love Somebody—Tod Goldberg (Timber Creek Review)
Parking Lot Hams and Other Acts of God—Becky Hagenston (Press)
Waste—Lisa Glatt (Columbia)
Badlands—Diane Glancy (Carolina Quarterly)

Salt Lake—Liza Wieland (North American Review)
Ashes—D. R. MacDonald (Epoch)
A Gram of Mars—Becky Hagenston (Antietam Review)
Whir of Satisfaction—Lara J. K. Wilson (American Fiction)
Third World Wolf—Jess Mowry (ZYZZYVA)
Roses—Sharon Booker Brooks (Writers' Forum)
Like Never Before—Ehud Havazelet (Southern Review)
The Myths of Bears—Rick Bass (Southern Review)
White Butterflies—C. L. Rawlins (North American Review)
The Letters of Heaven—Barry Lopez (Georgia Review)
Sailor's Valentine—Cary Holladay (Southern Review)
Love Story Without Words—Luis Sepúlveda (Grand Street)
Ropa Rimwe—George Clark (Zoetrope: All Story)
Live Bottomless—Lee Smith (Southern Review)
The Solitary Twin—Wally Lamb (Missouri Review)
Fezzini Must Have You Ever At Her Side—Leon Rooke (American Voice)
Moonlight—Marian Thurm (American Voice)
El Pulgarcito Express—Héctor Tobar (Bilingual Review)
Cojones—Adam Berlin (Bilingual Review)
The Rest of Her Life—Steve Yarbrough (Missouri Review)
What's Left Behind—Karen Outen (Glimmer Train Stories)
Twenty—Tessa Bridal (The Tree of Red Stars, Milkweed Editions)
Turn On/Turn Off—Jim Miller (Fiction International)
The Source—Elaine Romero (Alaska Quarterly Review)
The Blue Hour—Kate Walbert (Paris Review)
The Sin of Elijah—Steve Stern (Prairie Schooner)
Death Valley—Susan Moon (Witness)
Icarus—Susan Power (Story)
The Kitchen Window—H. E. Francis (Quarterly West)
On Balance—Tim Farrington (ZYZZYVA)
African Queen—Alyce Miller (Kenyon Review)
Self Storage—Mary Helen Sefaniak (Iowa Review)
The Shepherdess—Sam Roberts (Press)
Tilt-A-Whirl—Mark Jude Poirier (Laurel Review)
Street of Swans—Ann Harleman (Southwest Review)
Teleton—Tom LeClair (Fiction International)
How She Knows What She Knows About Yo-Yos—Mary Ann Taylor-Hall (Chattahoochee Review)
English As A Second Language—Mary Helen Stefaniak (Other Voices)

Kissing—Dick Green (Antietam Review)
Running to Ethiopia—Nancy Welch (Mid-American Review)
Lamp Soup—Tony Ardizzone (Italian Americana)
Three Hours & Thirty Years—David Conway (Antietam Review)
Field Notes—Jason Wilson (Northeast Corridor)
The Brilliants—Diane Williams (Gargoyle)
Squaring Up—L. G. Bateson (Whetstone)
Hunters—Laura Migdal (Other Voices)
Auden's Toothbrush—Lucinda Ebersole (Gargoyle)
Little Fur People—T. C. Boyle (Antioch Review)
A Neighborly Gesture—Alan Elyshevitz (Briar Cliff Review)
Kindness—Tamara Jane (Berkeley Fiction Review)
Rule of Snowman—Stephen St. Francis Decky (Literal Latté)
The Friction Point—Gretchen Comba (Greensboro Review)

PRESSES FEATURED IN THE PUSHCART PRIZE EDITIONS SINCE 1976

Acts
Agni Review
Ahsahta Press
Ailanthus Press
Alaska Quarterly Review
Alcheringa/Ethnopoetics
Alice James Books
Ambergris
Amelia
American Letters and Commentary
American Literature
American PEN
American Poetry Review
American Scholar
American Short Fiction
The American Voice
Amicus Journal
Amnesty International
Anaesthesia Review
Another Chicago Magazine
Antaeus
Antietam Review
Antioch Review
Apalachee Quarterly
Aphra
Aralia Press

The Ark
Artword Quarterly
Ascensius Press
Ascent
Aspen Leaves
Aspen Poetry Anthology
Assembling
Atlanta Review
Autonomedia
The Baffler
Bakunin
Bamboo Ridge
Barlenmir House
Barnwood Press
The Bellingham Review
Bellowing Ark
Beloit Poetry Journal
Bennington Review
Bilingual Review
Black American Literature Forum
Black Rooster
Black Scholar
Black Sparrow
Black Warrior Review
Blackwells Press
Bloomsbury Review

Blue Cloud Quarterly
Blue Unicorn
Blue Wind Press
Bluefish
BOA Editions
Bomb
Bookslinger Editions
Boulevard
Boxspring
Bridges
Brown Journal of Arts
Burning Deck Press
Caliban
California Quarterly
Callaloo
Calliope
Calliopea Press
Calyx
Canto
Capra Press
Caribbean Writer
Carolina Quarterly
Cedar Rock
Center
Chariton Review
Charnel House
Chattahochee Review
Chelsea
Chicago Review
Chouteau Review
Chowder Review
Cimarron Review
Cincinnati Poetry Review
City Lights Books
Cleveland State University Press
Clown War
Cold Mountain Press
CoEvolution Quarterly
Colorado Review
Columbia: A Magazine of Poetry
    and Prose
Confluence Press
Confrontation

Conjunctions
Connecticut Review
Copper Canyon Press
Cosmic Information Agency
Countermeasures
Counterpoint
Crawl Out Your Window
Crazyhorse
Crescent Review
Cross Cultural Communications
Cross Currents
Crosstown Books
Cumberland Poetry Review
Curbstone Press
Cutbank
Dacotah Territory
Daedalus
Dalkey Archive Press
Decatur House
December
Denver Quarterly
Domestic Crude
Doubletake
Dragon Gate Inc.
Dreamworks
Dryad Press
Duck Down Press
Durak
East River Anthology
Ellis Press
Empty Bowl
Epoch
Ergo!
Event
Exquisite Corpse
Faultline
Fiction
Fiction Collective
Fiction International
Field
Fine Madness
Firebrand Books
Firelands Art Review

Five Fingers Review
Five Trees Press
The Formalist
Frontiers: A Journal of Women
   Studies
Gallimaufry
Genre
The Georgia Review
Gettysburg Review
Ghost Dance
Gibbs-Smith
Glimmer Train
Goddard Journal
David Godine, Publisher
Graham House Press
Grand Street
Granta
Graywolf Press
Green Mountains Review
Greenfield Review
Greensboro Review
Guardian Press
Gulf Coast
Hanging Loose
Hard Pressed
Harvard Review
Hayden's Ferry Review
Hermitage Press
Hills
Holmgangers Press
Holy Cow!
Home Planet News
Hudson Review
Hungry Mind Review
Icarus
Icon
Iguana Press
Indiana Review
Indiana Writes
Intermedia
Intro
Invisible City
Inwood Press

Iowa Review
Ironwood
Jam To-day
The Journal
The Kanchenjuga Press
Kansas Quarterly
Kayak
Kelsey Street Press
Kenyon Review
Latitudes Press
Laughing Waters Press
Laurel Review
L'Epervier Press
Liberation
Linquis
Literal Latté
The Literary Review
The Little Magazine
Living Hand Press
Living Poets Press
Logbridge-Rhodes
Louisville Review
Lowlands Review
Lucille
Lynx House Press
Magic Circle Press
Malahat Review
Mānoa
Manroot
Marlboro Review
Massachusetts Review
Mho & Mho Works
Micah Publications
Michigan Quarterly
Mid-American Review
Milkweed Editions
Milkweed Quarterly
The Minnesota Review
Mississippi Review
Mississippi Valley Review
Missouri Review
Montana Gothic
Montana Review

Montemora
Moon Pony Press
Mr. Cogito Press
MSS
Mulch Press
Nada Press
New America
New American Review
New American Writing
The New Criterion
New Delta Review
New Directions
New England Review
New England Review and Bread
    Loaf Quarterly
New Letters
New Virginia Review
New York Quarterly
New York University Press
Nimrod
9 x 9 Industries
North American Review
North Atlantic Books
North Dakota Quarterly
North Point Press
Northern Lights
Northwest Review
Notre Dame Review
O. ARS
O·Blēk
Obsidian
Obsidian II
Oconee Review
October
Ohio Review
Old Crow Review
Ontario Review
Open Places
Orca Press
Orchises Press
Orion
Oxford American
Oxford Press

Oyez Press
Painted Bride Quarterly
Painted Hills Review
Paris Press
Paris Review
Parnassus: Poetry in Review
Partisan Review
Passages North
Penca Books
Pentagram
Penumbra Press
Pequod
Persea: An International Review
Pipedream Press
Pitcairn Press
Pitt Magazine
Ploughshares
Poet and Critic
Poetry
Poetry East
Poetry Ireland Review
Poetry Northwest
Poetry Now
Prairie Schooner
Prescott Street Press
Press
Promise of Learnings
Provincetown Arts
Puerto Del Sol
Quarry West
The Quarterly
Quarterly West
Raccoon
Rainbow Press
Raritan: A Quarterly Review
Red Cedar Review
Red Clay Books
Red Dust Press
Red Earth Press
Red Hen Press
Release Press
Review of Contemporary Fiction
Revista Chicano-Riquena

Rhetoric Review
River Styx
Rowan Tree Press
Russian *Samizdat*
Salmagundi
San Marcos Press
Sea Pen Press and Paper Mill
Seal Press
Seamark Press
Seattle Review
Second Coming Press
Semiotext(e)
Seneca Review
Seven Days
The Seventies Press
Sewanee Review
Shankpainter
Shantih
Sheep Meadow Press
Shenandoah
A Shout In the Street
Sibyl-Child Press
Side Show
Small Moon
The Smith
Solo
Some
The Sonora Review
Southern Poetry Review
Southern Review
Southwest Review
Spectrum
The Spirit That Moves Us
St. Andrews Press
Story
Story Quarterly
Streetfare Journal
Stuart Wright, Publisher
Sulfur
The Sun
Sun & Moon Press
Sun Press
Sunstone

Sycamore Review
Tamagwa
Tar River Poetry
Teal Press
Telephone Books
Telescope
Temblor
Tendril
Texas Slough
The MacGuffin
Third Coast
13th Moon
THIS
Thorp Springs Press
Three Rivers Press
Threepenny Review
Thunder City Press
Thunder's Mouth Press
Tikkun
Tombouctou Books
Toothpaste Press
Transatlantic Review
TriQuarterly
Truck Press
Undine
Unicorn Press
University of Illinois Press
University of Iowa Press
University of Massachusetts Press
University of Pittsburgh Press
Unmuzzled Ox
Unspeakable Visions of the Individual
Vagabond
Vignette
Virginia Quarterly
Volt
Wampeter Press
Washington Writers Workshop
Water Table
Western Humanities Review
Westigan Review
White Pine Press
Wickwire Press

Willow Springs
Wilmore City
Witness
Word Beat Press
Word-Smith
Wormwood Review
Writers Forum

Xanadu
Yale Review
Yardbird Reader
Yarrow
Y'Bird
Zeitgeist Press
ZYZZYVA

CONTRIBUTOR'S NOTES

RICHARD BAUSCH is the author of twelve volumes of fiction. He was recently elected to membership in The Fellowship of Southern Writers. He teaches at George Mason University.

MARVIN BELL is roving editor of this series and a past poetry co-editor. His books include *Ardor* (Copper Canyon) *Wednesday: Selected Poems 1966–1997* (Salmon Publishing, Ireland), and *Poetry For A Midsummer's Night* (Seventy Fourth Street Productions)

LOUIS BERNEY is the author of *The Road to Bobby Joe and Other Stories* (Harcourt Brace). His fiction has appeared in *The New Yorker, The Antioch Review, Ploughshares* and elsewhere.

MELVIN JULES BUKIET teaches at Sarah Lawrence College. His most recent novels are *After* and *Signs and Wonders.*

RICHARD BURGIN is the editor of *Boulevard* and the author most recently of *Fear of Blue Skies* (Johns Hopkins).

FREDERICK BUSCH's most recent novel is *Girls* (Harmony Books, 1997). He teaches at Colgate, and directs the annual Chenango Valley Writers' Conference.

JOSHUA CLOVER is author of *Madonna Anno Domini.* He lives in Berkeley.

GORDON CAVENAILE is a part-time writer who lives in Vancouver B.C., Canada.

BETH CHIMERA lives in New York City. "July" is her first published story. It began as a writing exercise modeled on Joy Williams' "Summer."

JOHN J. CLAYTON is the author of *What Are Friends For* (Little, Brown) and a collection of short fiction, *Bodies of the Rich* (University of Illinois Press). He lives in Amherst, Massachusetts.

MARTHA COLLINS' fourth collection of poetry, *Some Things Words Can Do*, is just out from Sheep Meadow Press.

TOI DERRICOTTE is the author of *Tender*, a book of poetry from the University of Pittsburgh Press, and *The Black Notebooks*, a literary memoir from W. W. Norton & Co. With Cornelius Eady, she co-founded Cave Canem, a workshop for African-American writers.

THOMAS M. DISCH is the author of many books. He lives in New York State close to the site of the Slaughter Rock Battlefield. He says that his story "belongs to a long tradition of fictions about inmates taking over the asylum, all descending from Poe's 'The System of Doctor Tarr and Professor Fether'".

STEPHEN DIXON's "The Burial" is part of a long work that Henry Holt is about to publish. Two collections are due soon from Coffee House Press and Rain Taxi Press will do *Story of a Story and Other Stories: A Novel*.

ANDRE DUBUS received the 1996 Rea Award for the Short Story. His collection of fiction, *Dancing After Hours*, is out in paperback from Vintage, and his essays collection is just published also (Knopf).

STUART DYBEK's short story collection, *The Coast of Chicago*, is available from Knopf. He teaches in Kalamazoo.

LYNN EMANUEL was poetry co-editor for the 1995 *Pushcart Prize*. Her latest book is *The Dig* (University of Illinois Press, 1995). She teaches at The University of Pittsburgh.

MARTÍN ESPADA won the American Book Award and received two NEA fellowships and other prizes. His five poetry collections include *City of Coughing and Dead Radiators*.

JEFFREY EUGENIDES is the author of *The Virgin Suicides* (Farrar, Straus & Giroux). His fiction has appeared in *The New Yorker, The Paris Review, The Yale Review, The Gettysburg Review, Conjunctions* and *Granta*.

KATHY FAGAN's second collection, *Revisionary Instruments*, will be published soon. It won the Vassar Miller Prize for Poetry.

EDWARD FALCO lives in Blacksburg, Virginia. He is the author of *Winter In Florida* (Soho), a novel, and two short story collections.

BECKIAN FRITZ GOLDBERG's poems have appeared in *The American Poetry Review, Field, Harper's* and elsewhere. She is the author of two poetry collections: *Body Betrayer,* and *In the Badlands of Desire,* both from Cleveland State University Press.

EMILY FOX GORDON's essays have been published in *Salmagundi, Boulevard,* and *The Anchor Essay Annual.* Her memoir, *Mockingbird Years,* is due from Basic Books.

MARILYN HACKER won the National Book award in 1975. Her books include *Love, Death and the Changing of Seasons* and *Assumptions.*

KIMIKO HAHN's books are available from Hanging Loose and Kaya Productions. Home is Brooklyn, New York.

PATRICIA HAMPL's book of essays on memory and imagination, *I Could Tell You Stories,* is due from W. W. Norton Co. in 1999. She has published two volumes of poetry and the memoirs, *A Romantic Education,* and *Virgin Time.*

JAMES HARMS directs the creative writing program at West Virginia University. *The Joy Addict* is just out from Carnegie Mellon University Press.

MICHAEL HARPER teaches at Brown University. His ten books of poetry include two that were nominated for the National Book Award.

JEFFREY HARRISON is the author of poetry collections from Dutton and Copper Beech. His poems have appeared in *The Nation, The New Republic, Poetry, The Paris Review* and elsewhere.

ROSEMARY C. HILDEBRANDT is the author of the chapbook *Brick on Silk.* (1997). She lives in St. Paul.

EDWARD HIRSCH has had poems and an essay in previous Pushcart Prizes. His books are available from Knopf—most recently *Earthly Measures* (1996) and *On Love* (1998). He just won a MacArthur Fellowship.

COLETTE INEZ is the author of eight books of poetry. Her latest is *Clemency* (Carnegie Mellon University Press). She has received fellowships from the Guggenheim and Rockefeller Foundations, and elsewhere.

MARK IRWIN is a poet, critic and translator. His fourth book of poems, *Quick, Now, Always,* is available from BOA Editions.

LAURA KASISCHKE's poetry collections have been published by New York University Press and Carnegie Mellon University Press. *Suspicious River,* a novel, was issued by Houghton Mifflin in 1996 and a second novel, *White Bird in A Blizzard,* is just out.

MARILYN KRYSL is director of the writing program at the University of Colorado, Boulder. Her poem originally appeared in the *Spoon River Poetry Review* as winner of that journal's 1995 poetry award.

MARY KURYLA writes screen plays and fiction. "Freak Weather," a film that she wrote and directed, will soon be released. She lives in Topanga, California.

PHILIP LEVINE, a past co-editor of poetry for this series, has received the Lenore Marshall Award, the National Book Critics Circle Award, the American Book Award, the National Book Award, and the Pulitzer Prize for *The Simple Truth* (1995).

WILLIAM MATTHEWS was poetry co-editor of *Pushcart Prize XXI.* His last book was *Time & Money* (Houghton Mifflin, 1995). He died in 1997.

JANE MCCAFFERTY is author of *Director of the World and Other Stories* (University of Pittsburgh Press, 1992) which won the Drue Heinz Prize. She teaches at Carnegie Mellon.

COLUM MCCANN's books include *Songdogs* (1995), *Fishing the Sloe-Black River* (1996) and *This Side of Brightness* (1998), from Metropolitan Books. He was born in Ireland and lives in New York.

RISA MICKENBERG is the author of *Taxi Driver Wisdom.* She lives in New York.

JENNIFER MOSES has had fiction published in *Gettysburg Review, Southern Exposure, Commentary* and other journals. She writes regularly for *The Washington Post,* and lives in Baton Rouge.

BHARATI MUKHERJEE teaches at The University of California, Berkeley. Her most recent novel is *Leave It To Me* (Knopf, 1997).

CAROL MUSKE's most recent book of poems is *An Octave Above Thunder: New and Selected Poems* (Penguin). Her book of essays was recently published by The University of Michigan Press.

MARIKO NAGAI's poetry has been published in *Gettysburg Review, Prairie Schooner, Southern Poetry Review,* and elsewhere.

KIRK NESSET teaches at Allegheny College. His stories have appeared in *Tampa Review, ZYZZYVA, Indiana Review* and elsewhere.

JOYCE CAROL OATES, a founding editor of this series, is the author of many novels including *Man Crazy* (Dutton) for which she received the PEN/Malamud award. She teaches at Princeton University.

LANCE OLSEN has published in many small presses. His selection here is from *Anyone Is Possible: New American Short Fiction,* edited by Kate Gale and Mark Cull (Red Hen Press).

ALAN MICAEL PARKER is the author of *Days Like Prose* (Alef Books, 1997). He teaches at Penn State University.

LUCIA PERILLO is the author of two books of poetry from Northeastern and Purdue.

CARL PHILLIPS is the author of three poetry collections, most recently from Graywolf. He teaches at Washington University, St. Louis.

FRANCINE PROSE is the author of *Guided Tours of Hell* and many other books. She lives in New York.

NANCY RICHARD's stories have appeared in *Prairie Schooner, Greensboro Review,* and *Crescent Review.* She lives in Metairie, Louisiana.

KATRINA ROBERTS, is a poet and freelance journalist. She graduated from Harvard, and The Iowa Writers Workshop and she teaches at Whitman College in Washington State.

PATTIANN ROGERS has published seven books of poetry including *Eating Bread and Honey* (Milkweed, 1997). She lives in Colorado.

GRACE SCHULMAN is the 1996 recipient of the Delmore Schwartz Memorial Award. She was one of the original poetry editors of *The Pushcart Prize* series.

ANGELA SHAW was raised in the mountains of West Virginia. She is working on her first collection of poems.

AURELIE SHEEHAN's story collection, *Jack Kerouac is Pregnant*, was published by Dalkey Archive Press in 1994. Her new book of essays will be *The Easy Blue Road to Love*.

JULIE SHOWALTER's stories have been broadcast on PBS radio's Fresh Air, This American Life, and Your Radio Playhouse. Her work has also appeared in *Calyx, ACM, Other Voices* and *Maryland Review*.

MARCIA SOUTHWICK teaches at the University of New Mexico. Her books include *Why The River Disappears* and *The Night Won't Save Anyone*.

MAXINE SWANN lives in Pairs, France. She is writing her first novel. "Flower Children" is her first published story.

JUDITH TAYLOR teaches and lives in Los Angeles. Her work has appeared in *Nimrod, The Plum Review* and *Crab Orchard Review*.

TARIN TOWERS is a freelance writer and editorial consultant. She lives in San Francisco.

BARBARA TRAN is co-editor with Monique T. D. Truony and Luu Truong Khoi, of *Watermark, Vietnamese American Poetry & Prose* (Asian American Writers' Workshop, 1998).

ALEC WILKINSON is a staff writer at *The New Yorker.* His books include *Big Sugar* and *A Violent Act*.

MARK WISNIEWSKI is the author of the novel *Confessions of a Polish Used Car Salesman.* His stories have been issued by *The Missouri Review, American Short Fiction, Indiana Review* and dozens of other publications.

MEG WOLITZER's novel, *Surrender, Dorothy,* is due soon. Her other books include *Sleepwalking* and *This Is Your Life.* She lives in New York.

MONICA WOOD has been published in *Manoa, North American Review, Tampa Review* and elsewhere. Her novel is *Secret Language,* and another, *My Only Story,* is almost finished. She lives in Portland, Maine, and grew up in Mexico (Maine).

CONTRIBUTING SMALL PRESSES FOR THIS EDITION

(These presses made or received nominations for this edition of *The Pushcart Prize*. See the *International Directory of Little Magazines and Small Presses,* Dustbooks, P.O. Paradise, CA 95697, for subscription rates, manuscript requirements and a complete international listing of small presses.)

A

About Time Press, P.O. Box 529, Redwood Estates, CA 95044
the Acorn, P.O. Box 1266, El Dorado, CA 95623
Acorn Whistle, 907 Brewster Ave., Beloit, WI 53511
Agni, Boston Univ., 236 Bay State Rd., Boston, MA 02215
Alaska Quarterly Review, Univ. of Alaska, Anchorage, AK 99508
Alligator Juniper, 630 Morrell Blvd. Prescott, AZ 86301
Amaranth, P.O. Box 184, Trumbull, CT 06611
American Letters & Commentary, 850 Park Ave., ste. 5B, New York, NY 10021
American Literary Review, P.O. Box 311307, Denton, TX 76203
American Short Fiction, see Univ. of Texas Press
The American Voice, 332 W. Broadway, Louisville, KY 40202
Amherst Writers & Artists Press, P.O. Box 1076, Amherst, MA 01004
The Amicus Journal, 40 W. 20th St., New York, NY 10011
Andrew Momtein Press, PO Box 340353, Hartford, CT 06134
Angelflesh, P.O. Box 141123, Grand Rapids, MI 49514
Another Chicago Magazine, 3709 N. Kenmore, Chicago, IL 60613
Antietam Review, 41 S. Potomac St., Hagerstown, MD 21740
Antioch Review, P.O. Box 148, Yellow Springs, OH 45387
Apalachee Quarterly, P.O. Box 10469, Tallahassee, FL 32302
Arkansas Review, English Dept., Arkansas State Univ., State University, AR 72467
artisan, P.O. Box 157, Wilmette, IL 60091

ArtWord Quarterly, 5273 Portland Ave., White Bear Lake, MN 55110
Asian Pacific American Journal, 37 St. Marks Place, New York, NY 10003
Atlanta Review, P.O. Box 8248, Atlanta, GA 30306
Aurorean, P.O. Box 219, Sagamore Beach, MA 02562
Avec Books, P.O. Box 1059, Penngrove, CA 94951
Axe Factory Review, P.O. Box 40691, Philadelphia, PA 19107

B

The Baffler, P.O. Box 378293. Chicago, IL 60637
Ballast Quarterly Review, 2022 X Ave., Dysart, IA 52224
The Baltimore Review, P.O. Box 410, Riderwood, MD 21139
Bamboo Ridge Press, P.O. Box 61781, Honolulu, HI 96839
bananafish, P.O. Box 381332, Cambridge, MA 02238
Bathtub Gin, P.O. Box 5154, Bloomington, IN 47407
Belletrist Review, P.O. Box 596, Plainville, CT 06062
Bellingham Review, MS-9053, West Washington Univ., Bellingham, WA 98225
Beloit Poetry Journal, Box 154, RFD 2, Ellsworth, ME 04605
Berkeley Fiction Review, ASUC Public. Lib., MLK, Univ. of California. Berkeley, CA 94720
Bilingual Review/Press, Arizona State Univ., P.O. Box 872702, Tempe, AZ 85287
The Bitter Oleander, 4983 Tall Oaks Dr., Fayetteville, NY 13066
BkMk Press, Univ. of Missouri, 5101 Rockhill Rd., Kansas City, MO 64110
Black Belt Press, P.O. Box 551, Montgomery, AL 36101
Black Warrior Review, P.O. Box 862936, Tuscaloosa, AL 35486
Blithe House Quarterly, ?
BOA Editions, Ltd., 260 East Ave., Rochester, NY 14604
Bordighera, Inc., Foreign Lang. & Lit., Purdue Univ., W. Lafayette, IN 47907
Borf Books, Box 413, Brownsville, KY 42210
The Boston Poet, 7 Speridakis Terrace, Cambridge, MA 02139
Boston Review, E53-407, Massachusetts Inst. of Tech., Cambridge, MA 02139
Bottom Dog Press, Firelands College, Huron, OH 44839
Bottomfish, De Anza College, 21250 Stevens Creek Blvd., Cupertino, CA. 95014
Boulevard, 4579 Laclede Ave., #332, St. Louis, MO 63108
Briar Cliff Review, 3303 Rebecca St., Sioux City, IA 51104
Brickhouse Books, Inc., 541 Piccadilly Rd., Baltimore, MD 21204
Bridge Works, Bridge Lane, Box 1798, Bridgehampton, NY 11932
Brilliant Corners, English Dept., Lycoming College, Williamsport, PA 17701
Brooklyn Review, English Dept., Brooklyn College, Brooklyn, NY 11210
Burning Cloud Review, 1815 15th Ave., St. Cloud, MN 56304
Burning Deck, 71 Elmgrove Ave., Providence, RI 02906
button, Box 26, Lunenburg, MA 01462

C

Cafe Solo, 5146 Foothill Rd., Carpinteria, CA 93013
Calyx, Inc., P.O. Box, Corvallis, OR 97339
Cape Perpetua Press, P.O. Box 1005, Yachats, OR 97498
Caprice, 420 E. 54th St., New York, NY 10022
The Caribbean Writer, Univ. of Virgin Islands, RR02, Box 10,000, Kingshill, St. Croix, U.S. Virgin Islands 00850
Carolina Quarterly, 510 Greenlaw Hall, Univ. of North Carolina, Chapel Hill, NC 27599
Carriage House Press, Carriage La., Barnes Landing, East Hampton, NY 11937

Chariton Review, Truman State Univ., Kirksville, MO 63501
Chattahoochee Review, Dekalb College, Dunwoody, GA 30338
Chelsea, Box 773, Cooper Sta., New York, NY 10276
Chelsea Green Publishing Co., P.O. Box 428, White River Junction, VT 05001
Chestnut Hills Press, see Brickhouse Books
Chicory Blue Press, Inc., 795 East St., North, Goshen, CT 06756
Chiron Review, 702 N. Prairie, St. John, KS 67576
Cities and Roads, P.O. Box 10886, Greensboro, NC 27404
Clackamas Literary Review, 19600 S. Molalla Ave., Oregon City, OR 97045
Clearwood Publishers, P.O. Box 52, Bella Vista, CA 96008
Cleveland State University Poetry Center, English Dept., 1983 E. 24 St., Cleveland, OH 44115
Coal City Review, English Dept., Univ. of Kansas, Lawrence, KS 66045
Confluence, P.O. Box 336, Belpre, OH 45714
Confrontation, English Dept., C. W. Post of L.I.U., Brookville, NY 11548
Conjunctions, Bard College, Annandale-on-Hudson, NY 12504
Connecticut Review, English Dept., So. Connecticut Univ., New Haven, CT 06515
Coracle, 1516 Euclid Ave., Berkeley, CA 94708
Crab Orchard Review, English Dept., So. Illinois Univ., Carbondale, IL 62901
The Crescent Review, P.O. Box 15069, Chevy Chase, MD 20825
Crow and Coyote Press, P.O. Box 10886, Greensboro, NC 27404
CutBank, English Dept., Univ. of Montana, Missoula, MT 59812

D

John Daniel & Co., P.O. Box 21922, Santa Barbarba, CA 93121
Denver Quarterly, Univ. of Denver, Denver, CO 80208
Dominion Review, English Dept., Old Dominion Univ., Norfolk, VA 23529
doublestar press, 1718 Sherman Ave., Ste., 203, Evanston, IL 60201
DoubleTake, Duke Univ., 1317 W. Pettigrew St., Durham, NC 27705
Duke University Press, 905 W. Main St., Durham NC 27704

E

Ekphrasis, P.O. Box 161236, Sacremento, CA 95816
Epicenter Press, Box 82368, Kenmore, WA 98028
Eureka Literary Magazine, Eureka College, P.O. Box 280, Eureka, IL 61530
Event, P.O. Box 2503, New Westminster, B.C., V3L 5B2 CANADA
The Ever Dancing Muse, PO Box 7751, E. Rutherford, NJ 07073
Exit 13 Magaine, Box 423, Fanwood, NJ 07023

F

Faultline, P.O. Box 599-4960, Irvine, CA 92716
Fiction CCNY, Convent Ave., 138 St., New York, NY 10031
Fiction International, English Dept., San Diego State Univ., San Diego, CA 92182
Field, Oberlin College Press, 10 N. Professor St., Oberlin, OH 44074
Fine Madness, P.O. Box 31138, Seattle, WA 98103
First Intensity, P.O. Box 665, Lawrence, KS 66044
Fish Stories, 3540 N. Southport Ave., Ste. 493, Chicago, IL 60657

Five Points. English Dept., Georgia State Univ., Univ. Plaza, Atlanta, GA 30303
Florida Review, English Dept., Univ. of Central Florida, Orlando, FL 32816
Fly By Night Magazine, P.O. Box 101, Harveyville, KS 66431
Flying Horse, P.O. Box 445, Marblehead, MA 01945
Flyway, English Dept., Iowa State Univ., Ames, IA 50011
The Formalist, 320 Hunter Dr., Evansville IN 47711
Four Way Books, P.O. Box 607, Marshfield, MA 02050
Free Lunch, P.O. Box 7647, Laguna Niguel, CA 92607
Frith Press, P.O. Box 161236, Sacramento, CA 95816
Fugue, English Dept., Univ. of Idaho, Moscow, ID 83844

G

Gargoyle, 1508 U St., NW, Washington, DC 20009
George & Mertie's Place, P.O. Box 10335, Spokane, WA 92209
The Georgia Review, Univ. of Georgia, Athens, GA 30602
Gettysburg Review, Gettysburg College, Gettysburg, PA 17325
Glimmer Train, 710 SW Madison, #504, Portland, OR 97205
Graffiti Rag, 5647 Oakman Blvd., Dearborn, MI 48126
Grand Street, 131 Varick St., Rm. 906, New York, NY 10013
Graywolf Press, 2402 University Ave., St. Paul, MN 55114
Great River Review, Univ. of Minnesota, Anderson Ctr., Minneapolis, MN 55455
Green Hills Literary Lantern, P.O. Box 375, Trenton, MO 64683
Green Mountains Review, Johnson State College, Johnson, VT 05656
Greensboro Review, Univ. of North Carolina, Greensboro, NC 27402

H

Hackett Publishing Co., P.O. Box 7, Cambridge, MA 02139
Haight-Ashbury Literary Journal, 558 Joost Ave., San Francisco, CA 94127
Hammers, see doublestar press
Hampton Shorts, Box 1229, Water Mill, NY 11976
Hannacroix Creek Books, 1127 High Ridge Rd., #110, Stamford, CT 06905
Happy, 240 E. 35th St., 11A, New York, NY 10016
Hayden's Ferry Review, Box 871502, Arizona State Univ. Tempe, AZ 85287
Helicon Nine Editions, P.O. Box 22412, Kansas City, MO 64113
The Heyeck Press, 25 Patrol Court, Woodside, CA 94062
The Higginsville Reader, P.O. Box 141, Three Bridges, NJ 08887
High Plains Literary Review, 180 Adams St., Ste. 250, Denver, CO 80206
Hodge Podge Poetry, P.O. Box 11107, Shorewood, WI 53211
Hubbub, 5344, SE 38th Ave., Portland, OR 97202
The Hudson Review, 684 Park Ave., New York, NY 10021

I

The Iconoclast, 1675 Amazon Rd., Mohegan Lake, NY 10547
Illumination Arts Publishing Co., Inc., P.O. Box 1865, Bellevue, WA 98009
Indiana Review, 465 Ballantine, Indiana Univ., Bloomington, IN 47405
Iowa Review, 308 EPB, Univ. of Iowa, Iowa City, IA 52242
Iris Editions, 1278 Glenneyre, Ste. 138, Laguna Beach, CA 92651

Italian Americana, Univ. of Rhode Island, 80 Washington St., Providence, RI 02903

J

Javelina Press, P.O. Box 42131, Tucson, AZ 85733
Johns Hopkins University Press, 2715 N. Charles St., Baltimore, MD 21218
The Journal, English Dept., Ohio State Univ., Columbus, OH 43210
Journal of African Travel-Writing, P.O. Box 346, Chapel Hill, NC 27514
Journal of New Jersey Poets, County College of Morris, 214 Center Grove Rd., Randolph, NJ
    07869
Jumbo Shrimp, 852 S. Logan St. Denver, CO 80209
Junction Press, P.O. Box 40537, San Diego, CA 92164

K

Kaya, 133 W. 25th St. New York, NY 10001
Kelsey Review, Mercer County Community College, P.O., Box B, Trenton, NJ 08690
Kelsey Street Press, P.O., Box 9325, Berkeley, CA 94709
The Kenyon Review, Kenyon College, Gambier, OH 43022
Kings Estate Press, 870 Kings Estate Rd., St. Augustine, FL 32086

L

The Laurel Review, Northwest Missouri State Univ., English Dept., Maryville, MO 64468
The Ledge Magazine, P.O., Box 310010, Jamaica, NY 11431
Lemonade Factory, 1678 Shattuck Ave., Ste. 267, Berkeley, CA 94709
Licking River Review, Dept. of Lit. & Lang., Northern Kentucky Univ., Highland Heights, KY
    41099
Literal Latte, 61 E. 8th St. Ste, 240, New York, NY 10003
Livingston Press, Sta. 22, UWA, Livingston, AL 35470
Lone Stars Magazine, 4219 Flinthill Dr., San Antonio, TX 78230
Lost Prophet Press, 330 3rd Ave. So., Minneapolis, MN 55408
The Louisville Review, 315 Bingham Humanities, Univ. of Louisville, Louisville, KY 40292
The Lowell Review, 3075 Harness Dr., Florissant, MO 63033
Lulu Press, P.O., Box 2344, Napa, CA 94558
Lynx Eye, 1880 Hill Dr., Los Angeles, CA 90041

M

The MacGuffin, Schoolcraft School College, 18600 Haggerty Rd., Livonia MI 48152
Magazine of Speculative Poetry (MSP), P.O., Box 564, Beloit, WI 53512
Main Street Rag, P.O., Box 25331, Charlotte, NC 28229
Mala Revija, 3413 Alta Vista Dr., Chattanooga, TN 37411
Malachite & Agate, 6558 4th Section Rd., #149, Brockport, NY 14420
Mandorla, c/o E. Allen, 59 W. 12th St., 9E, New York, NY 10011
Manoa, English Dept., Univ. of Hawaii, Honolulu, HI 96822
Many Beaches Press, 1527 N. 36th St., Sheboygan, WI 53081

Many Mountains Moving, Inc., 420 22nd St., Boulder, CO 80302
Many Tracks, RT.1, Box 52, Cooks, MI 49817
Many Waters, Empire State College, SUNY, Cobleskill, NY 12043
Marlboro Review, P.O., Box 243, Marlboro, VT 05344
Marmarc Publications, see Belletrist Review
The Massachusetts Review, Univ. of Massachusetts, Amherst, MA 01003
The Maverick Press, Rt. 2, Box 4915, Eagle Pass, TX 78852
Medicinal Purposes Literary Review, 86-37 120th St., #2D, Richmond Hill, NY 11418
Mellen Poetry Press, P.O., Box 450, Lewiston, NY 14092
Melting Trees Review, 2026 Mt. Meigs Rd., #2, Montgomery, AL 36107
membrane, 4213 12th St., NE, Washington, DC 20017
Michigan Quarterly Review, Univ. of Michigan, 3032 Rackham Bldg., Ann Arbor, MI 48109
The Mid-America Press, P.O., Box 575, Warrensburg, MO 64093
Mid-American Review, English Dept., Bowling Green State Univ., Bowling Green, OH 43403
Mid-List Press, 4324-12th Ave. So., Minneapolis, MN 55407
Milkweed Editions, 430 First Ave. N., Ste, 400, Minneapolis, MN 55401
Millenium Press, P.O., Box 502, Groton, MA 01450
Mind in Motion, P.O., Box 7070, Big Bear Lake, CA 92315
Mississippi Mud, 7119 Santa Fe Ave., Dallas, TX 75223
Mississippi Review, Univ. of Southern Mississippi, Box 5144, Hattiesburg, MS, 39406
The Missouri Review, 1507 Hillcrest Hall, Univ. of Missouri, Columbia, MO 65211
Mockingbird, P.O., Box 761, Davis, CA 95617
Moon Pony Press, 740 30th Ave., #78, Santa Cruz, CA 95062
Mudfish, 183 Franklin St., New York, NY 10013

N

Nassau Review, Nassau College, Garden City, NY 11530
The Nebraska Review, UNO Writer's Workshop, FA212, Univ. of Nebraska, Omaha, NE 68182
Nerve Cowboy, P.O., Box 4973, Austin, TX 78765
New American Writing,
New England Review, Middlebury College, Middlebury, VT 05753
New Letters, Univ. of Missouri, 5100 Rockhill Rd., Kansas City, MO 64110
New Millenium Writings, P.O., Box 2463, Knoxville, TN 37901
New Orleans Review, Box 195, Loyola Univ., New Orleans, LA 70118
the new renaissance, 26 Heath Rd., #11, Arlington, MA 02174
New Rivers Press, 420 N. 5th St., Ste. 910, Minneapolis, MN 55401
Nightshade Press, P.O., Box 76, Troy, ME 04987
Nightsun, English Dept., Frostburg State Univ., Frostburg, MD 21532
nine muses books, 3541 Kent Creek Rd., Winston, OR 97496
No Exit, P.O., Box 454, South Bend, IN 46624
North American Review, University of Northern Iowa, Cedar Falls, IA 50614
Northeast Corridor, Beaver College, 450 S. Easton Rd., Glenside, PA 19038
Northern Lights, P.O., Box 8084, Missoula, MT 59807

O

Oasis, P.O., Box 626, Largo, FL 33779
Old Crow, P.O., Box 403, Easthampton, MA 01027
One Trick Pony, P.O., Box 11186, Philadelphia, PA 19136

Ontario Review, 9 Honey Brook Dr., Princeton, NJ 08540
Orchises Press, P.O., Box 20602, Alexandria, VA 22320
Orion, 195 Main St., Great Barrington, MA 01230
Osiris, P.O., Box 297, Deerfield, MA 01342
Other Voices, English Dept., Univ. of Illinois, 601 S. Morgan St., Chicago, IL 60607

P

Palo Alto Review, Palo Alto College, 1400 W. Villaret, San Antonio, TX 78224
Pangolin Papers, Box 241, Nordland, WA 98358
Papier-Mache Press, 627 Walker St., Watsonville, CA 95076
Paris Press, P.O., Box 487, 117 West Rd., Ashfield, MA 01330
Paru Review, 541 E. 72nd, New York, NY 10021
Pearl, 3030 E. Second St., Long Beach, CA 90803
Peregrine, see Amherst Writers & Artists Press
The Permanent Press, 4170 Noyac Rd., Sag Harbor, NY 11963
Persea Books, 171 Madison Ave., New York, NY 10016
Phoebe, George Mason Univ., MSN 2D6, 4400 Univ. Dr., Fairfax, VA 22030
Phoenix, P.O., Box 317, Berkeley, CA 94701
Pine Grove Press, P.O., Box 85, Jamesville, NY 13078
Pivot, 250 Riverside Dr., #23, New York, NY 10025
Plains Press, P.O., Box 6, Granite Falls, MN 56241
Pleiades, English Dept., Central Missouri State Univ., Warrensburg, MO 64093
Ploughshares, Emerson College, 100 Beacon St., Boston, MA 02116
Poems & Plays, P.O., Box 70, Middle Tennessee State Univ., Murfreesboro, TN 37132
Poet Lore, 4508 Walsh St., Bethesda, MD 20815
Poetry, 60 W. Walton, Chicago, IL 60610
Poetry Miscellany, 3413 Alta Vista Dr., Chattanooga, TN 37411
The Poetry Project, 131 E. 10th St., New York, NY 10003
The Poet's Guild, P.O., Box 161236, Sacramento, CA 95816
Porcupine, P.O., Box 259, Cedarburg, WI 53012
Portable Plateau, P.O., Box 755, Joplin, MO 64802
Potato Eyes, see Nightshade Press
Potomac Review, Box 354, Port Tobacco, MD 20677
Potpourri, P.O., Box 8278, Prairie Village, KS 66208
Prairie Schooner, 201 Andrews, Univ. of Nebraska, Lincoln, NE 68588
Press, 125 W. 72nd St., Ste. 3-M, New York, NY 10023
P.S., 169 Garron Rd., Middletown Springs, VT 05757
Puerto Del Sol, Box 3E, New Mexico State Univ., Las Cruces, MN 88003

Q

QECE, 406 Main St., #3C, Collegeville, PA 19426
Quarterly West, 317 Oplin Union, Univ. of Utah, Salt Lake City, UT 84112

R

Raritan, Rutgers, State Univ. of New Jersey, New Brunswick, NJ 08903
Red Moon Press, P.O., Box 2461, Winchester, VA 22604

Ridgeway Press, P.O., Box 120, Roseville, MI 48068
River King Press, P.O. Box 122, Freeburg, IL 62243
River Oak Review, P.O., Box 3127, Oak Park, IL 60303
River Sedge, CAS 266, Univ. of Texas-Pan American, 1201 W. Univ. Dr., Edinburg, TX 78539
River Styx, 3207 Washington St., St. Louis, MO 63101
Ronsdale Press, 3350 W. 21st. Ave., Vancouver, B.C. *CANADA* V6S 1G7
Rosebud, P.O., Box 459, Cambridge, WI 53523

S

Salt Hill, English Dept., Syracuse Univ., Syracuse, NY 13244
Sarabande Books, 2234 Dundee Rd/ .Ste. 200, Louisville, KY 40205
Satire, P.O. Box 340, Hancock, MD 21750
Savannah Literary Journal, see Savannah Writers' Workshop
Savannah Writers' Workshop, P.O. Box 9561, Savannah, GA 31412
Seal Press, 3131 Western Ave., #410, Seattle, WA 98121
Seneca Review, Hobart & William Smith College, Geneva, NY 14456
Sera Publishing, 2685 Marine Way, Mountain View, CA 94043
Seven Days, P.O. Box 1164, Burlington, VT 05402
Sheila-Na-Gig, 23106 Kent Ave., Torrance, CA 90505
Shenandoah, Washington & Lee Univ., Lexington, VA 24450
Singular Speech Press, 10 Hilltop Dr., Canton, CT 06019
Skylark, Purdue Univ., 2200 169th St., Hammond, IN 46323
Slipstream, Box 2071, Niagara Falls, NY 14301
S.L.U.G. fest, Ltd., P.O. Box 1238, Simpsonville, SC 29681
Snowy Egret, P.O. Box 9, Bowling Green, IN 47833
Solo, 5146 Foothill Rd., Carpinteria, CA 93013
Sonora Review, English Dept., Univ. of Arizona, Tucson, AZ 85721
The Southern Anthology, 2851 Johnson St., #123, Lafayette, LA 70503
Southern Methodist University Press, P.O. Box 750415, Dallas, TX 75275
Southern Review, 43 Allen Hall, Louisana State Univ. Baton Rouge, LA 70803
Southwest Review, P.O. Box 750374, Southern Methodist Univ., Dallas, TX 75275
Sou'Wester, Southern Illinois Univ., Edwardsville, IL 62026
Spinsters Ink, 32 E. 1st St. Duluth, MN 55802
Sport Literate, P.O. Box 577166, Chicago, IL 60657
Stonewall, see Brickhouse Books, Inc.
Story, 1507 Dana Ave., Cincinnati, OH 45207
Story Quarterly, P.O. Box 1416, Northbrook, IL 60065
Sulphur River Literary Review, P.O. Box 19228, Austin, TX 78760
The Sun, 107 N. Roberson St., Chapel Hill, NC 27516
Sweet Annie Press, 7750 Hwy F-24, W., Baxter, IA 50028
Sycamore Review, English Dept., Purdue Univ., West Lafayette, IN 47907
Sycamore Roots Magazine, 205 N. Front St., North Liberty, IA 52317
Symbiotic Oatmeal, P.O. Box 14938, Philadelphia, PA 19149
Synaesthetic, P.O. Box, 91, New York, NY 10013

T

Talking River Review, Lewis & Clark State College, Lewiston, ID 83501
Talus and Scree, P.O. Box 851, Waldport, OR 97394
Tamaqua, Parkland College, 2400 W. Bradley Ave., Champaign, IL 61821
Tampa Review, 401 W. Kennedy Blvd., Tampa, FL 33606

Tar River Poetry, English Dept., East Carolina Univ., Greenville, NC 27858
Thema Literary Society, Box 74109, Metairie, LA 70033
Thin Coyote, see Lost Prophet Press
Third Coast, English Dept., Western Michigan Univ., Kalamazoo, MI 49008
Third Side Press, 2240 W. Farragut, Chicago, IL 60625
Thorngate Road, Campus Box 4240, Illinois State Univ., Normal, IL 61790
Thorntree Press, 547 Hawthorn La., Winnetka, IL 60093
Threepenny Review, P.O. Box 9131, Berkeley, CA 94709
Thumbscrew Press, 1331 26th Ave., San Francisco, CA 94122
Timber Creek Review, 612 Front St., E., Glendora, NJ 08029
Tomorrow Magazine, P.O. Box 148486, Chicago, IL 60614
Trask House Books, 3222 N.E. Schuyler, Portland, OR 97212
TriQuarterly, Northwestern Univ., 2020 Ridge Ave., Evanston, IL 60208
Tsunami Inc., P.O. Box 100, Walla Walla, WA 99362
Turning Wheel, P.O. Box 4650, Berkeley, CA 94704

U

Under the Sun, English Dept., Box 5053, Tennessee Technical Univ., Cookeville, TN 38505
Universities West Press, P.O. Box 697, Williams, AZ 86046
University of Arkansas Press, 201 Ozark Ave., Fayetteville, AR 72701
University of Massachusetts Press, P.O. Box 429, Amherst, MA 01004
University of Northern Texas Press, P.O. Box 311336, Denton, TX 76203
University of Texas Press, P.O. Box 7819, Austin, TX 78713
University of Wisconsin Press, 2537 Daniels St., Madison, WI 53718
The Urbanite, P.O. Box 4737, Davenport, IA 52808

V

Verse, College of William and Mary, Williamsburg, VA 23187
Voices From the Well, 402 S. Cedar Lake Rd., #2, Minneapolis, MN 55405
Voices Israel, Box 5780, 46157 Herzlia, *ISRAEL*

W

Washington Review, P.O. Box 50132, Washington, DC 20091
West Anglia Publications, P.O. Box 2683, LaJolla, CA 92038
West Crook Review, 14 Lantz Ave., Whitman, MA 02382
Whelks Walk Press, 37 Harvest Lane, Southampton, NY 11968
Whetstone, P.O. Box 1266, Barrington, IL 60011
Whispering Willows Mysteries, P.O. Box 890294, Oklahoma City, OK 73189
White Pine Press, 10 Village Sq., Fredonia, NY 14063
Wild Duck Review, 419 Spring St., Ste.D, Nevada City, CA 95959
Wild Earth, P.O. Box 455, Richmond, VT 05477
Willow Springs Magazine, EWU, 526-5th St., MS-1, Cheney, WA 99004
Wings Press, 627 E. Guenther, San Antonio, TX 78210
Witness, 27055 Orchard Lake Rd., Farmington Hills, MI 48334
Worcester Review. 6 Chatham St., Worcester, MA 01609
Wordcraft of Oregon, P.O. Box 3235, La Grande, OR 97850
Words of Wisdom, 612 Front St. -East, Glendora, NJ 08029
The World, see The Poetry Project
Wormwood Review, P.O. Box 50003, Loring Sta., Minneapolis, MN 55405

Y

Yale Review, Yale Univ., New Haven, CT 06520
Yemassee, English Dept., Univ. of South Carolina, Columbia, SC 29208

Z

Zoetrope, 260 Fifth Ave., Ste. 1200, New York, NY 10001
Zone 3, P.O. Box 4565, Austin Peay State Univ., Clarksville, TN 37044
ZYZZYVA, 41 Sutter St., Ste, 1400, San Francisco, CA 94104

INDEX

The following is a listing in alphabetical order by author's last name of works reprinted in the first twenty-three *Pushcart Prize* editions.

582

583

586

587

589

591

594

595

599

606